DIARIES

□ 1899-1941 □

BY ROBERT MUSIL

OTHER BOOKS IN ENGLISH BY ROBERT MUSIL

Young Törleß

Five Women

Enthusiasts (a play)

Precision and Soul

Posthumous Papers of a Living Author

Selected Writings

The Man without Qualities, Vols. I & II

DIARIES

□ 1899-1941 □

BY ROBERT MUSIL

Original German Version
of THE DIARIES Edited by

Adolf Frisé

Selected, Translated, Annotated,
and with a Preface by

Philip Payne

Edited and with an Introduction by

Mark Mirsky

BASIC
BOOKS

A Member of The Perseus Books Group

Library of Congress Cataloging-in-Publication Data
Musil, Robert, 1880–1942.
    [Tagebücher. English. Selections]
    Diaries, 1899–1942 / by Robert Musil; selected, translated, annotated, and with a preface by Philip Payne; edited and with an introduction by Mark Mirsky; original German edition edited by Adolf Frisé.
        p.   cm.
    "The present work is a selection from Robert Musil, Tagebücher, edited by Adolf Frisé (Reinbek bei Hamburg: Rowohlt, 1976)" — Pref.
    Includes bibliographical references and index.
    ISBN 0-465-01650-2 (cloth); ISBN 0-465-01651-0 (pbk.)
    1. Musil, Robert, 1880–1942—Diaries.   2. Authors, Austrian—20th century—Biography.   I. Payne, Philip, 1942-   .   II. Mirsky, Mark, 1939- .
III. Title.
PT2625.U8T3413   1999
838'.9103—dc21
[b]   98-36990
                                                                                  CIP

CONTENTS

TRANSLATOR'S NOTE

The present work is a selection from Robert Musil, *Tagebücher*, edited by Adolf Frisé (Reinbek bei Hamburg: Rowohlt, 1976). I am deeply indebted to Adolf Frisé for his help in the selection and allowing me to make use of the apparatus of his edition for this English translation—this use is so extensive that I have not acknowledged each separate reference to his notes. (Occasionally, in various notes I refer to Frisé's edition as follows: Heft 4, 23 [Notebook 4, p. 23].)

Editorial conventions used in this translation are broadly the same as those used in the German edition:

> Each new diary entry begins flush at the left-hand margin.
> Paragraphs within entries are indented.
> Editorial annotations appear in square brackets thus: [. . .]. A list of all the major points of abridgment in the text appears in the List of Omissions at the back of this edition.
> Musil's own brackets (to amend entries during composition or at a later date) are represented by open and close parentheses thus: (. . .).
> Musil's additions and amendments to his entries—he frequently returned to his diaries for ideas and inspiration and sometimes corrected or otherwise commented on his original text—are indicated by curly brackets thus: { . . . }.
> Very occasionally a word or phrase which Musil deleted has been retained in the translation and is enclosed in arrow brackets thus: < . . . >.
> A number of Musil's eccentricities in punctuation have been preserved from the Frisé edition, three periods where the American reader would expect four, two periods where usage dictates three, and a varying scheme of italicization.

Since I refer frequently to Musil's major work, *Der Mann ohne Eigenschaften*, edited by Adolf Frisé (Reinbek bei Hamburg: Rowohlt, 1978), this edition appears abbreviated throughout as MoE. A new translation of this novel, *The Man without Qualities*, edited by Burton Pike, translated by Sophie Wilkins and Burton Pike (New York: Knopf, 1995), is referred to throughout as MwQ. I would like to thank Burton Pike for his help and encouragement with the preparation of this translation of Musil's *Diaries*.

I also would like to acknowledge the help and advice I received from colleagues in England and Germany, particularly the following: at the Arbeitsstelle für Robert-Musil-Forschung at the University of the Saar, Professor Marie-Louise Roth and Professor Pierre Behar, Dr. Annette Daigger, Korinna Teschner, Patrik Feltes, and Silvia Bonacchi; at Lancaster University, Graham Bartram, David Craig, and Keith Hanley. My mother has undertaken most of the word-processing of this translation from the first manuscripts to the final draft and kept a watchful classicist's eye on my use of English!

P.P.

PREFACE

PHILIP PAYNE

ROBERT MUSIL'S LIFE, LITERARY WORKS, AND DIARIES

1880, Robert Musil Born in Klagenfurt, Austria

Robert Musil was born into the comfort, and stifling pressures, of a well-to-do Austrian family during the latter years of the reign of Emperor Franz Joseph I. The author's father, Alfred Musil (1846–1924), was appointed in 1891 to the Chair of Mechanical Engineering at the Technical University in Brünn (Brno), a center of administration, manufacturing industry, and culture. Alfred was a reserved man, firmly rational in outlook, without religious belief; he found it difficult to express his feelings. He waited patiently for promotion to a chair in Vienna but the summons did not come. His service to the Empire and his loyalty to the Emperor were rewarded with a hereditary peerage, just before the collapse of Austria-Hungary at the end of the First World War. His wife, Hermine (1853–1924), was made of different stuff—she was the driving force in the family and frequently quarreled with her servants and her wilful son. Alfred could not cope with her and tolerated in "his" household another male, Heinrich Reiter (b. 1856), whose function seems to have been to pacify Hermine. The permanent presence of this "uncle" aroused curiosity and suspicion in young Robert, at the age when the rivalry of another for his mother had begun to impinge as forcefully on the intellect as it had on his emotions.

Aspects of Musil's mental constitution had begun to emerge: a tendency toward critical detachment from and scorn for men; attraction toward women with strong personalities and strong sexual drives; respect for science and rationality qualified by scepticism toward their practitioners; hypersensitivity and an unpredictable temper; a predisposition to speculate about the motives and the private behavior of other people. In early manhood he became increasingly aware of the wider historical framework to his life: the social, cultural, and political momentum toward the dissolution of the Dual Monarchy.

Musil grew up a privileged, protected, lonely child. Vital early experiences were his friendship with Gustl Donath, the son of a colleague of his father, and a relationship with the young daughter of a neighbor that, well before puberty, stirred what he later would identify as sexual desire. His intellect was formidable and much was expected of him. Though under medium height, he was powerfully built; other boys learned to respect his strength and prowess in wrestling. He took pains with his appearance and later had some success with women. In his early teens he had already outgrown his father's attempts to discipline him; when the opportunity to go away to school presented itself he seized it, and his parents' regret was tinged with relief.

Military Boarding School at Eisenstadt (1892–1894) and Mährisch-Weißkirchen (1894–1897)

At cadet school he faced military discipline in a male community, homesickness, the passage through puberty, and—if we take as autobiographical the account of what happens to Törleß, the hero of his first novel—homosexual experiences with fellow pupils and heterosexual ones with at least one local prostitute.

Engineering Studies at Brünn (1898–1901)

Having graduated from Mährisch-Weißkirchen, Musil briefly attended a military college in Vienna from September to December 1897, evidently with the intention of joining the Austrian Army, but left disappointed by the species of human beings he encountered there. He was already a student of human nature, though he was later to develop more sophisticated analytical instruments with which to dissect the people he met. Engineering seemed to offer a potential that he had missed in soldiering, so he enrolled in his father's department at Brünn. Brünn was the location for a twin-track education: during the day he attended lectures in engineering; in the evening and night he read literature and philosophy, went to the theater and to concerts, and visited exhibitions. In compensating for the deficits of his philistine schooling, he overbalanced into the fin de siècle and became morbidly aware of the self. He read Nietzsche, Dostoyevsky, Emerson, Mach, and, to some extent under Nietzsche's influence, began to form relationships with women—some of whom were "eligible," some from the *demimonde*. Burning the candle at both ends and putting his health at risk, he qualified as an engineer in little more than three years.

Assistant at the Technical University in Stuttgart, Germany (1902–1903)

Musil's father, anxious to settle him in a career as an academic engineer, arranged for a distinguished colleague in Stuttgart, Professor Julius Carl von Bach, to take him on as an unpaid assistant. Musil had already become as disenchanted with the outlook of engineers as he had been with that of soldiers; having left his circle of friends behind in Brünn, he found time at Stuttgart hanging heavy on his hands and began work on *Young Törleß* [*Young Torless*], the account of his experiences as a cadet at boarding school. Even as he did so, he became intrigued by the prospect of yet another avenue of activity and persuaded his parents to let him move to Berlin to study philosophy.

*Studies of Psychology and Philosophy at
the University of Berlin (1903–1908)*

In this era the University of Berlin had an outstanding reputation for research; under the direction of Professor Carl Stumpf, it possessed what was then probably the leading department of experimental psychology in the world. Berlin, the capital city of a rapidly growing superpower, provided a wide range of intellectual, social, and cultural stimuli; here Musil built on the knowledge and skills he had acquired in Brünn: earlier fin-de-siècle experiences that had refined his mental powers were systematically extended. He felt acutely the contrasts between the actual and the potential; through study of those around him he became aware of anachronisms. He saw that most contemporary organizations—indeed, the psychic perspectives, the lenses through which contemporaries saw themselves and others—were more primitive than current scientific thinking could tolerate.

Musil, now in his mid-twenties, was still being supported by his parents. The student body in Berlin was relatively small and was recruited from the middle classes. Musil marked his belonging to this world of privilege by his dress and behavior (though the need to support his working-class mistress, Herma Dietz, whom he had brought from Brünn, forced him to economize on food and lodgings). The lectures and seminars he attended consolidated his rigorously scientific approach; they also brought him into contact with other students. Few of them became his friends, but Johannes von Allesch, later to become a university lecturer in psychology, was an exception.

Male acquaintances caused Musil to experience intense rivalry. As a child he had exulted in his physical superiority over Gustl Donath but had been forced to concede the older boy's leadership and powers of imagination. His response to his new friend at university followed the earlier pattern: while

Musil knew that in brute strength the other man was no match for him, von Allesch had scaled heights of aesthetic refinement that he had not attained. (The work under Professor Carl Stumpf helped Musil to identify the psychological processes that underpinned such relationships.) While men tended to bring out a strongly competitive urge in Musil, his relations with women were of a different order. Unlike his father, Musil expected to take the lead in his dealings with women. His tenderness and devotion to his working-class mistress, however, appear exceptional when compared with the attitudes of male contemporaries.

As a young man, his self-esteem was confirmed in part by literary success.

Young Törleß *Published (1906)*

Shortly after he had moved to Berlin Musil's first novel appeared; *Young Törleß* had been rejected by several publishers before it came to the attention of a leading critic, Alfred Kerr, who recommended it for publication. It is an account of critical stages in the life of a cadet at a military boarding school, based on Musil's own experiences. Though it records some details of the setting, it is primarily a study of the inner responses of Törleß to crucial experiences at school; these include stealing, the torture of a fellow pupil, the first sexual experiences with boys and a woman prostitute, awareness of the inadequacy of the concepts adults use to "contain" the world, and breakdown when his oversensitive mental and emotional systems can no longer cope with the demands on them. The novel is extraordinarily mature when set against Musil's earlier attempts at creative writing while studying in Brünn. It helped to consolidate his love of literature even though he continued to think his future lay in higher education. He was about to meet the woman with whom he would spend the rest of his life.

Musil Meets Martha Marcovaldi, née Heimann, a Berlin Artist (1905)

Martha Musil (born on January 21, 1874, and thus nearly seven years older than Musil, born on November 6, 1880) grew up with rich relatives in Berlin after the death of her parents and married her cousin when they were both in their teens; her young husband then died of typhoid fever during their honeymoon in 1895. In 1898 she remarried—her second husband was an Italian—and had two children; Musil was to help her to dissolve this marriage. Martha and Musil became, as far as outer circumstances would allow, physically inseparable; though their relationship was not without tensions and jealousies, they were intellectually and spiritually one organism.

She gave up her painting to devote herself to his career; he handed over to her complete control of the practical running of the household (to the extent that he was often not fully aware of the state of their finances).

Musil Turns Down an Academic Post in Graz (1909)

Musil completed his doctorate and was offered a post by Professor Alexius Meinong, an eminent academic psychologist; he sent a polite letter of rejection, explaining that he wished to devote himself to what he had finally decided was to be his career, namely, literature. The early years of his partnership with Martha were taken up with work on short stories and a play.

Publication of Unions (1911)

The two stories "The Temptation of Quiet Veronica" and "The Perfecting of a Love" in Unions amount to less than one hundred pages of text in all but took more than two years of unremitting work to complete—a rate of productivity that would not improve markedly for the rest of Musil's life. Whereas Young Törleß is based on a retrospective review of states of mind during Musil's own youth, the two stories in Unions analyze the inner world of Martha Musil at decisive phases in her earlier life. In Young Törleß the outer world remains broadly identifiable to the reader; in Unions each narrative is of hermetic intensity, focused in the inchoate, virtually subliminal, feelings of a woman under intense psychosexual pressure. What cost Musil so much effort was the reconstruction of mental states (evidently in continual dialogue with Martha) and the development of a prose based on metaphors that, according to him, are not literary tools but spontaneous projections from the feelings themselves onto the screen of the female subject's psyche. The stories require intense effort on the part of the reader; they were not received with the enthusiasm that had accompanied the publication of Young Törleß, which probably put Musil in a weak position when his parents demanded that he earn his own living. After years of waiting for Martha's divorce to be finalized, they married in 1911 and Musil found a "proper job."

First Period of Employment: Librarianship in Technical University, Vienna, Followed by Editorial Post on Berlin Literary Journal (1911–1914)

Vienna and Berlin are the two cities where Musil spent the major part of his life; they are also the axis of his interpretation of early twentieth-century civilization. He gave up the librarianship because it thwarted his commitment to literature; the second post—working for the publisher Samuel Fischer reviewing current literary production in Germany—did, however, offer both security and stimulation. Now living in Berlin (a city mounting a challenge to be the intellectual capital of Europe), married to a woman who satisfied his needs for love and companionship, in a job that brought him into contact with leading figures from contemporary intellectual and literary circles, with work progressing on a brilliant play, *The Enthusiasts*, Musil seemed to be on the threshold of the success his family had always expected of him. Then World War I broke out and Musil was torn from urban life, from intellectual dialogue, from the opportunity for sustained literary work, and from the woman he loved; stationed with his unit in the South Tyrol he awaited the outbreak of hostilities that came when Italy declared war in 1915.

Military Service in World War I

War seemed to offer the opportunity for a sea-change in European civilization; Musil recorded the initial euphoria, but the experience of the state of war itself was of boredom interspersed with moments of pure panic.[1] Musil was decorated for bravery and rose to the rank of captain. War brought him back into close proximity with the kind of men whom he had known at boarding school and it set up contacts with women "off limits" in local peasant communities. War at the front line meant being deprived of the comforts of civilization; it gave opportunities for casual sex but not for sustained writing—almost all he could manage was to record impressions in the small diary-notebook he carried with him; when Musil was later moved out of immediate danger to the Supreme Army Command for the South West Front in Bolzano he saw at first hand arrogance, incompetence, and intrigue in elite Austrian society to which hitherto he had not had access. Many years later it would provide experiences and ideas for scenes in his major work, *The Man without Qualities*. In private Musil criticized the social life around him but he knew how to behave in company and gained the respect and trust of senior officers; this smoothed the transition after the war to a responsible and well-paid post connected with the education of soldiers returning to civilian life. He later turned down the opportunity to join the Austrian civil service, preferring freelance literary work and the freedom that he needed for writing. He would, later still, have cause to regret the choice of creative work at the expense of security.

Peacetime Viennese society was at war with itself: the House of Hapsburg had fallen; Vienna, once capital of an empire embracing many countries and nationalities, was now the overlarge administrative center of the democratic rump which was republican Austria. But the difficulties faced by the new republic were as strong a stimulant to intellectual and cultural activity as the slow dissolution of imperial order in the prewar epoch had been.[2]

In the years after World War I Musil found support in a small circle of authors and intellectuals most of whom are now largely forgotten.[3] This loose-knit group provided an informal forum for debate and its members helped one another to find outlets for their work. In this phase of his life Musil wrote short pieces of polished prose—essays, reviews, literary sketches, and so on, which were informed by his very wide interests; from his "home" fields of engineering, psychology, and philosophy he had extended his reading into mathematics and many other branches of science, the arts, politics, religion and mysticism, anthropology, sociology, the philosophy of sport, and educational theory. His wide-ranging enquiries were pursued as so many avenues to understanding the individuals whose interests had spawned the research in question. From Musil's perspective each individual provides, through the life he or she leads, a kind of spontaneous "biological" commentary on the value of his or her contribution to the collective sum of understanding, skill, and knowledge in contemporary society. Musil does not simply study individual intellectual activity on its own terms; he asks the kind of questions the individual probably would have wished to avoid. What life does the moral philosopher actually lead? What example, what practical education, does the educational theorist provide for his own son? How does a lady of high culture treat her maid? Does the engineer make existential decisions with a slide rule in his hand and if not, why not? The answers to these questions are then worked into the fabric of the given fictional account.

In the postwar years the decision to earn his living from literature had at first seemed sensible. His work was in demand for newspapers and journals; though he had lost some of the freedom he had enjoyed as a young man he could move in the best social circles, as a leading reviewer he attended many cultural events, he had a steady supply of interesting books to digest, found time for stimulating discussion in the salons and cafés of Vienna and, not infrequently, Berlin too; and he was invited to soirées by the rich and famous. He had completed the play he started before World War I.

Musil's Play, The Enthusiasts, Published (1921)

The play was, within its genre, as uncompromising as *Unions* had been in prose narrative.[4] It involved imaginative extemporizing on experiences of Martha and Musil before the war—the central protagonists look back nostalgically on their largely unsuccessful attempts to break free from the world of middle-class values. They try to identify what inhibits the full development of personality, what blocks access to human wellsprings of profound feeling and condemns contemporaries to reproduce tired stereotypes of behavior rather than follow the promptings of creative impulse. The overtly lightweight and, in places, farcical plot centers on elopement, male and female jealousies, and outbursts from neurotics. Musil demands of his actors that they unlearn theatrical and extra-theatrical convention—it is the very *theatricality* of bourgeois life that Musil has in his sights—and that they speak, with detached passion, lines whose powerful imagery unmasks twentieth-century ritual behavior. A few performances of the play were put on despite Musil's protests about the substandard production—it was not a success in Musil's lifetime, though posthumous productions have prompted, at times, an ecstatic response.

It was not simply as a reviewer, essayist, and dramatist that Musil achieved success.

Publication of Three Women (1924)

The titles of this collection of short stories refer to women whom Musil loved: "Tonka" stood for his mistress, Herma; "Grigia" for the Italian peasant woman with whom he had an affair during the war; "Die Portuguiesin" was black-haired Martha in disguise. And the title might almost as well have been *Four Women*, since the mother of the male protagonist—modeled on Hermine Musil—plays such a vital role in the narrative of "Tonka." These simple and profound works deal, in the context of love affairs, with Musil's sense that two radically different modes of perception exist, one largely within the "male" domain, the other more "female." Each story charts the subtle interplay of reason and suspicion in love affairs; through the stimulus of love skepticism meets a yielding openness to the world and crosses the threshold of mystical oneness with the totality of created things. In the narratives the male "hero," initially embodying the rational, is initiated into another mode of experience. In the relatively brief span of each story Musil's prose achieves a level of poetic intensity that is scarcely surpassed anywhere else in his writing—as such, *Three Women* offers a route into his *oeuvre* accessible even to those who remain unmoved by his intellectual concerns.

For the full account of these concerns readers have to turn elsewhere. After the war Musil had planned to write a series of novels, some of them broadly realist, others critical-satirical. Eventually these merged into a single narrative that is modernist, realist, critical, and satirical by turns; this came to be called *The Man without Qualities*.[5] But the tension generated in the author by the expectation that a major novel would soon appear gave rise to the conflict that had occurred when he first tried to earn a living: work on a major literary project was incompatible with attention to minor matters even if these included earning money to support a family. In the course of the 1920s, as he began to focus more and more on the novel, the income from other sources declined and shortage of money became an increasing source of stress, especially whenever the date of publication was put back to give Musil time to meet the intolerably high standards he had set for his work. (In fact, Musil consulted a psychoanalyst about the inhibitions that prevented him from working.) When the novel appeared it was incomplete.

Publication of the First Two Volumes of The Man without Qualities *(1930 and 1932)*

As confirmed by the responses among the cultured reading public, this was no ordinary novel. Musil's major work may appear retrospective and historical—the novel is set in Austria in 1913—but Musil in fact had his eyes on contemporary matters: what was wrong with, and what could be done about, European civilization in this century. The work was designed in four parts:

Part I: a small set of introductory chapters entitled "A Kind of Opening";

Part II: "The Same Kind of Things Happen Again"—a retrospective view of a cross section of high society in the months immediately before World War I;

Part III: "Into the Millennium"—the account of a love affair set in the context of, yet separate from, the above-mentioned society (this part was not finished);

Part IV: "A Kind of End" (this part was planned but never written).

Ulrich von—, the central protagonist, a man of independent means, lives in a city that merges features of Berlin and Vienna; it is a kind of model designed to facilitate ironic detachment on the part of the reader-observer. This reluctant "hero" is and is not the author himself; he has explored different careers—soldier, engineer, academic in the mode of his creator—but unlike Musil he is removed from financial cares, has no family, and has long abandoned literary activity. At the outset of the novel he has resolved to take what he calls a year's "leave from life" in order to decide what he ought to make of the rest of his stay on this earth. His intellectual retreat is under constant assault—this is the source of delightful narrative play, particularly in part II of the novel when his mistress interrupts his reflections and he becomes hopelessly embroiled in an enterprise of stunning inconsequentiality; this involves intricate and often comical plans to celebrate the forthcoming seventieth anniversary of the Emperor's accession to the throne with a whole year of activities. This "stage business" brings the intellectual into contact with the stage world of Austrian high society that he would dearly like to avoid. Part I and part II of the work present Ulrich in a range of different contexts: in his private reflections on himself and the state of the world; interacting with men and women who represent, collectively, a typology of human activities (an aristocrat, a Prussian-Jewish man of business, intellectuals of differing persuasions, a woman who runs a literary salon, a banker, a civil servant, an officer, and many others); recreating in private psychological experiment the inner world of a murderer; associating with childhood friends including a woman who, in the course of the narrative, will slide into total insanity. It is only when the hero's father dies and he leaves the metropolis to deal with the family affairs that he has the opportunity to break free. In his father's house he meets his sister, a beautiful woman some six years younger than himself; they fall in love. Musil spent the last decade of his life working on this, part III of the novel; it explores the relationship of man and woman with unparalleled subtlety. Only one other important work appeared during Musil's lifetime.

Publication of Pre-Posthumous Writings (1936)

The title of this collection of short pieces of prose Musil selected from his many contributions to journals and newspapers expresses the author's concern about the state of his health, which had never been particularly robust. During an extended stay in Berlin from 1931 to 1933 Musil had watched the rise of Nazism at first hand (in Vienna in 1937 he made a celebrated speech entitled "On Stupidity" that the largely Jewish audience saw as an attack on the developments in Germany) and in 1938, after the Anschluß had grafted his native Austria onto the Third Reich, he left for exile in Switzerland. He continued to work diligently on the novel, and appeared to the last to be confident the work could be completed.

Geneva: Musil Dies of a Stroke on 15 April 1942

Musil's Diaries.   From around the age of 17 (about 1899) until a short while before his death in 1942 Robert Musil made notes in a series of journals; these have come to be known as his *Diaries*, though they contain many entries that are not usually kept in diaries, such as lecture notes, summaries of books, reflections on many different issues, essay drafts, literary sketches and plans, and other materials. The *Diaries*, edited by Adolf Frisé, were published in Germany in 1976; the English translation is based on a selection of about two-fifths of the German original.[6]

Running through this introduction, separated from my text through square brackets, I have added a few extracts from the *Diaries* themselves—I have thus tried to give the impression of Musil providing his own "commentary."

Fiction Out of Truth.   One of the strongest arguments for reading Musil's *Diaries* is that they are a storehouse for material that he intended to use in his creative writing. Perhaps the term *creative writer* is misleading when applied to Musil. Though he was more deeply concerned with the internal laws and processes of literary work than most novelists, he did not invent fictions and create imaginary people; he wanted rather to fit words closely to *existing* creation. His work is based firmly on experience—his own experience, or experiences borrowed from the lives of family and friends, from people he meets in Vienna, or Berlin, or on holiday, or at war, or wherever; and he also makes use of experience "at third hand," exploiting the writings of other authors. Musil would attempt to reconstitute the character and psyche of such authors from the traces in their writings of their attitudes and idiosyncrasies as human beings.

Such a figure is Walther Rathenau, son of the founder of the German electrical concern, AEG. Rathenau's range of interests and talents was extraordinary: successful businessman in his own right, polymath, intellectual, and, at the time of his murder by an extremist, German Foreign Minister. Though Musil appears to have met Rathenau only once, the encounter left a powerful impression—Musil made an intensive study of Rathenau's writing and evidently, too, via a kind of creative "daydreaming" (which we shall examine further in more detail), thought-felt himself into the mind and beneath the skin of the other man; thus, in MwQ, Musil was able to reproduce this unusual and imposing figure—barely disguised at all—in the character Paul Arnheim. In the novel, Arnheim, the Jew, is set against Musil's persona, Ulrich—Prussian drive and self-confidence meet Austrian style and subtlety. [Musil was gratified when he found out that Rathenau did indeed possess characteristics that he had identified "in Arnheim mode" while thinking out the relevant sections of MwQ: *The correct anticipation of unknown reactions of* Rathenau *from known ones of* Arnheim *is not a mystery but something like the prophetic gift of a correct theory.*][7] Or we might also follow Musil's reconstruction of the educational theorist Georg

Kerschensteiner through from the diary record of Musil's reading of a particular work to the point where Kerschensteiner emerges in the plot of
MwQ as Hagauer, the husband of Agathe, the hero's sister. Agathe is herself
the product of an analogous albeit much more intimate and complex reliv-
ing of experiences by Martha. The reader of the *Diaries* relives intellectual
and emotional processes of Musil's creative writing.

In these *Diaries* we have documentary evidence of the thoroughness
with which Musil prepared the ground for his fiction. He was, as we have
seen, a writer of epic slowness of production—the few dozen pages of
Unions took two years to write. (They present excessive intellectual and
emotional demands on the reader. Alfred Kerr, who had been so impressed
by Musil's novel, *Young Törleß*, rejected them.) Musil's speed of composition, measured at least in pages of draft, did increase and his writing became much less hermetic than in *Unions* but he often could not bring
himself to release his drafts for publication, and would start revising
again. Even before writing *Young Törleß* Musil had started work on what
he often simply called "der Roman" ("the Novel") that would ultimately,
after several abandoned attempts (successive drafts were entitled *The Spy*,
The Redeemer, *The Twin Sister*), become *The Man without Qualities*.
Shortly after World War I Musil mapped out no less than what he called
"The Twenty Works"—novels that would have been a veritable Austrian
"Comédie humaine" if they had ever appeared. But the first of what can
only with sad irony be called this "series" was postponed from one year
to the next (in November 1924, for instance, Musil wrote to Kafka saying that he expected his novel to be published the following spring), and
even though sections of MwQ did eventually appear in 1930 the work
was, as we know, unfinished at his death. The main barrier to publication
was Musil's striving for perfection. Having prepared the ground with ex-
acting studies of characters, ideas, context, Musil would map out a chapter to fit into the novel at the point that he had reached (often making
notes on what he had already written so that he would be in control of the
complex of themes that were to be alluded to, developed, modified,
rounded off in the new segment), would slowly write his way in, break off
in dissatisfaction after so many paragraphs or pages, then start all over
again (carefully filing away what he had rejected because it perhaps contained something that might come in handy later!). And this process
would sometimes go on for three, four, seven, eight, or more reiterations
until he had managed to create something that, in his own hypercritical
judgment, was half decent and could go off to the publisher. Even after
that stage the creative process had not finished—the galley proofs would
often trigger yet another revision so extensive that one can imagine the

dismay of the printers when their careful work was returned as palimpsest virtually obliterated by Musil's alterations.

The relevance of this process to the *Diaries* is indirect but important. Musil was unusually sensitive to the eyes of others resting on him. When one examines virtually any photograph of Musil, it is palpable how the author is uncomfortable at the present scrutiny from the photographer and the anticipation of exposure to those others who, in an unspecified future, would inspect the photograph itself. Even a visit to a café to meet friends might entail a lengthy wait for an acceptable seat to become available—one of the few that provided a panoramic view of what was going on around him but so positioned that the fortress of the self would not be vulnerable to an approach from an unexpected angle. Elias Canetti described the tension that emanated from Musil in the following words: "Musil was [...] always equipped for defense and attack. [His posture] may have seemed like a suit of armor but in fact it was more an outer skin. What separated him from the world was not something he had put on, it had grown there."[8] Similar considerations had evidently led to the choice of the Viennese flat where he spent some seventeen years, many of them devoted to work on MwQ. Adolf Frisé described this as follows: "Flat 8 in the building at Rasumofskygasse 20 [...] in the III District; formerly servants' quarters, over three-hundred-year-old, stone winding staircase, now under preservation order, outside, in each storey, the faucet, enamel washbasin, the larder-cupboard set into the wall, no entrance hall, one entered via a succession of several rooms, and right at the end was the study. In the middle the desk. [...] Martha Musil 'fenced him off,' this was what he wanted, every noise was perceived as an invasion."[9]

Musil appears to have felt that writing for publication was worse even than exposing face, clothing, posture to a cameraman. It was exposure of a more intimate kind—of the mind at work. In the *Diaries*, Musil works not for the public but for himself, his critical threshold is lowered, he writes fluently, spontaneously. He is no longer the buttoned-up, tautly organized author of essays, or reviews, or chapters of the novel, hyperaware that the eyes of the Viennese or Berlin reading public are upon him; this is Musil in relaxed, private mode—he quite often makes mistakes, misspells, gets names wrong; he occasionally lets himself go to the extent that he produces misshapen sentences, his syntax is awkward, even ungrammatical—in short, he is reassuringly human when no one is looking! Musil himself knew the benefits of spontaneity, knew that his writing was at its most powerful when feelings, perceptions, ideas were fresh. [*Something is well-written if, after some time, it appears to one as the work of a stranger—one would be incapable of writing it that way a second time.*][10] As impressions flood in on

Musil and he grapples with feelings and thoughts that, even now, possess him, his daimon dictates passages of force and beauty. Into the little notebooks that he carried with him on service on the Italian front, for instance, was poured all the energy of a writer in his mid-thirties at the height of his powers, torn away from work on novel and play. Given the quality of works that were the fruit of a slow process of literary ripening—*The Enthusiasts, Three Women, The Man without Qualities* itself—it may seem heresy to suggest that there is another Musil, kept in check by inhibitions, who had the capacity for a quite different kind of creativity. We glimpse this Musil in diary passages that are based on observations of Alice Donath, wife of his boyhood friend Gustl—these seem so fresh, so direct and vital when compared with sections where Alice's literary double, Clarisse, is at the center of attention—though in the latter writing, the requirements of the novel as a whole, the weight of internal allusion carried by every statement, necessarily slow down the flow.

Diarist as Observer of History, Society, Politics. The *Diaries* are not only to be seen as fine writing in their own right and as source for fiction; their importance is also extra-literary—they breathe life into our awareness of the things that preoccupied men and women of earlier epochs. Musil's observations and reflections on love, sex, morals, philosophy, psychology, politics, society, art, culture, science, human relations, and so on claim our attention in and of themselves. Some passages have an immediacy that makes a historical moment present to us in the most vivid way. [One of Musil's entries in the *Diaries* is an effective analogy for this observation: *On the Pincio, at the back, lie two sarcophagus lids of stone. Stretched out full length on them are the couple for whom they were made. One sees many such coffin lids in Rome, but in no museum or church do they make the impression as they do here under the trees where they rest as if on some trip into the country, seeming just to have woken from a brief siesta that has lasted for 2000 years. They support themselves on their elbows, looking at each other. (All that is missing is the basket with cheese, fruit and wine . .) The woman has her hair done in little curls—she is about to rearrange them—according to the very latest fashion before she fell asleep. And they look at each other {, smiling}, a long look without end. This true, obliging, bourgeois, loving look that has survived the millennia lasts for ever. It was sent out in Ancient Rome and in the year 1913 meets the eye. I am not surprised at all that it lasts till now. It thus becomes, not stone-hard, but human.*[11]

Musil was one of a generation that replaced the moral correctness and the stuffy hypocrisy of bourgeois parental attitudes with the aestheticism and urge to experiment of the fin de siècle. [He compared and contrasted the relationship of his to the younger generation with the relationship between his generation and that of his parents: *My generation was anti-moral or amoral because our fathers talked of morality and behaved in a philistine and immoral fashion. The present generation of fathers talked of the immorality (of the war) and behaved in a philistine and moral fashion (shoulder to shoulder). So, from the same oppositional stance that we had, children today are moral, but want people to be serious about morality.*][12] The outbreak of World War I brought a glimpse of what living might be like under a different dispensation, under conditions of sharing and giving, but the euphoria that swept over the rigid hierarchies of German and Austrian society soon gave way to harsh discipline, stress, privations, and daily casualties: [*The lists of those fallen in battle: . . ."dead" . . . "dead" . . . "dead" . . . each printed like that, one after the other—impression overwhelming.*][13] Musil looks for something substantial—something in, so to speak, the DNA of potential behavior itself—from which more lasting and fulfilling human and social relationships could be built. This urge is, in his own understanding of the terms, both ethical and moral: "ethical" in that it involves the discovery of human experiences so powerful that they demand radical change; "moral" in that such experiences require a substantial corpus of reflection to expound and legitimize them. Musil hoped that the war—the First World War—would detonate an explosion of social change; immediately after the war he worked with the radical activist Robert Müller in a group that tried to set up a publishing network through which intellectuals would influence the development of a new order in society. Both Müller and Musil were convinced that the old order was utterly redundant. But Müller committed suicide when it became clear that the anticapitalist venture had failed, and Musil then reverted to being an author-spectator on the sidelines of society and politics. [*Role of the creative writer "in politicis." Powerless onlooker.*][14] Occasionally he made speeches that had some impact. At an international conference of writers in Paris in the mid-thirties his liberal views did not find favor with the organizers, who were looking for a united socialist front against Nazism; in Vienna in 1937 his address "On Stupidity" found a more receptive response: one of the audience was a young Jew, Bruno Kreisky, who was deeply impressed by what Musil said and who later, as a post–World War II Chancellor of the Republic of Austria, was in a position to promote Musil's works and reputation. (The Nazis banned Musil's books and in 1938 he was forced into exile in Switzerland where, as the *Diaries* record, his financial problems deteriorated into ongoing crisis.) Though there is no means of assessing it objectively, Musil's influence on later generations of writers and intellectuals has undoubtedly been considerable. It is not only the German-speaking countries who need people in Musil's mold—he was open-minded but clear in judgment; critical of others but self-critical, too; both rational and passionate; willing to experiment but with profound understanding of the need for continuities; he was a vivisectionist of men and women who had first taken the scalpel to himself. This mind-set is apparent even when we shift the focus from the public sphere to the most private realm.

Love, Sexuality, Mysticism.   Musil's parents' injunctions on sexuality were problematical, perhaps even traumatic, though evidently well-meant. [*I know that I was always made to put my arms over the bed-covers when I went to sleep, and if I am not mistaken I was made to fear each and every contact with the region of the belly as something sinful. It may be that it was this that made every thought of the same parts of my parents' bodies quite horrific to me. And I believe that these precepts of moral hygiene came from my mother. [. . .] I was very easily influenced and all of this certainly left a very deep impression on me. Today it appears to me as much too powerful an intervention as if, over a long period, it had left me with internal injuries; it appears as terror.*][15] But his parents were not able to exert corresponding influence on him when he returned home after boarding school and began to take an interest in the nightlife of Brünn. [*21.II. Went to the variety theater with Jacques and Hannak. Jacques—what a character—no one could beat him. One of the chanteuses wasn't bad-looking. Underwear all in grey. [. . .] Flirted a little with the girl [. . .]. If she had come to our table I'd certainly have behaved decently toward her. [. . .] While I was deep in conversation with Hannak, Jacques beckoned to her and went outside. In the garden he had his way with her—genius!*][16] But he is no hedonist: he subjects each sensuous and sensual experience to careful examination. Even in the *Diaries* the writing is frequently more than simply a record—often Musil spins something out beyond the experience itself according to the principle "What would happen then if . . . . "; the actual happening may become a stepping-stone to speculative narrative and thus a training ground for the novelist.

The gathering of such experience is not without risk: Musil is infected with syphilis—a course of treatment effects a complete cure, but it may be that premature baldness was a side effect of the crude but powerful medicines then in use. While still a student, his allowance stretches—just—to keeping a mistress. Musil's grandmother had been looked after in the last stages of her life by Herma Dietz, a working-class girl, but when the patient died, the family dismissed the nurse. At this time Musil entered in a notebook, without any explanation, the simple statement: *She doesn't say "Yes," nor "No," nor*

"*Thank you*";[17]—it records how Herma reacts—or rather does not react—to Musil's offer of protection that led directly into their relationship. In "Tonka," the short story that grew from the affair, the sentence reappears—it gives expression to Musil's sense of wonder and astonishment at the way his proposal of support is accepted without a word. How different Herma is from him! In their affair Musil transcends the stereotype of the young bourgeois exploiting a girl from the lower classes. Tenderness and concern if anything outweigh sexual passion. It is certainly the case that Musil's jealousy and manic suspicions about a rival for her love intensify to the pitch of obsession when he discovers that she has a venereal disease and that, as doctors assure him, he cannot have been the source of this infection; however, despite her manifest infidelity to him, he remains faithful to her. It would be particularly gratifying to report that the love affair only ended—like the story "Tonka"—with the girl's death, but there is disagreement among scholars whether Herma died or was quietly set aside. Another affair, this time when Musil was a soldier whom war had parted from his wife, also leads into a story, "Grigia"; we feel through Musil's prose the pull of mutual interest between the local women and these alien soldiers and anticipate its adulterous outcome. [*The mistress squats in a field of potatoes. You know she has nothing on but two skirts, the dry earth touches her flesh (not unpleasant and unusual). Through her slim rough fingers runs dry earth. That is not the maid who with 20 others harvests turnips. That is the free peasant woman who has grown up out of the grey, parched earth.*][18] But, as in the relationship with Herma Dietz, here too the sexual is balanced by wonder at the power of other forces—the husband's soul-spirit feels the presence of the distant wife as "Fernliebe," "love at a distance." Reunion-union with her is central both to the story—where, incidentally, the name of Musil's lover is unchanged—and to the account in the *Diaries*. But even the most intense feelings are short-lived. [[. . .] *the mysticism is gone; does not keep in the city.*][19] How, Musil asked himself, could the transitory become permanent? (The literary works prove that, for Musil, this question was not rhetorical.) Later diary entries record flirtations, risqué conversations, sexual speculations,[20] but no more affairs.[21]

As we have seen, the borders between sexuality and love are fluid. As he makes entries in the *Diaries* at various stages throughout his life Musil looks back to events from the period of early manhood. Chiffres appear for things that intrigue and puzzle him. Many time he refers to "Valerie"—the name becomes a symbol of love as purest ecstasy. Evidence of who this was has only recently emerged.[22] When not yet twenty, toward the end of the last decade of the nineteenth century while on holiday in the mountains, Musil met a woman some eight years older than himself and fell passionately in love with her. This experience surpassed all those that had gone before. In the mountains Musil carried his copy of *Also sprach Zarathustra*; Nietzsche, mountains, love for a beautiful older woman—what was Musil to *do* about this, what could he *make* of it all? Following Nietzsche's prescription he turned his back on the impedimenta of compromise, pettiness, and disappointment that sexual fulfillment in an affair might well involve and returned to the valleys and to Brünn with ecstatic love undefiled and safely locked in heart and memory. This experience, thinly disguised as a love affair with a major's wife, resurfaces in MwQ.

Musil's mother appears in the *Diaries* and his creative work on several occasions. From earliest childhood, love and what in retrospect is identified as sexual stirrings focus on a fur that belonged to the mother. [*I recollect vividly a second memory attached to smell: that of the chinchilla fur that belonged to my mother. A smell like snow in the air mingled with a little camphor. I believe that there is a sexual element in this memory.*][23] Musil's mother was a much stronger presence than the father,[24] who tolerated her liaison with Heinrich Reiter, their permanent houseguest. Musil inherited her sensuality and emotional intensity, and there are hints of latent incestuous desire. [Commenting on his relations with Herma Dietz, Musil notes: *There is a hidden parallel between Mother and H[erma]. Mother was also a girl once and she would have suited R[obert Musil] better than H. did. [. . .] R. feels that he would have been happier with her than with H.*][25] Once, as a young man, Musil inadvertently caught a glimpse of his mother's part-naked body on a diving board; his response was an anger whose intensity suggests an undercurrent of emotion that, surprisingly in one of such intellectual curiosity, he apparently did not explore further. [*I was probably 18 or 19 years of age already when, during a summer stay on the Wörthersee (in Velden), I had the following experience: I happened to be on the diving board of the men's swimming academy while my mother was standing on the diving board in the neighboring women's baths looking out over the lake. She was in her bathing-robe and had already finished her swim. She had not noticed how close I was. Without being aware of the movement at all she opened her robe in order to wrap it round her in a different way, and for a moment I saw her standing naked. She must have been at that time a little over 40 years of age and she was very white and full and beautifully made. Although, to this day, it fills me with a certain appreciation, far more vivid is the shame-ridden and, I believe, angry horror that transfixed me then.*][26]

Musil was attracted to mature women; Martha, born in 1874, fell into this category. Dark, attractive, passionate, Martha possessed the full figure that contemporary fashion favored and that also corresponded to Musil's taste in women. Though Martha and Musil were deeply involved with each other from virtually the first meeting, Martha had a brief sexual encounter with another man while away from Berlin. Musil's "revenge," if this is how it could be interpreted, was to interrogate Martha on her feelings before, during, and after her infidelity, making of them the extraordinary internal narrative of the short story "The Perfecting of Love" in which the woman protagonist feels her love for the distant partner reach its climax in the very act of adulterous betrayal. Musil's later affair with the Italian peasant woman is, at one level, a squaring of the marital account, at another, an exploration of feelings that parallel those in the earlier story (to judge by the narrative of "Grigia," in which they are set down). In Martha Musil had found his physical-spiritual other half. [Musil's survey of achievements in the period 1905–1910 concludes with the words: *Martha does not belong in this account—she isn't anything that I have gained or achieved; she is something that I have become and that has become "I."*][27] Martha gave up her painting; Musil set about negotiating her divorce from her second husband. Musil was later concerned with earning the money to support his new household while Martha became the keeper of the family purse and even paid the bills in the coffeehouses they frequented. Though never jealous of the man whom Martha had divorced with his help, Musil felt rivalry with her dead first husband with whom she had shared a union of youthful passion. [*The thought occurs to me: who, in the world beyond, has priority: Fritz or me? Why me then?*][28] So self-evident was the strength of the bond between himself and Martha that Musil even permits himself the luxury of daydreaming about what it would be like if they were to part. [*Walk along the Hauptallee. Martha was in a bad frame of mind and reproached me quite unnecessarily, which left me cold. "You will leave me," [she said] "Then I'll have no one. I shall kill myself. I shall leave you." In a momentary state of weakness, Martha slipped far beneath herself to the level of a jealous or neglected woman with a fierce temper. In personal terms, of course, this has no significance for our relationship. But I switched off this reservation, so to speak, and gave myself over to the impressions that would arise if this were a time of disappointment. And the juxtaposition [sic] was roughly as follows: I can't stand that, etc. Pressing matters—yes, she is amoral and you are immoral; and that amounts, in terms of the relationship, to something bourgeois. Your immorality has blinded me and is, fundamentally, of a bourgeois kind. Fascinating to watch how, in fits and starts, such ideas take on a clearer shape while one is listening to pleas and reproaches. (Of course, I personally knew all along, that this was only a game.)*][29] The diary entry in question was recovered some years after Martha Musil's death, sewn into the lining of her coat—one wonders whether she wanted to suppress the evidence of Musil's trifling with her feelings, or whether, by contrast, she treasured the lines as testimony of his actual fidelity.

If it were possible to request, retrospectively, that Musil add some more entries to his *Diaries*, then one might ask for more evidence of the ways in which Martha assisted with his creative work. It is accepted that many references to Agathe, the heroine of MwQ, are built from Musil's exchange of psychic evidence with Martha; various themes of his writing—"sister," "twin sister," even "Siamese twin" are evidently inspired by this symbiotic sharing with his wife. But Martha had another female rival besides Musil's mother: some four years before Musil's birth his mother had given birth to a daughter who died before he was born. [*Elsa [. . .] my sister [. . .] was the object of a kind of cult of mine [. . .] I sometimes used to wonder what it would be like if she were still alive [. . .] Did I put myself in her place?*][30] The "cult" was refined into a wider, representative search, through the medium of creative writing, for the path to human fulfillment, for individual oneness, with its wider implications for social harmony. (In MwQ the hero realizes that the fuel of self-regard has run out of his life, that he has fallen out of love with himself; Agathe, whom he meets shortly afterward, he recognizes as his philautia—that proper sense of one's own worth and birthright to existence.)

The loss of self-regard is perhaps connected with the way in which the cult of contemporary manhood demands that certain qualities be developed—the kind of objectivity, self-discipline, asceticism of body[31] and mind that are (sometimes!) found in the professions that Musil had followed as soldier, engineer, academic psychologist. But the expansion of this side of a human being locks away the potential of what Musil called the "non-ratioïd" side in which the bonds of individuality burst open, the soul breaks loose into undifferentiated feeling and merges with the totality of things. This is the realm of what Musil called "the other condition."[32] The "Valerie experience" is one of those exceptional instances where Musil, this critical/self-critical, inhibited, circumspect, anxious male, found himself lifted—involuntarily—into the other realm. It is significant that the experience is associated with a woman, for the women in Musil's life tend to be those who provide access to the non-ratioïd. One of the earlier attempts to come to terms with this world was through his reading of the work of a Swedish essayist, Ellen Key. [*At night in the coffeehouse I read an essay by E[llen] Key that had a profound effect on me—she speaks with the voice of my own past. Here is to be found a line of thinking that I once followed, the Valerie tradition!*][33] So vital to his understanding of the dimensions of human experience was the realm that she (and Emerson and Maeterlinck) had helped to open up for him that he felt it essential to protect it from exploitation.

Often when Diotima, the "grande dame" in MwQ, launches into rhetoric her sentences are collages of unattributed quotations from Key and Maeterlinck, but her mysticism is skin-deep, aura not essence. She condemns herself by choosing not the Musil persona, Ulrich, as her partner, but his rival, Arnheim, who is inwardly as hollow as she is. Musil intended that Ulrich would ultimately turn his back on the shallow world that Diotima and Arnheim represented and enter the non-ratioïd realm of sister Agathe.

What was Ulrich—and, by extension, his creator—trying to escape? Perhaps, quite simply, himself. There is a strong narcissistic side to Musil that the readers of the creative works and the *Diaries* cannot fail to notice. It would be difficult to imagine how Musil could have avoided developing in this direction: the claustrophobic security of his home, fond parents smothering their one remaining child with their concern, Musil's hypersensitivity, hyperintelligence, his domineering spirit, the expectations that weighed down on him [*My whole family set great store by my talents and when I was ten years of age I myself believed that I would be very famous by the age of twenty*],[34] the time he spent on his own as a child—all these predisposed to introspection, to self-preoccupation. [*A childhood trait was my brooding in the melancholy of the room.*][35] Some commentators have tended to see almost the whole corpus of Musil's writing from this angle. But there is another, and probably fairer, way to view his attitude—as a long passage from self-preoccupation into contact with others and the world outside.

Strategies for Observation and the Process of Maturing.   We saw Musil first as fin-de-siècle Narcissus; later, in Stuttgart and Berlin, as the young novelist he becomes detached from his younger self through the practice of creative autobiography; in the Institute of Psychology in Berlin under Carl Stumpf he takes another decisive step to maturity. In some ways, this latter stage is the most distinctive. Musil firmly resolved to use, as far as possible, only empirical evidence importing the ideal of scientific precision into his creative work. At one level, such an ideal is unattainable—no reader of fiction can repeat the author's "experiment" (whether this is short story or diary entry) and check the "findings"; but at least Musil, as author, could take with him into the given literary enterprise that sense of scientific integrity and hard-headedness that had emerged in the years he had spent under Carl Stumpf at a time when the University of Berlin was one of the leading scientific research centers in the world. [*It occurred to me, as I was listening to a lecture by an assistant of [. .] Schlick[36] [. . .] how, in Stumpf's institute, everything was done in a far more precise manner. All credit for the sober, scientific atmosphere was due to this teacher and it was not by chance that his were the most important pupils.*][37] Stumpf taught his students to conduct psychological research via introspection and we can detect the effects of this teaching throughout Musil's *Diaries*. [*On association: I go outside, see that the stairway is wet and register a sense of unease. It is only then that it occurs to me that I have forgotten to put my galoshes on in the hallway.*]³⁸ Stumpf's effect on young Musil-Narcissus was to make him use his self-preoccupation for general human research. [Many years later, Musil is watching how mourning steals up on him: *On the psychology of deep feelings. About a year on from the days when Mama lay dying; we are in Brünn, with Heinrich describing exactly what went on a year ago today. "This is how it was, for three whole days." My feelings in real, deep turmoil; for the outside world, too, in deep mourning. Toward the end of the actual day of her death—Mama died in the following night—I become aware that it is almost more than I can take. I did not force myself to go through this mourning, it came about quite naturally, and yet it is like being bent double all the time, something that starts to become unbearable.*³⁹ Musil is recording a suffering common to human beings: this emerges spontaneously without his expecting it.] In other words, Narcissus metamorphoses into a more neutral human subject. This provides access to various inner worlds. [One of the entries from the *Diaries* that Musil included, with only minor changes, in his *Pre-Posthumous Papers*—under the untranslatable title of "Hellhörigkeit"⁴⁰—starts as follows: *Toward the end of November: I have gone to bed early, I feel that I have caught a slight chill, perhaps I've even got a slight temperature. The electric light is on; I look at the ceiling or the curtain over the door to the balcony. You began to undress when I had already finished doing so; I am waiting. I can only hear you. Incomprehensibly walking back and forth; in this part of the room, in that. You come and lay something on your bed; what can it be? You open the cupboard, put something in or take something out; I hear it shutting again. You put hard objects onto the table, others onto the marble slab of the chest. You are constantly in motion. Then I recognize the familiar sounds of hair being let down and brushed. Then cascades of water falling into the washbasin. Before this, clothes being slipped off; now the same again; it is incomprehensible to me how many clothes you take off.* [. . .]⁴¹ Of course, even here Musil is pursuing his enquiries beyond the range of academic/scientific work.] In other contexts, the technique of introspection is extended into realms that Stumpf would not have anticipated—into the regions of a meta-self where the dark inner world of a murderer, Moosbrugger—a figure present both in the earlier novel drafts and in MwQ—is brought into being. [It has been shown that the Moosbrugger figure is derived in part from newspaper reports on murders that captured the imagination of the public;⁴² however, the force of Musil's characterization is evidently taken from internal experimentation: *Unleash all* criminals *that live within us. The rage of Moosbrugger to plunge a curved knife into someone's belly is comprehensible when one sees these dolled-up forms go wandering past.*][43] And it is then a relatively small step to show a mismatch between the actual motivations of the psychopath and the theories and principles that the judicial system applies within the case. Musil's perceptions of society as a whole derive from precise observations of this kind. Thus there is an identifiable path from the hermeticism of the Narcissus-stage through to the mature author who, drawing on broad observation and deep understanding, produces a cast of characters representing a range of attitudes within society at large.

The young Musil is "monsieur le vivisecteur," a "fin de siècle" decadent. [*I love the night for she wears no veil; in the day, nerves are tugged to and fro till they go blind but, at night, beasts of prey take one in a stranglehold and the life of the nerves recovers from the anaesthetic of the day and unfolds within; a new sensation of self emerges that is like stepping suddenly in front of a mirror that has not received a single ray of light for days and, drinking in greedily, holds out one's own face.*][44] Love—the Valerie experience—breaks through the pose of indifference; later Narcissus becomes hermaphrodite—from around 1907 until 1911 Musil, as author, is as fixated on the female psyche as he was earlier on the male. In 1911, as a thirty-year-old, he takes the first steps toward earning a living with the post in the library of the Technical University of Vienna, though he resents the restraints imposed by paid employment. [*I've been in the Library for about three weeks now. Unbearable, murderous (all too bearable while one is actually there), I shall leave and steer out into the unknown.*][45] The post took up only four hours a day; however, Musil's frustration should be seen in the light of his commitment to literature that had, since the doctorate in Berlin, been unconstrained by the need to earn money. Marriage, making a living—after the librarianship he becomes an editorial assistant for the Berlin cultural journal *Die neue Rundschau*—all these come together into a new, more open-eyed, more objective involvement with outer reality.

Then came war. [*The five-year-long slavery of the [First World War] has [. . .] torn the best piece from my life.*][46] Any vestiges of fin-de-siècle decadence do not survive the ordeal of being thrown into rough male company, and being deprived of civilized living. [*Nothing to eat; wine that tastes like slurry.*][47] On his return to civilian life he has learned to study a broader range of human types. This, he promises himself, will contribute to the shelfful of novels he plans.[48] Yet the last two decades of his life—from just after the time when these plans were made—were taken up with the novel that eventually became *The Man without Qualities*. However, we should not overlook other literary productivity of various kinds, above all in the 1920s: articles and theater reviews for several papers, two plays, important essays, speeches, short stories—albeit fragmentary. The *Diaries* are full of preparation for the anticipated novels. The social panorama for MwQ is fitted together from interlocking, sometimes ironically mismatching perspectives, many of which Musil has retraced in painstaking study of a particular individual's attitudes, psychic habits, and emotional predisposition, some of the evidence for which is included in the *Diaries*.

After the end of World War I Musil was offered, yet again, the opportunity of secure employment; but, just as he had done when given the opportunity of the academic post in Graz in 1909, he turned this new offer down in order to have the freedom for substantial literary work. For some years he was in demand for contributions to newspapers and periodicals, and the literary world looked forward to the appearance of a brilliant novel; but the push in the late twenties to finish the novel placed a strain on some of the relationships that sustained his position in the literary world and society at large. The first volume of MwQ appeared several years late and the effort to complete it was gargantuan. The work on the novel placed great strains on Musil and his family, a situation complicated by accumulating health problems such as the removal of his gall bladder, the need for dental treatment, high blood pressure, and a stroke suffered in a swimming bath in Vienna in 1936. As the original subject matter of Musil's concerns receded further into the past and the messages he wished to convey lost some of their contemporary urgency (though none of their relevance), his rate of productivity slowed; his prose, in compensation, became if anything more refined—and the *Diaries*, in which some of the most important existential material had first been recorded—became even more crucial in the creative process.

SUMMARY AND PERSONAL NOTE

Musil acknowledged few contemporary equals: he respected Kafka but evidently felt that Kafka could benefit from certain suggestions on how to improve a piece he had submitted to *Die neue Rundschau* (Kafka did not accept this advice); his feelings for Rilke went through phases [[. . .] *represented without any mercy, my relationship to Rilke. The first love with the Worpswede book. The indifference later. Annoyance and love via Allesch. The indifference later. Love after his death.*][49] and he gave an address at Rilke's funeral that was widely appreciated. Other well-known authors he treated with scant respect: [*what is there for me in a world in which Werfel finds people prepared to promote him!*[50]; *Broch: leaning [on someone]. When one leans up against a wall one's suit ends up all covered in patches of whitewash—without plagiarism being involved;*[51] *There are two things that one cannot fight against because they are too long and too fat, and have neither head nor foot: Karl Kraus and psychoanalysis;*[52] he resented Thomas Mann's preeminence as "representative author" because he felt that Mann did not spend enough time on each of his writings for them to reach full maturity.] One has the impression that Musil felt that all these authors failed to put in the preparatory studies, the intense observation of human beings, the background training of mind and pen, the deskwork, the back- and mind-breaking effort that was the cross a creative writer ought to bear in order to achieve the standards demanded by *Geist*—that mental-spiritual continuum in which the greatest writing took shape. Vital to such preparatory studies was the regular work in the *Diaries*.

Philippe Jaccottet, the poet whose translation of the *Diaries* into French is both inspiration and admonition to those who would emulate him, captured the quality of Musil's writing in the following passage: "ce qui me frappe (et me touche) [. . .] c'est [. . .] une sorte de plénitude, une sorte de joie même à être simplement vivant au milieu des choses concrètes, observées certes avec une attention aigue, mais sans en être séparé."[53] Jaccottet was writing here about Musil's observations in his thirties when he was mentally and physically in his prime. But one meets work of such quality through the four decades of these entries that Musil's experiences leap across time and space and enter the consciousness and imagination of the reader intact and undiminished.

Over the years during which I have worked on translating selections from the *Diaries* I have had the impression of being a foreign linguistic apprentice to Musil, the master. The more sentences of the original I have reworked into English, the more the shape, the structures of the original sentences, and Musil's basic relationship to words have impressed themselves on me. By this I do not mean that my translation has become more German; it is rather that, in grasping some of the principles that guided Musil, I have tried more consciously to apply them in my English translation without losing sight of the separateness of the two languages. I do not pretend to have discovered via Musil any universal grammar of translation—each sentence, of course, presents its own challenge—but I visualize Musil looking over the shoulder of his English apprentice and offering gentle advice at different points: "There is a shape, a structure to this sentence that your first draft has lost—go back over it, keeping more closely to the way I have shaped mine"; "Watch the structure of this passage—the climax comes toward the end; don't go off half-cocked but wait as long as English allows before discharging the effect"; "Don't fill in the gaps in my exposition here—they give the German reader space for reflection. The English reader needs no less room for thought than the German; don't pamper him or her with a phrase, even a word, of surplus explanation"; "This word derives some of its force from its origin, its etymology, and I have fed some of the force into the passage—can you keep this effect in your version?"; "The idea is difficult enough in itself—at least keep the words simple!"

Philip Payne
Lancaster, 1997

INTRODUCTION

To introduce in a single, firm sentence a writer who left in suspense all possible solutions to the plot of his masterpiece, *The Man without Qualities*, is to take a first false step. A novelist both of this world—in particular, of Austria before the First World War—and of the "other" or spiritual world, Robert Musil requires not an introduction but a response, one that lies in that "other reality," the mind that turns his pages. The *Diaries*, a substantial portion of which follow in this first English translation, are more than a skeleton key to the riddles of Musil's fiction. They bring you into proximity with an imagination that often has a hypnotic effect on those who study to know it better. Frank Kermode, in his foreword to the edition of Musil's stories published in America as *Five Women* (combining the collections *Unions* and *Three Women*), observes that the "experience" of *The Man without Qualities* causes a "permanent change of consciousness in the reader." Burton Pike's preface to Musil's essays remarks on how the author "demands that the reader participate in their ongoing thought rather than simply observe it from the outside: the reader is expected to catch and be caught up in the emotional nimbus of ideas."

Both appreciations might be applied to the *Diaries* with one important distinction. Their author—ranked among the four or five most important European novelists of the twentieth century (for a novel that was never completed)—is above all a master of irony, of distance. Even when Robert Musil violates the personal space of his own characters and inserts himself, as a writer, into the narrative, his voice has a baroque omniscience tinged with mockery. Though immediately, one is forced to qualify this sense of irony; Kermode notes how the fiction woven out of a warp of autobiographical detail can seem so "personal." Qualification is a constitutional difficulty in matters pertaining to Musil, who worked toward an art of endless and contradictory qualities. Through the *Diaries*, however, in contrast to his fiction Musil often speaks without apparent irony. He is speaking to himself and responding to the echo of that persona.

The distance in these diary notations is the space in which he has stepped back to view Robert Musil. We go with him to the dentist as Musil tries to imagine the procedure. We listen as his wife undresses in the next room. He shares with us his erotic curiosity about the postwoman who delivers the mail; a Hungarian baroness he thinks of flirting with; the glimpse of his mother naked on a diving board; his father's bewilderment in the wake of her death. The sensation of the shells whistling by the novelist as a young officer on the Italian Front during the First World War; his tactile joy in the bursting fertility of a fig tree—in these passages and in many others the reader has access to a man who, observers testify, was addicted to privacy.[1]

Long before I saw the *Diaries* I wanted as a writer to meet Musil in this intimacy. My admiration for him evolved slowly. While his contemporaries Thomas Mann, Herman Hesse, and lesser German or Austrian writers were popular literary successes in the United States, Robert Musil remained a well-kept secret. The professors at Harvard and Stanford who introduced me at the end of the 1950s to the classics of modernism had not heard of him or did not include him in the canon, although Musil *was* taught at Harvard in History 149. The stories puzzled me at first, his essays more so. Musil begins what is acknowledged to be his most important work, *The Man without Qualities*, with a parody of the epic, the fanfare of an Austrian empire caught up in a baroque, comic-opera atmosphere. The book's first pages are deceptive, for the dimensions of the characters' metaphysical search become apparent only in the novel's second and third parts. I found my way to Musil through a few other writers—in particular, Harold Brodkey. Musil was on the edge of Donald Barthelme's consciousness as well. Harold told me that Donald was fascinated by the murderer Moosbrugger, a figure whose violence and naiveté in *The Man without Qualities* mesmerizes several of its protagonists. If you are curious about the forbidden, the taboos of society, and regard fiction as a way of exploring the boundaries of consciousness, Musil becomes irresistible. What constitutes evil? The reality of nationalism, the meaning in erotic and mystical awareness—these are the questions of his essays, shorter fiction, and novels.

Not just Musil's subjects but the way he observes compels attention. I can't speak for the voice of Musil in German, but through the English translation one feels the force of his surreal juxtapositions in the way he poses riddles to himself. What of a woman's identity, he wonders as a man, lies concealed in him? He listens for the sanity in the insanity of his friends. Is there a real racial characteristic to the German, to the Jew? Is it possible to create another morality in a secular age that will bring us into an experience beyond this particular time and age? Characters—and nations—imagine what they are. What they imagine becomes their reality. Imagination in Musil's prose is not an escape but the means, the "tool" with which the individual lights a way toward the furthest limits of what can be discerned of human reality. An editor of *The New Republic*, Leon Wieseltier, remarks as we speak of *The Man without Qualities*, "His mind glows in the dark."

Musil has become for me one of those very few writers whose work seems to hold wisdom, the secrets of one's own questions about Eros, political direction, and religion; what the pious of all religions would call "the Unknown" or "other reality" whose possibility or "quality" is of such importance to the author. (At an early stage in its writing, the hero of *The Man without Qualities*, Ulrich, was called Anders, or "Other.") Throughout his fiction, however, Musil holds the reader at arm's length. One doesn't get to know him until one has returned with the freight of the *Diaries*. The shy man whom Elias Canetti records in the Viennese cafés as watching silently, arriving, leaving "without having uttered a single word," no longer eludes us as he did so many of his contemporaries.

The eerie halo of Musil's prose can be felt in many of the *Diaries*' pages. Critics have noted the uncanny in Musil's language. One experiences it as a way of seeing the world, both abstract and concrete. His observations suddenly grow personal, touch the outrageous. "The negress: I think Somali or Abyssinian. In European dress, shallow bell of velvet, with hair darting out from underneath. Saddle-nose; speaks like a flock of starlings. The inside of the hands light-colored, speckled with pink. Mythical creature. I should like to kiss you under the armpits." In calling up the image of an adolescent girl's body, he asks what his fascination means.

"*The young girl, the woman-child in MwQ, has often given me pause for thought about whether inclinations like this are perverse. Today, as I observed children who were seriously disrupting my work, I have come to see things clearly.*

Girls between the ages of 11 and 15 have beautiful legs. They are long, good at running, and do not have the solidity that comes later when they will have to carry the heavy, voluminous sections of belly and buttocks. The hair has the sheen of youth. The face is pure and often indicates the beauty to come without being spoiled by the expression of pettiness, self-centeredness and retarded spirit. The eyes are full of dreams and fire. i.e., they still have the idealism of youth, while the emptiness of the idealism is not apparent. See the remark on art and infantilism. The thighs, though they already have some female fullness to them, are magnificent.

The weaknesses of the body., i.e., at this age the chest and the child's belly, are concealed by the clothing that suggests the adult shape.

In other words, these children are really lovable, and it is not in the least perverted that they provoke this feeling.

Perversity only makes an appearance if a person feels a desire to abuse this dream of form in reality. Then he has to disregard the spirit and inno-

cence {or helplessness} of the child, and also the absence of a sexual re-
sponse; it is as if he wanted to go to bed with a doll or like a rutting frog,
clasping a piece of wood."

It is difficult to quote only a line or two because one has to follow Musil to
the end of his thinking. He reaches past the conventional for an insight into
that "other" reality, whether it is an appreciation of the hysteria in the
streets of Berlin on the outbreak of World War I or the world of mice bur-
rowing in trenches under the brow of a cliff. These moments are not just
recorded but set down to be felt, smelled, lived through. His own humiliation is part of this experience caught like the fly in amber, an image he has
fixed in the *Diaries*. There are few lines more poignant than his exclamation
in Notebook 33, number 112: "now, finally, this experience of being thrown
out." Austria does not want him, nor Germany. In Switzerland as the
shadow of Hitler falls over the whole of Europe, Robert Musil is barely tolerated. Through his career he has noted, often with irritation, the attention
shown to Thomas Mann. When the latter joins the group of writers trying
to bring Musil to England, his gratitude—tinged with some guilt—is that
much more moving. At all times one feels his honesty, his directness.

The writers of diaries who are my favorites, Henry David Thoreau and
Franz Kafka, don't have Robert Musil's courage when it comes to their own
experience. This most indirect of essayists and artificers of prose fiction in
speaking and thinking of himself draws into a lifelong experiment the
writer's self-examination or surgery upon his own limbs. At the very beginning of the *Diaries* Musil names himself "*le vivisecteur*." Philip Payne,
translator of this edition, speaks of the "adolescent" quality of the first
diary entries. Quoting the passage "I love the night . . ." in his book *Robert
Musil: "The Man without Qualities"* spoken by Musil's "*monsieur le vivisecteur*," Payne sees a "neurotic self-preoccupation" and finds "the content
as pretentious as the form is awkward." Though the image of the "vivisector" is perhaps *portentous*, it is also self-aware—for a process of operating
on his own spirit is consistent throughout the *Diaries*. Robert Musil watches
and listens to himself, reviews his childhood sexual experience, his sense of
his mother, father, trying to take himself apart as precisely as possible.
Thoreau will be a naturalist of his backyard searching for the soul; Musil's
instruments of observation are brought to bear on his own mind, imagination, spirit (the English words, according to the critic David Luft, are all implicit in his references to *Geist*). Musil is a dissector of *Geist*, not only his
own but of those he knows best, above all his wife, Martha's.

Burton Pike chose as a title for his selection of Musil's essays "Precision
and Soul," a formula spoken half in jest by Musil's alter ego, Ulrich, in

MwQ, to conceal its seriousness. The phrase speaks to the paradox of the novelist's work. It is impossible to be "precise" about a phenomenon whose very existence is questionable—but Musil, in trying, brings us to a heightened existence in his fiction where we can, indeed, for a moment enter the "Millennium," this word that in literal translation has come to have such sinister undertones, "The Thousand Year Reich." It is the vision of where the human race might reach in the next thousand years. As we stand on the edge of that age as created by our own strange, religious calendar, Musil is one of the few major novelists to have looked into it before us.

It is a real world, this Millennium, and in imagining the possibilities for another life in it Musil hoped to alter its reality. He intended to use these *Diaries* for yet an "other" project, to which he no doubt would have written that "other" introduction the *Diaries* deserve. At the end of his life he left directions to himself, and so to us, as to this "other" book for which the *Diaries* were to be vivisected.

"127) (End of September 1939 in Geneva.) Yesterday while looking for something I leafed through many notebooks, and this ended in deep depression. Sometimes a good idea, hardly ever any progress. . . . But I have never taken anything beyond the opening stages (though I have finished the books that have the scars to show for it). It would have been so easy to arrange the reflections in proper order; these would have made treatises or books that would, together, have amounted to a modest life's work. But I didn't want to do that, nor do I feel capable even today of doing this. . . . Yesterday I had the impression of a person who is of no value and who was not destined to achieve anything of importance.

"128) [. . .] It occurs to me, that, if there is any chance of redemption, then it should come not by using these notebooks as a source for what I write, because I shall never be able to bring these thoughts to any conclusion, nor even to a state where they are of significance. I must rather write on the subject of these notebooks, judging myself and their content, depicting aims and obstacles. That would unite the biographical with the factual, these two plans that for long have competed with each other.

Title: The Forty Notebooks"

Since Musil did not fulfill his intention to use the entries of these notebooks to try to examine himself, the task is left to us. In many ways this parallels the space left in his fiction for the consciousness of the reader, the place for a response; it is the reason that reading Musil is not a passive experience but rather brings his auditors into a different understanding of the world. The *Diaries* or *Forty Notebooks* turn one toward their subject, the writer's mind, his *Geist*. (Luft weighs the many connotations of this word in German—mind, thinking, imagination, "the creative forming impulse in culture . . . rather than the more receptive faculties of *Seele*, Soul"—before settling on "spirit" as his translation.) The pages ask us to listen as Musil did, reviewing entries, hearing his voice speaking in a moment of time.

Time, and its metaphysical constituent, its antipode, *what lies beyond time*, is Musil's preoccupation. Even over the fragments of the first *Diaries*, where Musil has not yet matured into the writer he will be, there hangs that sense of the mysterious "other" that carries us toward a state of surreal consciousness. Burton Pike notes it in Musil's essays: "Language . . . is primarily referential, although in some mysterious fashion it also points beyond the empirical world."

Musil's prose addresses itself to riddles that cannot be solved in a purely "empirical world." What happens does not follow the logic of lockstep cause and effect. Turn the ghostly key of the *Diaries* in Musil's fiction and the bolt at times clicks open to that "other" reality. Something beyond both the fiction and the biography is revealed for us in the differences between the narratives in the short stories and moments recorded in the *Diaries*. In the story "Tonka" Musil's mistress of five or six years, Herma Dietz, appears in thin disguise as Tonka opposite a character sharing many details of the young Robert Musil's life. This unhappy fairy tale of a young woman from the working class and her lover, a son of the educated upper middle classes of Austrian society, has a grim reality that needs no biographical references to hypnotize us. Still the riddles remain unanswered: Does Tonka love the young man as she protests, or has she simply accepted his protection? Did she become pregnant and contract syphilis in a liaison with another man, or was it the young man, as Tonka insists, despite the medical improbability, who caused her situation? In both his life and his fiction Musil was seeking what was both real and unreal.

His diary entry for 11 March 1907 (Notebook 15), the spring in which Herma disappears from our records, is intriguing not in providing answers but in posing additional questions.[2] Herma has told Robert the story of an attractive widow who yields to the importunities of a man she hardly knows and becomes pregnant by him. A few moments later one finds the name of Martha Marcovaldi (whom Musil will marry), their meeting at the house of a Doctor G., who associates with "delightful characters of dubious reputation." The reference to Martha is offhand but it implies in that very tone an easy familiarity that hints at more. Musil's mind leaps on the entry for this particular day from a story of infidelity related by Herma to meeting Martha at Doctor G.'s. As Herma tells the story of the bride who uses a rival to force her admirer first into marriage, then into sexual intimacy, the reader—aware of Musil's narrative strategies—will pause. Why is he writing this entry?[3] He will say of Emily Brontë that the young woman who narrates the story of infidelity is more interesting to him than the tale of infidelity she tells. (Notebook I, "... if ever I want to depict a strong young girl who sees the world without moral diffidence and yet still in a girlish way, then I shall take *Wuthering Heights* [...] and show the girl who was able to dream up and analyze this.")

The romantic heroine of most of Robert Musil's fiction is his wife, Martha. This is a shock to the unprepared reader when it is spoken of by biographers. The author has artfully transformed her into different characters; the "quiet Veronica" who dreams of bestial encounters, the adulterous Claudine of the "Perfecting of Love," and, of course, the incestuous other, "Agathe," the sister of Ulrich. In the ingenious workings of *The Man without Qualities*, however, a number of the women beside Ulrich's sister—their characteristics drawn from very different life models—reflect the fascination of the writer for a wife who was his closest companion. Did this intimacy at times seem to him incestuous?

Musil "sensibility" has been characterized as "even beyond Proust's ... hermaphroditic." The author of MwQ in several paragraphs of the novel invokes the image of the hermaphrodite as a metaphor of the mutual identity of brother and sister. The figure of a person with two sets of organs, male and female, is misleading, perhaps, in reference to Musil. It does not represent, as I read him, his search for sexual wisdom. Ulrich's desire at moments to take on the identity of a woman—in particular, a sister—is a part of his will toward another existence, a life in which there are no boundaries of gender but an ecstatic wholeness, a submersion of two partners in a boundless Unknown. It is a marriage, however, of "Time to Be Found in the Future." "Sooner or later there will be an era of simple sexual companionship in which boy and girl will stand in perfectly tuned incomprehension, staring at an old heap of broken springs that used to be Man and Woman." [MwQ, 1020] In fact it seems to be a condition of the Millennium, as those "Thousand Years of Germany" are understood to be the earthly Paradise.

Payne, in his critical study of *The Man without Qualities*, quotes the critic Denis de Rougement: "Mightn't the fascinating prohibition of love between brother and sister have been the disguise—quite unconscious, I'm convinced—of a love too real to dare speak its name in a novel? Happy love has no history, as everyone knows since novels were first written—novels that arouse passionate interest. But wasn't this literary convention, condemning the fulfilled marriage, a taboo quite differently fearful, for both writer and reader, from any sort of incest of blasted passion? The eroticism of marriage is a terra incognita for Western literature. Perhaps Musil has unwittingly approached it closer than anyone else." Setting aside the question of whether Musil's brother and sister in MwQ's final draft would have consummated their spiritual incest in the flesh (Payne remarks that "in 1933 and perhaps later, Musil intended that brother and sister would physically make love as they had done in the drafts of the novel to 1927"), I think de Rougement has gone to the deepest levels of the novelist's irony. The forbidden is transformed into the permitted; the unhappiness of betrayal into the joy of fulfilled love. His own marriage reflects this, Musil remarks in Notebook 10, where he talks of writing a book about his wife. "The Crow [a reference to Martha's nickname, 'Raven']—novel of a child, followed through to womanhood, with all the characteristics that are considered pathogenic and disreputable—who becomes happy. Existing materials to be examined from the perspective of another moral system."

Imagining another moral system in which his sense of society's need for a new ethics could be defined, Musil stared into the Millennium. This makes it difficult to classify Musil's work in the "movements" of the twentieth century. It spans forty years, from 1902 when he began work on *Young Törleß* to his death in 1942, when he was still working on chapters of MwQ. *Young Törleß* is clearly in the tradition of the "moderns," as is Musil's story "The Perfecting of Love" from *Unions*, published in 1911. The ideas that led to *The Man without Qualities* were in Musil's head from the very beginning of his career, though the novel's serious development began in the 1920s. A large part of MwQ was withheld from publication as he continually revised.

Musil is not only a writer of the 1920s and 1930s like Gombrowicz, Schultz, Céline, Flann O'Brien, and others who begin the postmodern canon; he anticipates Borges, Beckett, Márquez, Kundera. Robert Musil begins to look beyond to the consequences of the cataclysm unleashed by the Nazis, even as they force him into exile. The shattering event of Modernism is World War I, but Modernism begins much earlier. The world that was disappearing before World War I is already caricatured in the works of Kafka and Virginia Woolf, who see its disintegration. The delay in publication of MwQ meant that slowly the novel was transformed from a critical appraisal of the Austrian Empire before the war into an anticipation of the disaster of the nationalism that overwhelmed the German search for a life of the "spirit" after that war. Hitler—and the bleak light of a German nation with no possible future, its spirit deformed—loomed. It is no wonder then that the posthumous chapters mock the German pedagogues as guardians of the national morals and pursue the idea of forbidden sexual unions, the private exploration of Eros and mysticism, in alienation from both society and the state.

All of which leads me to a second question about "cataloguing"—a subject of Musil's whimsical satire—that would situate his work on a particular shelf of historical or literary tradition. Musil's unfinished novel, which for me places him among the postmodern writers, is also a deeply religious work. A hostile witness to this as a literary phenomenon, Gertrude Himmelfarb remarks: "The mainspring of postmodernism is a radical—an absolute, one might say—relativism, skepticism, and subjectivism that rejects not only the idea of the canon, and not only the idea of greatness, but the very idea of truth. For the postmodernist there is no truth, no reason, and ultimately, no reality. Nothing is fixed, nothing is permanent, nothing is transcendent. Everything is in a state of total relativity and perennial flux. There is no correspondence between language and reality, indeed there is no 'essential' reality."

In the looking glass of literature this is only the surface of the mirror. Like Lewis Carroll's Alice, we must stare through it. The willingness to subject everything to doubt, to question its "reality," is not to abandon the search for truth but to insist that its boundaries, meaning, and substance will always lie beyond us. The great texts of Modernism also point in this direction: the ghost of Stephen Dedalus's mother who haunts Joyce's *Ulysses*, the moment of hallucinated spirit in *To the Lighthouse*, and the sense of an overarching horror orchestrating Kafka's *The Trial* are indicators. Still, there is a certain stark despair in the secular structures of Modernism despite their comic interludes. Musil, by contrast, is optimistic. Though language is inadequate to represent reality, both the writer and the reader can reach toward a new morality, a new ethics—one based on a fearless skepticism toward the conventional in all its aspects. Could adultery be the way to a perfect marriage? This question, despite its apparent facetiousness (and the pathos of questions about his mother's liaison with her permanent houseguest, Herman Reiter),[4] is sounded over and over in Musil's work, in both its corporal and spiritual dimensions. In *The Man without Qualities* and the *Diaries* Musil speaks to and thinks about the Unknown, God, in terms that must surprise most readers of contemporary literature. This aspect of human experience is usually assigned to a very private, unvisited corner. (If there are no easy answers in Musil, neither are there for the genuinely religious. The Talmud instructs the students, "It is not given to you to complete the Law. Neither are you free to desist from it.")

The award "greatest" European novelist of the twentieth century is a huckster's cry, but Musil is unquestionably in the pantheon that Kafka, Joyce, and Proust occupy. (Musil's epigram on the subject was "'He is the greatest creative writer alive today!' They ought to say: 'the greatest I can understand.'") Joyce was not appreciated by Musil (a prejudice he shared with Virginia Woolf) but he does accord respect to Proust. Musil, despite his parody of the polite novel, was an innovator to whom the questions of narrative were paramount. They were part of his attempt to use fiction to find that "other" world. In his search for precision, the notions of both the old and the new "naturalism" as to "causality" and "logic" seemed hopelessly outworn. Time in the novel was not realistic and therefore it was folly to try to create the illusion of conventional cause and effect, motive, for its events. In one of his late diary notations Musil remarks: *"How little pleasure I derive from dividing up the day I am describing into tenths of a second! Which is the reason why I have sometimes been compared with Proust. The optimum of essentiality is rather different from a maximum amount of time filled in, or from detailed analysis. The difference is similar to that between meticulousness and logical precision."*

On the other hand, Musil was frustrated by the limitations of his own craft as a novelist, never claiming mastery for his work, whose inadequacies were always before him. (Remarking on the Nazi strictures against destructive criticism he quips: *"Ironic introduction: since criticism is forbidden I have to indulge in self-criticism. No one will take exception to this since it is unknown in Germany."*) Musil was aware of his own tendency toward the abstract—"the dreadful style of Confusions," he exclaims, referring to his first novel, *The Confusions of Young Törleß*. One sees him in Diary 11 going back to this published work and revising, agonizing over a paragraph he wishes to make more dramatic and concrete.

Throughout the *Diaries* Musil makes notes about correct narrative technique in fiction and the drama. He knows that he violated the rules consistently. In MwQ he tried to provide himself with an excuse to make an exception. *". . . it is the norm that, in the novel, the writer does not himself speak. (This is only permissible at certain periods when an upheaval in taste or in the way of thinking, etc., is taking place—in times of 'Sturm und Drang' such as accompanied the birth of the Modern movement. Such novels are concerned with 'content,' they lack 'art.' . . . The limit of what is allowed is the point of demarcation from the essay.) But even characters in a story are also not allowed to speak 'novels.' The 'art' of writing consists in creating situations that make what is to be said appropriate to the characters while at the same time selecting what has to be said in such a way—selecting the suggestive nodal points from the general flow of thoughts—that the characters do not have 'much' to say."* Again and again he states a principle that his own work will violate. In Notebook 5, admiring Tolstoy's Anna Karenina, he observes: *"The principle of the ministerial regalia carried out with wonderful consistency. . . . The reflections are always the thoughts of individual people. Thus the strong impression emerges of different world-images existing side-by-side with each other, without this being somehow overdone—one sees, for example, how Anna looks when someone perceives her with benevolence and someone else does so with malevolence.*

"*This high level of objectivity leads to the conclusion (this runs counter to what I used to assert and accords with what is said about Ibsen, which also conflicts with the view I held) that it is here that the essence of great artistry is to be found, and that such artistry is amoral.*" Musil contemplates new work in which he will be an "observer." "*In future, in my creative writing, put myself only in the position of a minor character, a spectator. In the novel I stand in the middle, even when I am not depicting myself, and that inhibits the 'telling of the tale.'*" In those pages of MwQ that go over the "limit" of abstraction where Musil is all too present, the authorial interventions are, however, not the pretentious interventions of a self-confident narrator but rather a struggle on the part of the writer to understand a reality that is eluding him. Frank Kermode refers to the voice of Musil's prose as "discursive irony." Musil in Notebook 32, reviewing his decision to pursue the ironic, makes reference to the pain that as he employed it underlies this mode of discourse.

"*In my serious mode—with the first group of books I wrote—I do not get through. To achieve this I need a pathos, a conviction, which is attuned neither to my 'inductive modesty' nor to my intelligence which moves in directions that contradict each other—an intelligence in which enthusiasm and vehement passion have, as their indispensable complement, irony. One might also say 'philosophical humor,' etc. {For the world itself is not yet ready for seriousness.}*

"*At that time, then, I made a decision in favor of irony. It is true that the work on Vol. II—which is almost entirely positive—and also the preparations for the aphorisms have not made me forget this decision, but have robbed it of its efficacy. Now it suddenly occurs to me again and affords me comfort as does every thought which sets things in order. Now the reversals of fortune are nourishment to me; now the feeling that I never quite fully belong either here or anywhere else is not weakness anymore but strength. Now I have found myself again and also my way of facing the world.*

"*Irony has to contain an element of suffering in it. (Otherwise it is the attitude of a know-it-all.) Enmity and sympathy.*"

If I read *The Man without Qualities* the first time, as Rilke confesses he reads, for "happiness," still I noticed how old-fashioned—deliberately so—the narrative structure was in comparison with the short stories. Others have noted, however, that these pages are a form of parody. They leave one slightly baffled. The *Diaries'* invocation to irony as a method makes Musil's intentions clear in MwQ. Considerable art is employed in this antique, almost baroque, structure; it is mirrored in the description of Ulrich's mistress, Leona, as the book opens, and in the peculiar stage setting of the first chapter. A description of Vienna that seems conventional is shot through with scientific observation, statistics of traffic deaths. In terms of narrative technique, Musil resorts to what one might call "head hopping," that is, jumping frequently in a single chapter from the perspective of one character to another, then to his narrator. In a lesser novelist this might seem like a lazy and convenient trick. For Musil it is a way of creating "riches of ambiguity." We are introduced to a character speaking ironically only to have this overwhelmed by the irony of the narrator—second thoughts are followed by third and fourth thoughts. The drama of the characters' minds is at the forefront of the plot, although at times, under the weight of Musil's ideas, the reader has to stop, exhausted. Once the method has been understood one can savor the subtleties of the drama of consciousness being played out in the novel. The moment in Diotima's bedroom when she realizes that under Ulrich's hostility is physical attraction and her thoughts drift impatiently toward wanting him to reach out and "make a move" (while he goes on talking) is both comic and profound. For she is not just a cousin but, as the language hints, a sister—though not as perfect as the one he will meet later in the book. The high drama of the love between Arnheim and Ulrich, even as they regard each other at the very end of part II with revulsion and attraction, plays on so many ambiguities[5] that it tastes of "life" as well as the "other reality" or "life of the spirit" that is the author's— Musil's—preoccupation. The close seduction of Gerda; the hatred between Clarisse and her husband Walter; the yielding of the maid, Rachel, to Soliman, the African servant of Arnheim; Arnheim's courtship of Diotima; all the book's glittering moments of pathos and comedy are strung along the idea of a dramatization of ambiguity until it becomes possibility. For the "man" who is "without qualities" is also the man of infinite "possibility" (*Möglichkeit*), a word that recurs throughout Musil's works. The plot in Musil is a means to the search for this "other life" that is possible. The debates of MwQ take us back to Dante's voyage and beyond that to Homer's Odysseus to the questions of the Bible, *The Epic of Gilgamesh*, the stuff of religious drama such as that of *The Book of Job*.[6] This is a very different idea of the epic from that of "Auntie Homer," as the *Diaries* sarcastically term Sigrid Undset, a Norwegian novelist whose popular historical romances represented the best of the modern epic in the imagination of the moment and garnered her a Nobel Prize in 1928.

For an intellectual historian such as Luft, Musil serves as an important representative of the transition from the nineteenth century to the twentieth. For a novelist like me, Musil is the writer who points beyond the modern into the abyss of the postmodern, precisely because he was so focused on a search for something that lay behind what he observed of the reality of his historical moment. In several of the great masters of "modernism" one can observe the sense of "fragments" and the unwillingness to order time through a conventional plot. Musil, however, is akin to "the great Comedian" Jonathan Swift in his sense of other worlds, and the belligerent intuition that what we grasp of and call "reality" is inadequate to our experience.

One returns to the comparison of Musil with Proust—two novelists among the very few who change consciousness, recompense for the effort their pages demand. Proust, whose mother was Jewish, is haunted by religious imagery. Sodom and Gomorrah, the Biblical Cities of the Plain whose sin was legendary, become the symbols of his aristocratic Count's struggles with sexual fantasies. The Dreyfus case, which forced the question of anti-Semitism into the open, is the moral and political drama at the center of Proust's *Remembrance of Things Past*. That title, more closely translated as *The Attempt to Recover Lost Time*, intimates Proust's effort at a metaphysical endeavor that recalls the wrestlings in Virgil and Homer with the world of the dead. *Lost Time* speaks to Proust's kinship with Musil, whose efforts were directed toward future time. Franz Kafka's apothegm, "Plenty of hope—for God, no end of hope—only not for us," sums up the despair leavened by humor in Kafka's enterprise to explore a world where meaning, if any, had retreated to an unbearable distance. Musil's politics—which are only incidentally intertwined with the Jewish question in Europe—will be discussed in a moment, but of this triad of "great" European novelists Robert Musil is unquestionably the one to whom religion promised an answer. Like Dante, Musil felt the presence of the Unknown, in the body of his opposite in gender. In his fiction he explores that possibility. His *Diaries* speak constantly to his open curiosity about the Unknown and his remark—again, close to the end of his life, about his father's repressed religious tendencies—reveals that he understood how deep the riddle of the sexual and the religious was fixed in the biography of his own family.

It is obvious that despite his marriage to Martha (who was born Jewish but who, like many assimilated German Jewish intellectuals, moved in a world with almost no traditional Jewish content) Musil felt at a distance from Jewish concerns. Still, stimulated by his constant scrutiny of his wife, his fascination is palpable. He did not have, as Proust did, a biblical and Jewish agenda—the latter's imagery of the Canaanite Cities of the Plain, the weighing of the French aristocracy on the scales of the Dreyfus case. In MwQ there is, however, a Jewish undercurrent through the early chapters. Musil shrewdly observes how Arnheim is tainted, even in Diotima's eyes, by his Jewish blood. Ulrich's antipathy toward Arnheim, which is mirrored as a repressed fascination, makes this even more complex. And there is a comic and yet pathos-laden repetition of this in Ulrich's near-marriage to Gerda Fischel, who is half Jewish. The maid, Rachel, to whom Ulrich is attracted in a quiet hypnosis that is never quite developed (though the narrator hints that marriage is not out of the question), makes us wonder to what end the novel's "Jewish question" might have been plotted. If Agathe dominates the last part of the novel, Ulrich's sister offering her brother both incest and a Christian liaison—the fact that Agathe is an idealized figure of Musil's Jewish wife—knots the riddle of religious identity in ambiguity.

One could easily assemble a short autobiography of Musil from selected passages in the *Diaries*, but there is also an essay on European anti-Semitism in its latter pages as Hitler begins to press that crown of thorns on *Geist*. Was there a solution? "Basic formula adopted without any concern: cross-breeding, assimilation," Musil begins one passage. In his portrait of the Fischel family in MwQ, the "cross breeding" has produced a deeply unhappy daughter, neither fish nor fowl, and drawn toward the society of committed anti-Semites, the forerunners of Nazi "intellectuals." Musil understands that the assimilated Jewish world of his wife, of most of his Jewish acquaintances in Vienna and Berlin, is not the world of "convinced" Jews to the east in Poland and Russia. The idea of the "Jew" fascinates him and he wonders if anti-Semitism is based on a perception of race centered in a human discrimination like smell.

"*A convinced Jew . . . values precisely what is specific. He dislikes the characteristics of the assimilated Jew and finds edifying the things that I may find antipathetic.*

. . .

"*Similar to cheese that, for one person is loathsome, for another a complicated pleasure. Like tea, laced with sugar (and rum), and bitter tea. Like the connoisseur's delight in decay. Similar to sexual-symbolical smells from secretions in tabooed zones of the body, according to whether they are perceived sexually or not.*

"*The last example leads to the connection between smells and the relationship to the self. Deviant forms that are frowned upon, sympathy for what is one's own.*

"*Smell as a sign of being in heat. Vanilla smell of the vagina. Is the beast in us to be overcome, or is it right to return to nature. Is preference for one's own smell degenerate or is it the basis for the awareness of race? Is it possible to answer these questions?*" And further on: "*These anti-pathies and sym-pathies are capable of sublimation and shape the spirit. Is it dangerous to examine them via reason?*"

The brutality of Nazi Europe bore down on Musil's "Jewish" family, and the *Diaries* record his surrender of the vivisector's detachment. Early on he copies down the anti-Semitic swears of a decommissioned Austrian officer watching a Jewish bourgeois sloppily riding, a business conversation between Jews in the street. By the end of the 1930s he has come to a fellow feeling. *"On the previous evening, Frisch (at Frau Schnitzler's) told of his stay in Poland, saying that each Jew has a completely personal relationship to God (a relationship involving responsibility, with God, too, being made responsible, if I am not mistaken)—something which a non-Jew could not understand. And even Beer-Hofmann was non-Jewish or non-orthodox in a Jewish fashion which only a Jew could grasp completely. I do not remember the content of these assertions, but what I do remember is that I said 'So the Jews, in your opinion, are a chosen people?' and that F. did not deny it. Postscript: throughout the whole history of the Jews, and only through their history, runs this moral relationship to God—I have just now remembered this fragment of what F. said. But they don't think about it at all, so self-evident is it to them."* As Musil senses his own forthcoming exile, one of his last notations marks the distance he has traveled in his sympathies. "Spirit [Geist] and Jew *are both 'stateless persons'; nowhere in the world do they possess a country 'of their own.'"*

Musil was an eager student of the mystics. Martin Buber's 1909 anthology *Ecstatic Confessions* was his "bible." Paul Mendes-Flohr remarks, "No one perhaps read [it] as carefully as the Austrian novelist Robert Musil, who kept a special copybook in which he transcribed numerous excerpts. . . . These excerpts later served Musil in the composition of the many excurses on mysticism in his novel *The Man without Qualities*. . . . close to three hundred citations." If he mocks the misuse of the word "soul" it is because it has become a trivialized cliché in the mouths of most writers. He seeks the final consolation of religion, union with the Unknown or entry into the "Other World." His intuition that it is to be sought through the erotic is one that the reader can find in *The Zohar*, that document of thirteenth-century Neoplatonic Jewish Kaballah, and perhaps in Dante's *Commedia*. The postmodern architecture toward which the building blocks of MwQ are being put into place did not allow Musil the structure of the latter. The *Diaries* make clear that unlike Dante, Musil had no political illusions and this was one reason that the final form of Musil's great work may have eluded him. Or did it? Genese Grill in her forthcoming book on Musil makes a convincing argument that *The Man without Qualities'* refusal to come to "closure" may reflect Musil's mystical belief, that its welter of possibilities may be his architecture of choice. *"Many Musil scholars, noting his scientific background and dislike of messianic Romanticism, are confused by Musil the ethicist's interest in mysticism, equating ecstasy with disengaged quietism and an all too Idealistic quest for union and harmony. . . . The em-*

piricist devaluation of objective reality in Musil's time had placed the science of reason in a dubious position. Science, in its attempt to explain the universe holistically, was revealed to be as romantic as poetry or religion. . . . Harmony and union are notions which, in Musil's context of radical empirical skepticism, were, if not altogether inconceivable, at least highly suspect. For Musil as for Meister Eckhart, the search for union is only of interest insofar as it may prove transformational in terms of the conduct of life. If momentary unions were the only purpose and consequence of mystical experience, then it would be correct to call traditional mysticism quietistic and a-political, and to deem, as some critics do, Musil's novelistic experiment with the 'Other Condition' a failure. . . . When Musil's protagonists Ulrich and Agathe drop out of society, it is with the express intention of experiencing more intense forms of life, of finding the 'essential' or right life."

Grill points out that the phrase "a man without qualities," in which Walther, Ulrich's friend, stigmatizes him as a person with no fixed ideas, characterized only by his rootless dissatisfaction, is in the traditional language of the mystics the mark of a state of grace. *The Man without Qualities*, Grill argues, dissolves into chapters with no logical order, chronology, or "time" because that brings its world into a transcendence beyond time. "'*Exploding the normal totality of experience' [a phrase from Musil's essay, 'Toward a New Aesthetic'] in mystical terms a breakdown of qualities, habits and constructions of normal existence, leads to the desired state of qualitylessness which is referred to in the title of Musil's novel [Der Mann ohne Eigenschaften]. The traditional mystical phrase âne eigenschaften, translated best as a combination without possession, without characteristics, literally, without the things which are one's own, transformed in the Christian tradition by Meister Eckhart in the 13th century to include, along with a release from material possessions, the other meaning of release from spiritual possessions or attachments in the form of beliefs, habits, preconceptions or hopes, is an extreme state of spiritual, material, and moral vagabondage. The Sufi dervishes, many of whom gave up riches, even kingdoms, security and family to wander about the world barefoot and penniless, are a perfect example of such liberation from eigenschaften. . . .*

"*The traditional mystical idea of timelessness, or the 'time outside of time' wherein the ecstatic experience occurs, is itself a deconstruction of communal reality, a far-flung experience of Kantian subjectivity which denies not only the objective measurement of time, but also its teleological progression. If, as Meister Eckhart writes, God gives birth to his son over and over and over again, and there is no beginning, no end, no middle, then there is, after all, no narrative, no historical biblical story, no traditional novel. Any Bible story becomes for Eckhart pure analogy, timelessly cir-*

*cuitous, ever present. For Musil this means a narrative novel which is em-
phatically non-narrative, which gives the reader possible scenarios and takes
them back again, which plays with plot and time-frame as if an infinite
number of other possible arrangements were equally likely to occur. The
small chapters of Musil's novel move back and forth from past, present and
future, asserting neither a set beginning, nor a middle, and never coming
even close to an end. The non-linearity is . . . a function of the mystical
Eigenschaftslosigkeit, which does not allow for closure."*

The skeptic may see the MwQ's confusion of possible alternate endings
for the plot as only the "fallacy of imitative form," to borrow Yvor Winter's
phrase. For Musil, however, leaving both his final novel and his *Diaries* as
a deliberate expression of his mystical intuition may well have been an irresistible irony.

Musil's often stinging remarks about "liberalism" and "socialism" have to
be read in the context of his distress through the 1930s as he watched democracy in Germany and its defenders in the center and left seem to give way
so easily under Hitler's hammering. "Democracy has been laid bare to the
very bone," he exclaims as the Nazis take over and begin to jail their opponents without serious resistance. "Dogs that bark don't bite." Later he
will be furious when the English Prime Minister Chamberlain defends a policy of appeasement over Czechoslovakia using the language of morality. "I
do not fight against F[ascism], but fight within dem[ocracy] for its future,
so I also fight against dem[ocracy]," Musil asserts with the panache of his
military training. The writer, witnessing the "heroism" of the French and
English political leaders "boldly capable of all kinds of surrender" and the
acquiescence of Germans in Hitler's regime, reserved his optimism, like
Kafka (and in contrast to Proust), for the phenomenon of human love. In
Proust love is a brilliant illusion. For Musil I would say that its full realiza-
tion is in another, further reality, one reserved for the Millennium, though
the Millennium always lies at hand—the possibility of union with another.
In the latter part of MwQ—at least as he worked on its chapters through
the late 1930s—Musil seems to retreat from the political questions he raised
earlier in the book to the personal universe of brother and sister, their intense absorption in each other. (This of course may be a very "political" reaction to a world around him whose reality, he felt, as a writer in German,
could only be escaped.) In the *Diaries*, however, he tries to understand the
power of Hitler to touch and direct the irrational in the German people and
his own identity as both a German writer and thinker dedicated to search

for the "other world" that lies beyond the boundaries of language and nationality. Musil's remarks about fascism, however, will make some readers anxious about their own commitments. "Long before the dictators, our times brought forth spiritual veneration of dictators. Stefan George, for instance. Then Kraus and Freud, Adler, and Jung as well. Add to these, Klages and Heidegger. What is probably common to these is a need for domination and leadership, for the essence of the savior." Musil was not a political activist, in comparison to Thomas Mann. But Mann was also married to a Jewish woman and I am not aware in Musil of a sentence as condescending as Mann's diary entry of April 22, 1933. "I could have a certain amount of understanding for the rebellion against the Jewish element were it not that the Jewish spirit exercises a necessary control over the German element, the withdrawal of which is dangerous; left to themselves the Germans are so stupid as to lump people of my type in the same category and drive me out with the rest." (In common, all too human, the two writers rejoice that their literary enemies have been driven out together with them.)

The sketch of Musil by Nobel Prize–winner Elias Canetti in his memoir *The Play of the Eyes* reveals just how different the Musil of the *Diaries* is from the one his contemporaries perceived. Canetti as a young man understood Musil's genius, recalling, "I could not get enough of *The Man without Qualities*, the first two volumes of which, some thousand pages, had been published. It seemed to me that there was nothing comparable in all literature." Musil's friendship and critical appreciation meant a great deal to Canetti, but the latter committed a dreadful faux pas at the moment when his first novel appeared. "*Musil came up to me. I had never seen him so cordial. He put out his hand, and instead of merely smiling he positively beamed, which delighted me because I had been led to believe that he didn't permit himself to beam in public. 'Congratulations on your great success,' he said, and added that he had only read part of the book, but that if it went on in the same way I deserved my success. The word 'deserved' from his lips made me almost reel. . . . The moment he stopped speaking, I said: 'And just imagine, I've had a long letter from Thomas Mann.' He changed in a flash, he seemed to jump back into himself, his face went gray. 'Did you?' he said. He held out his hand partway, giving me only the tips of his fingers to shake, and turned brusquely about. With this I was dismissed.*

"*Dismissed forever,*" Canetti adds. This is not the self-amused Musil we meet in the writer's own pages. Canetti's preoccupations have disfigured his image of Musil and influenced perhaps unfairly the way we read MwQ. I think particularly of the paragraph in Canetti when he refers to Musil's one meeting with the Jewish financier, Walther Rathenau, the German Foreign Minister assassinated in 1922, and the model for MwQ's international magnate, Arnheim, a foil to its hero, Ulrich. "A man who put his arm around him as around all he wished to appease or win over became the most long-lived of his characters and was not saved by being murdered. The unwanted touch of this man's arm kept him alive for another twenty years." Arnheim's rhetoric in MwQ may be "hollow," but Musil's fiction and his response to the touch of Rathenau are more complex than simple satire. In the scene where Arnheim offers Ulrich a position as a junior partner in his business, the tug of brotherhood between the two men is manifest and the affection implied in the magnate's embrace. Between Walther—who is modeled on his close childhood friend, Gustav Donath—and Ulrich, who in certain "qualities" certainly resembles Robert Musil, there is hardly a moment of sympathy. Toward Arnheim, the man of action, Ulrich, who remains committed to the world of thought, feels more than just condescension or hostility. For a brief moment the possibility of real friendship looms—though neither man can manage to bridge the gap. Musil's narrator invokes the word "brother" several times in regard to Arnheim, just as the word "sister" appears in reference to Ulrich's fascination with Diotima and Clarisse. It is part of Musil's wish to seek a symbiosis between himself through Ulrich and the other characters in his novel, all of whom are at once the objects of his ironic judgment, and of his sympathetic love. The touch of this famous man of action was not, I think, so unwelcome to the novelist. (One of the byways in Musil's biography is his correspondence with a second cousin, Alois Musil, a prominent Old Testament and Arabic scholar, who played the role of master spy in World War I, riding through the Middle Eastern deserts for Austrian intelligence in the same deadly fashion as his counterpart on the British side, T. E. Lawrence.) In the self-imposed isolation of the Austrian novelist the reader senses, paradoxically, a craving for the world of heroic deeds and enterprise. Burton Pike, in his pioneering *Robert Musil*, cites Gert Kalow, who "advances as a reason for Musil's social asceticism, the idea that he regarded himself as embarking on voyages of discovery toward new continents of the possibilities of life. This makes one think of Musil stepping onto the steamer in one of Baudelaire's poems about to sail for exotic lands—and in his last years, Kalow informs us, Musil did carry around with him a visa for China, not intending to go there, but simply as a 'secret part of citizenship.'" (In this context Pike remarks on the peculiar kinship of Musil and Thoreau. "Musil's self-sufficiency in isolation was extraordinary; the only comparable case, perhaps is that of Thoreau, with whose writings Musil seems to have been acquainted.")

The *Diaries* are, finally, an adventure too, an adventure by a man who wrote, "I consider it to be more important to write a book than to rule an empire—and also more difficult." Despite the flag that flies over his prose,

"Before my eyes hovered the law of the higher life itself . . . ," we are thrust into the perception of a meticulous writer of actions on this earth.

  "*On the beach a little hollow is scooped out by hand and, out of a sack filled with black soil, the fat earthworms are tipped; the loose black soil and the knot of worms make a loamy, uncertain, intriguing ugliness against the bright sand. Next to them is laid a {wooden} tray {that looks like} a proper table drawer, long, but not very wide, or like a money drawer {full} of clean yarn, and an empty tray {is laid} on the other side; the hundred hooks that are attached to the yarn are arranged neatly along a little iron rod at the end of the tray and are taken off, one after the other, and bedded down in the other tray filled {at one end} with damp sand. While this is happening 4 long, lean and powerful hands {as careful as those of children's nurses} are ensuring that each hook gets a worm.*

  "*Two men crouch down on the sand on their knees and heels. They have powerful, bony backs and long, kindly faces, a pipe in their mouths and incomprehensible words that issue as softly from them as the movements of their hands. One of them takes a fat earthworm in two fingers and, gripping it as well with {the same} two fingers of the other hand, tears it gently into three pieces, {gently and precisely} like a cobbler clipping off the paper strip after taking measurements, while the other one, gently, attentively, pushes these writhing pieces down over the hook. When that has been done they are {regaled with water and} bedded down into rows of small {dainty} trenches in the {tray with the} soft sand so that they will stay fresh. This is done silently, delicately, and the coarse fingers seem to walk quietly on tiptoe. The matter demands close attention. Above this, the sky has stretched a blue vault, and the gulls are circling high above the land like swallows.—(Fishermen poetry on U[sedom].)*"

  It is at moments like this that the *Diaries* flash into their own—they are no longer source documents for Musil's work or life, but the "thing-in-itself." This short but gripping description of the matter-of-fact chopping-up and threading of worms onto fishing hooks has all the cheerful brutality of a mass murder sanctioned by ages of use. It is a small fable that inevitably provokes disturbing second thoughts. Musil handling the satirist's pen extends the theme of the vivisector to human behavior in general.

  Musil utters in a sarcastic aside about his *bête noire*, "Th[omas] M[ann] and similar authors write for the people who are there; I write for people who aren't there!"

  In the final extracts chosen for this translation, Musil, from his rooms in Switzerland, watches the cats in the yard making love. He observes them with a scrupulousness that parodies his own skirting of the obscene, recalling his remark about the suffering hinted at in the ironic. From this he passes unexpectedly to a lyrical recall of his sexual life with Martha, as if writing on the stone sarcophagus, proof against several millenniums, an epitaph of their own mutual curiosity. The *Diaries* invite the reader to subject the living body and whatever might lie beyond the body to that same scrutiny.

Philip Payne reminds us that Musil never meant for these diaries to be published, at least in their present form. Their arrangement in a rough chronological order must be confusing at times, and the omission of three-fifths of the material (though much of this consists of alternate drafts of stories and the novel) also makes it difficult to grasp them as work in their own right. Still, they allow us to come face-to-face with the man, Robert Musil. Burton Pike says that Robert Musil's friends, whom Pike interviewed, spoke of Musil as seeming to stand behind a glass window in his relations with others. In the *Diaries,* angry, at times pathetic, but always thinking, aware, vulnerable, Musil lets us approach him. A line from Thoreau's *Journals* dogs my ear. "I would have the man who is coming to see me pause by the way and consider if he is prompted by a laudable curiosity—if he has anything to communicate and really wishes to stand over against me come what may. I shall be truly glad to ram him if he will not run." We can come close to Musil precisely because he is occasionally ugly, bitter, egotistical, but always watching himself as we might watch him if we could draw our chair up behind his in that Viennese coffeehouse. As we see him intuit the coming near of death close to the end of his *Diaries*, we feel how precious his breath is to us, his thoughts, how intensely he lives in the last entries.

Mark Jay Mirsky
Manhattan, 1997

A NOTE ON THIS EDITION

The casual reader opening these *Diaries* will have a number of questions. Philip Payne, the translator, sent me the following explanation for his choice of nomenclature: "The English equivalent to the German *Tagebücher* (which is used to describe a specific range of Musil's notebooks forming part of the literary estate) are, of course, literally *day-books* and we have two words in English, *diaries* and *journals*. I have kept to the former since *journals* seems a little pretentious. . . . Musil's word is *Hefte*, which are, precisely, *notebooks*, though he also does use the word *Tagebuch* at one or another point in the *Hefte* to refer to day-to-day entries of the kind that we associate with normal diaries."

Trying to follow the order of the *Diaries*—not to mention their chronology—the reader naturally will be confused. Why do we begin with Notebook 4 and seem to go backward to Notebook 3? Are there missing notebooks? Again, Payne elucidates: "The run of diaries in my translation corresponds precisely, both in ordering and in number, to those in the German edition of the *Tagebücher* by Adolf Frisé. Frisé omitted one or two *Hefte* from the *Tagebücher* edition: these were a notebook in which Musil records notes on a book by Walther Rathenau (*Heft* 2); one with drafts for 'The Temptation of Quiet Veronika' and 'Tonka' (*Heft* 15—the standard diary entries to be found in this edition were entered in reverse order, starting at the back of this *Heft*); several notebooks with drafts for early novels which eventually became *The Man without Qualities* (*Heft* 16, *Heft* 22, *Heft* 36); a notebook by Musil's wife, Martha (*Heft* 18); a notebook with notes for an essay (*Heft* 29); an unnumbered notebook that Musil used as an index for characters and themes from his creative work (called by his wife the Register—or Index). For completeness it should be noted that some notebooks were lost without trace after Musil's death but before Martha Musil died (*Hefte* 12, 13, 14, 20, 23, 27); I don't know what was in these. *Heft* 3 and *Heft* 24 have been lost after being transcribed by Adolf Frisé; *Hefte* 16, 22, 36 were stolen in 1970 but had previously been photocopied.

"Musil numbered the notebooks as indicated in the text. He was a librarian/archivist for a while and seems to have delighted in producing a system of his own. The arrangement of the *Hefte* in the *Tagebücher* edition was determined by Adolf Frisé; this was in chronological order of the date (in some cases the estimated date) of the first entry in each *Heft*—the dates at the beginning of each *Heft* are taken directly from the Frisé edition."

In explaining his principles of selection, Payne remarks: "The German edition of the *Tagebücher* runs to 1,026 pages. It is my estimate that the selection I produced is equivalent in total to around 420 of these pages. . . . The criteria I have adopted are as follows: i) Cut out most of the entries that summarize works of other authors or contain excerpts from such work. ii) Cut out many entries that are virtually unintelligible to all but Musil experts without detailed notes. iii) Cut out many drafts for works that were later published in a more sophisticated form, and others that, though not published later, are too fragmentary to be of interest to the majority of readers. iv) Cut out material that does not add anything of significance to our knowledge of Musil's life or ideas or creative work or is not of particular stylistic interest." Bound together with the *Diaries* in the German edition is a voluminous appendix that includes literary sketches, drafts of letters by Musil, letters to him, notes on the development of "Anders" (who was to be the protagonist of one of the earliest versions of Musil's novel when it was called *The Spy*), and runs the gamut of interest from medical reports on Musil's health to preparations for a sketch of Martha.

As a result of the translator's selection, this edition has a coherence that Musil's *Diaries* lack in the German text edited by Frisé. On the other hand, the reader striving to know Robert Musil will regret every lost lane end. The omitted pages in which drafts of stories, articles, and plays are reproduced obviously show us his meticulous mind working at revision. What Robert Musil read and how he reacted to that reading is a fascinating question. Burton Pike speaks of "the remarkable extent of Musil's knowledge," and dipping into the index of Frisé's Rowohlt edition, begins to quote at random from the list: "Immediately after Aeschylus and St. Francis of Assisi, Kemal Ataturk, Aubrey Beardsley, William Blake, Boccaccio, Böcklin, and Botticelli are followed at a respectable distance by Emily Brontë, La Bruyère, Buddha, and Byron; Carlyle has six entries to Hans Carossa's one; Enrico Caruso, Cervantes, the two Chamberlains (Houston Stewart and Neville), and William Ellery Channing form a series of strange bedfellows, perhaps outdone by the eleven immediately following them—Charlie Chaplin, G. K. Chesterton, Chiang Kai-shek, Winston Churchill, Count Ciano, Cicero, René Clair, Claudel, Clausewitz, Clemenceau and Colette. . . ." Musil's remarks on Nietzsche constitute a small volume in themselves. Musil's critical remarks about other writers, his practice of copying sentences, paragraphs, pages from them into his journals, is, again, an important part of the process of his thinking. The repetition in his entries, their variations—what he sets down and what his next thoughts are in these archives of raw musing—constitute that many clues to the enigmas he went in search of. I regret most of all the epigrams and short sketches that had to be sacrificed. As the audience for Robert Musil's work slowly expands, so I hope will this edition of the *Diaries* to include material that records more of the interests of this remarkable writer and of the moments in which he thought.

M.J.M.

This page (from the second volume of the Frise edition of the Tagebuecher) is from the appendix to Notebook 8 of the Diaries; it contains Musil's sketch of ideas for the integration into the narrative of MwQ of the important character General Stumm von Bordwehr. It includes the statement: 'Make him the focus of the satire on [. . .] the spiritual substance of the time.' Stumm is represented as drawing up a 'map' with the main currents of spiritual life represented as countries and the main intellectual personalities as rivers and lakes—this is Stumm's attempt to come to terms with what for him is the alien world of ideas by translating it into a more familiar idiom.

I

NOTEBOOK 4
1899? TO 1904 OR LATER

[This notebook spans Musil's time at university: he studied mechanical engineering at the Technical University in Brünn from January 1898 until July 1901, when he obtained the state qualification as an engineer; after military service from October 1901 until September 1902, he spent a year as an unpaid assistant at the Technical University in Stuttgart, then took his grammar school matriculation in 1904 (the military college he had attended in his youth did not prepare pupils for university entrance) and went to Berlin to study philosophy and psychology.

In the earlier years in Brünn Musil was making good the gaps in what he considered to be his "barbaric" secondary schooling by reading philosophers, including Socrates, Schopenhauer, Emerson, and Nietzsche. In this notebook he is searching for guidance on how to shape his life (having rejected the example set by his unemotional and tentative father); even Ernst Mach, the serious-minded physicist, is treated as a guru who promises a life under the heady influence of empiricism. Musil's reading of literature is also prompted by the concern to restructure his life: he steeps himself in Poe, Baudelaire, Verlaine, Mallarmé, Maeterlinck, and d'Annunzio, absorbing not only their ideas but also the mood of their existence. The day is devoted to science, the night is a sanctum of the fin de siècle. Whatever the activity or pursuit, all Musil's energy goes into the search for the "right life," the one that brings human fulfillment.

In these pages a number of people are mentioned who are of great importance in Musil's life and literary work: Herma Dietz, his mistress in Brünn whom he would later take to Berlin; Valerie, a pianist met on holiday, for whom he conceived a passion that burned briefly but with unforgettable intensity; Gustl Donath, the son of a neighbor in Brünn and Musil's *oldest friend; and the girl who would later become Gustl's wife, here called Bertha but later identified as Alice Donath, née Charlemont. Musil intended that these lovers and friends would inhabit his novel, early drafts of which are found here. Although the scenes he sketches out do not, as far as I can see, go directly into his major novel,* The Man without Qualities *(MwQ), or indeed into any of its unpublished drafts, there is an intimate link between some of the individuals mentioned and important characters in MwQ: within the license of literary re-creation, Gustl becomes "Walter," Bertha becomes "Clarisse," Robert (Musil) becomes "Ulrich." Details from this notebook that feed into MwQ include the Swedish fortifications near Brünn that provide the setting for a trip by Ulrich and Agathe, and the man who claims to be the murderer in the entry entitled "Variety Theater" will later appear as an acual murderer, the prostitute-killer Christian Moosbrugger, a character with whom Ulrich becomes obsessed. The brother of the central character in one of the novel drafts in this notebook (apparently a Dr. Jekyll to his Mr. Hyde) would eventually, in MwQ, cede his place to another sibling, the "Siamese twin-sister," Agathe.]*

Pages from monsieur le vivisecteur's[1] "Book of the Night"

I live close to the Pole for when I go to my window I see only still white surfaces that serve as a pedestal for the night. I am cut off from everything organic, it is as if I am resting under a blanket of ice 100 meters thick. The luxury of burial under such a blanket provides a perspective known only to him who has placed 100 meters of ice over his eye.

This is how it looks from the inside looking out—and from the outside looking in? I remember a fly that I once saw interned [*sic*] in rock crystal. Flies, from some aesthetic predisposition that I've not yet subjected to the scrutiny of the understanding, are something that offend—how shall I put it—my feeling for beauty. But the one that I saw in the crystal was different.

By being sealed within an alien medium it lost the detail of what one might call its "fly personality" and appeared to me only as a dark surface with delicately shaped appendages. I remember having felt this way about people seen in the tired light of some evening, moving as black dots on grass-green hills across an orange sky. It was a sense that these figures that would certainly, in some way or other, have offended me in close-up now awoke in me a certain aesthetic satisfaction, a reverberation of sympathy.

So now I look from outside to inside and, summa summarum, this moving from outside to inside and from inside to outside gives me the contemplative peace of the philosopher.

Today, for the first time, I register a sense that this room of mine, this dreadful jumble of stylistic blasphemies, is something uniform, a sum of colored surfaces, organically connected with the ice-night outside that forces upon me my {boarding school} perspectives; and I feel the room is connected to me as it makes me experience, on approaching the window, this January night in central Europe with its snow-covered roofs as a polar arch, an ice-grave, which throws a delicious pall of death over the inner eye. A kind of pantheism emerging from a physiological insight! I shall now write my diary and in gratitude call it my "Book of the Night" and I shall feel I have done what I set out to do if no word of totality disturbs the beautiful unity of my {present} sensation.

Book of the Night! I love the night for she wears no veil; in the day, nerves are tugged to and fro till they go blind but, at night, beasts of prey take one in a stranglehold and the life of the nerves recovers from the anaesthetic of the day and unfolds within; a new sensation of self emerges that is like stepping suddenly in front of a mirror that has not received a single ray of light for days and, drinking in greedily, holds out one's own face.

Beasts of prey with their strangleholds! There were once kings who harnessed panthers to their chariots and it may have been the height of pleasure for them to live suspended in the possibility of being torn to pieces.

Recently I invented a very fine name for myself: "monsieur le vivisecteur."

Of course, inventing such a fine-sounding name for oneself has to be a pose but, occasionally, in moments of profound exhaustion, in the depression of limp lassitude, it is necessary to recover one's poise by making a word do service for those major stimulants: strength, pleasure, striving. No shame attaches to such a ploy.

"Monsieur le vivisecteur"—that's who I am!

My life: the wanderings and adventures of a vivisectionist of souls at the beginning of the twentieth century!

What is m.l.v.? Perhaps he is typical of the human being to come, "Brain Man"—perhaps?—but all words are so ambiguous, so resonant in meaning, so double-edged in feeling, that one is wise to steer clear of them.

I approach the window to fill my nerves once more with the shuddering thrill of isolation.

Ice, 100 meters thick. None of the responsibilities of the day that rise with the sun and go down with the sun can penetrate this—for no one sees us then. Oh, night is not there just for sleep, rather it performs an important function in life's psychological economy.

By day, we are Mr. X and Mr. Y—member of this society or that, with this obligation or that, we are required to live altruistically by laws acknowledged by our understanding. In the night—at the moment when we close the door with its heavy curtain behind us, we leave all altruisms outside too, they no longer have any purpose, the other side of our personality insists on its rights—egoism. At this hour, I like to stand at the window. Far away over there, a black and mighty shadow—I know that it is a terrace of houses beyond the gardens. Here and there an isolated yellow rectangle—the window of a house! It is the time when people return from theaters or restaurants. I watch their silhouettes, black patches in the yellow rectangles, I watch them removing their uncomfortable theater clothes and thus, as it were, retreating into themselves. They lead a double life through all the intimate relationships that now come into their own.

In the rooms that have often been dumb witnesses of their solitude there rests a temptation to let the self go—to forget the moral promptings of the day.

The things which then awaken from their sleep are different—for the people over there it may be trivial instincts and impulses, a <simple> pleasure in the comfort of home or the sensuality that comes from a bottle of inferior wine.

<For me it is the delight of being on my own—quite alone. The opportunity to leaf through the not uninteresting story of m.l.v. without the obligation of being angered by this, or pleased by that; able to be my own historian or the scholar who places his own organism under the microscope and is pleased whenever he discovers something new.

And this, exceptionally, is not a pose at all! {One is one's own companion.}>

———————————

[. . .]

———————————

First Night.

———————————

Grete with her blond hair. Or the fragrance of blond-haired Grete.
    The distillation of blond-haired Grete!

———————————

I cannot help that she is the first, for when one comes from a garden where the sun shines warmly one is assailed by the fragrance of the strongest flowers. And women are a perfume that nests securely in our nerves.

Variety Theater.

It is rather curious to see how one works things into a pattern, into a silhouette marked out as if with a pair of compasses or into a memory, so that one always feels one must say: "Once upon a time . . ." For example: "Once upon a time there was a big, sober building in a broad, quiet street. In this building was a hall with undistinguished yellow-green wallpaper. In this hall, a small variety stage. On this stage a petite singer, in this singer a tiny, tiny, complex temperament, in this temperament a point with the label 'If only someone would pay for my evening meal tonight'— and all this is felt in the pale colors of a silhouette, so to speak as: 'Once upon a time.'"

. . . . This was what the man with the strange eyes was saying to the small nineteen-year-old chanteuse at his table—her name on the program was Rosa. She then looked up with an air of incomprehension from the menu that she was just studying because she wasn't quite sure if what he was saying was to be taken as an insult or as delicate flattery. But she found a way around her uncertainty by asking: "Do you mind if we have roast venison?" "Please order what you like—I myself have just eaten." Then the man at the table screwed up his strange eyes as if he were looking at a picture in an art gallery and then continued in a relaxed voice:

"Yes, you know it's really curious: that's what I was thinking earlier, as I told you—and then the four of you appeared on the stage and sang—what was it you were singing?—Oh, yes—'If you give me your love, you don't need to be true.'—with those well-written variations at the end—and then the other song—no, I can't just remember it now—it's not important. But it then occurred to me that it was in a large, sober building in a quiet broad street, around the end of the nineteenth century. Fates, people, moods—life washed all manner of things into a small yellow hall and then four women came into the hall who knew how to sing and how to wave their short skirts about so that people could see their beautiful, well-shaped legs. And the drink, the rhythm of the dancers' legs, and the hubbub of voices were making everyone there feel warm and excited—that all happened toward the end of the nineteenth century. Doesn't that sound like a fairy tale?"

"But" said the girl; and there was a whole sentence in this word that might have gone something like this: "You silly fellow, are you really mad or are you just pretending to be so?" But when the man with the strange eyes seemed still to be waiting for an answer she had to go on: "Yes, but—

no—no, you really are a one!"—Rosa burst out laughing—"You're reading far too much into it, it's just a variety theater—if you knew it better you wouldn't talk like that." "So you don't feel that the whole thing is like a fairy tale from the nineteenth century, with that alien magic that all fairy tales possess? Four women on a stage waving their skirts about and singing provocatively . . . ?" "Don't you go saying such things: they were just Gisa, Mizzi, Karolin and me—should I go and fetch them here?" She thought that, at last, she'd understood him but she was wrong, for the man at her table said, without a trace of pleasure: "Yes, if you like, please do so—{but} you won't be doing me any favor; I'd rather be alone with you." He seemed, on the contrary, a little put out by the misunderstanding. They ate giardinetto[2] in virtual silence, smoking the delicate Turkish cigarettes that the stranger held out to her in a slim case. But then the wine loosened the tension that both felt, leaving a delicious lassitude. "Have you tried these cigarettes before?" "No, I've never seen such strange, flat ones." "They're from Algiers, you can't get them here; a friend gave them to me as a present. They can't be sold here because they contain traces of a very fine poison— they're made by Algerian gypsy women and whoever smokes three, one after the other, falls into a kind of dionysian trance; the things around them are transformed, they imagine that they've seen them somewhere before that way—but they've no idea where and when it was, and eventually they sink back into a kind of sleep where they sweat profusely but none reveals what it was they experienced then, and finally. . . ." The stranger fell silent and his eyes shone with a strange light when he saw Rosa violently stubbing out her cigarette in the ashtray. "What are you doing? You're not smoking any more—you haven't started to . . . , or perhaps you have? Was that really your third cigarette {already}?" But Rosa was on the point of getting up and going home: "You play such stupid games!" She was about to burst into tears of anger when his mocking smile made her realize that he had been playing a trick on her. But now, suddenly, his mood changed. He begged her to stay, saying he hadn't meant to offend her and that, though the cigarettes were really of a kind that was rarely found there, she could smoke as many as she liked and that he, himself, had smoked at least six of them already that day—and, as to the poison, he hadn't meant to poke fun at her just now—he'd simply felt an urge to tell her that particular story, just that one. And finally, he was in such a mood today and simply made things up as a continuation of the fairy tale from the nineteenth century. So, for the love of God, would she please calm down again. Then he won her over with a compliment about her dear, angry little face.

But since she didn't want to stay any longer he suggested a walk; she quickly drank the black coffee as she put on her coat.

Outside, the night was warm and gentle, the quiet streets had an air of cozy familiarity so that Rosa gradually regained confidence in him. He asked her to tell him something and she prattled on—about her family in which she'd always been one mouth too many to feed, about her fear the first time she'd appeared on stage, about the way the manager deducted expenses from her fee, about a lighthearted group of people with whom she'd spent a night drinking the previous week. Each time she paused, the man at her side would encourage her with a solicitous word and he was wonderfully clever at striking the right note and making it easy for her to continue to talk. But what she found most astonishing was that he walked on so quietly beside her without even having asked for permission to take her arm. "Why don't you take my arm?"

"Well, if it will give you pleasure I can do so, but frankly it is of little consequence to me for, as we are now, I have much more from you than if I were to permit myself the indulgence of walking arm-in-arm; after all, anyone whom you don't dislike and who happens to possess an arm can have that pleasure." A pause. "Now, please tell me something more about that elegant and handsome young man from that lighthearted group."

"No, I'm not telling you any more. You really are the strangest person I've ever come across. Why does that interest you?"

"Why shouldn't it? You know that everything interests me. And then, I just find it a bit comical, I can't help it, you didn't want to believe me earlier when I spoke about the big sober building on the broad quiet street—and I've just thought of something else. Look at that house over there . . ." "Number 10?" "And that one there where the sidestreet branches off, and that big one there with all the balconies. I know all the people who live there. I paid a visit to someone at that one over there today and tomorrow I'm going to have lunch in that one—two young women live there with their mother—we'll talk about the theater, about the enjoyment of art too, perhaps, and in the third house over there they even think that I wouldn't be a bad match. Just imagine, all of them there are now asleep and here am I walking past their windows with a little chanteuse on my arm and no one knows a thing about it. But perhaps they're not sleeping either. One never knows. Do you want to tell me about something else? There's nothing to stop you. We're quite alone. One of the waves of life brought us together and will part us tomorrow, perhaps forever. That sounds like a tale from the nineteenth century, doesn't it?"

Gradually they had come as far as the suburbs. Rosa walked up to one of the houses and rang the bell.

When she thanked him she said: "What a foolish fellow you are—I've never met anyone like you before. Just who are you?" The man with the strange eyes stood still for a moment. Then he said quickly "Should I say that I'm a fool? A poet? No, I'll stay with the truth; but then you've got to believe me—I'm the prostitute-killer who was hanged yesterday."[3] The very next moment the man with the strange eyes had disappeared around the side of the house and Rosa, standing there dumbfounded, could only hear his laughter which sounded just as it had done earlier when he told the silly story about the Turkish cigarettes.

[. . .]

―――――――

<From m.l.v.'s Book of the Night

Occasionally one views the state one is in at the present moment as a single link in a long chain. Suddenly specific things appear in the memory and one has an intuition of an iron context in which, so it seems, something that has been overlooked up till then suddenly takes on causal significance.

This is how I now view all of my childhood. My whole family set great store by my talents and when I was ten years of age I myself believed that I would be very famous by the age of twenty. But when I then turned fifteen, sixteen, eighteen, without having made any particular progress, a strange depression took hold of me.>

[. . .]

Paraphrase No. 1[4]

"If fortune's hoard we ever find
Then back to thee we'll turn our mind."

The moon shines, pale and full, wandering as it does in storybooks through blue sky and white clouds . . . . . .

The express train roars through the night, tak, tak, ratatak. In one compartment is a young man. He goes from one window to the other, the night air blows in on him.

Like viscous silver the waves of the stream roll slowly on, over the meadows lies a blanket of mist. Everything else is dark on dark and the eye becomes more finely attuned and learns to make out nuances even here. On a black field stands the wandering players' cart, a small patch of its roof begins to shimmer. Big dogs set up a ponderous baying.

Romanticism—the life of a traveling journeyman—"There's nothing to hold me now!"

Like a chalk line, the road. To go walking here, with a sprig of heather in my hat that dances before my eyes. That is romanticism for the masses.

Kissing! And to see the other's eyes swimming with tears! Ah!

Diaries?

A sign of the times. So many diaries are published. It is the most convenient, the least disciplined form.

Good. Perhaps diaries will become the only kind of writing since everything else seems unbearable. By the way, why generalize?

It is pure analysis—no more, no less. It isn't art. It's not intended to be. Why waste many words on it?

13.II.1902

Today was probably the last time with Herma[5] in our old room—this confidential witness of her loss of "innocence." Herma was very pretty.

Before me on my table there are Christmas roses[6] in a chased metal bowl. Although this clearly sounds a very stylish note and though I have always imagined it as something very pretty I feel nothing, nothing at all.

And it's the second day that the Christmas roses have stood before me.

20.II.

Four days ago a group of us went off sledding to Kiritein. Besides Herma, Hauer and Hannak[7] were in my sledge. Return journey pretty. Fir branches against the bright {night} sky; singing in the telegraph wires. Because of the cold, drank a lot of schnapps and Herma got tired. Hauer recited all kinds of verse fragments. Herma and I were princess and prince. She lay in my arms with her eyes shut like a little child. A kiss—fleeting—secret—positively unnerving. [...]

. . . . . His eyes were like violets wet from the storm . . . (Ch[arles] B[audelaire])

The eternal formula, the key to this world and the beyond. (Oh, Robert, why do you use, for things that are so indifferent to you, such highly charged words!), did Kant, did any other discover it? Can anyone ever find it?!

I have never finished reading Kant but I don't let that keep me awake at night, nor do I feel that I shall die with shame because another man has already grasped the world in its entirety.

There are truths, but no truth. I can quite well assert two totally antithetical things and in both cases be right. It's not permissible to weigh ideas,[8] one against the other—each has a life of its own. Cf. Nietzsche. What a fiasco it is if one tries to discover any system in his work except for that spirit which the wise man chooses as his guide.

Another species is made up of those who loved greatly—Christ, Buddha, Goethe—myself, in those days of autumn when I was in love with Valerie.[9]

These do not seek after any truth, but they feel that something within them is coming together into some kind of whole.

This has something purely human about it—a natural process.

And such people can balance one idea[10] against the other, for that new thing which grows within them has fastidious roots.

21.II. Went to the variety theater with Jacques and Hannak. Jacques—what a character—no one could beat him. One of the chanteuses wasn't bad-looking. Underwear all in grey. After the performance, however, we decided against inviting anybody. Flirted a little with the girl with grey underclothes who had her mother with her. If she had come to our table I'd certainly have behaved decently toward her. Because of that. While I was deep in conversation with Hannak, Jacques beckoned to her and went outside. In the garden he had his way with her—genius!—

22.II . . . . . . It is very seldom that he achieves the musicality which creates in poetry the mystery of song, that sense of melody possessed by Racine, Heine, Baudelaire, Poe, Verlaine, and which vibrates in the remotest regions of our souls.

Nor did Hugo possess that mystical sense of harmony.

. . . . He possessed few of the main characteristics of the creative writer, the mysterious sense of melody and the gift for surrounding reality with an atmosphere of suggestion (Stéphane Mallarmé on Victor Hugo).

Books: Romanes, *Mental Development of Animals*

Conrad Lange, *Journal of the Psychology and Physiology of the Sense Organs*, Vol XIV (1897)—Thoughts on an Aesthetics based on a Theory of Biogenetics.

Karl Groos, *The Games of Animals*

---

* . . . I once wrote to Valerie that it was sufficient if one felt each day that a single thought had grown out of oneself to maturity—clear and yet {after Mallarmé} surrounded by the sensuous mysteries of art.

In these entries there isn't yet a single line that reaches that standard.

23.II. Today, during a military exercise, I stood on the Swedish fortifications.[11] Far beneath us, away in the distance, lay Brünn, huddled fearfully around the Spielberg as if it could be covered up with a single giant hand.

A sense that one ought to be able to reach it in a single bound. The Swedish barbarians may well have felt a similar delight in the anticipation of booty when, long ago, the voracious pack appeared on these heights for the first time.

All the way from Sweden! It's the first time that I understand this wolf horde and that I can grasp how it is possible that their souls did not starve to death on the journey.

"There's nothing can hold me now" . . . "Here today, there tomorrow" . . . Good old Godfather Death . . . . This affected me intensely once before, as I remember.

But in my case this was a refinement of the soul that required a whole complex personality.

Moreover, this is poetry that, apart from anything else, doesn't flourish on forced marches.

But it is as if the northern wolves appeared before my eyes. Human beings—yes—but yet real beasts of prey. Why not? The cerebral element notwithstanding. But sensitive. An animal must be able to sense things in a very similar fashion, must know the same passion.[12] What drove them over here from Sweden—wasn't it this passion?! From time to time to stand on heights such as these and, senses quivering with lust, to pick up an advance scent of the moment when, in a single bound, one is amongst the people?!

It's ridiculous to adduce sociological motives. Whatever may have been their reasons for heeding the call of the recruiting sergeant, what was it that gave them the nourishment of passion they needed each day? Why didn't they die for want of passion? The reason: these moments. And ones related to these. Horde of wolves!

It is the human being—in his great deeds—{or rather} in his voluminous deeds that ensure lasting effects by virtue of their mass [. . .][13]

The sure, fine actions of the mind are only like droplets of a fine scent. Even if they take intense effect the exquisiteness of their conception lasted only minutes, hours, days.

And the extent and volume of a sensation have a value of their own.

Even if one usually chooses to neglect this.

Our life, after all, lasts only for a certain length of time—and every hour is the same gaping hole, the same child of death, that we have to fill in.

And with fine things one fills nothing. The essence of fineness, deeds of the spirit,[14] they are moments of conception, an abstract from life, a kind of holy spirit, a sacred mystery, the touch of energy—they have no psychic dimensions.

This is why they don't fill out the hours.

To do so, they must first be transformed into life and what is crucial is the kind of ethical state into which they propel us and how long their effects last. In moral terms they do remain but, ethically, they fade away.[15]

They describe circles in the soul and the breadth of these circles, the extent of the movement, the hours in which we are still ethical—that is the volume-factor in our lives——

So this is the way to assess what happens when something drives a human being here all the way from Sweden. And, even after all the subtractions that one has to make, there is enough left over to cause disquiet.

It is horrifying for us to confront such a brutal insight. But do we have the right to be so proud. People like me? Can we condemn them without hesitation?

Whose lives are riddled with such despair and emptiness?

<To be human is such a precarious thing.> [. . .]

———————

4.III. An hour of our Sundays belongs to God, the rest to pleasure that has no relation to God whatsoever.

Religion has quite forgotten its base. [. . .]

Why do I love so much the illogical products from the early phase of the *Vienna Review*[16] era?

—They have the royal freedom of fantasy—after Emerson—

Their authors are often mediocre human beings but are appealing because they are so possessed. [. . .]

12.III. In the early morning I went for a stroll over the Franzensberg—on the path that runs past the whore-houses from where one can look down into their backyards. Turned over in my head those unnerving passages that I once heard Paderewski play.

Then I started reflecting that if one had somebody who could weave that kind of feeling around one's soul or if one was such a person oneself { = conception of another life. Related to the erotic dream. Turning away abruptly from life.}

I sensed that I would turn away completely from life and toward this person—because life is not able to offer me something of like value. And, even as my feelings were dreaming away behind the high walls of the garden, it seemed to me to be the park of a lunatic asylum.[17]

"Art is a form of sickness. Or rather it would be possible to treat art as a kind of sickness"—this was roughly how I put it in my *Paraphrases*.[18]

And today, one year later, this idea is reborn within me—so I can see that it really did die in me—just like the whole of that beautiful period.

This sensation of dying—that once led to the abrupt break with Valerie—is evil.

We cannot hold fast to a wonderful insight within us, it withers away, petrifies and then we find that all that is left in our hands is the impoverished logical framework of the idea.

The possession of an insight is of no consequence whatsoever—even if it was the greatest expression of genius since the world began (and the world doesn't exist, by the way). We have to make anxious attempts to transform insight into "deeds" (in terms of the terminology of either Emerson or Maeterlinck). Then we possess it.

(This contrast between insight and deed is, by the way, not without a certain psychological interest.)

22.IV. I've appended an article about the book "Goethe as a Thinker." With respect to an article that I wrote about fencing, my material showed that a characteristic of decadence in French fencing was a tendency toward aesthetic overvaluing of the detail, the distinct moment of beauty, at the expense of the goal-orientated, more brutal totality of the fight.

I couldn't help thinking of d'Annunzio and also of the exaggerated value that Gustl[19] and I occasionally attached to certain "refinements." And also of our recent denial of the notion of repressing each separate beautiful idea and everything that is transitory—in short, of the possibility that there is something here that has general significance. By the way, we have to empathize with decadent people! {Then one learns to see.} When one feels things subjectively one never reaches any conclusion. Subjective feeling cannot make a decision—it reconstructs sensations and, within certain limits, finds {even} decadent beauty pleasurable.

What is interesting about this case is that the criterion lies outside the bounds of our sense of pleasure.

One cannot {any longer} rely completely on oneself (and can hope only for instincts that protect us from errors). "I am no longer on my own at the center of things; something alien, with its own laws stands beside me."[20]

3.V. Style in novels, in its tendency to suppress details, has the advantage, over the novella and the psychological sketch, of a certain degree of nobility. This became apparent to me in three instances. In Wassermann's *Renate Fox*[21] it gives rise to distaste mixed, however, with a touch of cautious respect.

In a novel by Potapenko which is otherwise undistinguished it gives rise to a quite eminent passage. "When the train passed places where the sun shone, there was the scent of mountain violets . . ." or something like that. Succinct, a sentence that simply registers things with no painting and no effort to be expressive, presenting the mood as a whole. Finally, the first chapter of the *Foolish Virgin* by [Rudolf] Stratz.[22] One would simply have to extend it to produce an excellent and exceptional sketch. After the fashion of the "dissecting" method that we once valued so highly. One would simply concentrate on one or other situation and develop there the full range of psychological refinement.

The novel-style despises such a method. And there is no doubt that it makes on me a noble impression. It does not even imply; it simply involves. In comparison, the whole dissecting method seems immature or, if one wishes to borrow from the realm of recent sport-theory,[23] "decadent."

Of course I wouldn't write like Stratz did, I would give more weight to the fine points of psychology, and the value of what is said resides solely in the caution which it instructs us to adopt. [. . .]

8.V. Today I borrowed two large volumes of Nietzsche from the Franzens-museum. A mood of sanctity took hold of me; how much reading his work once meant to me!

What kind of effect will he have on me this time?!

At any rate he means to me: recollection, self-examination, all kinds of positive things. I've already read the preface to *The Gay Science*. It's a work that helps to put things in their place—I once noted down something to this effect.

13.V. Characteristic is the way he says: "this could be the case and that, too. And on that basis one might build this and on the other that."

In short: he speaks of nothing but possibilities, nothing but combinations without showing us how even a single one of them could be worked out in reality.

But it is clear that it is only then that one can judge the value of an idea, or indeed that one can see what manner of person one is dealing with.

This way of thinking is bereft of life—the brain is pursuing flights of fancy.

In this case, admittedly, it's the + + + [*sic*] brain of Nietzsche—but people exist in whom this kind of thinking is unbearable.

People with busy brains that are indefatigable in their ability to make combinations and who are unbearably smug about it.

Such people make one realize that these rich, quicksilver brains have no value at all.

Perhaps the judgment is too harsh in so far as it affects Nietzsche. He points out to us all the paths along which our brain can proceed but he doesn't actually set out along any of them.

Perhaps this {in itself} was a major contribution but it fails to impress me as such today because it already seems such a common, everyday matter and I've forgotten who it is I actually owe all these riches. {How droll one is when young! Nietzsche as someone who is barely good enough to serve as a step for a young rascal! How one tends to see only what is beneath one! How remote is the idea of entering Nietzsche's thought as a whole.}[24]

15.V. Fate: that I was only eighteen years of age when I first read Nietzsche. Just at the point when I left the military. Just in that particular year of my development.

24.V. At the moment my attitude to all kinds of sensuality is frivolous in the extreme—I accept and enjoy every kind of sensual experience without any form of restraint.

There was a time when the opposite was true. A certain mistrust of banal sexuality, etc.; not wanting to enjoy, etc. In those days I would have treated with suspicion, and rejected, much of what I now surrender to without thinking and which I am occasionally tempted to see as that alone which is firm, unambiguous, whereas understanding[25] is eternally erratic, eternally insubstantial.

The conflict between understanding and the senses that I traversed in earlier years has now been turned on its head without having yet led to any tangible result. So take care!

26.V. Today I came across Mach's lectures on popular science which proved to me at just the right time that it is possible to base an existence on the understanding, and for that existence still to be deeply significant.[26] In the final analysis I've never doubted this—but I'm here taking the precaution of reminding myself again.

When I turned my back on the understanding, this originated and developed after I made the following assumption: even if the content of the understanding increases and the sum of knowledge grows, the person who typifies understanding (scholar, researcher) has remained constant throughout. One example: the "human" factor in Mach remains today the same as in Galileo.

This type has both remained constant and has changed.

In precisely the degree to which lack of confidence in understanding is justified—and not justified.

No idea why the following thought has just occurred to me: was Nietzsche's theory of morals perhaps given its impetus by his relationship with R. Wagner? For here one would find, on the one hand, an egoism that would not admit its own existence and, on the other, the force of a personality that rescues the given theme from the philistrosity that adheres to it.

27.V. The paths of the intellect[27] are strange ones. One can say that, in the course of evolution, the intellect has made the greatest progress. But one could also express this as follows: in the course of evolution, intellect has shown the least degree of stability.

Intellectual progress has always simply consisted in correcting, at every stage, the errors that one produced {for oneself} at the previous stage.

On the other hand—looking around—it is the quality of understanding[28] that demonstrates the greatest capacity for giving shape and substance to any human life.

What impressed me in earlier times about Schiller's moralizing aesthetics was that one sensed it was completely adequate for all one's needs.

And as far as "the sensual" is concerned, the fiasco can barely be concealed. It is associated with a certain barrenness. What was the harvest that this method brought me in a full year? How few of the hours brought fulfillment. And the price paid for all of this was sloppiness of thought!

It is characteristic of this barrenness that the "great work" seemed to me attainable only via all the stimulants that loneliness, suggestion, and positively hallucinogenic isolation could provide.

31.V. ". . . . rhythm burst into speech as a force that rearranges all the atoms of the sentence, prescribes the choice of words and gives fresh color to thoughts, making them darker, more alien, more remote" (Nietzsche, *The Gay Science*, p. 114).

Nietzsche goes on to explain poetry in terms of its usefulness in conjuring up gods, demons, human passions. A rowing song, for example, exists not to help me row more easily but because the god of the waters is soothed by the song.

Similarly, according to Nietzsche, the purpose of the orgiastic cults was not to send the personality into ecstasy but to give sudden release to the "ferocia" of the divine in an orgy that was intended to make it feel freer and calmer afterward so that it left people in peace . . .

Extract from a letter to Frau Tyrka.[29]

_____

.. I'm experiencing that old conflict between brain and the rest of the nervous system, between the pleasure in logical speculation and that more "lyrical" kind I've practiced in recent times. In my last letter I was still very angry with the understanding—I'm always moving from one state to the other and will probably continue to do so for some time to come. It's a full year since I wrote a piece of any consequence and when I think back it appears to me like one of those many Sunday afternoons that I used to spend in my shadow-filled room—reading a sentence from some book or other, then moving to the desk or to the window to fetch a sheet of paper or a box of matches,[30] then stopping next to the desk or window and standing for ten, twenty minutes, the object motionless in my hand as I stared out vacantly—then another sentence, and so on until dusk and supper.

May I beg your attention, gracious lady? Here is something that needs your judgment, and I ask in all seriousness: can an organism that functions in such a manner still pursue some purpose, is this simply weakness or a form of male hysteria?

On the other hand, this has been the year in which I have experienced many mutually incompatible moods.

"Mood" is probably not the right word. What I mean is something far more incisive—a complex of views, hopes, aims—the prospect of a path that one wants to take because one senses that it leads to a goal.

Yes, indeed—many things of this type.

This is not the stuff from which good memories are made. Perhaps each path would have led to some achievement if circumstances had been favorable. Or rather, if I had set out on it at all, which I never did.

I don't know if you will find the comparison I have chosen sufficiently concrete—my room smells of turpentine which makes me express myself somewhat carelessly. By setting out on a path I mean really going down it with one's whole self, with flesh and blood—not simply flitting along it in a fleeting act of the understanding.

You know how much importance I attach to this and the extent to which "art" for me is only a means of reaching a higher level of the "self." Sometimes I took this to extremes, setting in the place of "self" sensuality in the broadest sense. I did not put my ideas down at all, I quietly forgot them—the main thing was that they left a pleasant mood behind them. Thus I often lay on my divan and slaved away at this kind of self-annihilation. This may well be very educative, but it degenerated into, so to speak, a moral underpinning and defense within myself of the lethargy that I mentioned at the beginning.

Work, I imagine, implies that the value attaching to one's self remains unchanged and—by dint of self-persuasion or other such influences—is simply caught in the spell of some lasting and penetrating suggestion, and really lives within its span, is utterly permeated by it.

I imagine that one later wakes up and is left with the feeling that something dark and no longer comprehensible has enriched one's life.

Enormous concentration is required and since I lacked this I simply did not work at all, which I did not consider to be any great loss. [. . .]

Nietzsche says that it might come about that wars are waged for the sake of an insight. He repeats this too often for it to be possible to take him figuratively, to see it as just a mental process.[31]

On the contrary, we must assume that the courage and joy in battle that constantly reappear in Nietzsche's work point in that direction and thus have to be taken literally.

In the final analysis, it is quite interesting to take this point of view seriously and to reflect whether an insight in general is worth that much.

8.VI. How we read Kant: we cope very quickly with his logical man-traps. We simply make judgments based on linguistic criticism—here as everywhere.

But there are two grounds for being skeptical about the cheap pleasure of criticizing Kant from the "biogenetic" perspective.

First, "biogenetic" explanation, proof, analysis, etc., is the habitual way we think. It has been in the air over the last few decades. And such habits of mind are the most invisible and most rigid barriers.

Second, our "critique" has no point if we do not take leave of our habitual way of thinking, using it simply to criticize Kant. Rather we must criticize our way of thinking from Kant's point of view if we want to derive any benefit from the exercise.

How we sometimes seem to be moral:

Envy, greed, etc., are not bad in themselves, they are not unconditionally bad. But in each case we have to be persuaded by our understanding which reminds us that this holds true.

For we are used to evaluations that are held to be generally valid. And the reason for this is that in envy, in greed, etc., there is always a tendency that is distasteful to us—and rightly so. And this impression is always the immediate response and makes it easier for our sloth to keep silent in the face of the general judgment.

Today I did indeed feel shocked, while reading *Beyond Good and Evil* when I came across a passage where Nietzsche propagated the above characteristics,[32] and I felt repelled by them and had first to reflect before conceding he was right.

———————————

Summer in the mountains.

While, down in the valley, the air is soft and cool, as if it came from hidden tracts of snow, the moon above wanders in the glacier-landscape of white clouds at the edge of black sky-lakes.

And while, soft as a cat, you sit beside me, and it seems as if your sensuality stretched itself out over enormous hidden surfaces of snow, my soul becomes reflective, sad, desirous, ephemeral, and trembles like a note that has been played too long, with nervous tenacity—and though, in my desire, I am so small, so whipped and wretched beside you, it seems to me at times as if I were standing next to the moon by the abyss of white cloud-glaciers and looking into the black water of the sky-lakes—a long, mindless gaze— and suddenly lifted my head and strode off across open country . . .

it seems to me at times as if I were standing next to the moon by the abyss of the white cloud-glaciers, gazing like the moon in deep and vacant sadness into the black water of the sky-lakes.[33]

———————————

30.VI. First Treatise of *The Genealogy of Morals*, 7.

. . it is well-known that priests make the worst enemies—why?—because they are the least powerful.

Nietzsche, I believe, is guilty here of the kind of oversight that he warned against on the previous page.

He takes the notion of priest in a much later form, where he had undergone a spiritual transformation and, as it were, become charged with symbolism. He doesn't see the priest in a sufficiently primitive way. The princely priest, the warrior-priest, the sturdy hunter-bishop, was himself, in respect to the way he lived, a knight, he simply performed the functions of a priest for various reasons, none of which were particularly spiritual.

Admittedly it may be the case that I, too, have a later type in mind—what I have said somehow conjured up the priest of the Middle Ages—and is not necessarily valid. At any rate it has to do with who was active first: the essentially hysterical type who founded a religion—the kind that Nietzsche posits as priestly-hysterical—or the type who was an average member of a caste of priests—which I posit.

It must be borne in mind here that religion is the product of both—the only thing that I am able to assert from the outset.

During my reading of Nietzsche I felt the need for a different arrangement of the material, for a grouping around the questions that are closest to my heart.

On the other hand, one can read Nietzsche in such a fashion that one infers what is closest to his heart or rather what is most personal to him from his arrangement of the material; one attempts to get to know him and not just his philosophy. [. . .]

Evening in an elegant street.

July night. A piano and a harmonium join in a lament to Tristan. This imparts to suffering an exquisitely painful range of colored tints that simply do not exist in reality. The unending intensity, the sweet agonies that their notes would have them believe they feel are simply beyond these people's range . . .

Then the piano falls silent and the harmonium wanders on alone as if in old-fashioned arabesques between golden brown cornfields with girls in loose-fitting dresses and wide-brimmed hats.

Seduction.

Well then, draw the curtain to one side: what do you see? Oh, besides your fear! Stars? Come now, stars!

And do you still dare to speak of sacrifices? Of the sacrifice of your soul's peace? Of the sacrifice of your purity? And have you not yet learned to smile at the "size" of the loss that you are about to sustain?

What are all passions to us, what do all sorrows mean to us when set against this one passionate sorrow with which we try to read in the stars the mystery of their size, their incomprehensibility, their remoteness!

That stubborn passion that persuades us that only when the mystery of these stars is revealed shall we discover the secret of our souls.[34]

And until then . . . . . .

6.VIII. A major source of vulgarity is our sensuality. On occasions it still feels a sense of shame if it does not come across with the swagger and dash of a smart lieutenant—as happened, for example, with me and the two Viennese women.

And in just the same degree it delights in orgiastic excess.

It must become pale, elegant, discriminating. Sensualities clothed in the timeless color of autumn! With a very, very fine line marking them off from—I wanted to say, decadence, but such distinctions are so worthless!

"Sketchbook of a sensitive man" {Sensitive Sketchbook} would be the title that does not promise too much and that expresses precisely the degree of arrogance toward myself that I find appropriate.

These thoughts are often as thin as the plait of a little schoolgirl . . . a passage from the Preface.

---

3 October.

On the concept of décadence [*sic*]: in the first instance, the concept of décadence is not firmly fixed, taking its cue from the kind of person who happens to be passing judgment; so I may find, with Nietzsche's work for example, that he tends to present as decadent whatever is harmful to the understanding (for example, his healthy music—whereby it is still perfectly apparent how far he pushes this).

A further question: are there other passages in Nietzsche's works that allow us to deduce that an absolute notion of décadence exists—a notion of absolute décadence?

A general observation can be made here: there are roughly as many types of décadence as there are ideals. Almost every human being possesses not only his subjective ideal but also its negation, his subjective conception of décadence.

Is it not perhaps possible, despite this, to conceive of the concept of décadence in a more objective way—as the ideal? (Fencing in France.)

A further question: is the art of a politically decadent time necessarily decadent itself?

[. . .]

décad[ence]. Socrates' problem: Athens in decline and aware of its decline. Anarchic instincts, always on the verge of excess, the "monstrum in animo"[35] as a danger for all.

The drives want to act the tyrant, one has to invent a counter-tyrant, who is stronger than they are. All the world has need of him—his drug, his cure, the artifice he has personally evolved for self-preservation.

Reason = virtue = happiness.

With him the dialectic came into its own. In the agonal drives of the Hellenes it finds fertile ground. Nonetheless this marks the end of the nobility of taste that until then had rejected the dialectic as bad manners. One "issued commands" rather than "gave proofs" {(Dialecticians: Jews, *Reinecke Fuchs*, Socrates)}

Resumé—the one-sided overemphasis on reason points toward {undermined} conditions, toward lack of trust in instincts. A symptom of décadence.

In addition, Socrates' new method ran counter to the Greek tradition—however, this only provides proof of decadence when allied with the pathological character of this philosophy. [. . .]

Conduct of life.[36] At the age of thirty, in terms of high culture, one is a beginner, a child. One has to learn to see, one has to learn to think, one has to learn to speak and to write: the goal of all these is an aristocratic culture. To learn to see—to accustom the eye to be calm, patient, to be practiced in "waiting-for-things-to-approach-one"; to defer judgment, to learn to examine, to comprehend the individual case from all sides. This is the first schooling in spirituality: not to react immediately to a stimulus but to get a hold on those instincts that stall and inhibit. To learn to see, as I understand it, is almost the same as what is called—in non-philosophical terminology—"strength of will." The essential thing here is, precisely, not "wanting," suspending the decision. All lack of spirituality, all baseness, rests on the inability to resist a stimulus: one is compelled to react, one follows each and every impulse. In many cases such a necessity is, in itself, a susceptibility to illness, decline, a symptom of exhaustion. Almost everything that is crudely and unphilosophically branded with the name "vice" is nothing but the physiological inability *not* to react. One use to which one can put "having-learned-to-see": as a learner one becomes slow, suspicious, reluctant in all things. Anything alien or new one first, with hostile composure, allows to approach—one pulls back one's hand from them. (Doesn't this image vaguely remind one of the little dog whose hair stands on end and that puffs itself up when it faces a big one? M[usil]) Standing there with all doors open, the obsequious "lying-down-on-one's-belly" before every petty fact, the all-too-obliging "putting-oneself-out-for," "putting-oneself-into," other people and other things, in short that famous modern attitude, objectivity, is in bad taste, it's non-aristocratic in the extreme. {Path to Express[ionism]} [. . .]

Re Hartmann: mistrust of the thinking artist.

H. is quite right to give prominence to something that was emphasized by Schopenhauer already, namely the factor of the unconscious in artistic production. In its consequences, however, his distinction between dream-consciousness and waking consciousness goes too far, for a scientific thought is perceived in precisely the same way as one relating to a work of art; Hartmann's concept can only relate to "thinking" not to the individual thought.

But it is probably misleading anyway to take everything that is not discursive about thinking and ascribe it automatically to a dream-consciousness.

Later H., too, simply calls it "the unconscious factor."

Servile and liberal arts: according to H. it is decisive for tectonics that only when buildings are reproduced in the form of paintings that they take on an aesthetic aura whereas in the liberal arts such a reproduction would produce only a copy.

The following can be said against this viewpoint:

1. H. himself cites in another passage the little temples to friendship, ostentatious chimney-pieces, blind portals, etc. How are we to interpret these other than as attempts to provoke a response to the aura of the aesthetic.

2. It is perfectly possible, and would amount to an interesting psychological and artistic experiment, to make new versions of some well-known picture, or more specifically a portrait, with different lighting and different expressions, treating it as if it had an independent life of its own.

It might be added that, in terms of its actual structure, a building might well be described in many respects as being of "servile beauty" whereas this is decidedly not the case with regard to the original architectonic conception.

This example on its own shows how, with a change of point of view, judgments change too.

Thus one is forced to say that, in reality, a compromise is always reached between the liberal and the servile and that, in each case, a variable "plus" is decisive for the interpretation. [. . .]

H. Bahr: *Dialogue on the Tragic*[37]

Development of Greek tragedy: antisocial drives are tamed by human beings in the mold of Theseus—priest-people; in order that the drives were not transformed into malicious instincts the tragedy was invented as a means of "abreaction."

This may be so. But either the first taming took place through violence, then, after the death of the ruler, a reaction set in, as happened with the German Middle Ages, for example. Or the first master gained his following not only through simple "political" interests but through "ethical" ones that are based on some "new species" of human needs. Then the work, of which the master was merely the agent, will remain—but this, in the same proportion, reduces the need for tragedy.

If one replaces violence (whether the violence be that inherent in the promises and threats of politics or whether it rests on interests held in common) with a priestly lie like the one that was Homer, a fertile soil must be available for the lie to be credible. It is also scarcely possible for this to be the work of one single person; with particular regard to Homer this runs counter to what is generally held to be true.

So, even if Bahr's view cannot be turned down flat, it hardly provides a convincing explanation and has scarcely more weight than that of a chance "aperçu."

I would tend to support the following modification to his explanation:

As long as one has to work on a culture one sees it as being of importance to oneself. It is not suited to "play." But among the stages that culture has traversed there is one that is sufficiently removed from us in time to permit us to play with it and that is yet so close that our game can still have significance for us. This is the sphere of the Tragic.

This is also the realm where the concept of the "aesth[etic] game" is most applicable.

Why doesn't our culture produce any games for adults? {card games!} Why can't we have our fun? And when we do have fun, why in our games—in a stylized, nostalgic fashion—do we sate our appetite on earlier times. Dance? Blind man's buff? Games in a circle? We play at playing games; we never play our own game.

Preparations for the novel.[38]

While the older brother was alive, members of the household treated him with the respect due to someone with prospects. He had his own study next to his father's, his own books. R[obert], on the other hand, who was already 20 years of age on the death of his brother, had to make do up till then with the former nursery, spreading his work out on a disused dining-table; he had to put up with the large wardrobes and linen cupboards in his room. People were always coming to unlock them, disturbing him with their noise and shutting the doors again without much consideration for him.

In this way a sense of anxiety, unease, persecution grew up with R. No stable relationship had been established between himself and this room in which he had spent the greater part of twenty years.

The room was large, with two windows onto the garden, and the tall trees left it in almost permanent shadow. Linoleum covered much of the parquet floor, its pattern worn down. The idea of touching this covering with his fingers, of kneeling down or rolling around on it, was quite out of the question for R. A feeling of discomfort, of repugnance, resisted the idea. He didn't even like walking about on it and he felt, as it were, compelled to restrict all contact with it—even with his feet—to a minimum. Often he stood for a long time—for half an hour or three-quarters of an hour—at one of the windows, looking at the garden. But this, too, was more an inexplicable spell than a pleasure. And, in any case, one could see no more than a short stretch of the gravel paths and thousands, tens of thousands of leaves in the most varied tones of shadowy green, in a complex tangle of superimpositions. But R. didn't see this either. He saw only a dark mass, a slowly moving, breathing mass, and something dark spread out within him, something uniform and featureless filled his soul. And when at last he tore himself away from the window, he was invariably tired and prone to tears. But not disposed to any kind of actual outburst like sobbing or weeping.

The larger part of the time he spent at the big table. He was quite indifferent to the things he learnt there, never asking what purpose it was supposed to serve—of itself, the compulsion to learn gave him enjoyment. It was like a strong rope binding him fast to his chair and preventing the giddiness that was prompted by the emptiness all around, with its free fall into boundless space. If he had a German essay to write this intensified the feeling. The teachers were astonished at the length of his assignments and at the richness of the views and images that he worked into them. He felt as if he was running with glowing cheeks along a tightrope and that it was only the speed with which he piled up his thoughts that could save him. But even when this lasted sometimes for two or three hours, when the last word had been written and all had been read through again, he finally fell off headlong again.

If at all possible he stayed away from his room. Usually in the garden. There he would sometimes spend a long time watching a snail crawling over a leaf—once more vacant and spellbound. On several occasions he was observed by his father in this state. But he could not answer his father's questions about what he was thinking. So his father believed that he was interested in observation—and gradually such inconsequentialities gave rise to the intention of making a scientist out of him. R. spent most of the time in the lowest part of the garden where the ground fell away sharply, where it was very damp and the lettuces and hog-weed grew in abundance.

Once he was sitting, hidden deep in the bushes, next to the wooden fence that marked the boundary with the neighboring garden. There, on the other side as well, something was moving in the thick shrubs. His heart pounded in fear but he stayed sitting quietly. It was a small girl called <Bertha> Clarisse,[39] the youngest of the five children of the painter who lived next door.

{First with a girl-friend, then alone in the scene. With regard to the tale that Clarisse later tells.}

Then they would often meet in great secrecy. And on every occasion— even as he cautiously parted the bushes to creep in—his heart beat as strongly as it had the first time.

But it beat with particular strength when Bertha told him how her father, who was very quick-tempered, would hit her. And once when Bertha arrived, with tears still in her eyes and the skin of her cheeks, softened and swollen by the salty drops, gave off a strangely warm scent, his heart leapt up into his mouth so that he had to take hold of the wooden bars of the trellis and choked on every word while he felt a trembling and tugging in his eyes. Finally he managed to stammer out the words: "Show me where he hit you" and he was frightened at his boldness and had an unclear feeling that he had done something bad and was frightened that Bertha would run away and tell how bad he was.

{Why does he say that? Because an instinct tells him that this is something new and not so boring! (That's the main thing!) The emptiness, unhappiness, of being a child! Walks, etc.} {Take this overall as the basic mode.}

For at night he always had to sleep with his hands over the covers and it had repeatedly been explained to him that certain parts of the body were indecent.

But Bertha didn't run away. She knelt on the other side of the fence and seemed to be frozen in this position. A slat could be pushed to one side and Robert slipped across [. . .]. But then suddenly he knelt down not knowing what to do. Bertha kept looking hard at his face. Quite without expression. The eyes of a child. She was frightened, not knowing what he wanted. {The snake of paradise is throttling them both.}

"Why do you want to see it?"

"I want to look at it."

Bertha sat down on the ground and Robert crept up to her side. It had rained and his fingers sank deep into the damp leaf-mould. A smell of foliage rose up. Then they sat beside each other.

"I've never been beaten," said Robert, "does it hurt very much?" With the memory, tears came back into Bertha's eyes. He would have liked to stroke her. But something held him back from this small girl. Something like disdain. She wasn't pretty and the shame of having been beaten made her seem even uglier to him. She would have to answer; he waited.

{This Clarisse then turns completely away from the suffering and sexuality of her childhood and becomes Walther's[40] bride.}

"Yes, it hurts" she said at last.

"Show me!"

And again Bertha looked at him uncertainly. Several times the arm with which she was supporting herself moved, then tensed again.

"But you can't see anything" she said, both disconcerted and attracted by Robert's definite wish. But he forced her onto her side. And she did not offer any resistance. When he undid the buttons on her little white drawers both of them felt a rush of blood.

After this, they sat in silence for a while; there seemed to be no appropriate thing to do next. It was actually something of a disappointment. Robert had vaguely expected something to happen: as if he would be able to see the pain that had been inflicted there; while he had been performing the action, listening for any noise around them, the hot, urgent feeling that had impelled him to do it had vanished. And Bertha felt this and was suddenly ashamed.

"Goodbye, then" said Robert, crawled quickly back and ran up to his room.

Once there, however, his memory gradually changed color; he became uneasy again and went into his parents' room. He sat on a stool in the corner and closed his eyes. He wanted to call everything to mind again—from a place of safety—but he couldn't remember in detail how everything had happened; all that remained was an uncertain feeling of having experienced something that had brought happiness.

Later he had frequent meetings with Bertha. But the only effect these had was to excite his whole being, to subject it to an uncanny acceleration—he couldn't keep hold on anything for long, the words came tumbling over each other as he spoke, when he lay in bed his thoughts raced so quickly that he couldn't hold on properly to a single one. But this state did not lead anywhere. It heaped up in him the most fevered imaginings, each of which started out in a more monstrous way than the last but constantly broke off at a certain point. So Robert later stopped meeting her.

This was also partly because he had now found a friend. Professor D[onath] had accepted an appointment at the University and had moved into the apartment above their own. His son, Gustl, was only about two years older than Robert. But they were in the same class and Gustl was rather weak—so this evened things out.

They played at being cops and robbers, they wrestled and boxed. But often Gustl became exasperated at always being beaten by R. and then they told each other stories. Gustl was better at this; he could tell the most monstrous tales whereby he would always set out from a real person or real event familiar to them both. He was an inveterate liar. He wasn't treated badly by his parents—they showed no interest in him, concerning themselves exclusively with his elder sister, an invalid; he simply received the prescribed punishments when he had performed poorly at school or suchlike, and he did his best to avoid the unpleasant formality of such treatment.

Once R. was sick in bed. He was recovering but still very weak and could scarcely move. Gustl sat next to the bed, reading to him. About Vineta, the sunken city. Then Gustl suddenly shut the book and began to tell a fairy-story. About Clarisse.

About a girl who loved both of them and to whom—in intimations that he had made to Gustl—R. had transferred his experience with Clarisse. His only lie. And not in order to boast about the girl but because he wanted to tell the story and could think of no one else to tell it to.

{And so Walter exaggerates later, too, and with these lies drives Hugo[41] to extremes because of insatiability toward Tonka.[42] The "capacity for stimulation" is prefigured here.}

He had placed himself at the foot of the bed from where he could follow precisely every move that Robert made and, after a while, he asserted that what he was about to narrate was the truth. He described an experience identical to the one that Robert had had. But in his mouth it sounded much more seductive. {Leitmotif!} Robert began to yearn for what he had treated so inattentively; he became envious of Gustl. But he did not believe that Gustl was speaking the truth. Then he suddenly looked at him. Gustl's child's face expressed "Schadenfreude," he seemed to be lying in wait, he was triumphing over Robert {Leitmotif for G[ustl]!} who had to come to terms with the way another rooted around in his possessions—and Robert understood all at once that Gustl was now taking his revenge for always having been the weaker in their rough-and-tumble games.

When Gustl took pleasure in painting the scene in greater detail, R. thought no longer of whether it was true or false—he looked for something that he could throw at Gustl's head. But the fever attacks had exhausted him and he had no strength. And Gustl calmed him down. "What's so important about it? After all, you've always told me everything, haven't you?"

"Yes, but that was me—and it wasn't for you to interfere with it at all."

But Gustl merely smiled—he had kept something back and this was about to be brought up.

"Don't get worked up," he said, "I haven't finished the story yet. Pay attention instead. Do you know where children come from?"

"That business with the stork is only a fairy-tale, so Papa once told me—in any case it's quite impossible—but, apart from that, I haven't thought about it."

Gustl then gave him an explanation. In a vague, mysterious manner this went circling around something that Gustl himself could not imagine precisely but that he described, in words that were all the more passionate, as something wonderful that he alleged he had done with the girl. While Robert was sick, a friend at school had told him the facts of life.

It was only after Gustl had left and night had come that Robert grasped the full weight of what he had heard. He tried to visualize all that Gustl had told him. It was no use—he got no further than he had with Clarisse in reality on that previous occasion. And the fire that his imagination lit always turned inward at this point and his brain failed—as if consumed by flames.

At last R. got dreadfully tired. A sweat had broken out and the linen sheet that pressed against his body in a hundred folds was soaked—his hands were dry and his senses raw. He saw figures coalescing in the dark and heard with unusual intensity the creaking of the furniture at night. . . . .

When he had recovered, the first thing he asked Gustl was whether he, too, could try it out with that little girl. But Gustl, the liar, had excuses that made it impossible. No girl dares to do something like that a second time and he had promised that he would not breathe a word about it, etc.—and finally Robert had also to swear that he wouldn't betray a single word.

But in the meantime Gustl had been initiated into the most quintessential school secret.

Now the garden lost its attraction; its place was taken by the attic. Admittedly they still wrestled, boxed and ran races—but those utterly dead hours, such as the ones after walks with parents, no longer existed. Pretending to play a game of robbers they crept off into the remotest parts of the attic and crouched in a dark corner.

Here a remarkable difference between the two friends came to light. With Gustl it was more a pleasure, with Robert more a vice. Gustl's capacity for illusion knew no bounds. Robert was aware only of a dark burning sensation {without imagination} that forced him down to the ground and drove him to exhaustion. Afterward he felt as if nothing had happened; with the exception of the inevitable shame, he felt light and free whereas with Gustl everything was still trembling, and extremely intense but sickly pale fantasies were pursuing him. {Anders[43]—Walther; important characteristics}

He had by now confessed to Robert that he had deceived him on that earlier occasion. So the question of what it might really be like preoccupied the two of them. They brought exciting news back from school. Girls were supposed not to be able to resist certain signs, and other similar things. Giving the excuse that they were visiting school friends, they crept out onto the street in the evening. They made their way to the suburbs where there were obscene chalk drawings on the boarding and there were fewer street lamps. {It was just there that he met H[erma].} They allowed three, four girls—workers from the factory, girls from middle-class households, fetching beer—to pass without summoning sufficient courage. But at last they made the infallible sign to a girl as she passed them, then waited. But she would go on, or would turn around in anger, and once when this happened both of them got frightened again and ran away. But this hope and this fear, these hot lips and cold feet, this cloying mist that rose up from the empty building sites—it was all simply wonderful.

And because that was basically quite a different feeling Robert gradually began to feel ashamed of the secrecy. Once they were caught in the attic—they were not completely compromised but at least under deep suspicion. And Robert had to make a firm promise to his father that he kept.

That was in the summer of the fourth class of the grammar-school and that autumn he left home. He went to a naval training establishment. The endless tracts of land, countless adventures in foreign ports, the aura of distinction of the man who has traveled to distant parts—all these things were now to take the place of those indescribable shivers down the spine, that sense of perpetual unfulfillment, between the boardings in the streets of the suburbs.

When he returned from his travels, his elder brother was at university in Berlin and Gustl was due to move to Vienna in a few weeks to study law.

Robert moved back into the room he had had as a child that had been slightly altered, while the small room next to his still belonged to his brother who worked in it during the vacations.

He had returned with a disappointment. It had happened during the voyage on the training ship. He had begun to find the close spirit of comradeship and discipline oppressive. Adventures did not have their earlier charm once it was not possible to experience them in freedom. The fatalism of a hierarchical profession was a shock to him.

This had happened quite simply. In an hour of leisure he had written a novella in which he depicted his life. It then became perfectly apparent to him that he had to leave. To begin afresh from a point of freedom.

He came home in a state of great calm. The precocious masculinity of the military profession gave him superiority over Gustl who was still the very type of a grammar-school boy. His body and his desires were overdeveloped for his age.

But he was serious-minded. With iron endeavor he made up the necessary ground and, six months after Gustl, he too passed his matriculation.

There followed four years studying earth sciences. In the course of these four years he became very {serious and} melancholic. Fate was remarkably ill-disposed toward him. His yearning for adventure and for an expansive style of life had changed. In the place of the wide-roving romantic had stepped the ideal of the elegant and witty rake. Study was a means to an end; he worked in the big mine-fields around the globe in order to earn a fortune as a mining engineer.[44] And he worked very assiduously, with that iron-willed, yet indifferent, diligence that he had already shown as a boy.

Yet he was drawn not to this but to literature.

At university he had had the opportunity to listen to lectures on this subject. The arrogance that he felt as a modern person confronting these outmoded tendencies made him keep his distance both from literature and from student life. {Pupils from technical schools are more likely to become revolutionaries than are grammar-school boys} He read many books, including works of philosophy—but he read to no plan—he possessed a great disorderly heap of knowledge—and tended to be awkward in his approach to the problems that he encountered. He immersed himself in books that were difficult but that led nowhere, he read them through with painstaking care and there were times when his mind[45] was thereby tempted to stray into quite barren realms, into metaphysical speculations that were terrifyingly insignificant but difficult to unravel. And he felt bored as he did so, he was thoroughly skeptical of the value of all these efforts, but an overpowering thoroughness held him fast to what he had begun. He suffered under this thoroughness, it had a pathological side or even an element of vice about it, for it disadvantaged the whole human being merely in order to satisfy its {the one} ambition. But he bore it within him like a fate, like a dark and ignorant drive.

His father, as a man of science, supported this drive with the most intense inner joy.

And Robert was exceedingly arrogant. When, yet again, he had read a book without gaining anything from it, indeed even when he seemed fated never to find the right way, he was ashamed to confess this to a comrade.

Often he came home, firmly determined to give up reading altogether rather than to read the kind of books he had studied up till then—when he went into his room he was seized by a sense of sadness and pointlessness and, as if to rescue himself, he forced himself down on the chair at his desk to work at his books in the place where he had sat as a child.

His room still had the same effect on him as it had then—a kind of dreadful emptiness that filled him with fear. He once compared himself to a fly shut up within a piece of amber. He felt no less rigid and motionless. And yet he loved this prison. With a listless love forced upon him by exhaustion.

And still he took pleasure in standing at the window for long periods, motionless, vacant, spellbound. When he tore himself away he felt pain, lay on the sofa and was sad to the point of tears—for no reason at all.

Sometimes, in the evenings, he felt compelled to go out. He sought company, fellow-students, harmless people. And he only came home in the morning. His manliness, his strength, was seeking escape. He liked to sit in the little nightclub, drinking beer with the singers according to provincial custom. But he was happier to relax in company to getting close to one of these women. He persuaded himself that he did not have enough money, simply in order to conceal from himself that he was frightened of not being able to start anything with this kind of woman—that his room extended its spell of immobility into this sphere, too, and that although he liked the milieu of pleasure he was not made for pleasure. {And with Anna,[46] are things different then?}

Yet he was sensual. But—and it was difficult to say if it was chasteness or awkwardness—to demand even as much soul as the surrender of a chanteuse requires was in itself too much.

When all of them had gone home he first sought out one of those dark sidestreets where the narrow crooked houses had their curtains drawn. Always the same sequence ran its course within him. An idea rose up abruptly. Not a sensual one but that of a narrow, brown, winding stairway, with a smell of the kind that fills every corner of these houses, the image of the whore climbing up the steps in front of him and, strongest of all, the moment when she turns around in the doorway and looks the unknown guest in the eye. This bored scrutiny that is not sure whether it should veer—for sheer boredom and disgust—into cynicism or into a plea for mercy.

And that was always the end of things, a brief greeting, a hasty return home and, only the next day, a reaction on the part of the imagination that dissected each word spoken and that touched in each chance, fleeting mood with delicate tints.

The same behavior whenever he happened to enter into a fleeting and superficial relationship with some other woman.

He became accustomed to take note of all the minor details of life. The low-pitched sounds in the walls, the dialogues of the furniture expanding at night, the heavy carpets of dusk and the delicate grey veils of the first morning light became familiar to him.

And he yearned for the woman who would be able to transform all this into beauty and happiness, for it was anything other than that.

Only once in all this did he come close to his brother. He was in the penultimate year of his studies and his brother was working on his post-doctoral dissertation. But they weren't able to say very much to each other. The brother was quiet and reserved and it was this, remarkably, that drove Robert to excessive heartiness in expressing his views and to put on a show of bumptious cynicism.

They both got to know an actress. And Robert violated her with malicious remarks after she had granted him a hearing. "Listen" he said—it was in the room he had had as a child—"she isn't much. One always has to provide the flame-bath oneself. The woman just sweats and smiles: is that love?"

But there was no answer and his brother went off in a few days. It was only then that Robert realized how basely he had hurt him. But he had no time left. His affair began to take hold of him. What he had said to his brother was only the baseness that passion drives before it when it first fits out the soul as a bridal chamber. Love often begins with such words of cynicism. He had already taken the first steps down the track, had won the first kisses and still did not know whether it was a game or something more. He felt an obligation to adopt as skeptical a view as possible. But at a deeper level than his reason the threads were being knotted together and what he said and thought was only resistance to this entanglement. Just as young girls at the moment of decision strike out at the lover toward whom they have been driven for many weeks, so he still made play with remarks that violated her while inwardly he was already totally in the woman's possession.

A monstrous storm came. For the first time, his sensuality wore the red, gold-embroidered mantle of love. His whole being was changed. A mood of benevolence and generosity swept over him. Far-reaching thoughts, interweaving their way artistically through each other, took clear shape. In a few weeks he acquired a maturity far beyond his years. {His thoughts and feelings set themselves in order; the philosophy of tranquillity and maturity takes shape.} Then came disillusionment. Simple, brief, necessary. They had finished with each other. "It is immoral to stay together for any longer, unless every single hour brings growth to the soul," he said. "Farewell."

He had seen her the day before in a role in which she had seemed tasteless, inauthentic and banal. There were moments when he woke as if from a dream; like a breath of fresh air, like a new unfamiliar vista.

The following night their sensuality reached greater heights than usual; *vitriolic* {Why is it impossible for a young person to find an expression that is unaffected when one is young?} in their caresses. In the morning he said nothing and in the afternoon he came and said farewell. In the intervening time he had not thought much; it seemed as self-evident and necessary as the time when he had returned to his parents' home.

This was the time when he embarked on the intimate friendship with Gustl.

———————————

{A day just before the start of spring. R[obert] is sitting by the open window in the room leading to the chamber where Grandmama lies dying. R. is thinking of his childhood, the mood in the room suggests it, Novalis[47] suggests it, the girl who comes through the room suggests it. The narrative is his thoughts, but it is to be transformed into a technique of memory. Questions interspersed, why am I thinking of this at this particular moment? A quiet sense of shame in the face of death.}

2
NOTEBOOK 3
1899? TO 1905-1906

[Notebook 3 covers approximately the same period as Notebook 4. Its main concern is with intimate relationships. In one or two, Musil has no direct personal involvement: the liaison between a schoolboy and the mother of a friend who has seduced him, or the chance meeting with a fellow student from Berlin whose female companion Musil subjects to intense scrutiny, noting the lack of dress sense and the inattention to personal hygiene. However, the majority of the relationships touch Musil's own life directly and he plans to exploit them in his creative writing.

One of these is with the mistress of an acquaintance: Jósza inhabits an uncertain realm between the respectable and the tainted; she is discreet but sexually available to men like Musil himself who have standing in society. Other people here will be literary subjects throughout Musil's life. Musil's mother appears in a scene of delicate flirtation on an excursion to the country (which will be used in an MwQ episode where the mother's place is taken by the "grande dame" Diotima); she also haunts Musil's relationship with Herma, in her role as mother reproaching her son for immorality and lack of discretion but also as the woman who makes her implicit claim to be a more compatible partner than the mistress herself. The relationship of Musil to Herma is also worthy of attention in its own right; presented from the man's perspective, it details his awareness of changes over time—Herma's physical flaws, the moments of awkwardness or ineptitude—but continues to radiate the depth of his love. Further evidence of the extent to which figures from childhood preoccupy the adult Musil is seen in the parallelism between Musil's anxieties about Herma Dietz's faithfulness to him *and his unending speculations about the relationship between his mother and Heinrich Reiter. He constantly asks, "Have I been deceived as my father (possibly . . . , probably . . . , certainly!?) was?" but is never content with the answer that the given constellation of evidence provides.*

Musil extends his studies of sexual intrigue and the strange bonds of love into the lives of his friends; Gustl Donath and Alice Charlemont must each have taken Musil separately into their confidence about the early stages of their relationship, with its inhibited, stop-go lovemaking. He is intrigued by the way in which a third party influences their bonding. Through a thin fictional disguise we identify the philosopher Ludwig Klages (who lived with Gustl and Alice for a while), the catalyst of their relationship. Musil is intrigued by the triangulation of feelings that operate within these relationships—the constellation Gustl-Alice-Klages will reappear in MwQ as that of Walter-Clarisse-Meingast—and the hero, Ulrich-Musil, will provide a further element of complication in this fluctuating force field of desires and wills.]

Black exercise book no. 3

1898

Re. Jósza

Met her in October 98. A slippery misty evening in autumn—I was introduced to her on the street by Pigi[e]. Afterward he told me about her. Mistress of Dr. S. Perhaps available for a circle of intimates?

In the course of the next few days I visited her with Pigie. We spoke about the theater, literature, not very much, nor particularly witty things. She seems to be fond of Pigie, in the way that she is fond of her cats. Her apartment very shabby—her clothes fortunately simple and elegant. After about 14 days I visited her on my own and was taken up into the circle of intimates in such a way that the transition bordered on violence.

I was content. By the way I was then already confronted with a puzzle. {fin-de-siècle demonology} There are definitely two sides to her sexuality. While we were embracing something within her suddenly lit up with joy as if someone else had occurred to her. {Modesty of the young person who still feels insecure.} I told her this afterward. She then dismissed me rather quickly although I had clearly flattered her vanity. {The good woman didn't know how to deal with so much cleverness.}

Soon afterward I fell ill. After my recovery I visited her a few more times, but was then prevented from going again by a relapse.

I had already adopted a special tone in my dealings with her. I spoke gently and sympathetically as if with a woman friend whom one wants to possess although one knows it is impossible. From a superficial perspective she gave me everything a woman has to give. But, given her twofold sexual character, this did not mean much, and it was precisely the awareness that she was, in this respect, capable of reaching immense heights that made her an object of desire.

Each time I was with her I fell under the close personal influence of a charming woman, but at other times I hardly thought about her at all. In the spring someone pointed Dr. S. out to me. I had imagined him to be young and, though not witty, precisely because of that all the more dangerous for an average woman. I was pleasantly disabused when I found him to be in his thirties, very tall, *embonpoint* and with the beery face of a German philistine.

Immediately a vague notion of my tactical approach to Jósza took shape. I still had no definite knowledge and had not yet discovered any of the possibilities at my disposal, but I suddenly felt a great pleasure in experimenting with her. (Amusing that sexual possession comes first and has no particular significance and that only then is a search made for a tactic for conquest.)

We were planning an outing on our bicycles. I went to fetch her but she wasn't ready and then she had to go to buy carpets with her aunt. We postponed our meeting to a later hour. I waited for her in a coffee house—she didn't come.

I stopped visiting her.

After a few days I receive a very charming note in which she begs my forgiveness and asks me to visit. As luck would have it I had to leave on a journey at just that time. I informed her of this and promised I would visit after my return. I was full of anticipation when she wrote to say that she wanted to tell me something.

I visited her a few days later. We were rather stiff. I told her that my main concern was not to be a burden to her. [. . .]

Something on Nietzsche.

He is called unphilosophical. His works read like witty frivolities. He appears to me as someone who has found access to a hundred new possibilities but who has not executed any. For this reason he is liked by those who have a need for new possibilities while those who cannot forgo a mathematically verifiable result call him unphilosophical. In himself Nietzsche is not of much value. {The presumption of youth!} But Nietzsche together with ten energetic workers of the spirit who carry through what he only indicated would give us a thousand years of cultural progress.

Nietzsche is like a park given over to public use—but no one goes in! [. . .]

"Any more highly developed organism does not merely possess a single center or a single group of centers but a range of local centers, the ganglia-groups of the sympathetic nerve, the different segments of the spinal cord, the individual parts of the brain. These different central organs are relatively independent of each other and perform their separate functions themselves; on the other hand, they are subordinate to each other: their totality is not a republic of equals but a hierarchy of officials, and the system of nerve centers in the brain and spinal cord resembles the system of administrative authorities in a state. One might visualize the spinal cord as a row of rudimentary brains. The ganglia of the sympathetic nervous system as a network of even less perfect ones,——

And, from the years when no further growth in the volume of the brain takes place, what we call mental[1] development corresponds to a more extensive branching of the fibers that run out in groups from the cells, particularly in the cerebral cortex, and this links nerve elements that up till then had no connection with each other.

The further one moves down the ladder of animal life the looser does the mutual dependence of the nervous centers become. The monarchy of centers which, though they developed differently, are closely linked to each other and subordinate to a main center, becomes a republic of quite equal, indeed almost independent, nerve centers. Every single center is less affected by being separated from the others; if it is isolated it functions for a longer time and in a more perfect way. On the bottom rung each segment becomes a complete brain and the animal as a totality is formed of several elementary animals, arranged in a row one after the other——"

What is one to make of these facts if one is training oneself in the direction of a development upward and is striving to find a new kind of sexual life?

In truth one does not function in this mode or that; the way things actually happen is that, when one comes into contact with other people, they strike within one a quite specific (or quite unspecific) note—and this then is the mode in which one functions.

———————————

The law of crooked paths. It would almost be possible to believe that, in nature, the law of maximum economy does not hold sway. For, if we take this point of view when we examine the case of a little child, for example, who is scalded as a consequence of negligent supervision, then the state will punish those responsible because they have ruined one of its future citizens. In the process of punishing and evaluating, however, it will always be the "poor child" factor that predominates and the degree of punishment will always take a lead from the extent to which the victim was a "poor child." Thus nature here makes a detour. She does not show, for example, the bare iron structure but attaches a plaster ceiling to cover it up.

———————————

Re: What do you think about women?
What Schackerl told about Frau H. Ali:[2]
    "At that time I was 17 years of age and still unspoiled. It is almost distasteful to me to relive the experiences I shall relate because I'd like to spit at the woman. Her son was then at the grammar school. I had a bicycle and was teaching him to ride it. He wanted a cycle, too, so he invited me to visit him at his villa saying he would ride my bicycle for his mother to see, hoping to impress her so much with his skill that she would grant him his wish. So I rode out on my two-wheeler, the road was bad and my whole outfit was spattered with filth. When I arrived at the villa he was just getting off the electric tram with his mother. I dismounted when he greeted me. He immediately got on my bicycle to show off and forgot to introduce me to his mother. Frau H. looked my dirty suit up and down so that I blushed and stammered a few words of apology. I was brushed down at the villa and spent the afternoon there.
    "The next occasion I saw her again was in the theater some considerable time later. She was sitting in a box with her husband and, though I didn't dare to look at her, I felt her gazing at me repeatedly. I was dressed in a smart jacket. Then, after some more time had passed, I met her on the street. She stopped me and asked why I never came to visit her. I had the presence of mind to reply that I had never been asked. 'So you'll visit me soon in the theater—why don't you ever come to our box?' At that time I was incurring my first debts behind my mother's back. Dressed in this I went to the theater again and visited her in her box. She introduced me to her husband and

I was vastly amused by his jokes and the anecdotes he told about some of the ladies from the theater.

"I had an intuition that something was closing in around me. I was on terms of friendship with her son; he didn't like his mother and told various stories about her. Once he said: 'Today, W. the actor was with her and she locked the door of her room.'

"Soon after that evening at the theater I met her on the street when I was walking with my friend Siegmund. She stopped me and said that she had to send her son in Weißkirchen[3] a sum of money and didn't know how to set about it, so would I be so good as to do this errand for her? She arranged to meet me at three o'clock at the barracks to give me the letter with the money. I was vaguely aware that something was going on and in my youthful anxiety I asked my friend to accompany me.

"I stationed him in some bushes and went to meet her. She was carrying two letters. The letter with the money and another in a fine violet envelope. This one is for you, she said, but you must promise me only to open it at home. I promised and we parted. I immediately fetched my friend Siegmund from the bushes, we found a quiet bench and read the letter. The only words in it were: 'Dear, dear—a thousand times, dear! Resi.' I didn't know what to do. My friend Siegmund who was always cleverer than I was, finally explained to me that I had to visit her and use this occasion to declare my love for her.

"I chose a time when it was unlikely that her husband would arrive home for three hours, and went there. She received me in her nightgown and was charming to me. I stammered something about feelings for her that I had long cherished and which I now at last believed were returned. She just smiled in an infinitely endearing fashion and I left with the feeling that never in my whole life had I behaved so idiotically.

"We remained on platonic terms for some days. Then she was going with her husband to visit her son at the school for cavalry cadets in W. and said to me: 'You're coming with us, or rather not with us but after us. I'm going on Saturday evening; the next day, at 5 a.m., my husband is leaving on a business trip.' I told my mother that I was going to visit my sister at an estate near W., went there, but left on horseback the following day at 3.30 a.m., since I didn't want to wait for the train.

"When I got to W., the train in which her husband was traveling was just departing. In the hotel I asked to speak to Herr H. on a matter of urgency and feigned intense annoyance when I was told that he had just left. I pretended to have important despatches and demanded to see his wife. After I had been announced I had to wait for a while, then she herself opened the door. She had thrown a green loden coat around her, she locked the door behind me and went straight back to bed. Without any question or answer I got undressed. There was a frightful sensuality in her eyes.

"We had lain in bed for three hours when there was a knock at the door. It was her son who had obtained leave from school to visit her. She quickly locked me up in the adjoining room where her husband had slept and opened the door. I heard her telling her son to be quiet since his father was asleep next door and didn't want to be woken. When she was downstairs with her son I followed quickly and entered the room, pretending to have just come in from the street. In spite of this I had the impression that the son had some inkling of what was going on. During our meal we drank champagne. Afterward he took me to one side and asked me to tell his mother that he had no money. She gave him 5 florins as soon as I asked her: 'Go on, make Adi happy. . . .'

"This was how our affair started. We rented a room in Brünn—I had to go into debt on her account. Finally, for the sake of my health, I had to restrict our relations to once a week. This was evidently too little for her for soon afterward she was unfaithful to me with another of her 'son's friends.'"

Fantasies of a Realist by Lynkeus.[4]
    Classics of Philosophy—Frommann.[5]
    Development of German Speculative Thought since Kant -Joh. Eduard Erdmann.
    Philosophy of the Unconscious—Eduard von Hartmann.[6]

What is impressive about theoretical structures of fields such as psychology is the terminology. This has something of the smoothness of stones that have been rolled round and round in water, something of the untouchability of technical designs in their simplest form. [. . .]

Journal.
While I'm in bed with a cold my inner self is at times frenetically active, at other times it's not active at all. I had dreamt during the night. A kind of Christmas scene with snowflakes and people walking in pairs—the way that midnight masses in winter are represented in the theater, that kind of thing. I was arm-in-arm with Herma.[7] But details are of almost no consequence. It was simply one of those dreams I dream two or three times a year that, each time, fill me for several days with an intangible, indefinite yearning for love.

With this yearning I woke up.

Before my windows there is an inexpressibly clear winter sky and the windows are like white sails in its bright blue—?—No. A quite normal waking without any mood. Blunted nerves, everyday feeling of ease. My dream was not intensified—the indefinite, dull yearning remained.

After breakfast I began to reflect—in the way that one might pick up any kind of activity at all. [. . .]

Family dinner

The families of Hofrat[8] X and Hofrat Y. have somewhere met a painter; Hofrat X. is very interested in painting and an invitation to the "modest abode" is accepted.

The painter is a big, powerful man with a full black beard that is turning gray and a fat, thick-set neck.

He displays his pictures in a courtyard behind the single-storey house. Everyday hack paintings of the postcard variety, but among them the head of a young man with a black beard, like an Arab, of singular beauty.

Hofrat X.: ". . . it is a perfect painting, most singular . . ."

Painter: "Yes, occasionally something comes out successfully, one never knows how . . ."

Son of Hofrat X.: "I can't stop wondering where the charm, this particular quality of the painting, actually lies. I think it is in the line which rounds off the head."

Painter: "I think it's where the neck joins the body."

Son: "At any rate it's in the actual drawing. In some quite simple line as in Böcklin's 'Sanctuary of Heracles' where there is a similar difficulty in deciphering the secret causes of the impression that makes any addition appear profane . . . . ."

Painter, to his wife: "Is the meal ready?"

Wife (very full figure, in loose-fitting blouse that is not done up at the neck) "The first course is burnt, I had to prepare another quickly."

Lady Hofrat gestures that this is not necessary.

Painter: "Oh, that happens. Often the whole meal is ready and if I don't like it another has to be cooked."

The son has meanwhile recognized the house as a corner brothel run by the painter's wife, where he often used to visit Jósza. Jósza, the mistress of a provincial lawyer and prostitute by vocation, like her uncle knows how to put on airs; she deceived the young man at the beginning until he was so firmly enmeshed in her net that it took him a long time to get away from her again, even though he was fully aware of all her affairs. His parents had afterward learned of this and his mother in particular had been deeply concerned about him.

They go to eat. The table is set in a room into which two steps lead down from the courtyard. The room has the usual sanded wooden floor and has been completely cleared of furniture with the exception of a big table laid for a meal, in front of which stand a sofa and some chairs. The room is filled with an oppressive vapor. When they enter Jósza is already sitting at the table. She is also wearing a loose cardigan over her shoulders and her hair has not been attended to.

"My niece, Jósza—Frau Hofrat X, Herr X."

They sit down. The Y. family has not appeared and there is a good deal of space between the people at the table.

The son: "I have already had the pleasure of making your acquaintance, Fräulein, somewhere or other. I believe it was in the winter on the ice-rink."

(When Frau Hofrat X, who has been staring fixedly at the two on the sofa, has to speak to the painter's wife for a minute, her son whispers to Jósza:) "For God's sake, don't give anything away."

Jósza shivers nervously with suppressed (sensual) excitement. In the meantime the painter's wife is feeling more and more at her ease with Frau X.: "Do you know, the two have already met. The young gentleman has been here quite often already, but you don't need to be worried, my niece is a sensible girl."

Dinner is served. The servant is a woman who often works in the house and who has already had M.⁹ with the boy.

Frau X., with a sigh, expresses good-natured agreement: "Yes, indeed, at least he won't have one of those accidents that are a constant threat." As she says this, her eyes are bright with all the sufferings of a saint.

I dreamed this in May 1903. [. . .]

Thank goodness, I have an hour of redemption; the first for a long time, I've no idea how long. One of those exquisite hours when one realizes that one has missed one's whole life, that formidable, dominating peaks rise up high above one. That everything one has done was bad, that one is further away from the goal than ever. I have hours like these at most once or twice a year. The determination to start out afresh from this point is so far away; one stands still, idly looking out over a broad, icy plain. One will never traverse this again—the path will lead down and down for good—but it is so beautiful, so sad, so wonderful, at least to wander over it for one last time with one's gaze . . .

I know that I was a disappointment to you in Schladming[10]—I was so wooden, angular, rational—I don't even want to think back on it; I was—well, not I.

In the first few days in Berlin I had one or two flashes of insight. When I was looking at rooms. Some small, some big, dark, elegant ones, and bright, patriarchal ones. I was looking for something, but didn't know what; not a study, not a work-room, not a room for living, a room of the kind that might have been occupied before me by the person I would like to have become.

It sounds so ridiculous, but it made me walk the streets for days. That, too, was in vain.

Today I have been leafing through my old notes; then I felt once more what a strange path Robert Musil's life has taken, how the path led, slowly, ... into the sand.

4 October 1903 [from a letter that was not posted] [. . .]

It is said that a thing is the sum of its qualities, or some such statement. But there are instances of relationships that contradict this. Perhaps in all things that pertain to sympathy.

I have had an old armchair for years. I cut a notch into its armrest, or I rip one of its cushions. In other words I take something away from it. And yet it doesn't seem new to me at all; rather it only really becomes that which I feel my old armchair to be, when I take something away from it.

This often happens with love as well.

Dr. Pfingst[11] was a classical philologist by training. Then he found a post in a library where he fulfilled his duties conscientiously and punctiliously. He seemed born to the role of a subordinate civil servant; he was awkward and submissive in manner, and his colleagues took the occasional playful liberty with him and also found it quite natural that he was passed over when some of the better posts were filled. He possessed a sensuality that consumed him from within. For a while he worked in the reading room; this put him on the rack.

In those days no one could have foretold that he would go insane. Nor could they have done so for a long while after the time when, with the help of an inheritance, his fate started to be fulfilled. He left the library service and then an interest emerged. He began to study the Greek and scholastic mystics.

A day in Trento {Brixen} of blue and searing white. Two elegant young men were looking around the city. A day of the kind that leaves one parched within. In a square they meet a couple. A woman in her thirties with a long narrow nose and hair dyed red-blond with the original black showing through. Her upper body is a fraction too long. One of the young men looks down at her shoes—how dreadful that in all that dust she isn't wearing a dress that leaves her feet free—, the shoes seem pointed and too narrow for her feet. She certainly does not feel that shoe-trees are essential—she has no sense that it is unhygienic, in the morning, to step into a shoe that is still creased from the evening. She exudes something for which young girls have sharp instincts: a kind of soul-sweat—something unappetizing, unclean. The man who accompanies her has newly ironed trousers and German shoes and, of course, an imitation Panama hat. It is Dr. Pfingst.

The two young people walk on. They do not say a word. One of them would like to say something and knows that the other would not find that proper—something sexual, mocking or something about the heat that is death to everything that offers moral and intellectual support.

This all stops suddenly in the church. It is a church like the one in Salò.[12] A wonderful building. The one who a moment ago wanted to pass some comment explains some historical details. Why? He was interested in Nicolaus of Cues.[13] But it is as if carpets were hanging in front of the green niches. The image of that woman pursues him.

In the evening they sit on a terrace above the town. They speak of their relationship with each other, about their reconciliation and of Skal. About the stay in Laus. (Spa, air, aesthete's whiling away the time.) At midday the unknown woman is sitting with a first lieutenant whose trousers are too short and who has that air of neglect typical of a company garrison. She ignores the pair of them neither of whom, it appears, looks sufficiently manly and mature. Robert studies her—the dyed hair, the thick layer of powder.

But then there is a day of rain. The stranger asks them for some piece of information—they are very reserved, almost shy, in the face of women like this, but finally they have to introduce themselves: Dr. D[onath], Dr. M[usil]. An afternoon game of tarot is arranged with the motive—which she provides—that this offers neutral ground. Before that she shows them pictures from museums. Later, the first lieutenant and Dr. Pf. come. Robert studies the changes in tone; he and Gustl eventually feel extremely uncomfortable.

Sensual contact.
She unexpectedly pricked him in the arm with a toothpick.

One could put in the first place the sketch with Gray-Eye's[14] parents in order to illustrate his theoretical approach and his painfully respectful relationship to soul in all its diversity.

Herr von Allesch[15] arrived with Dr. Pfingst. His type: blend of hyper-aesthesia and scholarliness. Is sensitive to everything and knows all the reasons behind things as well. Encompasses the vices of a "feel-all" and know-all. One only really likes him on the occasions when he becomes conscious of what an unfortunate hybrid this makes him.

He has come here to do research into some painter or other. Robert knows him from Berlin.

The first lieutenant embodies the superiority of the "human being" even in a degenerate type.

The woman is receptivity personified, a lesser type of "Tyrka."[16] Allesch makes himself look ridiculous by being taken in by her.[17]

All of them without exception—Robert and Gustl as well—are so starved that even the vestigial existential flair that this woman possesses holds their attention. [. . .]

Relationships. Cf. diary note of 13.VI.[18]

The words Gustl and I exchanged then are to be used directly for the novel.

Without any intention on our part, a certain culture of personal relationships has developed that is no less important than earlier ones.

When Alice[19] comes back from Robert she appears to Gustl to have an air of dark hostility. The jewelry she brings with her fascinates and irritates him. It only gradually merges into all his other household objects. In this merger there is "relationship" (in the absolute sense).[20]

The actual plot of the novel can consist of the loosening of the bond between Robert and Gustl and the first steps in one between Robert and Allesch.

Earlier—looking on from without—it was incomprehensible to see the cruel single-mindedness with which Gustl terminated his relations to Skal, for example. It seemed to Robert—looking on from outside—that there was something of the instinct of a woman or a genius about this and it fascinated him, though others only saw it as a lack of character. Now he gets to know Allesch. From the outset, relations were awkward. Each saw in the other only the hedonist whom one surpassed by innate disposition—by "Austrian culture" or "poetic gifts." Each wants to outdo the other. The arguments become vulgar and scholarly at once. Robert is ashamed of this. But the way A. vacillates when he expresses things frustrates any outcome. Conversation on [Oscar] Wilde, conversation on silver jewelry with blue stones. R. sees sentimental Baconism in A. And he feels how he, himself, because of his defense of all that is solid and real, appears to be quite a different person than he actually is.

Then comes the day in the gallery. R. sees that he can learn something from A. He is surprised that A. is younger. But there's nothing to be done. A. is a more rounded person. He recognizes in A. the type of man who has been missing in his life, a mobile, emotionally labile mind. The kind he rejected in books as a snob is now an open question for him. Is there something to A. or not? At the same time—this he now realizes—he sees clearly that he, himself, has achieved too little.

And he moves correspondingly away from Gustl so that he is acting in a perfectly natural way just as Gustl once did, while the other now represents "fidelity."

The woman with a past is "soulful" à la Ell[en] Key.[21]

A conflict between the first lieutenant and Dr. Pf. is the trigger for the latter's crisis.

Alice—American girl transplanted to Viennese culture and an artist's family. Describe the young girl of today who knows very clearly where she is going, with a certain disposition toward social commitment (young girls enjoy—for some charitable purpose—being an omnibus driver or the like), but whose soul grows to maturity far from where we are.

Describe, how Gustl's wide-ranging requirements home in on her, how they are reshaped under her influence because she has the authority of something alive, because something that one intuitively felt, since it never took on the substance of actuality, recedes ever deeper into unreality, etc.

A[llesch] and Robert both enter into relationships with the woman. In A.'s case it is his emotional disposition that has not yet borne fruit. This, together with all that is growing within it, is transferred to her, a spectacle that is for Robert at once ridiculous, comforting and melancholic.

Robert is not expecting anything for himself—his relationships are purely sensual. Originally he worked very hard and achieved a great deal; but now he can't make up his mind to follow any profession because things have reached such a pass today that virtually only someone without a job can be perfect. {(After logic, he ends up with mathematics.)}

By means of his extraordinarily supple understanding, by means of the liberality of his understanding and through the absence of the kind of predispositions that tend to attach themselves to men, Robert does not need any particular expertise in the art of living in order to get on well with his people. But sometimes he still succumbs to doubt. As in his relationship to A. He is entirely uncertain about the effect he has on the other. He argues with A. and feels hurt, but does not know if he has also been successful [??] in hurting A. If only he were able to watch himself! It's exactly the same with his muscles: when he has looked at himself in the mirror, he feels strong.

In the form of a draft: throughout the whole story the "Brother's Book"[22] is in the background. Rob is a philosopher; this determines the element of passive expectancy in his character, that best-concealed form of cynicism that is the obverse of his understanding of how all things are what they are.

His younger brother was soft and tranquil like the page-boy in that English picture. He was like Re.,[23] who now is again going to appear at the beginning of the story and who spoils Rob.'s relations with his mother. Perhaps his literary gifts came from him. These were extraordinary. He had the relationship with Valerie and wrote the *Paraphrases*: "The Revolt against the Husband." When his soul lay dying, she was to save him. Success would have thrown him onto a new track of refinement. When hope was dashed his soul went to pieces. For Ro. his brother was part of himself. His relations with Val. were always indecisive on account of his brother. They vacillated between betrayal and the most delicate solicitude. Ro. himself had in many ways guided his brother's thoughts. Through him he was able to awaken the finest things in his own self. The brother's death brings a crisis in his own life.

That kind of sympathetic liberality, that compliant ability to understand all things that is incapable of creating anything whole anymore—Gustl represents this to one decisive degree more than Robert. More characteristic, however, are the ethical complications because Robert is in fact more liberal. Robert has creative blood. As long as A. is incommensurable for him he feels irritated. When he sees through him it is all over. A. is a humanist, a mixture of sophistication and misrepresentation. And Robert is like Lorenzo d[e] M[edici] in Mann's *Fiorenza*.[24] He senses that the substratum of this path is missing. When he reads through the naive sentiments in his brother's book, it is as if a mist descends before his eyes. Indistinctly he senses that, beyond the sophisticated grasp of things and beyond the constructive strength that he, too, possesses there might be a third element, something profound that is kin to Savonarola. This is the man he would like to get to know. But Pfingst is only a caricature of him. This is the relationship between Pfingst and Robert. (Longing and self-irony.) In his capacity as the "pure fool" he might please someone like [Ellen] Key but Robert feels too much loathing for him (this too must be examined to see if it is correct); it is only toward the end when Pfingst has already ceased to be normal that he seems to be an image with some hidden meaning and he sends Robert on his way with that skeptical longing.

The women—Gustl and Robert's mistresses—are surrogates. It is more dangerous in Gustl's case because this releases something fine with which one can easily learn to be satisfied. It is true that she is more cultured but only to the extent that $\_ + 1 = \_$. Whereas Robert is basically outward-looking. His mistress affects him by the "strength of her emotional disposition."

Only the younger brother seemed to have had perfection fall into his lap, whereas Rob and Gustl could not wait and felt compelled to make a quick move.

Ways of behaving toward each other: R. needs only to say to G.: "I sometimes feel that I'm perverse," and that is the signal for G. to tell the most intimate things; it is a ruse of R.'s to belittle himself in order to make the other confide in him. [. . .]

A *touch of piquancy.* The relationship of G[ustl] and A[lice] is described in detail with all its excesses; the delightful and endearing side of their shameless behavior is given the appropriate emphasis. That, in spite of everything, this novel—like every decent one—finishes with an engagement, is a piquant touch. Bridal music, family happiness, mother's blessing, warmth expressed on all sides—all this now has an ironic quality and yet it also seems cozily familiar and indeed self-evident; something one can expect despite all that has gone before. And it only has an ironic hue because, in the soul's terms, it is less fine than the feelings that accompanied what happened earlier.

It is so natural that one becomes engaged *after* such things, not *before* them.

The relationship between G. and A. At the outset, the situation was as follows: with the Ch[arlemonts] sensuality runs in the family. They live in the capital city of a country in decline and full of party quarreling, in a city like Madrid or Vienna where society no longer functions properly, but the individual and the elegant class have reached the heights of sophistication. Their parents' house is elegant and of dark splendor. The father produces art that is intended purely for the eye; he paints landscapes, still life, robes—the furnishings of palaces and mansions he does brilliantly.

This happens to prompt his passion for Fr. Gintskay; it intoxicates him to work with the most precious material; he is prone still to the kind of frenzy experienced by artists in former times. This is in marked contrast to Gustl who is as simple as English furniture with clear lines and who dreams on a small scale—in the gently suggestive, curving lines of Middle Germany's decorative style. In this contrast, Ch. is by no means always the loser. G.'s lack of pictorial splendor and his one-sided simplicity are a great handicap to him in the sphere of music. Fr. G., though she is bowled over by Ch., is too susceptible to someone like Gustl for her not to be taken aback by the small measure of intellectual consistency in this relationship.

In this way Gustl becomes a force in the life of his father-in-law.

{(How quickly this life of Alice has run through phases!)}

The relationship between Frl. G. and A. is also richly allusive. They share the same origins as modern "English girls." With one there is the additional fear for the father and the fantasies of curiosity, with the other the sense of superiority about having an affair with the friend's father. These relationships do not succeed each other, rather they produce a single state of high tension . . .

With the Ch.'s then, sensuality runs in the family. When Lili[25] was still a little girl and believed in the stork, she masturbated so often that at night her fingers had to be tied. (From sheer love of pleasure.) A. has always known everything that was going on. The father married the mother only for her sexual attributes; now there are constant quarrels and they get on well with each other only when they have had sex the night before. The very quarrels, loathing and barrenness of the day drives them, at night, to excess. A. realizes this at an early stage, she sees the conflict and, at the breakfast table, she sees her father's gentleness and the extra efforts her mother makes when she serves her husband, and the tired (stupefied) gaze of both. But this brings her to hate only her mother because she makes so much of this twenty-four-hour possession, speaks about "good Papa" who is only irritable and difficult to handle but is all the same a "good person," etc.

But she also suffers from her own inherited sexuality. She was corrupted at an early age. When she was in Klosterneuburg with Hilda Darnaut, young Rössler[26] once came into their room. He goes to Hilda's bed first but just looks at her, then leaves her for some reason or other and goes to A., and sates his lust on her.

A. kept quite still, she couldn't say a word and just let him do to her what he wanted. The main thing on her mind was why Rössler had only looked at Hilda, and then turned away from her. She thinks that it was from that time on that she was aware of having always made an impression on men even as a little girl.

Thus she gained the impression that sensuality was an arbitrary and abrupt force that could not be fully comprehended. {An inconvenience to which one is forced to submit.} Her relationships to S.[27] and to her father move in the direction of this impression, and Gustl is the first to provide a strong contrast to it.

Even though, from an early age, she has felt that men desire her, she nonetheless feels indifferent toward them. She surrenders to secret amusements with Hanna.[28] But they never caress each other; on the contrary, A. has always felt antipathy toward sleeping with girls. They do sit together on the dark wooden steps leading up to the atelier, or behind one of the big cupboards or other, and play with each other, but apart from the shivering thrill of the forbidden and the first sexual stimuli they do not feel anything.

Here already can be seen that unimaginative, purely sexual sensuality which A. constantly had to cope with. This naked joy in physical pleasure that, in the case of Lili and the others, she could only regard as part of the family inheritance, seemed to her a dreadful destiny—particularly when later mental complications occurred—that she would never be able to resist.

As an outward sign she had a black birthmark the size and shape of a medallion in the pubic region, at the place where the line joining belly to hip runs down into the pubic hair. At this point the hair had receded a little and the mark shone like a black eye. (Like a sad, shameful eye.) She speaks of this in her confessions to Gustl and it is a moment of redemption {redemption motif} when he kisses her there for the first time.

The development of the relationship between A. and G.

A. was in her sixteenth year when G. came to the house. From the beginning they always exchanged long glances. In those days G. had the relationship with Hilda Gutmann. Just to look at her was temptation for him since this was a scarcely perceptible act of infidelity toward Hilda. Alice was then just an highlystrung teenager and it was the time when Rudi Urbantschitsch[29] was covering her with kisses. G. becomes the gospel; when he talks about Hilda or Bertha[30] or starts philosophizing (infidelity with regard to Robert's privileges) A. is standing behind the curtain. She and her friend are in love with Gustl. When G. has left they kiss his footprints in the anteroom.

This is on the one hand an attempt to give pure sexuality some backing. To bind and legitimize it. Instinctive, of course. The intention is to objectify it and thus make it less disturbing. On the other hand it's just the usual schoolgirl crush—the wish to mean something to someone. Or rather, the latter aspect is given a keener cutting-edge by the former.

G. develops in her an awareness of nature. The father, too, is a great nature-lover. But, with G., it's the "life of plants" and similar things. Apart from this, their relations consist of squeezing each other's hands. This binds them together. Some kind of power was in the hands—a power, by the way, that was not yet admitted. If the way he offered his hand displayed a degree of coolness, she begged him not to do it again. "You don't know how much it means to me!" she used to say.

There followed the first few inept kisses in Seeboden.[31] ("I've promised Mama never to do such a thing.") {(Although this idea never occurred to her with the other man!)} Moonlight parties at the lake. As she told G. later, she used then to snuggle up to S.'s chest. Later, for the first time, she touches G. under the table with her feet. But S. probably did the same thing.

It was about this time that the conflict started about S. and G. which causes A. an extraordinary degree of suffering. It was G. himself who introduced S. at Chs. on the basis of a number of aphorisms with marginal drawings inspired by Nietzsche. (R. always loathed S. But this was a kind of rebellion against R.'s[32] influence. It was also a consequence of G.'s many-sided character [. . .] whereas R.'s loathing was a consequence of his fine-tuned feeling for great intelligence. So, at root, it was already the thing that led to the rift between G. and R.)

They had reached in those days the stage of pressing each other's hands when Hanna and A. were in love with G. and masturbated. S. is a splendid socializer and a man of experience [. . .] and is also surrounded by the aura that women generally recognize in unbridled men.

A. is, in any case, sexually in fear of him; she is frightened of being abused and, on the other hand, this is precisely what impresses her. From the beginning he has had a sensual power over her. A little later she is unable to say "No" to him when he remarks: "You will permit me now to kiss you." She is anxious not to seem stupid. S. gradually begins to show how unbridled he is. She knows all about him. Knows that he's lifted up Hanna's skirts. She tells him off. This itself gives her a sense of satisfaction, it lifts her, makes her feel maternal. It also gives her pleasure to use expressions such as "You are a swine" when talking to a man.

So, at this time, she is sensually closer to S. But the other side—the desire to be seen to be somebody—keeps her close to Gustl. She has the urge to surpass the others, her family and girl-friends, and feels that this is most likely to happen if she pleases G.; she pins hopes on him. This is why in Seeboden she feels more attracted to S., and why she stiffens at G.'s first inept kisses—in fact she appeals to her mother (without deviousness, or any kind of will to manipulate—simply something that flows from how she feels) whereas, of her own free will, she snuggles up to S.'s chest during the trip in the moonlight. She has the one sensation: it is out of the question to give up *this* relationship; how things turn out with S. I have no idea. Perhaps she is already determined to marry G. (Perhaps *because*, for the moment, she can't love him in that way.)

Remarkably, G. at this time believes she is not sensual. He still thinks this when once as they are going out he seizes her from behind and covers her with kisses.

Then comes G.'s visit to her sickbed. An evening of snow. He kisses her breasts. Without any coarsely sensual excitement. For her this marks a transition to a new phase. The first sensuality which does not shock her. Quite simply, love. This is not, of course, something without parallel, or even something asexual. She feels the sensuality in these touches, too, but here sexuality is the basis of a new kind of feeling, it gathers this up and is brought together in a melody—it points into the unknown. It is precisely for this reason that the old is far from being expunged yet. The new has as yet scarcely any mass. There follows a relationship rich in sensation in the manner of Lepage.[33] G. feels himself to be an artist. Despite this, at precisely this time, she is being kissed by S. His nearness makes her nervous still. She finds it impossible to speak to G. when she knows S. is in the next room. She cannot bring herself to forget that he is near. (Just as Gustl is still irritated by Lili's nearness today.)

At the same time, however, the relations to G. also take on a degree of sexuality. (It is not a new feeling but the old one that has taken on a direction, an ethical value.) The exclusivity of their association affects her. There follow the eccentric walks to Klosterneuburg, in the Prater[34] and like places. It is the time of confessions, of steps toward spiritual possession. The attitude toward sexuality is characteristic. The ideal, the purely spiritual element, is the anti-S. position and was originally necessary. Now, however, a new transition toward sensuality is necessary. So when they vacillate between extremes it means that they are, in part, building a common future, in part that they have not yet quite rid themselves of S. What, earlier, was moral (struggle against sensuality) has now become immoral; as soon as the thought of S. forces itself upon them, the disposition of the moral opposites springs back to the original position.

The decision is taken in M[aria]zell.[35] It is the decisive struggle between S. and G. S. has now really fallen in love with A. That she is no longer at his beck and call has improved him. In actual fact he's a poor devil because he's insignificant. He always needs some kind of justification. The frivolous literary pieces were an instance of this. [. . .] This, too, is a kind of antinomy. Thanks to a high degree of adaptability (similar to v. A[llesch]) he really does develop, through the struggle with G., a fine susceptibility. He is serious, behaves toward A. as a real friend, does not do G. down. A. feels naturally that she is making him "good" and this holds her captive. Since S. is not jealous he has greater freedom and does not behave in such a vexatious way as G. does. When the three are together, G. is unbearable. G.'s awareness of this makes him even more unbearable. Whenever she has a conversation with S., G. runs away. She runs after him, hugs him and tries to comfort him. So, on one occasion, she goes to his room when he is lying on the sofa in the depths of despair. G. pays no heed to a sense of aesthetic shame at states of high feeling (a remarkable vestige from his youth with R.). He does not hold back his despair. Ethics as a means of struggle and ethics as self-preservation have now both become necessities to him. He storms A. He will permit her to love S. as long as she does not suspend her love for him. Only under those circumstances is she forbidden to love S. She feels only the need to keep G. {If she wants to achieve something she has to keep him.}

G. has to go away. They write each other passionate letters in which A. denies that she has any relationship with S. although on one occasion after her departure she was again kissed by S. For the moment G. believes these protestations. But as soon as S. arrives, he believes he sees how well they "suit" each other and he knows that she has lied.

Then S. writes her a "long letter"; he says he feels incapable of destroying so much, and suchlike. To strengthen his resolve he begins a couple of other affairs and after three weeks' stay in Vienna tells her all about his girl-friends. He has lost his temporary ascendancy [. . .]

According to a more discriminating evaluation he has lost. But it is doubtful whether he is not, after all, from a normal standpoint, the victor. Things have become too insipid for him, in the long run the tragic toga is an encumbrance, storms he can do without. In a perfectly normal sense he is tired of the whole thing. His abdication is no more than a fine exit. It is pitiable only to the extent that he lets himself be affected by it again. G. now has A. secure simply because the other man no longer likes her. If he hadn't rushed into the new affairs, who knows?

It is also the case that A. is determined to maintain some kind of friendship with S. although she knows that G. would like to see her reject the other man. G. interprets this as a spirit of conciliation that refuses to be denied and he reveres her deeply for this; but it may also be seen as her holding firm to an appearance of high motives in the manner in which she dissolves her relationship with S. because she herself wants to believe this and so enhance her own value—she feels the pull of the actual relationship but does not want to give it any weight.

An unbearable year follows because G. does not believe her. In M[aria]zell Ch. had the affair with Frl. Gintskay. After she has left he behaves as if he's gone mad. At night he comes to A. She will only let him kiss her breasts. (A Renaissance trait.) On a second occasion he plays with her while they are traveling together. He is a very attractive person. A. feels physical disgust for him and yet likes him terribly.

In this unbearable year, G. is only successful in stopping A. from striking a frivolous note with S. When he is in certain moods, however, he adopts this himself. He takes a desperate pleasure in revealing everything. With time they become closer again. Gustl regains the spiritual upper hand. In conversations on nature and ethics their effusions bring them together. She gains a sense of life's seriousness, setting herself the goal of being "his woman." Occasionally he shouts at her when they play the piano; everything seethes within her but it is pleasure that predominates.

A sensual familiarity ensues, the immorality of brother and sister. An undercurrent of brutality, overlaid with the accompanying shame, binds them more closely. The affair reaches its climax. There are no limits. In seeking out forms of indulgence there are no scruples—this is possible given the spiritual security that prevails. Now all the sexual details have to be described on account of the fine soul-values that are attached to them. After each contact she seems more youthful, more modest, more untouched.

Engagement: G. is considering publishing the *Letters,* so achieving success and vindication in the eyes of the family. Through a misunderstanding on the part of the governess the idea of marrying A. suddenly overpowers him. (With a view to concentrating the plot, the woman with the overlong upper body might be divorced and a companion at the Ch.'s house.) For he says: "You will see, madam, that I shall shortly make everything good" and she naturally interprets this as his wanting to marry A. Once this has been said new perspectives open up. The marriage opens quite new realms of life; one has not exhausted life's possibilities unless one has had children, and suchlike.

On Robert: R. has not sufficient aptitude for magnification to relive all this. But he understands everything.

Every time he sees G. he studies the changes in his body. Now he is lightly tanned, his shoulders slope steeply but are comparatively broad—rounded, somewhat sagging stomach. [. . .]

The affair G–A confirms that it is madness to doubt the fidelity of a woman. For most of the time A.'s attitude is one that gives rise to doubt. And yet something really good comes of G.'s finally letting himself be deceived. There are other values between man and woman besides fidelity.

On technique: the story of H[erma's] youth only takes on value in terms of the sympathy she arouses in R. So this is not to be expounded in all its existential fullness but in the foreshortening that corresponds to the ethical perspective.

One might equally well execute the story of her youth in all its detail, in such a way that the sympathy that she will arouse in R. can be felt even in this narrative.

Moreover, it is wrong to make H. a figure of utter suffering, one must always keep open the possibility that she finds the conditions rather appropriate; i.e., constantly keep an element of reserve with respect to how things are "in reality"—in that crude reality of everyday psychological speculation. What is sad about the story is that it all appears so sad.

On R. and H.: the following arrangement might be used: R. leaves H. because he is jealous, at the time when she goes into hospital.

But then he hears the doctors talking and the thought of how wretched it is to be at the mercy of such people makes him feel sympathy. The defenselessness of all creatures, poor girls included.

Here he is on the same ground as G. (Poem) But R. and H. also have moments when they transcend their passion. "You must console me because I'm jealous of you, too" each of them then says, with that curious mixture of jest and earnest.

On R[obert Musil] and H[erma]. Sometimes she has a peculiar kind of sadness. A deeply moving, tender sadness without words. On such days R. feels an extraordinary love for her. And yet: if he asks himself for the reason for this sadness, among the possible explanations there are ones that give rise to jealousy. Perhaps she loves him, has to deceive him and then loves him all the more, and this is behind her sadness. [. . .]

———————————

Mother: she was by turns as good as an angel and hatefully malicious. Is this simply caused by neurasthenia? She is always stoking up the "tragedy."

Isn't it also possible that she is jealous?

Mother and H. There is a hidden parallel between Mother and H[erma]. Mother was also a girl once and she would have suited R. better than H. did. The need to be "swept along" was linked in her case with powerful emotional qualities. R. feels that he would have been happier with her than with H. She would also have deserved a high degree of "sympathy."

This comes to a head in the scene where she admits to him how H[einrich?] has become the sole content of her life. Up till then there had been bad feeling between R. and her (mainly on account of H[einrich?]). Now these feelings dissolve because he is forced to see her in a different light. Chronologically this occurs when the tragedy with H[erma?] has become inevitable. They avoid each other henceforth because they can't hurt each other any longer but there is already too much between them. At this moment of recognition there is a good deal of skepticism because it is evident how little there is in the realm of morality that is not ambiguous and how much everything depends on the allocation of a point of view and on the perspective from which one is examined.

———————————

On the main theme: facts prove, in this realm, nothing at all. I'm thinking of a short piece by Auernheimer[36] that I read in Munich: a young woman is crying and making a scene because her husband is neglecting her, or so she tells him. In bed, at two o'clock at night, it is touching to find one's wife in tears. One can literally see the chasteness of soul that, not finding words to express itself, was brought to such extremities. But, in fact, her state of arousal comes from having been jilted by her lover. What has happened here is a genuine transubstantiation of the pain to her husband. The woman is sincere. (Auernheimer did not realize this.)

R., of course, understands such things. Acts that speak most forcibly of fidelity may indicate an infidelity. Thus he sees what is questionable in A. as well. But he doesn't say anything to Gustl, for one has to live with appearances. It is only for him, for his relationship with H., that such thoughts are a steady drip of poison.

R. and Mother: being good-hearted is by no means a lasting trait. One may be this with regard to some people, but not to others. Indeed even situations that are very difficult to assess will either show this quality to be present or absent. Thus a person may be touching for one moment and otherwise insipid. Good-heartedness, after all, is only the capacity to be mild under certain circumstances; as a general rule it is hardly possible to assume that it is not there at all.

Mother is scarcely ever affected by it. As I've said, this depends only on the point of view.

That is, apparently, the mixture that is always to be found in R.: heartlessness and mildness, cowardice and courage, etc. However, at a deeper level, these apparent opposites form a moral unity.

Scene: R. is constantly irritated by the relationship between R[eiter][37] and his mother (Re. and the first lieutenant might perhaps be drawn together in a single figure.) In the case of other people he would definitely draw the diagnosis that an affair was in progress, but he cannot do so here either; this makes the inner connection between this relationship and his own with H[erma]. Indeed with the former it is even clearer; at least, he is forced to say to himself, it is a kind of affair, but he cannot believe it, i.e., he cannot act upon it. (Curious anchoring of the will in thinking.) Something he cannot grasp that would have to be added to the conviction, is missing.

Thus it throws him to and fro. From his jealousy, springs of meaning well up; he sees how far delusions can reach.

When his mother falls ill, he does not know if he should help her or should knock the man down.

When Re. says "What shall I write to him?" (referring to the father) whereas he writes letters many pages long to the mother, R. is deeply hurt. But when he pushes Re. away and the latter, with genuine unhappiness, asks "Why are you always pushing me away?", he is moved again by this man who has suddenly been excluded. [. . .]

On technique: the uncertainties of all inferences about fidelity and infidelity can be impressively demonstrated as follows (in the manner of the plot of a bad play): two couples and a male family friend and lodger are staying in a hunting lodge. From the outset it is known that one of the women is having an affair. And it can now be made perfectly apparent how difficult it is to conclude from the behavior of the two women which of them is unfaithful. (A. and Hanna {Herma?} in M[aria]zell!)

On technique: we have now almost completely forgotten something that former novelists were good at: creating tension!

We merely capture our listeners [*sic*]. That is we try to write with wit and to avoid boring passages. Wherever we go, we pull the listener along with us.

Creating tension, on the other hand, means making the listener anticipate what is coming. Making him think along with us, allowing him to go on his own down the way we point out for him. A certain cozy feeling of being there with us. The comic novel lives off this feeling. One points toward a situation that is about to arise and the thought emerges: what will good old X do now then?

This requires a good deal of miniature painting with the various types. But, however antiquated it seems, it is still an instance of artistic effect in contrast to the effects produced by philosophers and essayists. [. . .]

"What have I done then?" This motif, which would be sentimental if it were not lapidary, is H[erma]'s motif. H. is quite innocent, i.e., touching and yet often ordinary. Precisely her weaknesses must be emphasized. But wherever she appears a simple melody and a breadth of substance must dominate. Her fateful liaison with R. gives symbolical form to the fact that, from a certain perspective, one cannot place faith in the understanding. This is what relates to the basic idea. At the beginning and end of the story stands death.[38] That also has something lapidary about it and thereby provides a symbolical framework. This is the way to depict death: great when out of reach; within reach, simply banal. And the way in which, at the end, the beginning seems to be repeated provides an opportunity to sum up all the changes that have taken place in the intervening span.

R[obert] and G[ustl] met in Vienna again. R. is to take up a position in a factory near W[ien]³⁹ and still has time which he spends at the bedside of his grandmother who is slowly dying. H[erma] is employed to care for the grandmother. She dies and the relatives pay H. off in a shabby fashion. {After all, she's just a simple girl, they say. For the first time this vague suggestion of a fabric shop.} R. sees the silent girl for the first time. Perhaps just before this he has had a very lively scene. Awkward, just like in an old German painting.

During this period G. starts work with Ch[arlemont]. R. shows H. around Vienna. A walk in the springtime is just like H. One doesn't know if one should surrender to its charm or find it banal. {Here nature must be subjected to an exact, microscopic investigation.} Then R. takes the decision to move closer to H. Starting out from this feeling—taking a deliberate risk.

By this time he is in the factory near Vienna. The idyll follows. G. and A. have meanwhile reached the stage of self-abandonment. Then R. goes with H. to Berlin, and G. and A. reach the stage of sensuality. [. . .]

———————

On the plot: during the burial she didn't cry once, says Mother of H., but it is precisely because she, too, doesn't know how to deal with the situation that R. is drawn to her.

Life together then brings the following development: we actually know least of all about ourselves—our bodies, for instance. If we do not have others in whom we can see reflected the effects we have on them, we are fearfully alone. "If we could just once see ourselves through the eyes of others" is an expression of this. Then there is also the fearful sense of being alone at the end.

This occurs to Robert when he sees H. for the first time in the awkwardness of her nudity. This gives rise to a remarkable situation. The desire that is otherwise present is missing or has completely changed its hue; he feels positively timid and treats H. with painful tenderness. After this the bed becomes a symbol of flight and concealment which later gives it its power. {But that already presupposes a certain development in the relationship of G. and A. in order for it to have such a strong effect on R.}

In the opening situation R. is reading Novalis in an anteroom, thinking of Gustl! (This introduces Gustl in the story.)

———————

She doesn't say "Yes," nor "No," nor "Thank you."⁴⁰ [. . .]

It is said that feelings are the only evident things in us. This is partly right, for feeling is evident. That I "feel" "something" when I'm jealous, for example, is evident, but that I feel "jealousy" is not evident at all. That is based on ideas and accordingly all the uncertainties of ideas attach to it and these can reach as far as dream-idealism. Each feeling points toward a single fixed spot within me (which I can never get any closer to) and shows, moreover, how we hover over empty space.

It is distressing to reflect that we hurry like little hunted dots along the line that is our life and finally disappear down some unforeseen hole. And that, in front of us and behind, at intervals that nothing can reduce, other similar dots go racing along, which have some kind of temporary link with us, like the next links in the chain of a paternoster lift that goes racing on round. Anniversaries, birthdays, etc., are a cruel refinement. You have now lived a third, a half, two thirds, of your life . . . Finally chronology as a whole, if one assumes it to be a product of mankind, is something terribly shortsighted.

This is the backdrop of the empty hours.

On jealousy.

The scene with Friedm[ann][41]—H[erma] seems to go red. A certainty shoots up in Hugo which, the very next moment, he cannot grasp from any angle, and which leaves him quite helpless. [. . .]

Tonka. Half our life is expression. Walther expresses himself through his moral self, Helmont the Elder[42] through intoxication, Faust through his aestheticism. Hugo searches through all of these without finding satisfaction. Only Herma has no expression at all. That is why she becomes Hugo's fate!

R.: he can only suffer physiologically. Even his energy, etc., is not psychological.

The particular nature of love is clearly visible in the dream. One dreams of the loved one. She looks quite different, her voice has a quite different timbre and cadence. She does things that the other would never do. One is constantly aware of this non-identity. Despite this, one is forced—this is similar to pathological states—to consider the dream image to be her. To some extent it is attached to the name—and, in fact, in such a compelling fashion that the most unfamiliar movement becomes her movement, and in fact this once happened even with a flounce of white petticoats of the kind that H[erma] never wore. And with the name the whole insubstantial affection is linked to the arbitrary figment of the dream. This gives rise to rather curious combinations between thoughts that attach to the individual experience and those linked to the name. An inexpressible intensity is associated with the name. It is not produced by the real loved one but is simply prompted by her. (For we can draw such a conclusion from this observation.) But the real loved one is wrapped entirely in these spontaneities whereas in the dream there is a fine tear; there, too, one feels strangeness, one feels that it is merely an association.

A few details about the real Walter

Task of the lover: to maintain oneself as the being one was for her. In spite of the changes in her and in the circumstances.

Crisis: one takes note of every statue and every architectural element of the rich city, one takes note of every book one has seen on display in a window, one is pursued by every thought that occurred to one, wherever that was. But one does not take note of a detail in an opera. The visual memory is frighteningly powerful—but one's essential talent, itself, keeps its own counsel, as if sated. [. . .]

Illusion: Clarissa [*sic*] says in the theater: we should perform our story. What she means by this is: our experiences are the stuff of miracles. We are chosen people, etc. But one could take this to mean overall: real couples who are in love should act out their love. It would be useful for them. A new kind of love would evolve.

Thus this sentimental aside becomes, for Walter, a fruitful idea for which, of course, he is grateful to Clarissa. [. . .]

A detail: Hugo prefers not to imagine even the men whom he likes without any clothing. When he imagines the clothes have been removed from a seated figure, or when he imagines a longitudinal section through the body, they become loathsome to him in the area of the midriff. Women become purely sexual beings at that point, fornication rears up, taking the place of all values of the soul.

But when he imagines H.[erma] cut open, he loves her, feels sorry for her, the horror is transfigured——

So loneliness pursues him; only with her does he escape it. [. . .]

Dream: she, too, wears the brown dress and has all Herma's features. But somehow or other she is rejuvenated.

(The scene is 60 years back in time, reminds one of those simple chambers drawn by Schwind.)[43] He no longer remembers the way he seeks to persuade her, there is just a strong gentle sexuality that lingers on. Then an enormous sense of possession, a sense of anticipated possession to some extent, because she is still strange and new, yet, as double-image of H., already under his dominion.

Love demonstrates this same puzzling capacity for transference in waking life, too. Here, too, it seems that it is something totally detachable, and transportable. My knowledge and my judgment of A.[44] have not changed in the least and yet I love her. Something that I cannot identify anywhere has been added. Like a light illuminating the thoughts.

Love: we are those beings who must, at all times, give our all. To be deceived has no real meaning for us, for we act under immense inner pressure and the object has the sole function of unleashing this. Thus we are as naive as children when it comes to judging the loved one. Even when a lover only desires flirtation and a touch of sentiment we are so dazzled that we want to give her everything—our very soul. We are ridiculous, but for good reason.

One end to the novel. Mother-love is the strongest feeling of sympathy that there is—not from the reasons that are usually given but because every love is eaten away by the element in the other that eludes identification, by vital idiosyncrasies and by the worst possible interpretation being always to hand. And because no love can reach its full intensity unless some kind of external compulsion such as marriage or habit provides protection from the factors that seek to break it apart. It is only when the two lovers are penned together in their feelings in a narrow stall that they are assailed by the boundless will to bite into each other.

A similar bond that is always available is being closely related to one another. It is perhaps "mindless" but just for that reason can be used again and again. If one is quite on one's own, looks around and there is nothing there . . . one cannot escape it.

This is how, eventually, Hugo and his mother find each other.

. . . . Every day they took the path from the villa between the gardens down to the place where the trees had been felled and one had a bright clear view over the lake.[45] There he gallantly helped her to climb over knee-high branches. With smiles and little low shrieks that seemed like a merry flower-hat which you know is much too young for you but suits you, and, well, after all, the summer is so hot . . And the smile was like a soothing veil over these little, low, shrill shrieks.

Then they read. Read the memoirs of Stendhal, the love letters of Abbé . . . the stories of dark, sick Rétif[46] . . . He read to her and made comments on the reading just as one explains a past art—as something that helps one to outwit life. Then once there came a day of rain. It was evening before it brightened up—only the lake was still gently disturbed; the air was too strong, too pure, like someone who has overcome some malignancy and whose every fiber is now bursting with superabundant health; and the fragrance in the gardens was like the passion of a woman who has only just risen from her bed of confinement.

On this day they neither wanted to go out, nor to read. Her eye was troubled and each moment the tears seemed to be ready to break, just as they are in a little girl who's bored. And nowhere could he find peace, the images of his loved ones surfaced and merged one into the other.

They sat on the balcony, wrapped in soft blankets, not saying a word.

Then something pleasant occurred to him. He offered to make a grog in the way that Antoinette had taught him. It is quite a feat to get the measures right. And his mother smiled. The strong drink surged through her blood as if she were breathing in the warmth of Antoinette . . . And he started again to tell her something. In his words could be felt the deep and singular resignation of the man who possesses everything. But what he said was not direct. It was as if he were paying court to his mother. He chose polished words and gentle words of gallantry—only now and again did the words tell of Antoinette and of Margarite and of himself remaining as motionless as a fine mirror that is unable to hold these moving images . . . And he also spoke of her. He compared. Held up the fine, pale colors in them both, one next to the other. It was just as if he were speaking of her when he spoke of himself.

Then he began to question her: "Tell me, are women like this . . . . ? Or are they like this?" and "Could you have been completely faithful?" "To me?" And suddenly he asked her: "Tell me, how old are you, Mama?" "Oh, nearly fifty."

Thereafter there were few words.

Warm sun on the shore. Evening. Evening. In the damp sand, people busying themselves with the boats. Couples.

And the fragrance of the grog wafting upward ever more strongly. The people below become more and more like marionettes and their own movements seem to be caused by someone pulling on threads. Then she makes a remark that might have been made by a young lad—she shocks herself—and feels that she, an old woman, is no longer mistress of the notions and gestures that come streaming in on her from all quarters of her life. And they snuggle down into their rugs and the grog surges and laughs within them, but they can no longer trust themselves to say anything more to one another. [. . .]

The main theme is probably the connection between the motives of jealousy and loneliness. If one once starts to doubt a woman, one can question everything, even the most touching proofs of devotion. For precisely such proofs may conceal a subtle form of infidelity and one develops an acute sense for such subtleties. On the other hand, at a certain level of these feelings, a general skepticism takes hold. And this is equally directed against the things that motivate suspicion, so that we reach the same point of view as that which I have toward H. [. . .]

Tyrka's Samurai and Allesch's Catholic both have something linear—rhythmical, something two-dimensional, something monumentally rough-hewn, something finely colored and yet silhouette-like . . . . A samurai does not touch a woman he does not know, an aristocrat does not do certain things, a stoic does not let anything disturb his equanimity . . . it is always the same, always a class gesture that is very fine, very noble, very admirable. I was really ashamed for a moment about our tendency to overvalue the erotic. But how would it necessarily appear from close range? This agglomerating of nobility and the measures of convention? And even the Catholic, on his own, is only a drop in which nothing of the river can be felt. Wouldn't it be just a little bit, very, very boring? [*sic*] [. . .]

Like a doctor who investigates the innermost mechanism of the vagina and yet, one hour later, overcome by passion, lies in its thrall. .
    This is one of the characteristics I have given Hugo.

Style. Keep the novel humorous. Moralizing. Narrating the self.
    Tell the story from the point of view of hard-working Berlin, starting out by apologizing for the story.

Detail. H[erma] told me about home. The women from the prison, most of them prostitutes (—the prison had to be moved because they worked with convicts on construction sites and had a lot of children—), were hired out for household work. They were very good at doing the washing, for example. Grandmother was one of those who arranged for such women to help with the washing. They were given coffee—no one felt embarrassed with them, people spoke to them. At midday they had to be taken back. H., when she was a little girl, would walk along the street with them—they wore the gray prison clothing and a white headscarf—and did not feel embarrassed. [. . .]

Tonka I was suddenly given a reason to suppose—through a new medical diagnosis of the symptoms of her sickness, or some such thing—that she had, after all, five years ago, been unfaithful to me. But instead of its arousing in me the high degree of tension that I felt in those times this information merely makes an almost piquant sense of surprise stir gently within me. Tonka becomes for me an object of interest, I ask myself with almost artistic interest, what it must have been like then—poor Tonka, how this made her suffer then! There is not the slightest hint of loathing for the other man, I feel very close to Tonka. (Against this: being the first is everything!)

Tonka: the protozoon encapsulated within. One bears death within one, one only needs some chance thing to happen and the protozoon is released from its capsule; it is as if, somewhere, death were standing, waiting for one to pass by, quite by chance. [. . .]

———————————

Division between introduction and first scene.

It is the function of the death to adjust the mood of the scene to the empty hours. The sun was still very weak. Like someone who has got up for the first time after a long illness, she went outside and walked on the meadows and out among the trees {unnecessary digression!}, pressed herself fearfully along a row of houses in the street, and in the rooms she stood idly among the pieces of furniture, caressing with soft fingers, here the surface of the table, there a cabinet, or crouched down near the floor next to one of the broad, chocolate-brown armchairs, like one who is too tired to stay upright. And when she stood up and moved on, there remained on the parquet-flooring a dull sheen as if she had lost blood—her sick, colorless, weak blood . . . . .

The sun, too, was unable to throw a shadow. The colors of the fabrics simply turned a little darker, became more subdued, but were not extinguished. Nor did they shine brightly in other places. An unnatural calm seemed to press down on every separate object, to move all contrasts more closely together, as if with the dogged will of a sick person who is led by some vision encountered at the limits of life.

A state of unhealthy arousal, small watery drops of blood, seeping from a wound that may break open at any moment, something that has not yet become firmly atttached to life again, which tries to regain its strength and yet cannot purge the memory of glimpsing another world (not a new world but rather a glance from some outermost limit back at the old accustomed world)—a sense that a synthesis of all these things, something unquiet and evil, was hidden behind this seemingly tired, kindly, early spring sunlight, all this did not escape an observer as sharp as Hugo.

It was a mood of dissolution and decomposition, a mood in which, just as in serious illnesses, one changes one's point of view with lightning speed and, rushing each time through the new one, sees one's life passing by. An extreme skepticism as a consequence of this capacity, a skepticism that is prepared for anything, that would be no more surprised by a miracle than by the falling of a stone [. . . .]

3
NOTEBOOK 24
1904 TO 1905

[Though the opening entry was recorded while Musil was on holiday with his mother—he was recovering from a nervous condition of the heart brought on by overwork—most of this notebook was written while Musil was studying in Berlin. He called this his "book with scientific notes." Quite a few of the entries reveal Musil's interest in the work of Edmund Husserl, who was one of the assistants to Professor Carl Stumpf. (Husserl was the founder of the school of phenomenology—his most famous pupil would be Martin Heidegger.) Though Musil's reflections here are derived from the work of various lecturers or authors, they reveal his independence of mind. He does not simply absorb the subject matter but thinks through its implications and gives it his personal stamp. This is the case, for example, when he tries to work out the processes through which sentences become meaningful, using a statement about his friend, Johannes von Allesch; similarly, he breathes life into a philosophical issue by inventing (at least one assumes that this is an invention) a dialogue with Gustl Donath. Students in Carl Stumpf's Institute of Experimental Psychology were encouraged to take every opportunity to test out what they had learned and experiment within the realm of their own psychological experiences.

Musil's catholic tastes in serious reading are illustrated by his entry on Maeterlinck and Plotinus that deals with the soul and the mystery of light. These authors were outside the curriculum of Musil's prescribed studies— Musil is interested in areas that most of his contemporaries engaged in scientific work would have dismissed as "mystical humbug"—Musil approaches these with critical caution but an open mind.]

They had arrived at 11 o'clock; at one o'clock already he was sitting with his mother at the big table d'hôte. Thank goodness that old Countess Mannsberg was sitting on his mother's right; an acquaintance from her youth, met by chance at this summer resort—at least Mama was catered for. For him that meant a patent of freedom, a sense of positively physical well-being, he thought; one has no idea of what will come, but at least something can happen, one won't be locked up for a full four weeks. One is more than just a son, one has one's own nerves and can use them. If mother has nothing to do but keep a constant eye on one it's really embarrassing.

Four weeks! Why did he tell the whole story today to his traveling companion—a person who then continued on his journey, having told him to take things really easy and wishing him a speedy recovery; two stops later the man was probably swapping intimacies with another fellow traveler. From a psychological point of view, the railway is really no better than a brothel!

What had he actually told him? Everything! But why? Why had he done that? It's the fault of these doctors—these damned three months of absolute rest! As if any human being could stand that! And now of all times, just when he'd dynamited the gate to his authentic life.

".... Now listen to me. I'm 24 years of age and for the last eighteen months have been plaguing myself with something that is of complete indifference to me. An invention.[1] At the age of 21 I was already a qualified engineer.[2] I wanted to give it up and study philosophy. To do so one has to have complete financial independence. So all that needed to be done was to invent something and to buy freedom that way. Even as a technologist this was my main idea. Various ideas turned out to be unsuitable; loathing of everything that had to do with technology, and preoccupation with study of the humanities. Only half-time, of course. At last—I'd already spent a year and a half in the factory—an idea that stayed with me. I spent three months working on calculations for it; it demanded a good deal of theoretical knowledge and I had already forgotten half of what I'd learned at school. Time and again I threw the whole thing under the table. Hours of struggle within myself. This constant trying seemed to have no sense whatsoever. Good inventions have to be earned, one doesn't stumble upon them quite by chance. Otherwise, I thought, give up technology completely. Become a clerk, bootblack, servant, something American, and work your way up the literary ladder.

After 3 months I became confident that my approach, this time, was a good one. As far as I was able to take my calculations, the idea was right.

I was tremendously excited. It would by no means be right to conclude from what I had done that success would follow. On the other hand, I couldn't dismiss the idea out of hand either. At best it would take a year until everything worked. Tests, trial runs. I decided to risk this one year. With the firm intention that if it failed I would put an end to the matter.

It worked and buyers were found for the patent which brought me in quite a nice sum of money.

But what a year that was! Just imagine such a person in the first years of full maturity who, in order not to dissipate his efforts, cannot spare a single thought for what he considers his vocation. For a full eighteen months—then the sale and all kinds of related things made similarly heavy claims on me.

Eighteen months ago I was talented and my [literary] drafts were well received. But what does it mean to have eighteen months cut out of one's development! Will there be anything left there to justify having made this sacrifice? . . . You can imagine how one burns to test things out.

At the start, one feels deep discouragement—but this is something one anticipates. It has to be this way. The nerves are like ropes that have gone brittle and the first thing that needs to happen is for the association centers in the brain to be replaced. But in a fortnight one begins to pick up the threads again.

Then some family doctor or other runs across one's path and diagnoses a nervous condition of the heart as a result of overexertion, orders complete rest and paints the blackest picture of what will happen if one disobeys him.

Of course, one has lived too intensely—it's no wonder at all if, not having had a single finer idea throughout the whole day, nor any sense of one's own spiritual existence, one wants to experience stimuli at night that positively tear at the nerve-endings . . . . ."

Perhaps the man to whom he told his whole story was himself such a doctor. The answers that he had given showed sufficient lack of comprehension for that to have been so. [. . .]

———————————

There exist functions of understanding, thinking in categories, logical categories. Space and time, however, are not "a priori." They were thought to be so because they were considered as mental continua. But they are not. Space is a representation derived from something else and time is not a continuum but, in sense perception, always something singular. We don't think discursively at all; instead, we think in leaps. The illusion is the same as with a ciné-film. All active attention is discontinuous. The passive form is seemingly continuous. Since the capacity to notice something, to feel oneself thinking is the root of all "cogito-ergo-sum"–type theory of perception, these psychological tasks are of the greatest importance.

A wish is a will that doesn't take itself quite seriously; why not? [. . .]

What we unconsciously use as a measure of the degree of civilization are the value judgments of bourgeois life. Ancient Greece would still seem less civilized than the present day because, for example, an Anaxarchus was pounded to death in a mortar on the orders of Nicocreon, even though we would not be capable of producing an Anaxarchus.

Dead and living thoughts!

A thought is not something that observes something that has happened within us, it is, itself, what has happened within.

We don't actually think about something, rather something "thinks itself up" within us. The thought does not consist in our seeing clearly something that has developed within us; rather an inner development stretches out into this bright area. This is where the life of the thought is found; the thought itself is arbitrary, a symbol—this means that, though it is often the case that the thought is dead, as long as it is the final link in some inner development it is accompanied by a feeling of completion and certainty. [. . .]

The unsolved problem of naturalism.

We no longer think from the perspective of naturalism, we have different systems of coordinates to which we relate all mental life.[3] But I can now see clearly what it was that used to fascinate me about naturalism. This runs as follows: when we speak today of "human beings" we do so again in an idealistic fashion. The beings whom we create are far happier than we are. They are born into a system of forces that we can only posit in an abstract prolongation of our lives. They are tuned to a rhythm that we can only long to reach. The objects in their rooms, their words, their emotions, are valences in tangible shape. What we can only dream in shadows and fragments saturates each movement they make. As in music, we build a gigantic structure that relates to us like a fourth dimension, resting on unseen buttresses, something that is there, and yet is not anywhere at all.

But no one has yet successfully developed a facility for presenting the real naturalistic life around us—this life that fragments into hours without any context and into pitiable indifference—in such a way that it does not reach way beyond us and is yet still beautiful. [. . .]

1906 [sic]

Something is definitely holding me back from literary work. It is the need for style. Recently I have placed too much value on what I say. But is it just as important how one says things? Kerr's[4] remarks on dramatic art are very fruitful. I now know where to look for style and what literary impressionism means.

Note on Husserl:[5]

On one point nominalism would, after all, seem to be partly correct. To be specific: when I express an idea in the form of a sentence, I certainly don't think out the intention of each individual word, but have a merely half-conscious intention for the sentence as a whole and the words seem—from the perspective of consciousness—to come into my mouth mechanically. The intention may be posited to be unconscious but the words often come of their own accord and it is, as it were, tentatively, and often with corrections that the sentence intention develops in them, and with their help. [. . .]

Working with the tachitoscope:[6] from a certain speed upward, the pre-central processes start to become confused.

Purely optical afterimages are, in fact, excluded because the letters are seen one after the other at the same point.

But investigations need to be carried out into the question of whether it is possible to see a word, or at least the mid-portions of words, as a whole unit—so that the letters in the middle are more firmly fixed. (Either the letters leave behind two impressions—on their own and as a unity—or it is merely their interrelatedness that is more vivid.)

It is easiest to forget the first letters. When the whole visual field is full, the attention is under the least stress—this is why it is precisely the parts in the middle of the range that are registered together.

The mistakes that are made may be traced to the following things: optical process, apperception, reproduction. According to the particular mistake different conclusions will need to be drawn. [. . .]

The word needs its completion in the clause, the clause in the sentence, the sentence in the whole. A context for impressions runs through everything that probably varies in each case according to the particular whole that is involved.

It is only the way in which each points beyond itself that makes possible some sequences of ideas. Scientific thinking is only one special case.

The immediate question to be answered is this: Is logic to be dealt with psychologically? Or metaphysically? Or is there a third possibility?
What I consider to be characteristic of logic is that, though it does not function with fixed values, but has a tendency to move in their general direction, i.e., it operates as if . . .

Let us take the example "Peace is secured."[7] Here "secured" is a word with several meanings; a balance sheet, a nut on a bolt, etc., can be "secured." And in each case "to secure" has a divergent meaning even though one has to recognize something common which itself led to the equivocal term chosen.

Via the word "peace"—just as in cases where "balance sheet," "nut," etc., are used—a single possibility is separated off from this restricted number of others. The definite meaning of "to secure" appears only in some judgmental context. Now it will be said that this multiplicity of meanings has to do with the linguistic expression. There is no such thing, in a general sense, as "securing," only something that relates to a specific object. According to this view, in our example the logical predicate would be: "to secure in a context of peace." The question of the general meaning of such expressions is something we shall have to examine later.

We can, at least, make the following statement at this point:
1. Whenever the predicate has a general meaning this is modified by the subject when it passes into our judgment.
2. Whenever such a meaning does not exist, then in cases such as that of the example, a meaning emerges not on its own but in fusion with the meaning of a subject, in other words in functional dependence.

But then the further issue is raised that there is still a certain multiplicity of meanings present. The clause may be a general statement that these are times of peace, but it might refer, on the other hand, to arrangements for a peace that is about to be concluded. In both cases it is in the present tense but points, in the one case, into the past, in the other into the future. The clause is indeed subject to chance modification, for instance, when it is given a specific relationship to the Russo-Japanese War by being shouted out by a newspaper vendor, or by pointing to some specific historical relationship through some other context. Is it then the case that the meaning of "secured" which was strengthened and at the same time limited by the word "peace," is further strengthened and further limited by the process of individualizing this to a specific peace?

It cannot be denied that this is indeed so. Yet one will still have reservations about it. What is this apparently baseless reservation based on then?

Let us compare this with a second example: "A. is traveling to Vienna." If I know A., if I know the way one travels to Vienna, I may know that A. was still in Berlin this morning and that he therefore can only have taken the morning train. Does the expression therefore mean "A. is now probably in Dresden?"[8] One will reject this unreasonable assumption both here and in the previous example.

We could, by the way, take the analogy further still and say: In the clauses: "he is traveling" or "A. is traveling," "to travel" has a different meaning according to who A. is. My friend travels first-class on the express, Pope Julius II traveled in a litter, and suchlike.

Here, however, a difference is immediately noticeable: Is it not the case that there exists a much more intimate connection between the various kinds of meanings for "to travel" than between those for "to secure"? Do not the various kinds of traveling have conceptual features in common, whereas those of securing are merely equivalents? Certainly the latter is the case in an example such as "A. is a cur."

So we can say: a) at any rate there are some cases that correspond to those under 2). So, for example, "A. is a cur."

We have here a number of possible P[redicate]—meanings, from which one is selected by the S[ubject]—concept.

b) At any rate there are cases where P. has one general meaning which is merely modified when it passes through our judgment, for example, "A. is traveling."

c) We do not make decisions on intermediate cases among which "A. is secured" would fall.

To b) the following reflection attaches: it is possible to say that in the judgment "A. is traveling," it is not the traveling that A. is doing that is the predicate, but traveling in its general meaning, so the concept of the predicate is not modified. The meaning that we assigned as such was rather the meaning of the act of judgment as a whole. For A. as well was, after all, modified into a "traveling A." So we would simply do the same thing in two ways and with this double modification there would be nothing left for the meaning of the judgment as a whole.

This last assumption is definitely right. We have to say that the meaning of the judgment rests in a mutual modification of S. and P. In the final judgment it is wrong to talk of S. and P. as a prior condition of the judgment; in the final judgment P. contains something of S. and S. something of P.; in the final judgment they cannot be separated one from the other. What we usually call S. and P. are in no sense the meanings that are inherent in the judgment, but rather the meanings that ought to pass into the judgment.

We will conclude that both S. and P. are equivalent to a number of "valences," judgment-values, possible connections. In the judgment process, one of these becomes the real one. S. and P., in the final judgment, consist of a range of possible valences and one realized valence.

So the judgment "A. is traveling" does not mean "The traveling A. travels as A." but only "A. is traveling."

In other words: the judgment is not some third element in addition to the mutual modification. [. . .]

After all "act of judging" is a *psycho*logical concept.

Note on Husserl I [pp.] 62/63.

When we think "all As are Bs," "all Bs are Cs" we have to think "all As are Cs" (bottom of p. 62). That is a fact, not a law. The psychological explanation makes an unsuccessful approach from one side; we cannot find a satisfactory, an exact explanation. The "logical law" does not attempt to align the logical matrix of facts with the psychological matrix, it is content with registering the regularities that prevail within it; it establishes facts. That is the difference. Vague psychological laws cannot explain in an exact way logical (or psychological) facts; this has to do with their imperfection. But the exactness of the logical law follows on from the renunciation of a higher, or at least more comprehensive, mode of explanation. The logical explanation makes itself at home in its realm, the psychological one makes a vain attempt to adapt itself to another area.

The question will be whether Husserl can justify saying that the logical description of facts is one that obeys laws.

On objective truth: an objective truth, truth in the absolute, does not exist. There are only thought-contents that are true. To these contents is attached the feeling of evidence, i.e., whenever they occur, they *must* be true.

{But that means that only "if" they occur they must be true. For creatures that have such thought-contents the thought of a "subjective" truth is absurd, i.e., it is absurd to posit the thought-contents and not the truth. But from this situation *no* conclusion whatsoever can be drawn for a case where such thought-contents are not posited.

There is a similar case with the geometric axioms of perception.}

Here H. will say: "must?" But people think illogically, too! The answer will be: this compulsion is an inborn disposition, a condensation of the experience of earlier generations that reaches into the aimless associations of the present. To what extent is this tenable? Wherever thought occurred, logical thought was present. The point where logical and alogical thinking diverged must have happened as early as prehistoric times. But now we can observe in ourselves how very often we think alogically; and often incorrect thinking leads to the right result. So what kind of conditions must they have been in which the logical thought process was distinguished from the unlogical one, took precedence and was imprinted on the memory?

The "constancy of representation" is something pre-logical; it must even be behind the actions of animals. Here lies already the germ of logic. At this level it is decidedly beneficial. Where this becomes conscious the principle of identity is present. This principle is never breached; it is just that, in many cases, identity is not recognized. [. . .]

G.[9] "Tell me, what is this notion of the parallelism between the psychical and the physical. Isn't that just a hypothesis?"

R.[10] "Yes."

G. "Is that something which has been substantiated in many individual cases just as, for example, a mathematical equation is the overall expression for many individual cases, or if not how has this hypothesis come about?"

R. "I sense what you're getting at; you're quite right. It is more a necessity of thought than an inference drawn from experimental observations. In the first instance what we have here is our demand for a consistent causality that we feel inwardly compelled to generalize, extending it to this realm as well; otherwise, however, the determinants are predominantly negative. The untenability of the opposite, of all spiritualistic theories. But things aren't as bad as all that. In experiments, psychophysical methods of measurement indicate a connection."

G. "A connection, yes, but a parallelism?"

R. "That's just an image! But it is true, nonetheless, that one doesn't pay enough attention to it."

G.   "I'm pleased that you, at least, are prepared to admit that there is possibly a problem here. The medic and the lawyer simply shrugged their shoulders: consistent causality, but no metaphysics, please."

R.   "Metaphysics?"

G.   "Certainly. That is precisely my conception. Not a theory, merely individual experiences that I've had recently; it is questionable whether I'll find a comprehensible way of expressing this at all."

R.   "Let's try then."

G.   "All right. Let's stay with our image. I think of a ladder. The main thing is the two parallel bars; but the ladder needs the small transverse rungs. These are—the metaphysical."

R.   "Speaking non-figuratively, without the image?"

G.   "Speaking non-figuratively I have the impression that the parallelism is not sufficient to explain certain phenomena. Between mind and body, between averse and reverse, there is a connection that I can only think of as metaphysical."

R.   "We shall have to keep to specific examples."

G.   "A cold-water cure." [. . .]

———————————

The Aeneid, translated by H. F. Müller 1878–80, 2 vols.

Johannes Ruysbroek, *The Virtue of the Church Wedding*, French by Maeterlinck, Paris 1891. [. . .]

According to M[aeterlinck][11] it is only the contemplative soul that holds sway with R[uysbroek] whereas Plato (*Timaeus*) and Plotinus give a dialectical explanation for the soul. "The mirror of human intelligence in this book is something completely unknown; but within it there is another mirror . . . which is concealed in the innermost core of our being; in this mirror no detail can be clearly distinguished . . . ; reason would smash it if its worldly light were to fall upon it for one moment."

Something is manifest. The soul? God? M. does not know. He insists that he is able to empathize with all mystical thoughts with the sole exception of this one. Nonetheless he has a sense of ineffable certainty.

M.: ecstasy is: "The beginning of the complete discovery of our being."

Plotinus gives the following directions: "With intellectual contemplation the intellect sees the intelligible objects by means of the light that the primeval unity pours out upon them and in the contemplation of these objects it sees in truth the intelligible light. But as soon as it turns its attention to the objects on which the light rests, it no longer sees the principle that illuminates them with full purity; when, on the other hand, it forgets the objects that it contemplates and only looks upon the clarity that makes these visible, then it sees the light itself and the principle of this light. But the intellect does not contemplate the intelligible light outside of itself. In this respect it is like the eye which, without . . . perceiving any external . . . light, is suddenly struck by a clarity which is of itself, or by a ray that springs forth from itself . . . or when, from the pressure of a hand, it is aware of the light that is within itself. Then it sees, although it sees nothing external to itself; indeed it sees more than in any other moment since it sees the light. The other objects that it saw previously when it was illuminated by them were not the light itself. Similarly, when the intellect closes the eye somehow to other objects in order to concentrate on itself, it sees, even in not seeing, not an alien light shining in alien forms, but its own light."

"The soul which God examines must sink down, in the full knowledge of the great being with which it is fused and in the conviction that it will find bliss in this union, into the depths of the godhead to the point where, ceasing to contemplate itself and the intelligible world, it becomes itself an object of contemplation."

Intuition. Maeterl. says that, when one has talked to ordinary people about their pears or the frost, one returns home with no less buoyant a step than if one has spent these hours with Plato, Socrates or Marcus Aurelius—a scientist will argue that this is the effect of having one's mind taken off one's work.

4
NOTEBOOK II
2 APRIL 1905 TO 1908 OR LATER, CIRCA 1918-1919

[This was another of the notebooks that Musil used during his student years—at the time when he starts writing it he is apparently becoming more intensely involved with his formal studies, having spent some of the earlier months in Berlin finishing Young Törleß. The first entry indicates his determination to find what would be called in MwQ "the right way to live." In this entry Musil refers to what he calls the "Science of Man"; although he does not expand on this concept here I believe that it refers to the notion that an individual should approach his own life in the detached mode of a scientist faced with a problem—rejecting all theological or moral systems based on commandments or "a priori" assumptions about the nature of Mankind or God, he approaches human emotions and the realm of existential decision making with cold, rational precision, with the inductive, step-by-step approach of the engineer-intellectual. The "Science of Man" project is perhaps implicit in those self-reflective passages when he analyzes his anger at Hermine Musil's treatment of a servant, and when he confesses to himself, if to no one else, that he has been jealous of von Allesch: his friend and rival had revealed that he had read an author in the original French and therewith established a competitive advantage over Musil. (It is a tribute to Musil's objectivity that the literary high point of this notebook is an entry in which Musil rerelates one of von Allesch's experiences while on holiday in a remote part of Austria.) Later, the narrator of MwQ would treat an enterprise of the hero analogous to the "Science of Man" project as *the folly of an enthusiastic but misguided young intellectual; in this note-book, however, the enthusiasm is fresh and vital.*

Musil deplores the "elimination of the soul from scientific thinking"; at the same time, in making a proposal, as he expresses it, to "apprentice my-self to Romanticism and mysticism" and thereby experience the gamut of passions of mystic and Romantic alike, he leavens the enterprise with the skepticism of a scientist. (This ability to experience to the full while, at an-other level, dispassionately recording the experience for later analysis is seen in the entry for 30 June [1905?] in which he notes how moods ebb and flow like tides through his psyche within the span of a few hours and how he seems to have as little influence over this relentlessly regular, natural process as he has over the pull of the moon.) He hopes that Ricarda Huch, Ellen Key, and Novalis will provide access to the realms of feeling.

He is strongly aware that the existential task he has set himself falls un-comfortably between the work typical of an academic philosopher/psychol-ogist and that of a creative writer—this incongruity, at one point, is embodied in an imaginary conversation between two personae within the Musilian self.

In this notebook, too, there are reflections on the craft of novel writing, particularly on the technique of creating a narrative mood. At some point during the period when the notebook was being written, Musil met Martha for the first time. Perhaps the entry entitled "Calendar of love" records his feelings as this new relationship takes possession of him?]

1905

11.

Today I'm beginning a diary; I do not usually keep one but I feel a distinct need to do so now.

After four years of diffusion it will give me the opportunity to find that line of spiritual development again that I consider to be properly mine.

. . . I shall try to carry forward into it "the banners from a battle that has never been fought." Thoughts from that time of great upheaval are to be re-examined, sorted through and developed. One or other of my scattered notes is to be taken up in this process but only when it captures my atten-tion again.

I shall seldom make notes on personal matters and then only when I believe that it will at some time be of spiritual interest to be reminded of the matter in question.

All thoughts on the "Science of Man"[1] are to be entered here. Nothing from the field of academic philosophy. But drafts [of creative work]. Here and there a poem that seems worth remembering. Particularly any with halftones and shades of meaning. Absolute expressions. The important question here is that about style. Interest centering not only on what one says but on how one says it. Search for my own style. Up till now I have tried to say the unsayable with words that reached out directly. This betrays one-sided intelligence. The will to forge expression into an instrument shall stand at the entrance to this book.   2.IV 05, Brünn.

3.IV. I'm reading Ricarda Huch, *The Blossoming of Romanticism*,[2] by the way a real woman's book! A passage from Novalis occurs to me: "What can I do for my soul that dwells within me like an unsolved riddle? That leaves the visible man in large measure an autocrat because it cannot dominate him in any way?" A curious conception of the soul underlies this. This kind of thinking, in terms of form without regard to content, is found in the Gustl type.

Moreover the consequences drawn from Kant are remarkably eccentric.

I shall take a look at Baader[3] with respect to his role as intermediary. By the way, Huch's concept of the man-soul and the woman-soul is not unfruitful. [. . .]

One point of view that I take from this book (without knowing if it is that of the author):

"One can recognize oneself only in one's actions. Not in one's consciousness. They stream out from the unconscious." (The right mixture of conscious and unconscious is the ideal of Romanticism. Its fate was to dry up under the hot gaze of the conscious.)

. . . If, in the place of the unpsychological or at least rashly formulated conscious-unconscious, we put reflected-unreflected [. . .] we come to a train of thought that, though familiar, is worthy of further consideration.

The true human being is only found in actions—all else within us is never to be recognized as "true," one can never get this into sufficiently sharp focus.

The experience that lies beneath this is the historical perspective, e.g., "the uneasy delicate dreams of the Middle Ages and the bloody deeds in which this dreamer tosses and turns." [. . .] The lack of any common ground between them.

The same holds true for the present seen from a historical perspective.

Need to read Maeterlinck on this matter: "There are times when the soul is closer to waking than at others, where it rises toward the surface," and similar passages.

By contrast with these, all those trains of thought that relate to the "cogito ergo sum." Finally the elimination of soul from scientific thinking.

The "I" of Descartes is the last fixed point in the empirical-critical train of thought, it is the certain momentary unity.

The "I" of which the mystics speak is the complex "I."

The former is the most certain, the latter the least certain. In such a way is it possible to form an opposition. The question is only how far the mystical conception is justified. Of course, prior to any historical experience, it is based on personal experience.

"Influential actions that bring about decisive change in our lives usually arise in a kind of fire of passion. They take shape within us without our knowledge and we often have to be satisfied with registering what has happened, without, at times, having any complete overview of the context."

"Up to a certain extent one can predict the actions of a person—one knows him." When one goes up beyond a certain average one does not know a person. "In practical affairs, an average perception is sufficient. For more subtle ethical relationships this is not the case." One only knows the general tendency of a person's nature. But then on occasions something else breaks through what we might call the person's "good will." These really are impulses that rise up from the unconscious.

But the unconscious is partly shaped by the conscious. It consists partly of predispositions, partly of traces. The predispositions, so it is stated, are to a certain extent what remains of the species-consciousness {and family consciousness.} With respect to the traces that have been acquired there is only the central question [. . .]: "Do the traces equate to what has caused them?" Or has some kind of proportional transformation taken place? In other words, if a good impulse of the soul leaves a trace behind it, is that trace of such a kind that it becomes the same deed, or a good deed, or an evil deed? Is what happens only a transformation from the kinetic field to a potential one, or is something more happening? In a word, is our conscious person a guarantee of the unconscious one?

{What does pedagogics have to say on this?}

6.IV.

[. . .] It will at some time be necessary to take correct stock of conscious and unconscious and it is possible that the result (if one contrasts the proportion of the reflective and constant factor with the "other"[4] within us) will be a surprising one.

But first it will be essential to be certain of the data under discussion. Since for the present I do not possess much insight into this area, it is my task to apprentice myself to Romanticism and mysticism. The only critical activity to perform here is to reduce their ideas to the pure "senti=mental" [sic] core,[5] i.e., to cut out anything that is only possible from a specific metaphysical point of view, for example in terms of Schelling's[6] philosophy of nature.

With respect to the comprehension of the Modern, the following question also occurred to me in the course of these thoughts: what would be the attitude of Jena [Romantics][7] to d'Annunzio[8] for example? They would feel that the mental was missing in his work. They might possibly find that his sensuality was plebeian.

Here the modern view has clearly taken another route. The much-admired pagan joy in sensuality is to some extent a culture of the physical in order to bring relief to the spiritual. A dualist practice. Not that far removed from religious feeling. At least the body is cultivated in order to give the spirit a good foundation (sport), whereas in sensuality it is an escape valve. After all, with the renaissance type, it is also only a release. Without this perspective, sensuality in the Modern movement[9] is considered to be decadent.

So far little has been done to throw the light of the spirit[10] onto sensuality itself (rather than exercises that involve extemporizing on, and clever play with, sensuality). As sentimental sybarites, the Romantics from the Jena period would still find themselves rather isolated.

On the other hand, they would probably not be a match for the Moderns either with respect to sentiment or with respect to mind.[11] [. . .]

8.IV. Couldn't sleep until around three o'clock at night. Read Grillparzer's autobiography[12] and marked some passages. [. . .]

14.IV. Didn't sleep at all last night. First hot, tormented, then, after I had opened the window, wonderfully calm. Birdsong from the garden—like the touch of soft, busy hands. Indescribably delicate morning tints over the objects in the room. The black of a mirror sucking up the darkness—simply beyond description. It is not black at all, cannot be captured with expressions for color; rather with ones for materials such as velvet, etc.

At the dentist's over the last few days I've been dipping into Schick's[13] sketchbook. Again: observation is an art. And writing is an art. One has to make an effort to learn it.

In the dreadful style of the *Confusions*[14] I had written, for example: "he thought that he did not actually have any reason to make himself so dependent on this girl. He thought, moreover, about the way that his life had, thereby, become abstract and thin. And finally that [. . .]," etc.

An alternative way: "'These girls!' he thought 'Loveable? Good? Beautiful? Yes, indeed. But how deeply I'm entangled in all this love, goodness and beauty! As if in cotton threads! And beyond this warm tangle hasn't everything become thin, abstract, colorless?! Will I ever dare to leave this sweet nest?'" etc.

20.IV. Semmering.

A demarcation of this tendency from another angle—and the need for this can readily be perceived in my truly unfortunate text sample—came up during a reading of Huysmans' *À rebours*. For there is nothing that has a more wooden effect than when one puts long tirades into the mouths of one's characters, making them into phonographs playing back what the author has recorded earlier.

So it is important to say: it is the norm that, in the novel, the writer does not himself speak. (This is only permissible at certain periods when an upheaval in taste or in the way of thinking, etc., is taking place—in times of "Sturm und Drang" such as accompanied the birth of the Modern movement.[15] Such novels are concerned with "content," they lack "art" (in the sense used by Hardenberg[16] in his judgment of Goethe's [*Wilhelm Meister*][17]). The limit of what is allowed is the point of demarcation from the essay.) But even characters in a story are also not allowed to speak "novels." The "art" of writing consists in creating situations that make what is to be said appropriate to the characters while at the same time selecting what has to be said in such a way—selecting the suggestive nodal points from the general flow of thoughts—that the characters do not have "much" to say. A rather successful example of this is the lawyer in Huysmans' *Dilemma*.[18] [. . .]

Supplement to the stay at Semmering.   Berlin 28.IV.

Christmas weather; off the paths the snow is up to one's hips. Gustl came to visit; we were on completely different wavelengths. Heinrich[19] is deeply neurasthenic and has disturbing symptoms. (Particularly noticeable that his qualities have been turned on their head: earlier self-assured, now hesitant; earlier, careless in his dress, now anxious to choose clothing that conforms to the requirements of a particular environment; earlier, often contretemps with Gustl and me, now, something approaching tenderness on his part.)

On the last day of the stay met Gustl at Alice's house in Weissenbach.[20] Saw for the first time that Gustl is suffering like a lovesick student, without any sense at all of propriety. The psychic[21] background is a matter of speculation; it is not visible at all. I was good; there were only two areas where I failed to strike the right attitude—in keeping my own counsel and leaving them alone.

Here I feel walled in and on this first day my nerves are already on edge.

2.V. Written to J.C.C.B.[22] All literary thoughts as if obliterated. A certain passive philosophical interest is present. More so, a pleasure in good food and drink. (What was the point of my writing the prologue to this diary?)

3.V. I'm now reading Novalis, *Heinrich von Ofterdingen*.

4.V. On technique: describe a girl with sexual attributes, e.g., the one in the restaurant today with the chin that was a touch too prominent—and then suddenly remark that she was the same type as one of his aunts.

If this is done skillfully it releases some undertones that have a touch of perversion about them but does so in a perfectly proper fashion—like Jacobsen in *Niels L[yhne]*.[23]

This kind of technique can generally be expressed in the following offhand way (and I'm thinking now of the scene between N.L. and Frau Boye—oppressive inner intensity and the rattling of the door handle as it is cleaned, or footsteps on the pavement, or the conversation whose sound waves enter the room on a dense current of air that conducts them with exaggerated distinctness): observe the difference between breaking a door open and inadvertent pressure on a nail head that causes it to spring open. It is wrong to say that such and such a feeling is registered, one must mention something as unobtrusive as possible, like the sounds in the example above, something that through association is infallibly suggestive of the secret thought.

In the course of the evening, in the tram: when actors are not on stage they can hardly ever leave their mouths alone: with the most inconsequential words they make faces, and their lips in particular never take on calm, personal contours. They are ashamed—this is their organ of reproduction. [. . .]

13.V. "Let's spend a little time talking to ourself, Herr Musil. It is true then that you have days when you do not like artists?"

"Yes."

"And also days when you avoid philosophers?"

"Indeed. Sometimes the former are too unphilosophical for me, sometimes the latter too lacking in humanity."

"And today?"

"Today I'm on the side of the artists. I got annoyed at the Institute[24] and by way of compensation was delighted, in the course of the evening, by the harmless merriment of artists sitting at a table next to mine."

"'Harmless merriment' is virtually a slogan; it expresses what used to be the prevailing judgment of artists."

"Well, you're probably right, but you've put your finger on an awkward point."

"Forgive me."

"Please don't mention it. We shall have to talk this over thoroughly one day. I must admit that, although I believe I'm an artist, I don't know what that means. I'm irritated by things philosophical. I suffer from this mixing-up of the two elements. I do actually suffer. My notion of who and what is a philosopher has become more demanding; it lays forceful claim to things that I used to see as essential features of the artist."

"You have intimated what you thought about this matter once before already. You said that the philosopher is unwilling to concede that any artist can be profound."

"This is so. The artist's profundity cannot go deep enough, cannot be exact enough."

"But that charge would, at first glance, only be directed against the Maeterlincks, Hardenbergs, Emersons and others like them. Such artists do not do justice to their insights, they allow themselves to become too spellbound by them, etc. But a creative writer is simply someone who places such thoughts into a person, describes their effects in human relations, etc. Surely a philosopher lacks the talent to do things like that?"

"Certainly; but the creative artist lacks the thoughts. He cannot shape the thoughts with the delicacy that the fine palate of the philosopher demands."

"But is this necessary? Shouldn't the creative writer seek out his thoughts in the middle ground, so to speak, and then breathe life into them?"

"I have given this matter some thought, too, specifically with respect to psychology. Nowadays this discipline has very exact indirect methods that it uses to lay bare processes that would otherwise be quite inaccessible to observation—a kind of mirroring of the brain. This will probably be developed further. Elements from ever deeper levels will be revealed. But does this have anything to do with the way the writer describes things? He has always to work just with the complexes that are evident at first glance. Just as the painter represents not atoms but bodies wrapped in air, so the writer represents thoughts and feelings that are on the surface and not psychical elements."

"But people praise the kind of writer who penetrates into the depths!"

"And it is precisely here that I am searching for what is distinctive! And it is perfectly apparent that self-observation is an inadequate instrument! It is futile to turn one's ambition down this false trail! For this reason those jaded theories about the play of the powers of the imagination, about the mere appearance of beauty, etc., have taken on new meaning for me now. But I'm tired, we shan't finish this now. Good night, Herr Musil."

"Good night, Herr Musil."

30.V. With the regularity of some law at work the following process runs full circle within me:

I am arrogant, dismissive, reticent, refined, happy. Some or other sense of power takes territorial hold. I have taken too much pleasure in my muscles while I was rowing or I am working at philosophy with an intensity that blunts the senses. I feel first that my arrogance, with its conciliatory frontage on the outside world, is deserting me. I am no longer so friendly; I am less witty. I feel empty and work out of sheer desperation. My behavior in company deteriorates. I suffer a defeat. I feel that, by comparison with some other person, I am stupid. I behave with spectacular ineptitude, I cannot find an appropriate rejoinder to some insult. A few hours later I am, once again, arrogant, dismissive, reticent, refined, happy.

13.VI. From a letter to Gustl:

Tradition: Has it never occurred to you that we believed that we had boundless talents and that now we scarcely believe that we have moderate ones?

Where did they go to?

Of course, they were not actually present, even then; but, despite all skepticism, do we not believe that, though we later lost all intuition of where they were, those paths really did exist. I mean, for example, those recondite habits of thought. We didn't actually possess them, but we knew their perfume, etc., and we now still believe that there really are trains of thought that generate this perfume.

Alice:

> To *wait beyond the door with bars of gold,*
> *Until the other's footsteps come again,*
> *And breathe the heavy fragrance, rich and deep,*
> *Each, from his garden, brings to me . . .*[25]

Shouldn't we try in such a way to bring solitude and dialogue into harmony? Doesn't success mean a great deal? The verses are valid for each of us. Everyone, in the effect he has, cannot be compared to others. Is it not wise (in the rose-garlanded sense of the word) to unfold all the possibilities of such relationships? Can Alice not also bring from me something for you? Can you not bring from me something for her?[26] Is it not, of itself, something verging on excessive refinement to touch each other on occasions only through the medium of a third party?

19.IV. What is there to report? At night in the coffeehouse I read an essay by E[llen] Key[27] that had a profound effect on me—she speaks with the voice of my own past. Here is to be found a line of thinking that I once followed, the Valerie tradition![28] I bought a copy of this journal; now it's been lying on my table for such a long time and I still haven't found the strength to start reading it again.

Instead I have been reading *Buddenbrooks.* Very fine and boring; perhaps an al fresco masterpiece, but boring; in parts, to my surprise, it possesses sovereign power.

I am also pursuing my studies in logic, apparently with some talent.

Why don't I read the essay? Why don't I pick up the threads when I so deeply regret that they once broke?

It's possible to get by this way, too—that's probably the explanation. I know that I'm "hard-working" and feel a release from embarrassing reflection. But yet all I do is to live off notions, off ideas that choose me as their vessel, without my feeling any sense of fatherhood, any sense that they are "fruit of my loins."

If I think back to the time two and a half years ago in Stuttgart?[29] The decision that I have long since put into practice seemed madly attractive. The future that I am now living through seemed so rich then. Every day offering something refined, a further deepening of the personality. I must try all over again. [. . .]

5.VII. Today after a colloquium with Schumann[30] I spent a few minutes talking to v. A[llesch] and two others. Discussion moved from the Renaissance to Catholicism and thence to Huysmans whom A. praised highly. I said that I had not enjoyed *À rebours*. A.: "Oh, it is very fine, above all stylistically. It has such fine stylistic beauty in matters . . ." I replied: "But this fineness has a touch of artifice about it; it is not 'real'." A.: "What do you mean by 'real'? And since when is it a mistake to practice artifice?"

This short conversation spoiled my mood for the whole day. It had looked as if I did not know the aesthetic worth of artifice. But the main source of my discomfiture was that I have been suspended in a kind of unease since the day in the gallery. I coined the term "Baconism of the sentiments" and tried to console myself with it. But the situation is undeniably the following: a type of person whom I have never actually understood is now getting close to me. The type who is aesthetically sensitive. I am morally sensitive. Decidedly so since the time of Valerie. Earlier I went with the aesthetes. Later I came to see those of them who had reached a particular level of intensity as a hothouse species. Imperfect types like Strobl[31] confirmed me in this view.

Self-constructed sentiments, paper emotions. Now I have a person before me who demonstrates his versatility across a wide cultural field. Sentiments that to me are mere words he professes to experience. I must discover what lies behind this man; I feel the kind of excitement that I experienced in the days when I first found myself a half-barbarian among the grammar-school boys.

6.VII. Before one of Stumpf's[32] lectures I said to Allesch: "To tell the truth I'm annoyed with you—how is it possible to take pleasure in Huysmans' work?" "Oh, it's the refinement of his style as chronicler; his narrative is so calm, it's really just like old Latin chronicles, and then there's the way that, with such understatement, he suddenly points to a new aspect to the plot." I objected: "if that were so I would really value his work. But all I know is that he was held in esteem about ten years ago when it was seen as meritorious to parade decadent or contrived emotions; but today? He parades fine things, but that is all that he does with them." "Oh, he doesn't just parade them, this is what he really feels—quite 'real'." "'Real'? That's precisely the word that yesterday you said you didn't understand; that pleases me." "Well, I simply couldn't understand how you could deny that his work was 'real'." "Indeed I do deny it. Even admitting that he has read all these chronicles—and that is far from being the issue here—and admitting that he really likes them, my understanding of the term 'real' goes somewhat deeper than that." "?" "Yes, I can imagine a person for whom all that is indeed the case but to whose sensations I would not attach the description 'real'." Here I had won the more favorable position; did A. feel this? Unfortunately our discussion moved on again to the question of style since I cast doubt on whether Huysm. was really successful at reproducing the style of a chronicler. I put forward the view that Hofmannsthal, Schaukal[33] and many others wrote better than he did. A. was by no means willing to concede this. It eventually emerged that he had read Huysm. in the original. That spoiled my whole mood. Of course, the young man who reads French authors only in the original! Hadn't that instantly made me lose everything?

After the lecture, our conversation turned to Altenberg[34] whose work he does not value highly. I praised Altenberg as a fine stylist. Compressed style! Of course I didn't forget to remark that, when applied to A., this was in fact a cliché. But we avoided any argument.

I haven't yet told him what I hope he will mean for my life. But I have already flattered him, and only half intentionally. I mentioned how widely his interests range and how, in this regard, I have committed many sins of omission over the past few years. He was clearly moved. But of the doubts that, in my view, attach to his breadth of interests I said nothing at all. I'm feeling rather ashamed on this account. Having to learn things from this man, in order to be able to tell later whether there is really something I can learn from him or not, is not something I can take any pride in whatsoever. [. . .]

––––––––––

It is possible for one quality[35] to predominate, but not to such an extent that the other qualities cannot be sufficiently strong to magnify, deepen, etc., each other. The reciprocal effect of each on the others is the aspect that is essentially indefinable. But in some geniuses and some people of limited abilities this element is equally lacking. For all their culture they are incapable of achieving the synthesis that is the precondition for fullness of soul.[36] [. . .]

In the meantime Gustl is off on a [. . .] cycling tour in the Alps, on the way to Velden[37] to see Alice. No doubt he will drink milk, eat salad with it, and take Goethe's *Conversations with Eckermann* along with him. He is looking for his character and almost has it already. In describing him and me one has to trace things back to the common point of departure. Then back to the conditions in the respective families. The similarities we share today have come along different routes.

He suffered from sexual confusion—R. shares this condition but does not suffer from it—and from imagined physical illnesses. Or, to be more precise, he suffers from the hesitant attitude to the events of his life that is made up of both these factors. The friction at the Charlemont[38] estate forced him to find something within himself to hold fast to.

I now feel the same need, at a time when I find myself unable to be superior to a younger person, partly because his field is not mine to any great extent, partly because I am all too ready to turn against myself.

I feel the need to secure, through the way I present myself in public, a degree of superiority. [. . .]

21.VII. In haste a few notes on the essay by Key.

Although her essay had the most profound influence on me, I am now sobering up again. Her basic idea—more soul, or nothing but soul—is excellent. Her idea of making soul the subject of study brought me redemption. What she said about school and about harmful ways of living is absolutely correct.

Beyond these things, however, she fails. What soul is and how soul is to be nurtured are full of contradictions. She has simply gathered together, in a rather uncritical fashion, what has been written on this subject. Let me review here a number of these points of view, which cross over each other.

Key demands a complete and harmonious unfolding of the soul. A harmonious unfolding through a fullness of life is the view of Walt Whitman, while unfolding through a simplifying of life is the view of Thoreau. As far as fullness of life is concerned she repeatedly emphasizes that it is necessary to unfold "all possibilities." She fails to recognize thereby that fullness of life and harmony are things that by no means have to go hand in hand. She herself talks of simplifying life. Of course it would be wrong to understand this to be the style of life that poor people lead; rather that, in order to achieve harmony, it is necessary to make a choice from among dispositions all of which are good. Often it happens that some of these must be repressed in order to make way for better ones. Fullness of life, on its own, gives rise only to a beautiful animal, a Renaissance animal. Fullness of life with a simplifying of life is the required combination, but Key does not say this. And even if this was what she wanted to say, the real question is "how?" {Who needs fullness, who needs simplicity?}

Delight in "good work," avoidance of excess in work and of self-indulgence belongs under the heading of harmony.

But the most fruitful source of contradictions in her case is her position on reason. She calls for a life of intoxication (cf. fullness of life), for reverence for, and belief in, life (cf. simplification of life). Two directions that can be unified if one understands by "reverence for life" receptivity even to the most unobtrusive things. But she means more than just this. The notion of reverence for life rests for her on a pantheistic sense of belonging to nature. Now this is not to everyone's taste and it is not good to place some important matter at the very leading edge of a philosophical opinion that is under fierce dispute. No doubt even soulful people exist who are devoid of pantheism. But the following additional point is more important still: what kind of people are they in whom this sense of belonging is strongly developed, or, more precisely, in whom this is the determining factor? They are the type of the pure fool that is quite common in literature and history. Of course they are merely the extreme cases, but Key demonstrates a questionable leaning toward this extreme. The child and the animal are frequently the models she cites. The soul of the animal is, admittedly, merely a tendentious postulate by Key, but with reference to the child she is right in one respect—surrender to the moment, losing itself in the play of forces. This may be something that appears enviable to the adult. But it cannot be a model to the adult since it is not possible to wind back a more complicated constitution to a simpler one.

Key doesn't take account of this either. However, what she says is even more questionable when she tries to transfer the advantages of the child to the adult.

There is no more talk here of the reverence for life in the sense of Goethe, but of the pantheism of those simple people whose heart is heavier than their head. Key polemicizes against reason.

At the outset she is right to do so. After all, Nietzsche has repeatedly analyzed the people whose heads are so heavy that they constantly topple over and bang them. But hardly has she started than she overshoots her goal and seems to have no notion at all of the difficulties.

———————

24.VII. In the evening I leafed through Nietzsche. In Menschl. II, p. 177 Aph. 383[39] there is something relevant to my note of 6.VII.

Nietzsche describes someone he wants to praise as "a logician from sheer loathing." As long as a field of knowledge is less than completely exact it has nothing at all to offer the "human being." For it then suppresses subtler forces and this, in time, takes its revenge in a terrifying reaction.

Consider the way in which logic is usually handled. One has a sense of how people lose themselves in the object of their attention. All versions of psychological processes presuppose an element of passion. For, given the present state of knowledge, they are nothing more than hypostatizations. The good ones read well, even when they contradict each other. What fire, momentum, ambition, are necessary to make people who are schooled in some critical methodology capable of doing this. Hard though it is to believe, logic is a passion; what appears to be sober is only possible as the product of the mist of enthusiasm that swirls around it. So this also holds true for the scorn for Aristotelian syllogistics as representing the only thing that is fixed and sober. As long as it is necessary to enthuse, one gets into impossible company where logic is concerned. It will only be when logic has become exact, mathematical, cool, that it will mean anything to us. Like getting up on one occasion before the others do and going for an early morning walk.

25.VII. In *Essays,* I, Emerson says: "A human being belongs only half to himself—the other half is expression. For all people who, in their anguish of soul, demand to express themselves. In love, in art, in greed, in politics, in work, in play we all seek to give voice to our painful mystery."

5.VIII. Wagner wrote in a letter that he could not stand unmediated extremes. He said it was true that he could not dispense with contradictions but that he always felt it essential to build between them an artistic bridge with widely spaced gradations. In company he often speaks for too long.

Perhaps this is the only way to write an opera?

By the way, he has a remarkable feeling for the formal. Perhaps someday I shall be able to connect this with people of the kind that A[llesch] represents for me.

Here only one subject has so far engaged my interest, little Tino. He must be very delicate. I would like to keep some hold on him but see that I am too ham-fisted. He is melancholic and asks after every flower in the meadow; but what is a name like "melancholy" with respect to a child and what are meadow flowers to him and to me? He reminds me of Hanno Buddenbrock.[40] He loves my mother without a trace of shyness. If he retains this capacity he will become very dangerous. "I'm composing a fairy tale," "I love the carnations" he says with an emphasis that is completely literary. I asked him "Did you always love a certain kind of flower above all others and did you only then learn that they were called carnations? Or did someone talk to you about carnations and did you already like them before you were shown them for the first time?" He vigorously affirmed the former. However, he hadn't understood me but had probably only sensed that I was setting some snare for him.

A most remarkable little girl came up to Mama and said: "My name's Hildegarde; I very much enjoy playing with children." "Here in the hotel you'll find lots of them." "Oh, not with all the children, only with the little one and the big one." (Tino and his brother in the uniform of the Theresianum.)[41] I should like to protect this liaison. But first I must make him unfaithful to my mother.

———

27.VIII. It is characteristic of a particular social stratum of girls that, the first time, they do not give away their innocence but are robbed of it. They cry and beg one not to do anything to them; but then they give in, partly out of respect, partly because they are disarmed by the charm of the higher caste, partly from the sweet shock of awakened sensuality.

The way in which they are "taken" at the inception of their love life is something that draws into their life the consequences of a stigma.

———

To be used with reference to R.[obert]—H.[erma]

There are women whom one should never observe when they are not moving; in photographs they look unpleasant. But in life they have an effect on us through the constant motion that they impart to our soul. Like a snake dance, a can-can, a bolero, they are not fixed but a line that is far longer, more bizarre and subject to change than what it "actually" involves. Not asking any questions about this belongs with those existential skills that one must follow in one's treatment of these women. [. . .]

———

28.IX. On the theme of the advisability of building a marriage on infidelity: Canaletto. White wigs and these skirts with twin humps give every woman the option of a love life. Wearing these it is permissible to be ugly. The woman becomes pure sexuality and pure wit; there is no thing called "beauty" to serve as the mean. Canaletto's women are pug-faced and thin as rakes. But their clothing makes of them something quite unnatural over which the spirit can range freely. And when one practices another form of intercourse with them one snuffs out the candles.

––––––––––––––––

11.X. The sketch that I have just started for the novel—which opens with the childhood story—is schematically similar to the *Confusions*. Here again a basic chord of sensuality is struck in those scenes that do not belong to the plot proper and on this, as things progress, moral complications of a predominantly intellectual kind are based.

Undeniably this approach is a dangerous one. I am too young to adopt a particular type of technique.

However the childhood story is certainly very suitable as an introduction to the character of both Gustl and Robert.

Finally, I'm hesitating about whether I ought not try to steer a way around the sexual segments of text and, for this reason if for no other, drop the childhood section.

But, since it is precisely the difference between sentimental love and the love that Robert feels which forms one main problem and since this indifference is prefigured in childhood, one cannot easily avoid it. But it is clumsy to start out from a point that is so fearfully far away. Dostoyevsky never does anything like that!

––––––––––––––––

16.X. For all the riches in characterization and detail the basic ideas are very thin. What do they consist of, anyway?

First: sensuality is a force holding sway over all the characters. It is nothing at all in itself; from it, however, the widest variety of things evolve. The effusions of Gustl and Alice, the reserve that Robert brings to bear on all things, and, in Gustl's case particularly, more and more is built up on it.

Second: relationships between the sexes have to be built exclusively on the basis of illusion; the same holds good for fidelity. It is through fidelity that the fate of Herma becomes a tragedy. This fate is a sacrifice to necessity.

And, even with respect to her tragedy, full sympathy is withheld. The "skepticism," the "reserve," still press down on her memory.

Third: the relationship of Robert to G. and to A. This is our drama. Robert must show the simple opposition of this relationship to the one between R and H through his spiritual manner.

Fourth: the "poor" girls. The song of the herdsman.

5. The book and what is connected with it.

6. The "senti-mentals"!!!!! [*sic*] The relationships with A and H and G are only objects with respect to which R. states his views.

What is R. himself? An intellectual nature. Virtue a consequence of understanding—this holds for him. That is his formula. But what is this without the particular form of his understanding? In reality, what shaped me was the practice of always thinking the "other" way.[42] But this is inaccessible to direct representation. It would require a precise record of the period of youth.

A second method would be to keep the figure constantly in a tendentious and oppositional mode—keeping a continuous contradiction in the figure's own name and in that of the author—offering scenes that show his dissenting approach to moral issues

[. . .]

But perhaps the best approach is to have the figure emerge from the dark as Dostoyevsky does. Avoid introducing him from the beginning as the main character. Against this method is the consideration that the character has too much of a past (coloring of sensuality, change of occupation, H[erma])

{Becoming serious is, after all, a main theme}

1906

Wrongdoing: I had a row with Mama. Am now alone with the maidservant who is always attentive and polite toward me, but who is always quarreling with M. I feel the urge to say: M. is dissatisfied with everybody who does not unconditionally bend to her will; M. is quarrelsome, disagreeable, etc.

As I try out this idea—it has much to recommend it—I feel that it will be useful to me. It completely soothes my inner turmoil, makes me receptive to new impressions. But I know that, by thinking this, I am doing M. wrong. The maidservant really doesn't work hard enough, etc., for her. My intellectual situation is one of doubt. Should I now do wrong or not?

Morality: in certain cases it is useful to insist on steadfast resistance to the onset of temptation. Observation of pathological cases does indeed reveal a tendency for a transgression to accelerate like an avalanche. All conditions of high mental tension,[43] such as a struggle against a vice or mania, a state of fidelity to a distant loved one,[44] are ones of labile balance. At the first moment of surrender the whole disposition is annihilated, one has not merely taken a single step, one has become completely another person. So, for example, the simple act of noticing the smell of a strange woman, or a situation where one is seeking a chance meeting. An uneasiness affecting the will, disenchantment with all the thoughts that were occupying one a moment ago, form the introduction. This on its own breaks the state of high tension, and this happens even before it is possible to make any moral countermove. Any rescue would entail a totally new moral action making its appearance. It is sheer good fortune if such a disposition is present at just that moment.

By the way, in the example above a simple involuntary attention to the smell possibly involves a drift into temptation.

In all such cases, any conscious willing is in a precarious position.

———————

Willing: one has tended to identify mind[45] with consciousness and assigned to it, as its most noble attribute, the freedom of the will. It is scarcely possible to conceive of anything more erroneous than this. Perhaps in this context individuality is involved: I have never caught myself in the act of willing. It was always the case that I saw only the thought—for example when I'm lying on one side in bed: now you ought to turn yourself over. This thought goes marching on in a state of complete equality with a whole set of other ones: for example, your foot is starting to feel stiff, the pillow is getting hot, etc. It is a proper act of reflection; but it is still far from breaking out into a deed. On the contrary, I confirm with a certain consternation that, despite these thoughts, I still haven't turned over.

As I admonish myself that I ought to do so and see that this does not happen, something akin to depression takes possession of me, albeit a depression that is at once scornful and resigned. And then, all of a sudden, and always in an unguarded moment, I turn over. As I do so, the first thing that I am conscious of is the movement as it is actually being performed, and frequently a memory that this started out from some part of the body or other, from the feet, for example, that moved a little, or were unconsciously shifted, from where they had been lying, and that then drew all the rest after them.

———————

A conclusion drawn about philosophy from the perspective of a student.

As a student of philosophy one has an experience that indicates that this realm of thinking occupies a curious position between objective knowledge and creative writing, whereby it has the advantages of neither one nor the other.

The literature of all three areas is immeasurably vast. With regard to poetry, simple contemplation of what is produced in a single year could drive one to despair, yet with the certainty of instinct one finds, from among this eternity, the few books that will become important to one. The literature of the exact sciences has, by contrast, the advantage that each book modifies its predecessors and, by taking the subject further, renders them superfluous. In philosophy, however, one does not know who should be one's teacher. [. . .]

23.II. {07} Allesch today gave me a wonderful account of his adventures. He was able, for a moment, to give me a perfect intuition of a country road. . .[46] No one knows who I am . . the straight . . whiteness. . I breathe a sigh of relief when I'm back on the country road again. A person who knows how to disappear without trace! Someone who really does feel the urge to go off and away,—not simply the idea of doing so. . . .

Adamsthal—the black, marshy path from the railway—the high dark mountains closing in all around—the inn that does not open—the house of the watchman—[A.] knocks on the window—a lamp is lit, the curtain is thrust a little to one side. A naked woman becomes visible behind the pane. She lets the curtain fall back quickly. After a while the door opens. What, he is asked, does he want?

The way into the village is pointed out to him.

The houses sleep—the gates of the inns are shuttered and barred—he knocks—no answer at all—he beats against the shutters with his fists—but nowhere is there any sign of life. At last a dog starts to bark. Gs—Gs—he teases it. The dog goes wild to the pitch of madness—Gs—Gs—until all the dogs go mad. This alerts the night-watchman who then arrives. He is carrying a long pike with a crosspiece for parrying. A. makes himself understood as best he can. The night-watchman guides him to one house, to another. Everywhere he gives only a gentle knock, tapping carefully with just one finger against the windows. And straightaway people inside are awake. The curtains are lifted. A. has a glimpse of naked women who are peeping out, then the curtain falls—then it is lifted again and the watchman speaks with the people. They have to walk on. At last a house is found that is prepared to take the stranger in. But they have to wait. The window is closed once more. The watchman stands—leaning on his pike—calm—in his face nothing moves—like a statue—throughout the house one sees the lights moving to and fro . . . [. . .]

———————————

Calendar of love. A cold mist has come down like a curtain and the new act begins. I love this one, too. The feeling of banishment in winter, of being confined to one's room. On the street the cold surrounds one like an icy sphere. This protects against alien influences. At home, in one's room, it gradually dissolves, leaving behind it a mood like a thaw in early spring, so fresh, and yet so tired and tender, too. For lovers it is as if they were winning each other anew each time, as if in the pure element that surrounds people resurrected from the dead. For in such moments nothing is alien. The soul breaks open and the body is fragrant with the departing cold.

Often when I turn a corner of a street I feel as if I must see you wrapped in fur and cold. Then my mood is mild and still, as if I had dipped my hand into soft snow water.

These are the kind of images with which I now support my life and for your sake—for thy sake—I love this season that always used to fill me with horror, and thus I come to love all seasons.

———————————

Some notes

Some of the things that Gustl told me in confidence are very interesting: 1. the rebellion of egoism before the wedding—i.e., a certain spitefulness in one's view of the other who is perceived as an alien "I." 2. After A[lice] came back from England in such a state of decline, and he would often wander around the Prater, wishing she were dead, so boundless was his love for her. So he, too, felt this mixture of tenderness and wanting to escape. [. . .]

———————————

From a report on psychasthenia [. . .]

Ti. used to masturbate. In school he was preoccupied with supposedly philosophical problems: why does 2 + 2 = 4 ? The feeling that this is self-evident is simply absent—staring right into questions—telling himself that the answer is the right one but not being able to feel that this is so—the same situation each time he masturbates: what is passion? Masturbation to capture the moment on the wing, staring into the masturbation but being cheated each time.

On one occasion, a sudden alienation from the outside world, all sensations at full strength and in complete clarity but a feeling "as if the pelt of an animal skin were drawn over my head" (one might say "like warm glass," "like a woman's skin" . .). I believe that Ti. perceived this as a misfortune, but as soon as he met the boy he recognized that his condition was a desire to include, to demarcate, to secure, and involved immense secretiveness. He loves the boy, goes to the school to be able to watch him from afar, feels perturbed, gets palpitations when he thinks he recognizes the boy from a distance simply by the way he walks. Vows to love him as an image of beauty and purity, believes that this condition is his destiny, that he is a chosen one, as if fate had thrown him back on his own devices and had locked him away in himself . .

Another episode took place at the grammar school. He felt completely drained, could speak to no one, and concealed this behind a welter of quotations.

2.I.1908

[. . .]

Then A[llesch], the human being, someone who is truly open to question. He could be a painter, he could be a creative writer; why isn't he, then? He must not be one, he tells himself, he must be the man who embraces all things. At home in Amsterdam, as in Rome, taking no one seriously, destroying everything. A model for novels not a writer of novels, in a single small experience embracing more than a generation of creative writers, always conscious of this. A poser. Why a poser? He could really be a creative writer, he cheats himself out of everything. And yet seems to act correctly. Again it is breadth that is lacking. He becomes petty and underhand, because he feels this lack and because he wants to act out his goal using violence. One can scarcely reproach him at all when, only by the breadth of a hair, he . . . . misses what is right.

At the end, Marsilius[47] and A. feel the need to be free of each other for a certain time. And when M., for the first time, has the southern sea before him, he breathes a deep sigh of relief, and feels how he is outgrowing A. in the act of finding himself. But A. feels just the same under the damp sky of Holland that rises up over the plain—and who is right? Only sun, wind and rain. [. . .]

Hanka.[48] One line [of development]: the stuff of dreams in real life. Starts with the memory of the boy on the bridge in Steyr—then the many dreams by Hanka's side while the intellect is always unsure of itself—{!}. Then the ending with the mother—A narrative of the self, as one whose whole life appears behind him in a strange light.

"When he looked around the room was always, precisely, in one state or another, . . all seen with clarity, etc. But when he thought back in time, etc."

Throughout all this Tonka is in hospital. Only comes out to die. He is united with his mother—only this last stage is part of the narrative.

The story line is quite simple. Two people—he and his mother—who, simply because of the impossibility of communicating intellectually on a particular matter, parted and caused each other pain. This was brought about by Hanka's sickness.

A "critical condition" blend of dreaming and waking, past and present, out of which comes the narrative. He sits in his room with the red plush furniture, the housekeeper brings the coffee service with the flowered pattern. A person that sits at home for days on end and sits in the nebulous "status nascendi," wandering through the mists of his mind.

This man sitting in this room waiting for the coffee, making breadcrumbs of each day, was tall and lean, and had a pointed brown beard and red slippers. At the end he then appears clean-shaven and in elegant clothes.

He also goes out and thinks he sees Tonka "waiting" at every street corner. [. . .]

———————

There are those who are drawn by a kind of carrion stench in love. They are attracted to prostitutes, and it is their fate, after a time, to fall in love again with women with whom they once broke off a relationship. The reappearance of someone they once loved attracts them in a quite peculiar way—like some morbid fragrance. [. . .]

5
NOTEBOOK 15
11 FEBRUARY 1907
TO 24 APRIL 1907

[This short notebook covers a brief span in the latter months of Musil's studies in Berlin—he is working on his dissertation on Ernst Mach. Women are much on his mind: Herma, his mistress, is mentioned, but of more immediate concern is the relationship with "Anna." In the 1950s Adolf Frisé interviewed Gustav Donath, who spoke of Musil's acquaintance in 1907 with a woman called Anna; she was considered by family and friends alike to be a most advantageous and suitable match for the author. Those who knew Musil were amazed and disturbed when he turned this opportunity down. Perhaps the main reason for his decision was his love for Martha, whose name appears here for the first time in the Diaries. Martha was a painter; a shared interest in the plastic arts (in this notebook Musil mentions both Aubrey Beardsley and Gustav Klimt) may have helped to bring the couple together.

Here Musil relates everyday experiences, including gossip. Johannes von Allesch and Musil, apparently at the guest house where the latter habitually took his meals, speculate on the relations of two women who live together there; Herma Dietz tells Musil about a dressmaker whose pregnancy came about in an act of scandalous opportunism. Musil rehearses themes that become central to his creative writing from this point in early manhood until his death some thirty-five years later—for example, he discusses with a woman acquaintance the question of illicit love between brother and sister, an issue that will become central to the plot of part III of MwQ.]

15.

The preconditions in childhood.

1907.

11.II. Monday:

Answered Anna's[1] two last letters. As usual, experienced difficulty in finding the appropriate tone. In the midst of this a heavy sinking feeling. It is your vocation to make me—this intellectualized monster—whole. Suddenly a relaxation of tension. Abrupt transition. The importance of a shoulder tie for a shirt and of the way the loving couple are shut away behind closed doors. When I wrote this I was thinking about it in an objective manner, then I began to think of my efforts with a touch of irony. However, in the midst of this came a moment when it seemed to me as if Anna were sitting opposite me on the other side of the table. Wearing only a skirt and a chemise. As we sat there we seemed to be discussing something serious in a very lighthearted way. Much matrimonial winking of eyes.

12.II. Tuesday.

This morning another letter from Anna arrived. I only gave it a cursory glance. Don't these letters make the word "morality" too central an issue for me? Even when one remains cool toward it, its proximity is dangerous. How would it be if she behaved in a rather playful way, juggling with feelings? She wouldn't be such an excellent comrade but she would be more stimulating.

Yesterday with Allesch looked at Munch[2] and Corinth[3] at Cassirer's[4] gallery. No responses that registered on the soul. But a picture that left me quite cold (an elderly lady walking toward the foreground) seemed to say something to him.

In the evening read about the history of the German language. The old language with its full vowels seems to have been more beautiful. Replacing them with the unstressed "e," the loss of vowels, etc., looks to me very much like murder of the language for the sake of mundane interests. Given the increase in the numbers of concepts that accompanied this process it is probably irreversible.

13.II. Wednesday. In the evening listened to the first lecture by P. Waß-mann.[5] Made no particular impression. Afterward with the Hornbostels,[6] A. and Frl. G. in the Rheingold. Drank a pink Burgundy—effervescent and extremely animating.

14.II. For some time, two women have been living with each other in the boarding house.[7] A Frl. von Oertzen from Russia and a Dutchwoman. Today, as he left, Allesch asked me what I thought of such relationships. They live very quietly in one room. They're also probably still quite young. Rather naive and without taste. One of them is always having to go through the dining room to the toilet while A. and I are still sitting drinking our coffee. This activity has about it an air of decisiveness of doing what simply has to be done [. . .]

It would be interesting to know which of them takes the lead in this relationship. The one with the Egyptian bird-face or the one with the calm, almost satiated expression? I resolved to put out feelers.

17.II. I'm very depressed. Can't get on with my work, my day is over so quickly without any results. I am concerned about losing myself. Added to this the eternal disputes with A. on scientific matters which make me heartily sick. I need a change of air. Meadows. Walks. Books and the corresponding ideas. But I can't get any closer to reaching the precondition, the doctorate.[8] As far as the altercations are concerned—with Pfingst[9] in the Romanisches Café[10] after Waßmann's second lecture and others at table with A.—I must remember that A. puts forward an aestheticist ethics in that he denies the existence of emotional responses of an ethical nature. He argues that introspection cannot identify any such responses and he wants to find a way to support his view through genetics—starting with muscular cavemen or some such example.

Seems to me to be academic hair-splitting.

A certain Herr Peter Baum dedicated his novel to me with a somewhat pathological accompanying note.

Herma put me in a really sympathetic mood, like fresh water and all things hostile to conceptualizing. I'm not thinking of Anna.

Made a resolution to study literary history and the psychological processes concerned with judging and feeling.

22.II. Spend some time with Frau H.[11] at Keller & Reiner's[12] looking at Klimt's[13] paintings for Vienna University. I like the one entitled "Jurisprudence." The unhappy old man and around him the three girls preoccupied with themselves. In decorative balance. Intangible. Lyrical. And some other things too. Two days ago alone with Herma. No particular mood; just satiation. Wrestled in vain with my thesis trying to find a way of dealing with the formulae of dimensions that would be without logical flaws. Finally reached a compromise today and drafted a version that is about halfway toward being complete.

While traveling in the evening thought of the coming military maneuvers. Looking forward to nights with my collar turned up.

5.III. Tuesday. Wrote a good letter to A.[14] Looked for flats with Kerr.[15] Was bored at the Hornbostels. Before that, together with Herma. Splendid, splendid weather. All. has broken down completely and yet still cannot decide to take a complete rest.

I have to add that the mother and sister of the Dutchwoman[16] drowned off the Hook of Holland. This destroyed the love-idyll.

6.III. Wednesday. Today, at table, something was said quite by chance. All. was making something of a show of being decadent, I did likewise with my health (I did so first, which will probably have irritated him). It came across—unintentionally—as if, by paying this high price, he had come into the possession of greater sophistication.

I said nothing. After all, one cannot quarrel over who is subtler. But I was annoyed because I had to stay silent. This mustn't happen. One has to avoid it via style. He also believes that his need for a personal style derives from this source and no doubt holds the view that this is where I am most lacking. And, until now, I myself had only tended to confirm this. Today, however, I leafed through old notes and find that much of the style is, after all, my own. It is simply a question of finding a means of focusing it. The outward impression of negligence is all of one piece with this, but it must be given a clearer and more attractive emphasis.

11.III. Monday. Day after day spent wading through this thick gruel. I am nothing but an Egyptian mummy that goes into work spasms. Heinrich Geyer, my uncle, has died and it is difficult to write two letters of condolence that strike the right note.

Yesterday afternoon I was sketched by Allesch and Fräulein Pfund. The conversation was very amusing and I was rather frivolous. In summer she is going to Brittany with her niece, the countess, and that tall man whom no one knows. [. . .] The evening at Hornbostel's place started off dreadfully badly. There were four of us. Susi [Hornbostel] had had trouble with a servant and behaved terribly badly. My relationship with her is bad at the best of times. Round about half-past midnight we started a discussion and A. and I stayed until half-past two. It was about the way that certain kinds of life are emotionally uniform (peasant, Catholic, etc.).

Today Herma told me a nice story that she heard from Frau Prawdzik. A dressmaker had come to see her. Unmarried woman in her thirties, pretty, with a very beautiful body. Poured out her troubles. Already had one child and now something had happened to her again—for the love of God, could Frau P. help? A gentleman spoke to her on the street, invited her to a restaurant. Accompanied her home. Begged so much that there, behind the front gate of the house, in the hallway by the staircase . . . standing up. . . . She tells her all this! The poor woman doesn't even know his name for he hadn't even introduced himself to her. Now she is embarrassed about what her sister, whom she lives with, will say. Quite understandably.

It has just occurred to me that I visited Dr. G. the day before yesterday. Had rushed past him on the street. He seems to associate with some delightful characters of dubious reputation—at least I assume this from what he says about his dealings with people (Mr. X from Cincinnati who takes money from people for patents and then spends it himself, a fortune every year, etc.) and judging by the calm way with which, in the middle of a telephone conversation, he touched someone for a hundred marks and, when this was rejected, didn't turn a hair.

As arranged, I also met Martha[17] there.

18.III. Monday.

Have just read Beardsley's[18] fragment "Under the Hill." Delightful. But it's hard work to identify, in the ideas that occur to him, the hidden visual element that appeals to him. There were many passages where I was able to imagine how he would draw things; this would be different from the way he writes it; inexpressible; it does not correspond to the words he uses.

But he isn't just visual; a particularly beautiful example of such a passage is the following: Helen—before she goes to supper on the fifth terrace, dressed only in her underwear—makes her choice from among the shoes she is offered. Among them is a pair whose soles are fragrant with the scent of July flowers . . .

I do not know what they are called, those burning flowers whose scent is only bearable in sunshine with cabbage whites and brimstone butterflies, but is then quite unsurpassable . . But, walking in silk underwear and with a painted face and with the fragrance of peasants' gardens beneath one's feet . . . What a surprise for the art-lover in the act of undressing.

Hornbostel lent me the book. It was really pleasant there yesterday. He played Lanner[19] and the gracious chansons by [Yvette] Guilbert. Interspersed with a few bars of Beethoven. The conversation was nothing special but a great deal of laughter. (Last Sunday the songs of King Thibaut[20] and Old French chansons that he set to music were among the pieces performed.)

In the afternoon—trapped by rain in the entrance to the house because he didn't want to come up to my place for some Dutch courage—I talked to A. about relationships with women. It is the first time he has spoken without much discretion about Frl. G. This double "I" seems to mean a great deal to him. It is not clear to me how profit and loss are apportioned in such convoluted internal arrangements.

14.IV. Friday

On the evening before my departure I discovered a strange key at A.'s place. He then wrote a special letter to me in Brünn, telling me not to attach any importance to such clues. On the day before he had echoed my praise of monogamy and spoken for the first time without discretion about Frl. G.

In the days before my departure I had some detailed discussions with Frl. Pfund. One of these was really quite special. In the room in Berlin—it was terribly dark because of the rain—someone left the door open and I shut it; I shut us up in the dark. "Lottchen" was so visibly frightened that I had to say something or other about the mood of a particular location.

She confessed to me her love for a man with whom she wants to live "as if in a blue room"—I asked her lots of questions. She says that she sees everything as if on his behalf. She sees us, too,—namely A. and me—in this way. She weighs up advantages as one might assess furniture for the flat one will share; this does not have any erotic effect on her.

I also asked her about love between brother and sister;[21] she considers that such a thing is possible. When a brother marries this is supposed to awaken certain thoughts in young girls. He is surrendered grudgingly.

At a social gathering in the Hartmann household, I approached Frau Medical Councillor K.[22] She's probably somewhere in her forties. Great deal of makeup, but she has a delightful way of making conversation and is coquettish in a decent and tasteful fashion. I said many very risqué things to her.

Had a really fine time in Brünn. Gustl was with me for three days. We did a lot of walking. I shot a snipe; the hunt was marvelous.

Unfortunately mother was severely affected by trouble in the static organ. I lived in the lap of luxury.

I now eat in the Pension Stolzenberg on Viktoria-Luise Square.

24.IV. Wednesday.

I can't think of anything that stood out particularly in the course of these ten days. Only two tiny little anecdotes stick in my mind. One of these was told me by Herma. Two twenty-two year olds who marry in secret, against the will of the man's parents. He resolves not to touch her until the time when he can offer her a home. She wants to so much. Buys "enchanting" negligés. He asks "What are you doing? Oh, I know! But I . . we . ." he reaches for ideals. If it were left to him, she would still be a virgin after six months of marriage. But then a Rumanian attaché arrives. Had already served as a lever to propel the other into marriage, for he, too, would marry her, she says . .

The other one All. told me yesterday. It was about a woman who runs an inn in Carinthia and is well known for her intimate relationship with her mastiff. In the angry arousal of such an animal there is something that may well stimulate a woman. It is also possible that one feels loathing for men and prefers dogs—such a feeling is possible, precisely with women who love their integrity.

In the evening I read Per Hallström's *An Old Story*.[23] There were two passages I wanted to note down: ". . but a girl loves only her fiancé or her husband and does not even talk about it if she respects herself."

"Yes, but I simply felt that, that this is the only thing that I can think of doing . . ."

—Is this last sentence not the whole essence of love? The only thing that one knows about it?

. . "And it was after all a very serious matter to give oneself to a man, but a fine one all the same. Above all the sense of being allowed (!) to feel such indescribable tenderness for someone, to give oneself over completely to this state, to have the right (!) to lose oneself entirely in him and to concern oneself only with whether he was happy, not at all with how one fared oneself . . . ."

—The old fact that a knotted handkerchief can mean more, in relative terms, than the most precious mechanical doll.

6

NOTEBOOK 5

8 AUGUST 1910 TO OCTOBER 1911 OR LATER

[Some three years have elapsed since the entries made in Notebook 15. Though Martha and he have not yet married, the relationship has become intellectual, visceral, vital, permanent. Martha is, in fact, still married to Enrico Marcovaldi, who is continuing to make difficulties over divorce—these give rise to acrimonious negotiations and complex stratagems that include Martha's taking out Hungarian citizenship and Musil converting from the Roman Catholic to the Protestant faith. Musil is now devoting himself full time to creative writing—in the earlier pages of this notebook he refers frequently to the stories that will become Unions; *later he works on themes that will ultimately become part of* MwQ. *(A particularly important one is concerned with Alice von Charlemont, who has now married Gustav Donath and is already slipping into insanity.)*

This notebook contains entries in which Musil sets down his doubts about, and dissatisfaction with, the texts he is writing. His literary interests are, albeit within a quite narrow field, comprehensive; he analyzes emotions that form the experiences on which some of his creative writing is based; he examines the processes of literary production as well as the inhibitions that can cripple it; he tries to enrich his writing by studying the techniques of other writers—particularly the Naturalists, Zola, Hamsun, Hauptmann, and Ibsen, but also Tolstoy. Later entries contain references to work on a play; this will develop into The Enthusiasts *but will take more than a decade to complete.*

Musil is under pressure from his parents to find paid employment—perhaps this explains his plans to found a literary journal. Eventually he takes a job as a librarian at the Technical University in Vienna but, since this post interferes with his creative writing, he leaves it after working for less than a year.]

5

{8 August 1910. *Berlin*}

We are not in Italy, or Holland, or the Tirol, but in Berlin. This has meant that the children[1] have caught the measles, to which the cold weather has made them more susceptible. And once again negotiations have foundered at the last moment and our immediate future is uncertain.[2] After the tension of making concessions we have both experienced the re-emergence of open warfare as a relief.

I have just come from Martha's; on the street the air and the light are like those of early spring. I had the idea that all expression depends on the light—I had seen a coalman in profile. The cheeks dissolving, their colors as if ravaged by the light and then abandoned; forehead, bridge of nose, hair lit from the front (but a diffuse light coming only from over the rooftops)— I can find no word for the expression of this man's face.

I have been working recently on the alterations to the "Enchanted House"[3] for the version entitled "The Temptation of Quiet Veronica." I enjoy the work that is going quite easily but sometimes, it seems, too easily; I don't know if it will turn out to be substandard.

I am very irritable, and a single unreflected remark of Martha's can make me unhappy.

---

12 August 1910.

In the afternoon I read out to Martha what I have done so far of "The Temptation of Quiet Veronica" and it pleased me greatly; what remains to be altered seems not too difficult to me. (Veronica still speaks too much for the sake of the ideas, too little in terms of the situation.) In the evening at Martha's I read out the "Completing of Love"[4] and am very disappointed, even though it seemed so good to me only a few days ago. This time, too, I found the first part very good, it is completely calm and simple (Martha says "serene" and I think that the word fits well here). The second part I read without paying attention, but the third still seemed bad to me. Some fine sections but too much of the essay about them, observations strung together one after the other, intellectual paraphrases on what is only a pretence at subject matter. Felt very downcast. On the way home I resolved that, while working through it for the final time, I would bring into sharper focus the strange intellectual perspectives that form the nub of each individual scene, that I would be more intellectual still in order not to allow any fatigue to set in through the heaviness of the images (making them deeper and even making them more oblique!); on the other hand I would pull together the individual parts more sharply around the development as a whole. (Vague thoughts right up to the point of recognizing the value of the lie, of loneliness, of infidelity in love.) Third—and this is something that I resolved to do earlier—I must start to offer a little more of what is generally seen as narrative; when one is developing some inner process it is not enough to be fully involved from sheer inner necessity, but see how a person moves in stages of increasing intensity from one situation to another.

Since I have set myself all these targets, I am now curious about what I shall actually do, for until now my giving notice of some theoretical intention always preceded the execution of something that turned out quite different.

As far as external matters are concerned, the only thing to note about the last few days is that M[artha] and I spent an evening at the Caspers' house.[5]

---

13 August 1910. Before I went to sleep, one or two other things occurred to me about my way of working (in the novellas).[6] What matters to me is the passionate energy of the idea. In cases where I am not able to work out some special idea, the work immediately begins to bore me; this is true for almost every single paragraph. Now why is it that this thinking, which after all is not aiming at any kind of scientific validity but only a certain individual truth, cannot move at a quicker pace? I found that in the reflective[7] element of art there is a dissipative momentum—here I only have to think of the reflections that I have sometimes written down in parallel with my drafts. The idea immediately moves onward in all directions, the notions go on growing outward on all sides, the result is a disorganized, amorphous complex. In the case of exact thinking, however, the idea is tied up, delineated, articulated, by means of the goal of the work, the way it is limited to what can be proven, the separation into probable and certain, etc., in short, by means of the methodological demands that stem from the object of investigation.

In art, this process of selection is missing. Its place is taken by the selection of the images, the style, the mood of the whole.

I was annoyed because it is often the case with me that the rhetorical precedes the reflective. I am forced to continue the inventive process after the style of images that are already there and this is often not possible without some amputation of the core of what one would like to say—as, for instance, with "The Enchanted House" or "The Completing of Love." I am only able at first to develop the thought-material for a piece of work to a point that is relatively close by, then it dissolves in my hands. Then the moment arrives when the work in hand is receiving the final polish, the style has reached maturity, etc. It is only now that, both gripped and constrained by what is now in a finished state, I am able to "think" on further.

There are two opposing forces that one has to set in balance—the dissipating, formless one from the realm of the idea and the restrictive, somewhat empty and formal one relating to the rhetorical invention.

One only says what one can say within the frame of what is available; since the point of departure is arbitrary there is an element of chance about it. But the point of departure is not absolutely arbitrary, for the first images are after all products of a tendency that, hovering before one's eyes, sets the direction for the whole work.

Tying this together to achieve the greatest degree of intellectual compression, this final stepping beyond the work in accordance with the needs of the intellectual who abjures everything that is mere words, this intellectual activity comes only after these two stages. Here the effect of the understanding is astringent, but here it is directed toward the unity of form and content that is already present whereas, whenever it is merely a question of thinking out the content, it dissipates. (Even in cases where one already has the basic idea around which everything is to be grouped, as long as the capacity for creating images is missing it will not work; if one restricts oneself in the extensive mode one goes too far in the intensive mode and one becomes amorphous.)

---

14 August 1910 (or it might be anywhere between 12th and 15th)

Yet again this dreadful lack of energy and unwillingness to work. (Yesterday afternoon . . . Take note: a little too quick. You mount me as if I were an animal, how could you . . . . Outside, a Sunday like those in spring.) I am afraid that I shall not have enough time for a vacation, a yearning for that surge of energy that massages away self-reproach. Unpleasant letter from home;[8] I'm supposed to be in Vienna in mid-September, "on the way home"; when am I to take that break?

Yesterday I continued with my reflections. What I said is only true for works of the same type as the two novellas. The role of the images, which I was trying to account for, is taken over in other cases by other things, as in *Pan* by Hamsun,[9] for example. There, as in first-person narrative in general, the selective, unifying momentum is dramatic in nature. A personality forms the starting point, as well as the vanishing point, for all that is said and for the way in which it is said. The creative author has a feeling about a particular person and speaks in the way this feeling dictates. (The basis of portrayal is never of an all-round view of a person, but always, and only, a feeling of who that person is. The "dramatic personality" that radiates from the style and diction of *Pan* is itself something that has been much reduced, it isn't a body with many parts but a patch and this is why it is suited to its formal unifying role.) (So the element of "how it is said" in a certain sense dictates, here as well, what is said.)

{20 I 1911.

In *Törleß* the unifying momentum comes from the desire to narrate a particular story that has been thought out in advance. That is the backbone around which all other things—my interpretation and conception of the story—are grouped.

The feeling about this person "Törleß" is here, too, a secondary matter.}
[. . .]
Another type: *Hunger* by Hamsun, Zola . . There are works that have only one idea, and that one comparatively simple and well known. A social idea—misery, depression, some kind of horror, imaginings prompted by hunger, {etc.} Now this idea is shaped to generate the strongest feelings possible. Support for a cause, indictment of society, shaking the reader to the core. The aim is to make the experience as incisive as possible. The means: as plastic a portrayal as possible. Quality in the construction and in the rhythm of the narrative are definitely of importance. The strongest indictments made sotto voce, or in silence. The corpus of such reproaches {themes} is immense, any book can only give it, here or there, a slight twist. There exists no epic work of hunger, of social misery, but here and there one can strike down upon these things with a hammer so that they reverberate. The only way to compare such works—and even then without precision— is in terms of the brute force that they generate; a version that cuts to the quick, qualities that establish the formal superiority of one work over another—these simply do not exist.

And this all points, despite everything, to a flaw in this whole genre as it exists at present. One would not need to be satisfied with being shaken to the core by the state of affairs as identified. It would be possible to show, even in the contemplation of hunger and misery, what is miraculous and worthy of imitation, the new sensation. The new hunger. People call such books "perverse." The error lies not in their teaching people to love misery but, rather, a sensation that is only supposedly linked with it, but that in truth is directed toward a nameless object that is represented for the first time. A poem of conquest, not a paean of praise. It is perhaps the case that even in Zola just such a dark, heavy, scarcely visible mass takes shape; in some parts of his work Hamsun has a definite tendency to enter this second region. To admit as much would be the decisive flaw of these works, a lack of awareness of their actual goal.

––––––––––

Naturalism: When I recall my first impressions of modern literature, this word seems to me to be a promise that has never been kept. This thought occurred to me just now when I was speaking of the "dramatic personality" that in reality is only a particular state of feeling in the creative writer: the extent to which a real person is a uniform phenomenon (from a purely practical perspective, approximately, regardless of the epistemological and metaphysical treatment of the question) is something that one experiences as his character, as his style, etc. One should simply record what such a person in real life—a person who is felt to be uniform—actually thinks and says. The effect is totally lacking in uniformity. Then in the portrayal one inserts some kind of central point, a point of reduction. [. . .]

––––––––––

15 August 1910. Yesterday I leafed through the *Silhouettes*—the remarks by Frau Tyrka[10] are dreadful. But the excerpts from Hamsun I found very interesting. Remarkable how "he doesn't mince his words." The novel is a means that he uses to express his views on all kinds of things: Tolstoy, socialism, religion . . But in doing so he has a wonderful knack of avoiding being essayistic: the style and diction is always lively, personal, issuing from the person who happens to be speaking. The thoughts are not fully rounded out, but one has an intuition of how they would look when complete because one has an impression of the people to whom they belong. This method is eminently suited to creative writing . . . [. . .]

19 August.—For three days now in a state of deep depression. I am tired, I sometimes feel dizzy. Above all, I've little confidence in the work. Am now setting Veronica[11] to one side and want to see if some progress can be made with Claudine.[12]

What I noted down on the 12th on Veronica has intensified to an impossible degree. She speaks like a book. And I can now see that this can hardly be helped as long as I insert the middle portion from the "Enchanted House"[13] as a totality. But dividing up this middle portion without ruining it is next to impossible. [. . .]

20 August 1910

However hard I try, nothing seems to work; I've already become quite apathetic. Card from Alice asking whether I received the notebook from her, she seems to be rational.[14] Damp, cold, stormy weather— [. . .]

29 August 1910.

As late as 20 August I took the decision to write in the form of a narrative. Redrafted the first part of the novella, wrote a fair copy. Spend eight days of torture on this and have nothing to show for it, it is still nothing— it's almost something and yet it's nothing. Deepest depression. Admittedly something tells me that this is sometimes how things are just before they start to go well. But these two novellas have taken so long already that I've no more time and no more heart for the enterprise.

I can hardly bring myself to write that M. and I, in the meantime, once . . so deep is my depression.

Half-past midnight. Have just come from Martha's. Have discussed the first half of the work with her and now it's all right up to that point. Martha promised to come to me around 11 tomorrow. Cholera in Spandau.

2 September 1910.

Half-past one at night. Have just come from Martha's; from half-past nine to 11 at the Hartmanns'; he promised that he'd go with me to see Bernhard about a position as literary critic with the *B.Z.*[15] He doesn't think much of my idea of the Pasquill—if the publisher takes on a risk of this kind he will also want sole ownership.

Wrote home explaining my opinion about Vienna, telling them I'm going but that I don't want to go. Emphasized once again that I will not have anything to do with anyone on a social level when I'm there.

Provisionally concluded the first part of "Veronica" today. Worked hard the whole time—with Martha's help.

———————————

5 September 1910.

Read Kerr's critique of *Törleß* again—it gave me a jolt.[16] He says: "Nothing about Musil's story is flaccid. There is nothing in it that one might call 'lyrical.' He is a person who sees in terms of facts—only by giving shape to these does the measure of 'lyricism' emerge in the work that is part of the things themselves . . . Free from sentimentality. Representation of facts. The mood is not 'painted on,' rather what is represented gives off the mood."

In "Claudine," the narrative must not read as follows: "Somewhere a clock began to speak to itself about the time, footsteps passed by," etc. That is lyricism. It must be put as follows: "A clock struck. Claudine felt that somewhere there was beginning . . . Footsteps passed by . . . ," etc. In the first case, through the deliberate choice of the metaphor itself, the author is saying: "How beautiful." He is emphasizing that this is supposed to be beautiful, etc. Maxim: the author should only show himself in the formal ministerial dress of his characters. He should always shift responsibility to them. That is not only more sensible it is, remarkably, also the way that the epic mode emerges.

I was vaguely aware of this when, writing about "Claudine," I said that I would have to become more of what is commonly called a "narrator," and when I noted, with reference to "Veronica," that I didn't want to explain the problem of sodomy, but merely to tell what she feels about it.

———————————

8 September. Went with Hartmann to see Bernhard. Nothing—just kindly excuses.

I think that the—"lustrum" is perhaps the right term—of 1905–1910 has closed with a deficit of goals achieved. 1905 still had *Törleß* to offer, 1910, on the other hand, had nothing—Vienna, career as a civil servant.[17] What hopes of mine have proved to be unrealizable! (Martha does not belong in this account—she isn't anything that I have gained or achieved; she is something that I have become and that has become "I" . . That is not what I'm talking about.)

---

9 September 1910.

One must simply invent stories and narrate things that can be expressed in facts—today this, tomorrow that—give oneself time to do so. Just like writing a novelette. Then work in the other. I think that the next time I do it this way it will be successful again. But one must persuade oneself, after all, that every scene would fascinate even a dull-witted reader, and not rely on the effect of the subtler things. Remarkable.

---

10 September.

Maxim from *Törleß*: when one narrates something always narrate a scene that illustrates it.

---

14 September. Vienna.[18]

When Gustl came to Dresden, Alice was sensually aroused for the first time in their marriage. Insatiable. Gustl injured himself immediately during the very first night and could not satisfy her; as brutal as that: could not satisfy her. After his departure she suddenly falls in love with a Greek who is staying in the sanatorium. Propositions him. He is a homosexual. A jolt. Damming up. He travels to Munich. She sends him long telegrams, copies of which Gustl finds in the hotel. She, in the meantime, off to Venice on the trail of the Greek. There, feelings of immense tension. She has a sense of greatness, of hovering. Distributes her money, her jewelry, among the gondoliers. She still remembers wanting to make a speech in St. Mark's Square. But she draws attention to herself before she can do so and is taken to hospital. There she is fetched by Faust.[19]

At Kräpelin's[20] clinic, Gustl has someone tell her that he wants a separation. From then on she is devoted to him. Gustl loves Lilli, one of two sisters with whom he once worked in the Court Library. She is with him in an office at the Conservatory. "You know, she's simply feminine"—this is roughly the way he explains the situation. In the summer he spent a fortnight in the country at the place where they were staying. They are the daughters of an officer. No question of marriage. But he wants a separation.

He is not yet sexual. His tensions are still released with {into (like bolts of lightning)} Alice. Coming to with immense disillusionment; bestial, he says, this raging sensuality over a mentally sick body. He feels very sorry for Alice. He does not yet know how he will behave toward her. Probably her next attack will bring total dissolution. For the time being he has told her everything. With his head in her lap. She shed tears of shared joy. But she feels ashamed. And in the evening he goes home and spends the evening with [her], they make music, everything just as it always was, in the tone of their relationship not the slightest alteration can be detected.

What was remarkable about Alice's illness, so it is said, was the enormously heightened symbolism. Everything is related to everything else—but this is something that healthy people just cannot see. Today she probably has only a vague idea of how things were.

We talk about these things as if they were a common cold. We discuss what Gustl insists is the inferiority of modern painting when compared with Renaissance painting. We argue about psychology and Dr. Klages. Gustl enthuses about Stifter[21]—memories of youth are a not unlikely backdrop to this as are, probably, the unconscious opposition of this simple warmth to all that is tense, sick, riven.

———————

10 June 1911. Alice saw "the Greek" at Lahmann's.[22] She pointed him out to Gustl. At that time the high-calorie diet that she had been prescribed had left her in a state of heightened tension and sexual arousal, but Gustl was prevented by his injury. Then she heard in passing the Greek say to a lady: "Someone who has traveled a great deal is quite unable to love a woman." The same evening she wrote him a letter approximately along the lines: "I am the only woman you will love." The next day he brought the letter back to her. I think that she immediately propositioned him and became aggressive. She felt he possessed immense purity. And amidst all the acts of indecency that she performed she had the feeling that what she was doing was very pure. He told her he was homosexual; on a trip to the theater at Dresden he pointed out to her the policeman with whom he said he had a relationship. (Probably this was what transformed her sexual tension into fantasies.) But he let her do what she wanted to him. He only said once, in three languages, "Cette femme est folle," quietly and repeatedly. She thought that she immediately detected bisexual peculiarities {in her body}, describing herself in poems as a hermaphrodite, and felt that she and this person formed a divine constellation of love. ("I am descended from a line of bright gods . .") She goes for rides in carriages and can't keep her hands off him. He is anxious about the coachman. They are surprised by a storm.

("I imagine that I'm a witch from Thessaly" . . . The poor animal body shivers with electricity . .) He goes away; she wants to persuade him to travel to
Berlin with her, obtains money; but she sees that he doesn't want to; on the
last day he receives a visit from his male lover (it is uncertain whether this
really happens) and goes away.

She travels to Vienna. Spends a few days with Gustl and Klages. Already has
a sense of her mission and her divinity—i.e., Gustl and Klages seem to have
been placed there as if for her use. On some pretext, Gustl takes her to the
psychiatrist; during the evening in the inn she pretends to go to the toilet,
takes a carriage to the station. Travels by sleeper. Says straight away to the
sleeping-car attendant "There must be three gentlemen here, go and look, I
have to speak to them urgently!" They are all, so it seems to her, caught totally within the personal influence that emanates from her, and follow her orders. The waiter in the dining car as well. In the mirror she has a clear, sensual
impression of herself now as white she-devil, now as blood-red Madonna. In
Munich she lives in luxury in the "Four Seasons," smokes the whole day long,
drinks cognac and black coffee, and writes letters and telegrams.

Then she wants to go to Greece, via Venice and Trieste. In Venice she lives
the same life as in Munich. But she covers the walls of her room with paintings; as she does so, has the feeling that, in a hundred years' time, people
will be standing before these drawings and inscriptions. Distributes money,
etc. Buys a ticket for a passage. Takes on board with her the bedspread and
a piece of cloth that she winds into a turban—these are her imperial regalia.
Her landlady tempts her back with the fiction of a telegram. She is no longer
strong enough for the journey. Then comes the ride in the gondola. In the
hospital they strap her down straight away . . .

In Munich, where she begins to have some inkling of her situation, her first
firm decision is to get out again as soon as possible at any price (Perhaps this,
precisely, is the attitude that makes it impossible [for her] to grasp what was
different about the state she was then in, so that she might subsequently avoid
it.) On the advice of the doctors she concentrates on herself and writes. She
does not fail to notice both that, and why, the doctors consider it important
to bring her back together again with Gustl. Also that they interpret the
sodomistic remarks of another woman patient as a symptom that is still acute,
without thinking that as a child she had sodomistic impressions.

---

21 September, Lido.

The hospital to which Alice was brought lies close to Colleoni. She dis-
tributed her jewelry among the female warders and they accepted it. She
was strapped tight to the bed, she shed tears. The warders said "poveretto."

A gentleman fetched her from the pension for a ride in a gondola before she left. In the gondola she had the feeling that he was shy of her. {She fixed him with a stare.} {She tells this in such a way that one feels that this idea, uncorrected, still remains within her.} Near the church, he said to her: "Shouldn't we go into this place here on the right, there's something beautiful to show you." It probably seemed a little suspicious to her but I believe that the suspicion had no valence, it had no causal weight. Seen through Alice's eyes, madness may be nothing more, perhaps, than the act of dropping out of general causality. Not unreason, but merely a failure of one thing to mesh with the other; if one takes the intellectual element[23] as the main thing it is virtually nothing more than a disturbance in some ancillary function (seen through the eyes of my story).[24]

I envisage the style of this story as factual, pragmatic, with many conversations, much activity. When I looked through the notes for "The Completing of Love" today it occurred to me how one could have Alice make these remarks about the apperceptor,[25] etc., in direct speech. How much of this is the theory of her sthenic[26] states of mind, how she had to put herself in order, etc. I shall go through all these notes again.

I am thinking about setting a part of this story in Venice. In a salon like the one in the Hotel Lavigne in Rome, with crystal chandeliers, mirrors with glass frames, etc. In this crooked, out-of-focus, gap-toothed city, this deranged city, that sometimes stands up so straight again, with its far too many windows.

Only when placed in the context of causal observation is such a person irrational, the things he does are irrational, too; the way things happen indicates sickness, etc. But such people are aware of the open countryside around. After all, knowing that melancholy is caused by a sluggish digestive tract doesn't tell us anything about it, unless one wants to destroy it—i.e., to heal it.

Rome, 14 or 15 November.

[. . .] Literary people who speak scornfully of the work of their spirit. Kerr: "Literature takes up only a corner of my life." Set against that: literature is a bold life arranged in a more logical way. It involves the creation or distillation of possibilities,[27] etc. It is fervor that pares a human being down to the very bone for the sake of a goal in which emotion is in an intellectual mode. The rest is propaganda. Or it is a light that originates in a room, a feeling in one's skin when one looks back at experiences that at other times remain muddled and indifferent.

I am thinking now how intensely personal I am here. The theoretician opposed to the literary practitioner who does not conduct any analysis of the systematic significance of events, but who recognizes them immediately, if only approximately, then fleshes them out in approximate representation.

I have to remind myself how I invariably found all existing literature unsatisfactory from an intellectual perspective. But then all the more subtle and more powerful thinking about what is represented in the work must not take place within the work itself but before the work is written.

---

18 Nov. Five minutes past three in the afternoon: finished "Claudine."[28]

Beginning of December, [1910]

As part of the effort to earn money, looking for opportunities to write for newspapers and journals. Working for literary periodicals—even the *Neue Rundschau* or *Pan*—seems to me too loathsome. If some stranger, someone like myself, were to find my name beneath this or that redundant piece I would feel ashamed. I must set this down; there is a resistance here, which I *ought not to* overcome. The only excuse: for the time being I have no definite employment.

The scattering of pieces one writes in this way must be fragments, or at the very least off-cuts, from a broad stream of non-arbitrary exertion.

{Stayed in Rome until 21 Dec., then 22 and 23 in Florence, met the Bleis,[29] 24th spent on the train, 25 Dec. arrived in Vienna, took up residence in the Pension Seleschan; not satisfactory, looked for alternatives, moved to the Pension Lehner.}

Vienna, end of December.

Was profoundly affected once again by an essay by Kerr in the N[eue] R[undschau]. Here the unity lies in the way he feels secure within himself. If I understand him correctly, he is saying the same thing here, too: one must offer events, things, etc., not moods. The lyrical must not be something added on afterward.

a. Things that so far have been inexpressible are given shape in ideas and words.

a. [b?] One only handles things that one could discuss with every sensible person. This is how Ibsen handles problems. This is how problems are handled in the books discussed in the December issue of the Rundschau.

After the *Unions* have been written I shall definitely favor the second as a foundation to which the first can perhaps later be added.

---

31 December. Yesterday evening completed Veronika up to the final revision for the fair copy.

Impressions during the revision of the middle section from the "Enchanted House": Kerr says, on 5 Sept., that one should not paint mood but allow the desired measure of lyricism to grow from the shaping of facts. In "The Enchanted House" mood is painted. Occasionally one finds there an intolerable breadth; something that is already there in one sentence is clothed in new garments in three more sentences. It seems to me that there is a connection here with the following observation: (and also with what I have already written about the need to provide what is called, in everyday terms, narrative,[30] that one must describe the situations that a person experiences, one must hide each idea behind a situation, etc.) whatever one says must be capable of being understood even through the use of everyday words. It must also have a value in real life. In other words, it must be, quite simply, a real thought and not a vague stammering. An idea that connects with real situations, with relevant inner states. It must be something that is really important to me personally, important to me in my waking personality.

---

2 January 1911.

In other words, one must not sit down and wait for the particular kind of mood to arrive that is difficult to express; using one's understanding, one must write the kind of things that one can write about at any and every moment.

{7.6. In other words, one must never believe that one is not in the right mood. One is always capable of incisive thinking. If something that happened earlier will not come alive one should take this as a sign that it has not been thought through in a sufficiently sober and comprehensive fashion.}

11 January 1911. Finished Veronika at one o'clock in the morning.

Following on from a conversation with Gustl in the course of the last few days: he says that he has the impression that this novella—"The Enchanted House"—was written by someone whose brain is badly nourished—physically and spiritually undernourished, no less. The spiritual side implies that it was written by someone through whose brain life does not flow as it should in a broad stream. So this goes beyond the point that I have tried to express up till now, namely that one has to write with an understanding that works at normal temperature, etc.—that is not the nucleus of the problem. The problem lies in the very mode of experiencing itself. I experience terribly little, i.e., a short time afterward very little of the experience is still caught up within me, and only a very abstract selection that, incidentally, is not characterized by any lack of sensuous detail but by the reduction suffered by the intellectual part. I find it impossible to retain an intellectual grip on many of those things which, when they happen, I feel to be fine problems—the breadth of reasoning is immediately restricted to correspond to my personality and the area of focus within me is a narrow one. I remember having had this impression many years ago when I was still living in Brünn and when Gustl arrived from Vienna.

By the way, Claudine and Veronika are still giving cause for a special kind of concern.[31] Recently I have aimed at a maximum astringency in representation and at pursuing the problem down into the depths. I was seeking the true (ethical, not just psychological) determining factors of activity. For Hauptmann's and Ibsen's people are not determined; what impels them does not impel me. The danger—and this is not avoided here, at best it is excused by the character of all novellas—is as follows:

When one says that a feeling of attraction toward an animal[32] can, in part, resemble self-surrender to a priest, or that an act of infidelity, at a deeper level within, can be a uniting,[33] then one has found a new way of putting the basis of "Veronika" and "Claudine." There is no more to it than that. Admittedly the inner realm is now filled with a whole range of subtle things. But, from an ethical perspective, this variety is always characterized by being seen through what is draped over it. The influence of the book, giving shape as it does to the inner life of another person, will always be the drapery and no more, etc. The way in which the problem is pursued in depth is, from an ethical perspective, inconsequential. It is ethically impoverished. Provided that it is somehow possible to show that the basic problem does indeed have an ethical dimension, but that the work also takes effect on another level with the idea that, because one is not able to make contact with one's own inner being, it is possible to despair (and thereby be unfaithful). And also to show why this happens. Then one could postulate another kind of art in which one might operate with many such unities—one of which is subdivided here—in an undivided fashion.

---

15 January.

Yesterday evening we were at Gustl and Alice's house. [. . .] I quoted: "Your God is like a fat woman."[34] etc. and said "If that has no effect on you then the totality will not have any effect either." I said also: "If I read such a sentence in a creative work I would be fascinated . ." And Gustl, of course, wasn't in the least fascinated. It occurred to me then that I still tend to place too much emphasis on a particular detail. After all, I know that my imagination is capable of producing hundreds of such notions. And even if there is perhaps no other person who is capable of producing them, I must not see them as being anything more than architectural pinnacles—points that are allowed to extend beyond the main corpus but in which the energy of the whole must not be allowed to pause for even one moment.

---

16 January.

Today, while making further corrections to *Törleß*, it occurred to me that the right approach here is found, for example, in the narrative section on the relationship between *Törleß* and the prince. One does not build a story from such things, but one occasionally reaches for them, without looking, as if dipping into a full sack.

---

17 January.

I really think that the sack was full then and I took everything that came to hand without attaching particular importance to any individual thing. Afterward the sack was empty and the novellas were written partly using the same reservoir as *Törleß*. And at the same time I tried to fill up this reservoir again and searched for details as ends in themselves. And the novellas lack something that is perhaps present in *Törleß* namely a sure-footed terseness, which gives access to many things without using many words. A matter of attitude.

Re Kerr: "There is nothing soft about Musil's narrative . ."[35] etc., cf. the opening of *Törleß*. Here only the facts are given, the appearance of the street, the station building, the conversation, etc. It is not stated that these things had such and such a mood, but they do have one. The attitude within me was one of soot and strangled sadness, or something of the sort, and then I saw things in that particular way.

19.

One can also say: work with the things that lie immediately to hand! By the way, in *Törleß* I have made use of the ideas noted down on paper, in transitional passages, explanations, etc.; in the novellas I tried to use them to build the narrative itself. This is the reason for the impression that *Törleß* is richer, because its focus lies in the periphery.

Everywhere in *Törleß* an effort is made to take all that is incomprehensible, that is veiled in mystery, that virtually outstrips the powers of imagination, and wherever these things appear to seize them in the grip of understanding, to identify their genesis and psychology. [. . .]

---

30 January. Our life is very strange and beautiful; it seems wrapped in mist, gliding like a sleepwalker, an unreal and completely calm brightness lighting it from within.

We have nothing to do with anybody. (Gustl and Alice haven't even displayed the bare minimum of conventional politeness; we have time and no needs, we are considering whether at some point I should go to see Gustl and tell him what we think.) Each morning we walk for one to two hours with the children,[36] in the evening we usually go for a short walk on our own. The children are like small delicate things in this barely transparent and soft confusion that is our life.

I have finished an essay for *Pan* up to the point of the final, decisive reworking, on indecency in art.[37] I've begun a tender satire on *Pan* for the *Vagabond*.[38] Tomorrow or the next day I shall write to Herzog.[39] I haven't any answer from Kerr to a card in which I asked him for his review of the *Rats*.[40] What impressed me very much about the *Rats* was the precise modeling, the psychology in the words and grammar, and the way that all the mechanisms that are similar to those of human beings are presented without words. Everything about von Allesch's article on Grünewald[41] pleased me: the way he expounds Grünewald's mysticism, the way he makes academic psychology fruitful; it is only when viewing it as a totality that I have the impression that it is an impossible synthesis. The emotionally charged attitude of the committed Christian and the factual one of the scientist do not seem to me to match up properly.

For Kerr I have thought out a letter with a brief statement of account. Kerr and the socialist direction of *Pan* are probably the most powerful experience. With Kerr, "Young-German" traits are becoming more apparent. They complement his earlier disregard for the world of letters and his liking for Heine. He is, for me, a fateful personality. When I am confronted with him I realize that he is the only antipode that sometimes makes me anxious about whether I am right. With respect to his present political agitation I catch myself behaving as laymen do with books they read: "I have always thought that that needed saying . . ." But I know that fate is involved when one feels such things after someone else has given them an airing. And to have always been forgetting them beforehand . . However, I pulled myself together to catch up his lead, and this is the reason for the two articles: the one for *Pan* representing the wish to contribute, to advance the cause, even though this is without any merit on my part because it comes about through the initiative of others [. . .]; the other for Blei arises from the hope of being able to shore up adequately the substance that is threatened with collapse, securing my own position in the face of the bridgehead that Kerr has secured within me.

With my parents, a tense silence has descended. They had the incomprehensible idea of inviting Martha to come over to Brünn on Sunday while I was involved with my military exercise. I wrote gently pointing out that I would be spending the whole time in Brünn with M., and I also chose a different time for this than that which my parents wanted. Since then I have only received one letter from Mama about other matters—here she made the excuse that she was feeling exhausted—and have written a brief note myself saying that, given the circumstances, we would drop our plan.

In addition to the articles I am trying to find the direction for a drama. I feel that it may be possible, but still haven't any definite notion of what it should be. I'm writing notes instead of thinking about the drama as I'd intended; I was suffering from a bout of nervous tension this morning, but I'm now better.

11.2. Card arrived from Kerr in the meantime with the request to write for *Pan*—he's on its editorial board. Also a positive reply from Herzog. But the article isn't finished. I can't believe that as early as 30 January I wrote that it was as good as finished. I felt about it just as I normally do—I suddenly came to a point where sheer loathing held me up. Then I read Kerr's letter-articles to Jagow[42]—tremendous capacity to hit the mark—my article, for all its attention to style, was so geometric in a finely scientific fashion, so very 1.2.3.a.b.c. . . , but that is only permissible when one really is building a castle, otherwise one yawns and, out of a sense of scientific duty, ticks off all the self-evident points, but doesn't get round to adding the upper storey on top. Now I've started something more colorful.

Papa was here. Tension with home was a misunderstanding. There had already been an invitation from Mama that we should now all live with her. Of course, this is effusive optimism; I'm convinced that it will all end badly, but she is very hurt by my refusal.

Provisionally, the play has the psychological alias—*The Anarchists*. My latest idea is to set it in Berlin in student circles.

25.2. News from Mama and Dr. Maager that Papa has only another ten years to live,[43] and even then only if he takes things very easily, but that one has to be prepared at any moment for the rupture of a vessel releasing blood into his brain. This preceded by a seizure.

5.3.

To live, to live . . . to desire nothing but beautiful experiences—with such an attitude one can invent a novel.

Easter:[44]

I've been in the Library for about three weeks now.[45] Unbearable, murderous (all too bearable while one is actually there), I shall leave and steer out into the unknown.

Relationship with Kerr as good as finished. I found the honorarium from *Pan* minimal, felt offended, wrote to him—no reply. Wrote another short letter to him, ending something like this: "I was unaware that you think it appropriate to treat me in this way—had I known it, I would not have asked you, on several occasions, for small favors."

Frau Rudolph[46] was there. I gained insight into Allesch; confirmation of what I had supposed, deeply disturbing, in fact.

Since the start of my leave I've started work on the play again. Now it's become more concrete and has changed greatly, but I can't quite get at what I want. I'm noting here some impressions from *Michael Kramer*.[47] With utter single-mindedness, the consequences of each thing that the author assumes are portrayed, the effect of every individual on every other individual, the statements by each person who is introduced in a specific way, never statements about themselves or, at least, only very sparingly and then followed straight away by something of an everyday nature. All the people say only those things that are wrung from them by the day's exigencies. And they never say quite what impels them, but only that something is indeed impelling them. [...]

---

23 May. The problem with Kerr[48] turned out to be a misunderstanding.

Each day thoughts grind back and forth in my mind, wearing me out, all on account of the Library. It is virtually certain that I'll leave.

Today, during a walk, Gustl said of Wolfskehl,[49] in response to my remark that I assumed that his spiritual constitution was relatively underdeveloped: "Oh no, these are very fine people, of the most delicately nurtured intellectual qualities." Remarkable! With a single bound I was in a mood to work.

One must invent feelings, new feelings—the nice thing about this is that, in so doing, one invents the action. In its present form—for example, the lack of dénouement at the end—it may be quite interesting from an intellectual point of view, but as a feeling it simply fades away in the fashion one recognizes from a hundred other situations.

Apart from the self-analysis and conversation, a situation is the only expression for feeling. Feeling has to create certain situations. On the other hand, the desired feeling must radiate out from situations. {This also means that people who are capable of specific feelings create precisely the corresponding situations.} In both cases, the first step is to ask oneself: "What feelings?" And: "What kind of situations do they lead to, what kind does one seek to produce with them ... ?" [...]

12.7.1911. Steinach (arrived yesterday after four weeks of military exercise in Brünn)

Novel: like an autobiography. A representation of how one can arrive at this point of view of mine that others shun, expounded in scenes. Raven[50] is the last phase but one. The last is a room in an Alpine inn. Whitewashed walls with wretched paintings. Clothes stand, a broad cross with a curving transverse beam, and four hooks beneath. The little bedside cabinet next to the cupboard is in an impossible state of disrepair. Such things invent people. And he becomes sensual; but there is nothing in the whole world with which to satisfy this errant corporeality.

Vienna—Florianigasse 3[51]

31.8. You make your way through this nation of people to whom, in spite of everything, you belong yet who remain strangers to you. You see how they amuse themselves, what they do; they have erected statues. The opposition you feel is not merely that general mood which lies beneath all that we do, it is an intricate kind of opposition attached to life by many delicate fibers. Perhaps your perceptions lack some of the wit and spirit that are present on walks with your wife. I believe that, even in physical terms, the world seems broader, because at other times the right side is otherwise always screened off;[52] now, all at once, one is astonished to find oneself standing in a wide semicircle (Gentebrück[53] in the process of transformation).

---

6 September (from a note made on 25. 8. [1911] at the station, while waiting for Martha to arrive from Rome.)

One must never lose oneself in the deduction of ideas. Such a process is preparatory work. One puts the ideas—which have gradually formed a unified circle—into the characters' mouths or makes them act in a way that illustrates, or is derived from, such ideas. In so doing (this is the act of sacrilege) it is preferable to cut a little off from the idea and its consequences and eventualities rather than to sacrifice the liveliness and the practical possibilities of the situation.

But it is not permissible to want to transform "perspectives" into scenes, one must rather:

1. think things through philosophically (and objectively).
2. think in scenes (whereby one only keeps the elements of theoretical thinking around the edges at a subliminal level).
3. edit in the thought-content.

16.9

Wherever possible, one ought to let facts speak rather than feelings. This gives rise to a fine dryness of tone—i.e., things that have claim to objective, not just subjective, validity. Perhaps as a way of regulating this—statements that one can prefix with the pronoun "we."

———————

21.9. Yesterday evening while working, a sudden feeling that I last experienced in the days before Martha arrived. An approach that involved writing scenes down provisionally, without giving the process much thought.

I then gave some consideration to the question of how I came to lose this capacity and whether this was a sign of exhaustion. But the fact is that I approached things then by making scenes out of the material that lay to hand. In the process of writing, this material naturally grew a little and thus emerged the impression of an effortless creative élan. I was then left with a few remnants of notes that I couldn't shape into scenes without being clear about where they would fit—but that demanded reflection about the construction as a whole.

This, then, was what had held me up. And now is the time for a new push forward. I resolved to start out from two things: 1. An idea of the tenor, the factual core, of each individual scene. 2. an idea of the mood of each scene. Think about these two things and then write!

———————

3.12. The following is an explanation of the objective, and not merely subjective, meaning of spoken comments that are based on experiences: yesterday, as I began to design the scene between Lisa and G[entebrück], everything would have come about through the appearance of a few moods and ideas that, in themselves, can probably be understood in terms of the situation and that, in turn, of themselves, motivate what happens later, and that yet are no more than notions that might this time just as well not have happened.

The case would be different if G[entebrück] had tried for a long time to bring his relationship with Maria into balance, if everything that he suffered through her and everything he made her suffer (for example, if it is good to save a person by adapting oneself to his weakness. Maria accuses G. of {demanding that she display} such adaptability) was finally producing a particular reaction here. When done this way, this one scene with Lisa contains the whole of his life. And the feelings, too, do not have the air of cold chance, which is an attitude that I sometimes accuse myself of displaying.

1 October.

Remarkably I have really managed it. I have finished a framework of scenes for three acts, with the possibility of extending it to four acts, should this prove necessary.

I was unwell—angina—spent two days in bed and had a temperature for probably a week before that. Perhaps it was precisely this condition that made me more impetuous.

At the beginning of this period, together with Hornbostel and Wertheimer[54] on one occasion, felt a touch of homesickness for psychology.[55] Today, feel very weak and rather low.

7 October.

Slight temperature wouldn't budge, I had to go back to bed on doctor's orders and am still not allowed to go out. I'm reading *Anna Karenina*. Beneath the level of a shallow good humor, I feel rather wretched.

It occurred to me to portray a person who has grown up within Christian morality and to examine whether he comes round to my morality. But do I have one? (Do not forget: embody this Christian morality in the soft, undogmatic, kindly shape of a mother who inspires love.) I think that I have no morality. The reason: for me, everything turns into fragments of a *theoretical* system. But I have given up philosophy, so any justification for this has fallen by the wayside. What remains are—just notions.

"Love thy neighbor as thyself"—this gives a clear certainty of feeling. In addition, it offers a perfect regulator for behavior. Finally: the calm act of adapting to objective relations of the kind demanded by the psychiatrists as well as the Catholic moral theologians.

Thus the state is right in wanting to be Christian, since the Christian disposition contains all that is necessary to it. Christian education is education for a vigorous life within the community.

However, mistakes make their appearance as soon as one tries to force others to reach this happiness. {For example, when Karenin doesn't want to agree to a divorce {{Martha's husband}} in order to keep the woman safe from the sin of an illegitimate shared life.} Despite this, it runs completely counter to the laws of evolution to see Christianity as offering the only context for the health of a state.

The distinction between altruistic and egotistical feelings, and the old objection that the altruistic are basically egotistical are probably wrong. Both basic concepts are not sufficiently differentiated. Some make the assumption that, principally in the emotions,—and thus in every separate feeling—there exists something that is subsumed into the process whereby an idea of the self, an idea of "I," emerges and is sustained; but this {, too,} is not a proof. It seems to me that the two concepts of "ego-fugal feelings" and "ego-petal feelings" better denote the real distinction; but here feeling does not denote a simple act but, so to speak, a whole cross-sectional slice through consciousness. One of its points of attachment—speaking figuratively—may still be the "I," but what seems to be important is the second point. And the complex act may have the quality of the ego-fugal although, of course, with the act a relationship with the "I" is thereby established. The emotional quality of ego-fugality has various nuances, a subspecies is the Christian and no doubt there will be pathological ones, too. [. . .]

A Christian—I am tempted to say, a Christian Socialist—will preserve his advantage, even in the face of the advantages of others, within the bounds of what is right and proper; befuddled emotional states are alien to him. He doesn't always only think of the other person. This healthy activity within the context of what is right and proper is perhaps a second nuance of feeling—ego-fugal, too, but not altro-petal, but rather accompanied by the sense of being part of a larger whole. Or simply by the feeling of behaving in an upright manner and, beyond this, a consciousness of duty.

It will not be possible to get by with an exclusive morality of duty without also including as a goal the emotional state of individual people. For, so it seems, this is an indispensable feature that identifies general health and distinguishes it from neuropathic dispositions. For an exaggerated consciousness of duty can be just as sick as the lack of one. [. . .] It is also the case, of course, that sick or extremely egotistical and antisocial people can have, overall, a beneficial effect on the state.

But the decisive factor with respect to the value of all these possibilities would be whether one can be "ego-fugal" without any loss of sophistication.

9.10.

From time to time the little {round} birds let themselves drop down between the branches, and then, behind the glass of the windows and the thin lace curtains, they seem to be made up of cross-stitching. When they sit still one sees, through the small gaps in the curtains, extensive areas of their plumage. One sees their natural colors, bright, quite bright [*sic*] light that sometimes shines on beak or wings, but is somehow subdued, modified in some way for which there is no description.

By the left window the leaf-cover is still thick. Green with brownish-yellow patches. Likewise the transparent underside of the leaves. Where one can see the upper side it is grey-green through to off-white even where no direct light rests on it. For this impression, however, it is necessary to look up into the trees from below.——

He awoke and kissed her hand that lay on his pillow. A clear, warm sensation caused him to kiss her hand. At the same time, however, he thought of Frau . . who had sat next to him at supper, with her broad, warm, bare shoulders and her kindly smile that at this moment was associated with her hips in a way that he could not express. He felt the impropriety of the juxtaposition of these two ideas, though it was quite naive—and, guided by one of his favorite ideas, he tried to abreact the alien image and—inhibited, nonetheless—still focusing on it, motionless and seemingly deep in thought, remained lost in the sensuous present, his lips resting on his wife's hand. [. . .]

---

13 October

Anna Karenina:

The principle of the ministerial regalia[56] carried out with wonderful consistency. It is never the case that a person simply has a certain appearance, another always notices the way they appear. This is so strictly adhered to that Karenin's hands are described as clumsy and bony when Anna is looking at them, as soft and white when Lydia Ivanovna is doing so. The reflections are always the thoughts of individual people. Thus the strong impression emerges of different world-images existing side-by-side with each other, without this being somehow overdone—one sees, for example, how Anna looks when someone perceives her with benevolence and someone else does so with malevolence.

This high level of objectivity leads to the conclusion (this runs counter to what I used to assert and accords with what is said about Ibsen, which also conflicts with the view I held) that it is here that the essence of great artistry is to be found, and that such artistry is amoral.

The way that Tolstoy removes the cozy "family magazine" quality from those fortunate average people—Katja, Lewin, Oblonsky—is almost a trick, but it's overwhelming nonetheless. He does so by not glossing over slightly ridiculous, or evil, minor impulses—for example, when Oblonsky is moved to tears when he comes from Karenin and feels glad about the good turn that he is trying to perform, but, at the same time, is glad about a joke that he is working on: what is the difference between me, acting as a peace-maker, and a commander in the field, or something of the kind. In all cases he sees his people as a mixture of good and evil or the ridiculous.

––––––––––––

14 October 1911

It would be desirable to draft, besides the play, the comic novel. The barest program for this: a kind of satire on the conditions under which our souls exist by portraying unlimited other possibilities [. . .]

NOTEBOOK 6

29 NOVEMBER 1911 TO
7 MARCH 1912 AND LATER

[This short notebook is concerned with literary composition, including early drafts of the play that would much later appear as The Enthusiasts. *In the early part Musil is reading Nietzsche and reflecting on his ideas. He is already developing a theme that will be central to MwQ: the inner life of Clarisse (who is based on Musil's friend, Alice von Charlemont) revolving around her ecstatic reception of Nietzsche's philosophizing. He urges himself to produce living narrative rather than philosophy masquerading as literature. At least with respect to some pages on a Catholic priest—a draft for a novel that would not be completed—he follows this advice.]*

6

29.11.1911. (In the new flat. III. Untere Weissgerberstr. 61.)[1]

Since the move, I've lost all my sense of orientation with the play [*The Enthusiasts*].

30.11. Perhaps the best way is first to write down the scenes between the characters and then to shape the main plot from the situations and the actions that are contained in these conversations.

8.12. But one ought not to write scenes and put these together to form characters; one should have instead, at the very latest by the phase of the first revision, an overall idea of the characters who "make" these scenes.

---

13. 12. *Ecce homo* [2]—the parallel with Alice leaps out at one from the page! The way that she relives, in caricature, the personal insights and prescriptions of Nietzsche. But, to put this differently, the way that her ridiculous behavior is perhaps an expression of exactly the same earnestness that N. expresses but in a different, non-ridiculous manner. The point where the ideas originate is the same in each and every case as are also the physical factors that determine them.

{Here we find all the perspectives that Gustl and Alice take as their guide! Transcribe them, and the life of two such people is displayed before one's eyes!} [. . .]

4.III. "Just reach out into the fullness of human life and wherever you chance to lay hold of it, there you will find it interesting."[3] This warning sign was set up specially for me! Always start out from what is concrete! From whatever comes into your mind of its own accord. Never from the idea! If you do that you will immediately slow yourself down.

7.III. Whenever one hears a stranger expressing ideas one does not immediately tune in to the theoretical wavelength of the idea, but one asks: "What kind of person is this?" When one is at the theater one finds that this attitude is even more pronounced. The idea comes into effect far less in its own terms, far more as an expression of the life of the particular person.

1.1. Special characteristics!.

2. Provide characters with the strongest motivations of which they are capable, given the kind of beings they are.

3. Do not start with emotions but start straight away with the mature development.

4. In the preparatory reflections provide drafts, wherever possible, in the shape of dialogues.

5. One form of simplification is to present well-known figures but interpret them from another angle.

6. There is no such thing as getting stuck because one is not in the right frame of mind. One can always think. Getting stuck is a sign of having gone the wrong way. Give way immediately! Think up another approach.

7. Think through the situations and statements by the characters as one would for an essay. Only write the kind of things that interest one. Do not think of psychology; this comes of its own accord. Do not think of artistic arrangements for the dialogue; follow the idea ruthlessly, this always has the strongest effect.

[. . .]

---

cf. Modernism etc.[4]

Sometimes, at dusk, the two poplar trees in front of his window stand like the bushy tip of Satan's tail. The sheer mountainside to the left gapes (gapes open like) a bare, uncovered backside. And below, out of sight behind the little houses, flows—he knows this—the narrow stream, dark and dull; a limber, unceasing, dreadfully pointless snake of murmuring sounds, it has slithered along, probably for centuries, with the same senseless, quick windings, twisting at the same place, this hellish soul-vermin that he cannot shake off. And under the water luxuriate thick grasses whose names no one here knows, and bloated worms bore in the earth. But in the evenings, when the valley sinks down between the mountains, his eyes dig in this dark like women bent over mountains of waste; he alone feels that the yards behind are open, heedlessly displaying the entrails of the daily life of all these souls whose shepherd he is—the piles of wood, the dung heaps, the shirts hung out to dry, the actions without witness, a shovel, a barrow left standing, the little wooden privies. A dreadful fornication.[5] Whereas at the front runs a street where the village has a name.

Before he had the desire to come here, he studied for a long time at university, and not only theology, but also philosophy and quite a lot of science, and this is why he believes in the existence of the Devil, demons and angels. For these are beings whose existence science cannot disprove even if the nature of this existence is difficult to determine. So difficult, that—when he is on his own—he concedes that the merit of the Church lies rather in holding fast to their existence than in the manner in which it construes them. In hours of cold and limpidly intellectual ecstasy—and here lay for him the guarantee that he was not insane but called to unusual insights—, in the tension of nights of study in which no sound was heard save the hammering of his brain over all the roofs, he has bored out those channels that linked his knowledge-store with the possibility of his belief. It was, for him, easier than for those whose every need science meets because they are wholly shaped by the spiritual mold of their time, and it was more difficult than for those seminarists of peasant stock (who are told that, though Kant was very clever, he lacked a proper schooling in philosophy) who believe in the Devil because they have never heard anything else. But, although he knows that he shouldn't, he feels something like tenderness for that icy, narrow pride of science that is tuned to terseness and fact, and it always appears to him the last excuse for the spiritual sterility of scientific findings that they are true. Without this, his own life would have lost its value.

Two weeks ago he had buried his sixty-nine-year-old housekeeper. She had lain in her coffin, a withered figure with wrinkled brown hands and jaws with few teeth. Throughout her life she had been religious and dutiful: the sexton brought the inscription for the pious virgin's headstone for him to inspect. He read it and an unpleasant idea crept into his head. He is still not rid of it yet. It is {actually} not an idea; more the feeling of reaching into a bush, when leaves and little worms stick to one's hand.

Two weeks before that evening when he had told his housekeeper to prepare him a bath,[6] his old one had died; the sexton had brought . . . for him to examine. He had read it and an unpleasant idea had crept into his head whose afterpains he was still not rid of today. It wasn't really an idea at all; it was rather the feeling one has when, in spring, one rolls aside a great stone and looks at the yellowed rectal life beneath that has survived the winter there. The {notion of the} carefully guarded virginity of the old woman who had shared his house seemed as loathsome as sexual idolatry.

His new housekeeper has moved into his house only a few days later. She is the cousin of a female peddler from the village who has looked after him in the intervening period and arranged for the other to come. Previously {until up to approximately one year before that} she has been in service with the parson in St. Jakob up to the time of his death.

It is a pleasure that order reigns once more and {because he immediately turns to his books again} the only impression he gains of her is that the rooms, which in the days of the old woman had smelt of salves and herbs, now have another smell. And that, as she moves about in the next room or comes along the corridor in front of his room, the floorboards creak {with a different sound} than they did under the feet of the deceased woman. And that, when she steps beneath the low doorways, she nearly touches their frames with her shoulders and hips.

On the first day, he has given her the instruction to prepare warm water for him and to fill the trough that stands in the kitchen for him to take a bath. She has looked at him for a long time and has then said in a serious voice: "The parson, God rest his soul, never asked that of me." He has looked up briefly and the memory passes through his mind that the seminarists in . . . had to produce a doctor's prescription to their superiors in order to receive the exceptional permission to take a bath—, and he has given her the curt order to do what he said.

When Barbara brought him breakfast the next morning she has not left the room immediately, but has remained standing in the doorway and has informed him that in the night she has seen the Devil.

He remembers that it was an unpleasant sensation to hear her say that.

{He has the notion that the Devil is nothing to such people. He himself has never seen the Devil.

He has, rather, an indirect notion of him. When one walks through meadows full of leeks and lettuces, through undergrowth. The marrows and the old bed of manure behind his house.}

8

NOTEBOOK 7

30 MARCH 1913 TO 11 JANUARY 1914

[In the period covered by the notebook, in which he records things he is determined not to forget, Musil is at the height of his receptive powers. The period in question overlaps with the year in which MwQ is set, and some experiences recounted here will be taken up into the novel. One portrait is especially relevant: Walther Rathenau, the businessman and intellectual, has a prominent role in part II of MwQ (where he is given the name Paul Arnheim) as the intellectual adversary of Ulrich, the central protagonist. The sharp edge to the present account suggests that Musil is basing impressions on an actual meeting with Rathenau during this period.

In the previous notebook Musil explored the theme of the mental illness of Alice von Charlemont, a friend of long standing—here a visit by Musil and Alice to a lunatic asylum in Italy is recorded. Aspects of this account will be taken up and reworked into MwQ, part III, chapter 33, "The Lunatics Greet Clarisse." Most of the entries are fragments without context: a collection of experiences that register strongly on Musil's perception: workers relaxing with a simple game; sexual intimacies at first or second hand; Gustl Donath (who would marry Alice) staring at gutted fish; street scenes perhaps set down after one of Musil's habitual walks in the streets near his apartment; architecture sketched in words.

One such fragment is "Tanglefoot flypaper," the study of death that Musil published in several newspapers before eventually including it—together with one or two other studies from this notebook—in the anthology of sketches, Pre-Posthumous Papers.]

7.

Journal.
[. . .]

I don't want here to attempt once more to keep a diary, but simply to record things that I don't want to forget.

---

30 March 1913: In the afternoon I spent almost two hours waiting in a corridor of the Psychiatric Clinic for Dr. Pötzl[1] who was giving a course. I did so because this non-energetic wasting of time was a pleasant experience. Via an open court that let in the light, with two windows and a big glass door, I was able to watch him demonstrating. A pretty, plump young woman was sitting in an invalid chair and appeared both compliant and flattered. Behind her on the blackboard hung illustrations of sections through the brain. It seemed to me that she smiled a lot. He took her hand and lifted it up, held something up before her eyes, leaned gently up against her chair like an animal tamer, and other such things. Through the three panes of glass the impression was all the more compelling. I thought how good that must feel. What a curious sense one must have of humanity when one is more used to seeing it in distortion than in the norm. I also thought about how far away from the realm of literature is played out the inner life, ambition, happiness, spirituality,[2] etc., of our times.

---

1 April: Jella, the model, told my wife that she has two official lovers: Klimt[3] and the first lieutenant in Korneuburg. She has just spent a week with [the lieutenant] and when she poses in the nude one can still see the bites and scratches. She told Klimt that she had had to have an abortion during the time she was away and he gave her money for this. Mizzi is embarrassed about taking money but, after all, one has to live. However, she hopes that the lieutenant will marry her, and then she intends to behave quite differently.
[. . .]

1 June. Birthday of the deceased.[4] One suddenly remembers how, all that time ago, in that one year that seemed to stretch out like a whole lost life, one took one's walks—sickness of the eyes—only behind the hotel. It was a small sidestreet with a brothel. Between this brothel and another one there lay shadows, and it was here that one walked back and forth.

You lay on your side and I felt your {small, soft} breasts hanging in my hand like red currants.

A candle burns. The bodies are a pale brick-color. Looking down you at a shallow angle your breast seems to rise and fall excessively; the whole room moves with it, it's like being on the sea. The white border of the bedspread lies like a strip of snow on your skin. Broad strips of shadow run in curves over you but one cannot grasp where they come from.

A woman says: "You'll leave me." The man says: "No, no," this and that, "I love you so much." He becomes insistent. Suddenly the woman lets out a groan: "Despite all this, I can't feel anything of what you are saying."

5 June. The motion of a woman on a horse has—seen from beneath, from a bench—an immense sensuality about it. As if, with each step, she were being seized from below by a wave and lifted upward.

Walk from Neuwaldegg to Hütteldorf:[5] the meadows in the wood, when seen from afar, emerald-green. Everywhere full of people. They sit in groups, play ball and "piggy in the middle." Workers with women and children. All have removed their shoes and stockings. The women who are playing have also taken off their overskirts. Remarkable, the sight of these bodies, pared away by work, at play. Through the thin underskirts one can see the women's drawers. They are people between the ages of twenty-five and forty.

On another meadow there is a stall selling this year's wine. An accordion is playing softly. The people are standing around in a circle, not making a sound. A sixteen-year-old girl in stockings and underskirt is twirling around so quickly that one can see the red garters and the splendidly firm cones of the thighs above her knees.

10 June (Tuesday). Actors, directors: the tone only marginally different from that of the lowest nightclubs. Frau Roland[6] to Blei:[7] "Oh, you're no good for anything, my lad!" Sometimes "you" sometimes "thou." "Ohhh thou . . ." and he slaps her on the back. A Chinaman peddles his wares: "How's he got over here?! From so far away!! Buy something from him, won't you." The good-naturedness and solidarity of the lower classes. She appears pretty and inconsequential; full of nervous energy that comes across not as weakness but as electricity. Ostentatiously imbued with: "I want to achieve." I have the impression that she burns with fever, then suddenly the fever bores her and with utter indifference she slips away from beneath one—with some remark or other, "Oh don't put so much effort into it," or suchlike. I have the impression that she feels her vagina is like a funnel through which, now and then, she impatiently fills herself with stimuli; for herself it has no more meaning than that. {But for all that, a brave person.}

Be that as it may: in the morning, from my window, I saw a girl in her underwear; on catching sight of me, she hid. It occurred to me that this did not give me as much pleasure as it usually would. And, far away, I discovered something laughing within me, with the sense: "Oh, thou normal woman, I consort with tragediennes." Not me at all but, nonetheless, within me this ridiculous happening. Admittedly, it may be that it was only a possibility that I was trying to visualize and that then seemed to me to have actually happened. No doubt that was it.

Walk along the Hauptallee. Martha was in a bad frame of mind and reproached me quite unnecessarily, which left me cold. "You will leave me," [she said] "Then I'll have no one. I shall kill myself. I shall leave you." In a momentary state of weakness, Martha slipped far beneath herself to the level of a jealous or neglected woman with a fierce temper. In personal terms, of course, this has no significance for our relationship. But I switched off this reservation, so to speak, and gave myself over to the impressions that would arise if this were a time of disappointment. And the juxtaposition [sic] was roughly as follows: I can't stand that, etc. Pressing matters—yes, she is amoral and you are immoral; and that amounts, in terms of the relationship, to something bourgeois. Your immorality has blinded me and is, fundamentally, of a bourgeois kind. Fascinating to watch how, in fits and starts, such ideas take on a clearer shape while one is listening to pleas and reproaches. (Of course, I personally knew all along that this was only a game.)[8]

---

11 June. Medics' jargon

"An immaculate corpse." "Genital pipe."

One does bone transplants, amongst other things in order to correct saddle noses; to fill in the depression left by operations on the frontal sinuses; in order to raise the eyeball again after a fracture of the cheekbone. The periostal tissue of the donor causes new bone substance to develop in the recipient. One makes use of material from amputated limbs of other people, or takes this from "fresh, immaculate corpses." Most suitable are the corpses of healthy criminals who have been executed. (Amusing how a piece from a robber and murderer is inserted into a very sensitive and aesthetic woman.)

"Inhabitants of the vagina."

---

17 June. Gustl tells how fish have for him an attraction that is mingled with dread. When he is in the country he spends the first few days in a mad passion for fishing—hour after hour. Then this subsides and comes to a halt in a disgust that borders on horror. As a child he would take the bones of gutted fish, put them in a bowl and stand for hours, staring into it.

He insists that there are people who are attracted by birds and who themselves have something birdlike in their expression; every person, he says, has an animal-co-ordinate with which he is connected in some secret, inner way. [. . .]

Happened to see the end of the swimming race in the Danube canal. Weather and water very cold. When the swimmers came wading out of the water in the bay behind the "Urania" they could scarcely stand or walk upright. Some of them were quite unable to do so and had to be supported, carried, or dragged into boats. The rescue service took some away on stretchers. Their small barges, each with a two-man crew with red caps, were everywhere. A motor-boat tore up and down and turned in a great sweep throwing up a wide swathe of foam in the current. A swimmer crawled up near the "Urania," shivering with the cold, his legs covered with mud. A poor old man didn't hesitate to lend him his coat.

---

2 July.

Dr. Kr. L. took me into his confidence about an affair of the heart. He wants to live in concubinage and probably marry later. He considers concubinage to be more moral and will, "if he is satisfied," only marry in order to redirect the pension to his widow, that is, in order not to present it to the state. He says: "At the outset I hadn't given it any thought whatsoever. But it is scarcely possible to overlook it. She is young, elegant, has as much income as I do, f . . . s wonderfully . . ."

"You know what I mean, one may well get along very well if one meets for a f . . . once or twice a week. But when one is together day and night things may be different."

"At the beginning, of course, you know, I always used condoms; one can never know that she hasn't got gonorrhoea or syphilis. And it was only after quite a long time, when I realized that she is perfectly healthy, that I simply took contraceptive measures."

He tells me all this with a smile that says something like: "What a clever, circumspect person I am—no one can pull the wool over my eyes."

---

4 July.

Before the storm, the houses are brighter than the sky.

---

10 July.

How a person who is normally good-natured can become malicious! Annina[9] has a headache and is lying down. I come through the anteroom and, all of a sudden, find myself walking clumsily and noisily as she sometimes does. Why? Perhaps because I am annoyed that Martha is sitting next to her bed. Probably because I am irritated by her submissiveness. But, after all, it is I who would never let her be otherwise. I am almost shocked by the automatic way in which this malice in the walk started without my intervention. [. . .]

---

11 July. Met a married couple. She still has a child's face, a child's neck and shoulders, but already a woman's lower body.

---

3 August:

Journey to Mödling[10] a few days ago. City of Philadelphia Hotel. This is situated in the corner between Triester Reichsstrasse and the railway station, the

front is set at a slight angle to the station, a shallow gabled façade, in each
storey six to eight windows. Dates from Emperor Ferdinand's time. Stands
completely on its own; on the other side of the street, bushes cover the railway embankment; at a considerable distance, dispersed at irregular intervals,
the last few tall houses seem to look over their shoulders with their high, win-
dowless fire-walls. How does this hotel make a living? Probably off the people who travel on the Reichsstrasse. A strange form of life that, despite the
railways, still survives on a road like this. A strange place to stop for the night.

Between the forked legs of the telegraph poles children have set up their
swings.

The great plain was overcast with gloomy light.

In the trees, the leaves glitter, or are quite dark. This makes the masses of
foliage look rather like a lake when the wind just stirs its surface and tiny
waves flash.

Daydreaming: two months of love in a small town. The wife of some sick man
who is confined to his house, a teacher or businessman. She is quite thick-set
and powerful about the waist, and her knees are rather plump. When she is
naked, her hands seem not to move with her body but rather like someone
who stands aside in embarrassment. Yet so full of life, so full of the will to
enjoy, so womanly—in a provincial fashion, with a touch of shame, but determined to take what is her due. She smells of tulle and muslin. She knows
she doesn't do it perfectly, but she wants to do it nonetheless.

Summer resort. Man who has spent his youth working, wasting it away;
feels hunger on awakening and notices that, having already reached 35, one
seems comical to 17-year-old girls. Since one knows oneself only from inside, it is impossible to imagine that one is felt to be old. Excursions with
the young people. Their mother is 35 years of age as well. One belongs with
her. One walks with her behind all the others. One slowly surrenders to her
charms. But all the time one would like to leap into the midst of this pack
of girls. One girl starts to become serious, likes to listen, to receive advice.
Absolutely wonderful, the way that girls treat one as a comrade and turn serious before they fall in love.

---

4. August.

Between two downpours, the pavements, the carriageway blackish
brown. The people all seem to be wearing black clothes. They come out of

the factory, stiff hats, no collars. They walk, first two together, then three, and then one, and then four; and someone pushes on through at a quicker pace, passing this group, then that one.

Rain: a sense that the air has been slashed open, flashing. From somewhere comes a call: "Wal-di!"

Street scenes: a bend in the Favoritengasse: the Theresianum[11] in the evening seems covered with a pale varnish. When one catches sight of the Landstraße from the Rasumofskygasse[12] one can see the church with the illuminated clock as a theater set. The big gate in the Salmgasse takes up almost a quarter of the front of the little house. It is always half-open; one sees a courtyard that is higher on one side than the other; it is paved with round stones, grass growing between them. A light carriage stands there and a cavalry-man is cleaning saddle-gear that he has hung over the carriage.

The shopkeeper's apprentice twists a bit of brown paper into a cone and uses this to sprinkle the pavement.

Blocks of houses on the other bank: 3 storeys, 95 windows and 3 doors on the longer frontage, 50 windows on the shorter one. The houses are by no means all the same, not even the same height; one has a dark roof, another a bright one, but they give a uniform impression, appearing as a surface, as boxes set up behind trees that are even lower than they are.

The bank has a brown wooden barrier. A few houses stand there, just as they once stood when it was still a country road.

High spirits: workers tease an old man who is driving around with his cart looking for broken barrels, etc . . . "Oh, du lieber Augustin, everything's broke, everything's broke," they sing.

He: "You miserable, dirty bastards . ." and so on. When one looks him in the face, however, one sees that he isn't particularly angry. A factory girl lets out a scream: she sets her legs apart, and then bends forward, so that her rear is jutting upward, and only then does her laughter break out.

{To be used toward the end of the "Spy" when A.[13] is again starting to take interest in people.}

Steam-mill Schöller & Co. 126 windows in 6 shallow storeys set one on top of the other.

Windows after sunset. They look as if gold foil has been stuck onto their inner surfaces; in some of them this has rucked up and formed little waves; others look as if they have been covered with brown packing paper. Windows that are partly open, however, look as if they are papered with frayed and torn foil. Later the colors fade and become drained of blood.

The corner of a house leaps out into the tops of trees; next to them an arc-lamp on a wooden mast, looking like a bengal match.

---

7 August.

Shape of a square:[14] the street was raised at some time in the past so some of the basement windows of the old palais are half buried in the ground, some a quarter buried, some less than that. On the side elevation, a columned portal arches down to a neglected area of garden or courtyard below the level of the street. Corinthian columns. At the point where the Landstrasse is joined by the Rasumofskygasse it broadens out in just the way the flow of a river slows and stagnates forming a small lake, then runs off in two gutters. An island with brown wooden huts and two rows of trees, with a sidestreet cutting through the middle, positioned quite close to one of the banks.

Looked at approximately from there [. . .] chimney hoods on the roofs of the low houses looking like Dolomite towers. Somewhere among these old-fashioned roofs there must be a bakery or some kind of commercial enterprise—there are so many chimney hoods.

Behind many of these old houses there are gardens. One looks through an entrance onto a small cobbled courtyard, then comes a railing and, up a couple of steps, a garden with dark-green, spherical trees. Or one sees all this through a back gate that stands half-open and whose other half has brownish-yellow and blue panes of glass in the shape of a star or a cross.

Often there are "back-buildings" in the simpler courtyards. These are single-storey huts with green and grey shingle-roofs. Open doors. On the threshold someone sits mending an appliance. A coach-builder or blacksmith plies his trade here. Wheels lean against the walls, stacks of wood, bundles of kindling. A sawhorse stands in the middle of the long, narrow courtyard next to the well. And in the background, trees, gardens.

Right at the top in the Landstraße, the carriageway runs on at the same level but the pavement suddenly goes up four, five narrow stone steps and there stands a little inn with a trellis garden where a roast chicken costs a guilder and one goes along for about ten paces above the level of the road then gradually comes back to it via a kind of sandy sliproad. But, as it turns into a sidestreet, the verge is covered with grass. [. . .]

———————

Type: very muscular, athletically trained men who are timid.

———————

23 August.

Lavarone: the autumn is coming through the air, a part is left on the trees. Journey from Caldonazzo-Lavarone: groups of trees in the sun; dark shadows joined together as if in a water-color; above them, spreading out more extensively, are brighter ones that look like a glaze. The whole is covered in irregular stains, as if someone had squeezed out a paintbrush on the paper. A big, old, uncomfortable carriage: high wheels, brownish-white upholstery. The road leads through a ford—a dried-out riverbed full of gravel. Then, in very tight turns, it goes up a very steep slope.

Trento: Hotel Trento. Breakfast terrace with bright, striped marquee, palm trees.

In the streets one can scarcely keep one's eyes open for the glare. This time, the nave of the cathedral is very disappointing. In the shops, renew acquaintance with doors taken off their hinges and billowing curtains.

———————

End of September:[15]

Rome: visit by night to the Anthropological Institute. We have to go quickly through the door and into the dark because otherwise the bell rings at the porter's. Old Jesuit college (Collegium Romanum). Long hall, on both sides, covering all the walls, cupboards filled with skulls. The skulls simply look as if they are scientific preparations, but on top of the cases there are colored wax casts, busts of various primitive peoples taken from living persons; these busts, with their eloquent expressions, have a very eerie effect.

The room where Sergi[16] works: former Jesuit cell, roughly square in shape, window overlooks the quiet courtyard, a vault forms the ceiling. At the window, the microscope table with lots of chemicals in little bottles. A cupboard with countless little drawers with small white porcelain knobs—these contain slide preparations with sections of brain. A large, valuable microtom and a smaller one. Microscopes. A canary. Sergi works for about 14 hours each day, getting up at six. Has published a great deal. Looks like a smart young Roman hackney-cab driver, but has a finely wrought forehead, at once beautiful and ugly. This is crossed by long, sharp wrinkles. His soul seems to be that of a seventeen-year-old. From his science not the slightest influence crosses over into his life; it has no shaping effect whatsoever on him as a human being. . He is as naive as a blithe monk. Science in general provides a modern analogy to the monastic existence.

Even existential questions that abut his field of research do not touch him. He says: "I sometimes feel that I am of Sicilian race. My reason grants freedom to a woman but my feelings cannot tolerate this." He does not understand that this is not a matter of instinct.

His father, the free-thinker and anarchist, says: "A woman is there for the children. As soon as she is a mother, she must renounce a life of her own." (His name is Giuseppe and he seems to be a kind of W. Wundt.[17])

In the evening in the birreria, read the following in the Berliner Tagblatt: If, instead of the aesthete (who finds groups of summerhouses dreadful), someone with more profound insight comes along, he recognizes their value for the health of the people, etc. Atmosphere of around 1870. In the same issue, however, a (rubbishy) article in favor of Expressionism.

---

2 Oct. Idea: Signora Edith saying: "Give me a kiss," "Touch beaks."

Quirino is 27, she is in her late forties. All her teeth have now been extracted and she has an ovarian cyst. Quirino only refers to this in medical terms and as tenderly as if speaking of a young woman who, having contracted typhus, has been forced to have all her beautiful hair cut off. She doesn't have a bad figure but she has the face of a Jewish old maid and two warts on her nose. {He has a fine, clever forehead that looks like yellow-toned marble.} She always wears too much perfume and her clothes are quite impossible. She is completely uncultured and has pronounced views on all matters in the way that one does "in society." All the while she is very self-confident and "chuzbisch." Miserly, too. Has absolutely no respect for the opinions of more intelligent people when she is of a different opinion. And it makes Quirino happy simply to be able to speak of her. In spite of this he seems to be really an engaging, hard-working fellow. Given his age, he is already astonishingly mature as a doctor, as well. He obviously sees in her a higher world. At least a more beautiful and more human one than that of his famous father. There is perhaps a certain filial element in his eroticism. {Because he evidently does not have a spiritual relationship with his mother who is simple and pious.} And he does everything on his own, against the will of his parents; he is making a name for himself, he is working his way up as a general practitioner and doesn't want to touch a penny of E[dith]'s fortune. He is an idealist, through and through.

Visit to Sergio in Manicomio.[18] Via [della] Lungara. Staircase, lawyers' chambers, doctors' flats. A crooked corridor with whitewashed beams leads across the road into the complex of buildings that lead up the slope of the Gianicola. Before this, one opens and closes heavy doors. Pavilions in a very large garden that slopes upward and stretches out at the far end to the left. Viewing places. On one of these, patients with nurses in attendance—at first glance it is scarcely possible to tell them apart. We go marching through a women's ward; house, square surrounded by railings, trees, benches. All with hair let down. Their faces are all of repellent ugliness with fat, soft, stunted features. One is pulling up her stocking, a very white, ugly leg. An old woman gives us a letter for her husband. "Ernesto, beloved . . !" Quite coherent, as far as I can see. Always the same thing: "When are you coming? Have you forgotten me?" "You'll make sure he gets it quickly?," she says to the doctor. "Certainly," he promises her, and tears it up as soon as the matron has closed the gate behind us. He possesses a collection of such letters.

The Esperanza Pavilion: a quiet ward. The strongest impression made by a man from the upper classes, a paralytic. He is sitting in bed. White pointed beard, white hair. Well cared-for, noble and intelligent face. Idealized Cavour type. Perhaps late fifties. Very white complexion. Quite melancholic. He nods to us when we greet him and answers a question from the doctor quietly and melancholically in a way that is typical of his whole demeanor.

Then a merry, fat, old painter. His bed is by the window. He has paper and pencil and spends the whole day sketching. What I saw of his work was not the kind I associate with the insane, but just like the sketch a healthy person might make for a painting. Groups in halls—vieux jeux, perhaps, but healthy. Sergio, who seems to lack all feeling for art, does not know that this is what a sketch should look like. He clearly thinks that this, too, is a manifestation of sickness simply because he does not know enough about painting. He quickly filches a sheet—the old man giggles, behaving like a woman—and shows it to me. "Bellisimo," I say. "Oh, you see," says the sick man, "the gentleman likes it. Show him more, show him. He said 'Bellisimo'; oh, I know that you only laugh, but he likes it." He says all this in the easygoing fashion with which two people tease each other. I look at a few more sheets, then we have to go on. Idiots, the most horrific sight there is. They sit in bed, their whole posture lopsided, lower jaw protrudes and hangs down, violent, chewing movements with it whenever they struggle for words. Soiled. One old man—dementia senilis—like a thin leather sack stretched over a small skeleton. Little, sunken red eyes.

Ward for disturbed patients. On the corridor, already, the warders join up with us. One hears cries and gibbering, as if one were approaching an aviary. The warders are reassuringly big, strong, clean, friendly people. There are seven of us. One warder makes ready to open, I am about to go in first, Sergio holds me back. The warder opens up with the key-spike, then this big broad man listens for a moment in the doorway before pushing quickly through the gap. We follow. Whenever we go up to one of the patients, he is immediately tactically flanked by two warders, the other ones stand around us, giving us cover on the sides and to the rear. The patients sit in the beds, crying out and gesticulating.

Some of them have their hands tied to the bed in slings that leave them only a limited freedom because of the danger of suicide. Paralysis, paranoia, dementia praecox. As we come up close to one of them, he shouts at us. I don't know what he's saying. Big gestures, complaints, curses. The chief warder makes some comment or other, the doctor prescribes some treatment. With one of them Sergio talks for rather longer. "Who is the gentleman," the patient asks. (Many ask this.) "A doctor from somewhere else." "No, you are the seventh son of the German Kaiser." "That is not true," says Sergio, "It's just you who say this." "Non e vero radebreche ist. [*sic*] Ma tu [sei] il settimo figlio . . ." "No," I say. "You lie, you dog, pig . . ." and a bucketful of curses descends upon me. With great authority, the warders force him back down onto the bed and we walk on. Those we have passed shout out after us, others shout at us as we approach. An old man with whom I have exchanged a few words is in a good mood, tells little jokes, then suddenly he slips—one notices the way he slips—out of this quite sensible dialogue into obscenities; busily and communicatively, he points to something on his penis, begins to masturbate. "Non far porceria," the doctor says {sternly and} energetically and the warders take hold of him.

On the corridor, women and pretty little girls, who are visiting the patients; they greet us politely and with trust. It is Sunday.

A courtyard, locked, surrounded by a gallery. At the entrance, idiotic boys, smeared with snot. A young man presses up close to us, starts whining. {God knows how he had been spending his time up to this moment.} "I want to get out," he pleads, "when will you let me out?" "It is the Director who decides that, not me," Sergio says comfortingly. The boy goes on with his pleading, then gradually his voice takes on an urgent, threatening tone, something whirring, fluttering, some unconscious expression of danger. The wardens force him down onto the bench. Someone is sitting here, a simple man, still in his dark Sunday clothes. They greet us shyly, politely, they have modest little requests to make—here it feels more like a prison. Then the other courtyard. Care upon entering, the warder bangs on the gate with his fist and, at this sign, all have to line up in a row in the gallery or sit on the benches there. Once more Sergi impresses upon me the need to leave a distance of at least two paces as I walk past. We all do this. When one of them leaves his place the wardens grab hold of him. Everything depends on nipping any disturbance in the bud; we are seven against thirty, surrounded by walls in a quiet courtyard occupied only by lunatics; murderers among them. {The remarkable thing is that they do nothing to each other, they only get excited about strangers who disturb them.} Right next to the door stands one of them, medium height and build, with a brown Van Dyke beard and piercing eyes. He leans in the corner with his arms folded, says nothing, and looks at us angrily. I believe he will manage to break out. Then a small, stocky man. With the shorn head of a convict, pointed at the top. Teeth to crush stone. He gets up. Sergio exchanges a couple of words with him. "Ask him why he is here," Sergio says to me, "he speaks quite good German." "Why are you here?," I ask. "You know very well" is the answer. "I don't know," I insist, "Why are you here?" "You know very well!!" "Why are you so rude to me?," I say. "Because I want to be; I can do what I like!" "But surely it's not right to be rude without any cause?" "I can do what I like!! Do you understand? What I like!" I wouldn't like to be alone with the fellow now; he speaks very loudly, dressing me down like an NCO, laughing with part of his face; and I believe that, if he could, he would seize me by the throat and bite my face. "I come from Berlin," I say. "Ah, Berlin—a beautiful city," the murderer answers, quite altered; he starts to shine, to turn quite soft, but that only deepens the impression of an uncanny unpredictability. Sergi teases him, and he becomes angry, will not answer. A young negro is sitting there, powerful, with a dreadfully flat nose, squashed in at the bridge; he looks at us with a mixture of anger and apathy.

Individual cells: from a distance comes a cry, time and again the same cry. We open the door of the cell. A bare room, a toilet in one corner, covered over; in the middle, free-standing, a low bed. A naked man stands in the center of the room. He is as tall as I am, rather muscular. Brownish blond beard, light-brown pubic hair. Legs apart, he stands there, his head lowered, his beard thick with spittle. Repeatedly, he makes the same movement, like a pendulum, hurling his upper body just to one side, with head lowered a little and with a movement of the finger while his arm is bent stiffly at a right-angle and held close to his body as if he were playing mora. Each time he does so, he lets out a loud cry: "Ah!," panting and expelling the sound with a colossal tensing of the pulmonary muscles. He is beyond help; one has to wait until he tires. This lasts for hours. In another cell an imbecilic old man. He winks at us. An alcoholic. Dreamt his wife was deceiving him and killed her when he awoke. In another cell a doctor, apathetic, brooding, we go out again quickly. In the last cell, a lawyer. In street clothing but with no collar. He has a full black beard, black hair. He looks as if he could be off to plead a case at court. But in the way he speaks one senses how difficult he finds it to understand, since his spirit must fight its way through some tough substance; but one would scarcely be aware of this if one had not met him in this place. "Doctor," he says, "You're always bringing friends with you. Who is the gentleman?" "A doctor from Berlin." "You are always bringing friends, I want to come along too for once, show me . . . ," and he prepares to join us. "Addio avvocato," says Prof. Sergi quickly, and the warders shut the door with a certain degree of respect.

Mid-October:

Three weeks ago, when we were walking through the streets "fuori porta"[19] the people swarmed out of the front doors of the many houses like insect-pests crawling out of holes in walls.

Two female snake charmers fuori Porta Pia. Women about thirty to forty years of age. Dressed in bourgeois clothes. A circle [of people] around them. Some kind of naked light, flickering and bright. They direct the snakes with little sticks; the snakes creep through bags, etc.

Prof. Sergi senior: a face like a friendly 70-year-old baby; chubby little cheeks, framed in white beard, little hands.

The sons hold the father in extraordinary reverence. They are so anxious not to disturb him that when they want to speak to him alone they join the queue of the other visitors in the Anthropological Institute. They idolize their mother. She is strictly devout, the sons, like their father, are atheists. But when Quirino happens to be there he goes to church with his mother so as not to offend her. Even in their twenties the sons were not allowed out in the evening; it would have offended their parents. When Quirino was invited by a friend of E[dith]'s to dine with her and E., they ate at seven and then he ran home and pretended to eat another meal there. At table, the sons serve the mother as if she were a stranger. No one in this family has anyone to confide in; their lives are absolutely sealed off from one another. When E. came, she was actually just like a mother to Quirino.

The brothers respect each other, without love or trust. Sergio, when asked about Quirino's scientific approach, says: "Oh, he works as well, but in quite a different way from me." (Yet he says this with a degree of tender pride.) Quirino, when asked what Sergio thinks of his sister, answers: "I have no idea whatsoever, but I assume he sees her as I do."

When Qu. had got himself into some kind of terrible mess and, for the one and only time, confided in his brother who was nine years older than he, the brother said: "You've been very stupid, now it's for you to find a way out."

Their sister, a spinster of some thirty years of age, is kept like an old songbird in a cage. Or like the Dalai Lama—captive and worshipped. "We worship her," says Quirino. "I couldn't bear it if she married. I would perhaps kill the man." She is to remain pure. Untouched by life's darkness. He supervises her reading. Keeps her completely naive in sexual matters; no such shadow shall darken her life. "But won't she lose out by this?" "Chi sa, I can't behave in any other way, I worship her."

She plays the piano for hours. Her face is anything but peaceful. As if ravaged by nervous energy from things that have been suppressed. She grimaces when she speaks. Displays an exaggerated, impetuous gaiety.

But, after all, she plays Wagnerian opera, she reads the libretto after all, and in that there's so much eroticism? She probably understands it, but it cannot take root in her understanding and slips away. (It's just the same with children who have been told about sex.)

Frau Croce says she's an idiot.

The brothers will leave all their money to their sister.

––––––––––––––––––

End of October

The trees are in winter green, a durable green.

Vienna, for some days in winter, wears a light white fur of grey air. Sitting down; six steps ahead is a path to somewhere or other, an iron railing. Suddenly two hands appear, portions of arm, a head; somehow or other a person has come up from down below. The impression is not one of shock but of an experience without parallel. The heart constricts.

Room in the boarding house: midnight; a train has arrived; from Paris, or Berlin, or Vienna, I don't know where. The maidservant shows them to the room, brings in their baggage. They speak in loud voices; the brutal jolting, the giant energy in being shaken along for a whole day is still in their bones; they still have a remnant of briskness about them in the first few minutes that they spend in the room.

I hear the buckles on the belts around their cases, the key, the clatter of toothbrush and soap being laid on the washstand. I know the room, know where each piece of furniture stands. Tissue paper rustles, objects are unwrapped and put down. They are cheerful as they do this, they laugh. What are these strangers laughing about? How cheerful they are. With an effort, I make out that they are speaking French. I understand individual words and forget them. They take off their shoes. The door is locked. They wash. I understand from the sounds that they have used a great deal of water and are splashing lots of it over their faces, time after time. They soap their hands for a long period, brush them with water, rinse them, brush up the foam again, rinse. I can distinguish from the sounds that they have kept their vests on, but have perhaps got these {wide} open to the shoulder, for when the neck and upper chest are washed it sounds different. They repeatedly force water into their noses, on account of the dust of the journey, and snort it out. The woman has a slight cold, gives her nose a long, energetic, unembarrassed blow: they have been married for quite a long time already.

As they are doing this, he says something to her in a slightly lower tone, she gives a contralto giggle; something about this makes me guess immediately. {After a while} they go quiet, I hear kisses; eight, nine of them; three, four of these in quick succession. {They go about their business in silence.} The iron bed bumps softly against the wall. Then, lasting half a second, the female sound, half vowel, half breath. After this, absolute silence.

Next day: they are tall, fleshy people.

After a few days, disgust at listening to them.

November: the colors of things are pale without being weak. They are different without my being able to explain to myself how. I know only that the sky is often a light blue-grey.

Dreadful: that you[20] were pregnant here. Bearing your body through these streets. Acknowledging that you live here with this people.

Dreadful, too, that you felt no shame to bear your body like a board with the inscription: I have sexual congress with this person.

From everywhere it is just a single step into the metaphysical: in eight days you will be sitting here opposite me. I can see already the space you will take up. The upholstery will sink in a little beneath you. Everything will be just as it would be now, only time will have passed. We shall come in the carriage from the station, you will squeeze my hand, all this will certainly be, already is; only the time is missing. What is it—time? (The thought that someone then doesn't come after all!)

The negress: I think Somali or Abyssinian. In European dress, shallow bell of velvet, with hair darting out from underneath. Saddle-nose; speaks like a flock of starlings. The inside of the hands light-colored, speckled with pink. Mythical creature. I should like to kiss you under the armpits.

S. Spirito: it is a curious experience to see forty-five typhoid patients in one room. Well-nourished, (they are given a great deal to eat, semolina, chicken; no medicines, only compresses if the temperature reaches 38 degrees, cool baths at 39 degrees) just a skin that glistens slightly with the fever. The floor is wiped down every hour with carbolic, we clean our shoes on a carbolic mat and take care not to touch anything.

Most powerful impression: patients with tuberculosis in the final nights of their lives. They sleep propped up on five or six pillows, their long hands stretched out on the blanket. Their long, thin necks seem to crane forward. The lower part of the face is quite shrunken so that the heads look like a triangle in which the eyes shine when they look up and the skin is greenish- or yellowish-white. They die either when their breathing turns quick and shallow (the light flickering and dying) or after a particularly heavy vomiting of blood they fall exhausted into death-throes, or they die when a blood vessel in their brain ruptures, etc. They look, in fact, like dreamers. Like fanatical followers of some impenetrable concern.

The halls are tall and large, with the kind of beautiful ceilings one finds in mansions—it is almost as if beds had been set up in a church.

———————————

A faint shiver, is a cold on the way? Ringing and humming, not heard, but felt in some other way. When you are with me, my rooms will have red curtains with golden tassels. You are like chocolate in a silver cup. But I shall be as good and gentle as chocolate.

———————————

November:

postscript on the Lido: the vulva of a twelve-year-old girl is like a blind eye {The breasts: as yet they are mere form. They are still, as it were, without meaning. (They are rather disagreeable, like a bleak range of hills.)}

"Tanglefoot" flypaper:[21] one fly has dragged itself to the edge, two legs and the head are free but however far it stretches forward it is caught fast by the back part of the body and the other legs. Another sits upright, both front legs spread out away from the body in a gesture that resembles quite closely the wringing of hands. All of them first force themselves into an upright position on all six little legs, which are stuck fast, with their last segment bent over. {For this reason} they are all rather bandy-legged—the way one would stand on a sharp ridge. They are collecting their strength. Then they begin to whirr with all their might until exhaustion makes them stop. Pause for breath; renewed effort. Like a small hammer their tongue gropes out. Their head is brown and hairy, as if made from a coconut; just like negro idols resembling people. Then, for a moment, their energy flags and straight away they are stuck fast at a new place, by wing or body. And are gradually pulled in this way. Or they suddenly fall forward onto their face over their legs, or sideways stretching out all their legs. Often all their legs are stretched out toward the back on each side. Thus they lie there. Like crashed aeroplanes, with one wing jutting up vertically into the air. Or like horses that have broken down and died. Or with infinitely tragic gestures like those of humans. From time to time {(as late as the next day)} one of them still fumbles about with a leg, whirrs a wing. On the side of the body, around the area where the first leg joins the body, they have some kind of tiny, shimmering organ; this opens and closes, too quick to register; it [. . .] looks like a tiny eye that opens and shuts unceasingly. One is pregnant. One has seen the chosen partner, has flown toward her and, crash-landing, is stuck fast over her.

{They push themselves up on all sixes. Or, their rear legs outstretched, supported on their elbows, they try to lift themselves. One lies with head and arms outstretched into the clear. Quite a strong one is able to lift its legs, one after the other. It walks. But it cannot get off with all at the same time. Some are like peaceful sleepers. Almost all of them, at the end, sink over head-first.}

Young, rose-skinned girls come up the stairs past you, reading a picture post-card. Deferential and ashamed simply because you are a man, you make way for them. A smell of clothing, freshness and perhaps a little—but "sweat" is to say too much—is left for you as you descend the next few steps.

The young postwoman already knows you from your polite and clumsy questions about which was the right postbox. You can tell by her eyes as you greet her. You give her the recorded letter; she has you write name and address on the back. You feel that this is not absolutely necessary. She hands you her pencil. She looks at what you have written, makes a correction with an official air, and then first does something else with the letter. She only starts to read when she has to write the address on your form. She mangles your name. You cheerily point this out to her. She looks at you with her little face whose lower part is about to sharpen into laughter but she stops herself at the last moment. Then, in perfect parallel, you dip your eyes into her black and shining eyes—a favor that she grants you—, bid her a polite farewell, and leave.

Waiting: I look at my work. It is motionless; as if of stone. Not without meaning, but the sentences do not move. I have two hours, in round terms, before I can leave. Every fifth minute I look at the clock; it is always less, not than I had estimated, but than I hope—as if by some miracle—it will be. I see for the first time the furniture in my room standing quietly there. This way is different from the way one sees five points as a five in a game of cards. The table, the two chairs, the sofa, the cupboard. This is what it must be like for people without ideas when their day's work is done. An excess of joyful expectation rises in me. An excess of joy like the end of the day on 24 December before everything gets under way.

Someone is whistling on the street, someone says something, goes on by. Many sounds come at the same moment; someone is speaking; in the upper storey someone is playing the piano; the telephone is ringing. (While I write this down, time tears past.)

———————————

Toward the end of November: I have gone to bed early, I feel that I have caught a slight chill, perhaps I've even got a slight temperature. The electric light is on; I look at the ceiling or the curtain over the door to the balcony. You began to undress when I had already finished doing so; I am waiting. I can only hear you. Incomprehensibly walking back and forth; in this part of the room, in that. You come and lay something on your bed; what can it be? You open the cupboard, put something in or take something out; I hear it shutting again. You put hard objects onto the table, others onto the marble slab of the chest. You are constantly in motion. Then I recognize the familiar sounds of hair being let down and brushed. Then cascades of water falling into the washbasin. Before this, clothes being slipped off; now the same again; it is incomprehensible to me how many clothes you take off. The shoes. Then your stockings go back and forth without stopping, just as the shoes did before. You pour water in glasses, three, four times in succession, I cannot puzzle out what this is for. In my imagination I have long since come to an end of everything imaginable while you are clearly still finding something else to do in reality. I hear you putting on your night-gown. But that is not the end of things by a long way. Again there are a hundred small actions. I know that you are hurrying so evidently all of this is necessary. I understand: we watch the dumb behavior of the animals, astonished how, with creatures that are supposed to have no soul, actions follow, one after the other, from morning till night. This is just the same. You have no consciousness of the countless movements that your hands perform, of all the things that seem necessary to you and that are quite inconsequential. But they jut out prominently into your life. I, as I wait, happen to feel this.

———————————

Priest at the Lateran [Palace]. He preaches about the triumph of the Catholic Church. Young men lean their bicycles against the inside of the church door. He looks healthy, youthful. With these gestures and this enthusiasm, he might well be standing on the street, in lively debate about Gioco di ballone.[22] But it is just because of this that he brings the Kingdom of God incredibly close. The way there does not have to lead via civilian self-sacrifice.

Café Faraglia, figurine lamp: a broad, soft shaft of light, glowing {yellow}, (making no sound, but, half-an-hour later I think of my mother's good cook, Julie, with the frying fat crackling just before she put in the schnitzels) dips from her hip—from the hand that hangs down to her hip—into the mirror. Through this side {of her body} flows a narrow stream of light, down to below the knee. But the other side is proudly illuminated; down from her raised hand; bronze-colored; like the landscape of a circus ring; with soft hill-shadows at breast and hip; like a leopard skin around a naked body. At the back of the figure the two mirrors meet at a right angle. Coffeehouse music, no doubt banal, plays softly. Martha says: "Whenever you shout at me like that I'm always out of my mind with despair." When we stepped out of the café, the air was soft and mild; night-clouds of dark steel-blue were rolled up in walls, one on top of the other. Liking her so much brought me close to tears and I wanted to stroke her all the time.

---

1 December: in the Piazza Monte Citorio, in front of the Parliament, in the midst of the heavy traffic, I saw a baker with a bare chest running across the street on the way to the pissoir or on some errand or other.

Here, about four weeks ago, I saw a horse laughing. This was at the Viale della Regina. A small, elegant young carriage-horse. It was tied up to a wall (on the unpaved footpath, to the left, in a gap in the houses, was an "osteria" or a wagoners' workshop, a place with courtyard, bushes, sugarcane) being curry-combed by a groom. The inside of his thighs was his sensitive spot. The closer the man came, the further back it laid its ears, became restless, tried to move its mouth there—which the man prevented with his body—and stepped from one foot to the other. When the man had reached the actual spot the horse couldn't stand it anymore, tried to turn around, to force him away. And because the man was stronger and didn't let it change position it had to stand still but shook over all its body and bared its teeth. Just like a human being who is being tickled so much that he can't laugh any longer.

In the evening, Miss Frazer sits on the edge of the armchair, her upper body leaning back, straight as a board so that she only touches the backrest at the top, her legs stretched out straight, so that they only touch the ground with the heel (as in riding boots), and she crochets. Then she prepares her lesson. Then she plays her quick game of patience. And goes to her room. Her profile is like a knight's, as sharp as a rough nobleman's. With a comical (endearing) trace of girlishness beneath her white hair.

Carriage-way down from Pincio to the Piazza di Spagna: cactuses on the high wall. The way that a throng of people, on emerging through a gate, spreads out as they disperse—this is how these cactuses hang down, grey-grey-green. Other large ones, half like curved swords, half like a phallus. Like the narrow, prickly, giant cattle tongues. Like horns of prehistoric animals.

Trinità dei Monti—bronzed marble. When one comes from Pincio toward the via Sistina: this red façade.

The heaven bleach-blue.

The dark evergreen trees as if gold foil had been pounded among the foliage.

Big palm trees with trunks like gigantic pineapples. The leaves as if painted with dust emulsion. Their shape cubist, futuristic, ugliness unending: the same emotion that emanates from elephants.

One cactus at the upper stairway to the Pincio: completely turned to stone. With holes at the base of the leaf like the holes in paleolithic stone axes. But its life went on around these parts. The life here is as hard as this cactus.

In a hackney-carriage, a gentleman. Immense glutton-face. Spats and English suit. The face, with its immense culinary energy, appears grandiose, gigantic. When he tucks his serviette into his collar it is as if a hero of Homer is shaking his shield. [. . .]

---

11 January: Dr. W. Rathenau:[23] a wonderful English suit. Light-grey with dark vertical stripes framed with little white eyes. Comfortable, warm cloth yet infinitely soft. A fascinatingly arched chest and side-panels further down.

Something negroid about the skull. Phoenician. Forehead and the front portion of the cranial roof form a segment of a sphere, then the skull slopes upward and backward—behind a small depression, some impact. The line from the tip of the chin to the farthest point on the back of the skull is angled at almost less than 45 degrees to the horizontal, and this is further intensified by a little goatee beard (which hardly seems to be beard but rather chin). Small, boldly curving nose. Lips that arch away from each other. I do not know what Hannibal looked like, but I thought of him.

He likes to say: "{But,} my dear Doctor," and takes one by the upper arm in a friendly grip.

He is used to taking immediate charge of the discussion.

He is doctrinaire and, at the same time, lord of all he surveys. One makes an objection; he responds: "I am delighted to concede this premise, but . . ."

He says (and here his image flashed across my mind with brilliant clarity as the model for my great financier in the hotel scene):[24] With calculation you achieve nothing in business life. If you are cleverer than the other man, you are cleverer only once; for the next time he will pull himself together completely and outwit you. If you have more power than he has, the next time several will get together and will have more power than you do. It is only when you have intuition that you will outdo others in business life; if you are a visionary and do not think of your purpose, if you do not think about how to start this affair with a clever gambit (in fact, not noticing at all the inner foreground, as it were.) {(This might be a shattering experience for the other character in my scene, the impertinent one. "Is this necessary, too?," he asks himself. "Not only the external prepotency, but also this inner swindle? This bee in his bonnet.")}

Sombart stretches in his armchair and, as accompaniment, makes great, big, round eyes. Face like Jack of Spades, he sucks a thin cigar-butt that he puts to his lips in a metal holder. Just once in a while he pulls his whole body together with a shake (in a movement that starts with the fists then jumps to the head): "Nnnno!"

The old grey-black professor in the huntsman's frock coat: "Ifffff I have underrrstood you rrright, Herrr, Professorrr, (he shakes the words out like a dog seizing another by the scruff of the neck and lifting it bodily off the ground) then that means . . . . But, in that case, I must say that . . . The findings of psychology cannnnot overrrthrow the irrron necessities of logic . . . I rrratherrr take the view . . ."

Best figure—the young servant[25] who, from time to time, comes and goes about his duties.

He sees these worthy men, most of them old, engaged in a mad altercation about something completely incomprehensible and which seems to him of no consequence whatsoever.

One observes his pleasure and composure when, with eyes, his young master gives him an order—the return to normality.

9
NOTEBOOK 17
MAY 1914 TO
AUGUST 1914 OR LATER

[Entries from this notebook record scenes mainly from in and around Berlin in the period immediately before World War I, although one refers to a visit to Wenningstedt on the North Sea island of Sylt, where many Berliners used to go on holiday. The final entries give expression to the general mood among the German population as war breaks out.]

Journal II

[. . .]

Sunday before Whitsun[1]

A strange place, Grunewald near Eichkamp;[2] areas for gymnastics and games. Girls in blue knickerbockers walk arm in arm. On a sports field two young people wearing swimming trunks are sunbathing. People are running, playing ball games, volleyball, two pairs are even fencing, with the aplomb of gymnasts. It's like letting town dogs out into the open air; a senseless urge to rush around breaks out; what they are doing is full of idiotic happiness.

Conversation in the tram: "But my great loves—and I have experienced some, Fräulein—were all Jewesses. Remarkable."

"Have you not noticed that each kiss has a taste of its own? A nuance like one from a bath of developing fluid?"

"What did your last kiss taste of, Fräulein?"

———————————

The female dancer:

Her face, seen in close-up, as surprising as a landscape.

Her complexion is like very light milky coffee.

Her mouth is cut too big for her teeth. When she laughs both rows of teeth curve sharply backward and a delightfully pointless, sensual space is left in both corners of the mouth.

———————————

The nightingale: (but it was a blackbird).[3] After one o'clock the street starts to go quieter. Conversations seem to be something unusual. Around two o'clock the laughter and noise down below has clearly turned into drunkenness, the hour is late. Around three o'clock (in May) the sky starts to go brighter. I lie down to sleep. Between the green curtains, between the gaps in the green shutters, a certain whiteness appears. I am woken from my half-slumbers by something coming closer. . . . The sounds shatter against the windows like flares at a fireworks display. As one lies there, the first impression is of a fairy tale. A magic bird, a bird from heaven. Now one feels that one has to believe in a metasensory realm: "So this really does exist," one says to oneself, immediately at home in this magical world, like a child.

———————————

Wenningstedt, second half of July.

In the baths everything goes blond before one's eyes.

The young woman lifeguard who takes your tip in order to reserve a hut for you despite the crowd, then declares she cannot square this with her conscience, but keeps the tip.

The tall man who boxes his way headlong through the surf. Women into their forties, already broad around hip and belly, but with little rounded breasts.

The senior teacher, a nutcracker of a man with a spiky beard who shouts rather than speaks, and then when the war threatens becomes quite quiet and ill-at-ease, with eyes that glisten, because he is concerned about his brother.

Berlin, August, war.

Mood breaking in from all sides; see article.[4]

The uprooted intellectuals.

Those who after a while declare that they have recovered their equilibrium and do not need to change any of their views, e.g. Bie.[5]

Next to all the transfiguration, the ugliness of the singing in the cafés. The state of excitement that expects a military engagement for every edition of the newspaper. People throw themselves in front of trains because they are not allowed to serve in the field.

On the steps of the Gedächtniskirche[6] during the service of atonement and intercession, lay-people start to preach.

Most of the marriages by special license take place in the maternity wards.

The women's clothing is simpler.

I hang onto the roof of an automobile that is traveling quite quickly in order to get hold of a special edition of a newspaper.

The appeals from the various professions: "Apollo is silent and Mars rules the day" is how the one from the Actors' Association finishes.

Only one newspaper—*The Post*[7]—is still ranting against the Social Democrats and speaks of the "enemy within" that in the face of the enemy without, one must not forget.

On one of the very first days in the evening when, on the street, a crowd surrounded someone reading out a special issue of a newspaper and a tram was trying to drive through quite slowly, the tall man, in his late twenties, shouts out: "Stop, stop, I say!" and waves his cane madly. His eyes have the expression of a madman. Psychopaths are in their element, live their lives to the full.

Counter to, and in parallel with, what Einstein[8] says: in the barracks, disorder, loss of inhibition, except when on duty. Dirt several centimeters thick, temporary beds, drinking. Stealing is rife. Cases are broken open. One can't leave anything lying around for one moment. He says he doesn't know what it is, but it has got into him, too: he doesn't need a brush but steals two, sees a third and rushes headlong at the man: "You've got my brush!" and takes it by force. The breech-blocks for the rifles of whole divisions are stolen, hidden for no reason, scattered about. Even the officers only say: "At least, don't go stealing from your own comrades!" Judges and lawyers say to each other, as if it were a matter of no consequence: "Was it you that pinched my belt?" One has the feeling that if we're not careful everyone will fall upon everyone else.

Einstein is wild with enthusiasm; everything else is obliterated. When he is sleeping with his wife, he is interested only in the stuff he uses to clean his buttons. He never goes into his study.

The lists of those fallen in battle: . . "dead" . . . "dead" . . . "dead" . . . each printed like that, one after the other—impression overwhelming. [. . .]

10
NOTEBOOK I
CIRCA 1915 TO 1920

[This is a small pocketbook that Musil probably carried about with him during his service as a soldier during World War I. His creative writing has been interrupted by the war but in this notebook Musil demonstrates that his mind is still turning over literary material. One entry refers to a character from his play The Enthusiasts; some of the entries written in the South Tyrol will be assembled in the novella "Grigia." These latter entries, like the work in which they will later be incorporated, are a secular meditation on love in which sensuous-sensual details are entangled with memories and disturbed by pangs of conscience. When Musil had an affair in South Tyrol with one of the local women (whose name, Lene Maria Lenzi, is actually recorded in the narrative of "Grigia") this seemed to sharpen his awareness of the intensity of his love for Martha. Love focuses his sense of the metaphysical; one entry records an encounter (perhaps based on a meeting with Martha during a brief leave from the front) in which lovers come together in sexual and religious union. This passage is taken up, with barely any editing, into the narrative of "Grigia." The mystical dimension is heightened by a reference to Martha's first husband, who is presented without preamble as a potential rival for Musil in the afterlife. Musil notes that mystical experience is not sustained in an urban environment but instantly awakens when a piece of metal dropped from a plane buries itself in the ground close to where he stands—death has missed Musil by inches. The loneliness of separation evidently provides an opportunity for him to think through earlier experiences that have helped to shape his life and personality: the excessively intrusive attempts by his parents when he was a young boy to make him moral, memories of early childhood in Austria, and repressed sexual *feelings for his mother when he was in his late teens. Toward the end of the notebook he enters some reflections on plans for two novels—*The Archivist *and* The Land over the South Pole—*that were never to be written.]*

War. On top of a mountain. Valley as peaceful as on a summer tour. Behind the security chain of sentries one can go for walks like a tourist.

In the distance, heavy artillery in a duel; at intervals of 20, 30 seconds and more; reminds one of boys throwing stones at each other from a great distance. Even though success is uncertain they always let themselves be tempted into just one more throw.

Shells land in the ravine behind Vezzena; ugly black smoke, looking as if it has come from a house fire, hangs around for whole minutes.

Feeling for the poor encircled hillscapes of Lavarone.

Cannon fire in the distance: one can hardly tell if it wasn't, far off, just a gate shutting with a thud or someone banging on a wooden threshing floor. But the faint impression is more contained, more rounded, soft but distinct. With time, unmistakable.

1.IV. Life unchanged as always (with the exception of the two days of patrol), dealing with the post, conversations on the telephone. {Card game}

3/VI. When one said to her "Come into the hay" she gave a merry snort with nose and eyes. Movements like those in the Comic Opera.

4/VI. Friend Joh. Jobstreibitzer. Sharp brigand's face. Intense eyes. "When the Major comes I can then tell him everything that I have seen and heard." A kind of professional joy in his face as he says this. A hunter's cunning.

"Getting back is a tricky business; I got out of one pickle, and was stuck straight away in another."

4/VI. When for the first time for a week I see Martha's writing (the address on an envelope) something goes from my eyes right down into my legs.

Knowing your address like some possession of immense value. As if I knew much, because I know that you are no longer living in hotels but in a furnished room. Accompanying this, the old, familiar fear that this strange life could lead you astray to. . . .

[. . .]

Girl on donkey, riding up mountain path. Gentle rocking motion of the whole upper body. Sits in wooden saddle, evidently not wearing any drawers. The legs indecorously drawn up high.

{6/VI} As they wait, the women sit right down on the ground with their legs up on either side, oriental fashion. The one with consumption is as white as a wax Madonna with black hair. She is delicate and jokes with all of the women.

In S. Orsola, a young Italian rifleman has been left behind. The patrol brings him in. Since the major first wanted to have him tied up, one of the N.C.O.'s fetches a rope. Swings it playfully back and forth, then hangs it over a nail. The lad trembles all over because he thinks that he will be hanged.

Animals being herded up from the Val Sugana. Young whitish-grey cattle with narrow skulls. Peasants who resist and are shot at. An elderly peasant with a long broad chin and big mouth, clean-shaven—brooding after breaking his resolve to defend his property to the last. Still determined to defend every inch should any kind of opportunity present itself.

8/VI. Many of the women here are liberal with their friendship, upright and kind. "Please come in," they say, or "Won't you let me carry your coat?"

[. . .]

9/VI. White-violet-green-brown stood the meadows.

Fairy-tale wood of old larch trunks, with a delicate hair-covering, on a green slope.

The stream falls suddenly over a stone like a silver comb.

In this mysterious nature, as if connected, our belonging to one another. The scarlet flower: miraculous knowledge that this place in a woman is only there to unite you with her. For it is so senseless, so impractical, a religious folly no less. How long it is since we were together: such a disjunction of belonging to one another, a declaration of bankruptcy, so that afterward one can only feel humbled and start anew. Must woo and win you anew after allowing that to happen. Vow.

I thought—after all—that I shall soon be lying there among anemones, forget-me-nots, orchids, gentian and (magnificent greenish-brown) sorrel. How am I to take you across? To be able to believe that this here is not the end. Am beginning to turn mystical. This personal providence that has steered my fate till now in this war has long affected me. How magnificent now: reuniting. Youth regained. The little blemishes that the years have wrought on the loved one are now taken from her. With hope of the eternity of a relationship, love is unshakeable. Who will permit himself to be led astray into infidelity and sacrifice eternity for a quarter of an hour? That can only happen when one uses an earthly measure. Love from the perspective of a worldly man.

No question about where the greater power of love lies. In constancy. Courage in the battle.

One can only love when one is religious.

Infidelity means the loss of eternal bliss; it is a breach of the sacrament.[1]

———————————

10/VI. The thought occurs to me: who, in the world beyond, has priority: Fritz or me? Why me then?[2]

———————————

11/VI. On the ride to the station my horse gets tired; this means a journey by night on a ladder-carriage to Trento. Accompanied by a fireman who comes from Lavarone and tells of the positive attitude of the troops there. It is only the riflemen, he says, who shoot at friend and foe alike.

Searchlights: they issue forth from the hair-covered silhouettes of the mountains—which themselves seem to be products of a wild imagination—like the eyes of fabulous snails on stalks. Emerge somewhere out of the flank of the beast. Wander about. Rest for a long time on one place. Rear up in high spirits and light up the clouds. In the train even the modest luxury of the second-class compartment seems extravagant. Memories of culture awaken.

Arrival in pitch-black Bolzano. The headwaiter from the station guides me to the hotel that has been recommended to me.

12.VI. City: barber's shop. Glass, marble, bottles, phials; in the shop windows, the thousand dainty accoutrements of a life of ease; nothing that has on it still the crust of earth, the dirt and discomfort of nature. City: bathing in the tub, cherries, strawberries, cucumber salad, jam, Pilsner beer, wine that doesn't taste of goatskin; girls with corsets and breasts in shadow-outline through damp blouses.

You: you load the space that surrounds you with a charge of increasing strength. The difference in intensity between imagining and actually being there becomes a joy that I feel.

A great cloud of grace, fragrance, benevolent order surrounds me. I enter the nobility of your body like a peasant. I am happy to make light conversation with you. You are the only one with whom I can talk this way. Comrade. Sole human being I love. Who I feel at ease with, wander about with, lie abed with; without a shadow of dislike passing between us.

But the mysticism is gone; does not keep in the city.

In its place, something hasty, furtive. The quick theft of this short time spent together. Earthly; as hot as sun on a clump of strawberries.

And still some lack of trust: I want not to be unfaithful to you—without seeing why this is so, merely because you do not wish it—and you might be unfaithful. You would be capable of this without telling me. This conception makes me—for whole minutes, in the midst of happiness—malicious.

And then you were standing at the station as I went off on the train, with your arm bent, like a flag being held aloft, with no concern for the other people, by overcoming the pain of fatigue forcing fate to make some concession; and, in this moment, I loved to the point of tears you and your whole life.

Mornas[3] in the country: it starts the way a sex murder might take shape: an inner pathway, otherwise under lock and key, is suddenly, compulsively, thrown open. In the truest sense, abandon and, a quarter of an hour later, complete certainty that it will be—

He loves one woman and cannot resist trying another. Fidelity makes the demand that the first be moved "hors de concours." The form he chooses for this, ecstatic love. By loving ecstatically he can give free rein to base lusts. If this is not enough, the humiliation of the second woman follows.

If one wants to have a correct idea of the sexuality of the peasants one must think of the way they eat. They chew slowly, smacking their lips, appreciating every bite. This is how they dance, one step at a time, and probably everything else is just the same.

{29.VI.} The German lieutenant comes to Pontarso with the detachment; our gendarmerie sergeant reports to him and wants to explain to him where the enemy troops are positioned: "Don't bother, we'll find them all right," he says, and goes straight off without stopping.

"Now, we're going to make things quite hot for them." What in peacetime is sometimes just loud-mouthed bragging is now becoming a reckless religion. [. . .]

{30/VI.} A pretty sight, each time horses arrive. Stand on the meadow, lie down. Always form irregular groups receding into the distance (as if according to some aesthetic law).

30/VI. Arrival of the dogs. The soldiers lead them on ropes without collars, in pairs or in threes. Among them are valuable hunting dogs and mongrels that look like evil little monkeys. From time to time the dogs in one or other of the groups will set upon each other. Some of them are half-starved, some refuse food. A little white one snaps at the cook's hand as he is about to put down a bowl of soup for him to eat and bites his finger half off. Rustan, the dog that belongs to this house, runs from one pack to the other; the response to his friendly sniffing is sometimes a wagging tail, sometimes a threatening growl. The small white dog, in particular, growls up at his throat; Rustan opens his eyes wide in innocent fear but is unwilling to make a run for it. We feed them with meat soup and a lot of raw meat; but they prefer bread, which is in short supply.

The detachment is led in by a cadet. [. . .]

4/VII. 3.30 A.M.; it is quite bright already but there is no sun. Cattle are lying close [. . .] in the meadows, somewhere between sleeping and waking. Lying in pleasing postures. One has a clearly defined notion of this dawning bovine existence.

Saw the bombardment of the Monte Verena fortifications by 30.5 [cm] mortars. Wherever the missile lands a fountain of smoke and dust rises up vertically, opening out at the top like a stone-pine. The sensation is quite neutral. Like watching a clay-pigeon shoot. Precisely the same when one sees Italian patrols down in the Val Sugana, or their trenches, or the train that takes provisions to Gobo each day.

Around the Austrian fortifications the shell craters from the last bombardment are as bright as mole holes.

An Italian heavy-artillery battery is trying to locate our mortar with shrapnel shells. Dust cloud in the air, no other impression. {(Bright cloud of smoke)}

Work being carried out on the Fabonti, paths well defended: surprising how this mountain was taken.

Celebration of mass in the field. On a packing case, the image of a saint and two candles. The Major somehow finds this event of sentim[ental] beauty and takes a photograph. [. . .]

Making hay: strange to observe this from a distance.

Mountain meadow. The hay has already been mown and dried, is being bound into sheaves and carried up to the top.

The girl (all alone in the meadow) always shapes the hay into an enormous bundle. Kneels right into it and draws the hay toward herself with both arms. Lies down over it on her belly—very sensual—and reaches forward into it. Then turns over right onto her side, reaching out with just one arm. Slides a knee up onto it.

It looks a bit like a scarab beetle at work.

Finally she pushes herself right underneath the bundle that is encircled by a rope and slowly rises to her feet. The bundle is much bigger than she is.

End of July. Death of a fly: World War. The gramophone has worked away through many an evening hour. "Rosa we're going to Lodz, Lodz, Lodz" and "Come into my bower of love." Interspersed with these the occasional Czech folk-song and Slezak[4] or Caruso. Heads in a haze of dance and sadness. From one of the many long flypapers hanging down from the ceiling a fly has fallen. It lies on its back. In a patch of light on the wax cloth. Next to a tall glass with little roses. It makes attempts to get onto its feet. Sometimes its six little legs are folded together, pointing upward. It weakens. Dies quite alone. Another fly runs up to it, then away again.

Peasant women in the hay: they lie there resting like statues by Michelangelo in the . . . Chapel in Florence. If they are speaking to you and want to spit they do so in a very refined way. They pluck out a clump of hay with three fingers, spit into the hole and stuff the hay back in again.

A peasant woman whom I overtake on the path in the valley has a button undone on her bodice. Through the oval gap the belly protrudes from under the coarse material of her shirt.

27/VII. I stand next to a fence and rewrap my puttees that have come undone. A peasant woman passes and says: "The gentleman shouldn't bother doing up his stockings, it'll soon be nighttime." [. . .]

I ask about a strange peasant woman who looks rather like an Aztec: "She never knows what she's saying. One word here, the next over the mountains."

3/VIII. Vielmelti talks to a big tall peasant woman who looks like a German widow.

"Tell me, are you still a virgin?"

"Yes, of course I am."

"You're still a virgin?!"

(Laughs.)

"Tell me!"

"Ha, ha! Was one once!" (And she blows into his face.)

"If I come to you, what will I get?"

"What you want."

"Everything I want?"

"Everything."

"Really? Everything?"

"Everything! Everything!"[5]

/VIII. [*sic*] Prisoners. They turn the corner with something of a swing in their step, come to a halt, and there's something of a swing as they lean their rifles against the wall. As they do so they perhaps tend to turn their head away a little. They are friendly and concentrate on what they're doing. The officer salutes, the salute is returned.

They are dead-tired. The officer throws himself down on the bed in the little room. I bring him cigarettes; he jumps up, smiles. I feel I'm in Italy.

Sentries posted everywhere; I constantly have the feeling that we've locked up a bird.

14/VIII. A prolonged yell: "Fire!" Everyone runs for cover; behind the house a rock is being blown up in preparation for building the command barracks. The first few damp strokes of rain brush over the grass. Under a bush on the other bank of the stream a fire is burning. Next to it, like an onlooker, stands a young birch tree. Still tied to this birch by one leg that is suspended in the air is the black pig. The fire, the birch and the pig are alone. {And a long pool of blood like a banner.}

This pig was already squealing when it was led up by a single man who was telling it to come along. Then it squealed louder when it saw two men running toward it. These squeals reached a pitiable pitch when it was seized by the ears and dragged along. The pain forced it along in little jumps. At the far end of the bridge one of the men reached for the pick-axe and hit it on the forehead with the sharp end. In the instant of the blow both forelegs collapsed simultaneously. Another squeal only when the knife entered the throat. Convulsive twitching. Death-rattle; like a pathetic snore.

3/IX. What is left of all that happened between then and now? The autumn evenings that remind me of the chinchilla fur;[6] the rooms, so pleasant as dusk falls. First Lieutenant Samsinger's quarters with their large, horizontally aligned rectangular window. Beyond it the bright-grey mist and everything arranged in such careful gradations right up to the brightness of the dawn. The brief bang of the mountain guns. A hesitation in the step when I heard this at a few paces' distance around a cliff and thought that a shell had struck there. The path down from Portella to the meadows; Randaschl's[7] shape, non-reflecting black against the sky that is somehow brighter.

A night ride on Lago d'Ezze; great at the moment when one turns into the rocky canyon and the black mountains rear up into the black night. {Landscape of the dead}

The horses pull harder than usual on the reins during night rides in the mountains. Felt fatigued up at the top and slept for 3 hours among the soldiers; next to an old rifleman, grateful for the warmth he bestowed.

The skirmishing, deaths, etc., that took place in front of these positions have not, until now, made any impression on me.

5/IX. On the Schrumspitz and the Scharzkofel, snow. Below them, golden in the sun, a field with sheaves of corn. And the sky, white-blue.

22/IX.

The piece of shrapnel or airman's dart[8] up in Tenna: the sound has already been perceptible for a long time. The noise made by a whistling or rushing wind. Getting louder and louder. Time seems to pass very slowly. Suddenly something went into the ground right next to me. As if the sound were being swallowed up. No memory of any air-wave. No memory of any sudden swelling nearness. But this must have been so since I instinctively wrenched my upper body to one side and, with feet firmly planted, made quite a deep bow. Not a trace of fright as I did so, not even any purely nervous response such as palpitations that otherwise manifest themselves with any sudden shock even when there is no sense of fear. Afterward a very pleasant feeling. Satisfaction at having had the experience. Almost pride; being taken up into a community, baptism.—

Wind in the maize fields. As if something were constantly running through them. Whispering.

Nice gesture: with a playful word of flattery I reach out to touch the chin of a peasant girl. She grasps my hand to stop me but as it sinks down keeps hold of it, smiling.

Shells: probably it is a howling sound. But that of a strong wind, not a hurricane. A whistling with scarcely any note in it.

10/X.

The sound that the projectile makes is a whistling—in which the "i"-note is not fully formed—that gets louder and louder then, when the shot passes over one, fades away. With big shells that do not pass very high over one's own position the sound swells to a roar, in fact to a throbbing of the air that has a metallic note in it. This was how it was yesterday on the Monte Carbonile when the Italians fired from the Cima Manderiolo at the Pizzo di Vezzena and the [troops on the] Panarotta fired over our heads at the Italian positions. The impression was one of an uncanny turmoil in nature. There was a rushing and roaring in the rocks. Feeling of malignant futility.

17.X.

Rowed out in the boat, tied up, plundered the fig tree. One has to stoop to slip under its branches. Then one can stand up inside the tree, the branches hang down, and a strange, sensual smell floods over one.

23.X.

Skirmish on a patrol. Wrapped in a scrap of {news-}paper on the table where we eat lie the dead man's few belongings. A purse, his cap-badge, a small stubby pipe, two oval tin boxes with cut Tuscan tobacco, a small, round pocket mirror. A heavy sadness streams out from them . . .

Italian postcards taken from the prisoners: unlikely that the desire of this people for battle is exhausted already; they portray their soldiers in the favored heroic poses; they are still just playing at being soldiers. Particularly nice, one card—the obliteration of the Austrian boundaries. An officer stands—the squad of men behind him looks quite small—on an overturned black and yellow post marking the border. They are, roughly, in the position of a fencer when he lunges. In the left hand the banner, in the right the sword pointing downward: he is shouting. Simply shouting into thin air . . . Another sign of how they still love the war is that their depictions of "la patria" and "l'Italia" are very erotic; always a young, soft, rather sad girl who actually doesn't look Italian at all. Here some feeling breaks through that was hitherto unknown.

I have intended, on occasions, to write about my life; today, after reading the second volume of Gorky's autobiography,[9] I am beginning to do so. I ought to refrain from so doing precisely after reading such a work since, in comparison with this wonderful life, my own contains scarcely anything remarkable. The actual driving force is to justify and explain myself to myself; I'm reluctant to investigate how that is connected with Gorky.

The psychologists distinguish several types of memory; when I was a student these were "visual," "auditory," and "motor." None of these three corresponded to mine, even though in the standard experiments I gave a motor response. But these are elementary. I can get closest to the description of my memory (and also of the conceptions that are generated by my imagination) in the following terms: in each instance I conceive things in a non-representational fashion, in terms of how things relate to one another, for example. I also seldom take note of details but, instead, simply of some general sense of the matter in question. From the formless relationships of things that are almost not there at all emerge, in a way that I have not analyzed, the statements that I make.

I think that this is also the reason why I find writing so difficult.

I say this by way of introduction because it is important for the evaluation of my memories. In "general" terms, they can be relied upon, in terms of detail, they are not invariably accurate.

My oldest recollections concern my nanny. Her name was Berta, she was tall, stout, good-natured, and told me stories that I dearly loved. This I know from what my parents later told me. When I think of her it is as if I could smell her. A good-natured {dry} smell of sweat of the kind that sticks to clothes that are changed neither too often nor too infrequently. In those days I must have been somewhere between four and six years of age.

I recollect vividly a second memory attached to smell: that of the chinchilla fur that belonged to my mother. A smell like snow in the air mingled with a little camphor. I believe that there is a sexual element in this memory although I cannot call to mind anything at all that might bear on this. According to the nuance of my memory of the fur it must have been some kind of desire. I also remember that the remnants from the sewing room, these bright patches of silk and wool and the contents of drawers filled with bits and pieces of every hue, were connected with notions of love. In my earliest years these were very strong. Their connection with my mother, however, was certainly merely a negative one. I know that I was always made to put my arms over the bed-covers when I went to sleep, and if I am not mistaken I was made to fear each and every contact with the region of the belly as something sinful. It may be that it was this that made every thought of the same parts of my parents' bodies quite horrific to me. And I believe that these precepts of moral hygiene came from my mother.

It is bitterness that I feel when I think back to this process of influencing. My parents were for enlightenment in every respect. The resolution with which my mother imprinted these injunctions on me stemmed certainly from concern for my health and nothing more. I was very easily influenced and all of this certainly left a very deep impression on me. Today it appears to me as much too powerful an intervention as if, over a long period, it had left me with internal injuries; it appears as terror.

I was probably 18 or 19 years of age already when, during a summer stay on the Wörthersee[10] (in Velden), I had the following experience: I happened to be on the diving board of the men's swimming academy while my mother was standing on the diving board in the neighboring women's baths looking out over the lake. She was in her bathing-robe and had already finished her swim. She had not noticed how close I was. Without being aware of the movement at all she opened her robe in order to wrap it round her in a different way, and for a moment I saw her standing naked. She must have been at that time a little over 40 years of age and she was very white and full and beautifully made. Although, to this day, it fills me with a certain appreciation, far more vivid is the shame-ridden and, I believe, angry horror that transfixed me then.

I can remember many details of the room I had as a child. I see its shape before me, I know where the windows and doors were, that it [had] a polished rectangular table with bare, planed . . . .

Character: if ever I want to depict a strong young girl who sees the world without moral diffidence and yet still in a girlish way, then I shall take *Wuthering Heights* by Ellis Bell (Emily Brontë), published by Zeitler in 1908, and show the girl who was able to dream up and analyze this.

Wuthering Heights: It is not inconceivable that this English girl merely wanted to show that this is how far a person of good disposition will go if all moral influence is withdrawn. The way that examples of noble and obscure origin are placed in parallel argues this interpretation. But this unabashed, girlish evil goes hand-in-hand with the little moral plot through thick and thin.

If she had a bit more immanent philosophy this would be a novel by Stendhal. But a trace of Romanticism always sticks to the figures and evil simply breaks out of them with immense force.

A tiny portion of irony and this housekeeper with her righteous misdeeds would be a figure of global dimensions.

Autobiographical novel:

Born in Steyr.[11] In fact, not quite there. But in the age of transfers, business postings, etc., many people are born in places that are not the same as where they first enter this world. His father in Temesvár,[12] for example.

Steyr a place chosen with great circumspection. Arms factory—social issues and arms race. Enlightened home in which one believes in nothing and offers nothing in its place. Stendhalian experiences in childhood, abduction from the Kindergarten,[13] etc. All later influences—the Institute,[14] technology, Bach,[15] Stumpf[16]—were then directed toward making a normal contemporary out of him. The mathematical outcome is the position as librarian in charge of the archive of newspaper cuttings (sanctuary of {newspaper} filth) and the last smile of his existence, when he is about to cross the border to forty, is the secret acquisition of a canary for his office.

Marries Frl. v. P. "because one simply can't have them all." [. . .]

Looked like a jockey, a Japanese, a young Englishman. Finally only like a person who, beneath the office-mask of subservience, is deeply preoccupied but no one notices this.

Narrative both interwoven and running in parallel. The long life and the short Stendhal period from the fourth to the tenth year. To be presented as if this period were the cause of his never amounting to anything.

Title: *The Librarian*,[17] *The Archivist*. [. . .]

Work into the novel all the philosophical and literary plans that have not been executed. The language with no punctuation, ethics, epistemology, etc.

He, too, was once married and wakes up in the midst of quarreling among {incompatibilities between} characters. He gets divorced again. Another adventure à la Lilli.

He gives expression to some of his ideas and others make a career out of these. In spite of this he has the feeling that something was lacking in himself.

Politicians: in comparison with active people like big businessmen, they are literati. And in comparison with literati they are practitioners. They combine the mistakes of the practitioners and of the intellectuals[18] without having a single one of their advantages

---

The Land over the South Pole.

Possibly: Germans emigrating.

The sorceress. Relaxing at home she wears no satin gown sown with stars but a thin, light-grey dress with dark-grey flowers and a black pigtail. When she is like this he is in fear of her, of the helmet of her hair, of the beautiful, sharp, aquiline curve of her nose, this crow's head that is nonetheless the beautiful head of a woman. And she is a sorceress as well, after all. She lays down the cards and sits up straight in her soft robe with its Greek dancer's skirt (close-fitting with many pleats). One could take the female, and would then come hard up against a magic power.

Archivist. It is the age of shady business deals. He spends a great deal of energy in convincing himself that he, too, has a right to be involved. Tries this, and is immediately taken for a ride.

The Devil. As housekeeper not some gloomy maid, rather the same species of woman but as a down-at-heel representative of civilization. The widow of a county sessions' lawyer, or some such person. Ran a gambling club with a rather shady side to it. Likes to wear green satin trimmed with gold braid and has brown hair, slightly discolored and singed. Like grass underneath stones. If one did not look closely one would call her ugly, i.e., she doesn't come into consideration. Not once in her life has she had any pleasure from sex. Simply feigned the appropriate feeling, now one would just like to drink a cup of China tea again, and then it's nothing special after all. She has never been able to direct her will toward something in particular, always doing only what happened to be on offer at the time. Perhaps he takes her on because he is running an inn during the summer season and perhaps needs a person who can add up and has a touch of culture. She then takes all this on as a duty affording no pleasure.

He has come to the study of theology only in later life. As a doctor of philosophy shortly before completing his "Habilitation."[19] And it was prompted by a vague feeling of opposition, a lack of a sense of destiny. By discontent in the nerve fibers, lack of concord between spirit and the needs of his nervous system. Through this he has a free relationship with the Church. At first he has received a joyous welcome (a bishop like Becher, an officer from the general staff with fancy ideas) because they saw in him a weapon to use against science; then the new Bishop (or the Bishop's secretary) "dropped" him, he became disreputable, and with some difficulty managed to rescue for himself the living whose obscenely red, pointed tower he had once seen. It is here now that he studies and is steeped in speculation. Carries on his work against secular scholarship. There are 307 proofs for the existence of God and 311 counter-proofs. He abandons the path of rational discussion, proves only the possible existence of God and draws the appropriate consequences from this. He busies himself at the same time with the history of the Church and is not in any way orthodox. He prefers the original forms when there was no dogma, only creation in ferment. Then comes upheaval with everything turned on its head. Support is needed. A new bishop summons him to a post at the University of Vienna. Here then— he enjoys the city, barber, tailor—his fate confronts him as he is on his way to see the Bishop and, as if for the first time, approaching from the Graben, stands before the Cathedral of St. Stephen. This is the religiosity of another, quite different, era. Beforehand, while still in exile, he reproaches his house-keeper for playing cards (patience). She shows him, saying: "Don't you notice how remarkable that is—like a row of cockroaches, all these spades."

He thinks that he will not be able to take her with him to the city, but she makes arrangements herself via the Bishop's secretary. Now she has found her life and comes into her own. It grows into a Catholic novel. He is assigned to the living of St. Ulrich,[20] he hates all this Baroque with its stone clouds painted blue-grey and the gold decorations that look as if they are from a petit-bourgeois chiffonier. He becomes aware of the way that the whole of present-day Catholicism originated in that era. All the hymns and prayers that seem as if they were specially composed for Catholic journeymen's guilds. He senses how the personality of genius is excluded from the Catholic Church and stalwart mediocrity is preferred. The Christian-Social Party[21] becomes a dreadful symbol to him. From a religious perspective he has nothing against bolshevism, but clericalism and socialism seem to him to be the great movements of destruction. He gets to know types like Blei, Gütersloh,[22] Chesterton,[23] Newman,[24] *Hochland*.[25] They, too, repel him. Meanwhile the woman grows, as somber as the Church of St. Stephen.[26] [. . .]

II

LITTLE NOTEBOOK
WITHOUT A NUMBER

AT THE LATEST
1916 TO 1918-1919

[Like Notebook I, this is a pocket-sized notebook that Musil carried with him as a soldier probably during the second half of World War I. The peripatetic account records travel under wartime conditions, wounded men, notes on the civilian population in the areas where he is stationed, what it feels like to be under fire from heavy artillery, a spell in a Prague hospital where Musil was treated for a severe infection of the mouth and throat. His duties as an officer involved the censorship of letters sent home by his men; this provides insight into their private worlds. Transfer to the military H.Q. of Grand Duke Eugen opens the Austrian establishment to Musil's critical analysis—he plans to use this in a novel, Panama, so called in reference to the construction of the canal that was associated with corruption on a breathtaking scale. In Vienna (where he goes in 1918 to be editor of a military newspaper) he witnesses revolution at first hand—one of his subordinates, Communist Egon Erwin Kisch, was a leader of the revolutionaries. Musil himself had some sympathy with their concern to rebuild society, though neither at this juncture nor later was he a political activist. In this notebook there are fragments intended for use in literary works (among these, a reflection on the planned novel The Spy) and others that will actually be used (the sensation of standing thigh-deep in hay in a barn is reproduced in "Grigia").]

Retrospective glances:
Alarm in Christof[1] after a long period of calm and adjustment to peace is like being attacked with a fist. These short commands: "Battalion alarm," "Prepare to board wagons," etc. The nerves, not at present used to such things, tremble. I was pale and agitated, without feeling any reason.

Boarding the wagons. During the long wait, groups of people, a few here, a few there, go off unnoticed; in the evening many of the squad are tipsy, some of them are completely drunk. The brigadier with his cane is at the station; he makes a speech. In the wagons a menagerie of sound. Otherwise well-behaved people are like animals. Good-natured persuasion and threats have no effect. We have the sliding doors closed. From within fists drum against them. At some of the doors there is secret resistance. Lieutenant v. Hoffingott who takes charge of the door closing shouts "Hands away!" and, in the same instant, strikes against the secret hands with his hunting knife . . This movement of the hunting knife was indescribable. Like an electrical charge released in a bolt of lightning; but with no flash, no lightning or the like—something white, decisive . . .

Journey in a third-class carriage, a blanket to sit on, journeying slowly with many stops—magnificent. Not a trace of discomfort. This comes from the complete change of mood within. [. . .]

Disembarking from the wagons in Prvacina.
   During the latter part of the journey already, airplanes out in force. On leaving the wagons, artillery fire all around. The horizon heaves. Long files of wounded in carriages and on foot. White bandages with red stains. An eddy picks you up, a disturbance pulls you into it.

Cerniza: [. . .] For the first time, the house with the fireplace. About 75 cm above the floor, rectangle four by two and a half to three meters square. In the middle, the open fire, over this hangs the kettle. At the top covered over with a kind of chimney like a bonnet. All round its edges, a red curtain about two spans broad. The hearth built of Dutch-red tiles. Blue, green and yellow crockery. Around the fireplace runs a bench, and there are low chairs. A young woman suckles her baby, a pretty girl sits next to her, a third woman is the innkeeper's wife. All this at the front end of an elongated room that is entered from the street.

Nothing to eat; wine that tastes like slurry.

Type of women in this whole region: their faces have a trace of Raphael and something of a pig. Squat, strong-man build, yet good figures. Stone Age women. Their waistline at the back is not drawn in but forms a pure oval.

A certain human, natural friendliness.

In the north and northwest there is a constant rumbling.

March off toward it.

Idiocy of the march, brooding in base inns.

On the ridge before Britof, the first sight of where the shells are landing, the whole of the slope wreathed in a cloud. That's where we're going in a few days.

In Britof, around my house, shell craters, neighboring houses have been destroyed. Reflection: it is like lying down at night on the train in a sleeping compartment, a marginally reduced probability quotient that one will wake up again—the danger is a theoretical one, the fatigue is immediate, one falls peacefully asleep.

Everywhere the Croat women, sitting by the hearths.

March down into the valley: departure in the {evening} twilight. Ascent. Then uncertainty of the height at the ridge. Then lines of men snake slowly downward. Below, flares rise up, rockets, the river lights up, trees—a fireworks display. The way downward seems endless. After the bracing bora[2] of the previous days, the air is warm. Drugs the senses. With this the stubborn feeling: you are stepping into your grave. Single, melancholic rifle shots; occasionally heavier fire—melancholic in the night.

Bombardment: summary: Death {sings here}. It sings over our heads, deep, high. One tells the batteries from one another by their note: "tschu," "i," "ruh," "oh"—"puimm." When a shell lands close by: "tsch," "sch," "bam." It snarls, once, twice, and leaps at you.

(W., owner of a building firm, says: "Inside, every person is, of course, a socialist. But one cannot put it into practice. If the social-democrat youth organization finds it obscene that young boys are being drawn into the fighting, it is pleased about [this also affecting] the organizations of its nationalist opponents.") [. . .]

This singing and snarling has a touch of primeval jungle, one feels all around—as one walks alone—the whirr of hummingbirds and big cats about to spring. For example, in the morning, with clear visibility, when all are safely under cover, going for a walk for no external reason. Yet with every step it is necessary to overcome oneself. Then, at some point, something passes by at a distance of 100 meters, the next moment a sensation of joy floods one's being. Death is something quite personal. You do not think of it but—for the first time—you feel it. Then, the way that, when contrasted with the receptive state in peacetime, the will comes to the fore in war, also offers us a small gift of comfort. (Will, in times of peace, directed usually toward impersonal distant goals, money, studies, etc.; in wartime toward stretching one's legs, constant decisions that closely affect you.)

––––––––––

Turudya. He had influenza and, because of this, he is intoxicated. The service-jacket is open, his shirt is open, the Order of the Crown is hidden in a fold. He is small, ugly; his face hard and impassive. He speaks quickly and at length; at intervals, repeatedly: "Benjamin! A grog!" One of the most famous old warriors of the Isonzo. Croat. Successes without heavy losses. Is always talking of the Battle of Plava, of the Hero of Plava; it is his latest "idée fixe."

Says: when you touch somebody, through the coat, you can clearly feel the cold if he is dead.

Praises the Italians, shines when he says they leap out at you, rather like panthers, when they attack. But our people are superior to them. Throttle them, bite their noses off.

––––––––––

Fire:
The smoke stretches out for hours in a broad swathe through the valley (forcefully announcing everywhere the importance of the event.)

––––––––––

Waxing moon: the thin sickle lies on its back among the brighter stars. Whitish. The stars shine powerfully. The night is blue.

When A. insists[3] that a thick wire would conduct electricity poorly, and one objects that the thicker the wire is, the better it will conduct, he says, after some hesitation: "Yes, this . . . is what people assert . ."

A. says: "It is unfortunate that I have no children, for this means that I cannot make proper use of my rich pedagogical experience. (His spirit has a need to exert its power but insufficient means. Either dreamer or pedagogue.)

The tooting of the telephone, at night, is like a steamer on the lagoon.

Prague:[4] magnificent rooms in the Hradcin: contrast with Italy; here, a wooden staircase winds upward with tight turns—as if laboriously chiseled out of stone. The anterooms are small and of no interest.

St. Vitus Cathedral: the catafalque of Joh. v. Nepomuk makes the strongest impression on the Captain, because the guide says that 4000 kg of silver were used in making it. "How much?" "4000," "4000. Ah, that is very interesting."

Coats of arms in the guild chamber: dark blue, silver, black, red, white— these are the colors of the arms. The last vestige of vaulting imagination has taken refuge in the coat of arms; secret handed on down, finally no more than secretiveness; perhaps that is also what coats of arms are about?

Faradization.[5] Suspicion of shamming, the young lad is faradized every day. "Hu, hu, hu, hu, ayaya, ya," he wriggles. One warder and four nurses stand around him laughing, holding his arms and legs and pressing the contacts to his body. He pulls faces as if he were laughing.

Surgery: unexpectedly I arrive in the dressing station. Fifty people in a room that is not very large. Doctors and nurses in white coats; naked, half-naked, clothed patients. With frozen feet, bare behinds, stumps of thighs, crippled arms. In the midst of unclothed supine bodies, people hurrying to and fro, fingers reaching for instruments, women's hands holding brushes, preoccupied, it seems, with some kind of painstaking, degenerate painting, others hobbling out and carrying things in—jumble of naked and clothed.

Nurses: They talk to you about anything at all. Syphilis, urine samples, enemas. They dress and undress you and are prepared to touch you anywhere. They seem to be immune to the accumulated sexuality. And yet they remain completely feminine. Have favorite patients, walk up and down the corridors with the young gentlemen, bill and coo. Sometimes the corridors are a positive pigeon-loft of courting couples. Soldiers, it appears, tend to make coarse suggestions, lieutenants reach into the apron pockets.

Col di Lana. In the course of the quiet dark descent from the Campolungo ridge, suddenly the {famous} mountain with its snow-covered, moon-white peak, shining in the searchlights. Then the dark {blackened} ruins of Varda and Arabba.

Conversation: Lieutenant W.: "Excuse me and please do not take it as an indiscretion, but tell me, how can one marry a widow?" I reply: "Being the first is everything—being the last is everything. In all events the latter is the more difficult . . . ," and so forth. He continues: "The highest that one can aspire to is union with a perfect being. To engender a child from completely healthy organisms . . . ," and so forth. Suddenly he says: "I gave life to my daughter twice. She was dying with diphtheria. I wrapped her in damp towels and fed her sour milk and full-corn bread, after the method of Dr. [. .] in Dresden. Today, at the age of fifteen, she weighs 59 kg." (Before that: "Do you know, my wife has a heart of gold and she's pretty, too, but we don't get on well with each other. She has no sense of higher things. I always pursued the ideal. I gave life to my daughter twice.")

Dead men: if someone is lying completely covered up or buried in earth and snow and you can see only the nailed soles of their boots: by the soles you can tell that the man is dead. (This most rigid of things, the nail on a boot, is somehow or other more rigid, and this shocks you.)

Transport of wounded men. Coming from Poland, days, nights, nights, days; a goods wagon with cots carries the most severely wounded who are not expected to survive the journey. A man with a severe bullet wound in the lung, and another whose hip joint has been smashed are carrying on eristical dialogues. One is Tyrolean, the other Viennese. The Viennese insists that the Tyroleans were no good at all in the war, the Tyrolean gets worked up about it. The Viennese with the bullet wound in the lung is constantly chipping away at him. Often the whole wagon can't stop laughing. Thus some minor matter in the foreground can hold up death itself. On arrival, the Viennese is dead. {Even better: have them quarrel over which is better, the Viennese or Bohemian cuisine. That's what nationalism is all about!}

When the train stops most of them start to bellow like animals, feel unbearable pain, and relieve themselves. Officers and men.

Prague, tram: a simple young lad gives the conductor (with a gesture that has a hint of the man of the world about it) a tip. The latter feels embarrassed, takes it, but does not thank the boy. He ought not to have accepted it, but he couldn't bring himself to do that, and this was the reason for his comical way out of the situation.

Prague. Walking around with A.; this being-tied-down makes me so tired. Characteristic of the life of my mother: living in such a situation, living in constant exchange with a second being. The stuff of consciousness become conversation, not will, not decision. Life's warmth surrounded by clouds.

(A civil servant in a position of authority who is on friendly terms with the family of his subordinate and takes a hand in the education of the children.)

Novel:

A misshapen person, awkward, crooked: a magnificent nude! Not to be made fun of but presented seriously.

Censorship:[6] Letter 1: with pathos: "Your father in the field." Card 2: to Spezi: "Minasch[7] good," etc.

"The pains in my rectum have disappeared."

Recurring very often, anger: "You mustn't let that woman, XY, back into the house. It is your duty, for love of me, not to have any more to do with X. You know how much such things upset me."

A great deal of anger.

"Let's leave the blue of the sky up where it is so that it will stay beautiful."

"Two things no one can change: people talking and the stream flowing."

"Beloved, precious, good children! This is to tell you that, with God's gracious assistance, my sick body will survive a little longer. Warmly cherished, good hearts, yesterday yet again I received no dear letter from you . . . . . Dear, precious, good souls have you received any . . .[8] to put on your cabbage?—Beloved, precious children, now with heavy heart I close my letter with many thousand heartfelt greetings and millions of kisses to you, my precious, dear good hearts, to my father, brothers and sisters and my friend, and, if this is God's will, wait for reunion with your beloved, good husband and father who never forgets you. Your good heart, Filipp. Please send an answer. (Blasius Filipp) [. . .]

Novel: in a second part, deal with the war. Part I up to the {partial} mobil[ization] {against Serbia} in Austria. The anarchist reconciled to the life of the community.

Part II begins with a flashback to this last chapter. That was still (only) regimental music. Austrian. He experiences the general mob[ilization] in Berlin. Here already show how different, how serious this is.

The "great experience." Depict this without criticism; the intoxication. Something that brings God close, the feeling of having to defend a Goethe and, and, and . . . that causes the inversion of concern about death into surrender to life—this is not a trifling matter. Defend it against other conceptions.

Enlists as officer in home guard. Linz, Galicia. Vast gossip factory. (Failure of the leadership?) Is wounded. On a train for the wounded. In spring

1915 moves to Tyrol. Begins to feel that life together is unbearable. Depression because of the loss of S. Tyrol. Different from the more expansive feeling in Germany. War starts up again. Palai, death among the flowers. Tenna, the airman's dart,[9] etc. Falling ill. Poor treatment by doctors (different experience from Galicia where no better facilities). Assigned to the Panama-Command.[10] Sister back with self again.[11] But relationship completely non-sexual. Only, on occasions, jealousy (shadow on tree, ruin). She is a nurse. Draw together Bozen and Adelsberg. {Politics!} Then Vienna. Now the obverse, civilian side of the war. Profiteering, inflation, etc. Literati, people like Zenker[12] and Karpeles.[13] Lack of national feeling. Political problems highlighting the importance of questions of the community as a whole lead to deeper insight than in the intoxication at the beginning. At the same time, disgust. Reversion to anarchist. {Into uncertainty: is it different in Germany?} At the end he returns to his laboratory and picks up the threads of the life that he left at the beginning of Part I. [. . .]

On reading Balzac:

The only way that his types take on significance is because he believes in the significance of the atmosphere in which they live. (These politically ambitious youths who look for a mistress of high standing, these journalists, etc.) To write about, and for, Paris: same certainty as that of belonging in the best society. This certainty is the good conscience of the descriptive writer.

Such a life's work would not be impelled by that kind of motive power today. Its place is taken by the subjective, philosophical formula of life, for example, Cyn[icism]-Ideal as with the *Enthusiasts*.[14] Into this, each figure is to be dipped. Then an atmosphere emerges around the figures, as if they were types taken from characteristic aspects of life.

Diary of revolution.

2.11.18: Up till now, no worse than the chronic national-political demonstrations were.

"Once there was a tense moment when a soldier was seen with an army revolver. He was forced to take flight, was pursued and this caused unrest." This newspaper announcement about a "Council of Soldiers" conventicle of dissenters in front of the Parliament is characteristic.

If the Dynasty[15] and the authorities had not positively surrendered power of their own accord, there might almost have been no revolution at all. The representatives of the sovereignty of the people moved only hesitatingly into the abandoned positions.

At the beginning, the *Workers' Paper*[16] left one with the feeling that it knew what it wanted; for two days now its attitude has gone limp, it doesn't have any proper theme. The party seems to be compromising itself through cooperation with the Nationals and the Christian Socials. One also has the feeling that planning and will are nowhere to be seen. The German Austrians are facing bitter retribution for always having been the people of government; they are politically disorganized and without national will.

K[isch][17] is making efforts to inject Bolshevism into the situation. "Are you coming to watch me?" he asks my wife today before the gathering of the Red Guard at the Deutschmeisterplatz. "{This evening I'll have 4000 rifles at my disposal.} There's a lot of blood still to be shed" he says with an expression of serious regret. (Four weeks ago he declared that the death of every extra man at the front was a crime!)

He thinks that he has not eaten or slept for 48 hours (but he was seen eating a meal at a café). He is quite hoarse, volatile, and one can't get two consecutive sentences out of him. W.[18] is at his side; in these two days he's become pale, thin, and quite hoarse. Apparently has no inkling of what he is doing, thinks that he is influencing people to take part in a peaceful putsch. He is prodigiously comical. K., by contrast, gives the impression of hysteria. Concerned at any price to set himself at the center of an upheaval in the affairs of state. Spirit of the spirit of Expressionism. [*sic*] (But perhaps such delight in theatricals is a precondition for a role in history.) What will be said to him is at any rate of importance to him; to give the War Press Office goosepimples is, at any rate, an ambition of his, albeit one that he has not admitted. Two proper anarchists are pushing both him and W. on in front of them.

In the evening rumor spread that 10,000 Ital. p.o.w.'s are advancing on Vienna. The Röhrich sisters have packed already. [. . .]

Fig tree on Lake Cald[onazzo].[19]

As I step under the tree: like a green silk petticoat through which the sun shines.

And the figs burst apart, flesh-colored and red where they have opened . . . : oh, so long without a woman . . . !

Bees, glittering as with honey or gold dust, hum with me. {(In this green light the bees glitter . . .)}

Before this: rowing on the blue lake. The long-range shells from Cina. V.[20] fall in the narrow plain between cliff-edge and water. A little further and one might land full on the boat and smash it to splinters. We might also be hit as we swim—just like catching fish with cartridges of dynamite. {Then, with belly torn open, we would flash silver on the surface of the water.} The plain is not so narrow after all, but . . .

———————————

It is generally held that, when faced with death, one enjoys more wildly, one drinks life more deeply. This is what the poets say. It is not so. One is merely released from a constraint, like a stiff knee or a heavy rucksack. From the constraint of wanting to be alive, from horror of death. One is no longer entangled. One is free. It is the splendor of being lord.

———————————

On the Pincio public square in Rome, at the back, lie two sarcophagus lids of stone. Stretched out full length on them are the couple for whom they were made. One sees many such coffin lids in Rome, but in no museum or church do they make the impression they do here under the trees where they rest as if on some trip into the country, seeming just to have woken from a brief siesta that has lasted for 2000 years. They support themselves on their elbows, looking at each other. (All that is missing is the basket with cheese, fruit and wine . .) The woman has her hair done in little curls—she is about to rearrange them—according to the very latest fashion before she fell asleep. And they look at each other {, smiling}, a long look without end. This true, obliging, bourgeois, loving look that has survived the millennia lasts for ever. It was set out in Ancient Rome and in the year 1913 meets the eye. I am not surprised at all that it lasts till now. It thus becomes, not stone-hard, but human. [. . .]

———————————

Geraldine Farrar:[21] for once in my life I should like to describe this. A voice rises in a lift, a woman's voice, of course. And the lift seems to rush madly up into the heights with her {, reaches no goal}, falls, balances in the air. Her skirts billow with the motion. This rising and falling, up and down, this lying quietly pressed up against one note, and this streaming away—streaming away and then constantly being seized yet again by a new convulsion, and streaming away again: this is lust.

It is that common European lust that reaches the pitch of homicide, jealousy, automobile races—ah, it isn't lust anymore, it is desire for adventure.

It is not desire for adventure, but a knife, plunging down from space, a female angel. It is lust that never becomes living reality. War.

The laughing horse: {cf. Roman Diary 7/}[22] displaying every sign of profound shock, someone comes and asks: Can a horse laugh?

One says: it neighs, it shrieks out, it trumpets, when it is touched inside the joints at the top of the forelegs. And shrieks that are snorted out in quick succession can seem like laughter. Defined physiologically—stimulation of the diaphragm.

Yes, but then it simultaneously takes defensive action, strikes out.

But if, after each occasion, it keeps quite still, moves its ears back, moves its eyes back, and positively *waits* for the curry-comb to approach the spot? If it does not strike out but hops, keeping control of itself like a person who must take care to avoid hitting, in the mouth or in the eye, someone whom he has got to tickle him?

When it plays, quite visibly plays, with the young lad who is combing it . . .

Oh, that is dreadful. That is uncanny.

Gridschi:[23] going to our mountain pasture. What enchantment.

Hay-shed: through the joints of the beams silver light streams in. Green light streams out from the hay. Under the gate lies a thick trimming of gold.

The hay has a sour smell. Like the heady drinks of the negroes (made from the dough of the breadfruit mixed with spittle). This thought gives rise to a real state of headiness. In the heat of the narrow room, filled with fermenting hay.

In all positions the hay takes one's weight. One stands in it up to the calves, insecure and extra firmly fixed. One lies there as if God's hand, would like to wallow around in God's hand like a little pig. One lies obliquely, almost vertically, like a saint traveling up to heaven in a cloud.

The mistress squats in a field of potatoes. You know she has nothing on but two skirts, the dry earth touches her flesh {not unpleasant and unusual}. Through her slim rough fingers runs dry earth. That is not the maid who with 20 others harvests turnips. That is the free peasant-woman who has grown up out of the grey, parched earth.

No artificial naiveté, please! Something mysterious is only of value when it arises despite the engineer's aura of precision. [. . .]

The mouse on the Fodara Vedla Alp.

Who placed a bench there? Whoever sits on this bench sits fast. The mouth no longer opens. Breathing becomes alien, an element of the surroundings (becomes, not the breathing of nature but—when it impinges on consciousness {when one notices that one is breathing}—something that is not done but happens, like pregnancy) The grass is still last year's, as anaemic as if a stone had been rolled away. Brushwood, knee-high, and alp. From out of this surf the gaze is hurled {time and again} against the round, yellow reef of the cliffs and, shattered, runs off. It is not immeasurably high, but above it is only the blue void. So barren and inhuman was {is} the world {still} in ages of creation.

{In this} the little mouse has arranged a system of trench-runs. Mouse-deep, with holes to disappear down and reemerge from elsewhere. It flits around in a circle. Stands still. Flits around the circle again. The human hand sinks down from the back-rest of the bench; one eye, as big and black as a [darning needle?], locks onto it. Is it this tiny, turning eye or the immobility of the mountains?

God's will is done? Or the will of a little field mouse before which, trembling and unprepared, you stand: {one dismisses the thought of God as something literary. The exact question is:} mobility of the eye—immobility of the immense mountains. {And {helplessly one notices:} it is quite the same}.

Foreword to the new edition of the novellas:[24]

What is wrong about this book is that it is a book. That it has a binding, spine, pagination. One ought to lay out a few of its pages between sheets of glass, then change them from time to time. Then one would see what it is.——

The only recognized narrative forms are either causal—the nursery tale and horror story—or ostentatiously aesthetic. As a third there is, at most, lyricism that got lost in prose. This book is none of these.

My body turns me around.

Involuntary characterizing of Francis Joseph[25] by Graf Kielmannsegg[26] who hoped that he would thereby prove that the Emperor always strove for what was good and what was just:

Much-favored turn of phrase of the Emperor: "He has deceived me." This represents the constant mistrust of someone who feels himself to be stupid.

A baronetcy was awarded to a high-ranking general through the intervention of the Minister for War, then an even more senior general complains about this preferment and the Minister for War enquires of the Emperor whether, in view of these circumstances, he will agree to [another] baronetcy. Answer: "You deceived me (over the first), (so) now the other person won't get it." [. . .]

The Spy.[27] Develop the figure of Achilles[28] out of the context of his epoch—the time before the War. The time that did not know death. Rushing automobiles, flying as popular sport, this, by contrast, was quintessential vitality. Crime for pacifists to say: "You met him in the brothel." This was how the present was cheated of insight. And people continue their existence just as stupidly as before. Sister, madmen, spying, these were A.'s discontent. He, himself, already believed that he was a pathological being. All human impossibilities that came up in the War he knew in advance, that was the seat of his abnormality. Now he understands the kind of person who is hero and profiteer at once, and that, too, is his abnormality.

Link immediately with the matter of the execution.[29] This was the form in which all people in those days used to stare at death when they had the opportunity. Staring at its insouciance. For what were the experiences that people wanted for themselves? A white tennis coat and a brown arm. An automobile, etc. [. . .]

12

NOTEBOOK 8
1920

[The "twenty works" of the title refers to Musil's plans for twenty publications—among these are seven novels.[1] This notebook confirms that Musil has significantly extended the range of his subject matter as a creative writer. In his twenties he had focused on a handful of people: on himself, on Martha, on close friends such as Gustl Donath or Alice von Charlemont. Now in the post-war era he takes in a broader range of characters and issues. Earlier his approach was via individuals' own accounts of emotions and ideas; now he concentrates more on external evidence—actual words remain important but so too are habits and routines, attitudes, institutions, the material and immaterial things that are shaped by, and in turn shape, the minds to which he wants to gain access. The characters he assembles have a powerful presence in their own right but also make up a catalogue of significant types.

Politics, in the widest sense, has become a pressing concern. The world war has shattered society and in doing so has called into question the political, social, moral, intellectual, and spiritual fabric of European civilization. To rebuild society will involve, of this Musil is convinced, the intervention of thinkers like himself. Central to this project of "Geist" ("spirit," in other words, the collective effort of those who think through what is happening to society) will be what Nietzsche described as a "revaluing of values"— seen from Musil's perspective this will imply, among other things, examining morality and moeurs with scientific detachment and identifying the wellsprings of mystical experience as they appear within the very self of this

*astonished skeptic. Themes of MwQ are already appearing: the Jewish Sec-
tion Head referred to will develop into Tuzzi; the woman who leaves an
item of clothing at her lover's house may be an early incarnation of
Bonadea; the prototype hero already possesses the enviable physique of the
later one; paranoiac fury against women (this may have been Musil experimenting with feelings that he observed through his contact with the mentally ill) presages the murder by Moosbrugger.]*

The twenty works
8
General Entries
[. . .]
Balzac loves his women; that is why they appear so seductive. The small
blond whore from —Street might be drawn this way. The one with golden
hair in ringlets. Childlike. [. . .]

These times: everything that has appeared in the War and after the War was
there once already. {There was a tendency:
  1. simply to let things happen.
  Absolute cruelty:
  2. Only experiencing the means. For the same reason, egoism.} It is simply that the times have decayed like an abscess. Everything must be shown
to be there already submerged in the novel about the pre-war period. Remarkable are then only the two weeks of ethical resurgence in between.
  Town and country. Bourgeoisie and workers. Parliamentarism and court-
aristo-bureaucracy [*sic*]. The businessman who in those days already knew
how to take advantage of the situation, but where hard work and correct
behavior held the upper hand. The clerical parties {the Bishop on behalf of
M.}[2] and the spiritual ultras. The mad overproduction of books and journals, etc. {later notes.}
  It is probably typical of a time of decay, of an epoch of civilization. Here
the cause of the decay is to be seen in the inability to give the times any uniformity.
  Perhaps, in the midst of all this, a utopian figure of some kind who might
after all have the prescription. Who is listened to by nobody; everyone races
past him. A figure from a fairy tale. {(Ach[illes] However, only in terms of
his potential.)}

The officers among whose numbers the late White murderers[3] could be recognized. Also the Napoleons who may, or may not, be on the way. Probably not. Why is it, by the way, that I believe the "probably"? Do not historical epochs return again? But it is partly the case, in economic terms for instance, that they do indeed return. Is a particular evolutionary direction involved?

This City of Vienna which, in the old days already, only pretended that it was an imperial city, has now found her role.

Draw Slav and Hungarian politicians as well. Before mealtimes (decay) one heard things differently. {With Harrach.}[4]

But this grotesque Austria is nothing but a particularly clear-cut case of the modern world. [. . .]

───────────

Construct a person from nothing but quotations!

Make another one, a "Goethe-Man," to whom some saying by Goethe really does occur on all kinds of occasions, like Walther. Whose very life is arranged accordingly.

───────────

{K}[5]

Set up at least 100 figures, the main human types in existence today: the Expressionist, the Courths-Mahler,[6] the profiteer, the psycho-pedagogue, the disciple of Steiner,[7] etc. Then have these figures crossing each other's paths. {Find out the psychological method that will stop these figures' becoming blurred in the reader's memory.}

───────────

Basic idea: to set up the Empire of the Spirit which, of course, does not come about. (And does not even occur in Part 1 of the novel—or only in an unsatisfactory prototype.)

The times viewed it as if in a play. On the threshold of a new form. The old tragedies fall by the wayside, etc. [. . .]

───────────

Bureaucracy of a monarchy.

The lack of initiative and of a personal opinion within the monarchistic bureaucracy. To do what one considers right is a presumption. This right is the Monarch's alone.

Extract from Erich v. Kahler: The characteristic idea that one had of Austria before the War was the lack of any pronounced image. No particular flavor, no concept, no slogan was attached to it. "A form of diplomacy which, in subtle and circumstantial forms that had been tried, tested and revered over a long period, tended rather to defend what existed than . . . to promote something that was necessary." "A government governed a country which it was scarcely able to remember any longer." "The cupola of state blocking out the light of the age, of the world" lay over all independent efforts. "No people, no idea, no solidarity of the urge to press onwards and to engage in natural activity." [. . .]

{K}[8]

The task for Germany would now not be the League of Nations and compromised ideas of civilization, lacking any originality, but going beyond the state, critique of the state.[9]

All horrors of the War are excusable when set against the indifference with which one has left the states of Central States[10] in post-War misery. And the indolence (which is completely understandable given the way the superstructure that is the "state" switches off the moral initiative) with which one hides behind cash. Here once again, money shows its capacity to leap into the breach left by moral decision making. [. . .]

Program: 7 Vols.

Spy
Panama
Archivist
Catacomb
Devil
Buffer novel
South Pole

The following table from the *Enthusiasts* is generally valid:

Creative people	Uncreative People
Undetermined	Determined
Trans-truth	True
Trans-just	Just
Unfeeling dreamers	Empathizing
Metaphysically unstable	M[etaphysically] stable
Excluded	Included
Passive out of distaste for what exists and for improvements	Active
Despising reality	Real
Anti-ideals	Sunday-ideals
Anti-illusion	Illusions: realities
[. . .]	

Signature of the times: the average person is torn open to the depths of his being. (War, Red and White terror, imperialism, Czechs.) One of the most powerful epochs in world history. In the process, hitherto unparalleled potential for communicating what happens. If no "New Man" comes out of this then this hope must be relinquished for a long time to come. "Experimentum crucis"[11] for God. [. . .]

Miraculous rescue:[12]

Matthison has lost his way on a walk in the mountains, finds himself (in June) on a snow-covered scree-slope full of crevasses, cannot go any further, has his last supper—bread and wine, and lies down exhausted on a slab of rock. If he sleeps on into the night he will freeze to death in the night-frost. It is half past three. He is woken from his slumber of death by the loud cry of a bird of prey that almost touches him as it flies past. By the time he is completely awake the bird is already a long way off, but its cry in his ear makes him think it is an eagle. Chamois-hunters later confirm that the golden eagle is not rare in this region. Reinvigorated, he struggles onward and after an hour reaches the bed of a stream that takes him down into the valley.

(His supper reminded him of the last meal of the heroic host of Thermopylae. Perhaps this link comes via the eagle of Zeus.) [. . .]

German type.

Herr Mass, the very image of power. Chubby cheeks, nose with broad bridge. Figure of a heroic tenor. Head and shoulders stiff and erect. He holds a chemical patent, and has made a success of a small factory, intends to buy himself an estate in Upper Austria and, without doubt, will make it into a model enterprise run along the most rational, industrial lines. That is the man who, on his own, would reduce a primeval forest to kindling. And yet I have the feeling that behind all this power lies a nervous restlessness. A primeval strong man doesn't exert himself more than is necessary; at other times he is lazy.

She has one lung, two children. Pinched, and small next to him, scrawny. No longer young (older than he is). Everyone tells her how handsome her husband is. She thinks, lives, only for him and the children. Goes tripping along next to him. He is certainly faithful to her because, if he were not, a door somewhere that needed a bolt would not close properly. This, naturally, is scarcely protection against an occasional fling in male company. "The only books I have are good ones," she says, and lists authors whose names I do not know.

Viennese type: the Baronesses Glaser, daughters of the former Minister of Justice.[13] The younger one is dressed like the picture of a fashionable painter. Yellow in yellow [*sic*] with delicate violet buttons, or such like. They value that which is famous; Fulda[14] is just as interesting for them as Klimt— as long as it is someone who is being talked about. This tendency stems directly from socializing, from drawing up of lists, from the passion of the social hunt. From there, a path leads to the Concordia[15] that is an imitation of a society that imitates.

Eccentrics: A woman, in her fifties, inherits about 300,000 crowns. She uses the money to start legal proceedings against all the people whom she dislikes; the remainder of the money that has not disappeared in this fashion she squanders on celebrations, meals for children. Afterward she returns to living in a house with no furniture, sleeps on the bare earth, goes around dressed like a scarecrow and is very contented. [. . .]

The female nomad. She runs away from home in the spring and wanders the countryside for four months. "You can find something to eat everywhere you go," she says. She sleeps in barns—without asking first so that she won't be raped. [. . .]

Modern youth: girl, 14 years-of-age. Beautiful long plaits. Dresses like a Russian revolutionary. Has read *La Ronde*,[16] indeed has read everything. Kisch asks her if someone is in love with her. No, she says, a man means nothing to her. She is in the fifth class of the grammar school and will be going to a children's home as a tutor. [. . .]

The Jewish Head of Section: French jokes with a touch of smut. Oblique, ingratiating posture, jacket a little too long. His singing voice is a pleasant, very melancholic baritone. The release of sentiments through music allows human beings like this to stay as stupid in human terms as they actually are.

Lunatic asylum: Hungarian bolsheviks are accommodated in the psychiatric clinic, some as inmates, some as warders.

Another case: a patient unleashes a polemic against the lecturer who is explaining his physical symptoms and is clearly in the right. [. . .]

Achilles: it is best to have A. as a modern philosopher since this reflects what is unsatisfactory and unsatisfied about the times. He has successfully completed his "Habilitation" and this has exhausted his sporting instincts. He writes the *Unions*. In precisely the same way (excl. woman) that he is revolted by the thought of writing a novella of causal psychology—that he would do with much greater success and where it would be possible to demonstrate the extent to which such an enterprise is possible along scientific lines. Is unsuccessful. Does nothing more. {Thus} he retains his importance, but does not produce a work.

Technique: in order to anchor characters firmly in the memory of the reader, one must guide them into situations that make the latter wish, demand, fear, etc. It is best to set up such situations by starting out from the main characters.

———————————

Beginning possibly as follows: Achilles loves an ambitious woman. He doesn't actually like ambitious women at all but in his situation {of indolence} he has a feeling that it might do him good. In the process he sees all the striving and pretence behind ambition today. Constantly peering behind the makeup. And he says it. Thus it is a constant struggle. This provides the background for a quarrel over a treatise for the Academy with a professor who is the reason for his taking a period of leave. The woman would like to see him as a Humboldt;[17] he explains to her what science and learning are today. The woman sets up a salon: "Salon Apathy." This is frequented by creative writers and others. She is the widow of Erich Schmidt.[18] [. . .]

———————————

A *spiritual point of focus:* party in the evening at S[amuel] F[ischer's].[19] Begin with the visitors getting ready. A woman who is still irrigating [some matter of personal hygiene?]. Achilles gets to know the literati there. Describe the desperate inability to engage in real conversation, whether spiritual or pleasurable.

In the middle hangs the Van Gogh.

Heddie[20] treats Achilles in the rather cool manner that ambitious Jewish women sometimes adopt toward Christians because they are in fear of them.

The line from Sam's chest to his belly is like the white belly of a frog seen in profile, but one might just as well say "like that of a nightingale." Apart from A., he is the only well-dressed gentleman. A. is aware of such things and notices the minor departures from good taste. A tie that is a little too large, a cuff that is too narrow in relation to the arm.

In conversation, he displays the tastes of a man of science—this includes already the theory of the *Spy*—and loses touch because of this. Having got into a rage on the way home, he takes an automobile, finds his books lying open and feels disgust at them as well. He remembers that he has to pay the call the following day. Takes out the letter of recommendation, from some Geheimrat;[21] here he is described as an experimental psychologist, which is not correct; it is the first time he has noticed that this does not tell the truth.

In the living room a woman-friend has forgotten her bodice. He writes a few words for his servant in case she comes—he does not want to speak to her. Gets

his outdoor clothes ready, has a bath, spends the rest of the night. . . . . , while
Sami sleeps with Heddie in a sea of scents from the garden. [. . .]

Achilles: one of those people involved in individual sciences who have no
sympathy for this culture. With a head for facts and unbridled logic.

> A supporter of the diffuse.
> Clear about the nature of illusions.
> Animal with the glint of a star.
> A beggar journeying through chaos.
> Morality of creativity.
> On occasions passive.
> The sensuous experience is immediately integral to a spiritual one.
> > Things lose their color and shape in his presence. (And only re-
> > cover them in the perfect tense.)
> An "other" feeling of morality (Gliding)
> Inhuman. Heartless.

Good and evil are indifferent in themselves but, at the point where they
touch society with its diametrically opposed point of view, there develops a
difference in "electrical" charge and in moral movement. (Potential) Crime is
a legal concept but not a moral one. What people do is affected either by expansion or, as the case may be, by being pressurized by the world (The world
streams in or one streams into the world.): {Moral imagination is created.}
 Up till now, morality was static. Firm character, firm law, ideals. Now dynamic morality.
 Or: good and evil are only lower steps on the way to morality.
 The person who is absolutely bad is one who contributes nothing to creation.
 Someone who steals for the first time may be close to God as he does so.
 Difference in electrical charge, difference in temperature, difference in al-
titude—these release power, movement, work.
 This being-in-the-right or in-the-wrong in relationship to the world pre-
supposes that the relationship to it is a moral one. This must be introduced
in another way. Basic fact of sociability.
 Ideals: producers of illusions.
 One can view the "ought" of the individual as a function of society, or
view the "ought" of society as one of society: [*sic!*] this is a social viewpoint.
Or one can view the "ought" of the individual and of society as a function
of the individuals: individualistic way of seeing things. Or both as a func-

tion not only of the individual but also of society: a mixed way of seeing things.

There are virtues, goods, values that can only be explained as a function of the individual or only of society. And some whose value follows on from both.

The objection to be raised against this morality of creativity and of spirit is that it pays no heed to the happiness of "Im-pro-Visation" [*sic!*]. That which Müller[22] names "rhythm."

Mystics to be depicted in the *Spy* already. For rationality and mysticism are the poles of the time. For example, a mystic may, when still a child, succumb to an illness whose nature is never completely cleared up, like Pascal, for instance. Then he is told that he has been bewitched, then released from the spell, by some woman-prebendary who wants to take revenge for criticism that came her way because of some slander. Finally, Father slaps her face and brings about her moral volte-face.

Read the mystics.

Leave space to do so. Climax probably as late as *The Devil*.

Spy: don't forget that the execution of the carpenter[23] touches, as well, mystery of death.

Thoughts and people: "The wish is father of the thought." Profound wisdom! One only learns what one already knows. All learning is a relearning. Make someone enjoy a particular subject and you will give him knowledge of it. {Envelope of feeling around concepts. Sudden breadth of vision.} These, spread over millennia, are fragments of an insight that never became theory.

Collect! Possibly: understanding is not the only means of orientation and communication, there are older forms. Shared delight is related to these. Sometimes the older form breaks through. Those are mystical moments.

How does one incorporate? A person who has one of these thoughts also has similar ones. Just as, here already, a group has been hastily gathered together. A bundle of thoughts, then, with the appropriate ways of behaving, one doesn't need to offer anything more of a person. What remains of almost every person is quite normal. But, in the plot, one must depict that also in the following way: people only appear when their cue occurs and leave morality behind; they are tuned to a wavelength. [. . .]

Agathe: at school she found learning dull and difficult. Now she hears the sentence (wish . . .) in isolated emphasis and suddenly she becomes a seer, she understands herself, etc. Reads Maeterlinck. I say: M. is, in himself, much less than what he represents as the inheritor of a tradition. She does not read him as we all read him—poetically—but as a messenger from her homeland. Nor does she have all the possible interpretations at her fingertips, rather she is helpless in the face of the experience. She is not enraptured, but rather—in terms of my pseudo-theory—the person in whom the older level is less repressed. {At the end she marries a person who is not very spiritual at all.}

The Greek with whom Clarisse elopes: hypnotizer-type. In order to permit this type to come fully into its own one must place him in between the psychoanalyst and the others. That determines another beginning.

Devil-novel: Agathe at the height of mysticism. Her second marriage has not lasted either. [. . .]

Land over the South Pole:[24]
  Regeneration of the fresh water hydras. One tears them to pieces: sex-murder for the purpose of procreation. Or one cuts off the head of a tabularin polyp; according to the way one puts this in the sand (with one or the other end pointing downward) the body grows another head or the old head a new body. Means of experiencing variations on the sense of selfhood.
  The public prosecutor appears as missionary of European morality.
  A woman, parts of whose former brain were used to regenerate the legs. "Déjà connue" in the soles of the feet. Eroticism of such a woman.
  Those gentle people who, in order to avoid conflicts, leave their opponent not only their cloak but an arm or a leg as well, and then regenerate it.

In describing the landscape, etc., represent the external conditions as well in a way that corresponds to all this potential for variation.

We do not pay sufficient attention to the capacity of nails and hair to regenerate. In spite of this they are very much part of the personality. [. . .]

———————

Achilles: the following, too, would make a beginning:

Achilles was a logistician. But it is a very difficult task for any creative writer to expound to his nation what this involves without being buried in inattentiveness. Even explaining "logician" is difficult. . . .

. . . And now begin with Aristotle. [. . .]

Philosophy: at once the highest and the most indifferent matter. It is easier to describe A. in physical terms. His big, deep chest is the delight of every tailor. The materials sit well on him. The figure is Greek but with {stronger} muscles; and the muscles cylindrical, conical, and not dumplings one finds in the Renaissance.

That wouldn't be worth mentioning if fate were not involved. For he had, of course, all the success with women that he wanted; but success came much more quickly with women of a particular kind. Women that have the need to lean their cheek up against a strong manly chest; that need not to be able to get their arms around their lover. Decent and sentimental women as a rule; good, simple, upright women. His fate was overburdened with experiences of such kinds. There was nothing at all about him that was ugly, exotic or quenched the imagination.

Here, of course, the literature that is currently being read has a part to play. It is ridiculous when the newspapers, in their envy, want to make out that literature is—just literature; it is a ghostly form of life. [. . .]

———————

The influence of creative writers has declined, among other reasons, because in former times they were just about the only people who spoke to the public. [. . .]

———————

Bank manager: in order to have an idea of how he is when he is not at work and what is his attitude to such things as art, philosophy, etc., ask the question: "What mode am I in when I'm not working? How indifferent to me are art and philosophy whenever they are not related to my work?" With the exception of music which takes a rough hold. And here and there a book that touches upon a problem that happens to be personal. Everything else only goes via the medium of what is currently being discussed—society.

This is where the opportunity comes from for presenting art as a barrow-boy would, explosivity of youth. [. . .]

———————————

Present time: maliciousness of Fate that it gave Nietzsche and socialism to one and the same age. The ideology of race, cult of the aristocratic, the anti-democratic movement are tolerated on Nietzsche's account. If even R.M.[25] goes so far as to use an expression like "the new spiritual aristocracy of mankind" it is for this reason. The antinomy: "Society, like any organism, consists of brain and entrails" and the mistake is to believe that "the entrails could think and the brain could perform metabolic functions." (R.M.) On the other hand, however, the brain does not think as it should and the entrails are also the source of spiritual malaise. In fact no one has yet set this on any other basis than Nietzsche did—Anti-Nietzsche and individualism-socialism.

"The masses are dull and are beneath the level of any kind of awareness and so they should remain. I am against enlightenment; but I support efforts to create the best and most hygienic conditions for the belly-people. That is the duty of the brain-people but, on the other hand, the brain-people have, on their own behalf as well as Nature's, the right to an existence in which they are isolated, set above others and possess the power to command," *Council of Art and Culture*, Volumes 11 and 12.[26]

Since those who represent spirit would not be satisfied with Hiller[27] in command or, indeed, with anyone else, "Nature" has made an arrange-ment—a selective arrangement—that the people of spirit who She allows to take command must necessarily possess the capability of wresting command from the mob by subtle ploys.

What was there in France and Scandinavia in the place of Nietzsche?

Isn't it the case, after all, that all countries are more or less in the same state? So there must be a more general typology. This is probably the "mod-ern man."

Another very amusing thing in the *Council of Art and Culture* is the link-ing of activism and romanticism: "Next year's issues . . . . will . . . . . be de-voted to the romantic (border-)sciences that have already been taken into account and provide a layperson's introduction to the essentials of astral sci-ence, a short course on graphology, physiognomics, etc. Existential counsel-ing on all questions of inner culture . . . . ." It's still the same pot into which they've all been dipping their ladles for the past 30 years. [. . .]

{Panama}

If one had little confidence in humanity and considered that the only real possibility was to choose the lesser of two evils, then it was possible to envisage the project of Central Europe with a curtain of non-German protective states attached to it. Given the competition between rival super-states, that was the sole possibility. It was even possible to think of a German hegemony according to the principle: "If it is necessary for one of the two of us to be in a bad way then it should be you." It is certainly the case that we were guilty of all those mistakes that come about through a failure to make sufficient effort to put ourselves in the other's shoes; we behaved with a rather delicate indulgence toward the peace-generals of Brest Litowsk; we thought to ourselves: "It is not wrong to make the agitators do a little work then whistle them back into an evolution that has lasted for generations." We were careless at the expense of other people. But when we had a care and gave ground to them we made the mistake of the pacifists who conjured up our misfortune without being able to control it.

One may presuppose that the same situation obtains in all cultural states and no one has the right to make reproaches, with the exception of a bolshevik and he must not count his chickens before they're hatched.

The question of guilt is a different one with respect to the French, the Czechs, etc. We had to reckon with the sad case of old and seemingly incorrigible Europe, they had fresh clay to work with. We could find no way out of a situation of total constraint, they made nothing of an opportunity for creativity. The Czechoslovak state is far more immoral than the old Austria.

Wilson: with his 14 points came the failure of scientific-academic understanding that is fettered by counterarguments and finally dissolves in countless conferences. Versailles was intellectual history[28] from 1830 onward.

In spite of all the national reproaches that are made, one should not forget how Germany has failed too. A failure so great that here lies a justification for the Entente. So our position is not to accuse but, without deflection, to warn. [. . .]

Church in Gaaden.[29] Old stone nave with complicated cowl-vaults. Baroque as far as halfway up. Blackish-brown wood of the altars goes with the expanse of Baroque white in the statues, columns etc., to form a unity that is imperceptibly tinted by stained glass windows; tinted as imperceptibly as if one were looking through colored glass oneself. This shaping of space is impressionistic. Behind the altar, a big {narrow} glass window with Christ ascending. Blue background, the massive yellow gloriole like a garland radiating swords. Here, as it narrows, this artistically tinted space reaches the pinnacle of ecstasy.

Church chairs with fine inlay-work. Motifs from biblical history. With perspectives that verge on the Expressionistic.

Unleash all *criminals* that live within us. The rage of Moosbrugger to plunge a curved knife into someone's belly is comprehensible when one sees these dolled-up forms go wandering past.

The repellent effect this has on many people is toned down simply by making it comprehensible. In earlier times the narrator turned away in horror (and still related what happened); perhaps it would not be such a bad idea to do something similar today; for the better reader one can do this in an ironic way. [...]

Building style. Why doesn't our epoch have one? Because everything it covets is "anti-house."[30] Travel, automobile, spas, hotels, theater, sport, dressing well, sleeping cars, Pullman train. These are expensive luxury articles that demand money and, on the other hand, the place where they are enjoyed is anonymous, life in a hotel, for instance. What the hotel looks like is of no consequence, it must merely be "de grand luxe." Of houses, one only desires comfort. Man in former times, lord of the castle as well as city dweller, lived in his house; life and desirable objects came to him. In Biedermeier[31] times, too, people received visitors, today one just has a big comfortable place to live.

All efforts to create a building style are artificial.

Culture: the phenomenon of the blossoming and decay of great cultures has not been explained. Here Spengler has an excuse. The biological explanation that a race exhausts itself is not a persuasive one, for the bearers of culture are a varying mix of races.

But is it not possible that a culture collapses because its spiritual core is exhausted? After all, the individual person dies as soon as tension leaves his soul. (Pensioners, members of a toppled régime.) Then there would be nothing impelling one from within, people try out this, then that, without any sense of deeper involvement. This makes people weaker.

One cannot say that of the present day. Work, knowledge, inventions, technology, etc., are passions, tensions. Stupidity off-duty—and one asks for nothing more than that—is dionysian release. The conversation in the inn yesterday couldn't have been more stupid but everyone was doubled up with laughter—they had all come in order to double up with laughter. Our serious interests are remnants of an earlier epoch. The art of the working man is explosion, sneeze inducing: snuff. Hygiene for the soul.

It is only when this generation is faced with matters of life and death that it is capable of being profoundly shaken.

In the place of *Catacomb* one might choose the name "Trappists" for us. We stay silent when they bellow. We are monks whereas they work. (Would there have been monks if there had been much more "culture" in earlier times than in ours?) [. . .]

Heiligenkreuz[32]

In Fullenberg I lay in a field of clover under an apple tree—these two delicate pleasures mingling in my nose, an idyll of milk, butter, eggs inside me.

Romanesque: barrel vault. Gothic: pointed arch.

Aisles divided off by whole walls resting on short, heavy pillars. It was only in the Gothic period that all walls dissolved into pillars; in their place, the buttress walls outside.

St. Christopher on a gold background, but this is not smooth rather as a landscape of wonderful depth and delicacy.

Romanesque: big, smooth shapes. The oldest glass windows with figures but no color. This draftsmanship tolerates white light. In the wall, a hollowed-out secret staircase leading from the living space to the chancel. Somewhere hidden in the stonework and suspended like a cage, the wood-paneled area for prayer and hymns.

In the late Baroque period the heavy, tensed shapes dissolve. Magnificent ceiling in the library (adjoining room). Only one simple scroll traced over the white "plafond,"[33] as if by Mozart.

Plague columns: original shape an obelisk; draped; then all that remains is to twist clouds around it.

Draught-board made in black and white ivory with seal-shaped draughts, irregular discs of amber, the color of dark honey.

Silk Gobelin tapestry from Flanders, not of any special artistic beauty but of great rarity.

They preserve objects from ancient Roman excavations, hairpins, rings, little oil lamps like those in Aquileja. Old flooring put back together again to form ornaments, (3 rings and suchlike)—work performed with miraculous sureness of intuition. They have bits of kitsch such as a {silk} embroidery, displayed pretentiously (under glass with curtain), allegedly done by Maria Theresa herself. But, given this successive layering of generations, even I have the feeling that, if I were Abbot, I would not correct this lack of taste.

Many things by the lay-brothers Giuliani[34] and Altomonte.[35]

Library with endless precious things, manuscripts, and incunabula, the original editions of the Classics, in long rows next to them, give the impression of cheap trifles.

Wonderful notebook in black-white-red, its surface executed with Japanese assurance. Incomprehensible—the loss of such formal assurance. (Attempt to solve this puzzle: what an undertaking such a manuscript is! A work that takes years. One makes preparations, looks at precursors, in short, compulsion to follow tradition. Incunabula can scarcely be distinguished from manuscripts. As soon as things move quickly, as soon as the production process is accelerated, the work of preparation falls by the wayside and so does the tradition. But if an "artist" today wanted to make such a manuscript he would put in too much that is artistic, that is personal, it would be overburdened with imagination or simplicity, for the question would no longer be, "How is this done?" but "How am I to do it?")

. . . The brothers leave a partly intelligent, partly average impression. It must be difficult for them to get along with each other. The old {former} parson for whom the most interesting thing about the whole library is a Lord's Prayer in all the languages of the earth.

This life is so beautiful that nothing can be superior as long as it is sealed in with itself. As soon as it becomes exoteric—sermon or the Abbot attending a Catholic conference—imposes itself on others, tries to improve the world, etc., it becomes stupid and sinful!

Picture by Jordaens:[36] Moses striking water from the rock. Moses with horns of light (small, pale, fluffy), face rearing up toward the point where the picture explodes. Naturalistic faces, greed, longing, hope for water—in all possible variations.

A butcher rents a room that I can't afford. I don't let it trouble me. Suddenly it occurs to me how *enormously patient* we are as we allow ourselves to be forced down from the level of a spiritual elite to that of pariahs. [. . .]

Spy. Possible opening: Moosbrugger: Achill[es] in association with a person whose speciality is scientific enquiry into this pathological crime. Jew who can allow himself the luxury of such an unremunerative life's work. Ach[illes] knows full well where that leads, but show the impossibility of obtaining sufficient information about such an individual case in less than a year to satisfy the scientific conscience. Through this specialist he comes into contact with all the people in neighboring fields. This method makes it possible to offer a tenable representation of all this digging around like a mole in widely scattered fields. This case could make Ach[illes] into a Titan. He could blow into all these little fires, shake the public conscience from its slumbers, etc., even though he is only a young university teacher. Why he doesn't do this is interesting, too; reasons why he refuses to be the "man of enthusiasm," the "man with a mission."

After a storm that has not released the pressure in the atmosphere. Air superficially refreshed but beneath this a thick mass, as hot as a greenhouse, that positively stings; whether by chance or not, the animals seem freed from inhibition. In the matted undergrowth of the ditch, a snake, bigger than any I have seen in the wild. As thick as my wrist, grey-black warty skin. A deer on the road, twenty paces ahead of us, steps back into the wood but only to fetch her two young. Off into the cornfield. At each leap they spring over the ears of corn like fish jumping. Delightful shape of the deer; virgin mother. Countless buzzards or small falcons, plumage glinting with the patina of antique metal. One drops down quite close to a resting reaper. Another lifts a mouse or frog high into the air; the thing wriggles too much in its talons, it stops in midair and gives it one, two blows with its beak. In the wood a gigantic hawk, broad in body, looks like those big, furry butterflies.

Constantly the feeling: if everything in Nature is adapted to cruelty how can one *take responsibility for* the abolition of war? Melancholia that a defeated man must think this way. What a monstrosity that human beings want to emancipate themselves, unnatural, it needs a positively anthropocentric, metaphysical belief. [. . .]

Bolshevism: it is true that Tolstoy is considered a saint, but one admits that, if he were alive, he would be seen as a counterrevolutionary; for dogma has it that "who is not for us, is against us."

Three currents in questions of culture: requisition the positive values of bourgeois culture (probably as represented by older heads). Destroy and totally rebuild. Art, etc., is no subject for reflection at all.

I call this "barbaric." But these are young people. What was I like then? Neither in philosophy nor in creative writing did I consider that any predecessor had written anything to match my as-yet-unwritten works. The older I become the more I begin to appreciate. Give power into the hands of the kind of young people I once was and they will, of course, proceed with total lack of respect and no thought for tradition! It is very doubtful that they will later come to appreciate older things because this, after all, involves a degree of surrender, of compromise. It is clear that they will continue to believe dogmatically in the circumstances that formed the context for their power, in the political dogmas of bolshevism, that is.

Consequence: if you are convinced that bolshevism will come, then break with yourself, become young again and "limited-without-limits."

Not being able to decide to end up in personal nihilism, the condition from which one had started out in the capitalistically monarchic state—this might be the end of the *Catacomb,* the end of Achilles' story. This person exits the stage. New ones arrive. [. . .]

Coitus: the breaking of the eye, the convulsive letting go by the body, the lips forced open, letting the breath steal through—this whole mime is related to that of catastrophe. This is one of the disturbing charms of the process. Similar to the change that happens when a person stands there, healthy, strong, proud, then the next minute has a bullet in his body and belongs to the dust in which he is writhing.

Aging woman. Her reaction, "I have given you everything, you used me up, now I'm just lying here," is perfectly justified. She has given up her hope, her expectations and erotic imagination. She is reduced to utter penury, whereas the aging man establishes anerotic connections between himself and life.

Racial theorists to be sketched. Chamberlain,[37] for instance, to serve as a model. He and his kind were of great interest.

Technique for <u>Catacomb</u>: visualize the most general types and bring them into play—for example, the few ideas that motivate the times. (Nationalism, philosophical idealism, women's rights, socialism, etc.) In short, make an ideological image of the times sketched in the crudest terms. That is the mechanism. Everything else is just a ripple on the waters. [. . .]

Inhibitions in courtship where men of experience are involved do not arise as a result of uncertainty vis-à-vis the woman, but uncertainty about themselves. Will I be up to the consequences if I now press the button? He offers soul, breaks into the woman's inner prison and then hesitates. And looks into the eyes, at the skin, of a chaste woman, seeking there the only, oh-so-silent answers that can give him his bearings. It is like moving forward in the woods, rifle in hand, before the encounter.

Business people. Robert Müller, too, confirms from his own experience how stupid they are. They take weeks to comprehend some project and then ask questions like mad. Calluses on their hands from their greedy grip on money is all they have.

Cata[comb]: attitude of the creative writer in the political arena that of a powerless observer. What Becher once said (greater tasks), Kisch will say tomorrow. Account for the realm of the non-ratioïd; show its extent, its importance; let us call it "soul" without assuming that a "soul" exists. [. . .]

Spy—Part 2. The criminal develops into a normal person while the latter develops into a criminal.

Have Achilles do all those things from which reason and conviction hold me back. [. . .]

Cecil Rhodes.[38] Study this figure!

Bismarck Study!

South Pole. Men whose whole figure expands during an erection. Grows four times as long and four times as broad.

Spy: everything is done incorrectly. Starting with the incorrect view of classical writers and philosophers. One surrenders not to the authority of the dead but to their thousand living mediators. This leads to hatred of all the hubbub that is life. But at last take seriously the rejecting of all that there has been up till now! That would be Achilles, that would be the kind of setting I must find for him. The first phase lasts from the chaotic, from being unable to wake up, from the unexplained contradicting of people in general to the point of surrender to people in general during the mob[ilization][39]—in other words, another blunder, still another blunder. All his lapses belong here. The history of the times from naturalism to expr[essionism] belong here. [. . .]

[. . .] This woman: sensual, a drinker, monstrously jealous, beautiful. How is it that she captivates men? Probably first through the charm of the unusual, of life on a higher level. Sensual women are more diverse. She plays the woman of spirit, the misunderstood woman who has been hurt by life. Then she will make these average men experience loftier emotions. Simply being in possession of a beautiful woman acts as a tonic. Then she flatters by her passion. {Thinks this stupid man is wonderful.} Here she is in tune with a universal principle—flattery. Why don't these men marry her? Perhaps she would cost them their severance pay. Mysterious resources, an occasional mysterious disappearance, the link with the former life that has not been completely severed, give rise to mistrust of a kind that one doesn't even need to examine in detail.

How is it possible to understand her impetuosity? One possibility would be to conduct a pathological investigation: drinking, lack of inhibition, sense of inferiority. Another: simply to accept this; such people are facts. Those men, too, who brawl and stab.

Use her in one of three ways: either Achilles—who, after all, noses such women out—lives with her, she shoots at him, too, etc. This has the disadvantage that Achilles' series of adventures gets too long. Second possibility: a hero of the later novels? It's not suitable for *The Archivist* so, if at all, for *The Priest*. Third: a minor figure. Usually one who plays a role involving the inhibition of what is good, by being average. By the way, he came to a dreadful end. And now one weaves the story into the narrative like a digression. This has the advantage that all that needs to be said are things that really interest me. In sum, such stories should form the fabric of the world against which the story of the special people is played out. They stand, as it were, in the place of descriptions of landscapes. [. . .]

Wasp attacks a butterfly from the front, bending herself over its head like a tiger, her claws in the nape of its neck. The butterfly struggles, and tries without success to shake her off. The wasp's body just bends and stretches as she carries out her task. [. . .]

Meaning of the dinner jacket: men to whom quarreling and rivalry are natural indicate, via the mask of the dinner jacket: "We are one company, we wish to belong together (in order to avoid any quarreling)." [. . .]

Short woman who reaches only to my chest. Her eyes that are positioned so far below me are somehow merely objects, peer out of the bush like an animal, a prey. Immediately a note of cruelty is struck. Don't recognize as fellow human, as spirit—no such thought at all. Here is an access to the brutality of the man and to the woman who seeks out this brutality. The sexual is only secondary, primary are war, animal, hunt, hostility of alien biological species toward one another.

Frau Tildschi. Female aesthete. Has a theory according to which she applies a different perfume to every part of her body. Takes artificial flowers with her when she goes into the countryside. A low-grade aesthete is indeed a rewarding figure. Is masculine with a tendency to tyrannize women who please her, keeps men who have a tendency toward homosexuality. [. . .]

An old man in a threadbare "Emperor" coat picks up, on a sidestreet, a tattered shoe. Lads, playing football there, shout after him: "Hey, you, leave that shoe where it is, it's mine. Give that shoe back!" He tries to walk away, the shouts of the lads pursuing him: "Just look! He's taking my shoe . . . Hey, give back that shoe straight away!" They start to run toward him; then he comes to a decision and, with as casual an air as possible, brings the stolen article back. But now the owner says: "Mister, you can keep the shoe as far as I am concerned. Just keep it." He doesn't say thank you, turns around again, examines the shoe as he walks slowly away and conceals it under his coat. [. . .]

Role of the creative writer in politicis. Powerless onlooker. What B[echer] once said, Kisch will say tomorrow.

Expression: Strapping smell.

Spy: might also start in this way: I relate A 257[40] (The Inn in the Suburbs).
   Then I say: "This, precisely, in every detail, was what Ach[illes] dreamed."
   (At this stage he already knows about Moosbr.) This somehow makes for an uncanny, mysterious opening, one doesn't yet know how that communicates with the narrative. It is only then that there appears the rational problem of being alone on the "orbis rationalis."[41]
   Ach. drives in a friend's 90 horsepower machine to the execution. The delight of his epoch in technological records. But as he does so a feeling: the quicker he rushes, the more he accelerates the execution.
   Say before this: it was the dream of a logician.
   Ach. is a member of the bourgeoisie. His father was a professor, but his uncle and grandfather were factory owners, shareholders of big enterprises. But no longer so rich that imagination is not reined in by financial considerations. If death occurred during this journey: how unprepared! [. . .]

13

NOTEBOOK 9
1919 TO 1920

[Much of this notebook is concerned with the figures for later works. In fact Musil elsewhere refers to this notebook as "The 20 Works II (characters)." The figures, all drawn from life, include a bohemian artist, a university professor, a demimondaine, an aristocrat turned black-marketeer. In two of the preliminary sketches we recognize a resemblance to a person who will take on plastic form in MwQ: May/Meh, an aging prostitute, is forerunner to the much younger and more attractive woman who becomes Ulrich's mistress; Peppi will become Rachel, the serving girl. (Peppi, too, will appear in MwQ—but as a horse pulling an aristocrat's carriage!)]

—————————

Reports of battles; harmonizing with each other: the singing or whistling of the shrapnel; the deep howling of the shells, probably like a U-sound.

Everyone's former life seems sunk into the depths.

Soon jokes and conviviality are part of a routine.

An ensign goes for a walk outside the trench, he is struck by a shell—a direct hit—only the hands can be found; the experience is quickly forgotten.

To perform bodily functions, the opposing sides grant each other special permission. (Rifle butt raised)

Clouds of shrapnel like bright swarms of doves.

Civilians till the battlefield. Civilians and doctors are soon as courageous as the soldiers. An advancing line of skirmishers, seen from a distance, looks like a group of people who seem to be slowly looking for something.

When, in the tolerable security and conviviality of the trenches, the order to advance is given, this is like an order to calm, unexcitable people to become passionate.

9

We journey to Prad.[1] Sun is everywhere; the woods seem to blossom. Autumn glows.

Some three hundred paces away on the other side of the road the Platzer girls are leaving the church with their mother. Little black shapes. I do not know them, my companion is telling me something; we look up. Suddenly, in high, high spirits, one of the girls waves her arms in our direction.

Strange impression; I know that the girls here have rather a bad reputation and there are some illegitimate children; but something wells up and overflows in a person, sympathy breaks out, even if this is frivolous, and something human touches you.

We meet a peasant woman, perhaps in her late thirties; she is old before her time, as these women are. We look at her, she looks at us, all at once she gives an embarrassed greeting. It is very moving to see stirring, in this lifeless, stiff apparition, as neuter as grandmothers, a little trait of Eve.

	Contemporary figures[2]	1918 — 1920	
Anich		Fischer	
		Holitzer [sic]	
		Kratochwile	
		Kralik[3]	
		Meh[4]	
Servants			
Average		Neurath	Zerner

Holitzer[5] is behaving well. As if to avoid trampling on anyone. In truth, in order to hide his bestial egoism. Thinks I have some influence with Billy;[6] helps me into my coat, looks at me warmly when I speak; I know how pleased he will be when he has reached his goal, to be able to say: "I could have crushed him with one blow of my fist, and I was always itching to do so."

Gentleman in the region of 50. His father made a fortune.

Collector. Why?

Metaphysical formula: "I please; what I want I achieve."

What is his attitude to religion?

He boasts of his strength. Brags about boxing people on the ears. But also boasts that he was cowardly during the war.

Pleasantly filling out the place he inherited.

As philosophy a not entirely unwitty epicureanism. Talent ought not to lead to needless exertion.

Has seen a great deal in his discipline. Has a delicate relationship to paintings.

Has no love for the ugly spiritualities of the school of today. Wants to "give pleasure." Feels comfortable as an arranger of processions. He derives his right to do this from the sense that it is only those with much talent who are allowed to exert themselves. In an epoch like the Renaissance he would perhaps have made a good painter's assistant because his soul is at home in that epoch. Thus he is a real Concordia[7] type.

He is an Anti-Semite. Probably a touch clerical as well. (Fear of death)

Since Billy keeps him wriggling on her hook, he notices her attachment to her father and that her mouth is not soft but, if anything, rather unfeminine.

What led him to Kraus?[8]

He's a real Viennese type. Doesn't like the Germans. Speaks, for example, about how well the film "J'accuse"[9] was made, the two friends in the trenches have dents in their helmets and are covered in dirt. A German film company would have put them in shining new outfits.

Although his conversation is often clever and witty he talks about a film full of the worst kind of sentimental rubbish (a young student loses his wife to another man. When he is a famous professor she is brought to him—as the corpse of a prostitute—for a demonstration class; when the students see how deeply moved the professor is, they tactfully take their leave . . .) and says in all seriousness that nothing in life has touched him as deeply as this ending.

Was very happy when he was allowed to join Archduke Salvator's[10] social circle. Was not received anymore after he appeared in a nightclub.

Can't abide the Prussians and the Japanese, this Irish captain about whom H. is so enthusiastic. How much pleasure that gives when, in someone who comes from a completely different place one suddenly finds the same attitude and, of all the possible parts of the world, precisely this combination, Pr. and Jap.—"These unpleasantly busy people."

". . . . . . the princess, in rich regalia, was already lying in state. This youthful being shook me to the core in a manner that I am incapable of describing; to me she seemed to be not of this earth and later became my inspiration for Saint Ludmilla.

After I had paid my respects to the grief-stricken father, Prince Schwarzenberg, and his brother-in-law, Count Dietrichstein, who both desired to speak to me as soon as I arrived, I set about making the cast for the death mask, a task that went well. I was so painfully affected as I performed this task that I was unable to pay an evening call on Count Dietrichstein as I had promised." Though this is by the sculptor E. Max Ritter v. Wachstein (82 years of age, Prague, '93) it could have been by H[ollitzer].

Zerner.[11] When sitting, the young David. Broad, sloping shoulders. When walking, he is almost flat-footed, his legs slightly crooked, gait shifty and ingratiating, briefcase under his outstretched arm. Has already published several short pieces on physics, but no doctorate yet. Typical second assistant.[12]

Is bad at developing his ideas.

Why has he become a Communist? Ask him. What is it that drives him to politics? Probably Jewish eagerness for reform.

No: ideas! "We oppose those who think they possess the absolute," "creative man," "the only true revolutionary." "Our ultimate goal is permanent dictatorship by revolutionaries." "All thinking is ignited by the imperfection of existence and strives toward action." "Capitalism consists in the dominance of past work over present." (This youthful feeling in "past"!) Work of a given kind is valuable or unnecessary, with a common measure (money), different tasks cannot be measured. The revolutionary proletarian becomes a bourgeois after the victory: natural law whereby human beings petrify into specific shapes. "The nature of the bourgeois is his will to petrify into shape, the social expression for this is the state." His petrifaction is not the meta-natural one of the "Idea" but the natural one of death; this is why he cannot be dealt with by evolution but by revolution. Conservation of the existing culture (school!) means repression of the creative. "The scientific-academic way to express this is as follows: it is the task of the school to educate youth to aspire to the educational ideal. (For this, too, what was said about the state is valid: 'its unchangeability' is not the expression of eternal value but the petrifaction of death.)"

The preparatory revolution[13] must create a society in which, confronting the mass of the citizens whose formal expression is the given social order, is an independent group whose "raison d'être" is to overcome the existing order.

Der Strahl,[14] Vol. I, No. 2.

He came to the C[ommunist] P[arty] via the youth movement.

Main characteristic: a certain lack of respect, probably via the "Idea." [Idee] Or rather, a certain freedom despite respect, for this he does feel, toward Neurath,[15] for example.

"Brooklyn Bridge" by Müller[16] pleases him greatly.

Without any embarrassment he asks Martha to pass a card on to Fischer.[17]

Fischer.

A strapping lad, this Kant[18]—hasn't a clue about the "a priori." Now at last I'm writing my work on biology. Bring some order into this biological midden. "A priori" constructions of space in painting. Dreadful distortion of the subjects for the portraits. Probably calls this: "synthetic portrait a priori." Leaves his wife all the worry. Isn't debauched but as far as his needs are concerned—books, coffeehouse, smoking—he doesn't deny himself anything.

Buys and sells books. Dips into an enormous number of them.

Is for the war, communist, Prussian-conservative, in cycles of a few weeks. All absolutely honest.

For a week, gets up at 6 a.m. on account of some piece of work that he then abandons.

Was a great brawler and student duellist.

Anich[19]

Courtly, kindly, lazily absentminded. Cunning and "laisser aller." Sells cured tobacco, a cut of indifferent quality; but then, on the other hand, Southern Slav hospitality. Doesn't like the Jews. Likes "nice" people. Has a very fine instinct in this regard. Seeks out the best of these for social contact without then starting any proper spiritual exchange. But can tell very nice little stories. About his servant, about the "Green Cadre,"[20] etc.

In the golddigger situation after the formation of new states[21] he, too, makes something of himself; he becomes a politician; but has none of the silly pretensions that take the "legislators" more seriously than the artists and other mere mortals.

He looks so nice in his thick, laced-up fur with its many little cloth buttons that seem like the breasts of a virginal little pig.

Neurath.

A hint of the fighting stallion "ex cathedra." But explosively energetic. "After their spiritual collapse, they . . . invited Max Weber[22] and me to tell them what they could believe in. I wasn't able to help them either." In this there's a good deal about what it means to be a professor in Germany.

Has a notebook with very many energetic entries. Matters dealt with neatly struck through. Is apparently always somewhere else with his thoughts. Then he quickly pulls some kind remark out of his pocket: "Please give my regards to your esteemed wife" even though we were together with her only a quarter of an hour ago.

Is now up and about a great deal, setting up contacts in all directions.

May.[23] Here at last a counterpart to Balzac's courtesans. But she must be made younger.

She showers a man with sacrifices; if he did not deserve it then that was his fault. But this common change of polarity is not the characteristic feature but rather the kindliness with which she registers it. The same optimism in life that guides her business dealings.

According to Ea,[24] she says of herself that she has never heard any declaration of love because she couldn't wait that long.

It is said that her mother hired her out as a prostitute when she was still a young girl. In spite of this she loves her mother and declares that mothers can be whatever they like to their children. Perhaps because what her mother did with her was actually something she liked.

Has never used contraceptive aids; on a much-traveled road nothing grows.

If a man pleases her and then merely touches her, she's lost. Brothers and husbands of her women friends, however, trigger an inhibition that is stronger. (This may mean that not only physiological libido is at work here but also one steered by the imagination. This, by the way, is a question that requires *further study*.)

If she loves a man, she waits on him hand and foot.

She has no habits of her own, only those of each of the men. (This is rather amusing as an active counter-species to the Genofeva type.)

After the death of Lieutenant K. she remained chaste for a whole year.

{I could introduce her in an episode in the *Spy*. Excelsior. Still married to the Khedive. Episode of love with staring into the brilliance. [*sic*] Brilliance not yet been exposed as sham. Then, in the disillusionment after the collapse, becomes a bourgeoisie.}

Servants

Peppi accompanies the young ladies on a picnic, waits on them there till the early morning, sleeps for one or two hours, has to go back while the young ladies lie down, in order to wait on the pensioners, and is happy. She is the same age as the young ladies, as pretty as the young ladies. Takes pleasure in all the receptions that are given in the young ladies' honor, where she waits at table. Smiles radiantly when she sees the pretty costumes. Stands happily, peeping through the door. Such people are not to be helped in terms of material advancement but through pleasure. She is hugely exploited, slaves away the whole day but because there are diversions in this household she prefers it to another where she would not work so hard but which has no variety.

As a dog loves his master. That is really the position of the master. Marie[25] was also like that. But she also collected her trousseau by stealing and she was a socialist.

If the young ladies are to be all decked out in their finery, Pepi [*sic*] goes racing and shooting all over the place.

Kratochwile-Löwenfeld.[26]

Uncultured: nobility before the Counter Reformation. The "beautiful," frivolous person. The beautiful person is the human being without crutch or buttress who yet has a certain sense of who he is.

Example: how loosely it actually fitted—that old form of life that seemed so stable; those cavalry officers who have become racketeers.

Main vehicle of his career: the disinterested willingness to oblige with which he binds everyone to him.

Such people are like servants as soon as they have to write a letter. That is the difference between the "beautiful" people of today and those who belonged, for example, to the "ancien régime."

The splendidly true maxim: "racketeering is an educational experience."[27]

[. . .]

Power politicians. Civilian species: morality of duty. Treitschke.[28] History is made only by personalities, never by the mass. The mass is always common (even when it is made up of noble individuals). Ideals have to be raised up before it; must be there before it comes on the scene; kingship, order. There is only the one excuse for parliamentarism—that the kings are not proper kings. This type is not servile at all; in these circles there is much freer criticism of the monarch than among the bourgeoisie. In dynastic terms they are actually only "faute de mieux"; their ideal is the hero-king. Ideologically they are weak, the ideological imagination of the times is not working in their direction. This is why they have about them an element of mendacity, of aestheticizing. They are strong not when they portray their "Idea," but when they criticize the existing order. Distaste for the speechifying, the push and shove, of parliamentarism. "The lieutenant with 10 men,"[29] however annoying the maxim may have been, was not completely false. This is also the source of its anti-Semitism.

Naturally this type is also found among educated military men. The other type, purely a military one, is the Napoleonic. Philosophically less well-founded than the first type, it has as its sole principle a general disregard for all human beings. So to speak, that of speculation in a falling market.[30] Pessimism. In unrefined specimens, a natural roughness, in more sophisticated ones, an inborn skepticism. The stick is stronger than the idea. The pleasure in this can be primitive or complicated. Everyone imagines that, {with a few, but} good troops one can overrun the world. Despises the civilians, i.e., the powerless mass. This is the true man of violence. He grows up in the cadets' quarters. His weakness: if he is as rough as a boxer, he is usually stupid; if he is shrewd, he has {already} been corrupted by civilian influences. [. . .]

Clergy.[31]

Perfectly understandable train of thought. Making the members of the proletariat covet things without giving them the capacity to make use of what follows on from this is Jewish agitation. All that they can demand, Christianity already demands on their behalf. Human beings are brothers. They are not, however, equals. Order must prevail—at best, monarchy. This is also how things are in the Realm of God. Differences must remain. It is, however, essential for the mighty to incline toward the weak. Without authority everything disintegrates.

Morality, too, self-evidently. What, by the way, is the need for the categorical imperative[32] if one has the Ten Commandments?

Politics must keep to the middle of the road. Find support not only among the peasants but also among the middle classes. (and it is only because they afford too narrow a base that the artisans take their place). And oppose the extremes of capitalism above and below. The Parliament represents the wishes of the people in concert with, and {as} self-appointed corrective for, the agents of God's Grace.

Intellectualism, which has infected modern literature and which it cannot throw off, is Jewish.

For today's cultural convulsions, for the inability of civilization to become human, they bear a major part of the blame through their implacable struggle against materialism. [. . .]

German woman says in coit[us], "Give me a kiss!" There, for Austrians, lie all the borders in the world!

14

NOTEBOOK 10

1918 TO 1921
(1929, 1939)

[In order to fix, in his own mind and the minds of his readers, salient features of the characters in his works, as well as to capture significant aspects of institutions, shared attitudes, ideologies, and beliefs, Musil read very widely. It would be difficult to find an important area of intellectual enquiry that escaped his attention: experimental psychology, psychoanalysis, literary criticism, aesthetics, mathematics, politics, literature, ethics, biology, and education are only some of the areas identified in this notebook, which bears the title "On Books." One of the reasons why Musil took so long over his creative writing was the time he spent in studying the works of real-life characters he wished to portray. Instances of this are his preoccupation with Walther Rathenau, on whom, as we have seen, Paul Arnheim in MwQ is based, and the philosopher Ludwig Klages, whom Musil adapted into Meingast. Given this process, some of the elements of the character in the novel are supplied not by Musil but directly by the original subject. The portrait becomes part fiction, yet also contains a collage of authentic source materials, particularly quotations. Notebooks such as this were central to the process of matching the created world to the original.]

On Books

10

Enthusiasts; the novel.[1]

The Cigar Salesman and Our Dear Lord. The High Command.[2] The Nation of the Blind. The Stolen Fur. In the same direction as the Nation of the Blind (technique rests on ideas, anti-naturalistic, closely conforming to the spiritual tendency.) The Antichrist with, as opponent, the Christian and business-orientated epoch.

The Crow[3]—novel of a child, followed through to womanhood, with all the characteristics that are considered pathogenic and disreputable—who becomes happy.

Existing materials to be examined from the perspective of another moral system.

The Land over the South Pole—novel of moral experimentation.

The Life of Vincent van Gogh.

Fundamentals of Literary Criticism.

Development of Logic since Aristotle.

Questions pertaining to the Borders between Logic, Mathematics and Science.

Locke's Letter to Anna v. Musil.

Selected Objects of Literary Criticism. (Heinrich Mann, Stefan George, Zahn,[4] Bloem[5] . . .)

Political: The Fight against Censorship.

Piety and Enlightenment. The authors of the *Encyclopédie*, Mater[ialists].

The Poets of the Eternal. Paul Ernst,[6] Stefan George, Ed. Stucken[7] and Hardt.[8] [. . .]

———————

The Aesthetic Fundamentals . . .

The controversy over whether aesthetics can posit values or should be purely descriptive is not our immediate concern. Criticism should posit values and lead one to distinguish what is of value from what is not. That is why it exists. Thus we determine, in advance, that this shall be the purpose of criticism and investigate to what degree of general validity it can fulfil this role.

———————

To deny absolute beauty nevertheless does not mean that, *whenever* something is perceived as beautiful, this process cannot come about almost anywhere in a similar manner. Thus certain individual things (rhythm, verse-form, vowel-system, etc.) have quite a universal significance. But, in their own terms, they are hardly described as "beautiful."

<Is a scientific aesthetics possible? The only aspect of this question that should interest us for the moment is: "Is it possible to establish with scientific unambiguity whether a work of art is good or bad?">

1. Starting point: a book takes hold of me or captures my attention. It is a charming book, a book with spirit, a boring, an emotionally charged book, etc. Is this really so or is this only the case for those who are poor observers? Etc.: is it embarrassment or law that, in actual practice, we make such statements about a book and that these are the same statements we would make about a person?

When I read Raskalnikov,[9] Raskalnikov and Dostoyevsky take hold of me; when I read the *Papers of Malte Laurids Brigge*, only Rilke takes hold of me; when I see Hannele[10] only Hannele takes hold of me; when I read Mme. Bovary, Mme. Bovary and an insubstantial third element take hold of me; when I read *The Small Town*[11] it is only this third element that takes hold of me.

What takes hold of the reader of a book has some elements in common with the way one forms an acquaintanceship with a person and occasionally some that are not. I can think about the figures in a book in the manner that I think about the people whose acquaintance I have made without knowing them well. This is just the same in the case of the creative author. What the third element might be remains, for the present, an unsolved mystery.

There is one thing that is important and yet quite simple: the figures in a book are not alive and the author is not alive. They are totally at my disposal and the primeval hatred between living beings is switched off; they are completely suspended in a medium of warm involvement. {One can "surrender" to them whereas one holds oneself back in life.} One reason for the way that they seem so radiant if one does, indeed, love them. The hatred for a book, however, is the perfectly normal hatred for people and ideas.

Copies from life; segments of reality are copied and put together to form something that is entire of itself. {Ideography}

The intellectual relationship of the reader to the figures in a book is, roughly speaking, the same as that to figures in reality. The emotional relations are of a different kind. {The practical relationship is missing.} [. . .]

Drama: basic questions the same as with the novel, everything else merely technicalities? The performance of a drama could take 8 days; one could read Wisdom and Fate[12] on the stage with a few accompanying poses?

A theatrical performance is a social institution "sui generis." It has its laws of tension, of increasing suspense, etc., like a quadrille. [. . .]

It is advisable for the investigator to distinguish between the conventional means of producing intoxication and the individual content {and to conduct an independent investigation into the conventions.}

Intoxication = theater-state.

Death in the theater is one of the instruments.

The demand for the most suitable means: one could arrange Kant's study of space and time in the form of a dialogue and stage it. First, one would be disappointed because that is not what one expects on the stage. (No longer! The demand that it is not intellect that belongs on the stage but passion, etc., is a convention that, precisely, leads to our building of theaters.) Second, one would also do damage to Kant's thoughts. The object of art is that which can only be expressed in art. The proof for this principle is not one that is confined to aesthetics; I don't {go skating} on horseback.

What the poem is about is that which can only be expressed in the poem.

Experiment: words like "wireless telegraphy," "induction brush," indeed even just "brush" or "sausage" or "detonator," to be used in poems. Where does resistance to this come from?

Scientific aesthetics[13] searches for the universal building block from which the edifice of aesthetics might be erected. But, for us, art is that which we come across under that name. Something that is simply there and that has no need of laws whatsoever, a complicated social product.

Art: expression of an individuality.

<I can see a work of art already in nature and react to it in the way I would to a work of art.>
   The displeasure or pleasure that a work of art prompts in us is not aesthetic but quite a commonplace feeling. [. . .]

Literature that tells a story: I am reading . . . and it is a good read; that was the point of departure. {At a higher level, this is how Björnson's[14] peasant-novels are.}
   In all these books there is nothing more than a touching upon the complex of longing that lies in every person. {Such books are quite positive.} A handsome youth, women of wondrous beauty . . . not what is actually related in the story, but what is touched upon—the fairy tale. What is related can be quite stupid, quite worn out with use, one has no idea at all of what one is reading, one is young again, yearns, dreams. One creates the fairy tale oneself. (This is why, with respect to better books, the theory that the reader must have some space to maneuver is so dangerous.) The law that governs the very life of this kind of book is that complexity of any kind is kept at a distance. There are times when I find that this is even better than a complex structure that is flawed. I can now understand the desire to relax when one reads, bedtime reading. Where problems do arise they must be of a quite conventional kind.
   Quite understandable that the art of the Germans is that of practical or scientific people.

Time in the drama: naturalism ought to have explored this problem, but did not do so because it treated truth more as an attribute of character than as a technical problem. On the stage, what takes x hours in life is played out in 3 hours. This x should first be estimated in the case of different stories. In this process, the time that elapses between the acts does not count.

One can say: the coherence is not causal but rather one of motives. The individual scene is a telling moment, but the act is a sequence of motives for such moments, with the illusion of a causal succession.

{The meaning of the act: in the act, causal temporal sequence. In the totality of the acts, this is not the case.}

One might advance the hypothesis that the drama is outside time.

One might advance the second hypothesis that it is through this that it stimulates the imagination. And one might leave time out of play in quite different ways, leaping forward and backward in time and presenting different time-frames at the same time. Since, as time passes, there exists a certain ordering of external events for us, one would have to introduce a different principle of order so that "one knows one's way around." {That is just what one does. That is the actual artistic arrangement.} Perhaps the only reason for the illusion of a causal coherence is for one to know one's way around. This also comes into play through the way that passages of life are recreated. Realities are, in some measure, the infinite number of polygon lines that are drawn in, while the drama is the curve on the graph.

In his exposition (by the way, a bad expression, "laying the foundations" would be better) Ibsen does not show people, but rather the lives that people lead—for example, Oswald's mother[15] who has taken upon herself the reputation of being a cold mother in order to shift him away from proximity to the father. And he does not relate the lives of these people but he picks out a few characteristic details—as far as possible, ones that are unexpected. "The character is not what he seems" is a well-tried recipe for gaining the sympathy of the audience for them.

If only the critics would simply ask, when faced with the figures in a book and an author, "What kind of people are they?" If only they were willing simply to register new types of the human species, instead of concerning themselves with laws of art that they do not understand. They would then, in most cases, not only say the most sensible kind of things that can be said about a creative work, but they would bring about the longed-for miracle (at least its absence is a source of constant lamentation) of reuniting creative writing with humanity, fetching it back from its isolation into the warmth of the center. [. . .]

The following circumstance has also, as far as I know, never been given sufficient attention; the work of art is absorbed in the space of a few hours and produced over many weeks. This, in itself, puts any adequate comprehension out of the question. The work of art is not like *one* curved line but like one drawn with many separate pen strokes. It is not continuous but has fissures that are beneath the threshold of observation or that even radiate into the specific character. {But that is the origin of the effort to arrange for understanding to be possible within a single act!}

If one assumes that decisions about the value of a work of creative writing are taken in a similar way to the question of whether a person is important or not, then one understands that such value is, in the last analysis, not an object of perception but of struggle. With these parts of a work of creative fiction others are connected that can be the object of an aesthetic study in a narrower sense.

Consciousness = to stand in a context. The object one stares at is at best half-conscious. It is only the relationships as they are linked together—this is actually already what perception is—that bring about the conscious experience.

To pay attention = analyze and synthesize. Often involves only watching, listening.

Free will (par excellence) = being able to undertake something.

The sense impression is objective and not conscious. Merely that this is less than the totality that I am able to perceive immediately afterward if I so wish—this is what brings in the subjective, the element of what I know.

Something is more quickly at the center (and finds expression there in word or other kinds of notions) than at the periphery = I undertake something.

Action = a vaguely perceived accompanying condition.

In human life neither the facts nor the inner conditions are different, but their arrangement in time and space.

An individual is a process running its course, a variation. The course is run when it dies.

Consciousness, evolution:

| Central nervous system: function | 1): switch mechanism, etc., from outside to outside. |
| | 2): Ministry of the Interior. Hunger, anger, sexual drive. Transmits the internal affairs of the cell-colony. |

Would be conceivable without consciousness, automatic. Indeed, in many cases, is just that. {Is it not the case that consciousness only comes about through living together? What does Helen Keller[16] say? Through expression? Partly?}

Biologically important signs: biologically important stimuli are linked with particular inner signs. Would also work unconsciously.

{The theory that states that biologically important stimuli become so numerous in a higher order of development that consciousness is necessary in order to manage them, seems to me incapable of substantiation. Rather it is correct to say that consciousness (more correctly: thinking) is a kind of accessory that develops together with the communications.}

Is consciousness to be understood as something appropriate to a purpose? In biological terms this is actually not the case. But then one must express precisely what one understands by consciousness.

We can, for example, make quite clear distinctions ourselves between a state where the brain is simply receiving optical stimuli, and one where it is perceiving or recognizing.

An assumption: the objects release stimuli, they give signals. It is only then that these are interpreted. We can register quite well the experience of seeing something that is a quite indeterminate stimulus which is only then supplemented by further stimuli that stream on in. Misconceptions, illusions, etc., also, are easily explicable in these terms.

It may well be that this stimulus, this biologically important signal, has some sensation-quality for us, regardless of the circumstances; we know in advance whether it is optical or acoustic. But these are actually no longer qualities of the senses but really only stimuli. (We know which organ is aroused.)

In this way, gain access to the elementary phenomena of the soul. Those of higher order, then, in conjunction with language and discourse (and memory).

Method to be used here: narrowing down of what we consider to be specif[ically] human, to be an effort of consciousness belonging to a higher order, etc.

Objection to this: making oneself understood by means of a glance or an example. Influence of the context in which something happens. Married couples or friends are, in this respect, close to animals. Precisely the most intense conditions—ecstasies, mass psychoses, crusades, war, flagellantism,—develop in this way. Consideration of how little is conscious when we are on our own. Example of turning over.[17] [. . .]

A path that leads into the essence of creative writing is consideration of the fact that allusion is more effective than actual execution. Facts from life that touch on this point are:

Children playing with quite crudely fashioned dolls. Why do these stimulate the imagination more strongly than beautifully executed ones? Does this bear any relation to the way a dog pretends that a stone is its prey but doesn't know what to do with an imitation rabbit? Why? Because the latter is a reproduction of the original that has been toned down in all features to the point of being unrecognizable, whereas the stone is a reproduction only in one feature, namely the capacity to be carried in the mouth. The small size of the doll, over which one has control, is the decisive factor with regard to motherliness; it is, so to speak, the idea of the small child from which the fullness of the appearance merely distracts.

When I was a child, the lions and tigers on a circus poster excited me to an extraordinary degree before I got hold of it and cut them out; a sweet-box in the shape of a horse had a similar effect. I believe—I had always wanted to have horses—that what was decisive about the object was the sudden capability of possessing it; this would belong in the realm of speaking about things, etc.

Nature of rumor. Things of which one has no certain knowledge set the imagination alight.

Nature of the art of metaphorical. Comparison of a mouth with a coral {But coral is, however vaguely, the carrier of a notion of value} would be a degradation if it were not for the addition of an element of unclarity that produces the effect.

Magnification of a danger in the imagination. It is perhaps not magnified, but imagined in isolation.

The nature of phobias is certainly connected with the problem in some way.

Why do smells stimulate the imagination so strongly?

(On the nature of the artistic imagination)

Creative writing is not an activity but a condition. This is why it is not possible, if one has a full-time job and a half-day off, to pick the work up where one left off. Reading is transmission of this condition.

The tragic, in bourgeois terms, may be the individual's struggle against the law; what is tragic in poetic terms is the contradiction within the law. The difference in the way the conflicts are resolved is to be found in whether one calculates the world-formula to one further decimal point or not.

Another meaning of similes:[18] to alienate, to distance. Meant in the same way as in Klages' *Eros Kosmogonos;*[19] the only form of love is love at a distance. [. . .]

Subjects for Essays.

> Criticism or Aesthetics?
>> Publishing Circles
>> Why is Theater Criticism better than Book Criticism?
>> Creative Author or Work?
>> Human Warmth and Creative Writing
>> The Problem of Representation in Creative Writing
>> The "Best" Novel
>> Stage Effectiveness (and Theatrical Intoxication)

The Most Fitting Means, the Shortest Way
What is Lyrical?
Adequate Comprehending
Convention and Motives
Creative Writing—Essay—Philosophy
Allusion and Clarity
Essence of Artistic Imagination
Instruments of Criticism
"Psychology" in Creative Writing
The Art of Pathos
Motive—Causality—Reality

How long does one take to produce a work?

If the essay topics (e.g., as a series for Fischer)[20] are supplemented by critical pieces on individual creative writers, it will be necessary to preface these with a statement that they do not do justice to the subjects but represent rather a struggle to find a philosophy of art or a *Weltanschauung.* [. . .]

Theater criticism: a performance is a book being played on stage (in Vienna it is a theater play with a book-underlay. That is the difference.) In addition, of course, there is dissembling, dressing-up, having the feelings of other people, the whole complex of emotions that are peculiar to the theater. Even a very good performance could be based just on these. But the overriding stylistic leading principle remains that a book is being played. (Here lies the possibility of going beyond Berlin.)

This book[21] is, of course, a theater play. But all mistakes come from the belief that it is possible for a play to be good without it being a good book. Plays of that kind lead to smash-hits but they ruin the tradition. Vienna's decline as a city of the theater has to do with repertory. [. . .]

Remarkable that in England women write novels, that in Germany they don't. Expressionism.

Before I joined the army there existed an explosive form of intellectual lyric poetry based on imagination, poetry of intellectual intuition, philosophical ideas blasted into fragments to which were attached torn-off flesh-scraps of feeling.

I returned to find Expressionism.

Blinded by long absence I try at first to find my bearings using the word itself. Expre.— that would be the opposite to Imp.? But what is meant by Imp.? The sketches of Altenberg? One might call these "impressions," but one might just as well call them "little reflections" and, the older he gets, the more the receptive element retreats behind the reflective one.

Herm[ann] Bahr? He once wrote something that he called "Impressionism." But these were live interviews and, after all, one doesn't found a literary movement on the basis of opposition to journalism. The early Schnitzler? He was a moralist—it does not matter how deep he may have been. Ibsen was a moralist and critic. Hauptmann, an optician for German bourgeois movements with a German Spring as backdrop. Thomas Mann? He described himself as a pupil of C.F. Meyer and Storm so he wasn't an Impressionist either. Nowhere in the higher regions of creative writing was there an Impressionist. There were some who were of Impressionist hue but these were fellow travelers.

I interrupt this to record that I have not the slightest feelings of belonging to these {older} generations of authors, indeed that I oppose them even though I appreciate one or other aspect of their work.

———————————

Later: formation of a group like Naturalism. Ambitious people provided with the trademark.

———————————

Note: some also call it expressive art. But what kind of art would not be expression? "A piece of nature seen through a temperament." A piece of temperament looking out at nature—this is a simple shift of the balance weight. But probably one that hits the mark. But probably this matches the concept of Romanticism that already exists. (A very subjective art.)

———————————

T. Mann on Expr.: Pol. p. 192[22]
Each artist should have the feeling that everything that went before him was filth; if a movement shouts this from the rooftops that means: banding together, cowardice, sense of inadequacy.

All of them (the Expr.sts) follow the impression of the moment, so they're Impr.sts.

Hauptmann: monstrous phenomenon of brilliant surface movement with minimal movement within (ideological movement).

On the other side, a fluid border with the Impr.sts. *The Dancing Female Fool*[23] full of impression. Even more so the sketches by Däubler;[24] these might have appeared 25 years ago.

Re: the anti-psychologism of T. Mann, Pol. 505: "Apparently doubt has changed its spiritual-political role. Once, at the dawn of the 'New Age' at the time of Petrarch, doubt was the progressive principle that subverted belief, put authority into question, emancipated the individual, destroyed the basis of the unitary culture of medieval Europe. As things stand today, doubt has become the common denominator of all those outdated conditions of the spirit, that oppose and are harmful to, will, to firmness of purpose, to spiritual-political action in the service of the progress of mankind—I shall list once again the learned names that critics gave them but that are now on everybody's lips: these are Aestheticism, Relativism, Psychologism, Impression . . . whereas, previously, people wanted—and were allowed—to distinguish between spirit and deed, insight and deed, as elements that were very different from, and incompatible with, each other."

How did the Romantics define themselves?

How are they defined?

Something common is present. Only one or two aspects in common. It merely forces itself on (the artist) as the dimension of form. A poetic style, a mania. Sternheim was the first to dislocate language thus. This is, properly speaking, chopped-up verse because it places its accents according to the concept, without any regard to syntax. This has always been done that way, and indeed everyone has done it. But, in Döblin's case, it involves a constant reminder: "Just look how short I am!" which makes him very long. I have for a long time now privately called this "the demand for the shortest line." Must examine whether the overall path that these creative writers take becomes a shorter one.

Remarkable about these creative writers is the renunciation of the use of suggestion by the interpolation of factual elements. Wherever I wanted to achieve a certain nuance for a thought, I would not hesitate to try to achieve this in the novel by describing the situation of the person thinking. I would provide a brief, minimal set of descriptions for some behavior, for a particular setting, retreating completely behind a stance of pseudo-objectivity. "Cendrillon said . . ." And a little courtyard glows around the sensuality of this sentence as if it around a candle flame. I do not see why one should communicate through concepts instead of through notions. I would (perhaps prefer to) do so through notions if it were possible. I am waiting to be corrected.

But other creative writers are quite different—for example, Gütersloh in a fragment from The Ecstasy of Abstract Things. A long, balanced, solemn prose. Wolfenstein[25]—Hölderlin.

Edschmid.[26] Examine also with respect to the nature of his brevity.

Werfel—

Ethics: Ethics existed in every superior epoch. Here it is perhaps of a rather "Old Testament" kind.

My critiques of Sorge and Wolfenstein[27] are to be compared with those of Expressionist critiques to tell whether I see things in an "other" way.

Nietzsche toward the end of the first volume of *Human, All-Too-Human*:

Everyone who is still caught up in the net of the belief in which he first became entangled is suspect. He does not grasp that there are necessarily other opinions. N. calls these spirits "unscientific." As soon as they find the first hypothesis for some matter they attach themselves firmly to it. To have an opinion means to them: becoming fanatical about it and, henceforward, to take it to heart as a conviction. (In Mann, Pol., p. 511)

The further essence of Expressionism is that of a synthetic method in contrast to an analytical one. The Expressionist renounces analysis. Therefore, as far as the complexes that he recognizes to be valid are concerned, he believes in them implicitly. Therefore he leans toward dogmatism. He therefore tries to find a new "world-feeling" in the way in which a chemist tries to find synthetic rubber. What limits him is that no purely synthetic technique exists. [...]

Area of the non-ratioïd: that of singular[28] facts.

Theoretically we assert that they are subordinate to causality but this has no practical meaning. How an individual happens to be is, no doubt, something that has come about through some way or other, but the only important issue is the way he happens to be. (In other words, without any reference to all objections to the caus[ality] principle.)

But, second, there are facts that take up their place in science beyond any caus[ality] chain—the constants. They bring into the concept of the natural law that which is factual and pre-logical. In other words, the individual appears to us as something in which the factual is far more important than any possible law explaining the way he came about.

We may well, however, interpret individual decisions as falling into types; psychology is less helpful in this context than statistical observation that points the way. But we can also experiment with superimposed motives. That is the non-rat[ioïd] method.

In principle, perhaps, there is no non-ratioïd realm at all; or, speaking more cautiously, we cannot imagine any.

But there remains the difference in method or behavior.

To be specific, this changes according to whether I have recourse in my explanation to acts or contents. One mode of observation will always try to reduce to the minimum number of types.

The other mode is as inexhaustible as the possible kinds of content.

The difference in question is that between determining something and finding reasons for it. In an ideal case there is only one possibility of determination, but there are countless possible motives.

This person can only have this motive: the administration of justice always moves toward that goal.[29] Practical life, too, in general. The creative writer is always exploding this.

There are, of course, usual and unusual motives. That certain motives do really occur frequently marks an advance of the realm of the ratioïd. One might say that this is a typology of the individual. Those who profess to understand people are so dreadfully blatant and—they are usually right. [...]
Statistics would show that there are invariably only typical motives at work

and that their variations have no influence; here, too, we find a law that tolerates an exception. Then the creative author takes the side of those unusual motives that practically never come into consideration. Resist becoming petrified! (Now only in the struggle against unscientific-practical motives that are held to be self-evident.)

New motives are born, as well, for example, pleasure in driving automobiles. Is put together from old motives, but the new experience has a unique "timbre." Gliding away, motive of speed, of flying, of luxury. Some of these are picked out by the creative writer, colored in the atmosphere of a complex of ideas, are arranged in the interest of a particular goal, etc. He adds and subtracts. And at the end, something unique emerges. So now one has proved that motives fall into types. But there will always be something unique that remains outside the sum. [. . .]

Education for genius.

Thesis: the difference between a genius and a sharply critical gifted person lies not in their capabilities but in the objects on which these are expended.

For example, someone will work out with ease that the trams on the Ring in Vienna always have an 8 in their number; 8, 18, 118, etc. Something similar happens with a remark in the theater: "What a strange name this singer has: Mi Ehnepo." Without pausing to think, he replies: "Her name is Oppenheim." (Ability to establish connections, unconventional attitude.) Another example is provided by the often brilliant witticisms and obscene jokes . . . A further one: after the transition from scholasticism to "exact" thinking, scholastics (and some important ones will certainly still be found among the theologians, for example,) are no longer taken at all seriously.

Ability to make connections, capacity "to see with fresh eyes," i.e., to keep oneself independent of old ties, these probably constitute the genial essence of genius; capacity to notice, diligence, capacity for concentration and passionate interest are added to this, but are also found in the person of sharply critical gifts. But the latter also has the ability and the willingness to connect in his area of interest. Thus the decisive element is the nature of this realm. Science and art have their geniuses. If one were to take stamp collecting just as seriously, this too would have its geniuses. In this way, the question becomes an educational problem and a moral and sociological one, too. [. . .]

Untested aperçu. Origin of the world. That something comes from nothing is beyond the reach of imagination because all becoming is a change in something that is already there. That something is there for ever can readily be imagined; one can after all, also imagine that something is timeless; time can be conceived as a function of physical events running their course and matter can be, so to speak, older than time.

Ideology of socialism

    1.) All people are equal
    2.) Love thy neighbor as thyself.

    1) is a downright untruth. The real true meaning of this assertion has become apparent in the meantime. Trials by jury, councils, parliament, the pupil often cleverer than the teacher. Take, from time to time, a spiritual purgative to clear out all knowledge. Spirit is destructive, and only constructive through setting up a collection of solutions from which practice makes its selection. When left to its own devices, spirit is a feud without end. (From this follows the position of the creative writer and the philosopher in socialist society.)

    2) This principle has never been realized. It is not only unsuitable for the ethics of everyday life but also for the ethics of those who are most advanced. The only way it is realized, if at all, is in the exaggerated form: "Love thy neighbor more than thyself." But then it is no longer pure, for here an idea is loved, an issue. Moreover, it denotes a condition, that of love.

    This should be replaced by a principle that is, in ethical terms, of much less consequence but, in practical terms, more important: "Act in solidarity."

    Accordingly, the ethics of socialism rest on 2 practical maxims. That corresponds to the tasks of a political movement.

    Hatred of the oppressors, feeling for the subjugated—all these ideas so dear to the socialist, his élan? First of all, these ideas all belong to the "status nascendi" of socialism, not to the finished society. [. . .]

Animal—Human Being:
". . they are quite right to object to the uncritical overvaluing of the thought-life of animals, on the other hand these . . men who have been brought up to think and speculate do not seem to have any inkling of how exceedingly

small is the degree of consciousness and reflection in which the totality of mankind lives, and gets by with really rather well." Note to p. 57, Chamberlain, Foundations.

> Carl Vogt, Investigations of Animal-States, 1851
> Alfred Möller, Title not given, about the gardener ant
> Huber, Nouvelles observations sur les abeilles.[30]
> Maeterlinck, La Vie des abeilles
> J G Romanes, Essays on Instinct, 1897
> Fabre, Souvenirs entomologiques[31]
> Wundt, Lectures on the Mind of Humans and Animals[32]
> Fritz Schultze, Comparative Theory of Souls 1897[33]
> Bethe: Is it proper to assign mental qualities to ants and bees?
> Forel, speech on 13.8.1901, at the Zoologists' Congress in Berlin.
> (Ants act with conscious reflection.)

Every great creative writer was a philosopher, every philosopher of genius is a creative writer . . . Foundations p. 62.[34]

Ihering—Prehistory of the Indo-Europeans.[35] [. . .]

Theater and novel of illusion.

What really takes hold of the imagination are experiences. Not the "how," the nuance, but the coarse "what." Experiences, then, which anyone can have, but doesn't have. What takes hold is not even the hero, the suggestive figure, as I believed up till now, but the sum of his experiences that go into the making of this child of fortune.

E.g., the idea of the *Enthusiasts*: quite a normal plot, but one that is played out among important people, runs completely against the grain of illusion.

But what are these experiences then? The most fruitful insight that I have had into this up till now is: ones that have to do with society. The human being as a social animal would like to achieve distinction from the others, and be praised by them. This is where the suggestive power of the hero comes from in terms of courage, strength, achievement. This is also the basis for the preference for virtue.

As a child, everyone would like to be good, beautiful, rich, strong, etc.

The second major area is, of course, the erotic experience. Here, too, the desire to surrender oneself, to rescue, to abduct, to set free, etc.—this all comes from a more fundamental root than sex.[36] Germinating sexuality simply floods this with the rays of a provocatively incomprehensible light. Perhaps one can add the longing for a second person, for the being who is determined for one.

Here one has already entered the realm of the illusions of individuation, the antisocial elements within the individual that finds expression in the power for illusion that resides in utter evil.

The occurrence of precise, individualized ideas of beauty is a gross untruth. The young person puts these together for himself in a more or less violent way and finally the full magic ends in a person with all the wealth of nuances but the flame that flickered over the whole of the inner firmament has gone, even if the whole thing ends in a gigantic conflagration. (Everything has become concrete. No longer the desire to wrestle but to wrest the prize, etc.)[37]

Creative writer and practical person: people who shape life creatively. People who reflect about creating. [. . .]

Hans Cornelius, The Elementary Laws of Fine Arts, Leipzig, Teubner, 2nd edition, 1912
Kerchensteiner, Georg, The Concept of State Citizenship, Teubner, 1910.
  Concept of Character and Formation of Character, Teubner, 1912.
  Nature and Value of Science Teaching in Schools, Teubner, 1914
Foerster, Friedr. Wilh., Education for State Citizenship, 2nd edition, Teubner, 1914.
  Education and Self-Education, Schulthess & Co., Zurich, 1917.
  School and Character, ibid., 1912.
Kerschensteiner, "Basic Questions of the Organization of Schools," 3rd edition, Teubner, 1912.
  "Concept of the Work-School," 2nd edition, Teubner.
A. Lion, "The Book of Scouting," Verlag Gmelin, Munich, 1909.
Natorp, Paul, "Social Pedagogics," Frommann, Stuttgart, 1904.

Wyneken, Gustav, "School and Youth Culture," Diederichs, 1913.
Herbart, "General Pedagogics," 6th edition, Beyer and Sons, Langensalza
({1st.edition} 1806.)
   Outline of Pedagogical Lectures, 1835 and 1841.
   Idea for a Pedagogical Curriculum for Secondary Level Studies, 1801.
Müller-Lyer: Sociology of Illness[38]
Literary Adviser of the Dürer League: Neurath Lit. Notes on Social and Ex-
istential Organization. [. . .]

Dr. Alfred Adler, On the Nervous Character, 2nd edition, 1919.
   (Describes the Regine-type?)[39]
   Practice and Theory of Individual Psychology, Bergmann, Munich, 1920.

Rud. Steiner—The "Goetheanum" in Dornach near [Basle], half-way between a college and a theater—many supporters in England and America!

---

6 grams of potassium cyanide
8–10 drops of hydrochloric acid.[40]

The task influences the course of the reaction: H.J Watt, Experimental Contributions toward a Theory of Thinking (Archive for General Psychology,
Vol. IV—also Special Number).

Rudolf Hildebrand, On the Teaching of German in Schools, 2nd edition,
1896.

Also on liter.-artistic education in primary school: Ludwig Pfeiffer, Bavarian
Teacher's Paper, 1903 Nr. 27–29, 1902, Nr. 23.

Hesse and Doflein, "Animal Structure and Animal Life," Teubner, 1910/14.
O. Abel, Paleobiology of Vertebrates, Stuttgart, 1912. [. . .]

15

NOTEBOOK 19

1919 TO 1921

[At the start of this notebook—and the opening section may stand as an example of the whole—Musil is attempting to identify what marks him out from other contemporary intellectuals. He decides that this has to do with his training in science and the unsentimental and objective method this fostered. However, he recognizes that his subject—which is no less than the state of the world around the time of World War I—is far too broad to allow him to approach it as a scientist would approach the task of collecting data. He organizes his approach into five segments. The first is an overview of things as they enter his consciousness (population statistics, for example, and the impact of inventions that affect civilization over the period 1880 to 1914). Modern society is so complex, or, to use Musil's own image, the "horizon" the contemporary intellectual scans is so wide, so incomprehensible, that there develops a sense of (to use another of Musil's words) "incoherence." The second points to various responses to this state of affairs, including the transition to government by parliament and the formation of interest groups. The third identifies ideologies. The fourth looks at the isolated individual confronted by generalities. The fifth examines the processes that actually impose shape on society, namely, the collective mental response (the "metaphysical adventure of mankind" is Musil's term for this) and the driving force of material change or "megalo-civilization," as Musil calls it. The rest of the notebook contains reflections on morality, politics, culture, and religion as they impinge on people during and after the war. Here we sense the complex interrelations between events on the one hand and the attitudes of leading figures and the populace at large on the other.]

Clear-out!
19

I do not ever know if it is my good spirit or my evil spirit that speaks these words within me. But it simply has to get out.

Since I awoke to life I have always seen things in an "other" way.[1] That means: in places, clear criticism, in places, clear suggestions, well thought through. Some I have written down and published. But much more has remained at a level of dark antipathy. Half raised up, then sunk down into obscurity. Intuition sensing far-reaching connections that the understanding has not followed.

The understanding that has had the benefit of scientific training is loath to follow if it has not been able to build itself bridges for itself whose load-bearing capacity is calculated exactly. Here and there I completed the calculations for a single area of such a bridge; dropped the work again in the conviction that it is not possible, after all, to finish it. I could sit down and gather material in the way that it has been done in similar assiduous, large-scale experiments—Wundt,[2] Lamprecht,[3] Chamberlain,[4] Spengler.

But what remains when this is done? When the breath has evaporated with which one tried to bring such fullness to life, there is nothing but a dead heap of inorganic material.

The five-year-long slavery of the war has, in the meantime, torn the best piece from my life; the run-up has become too long, the opportunity to summon up all my forces is too short. To renounce or to leap, whatever then happens, this is the only choice that remains.

I renounce any systematic approach and the demand for exact proof. I will only say what I think, and make clear why I think it. I comfort myself with the thought that even significant works of science were born of similar distress, that Lockes . . . .[5] are in fact travel correspondence.

I want to develop an image of the world, the real background, in order to be able to unfold my unreality before it. I observe life since 1880, the decisive span of time for people between the ages of 20 and 60.

Oil lighting and tallow candle just been superseded, paraffin, gas, electricity, gaslight, further development of electric lighting.

> Penny-farthing,[6] safety-cycle, motorcycle and automobile.
> Flying machine.
> X-rays
> Anaesthesia
> Submarine
> Train travel in the year 1880 and in the year 1914. Restaurant-cars and sleepers.
> Numbers of inhabitants of major cities 1880 and 1914
> Density of population in 1880 and 1914.
> Book production . . .
> Number of civil servants
> Growth in trade and in the numbers of those employed in trade.
> Growth in numbers of factory workers.

([All the above] to be replaced by the structure around 1911. Prefer comparison, if possible, with the time around 1800.)

Result (apart from the shift in interests which is to be tackled later. One should read the Proceedings of the Chemical Society or such like; and the literary person who reproaches these people with their degeneracy—who appears like a dwarf of Jewish vitality facing giants—even if they are somewhat clumsy giants): an immense broadening of the horizon and with this an incoherence that is constantly increasing in magnitude in the course of its natural development.

II. We examine its symptoms and consequences and the attempts to counter this (with the exception of the ideological ones.)

One attempt was parliamentarism. Not too long ago it was a movement of souls. Probably, a form of reaction. Heine, Börne, the political literature around 1848 and before Bismarck. Soon after that it became nothing more than a (highly imperfect) means of communication. Earlier, politics was carried out by people of political will seeking and hiring party supporters. Today a scrutinium [sic] of the political will itself. It is no longer the means of implementation that are sought, but the aims. One must not be deceived by the party programs; those are atavisms. Much more important is the indifference of the voters. . . . percent are politically indifferent. {(Subtract the socialists from this figure)} Since one knows what the reasons are for a large part of the remainder coming to the party one can say that the enormous and venerated apparatus of parliamentarism does not work at all. So it is ridiculous (even if bolshevism gives this ridiculous show a tragic hue) to cling firmly to parliamentarism in the name of propriety and democracy. This is the place to remind ourselves of the discovery by Lagarde: . . {At this point the German distaste for western parliamentarism turns off down a sidestreet:} {(It is not that political personalities are lacking, but that the task of politics has changed.)} Another attempt is the newspaper. This forms public opinion but it is better to see it as a mirror of opinion at a later stage.

Court of law.

School.

Many kinds of inferior writing. Independent publishing circles.

In summary: a huge body of people, ruled by a caste of kings, feudal lords and financiers, or politicians and financiers. In groups that pursue particular leanings and livelihoods, each group with very defective knowledge of other groups {Times, char[acteristics]} People seem to have become rooted to their own spot. The organization of communication has not kept pace with the development of obstacles to traffic. On this soil grow the brilliant and unfettered achievements of individuals. That is the true picture. Not the one that was proffered by socialism of a bourgeois stratum that has established for itself a monopoly of all material and spiritual goods. It is incapable of making full use of the spiritual goods at all, and the material ones benefit only a few.

Make reference (perhaps later) to the second inadmissible simplification of Marxism: separation of the exploiters from the exploited while, in fact, between them, lies the gigantic layer of the bureaucracy in the most general sense, and this problem is today the thorniest one that socialism faces.

III. The ideological attempts.

Church	Church
Epistemology	Science
Public morality, customs, school.	Art.
Ethics (scientific and artistic)	Sordidness
Art	Nationalism
Sordid attempts	as pseudo-tie
The German historical school	(The German dilemma)

IV. The individual in the midst. His helplessness. The facts growing at enormous pace. The unbridgeable gulf between individual and generality. The constituents of a new ethics but only when this takes the actual situation into account.

V. New order: fastest possible implementation of the reshaping of society, the social corpus must reach a stable balance. Two firm perspectives as points of orientation: the metaphysical situation, so to speak, the metaphysical adventure of mankind. Not yet at the stage where decisions are made, all philosophical experiments very provisional. The real trends of development: increase in population; unquenchable curiosity about facts; increasing domination of nature; increasing comfort; megalo-civilization.

{A man of imagination who is offended by the lack of imagination of the Vienna School[7] has too little imagination.}

War as the crisis of this "Only-civilization!" It becomes insufferable to hear, time and again, capitalism-imperialism being held responsible for this. Capitalist and bolshevist are nothing but tiny, indeed scarcely noticeable, differences in the type of human being that has emerged recently.

Houston Stewart Chamberlain: The Foundations of the 19th Century.[8]

Sets, as the beginning of our era, round about the year 1200; from then onward a development that has not yet run its course today. The movements against the rape of individual freedom by Church and State—which was gathering pace—had already made a strong impact in the 13th Century (p. 19).

"It is . . . striking how very marginal the differences between separate individualities generally are. Within the individualities of their different races, people form an atomized, but nonetheless very homogeneous, mass." Seen from the perspective of the stars, humanity would appear as uniform as an anthill, all individuals obey a common impersonal impulse. All great and lasting upheavals take place "blind." From the biographies and the correspondence of Napoleon I, it emerges that he achieved none of his desires and dreams "and that he sank back into the undifferentiated, homogeneous mass, just as clouds dissolve after a thunderstorm." {Check this!} On the other hand, the transformation of the economic conditions and the most comprehensive restructuring of all human relationships "came about in the course of the 19th century by means of a series of technical inventions, without anyone having even the vaguest idea of the importance of these innovations." (24)

Great men are the blossoms of history, but not their roots. (26)

Believes he can exclude from this the genius, the creative spirit.

"Genius," both the concept and the word, appeared in the 18th century.

Ranke predicted that our century would be one of nationalism, pp. 28ff.

Chamb. calls it "a Century of the Races."

Rousseau: "Siècle des Révolutions" (he calls it prophetically).

Century of Natural Science (wrong—because the 16th to 18th centuries achieved no less).

Century of the rolling wheel is a term that Chamb. considers almost justified.

Century of (Exact) Science

Century of Philology (he has a lot of sympathy for this).

Century of the Emancipation of the Jews.

of Electricity.

of the Peoples' Armies.

of the Colonies.

of Music.

of Advertising.

of the Declaration of Infallibility.

of Religiosity.

saeculum historicum by contrast with the saec. philosophicum (Paulsen)

The Economic Century

Ch. pokes gentle fun at all these one-sided definitions. Ch.: "The 19th century is essentially a century of the accumulation of material, a transitional and provisional stage . . it swings to and fro." p. 31 (Empiricism and spiritualism; liberalism and reaction; autocracy and anarchy; declaration of infallibility and materialism. Worshipping of Jews and anti-Semitism. Capitalism and proletarian politics.) "It is not the ideas that are characteristic in the 19th century but the material achievements." p. 32 {I would give it the name: "The Century of the Absence of Organization."}

Ranke, "World History," Vol. IV.[9]

Cf. Treitschke, "German History," Vol. V.[10]

Paulsen, "History of Scholarly Instruction."[11]

Beer, "History of World Trade."[12] [. . .]

———————————

Germany suffered its actual collapse through being unable to seize the new. If one also takes a look at the victorious states one can say: Europe has never been at such a low ebb as now.

It is absolute rule by routine. Reaction as {human} inability not as ill will. Rule by the politicians of yesterday. Rule by the ideas of yesterday. (Because the Biedermeier face of today's Germany also belongs to yesterday.)

November-socialists: confirming with enthusiasm that one is a Nov. soc. Why one stood to one side, why one came. The Nov. practices will be assimilated; they will make as good socialist officials as they were clerical officials.

If one cannot take the economy into socialist ownership, one could at least prepare this spiritually. No question of this. We thought: as minds they are no more than mediocre, but they will be politicians, these socialist leaders; now we see to our dismay: they are minds. [. . .]

Important to distinguish between two kinds of spiritual nourishment; ingestion by personal processing (study, original research) and in form of an emulsion. In between, gradations of ingestion—secondhand, thirdhand, one-hundredhand. Even in university studies.

There are those who believe that, in history, certain ideas exist in a state of immanence. Who believe that spirit unfolds of its own accord. Who believe in progress. This belief, as the war propaganda of our enemies has shown, is perfectly adapted to banalization. I don't wish to say that it is itself banal or itself wrong. I merely would like to try to put another kind into practice.

I would put it roughly as follows: people are an enormously indolent mass in every moral question. I doubt if ethics in Western Europe is finer than in the South Seas, it is probably simply more rationalized. It is certainly no richer than it was in ancient times. I observe the monstrous degeneracies that the war caused to shoot up like mushrooms. The ruthless egotism of profiteering, of the peasants, of legitimate traders, the pompous presumption of the master caste with its Army General Staff, the hangman's composure with which the custodians of the new German order proceeded against anything that was alien to their spirit, the rejoicing with which the peoples of the Entente celebrated their Trojan victory (Wilson[13] as the Horse), the pliability with which the French give their Foch approval for the fortifications of Strasbourg.

I compare these degeneracies with the breath of a religious feeling (lying is of no help, even for pious, "independent" purposes) that, at the beginning of the war, wafted through all the warring peoples (something strange, not of the accustomed earth, for this reason quickly explained away either as hallucination or as ghost.)

And I come to the conclusion that I put forward before the war began—one of only a small number of Germans to do so—that in moral terms a human being is a misshapen thing, a colloidal substance that snuggles up to other forms rather than shapes them itself. {(This would argue in favor of rule by the few.)}

Putting this idea more precisely: the human being does not fix the shape of his own life. Two processes are at work here that run in parallel with quite a different speed {and phase-difference}. The causal chains of human development and those of the particular life-form are different.

Example: the life of the state and that of individuals. Imperial Germany did not give expression to what constitutes a German; a peaceful, busy type of person had acquired an enormous suit of armor (in a moral sense as well). I shall leave aside Byzantinism but how thin was the substance of what was assembled as (official) ideology. Categor[ical] imperative, fragments of Bismarck, a little "Germanistik," health, family, etc. One should compare with this the life between 1880 and 1914 (Nietzsche, the Scandinavians, Strindberg). {So it is also not the case that individuals shape the mass; a very complicated process is responsible for this.}

———————————

It is only permissible to be a conservative if one is creative. In order not to sabotage Wilson's peace initiative in 1916, Bethmann-Hollweg[14] (Workers' Paper of 18.11.1919) did not let the parties into the secret, so that it would not leak out that Germany was in agreement. In addition, one was frightened that the step would be condemned as antinational. In spite of this he resisted the submarine war and repeatedly informed the Party leaders of this view. The personal impression of Helfferich[15] was that, even without the sub. war, the course was set for war with America. Bernstorff[16] shared this view, {but} declared that the only countermeasure was to accept American mediation. Bethm. Hollw. declares this statement to be of decisive importance and gives it his support. "But if we had entrusted ourselves to Wilson then, we would have placed ourselves in the power of a president who, according to what Count Bernstorff stated, was not disposed to be friendly toward us. Given the {military} situation that existed at that time, was the German people in a position to subject itself to the terms of peace in the form that Wilson had announced? . . . . Was it not imperative that we secured certain guarantees against impossible peace terms? We had sent a telegram to the President on 30th January saying that we would stop the submarine war immediately if Wilson gave us serviceable guarantees for an acceptable peace. If Wilson had been willing, in his heart of hearts, to give peace back to the world from the highest motives, then what was stopping him at least from answering our telegram of 30th January?"

The following is clear: apart from the well-known damage inflicted by diplomatic secretiveness (but which cannot be entirely avoided anywhere even in civilian life), apart from the not entirely involuntary (for it had its origins in the circles around the Kaiser) overvaluing of national public opinion, and also apart from the speech by the Kaiser in Mühlhausen (on 13.12., Helferrich said of this: "A tactical oversight has determined the fate of the world."??) . . . So the following is clear: the inability to take possession of Wilson's new ideas, to free them from their vague ambiguity and even make them into one's own slogan. {In oneself one must harbor a part of one's opponent, even when he is only bluffing and one wants to take him in.} They all mistrusted Wilson but they were not able to force him to make a confession. They all felt the war with America to be an increasing danger, they recognized the value of "mediation" as a tactical instrument, but between Wilson and themselves there was no spiritual mediation. The "Idea" of world unity was so alien to "Realpolitik" thinking with its orientation toward nationalism and the state, it seemed so utopian to them, that they were obviously unable to give it serious consideration.

The same process was apparently repeated in Versailles where the leaders of France and England burdened themselves with the same guilt (and, in view of the greater clarity of the visible situation, the greater guilt). One can think of Wilson as a Machiavelli or the 14 points as a Trojan horse, but it is more likely that the collapse of Germany robbed him of all means of applying pressure on the Allies and that he merely made the mistake of not drawing the personal consequences from this. (But, since the game of diplomatic intrigue remains unknown, it may be that he could not do so.)

The same inability to shrug off the customs of the past is to be seen in present-day Hungary and the speech of Horthy[17] noted earlier.

One can say that the conservative human constitution has flooded the world with a storm tide of ignominy, stupidity, baseness and misfortune.

But one cannot absolve from the same reproach the diametrically opposite side. (Apart from bolshevism, for this is slandered too freely and we are guilty of not having informed ourselves on the matter.) The rule by commissars in Hungary has, in all probability, also brought a great heap of dirt, baseness, corruption, etc., to power. The murder of the hostages in Munich[18] presents (if one subtracts all the inflationary presentation by the bourgeois press which every good spirit has abandoned) a picture that one can consider, in terms of its inner probability, to be typical. And then one only has to call to mind "Revolutionary Man" as a type.

He flies, yet cannot walk; he swims under water but cannot breathe the air. That which for an important person is personal fate, a path blazed with difficulty through objections he has set up himself, is, for him, style. The creative person is—with respect to the issue of life and death, for example so constituted that both scales are heavily weighted and only an excess surplus weight is needed to tip the balance, the "ultra" is either aflame for the inviolability of every hair on the human countenance, or he condemns thousands to destruction with a mental pen stroke.

His radicalism is the monkey kept by the radicalism of the creative person, is in the same relationship to him as a loud yell is to silent resolution {(like a small, fierce dog to the momentum of the planets)}. Outdoes him, is always ahead of him. This is not reflective but psychological radicalism. {Flaubert sketched this in Mme. Bovary, Hamsun did so several times.}

(It is not coincidental that the reaction to this is anti-Semitic but it is an "Aryan" guilt.)

It is necessary. It is as necessary as war and social injustice. No more and no less.

It cannot achieve anything. It can only inaugurate achievement. The conservative person has to achieve. All guilt rests on him.

Austrian report of the Trades Union Commission to the Congress of German-Austrian Trades Unions contains documents about the terrorism that was carried out during the war against the workers. The workers were robbed of their rights (by the War Productivity Law, etc.) and delivered up to the capitalists {Mob.[ilization]}

One must also not avoid the question of what this war actually was. One cannot simply go away as if one had simply shaken off some state of intoxication, in which millions of people had lost their nearest relatives or their livelihood. This must tear the people apart, it is one of those repressed experiences that take their revenge in the form of hysteria. That is the great ideological crime of the independents and pacifists.

They are, morally, the victors in the War. Chance has played into their hands in leaving their views in the ascendant.

I am a pacifist, but not from ideological conviction since that has its limitations.

The enormous moral burden of radical politics is the certainty that it is unable to rebuild after the destruction. However much one may be outraged by the philistinism of the socialists in the government and by certain crimes that they have committed, one must concede one thing to them: they have looked into the abyss.

As an individual I am a revolutionary. There is no other possibility, for the creative individual is always one. But in political matters I am evolutionary. But it is necessary for something to be undertaken on behalf of evolution.

The failures of the socialists and of the bourgeois parties have balanced each other out. Criminal stupidity.

No political party can build up. But the clearing and preparation of the building site *does* devolve upon one party.

What first came out as a stammer and later degenerated to an empty phrase was quite correct: the war was a religious experience. What is left is, as always, the empty aura of the word. One must understand religious experience through the war and not vice versa.

The irrational, reason-flouting quality of the war. Tearing open the problem of existence. I do not bewail the way the war lasted too long to preserve this; retrospective attempts at interpretation would also have destroyed this. I lost it quickly myself; why? It only remained when one was alone with death, with the unseen enemy and with nature. Our community cannot grasp religion. Those who want to promote religion like saying this to each other. The organization of the future must simply leave both the individual and free groups sufficient room for religion.

Another element in the experience was the ecstasy of altruism—this feeling of having, for the first time, something in common with one's fellow Germans. One part of militant nationalism was nothing other than pacifism. This has been broken into pieces. Can we then, like Werfel, Rubiner,[19] and also bolshevism and communism, expect a regeneration on a world scale? Is the human being good? (For that is, after all, what they understand by "good.") He is good, and much more besides.

Cf. also, re the opposite pole, the black-marketeers: masochistic trait in cinema posters. Fetishism with items of female clothing. (Rich[ard] Guttmann, Morgen of [17.]11.1919).[20]

———————

Do not prophesy that the bourgeoisie is finished for good; it could still produce another culture. But do show how poorly organized it is for this.

And the obstacle is not the big capitalists but the small ones. It is not by chance that the parties of reaction, the Center Party and the Christian Socialists, are augmenting their numbers from the petty bourgeoisie.

On the other hand, do not keep quiet about how unpromising the radicals are. Fey[21] type: "Hang them all, the French will help, the essence of the German is threatened with destruction." The corruption in the C(ommunist) P(arty). If the bourgeoisie refuses to ally itself to evolution, it breeds this type.

———————

{Catac.[omb]}
I cannot say "brothers"; instead of this it is always "black-marketeer" that comes to my lips.

———————

It is not right to overlook the other side of what happened. There really existed an unparalleled willingness to make sacrifices, courage in the face of death, greatness (I am not one of those creative writers who bandied such words about and this is why I attach to them a specific idea) etc., which were displayed partly by the same people who later dealt on the black market or who today betray the Rhineland.[22] Between these two extremes there is an enormous moral space and quite a small psychological one. This is how the human being is to be understood if one wants to be of use to him.

———————

{Students}
The organization of German students did not take part in the celebrations to mark the Anniversary of the Republic.

———————

"Are those utopias"?

"Yes"   {Nat.}

"Can utopias suddenly become a reality?"

"Yes. Take the end of the war. An 'other' world almost came into existence. That it failed to appear was by no means a necessary outcome."

"So that, next day, our people may be equipped for the next day of the utopia, we must prepare them. We must accept that we shall not be writing for them any more 'Speeches to the German Nation'; that we desert it in its hour of misfortune. We must think ahead."

"'Our people'—we must mean by this: the portion of humanity to which we have access." [. . .]

On the 24.12 [1919] one could read the following in the Viennese evening papers: "In the Munich Chamber Theater, during the first, and also the 6th to 8th performances of Frank Wedekind's Schloss Wetterstein, there were riotous protests by the audience against the play. On Monday the riots became so extensive that they had to be put down by a strong contingent of police. These events have, today, caused the police to ban further performances of Schloss Wetterstein at the Chamber Theater. The Police Commissioner expressly stated, with respect to the ban, that this was not intended as any kind of censorship of the play. But the events on Monday had shown that it would not be possible, even under police protection, to hold public performances of this play, which has aroused such opposition among the public, without there being disturbances on a significant scale. It was definitely to be assumed, he said, that the disruptions to public order would be of even greater amplitude. Under these circumstances the Police Commission was not in a position, without the constant use of force *which would be out of all proportion to the significance of the occasion*, to take on responsibility for public order during further performances of the play.

In the same newspaper one read: ". . . the chess-master of genius . . ."

Over the same few days the play Tanja by Ernst Weiss was given the bird in the German Volkstheater and the "High Court of Art Critics" from the major papers found not one word of support.

Over the same few days the Jessner[23] production of William Tell became the butt of scandal.

It was through these events that I found the way to organize this book. If we were a people that lived for the spirit, all that happened to us in recent days could not have come about. We would then have been able to appear in our own defense. This is the context.

The others are not any better. This is the World War and the Peace of Paris.

In 1914 one was able to hold the view that these characteristics have no role to play, next to the following: the law, the Prussian spirit, German order, hard work, wide-branching scientific approach, etc. One might have considered these to be excesses. Today in the times of Ludendorff [. . .] murder of hostages, Eisner[24] and Ledebour-murder,[25] they mark the norm.

With the other great peoples it is probably no better.

How does such a people build itself up?

Powerlessness of the spirit. A priori.

———————————

The political future lies in the school.

The school-question is only to be solved as part of the question of how the spirit is to be developed.

———————————

Goal: philosophers' and poets' state.

Starting point: German feeling rumbles within us. But for whom? Can we love the nation? If we are honest we have to turn to very complicated explanations of what we understand by "nation." Examples.

But we are surrounded by nationalistic states (for the Czechs cf. A. Fischer, "Pan-Slavism up to the World War," Cotta).[26] We need a very powerful counterideology, otherwise we sink back into pre-Bismarckian respect for humanity.

Goal: despite all division of labor and profits we remain spiritual amateurs. Create institutions that give access to spirit. Do not relinquish the past to the schoolmen but rather to a vital discussion.

? The spiritual club? A comfortable place. One must be able to enter it from the street. Everywhere there are churches, coffeehouses. To what purpose?

A people: it consists of its papers, its civil servants, laws, schools, its military. And beyond that, it's actually no more than a nuance.

———————————

Very typical that revolutionary energy today finds expression only among the conservative parties. Count Arco,[27] Oltwig v. Hirschfeld.[28] I do not believe what is being said: that pan-German hate campaigns in newspapers are responsible for this. A young person needs more of a unifying "Idea." The responsibility lies with a situation in which the bourgeois have the stronger ideologies, the aura of ideology. On the other side there is only revolutionary romanticism.

Of the political parties, the following have ideologies today: clericals, conservatives. Socialism is formed predominantly from the ideology of liberalism—its positive parts—and beyond that from an insubstantial urge to revolt.

Liberalism has brought free trade to the realm of opinions. It has acted as a stimulant but with a centrifugal effect.

This is a major constituent of today's spiritual situation.

———————

One says, for example, that the German has broken down. That is only a literary phenomenon. He deals on the black market, the peasants gorge themselves, the Spartacists couldn't care less about Germany. So that is a chimera. The same is true of the benevolent, roguish Englishman, the egotistical Frenchman, the Russian who lives next door to God. Public spirit, who is that? Do not permit this chimera to rule any longer. Consider how it emerged. [. . .]

———————

Essay topics:
Stage prejudices (Shakesperitism) [*sic*] Against the . . . isms. [. . .]
  Soul. Understanding. Expressionism: Spengler article. [. . .]
  - intuition—Understanding: Eisler[29]
  The two psychologies: Spengler article, Münsterberg [. . .]
  - German Idealism and the Present.
  -The Problem of Spiritual Organization/School/:
  - Nation and Internationalism.
  - Dynamic Ethics. .
  Nietzsche—Socialism.
  In hoc signo vinces.[30]
  Socialism and Active Morality./Nietzsche, mysticism etc. diverge completely from each other with the exception of the desire for an active ethos instead of stasis.

  Stat[ic] morality can be derived from the economic order, from possessions.

  Workers, the only group of people who could break with this morality. [. . .]

16
NOTEBOOK 21
1920 TO 1926

[This is the third notebook containing Musil's plans for "The 20 works." It has entries on characters for the novels, brief details of their attitudes and the kind of things they do and say. It includes extracts from works by the educationalist, Georg Kerschensteiner, from Maeterlinck's The Treasure of the Meek, *from Ludwig Klages's* On Cosmogonic Love. *(Musil will incorporate ideas, and indeed text, from these and other authors into MwQ.) The notebook has entries on various aspects of narrative technique and elements of plots; it presents society as being in flux but still dominated by outdated views. One detects here that Musil is charting changes in the attitudes of successive generations—he notes, for example, how different are his views from those of Martha's children. Entries relating to Anders (the name of an earlier central protagonist) reveal the extent to which themes that later will be central to MwQ are already present in Musil's imagination: the brother-sister motif; the hero as scientist-observer, his desire to make his life significant, his self-perception as muscleman and dreamer, his associations with aristocrats; Leona and Bonadea, the hero's mistresses, and their respective appetites; the hero's fixation on the murderer, Moosbrugger; the Collateral Campaign involving preparations to celebrate seventy years of rule by the Austrian Emperor. The account of the funeral procession in which Musil walks behind the coffin of his mother will be used in MwQ (see part III, chapter 6, "The old gentleman is finally left in peace").]*

21

The 20 Works III—[. . .]

Spy: the generation of the fathers—for example, old Donath[1] behaved with indulgence toward Ach[illes]' generation as utopians whose (decadence) taste was rather difficult to understand. Kunschak[2] today would refer to the same word, "utopian" if one came to him with some or other question relating to the *Catacomb*. Utopia is a purely spiritual demand; but one must remain aware of how any rejection of it is accompanied with a measure of fatherly indulgence. {Kerschensteiner}[3]

To a certain degree the problem of the *Spy* is that of the generation since 1880. How full of élan was naturalism at the outset and how positive was the activity that was found even in the decadent atmosphere of the "fin de siècle." How much hope was to be found there! The tight-knit procession then broke ranks and, all at once, each stood alone facing the unsolved problems. Such was the spiritual situation before the war; it was without guidance from within.

People who participated in the various groupings belong in the novel. Also, representatives of the [Stefan] George type, etc. Apart from these spiritual spheres there are also the unrelated ones of science and academia, etc.

With reference to the war the following should be noted: before 1914, everything that was on the threshold of self-rebuttal, in other words, all of those born since about 1888 were, on average, for the war. Those born after 1895 were 19 years of age on the outbreak of war or in [19]15 and knew that their turn was coming. Apart from the ruffians among them, this young generation hesitates in the face of the machine as it was pushed ever closer to its jaws. These young people then became the soft-center pacifists. [. . .] A certain age is necessary for one to be prepared to put one's life at risk, if one is not subject to a powerfully romantic influence.

Girls who were 12–14 years of age at the time of mob[ilization] and accordingly did not count then, are 18–20 today. [. . .]

What is remarkable about the philosophers of Christian ethics like Foerster is that they actually say the same as what the politicians say: that skepticism is nothing but theory and literature. Whoever is really familiar with the facts, is less and less in doubt about the truths of Christian ethics.

Hopelessly defeated on the literary field, they retreat to this position.

How are such people to be woven into the fabric of the Achilles novel?[4] Where one meets them in literature outright enmity ensues. Usually in life itself each is a world, an enclosed entity, and there are few kinds of plot that really bring them into contact with each other. (Otherwise contact is restricted to protest resolutions.)

It would have to be the case that, for a moment, one of the two was in a much weakened state in order to permit the misty atmosphere of the other person to swirl about him and draw him under its spell.

Or alternatively, Achilles, in the mood of diffusion that is developing, feels a certain sympathy for this. But what about the other man? Here Agathe, in fact, could act as intermediary as someone who via mystical leanings (that in fact are repelled by Foerster's) has a relationship with them.

She feels drawn to these ethical influences and tries to follow them. (A person of today subject to influences from all sides.) The helplessness in which one finds oneself must make these often comical prescriptions seem quite serious.

"What attitude is one to take toward oneself?"—this question that all young people ask is one that the world does not answer; nor offer any form of instruction. One lives simply as it occurs to one to live. So this helps make it understandable that a person with maxims like those in Meyer-Förster[5] makes an impression on Agathe.

Her forlorn state of moral isolation is the counterpart to Ach.'s intellectual isolation.

The first meeting between brother and sister needs to be set in a context of powerful illusion; the first meeting of two heroes of a long and complicated plot.

If the duel remains:

Phase 1: As if through a mist. Ach. catches himself using attacks of the kind one learns first and that are usually automatic.

2. He is startled as if by an impending loss of all strength. Finds an opportunity to deliver a particular blow, then holds back for no apparent reason at all.

3. The opponent, who apparently has had a similar experience, becomes aggressive. Ach. receives a blow with the flat of the blade.

4. This makes him calm, full of hatred against humanity and he finishes what he has come to do.

Success with books and mass psychology are also, in some kind of way, connected. The gradations of mass, sects, etc. must also have their counterparts in a book. It is true that understanding is diminishing. The mean or average, which is the sum of several original people added together in a mass, is anticipated by the average novel. The non-individual aspect of its heroes is characteristic, the extreme abstractness. Perhaps even the speculation with well-tried emotional reactions matches those of the masses; nobility of mind, scorn, etc. with the exception {No. For it is constantly being killed off in such books.} of all acts of coarseness may well be in evidence here. Though it is true that the emotionality of the mass is augmented to a greater pitch, this is restricted to amorphous feelings—nobility of mind, anger, sympathy, etc. Where the comparison breaks down is with the preconditions under which a mass is constituted. This would mean mass psychology without the mass.

Two possibilities: either masses are constituted even without spatial-chronological unity (but then almost all physiological explanations fall by the wayside and also the impulse to talk of a mass psyche); or the mass is, after all, merely a sum. It is not the case that the reader is an individual under conditions of mass psychology but that the mass is a sum of individuals under similar conditions to those of reading. . [. . .]

Rousseau Island.[6] Martha H[eimann][7] went skating here. Glowing with passion for herself. Today it's a totally alien matter. If the artificial continuity of the "I" were not formed, death would not be any more frightening than life. There would only remain the momentary corporeal clinging.

Entrepreneurs in Berlin all insist: one person has to rack his brains and bear the brunt of concern for the whole company. That person deserves more profit. Socialism leads to bureaucracy.

Rousseau Island.

The bells of the Memorial Church are ringing. I am already no longer the person who, an hour ago, was waiting impatiently for the phone to ring. But if I had done something to be ashamed of I would still feel responsible. Or [sic] the things that touch the primeval substance possess continuity. Under this level of being is another. "I" is illusion. Beneath it something general, something that lasts. Substance. But no one can observe it. One deludes oneself. [. . .]

Types on whom the action is constructed must be constituent elements of life today. For example:

The chess player and the mathematician
The scientist
The researcher into the humanities.
The artist and the middleman-swindler
The businessman
The big businessman
The minor civil servant
The ministerial civil servant
The priest
The soldier
The technologist
The politician
The lawyer
The doctor
The worker
The peasant
[. . .]

Narrative technique Catacomb[8]

I narrate. This "I," however, is not a fictional person but the novelist. An informed, bitter, disappointed person. "I." I narrate the story of my friend Achilles. But also what has happened to me with other characters in the novel. This "I" cannot experience anything and suffers all these things from which Achilles makes good his escape and that nonetheless bring about his downfall. But without actually doing anything, without the capacity to come to a clear insight and activity, which is appropriate in the diffuse situation of today where an overview is denied. With reflection, starting out from my point of view. As if narrated by the last survivor—become wise, bitter and resigned—of the catacombs.

The narrative technique is, in general terms, objective, but, where this is desirable, ruthlessly subjective. It is possible for one to defend this as a person who would not do such a thing oneself, but it is doubtful whether it is right to do so. [. . .]

Agathe's husband (Kerschensteiner):[9] "When I set up a slide in an attempt to force desmids to take up new positions by means of some stimuli to which I subject them—this in order to help me to complete my studies on shape—or—when for the first time I angle my racquet in a particular way in order to give a particular direction to the ball whose flight had satisfied me until now if it simply made its way over the net at all, I interfere in the course of the phenomenon: *I experiment.*"

"An unhistorical attitude of mind sees in the present systems of society, state, law, moral order, and religion only a chaotic arbitrariness that is derived from the egoism, and the need for dominance and might, of individual classes and estates. The historical attitude of mind, on the other hand, teaches us to understand the world of values as a necessary process of evolution that is precisely analogous to the world of objective phenomena, and only then to judge the present and its conditions with greater accuracy and fairness."

"In history, in literature, ideals live in thousands of examples. . . . There they take on tangible shapes even for those millions of people who are not able to follow the arduous course of philosophical deductions."

Achilles: before he becomes a spy, a decisive moment occurs when he is confronted with someone called Winterstetten who prophesies the future of Europe for him. The aversion to this prophet becomes aversion to Europe.

A Jewish servant girl. Small, darting about, has come to Vienna on account of indeterminate ideals of freedom. Un-German person, ardent, always moving.[10]

Revolution and later: there is no leader available—many want something new but no one knows how to make it.

Foerster Fr. W. How to Live one's Life, Berlin, G. Reimer, very important for the *Devil-novel.* This philosopher of Christian ethics is counterpoised with the main character who has read Nietzsche before taking up the priesthood and in whom these differential calculations suddenly break through again after he had long believed that all interest in them had disappeared.

Dr. W., at a personal level a horrible man, is committed to social ethics and pedagogics and to loving solicitude for every other person.

Spy: Achilles saw the liberalism in social democracy. It has not progressed beyond this point. The scant training in logic among those who research into the humanities leads to a belief in Marx. The ethical impotence repels him. Aryan dogmatists become Catholics, Jewish Marxists? Etc.

My reform? But in *The Spy* it is simply kept at arm's length.

The times. We celebrate the festival of the coming of the Lord by eating twice as much as we do usually. (Foerster)[11]

Dehmel[12] says: In 3–10 centuries it will become evident whether or not I have succeeded with this poem. This tendency today to overestimate what it is possible to achieve through creative writing is something that Ach[illes] does not share.

The Catacomb technique of invention.
Situations of world literature.
Major ethical situations (sacrifices by a mother, fidelity, etc.)
I should offer these in my own revised form. Passion for the "Other"[13] of the kind that has accompanied me since my youth.

For example, Shakespeare: unscrupulous yearning for power, mania for revenge, ambition.

Socialism: The dialogues of Abbe Galiani,[14] translated and introduced by Franz Blei, Georg Müller, Munich, 1912.

There are interesting parallels between the period before the French Revolution and today. When one debated the corn monopoly in those days it was quite similar to now when people are writing for and against a centralized economy.

Quesnay[15] with his "ordre naturel."

This first confrontation with the enormous difficulties of organizing mankind! [. . .]

Catacomb.

Redeemer[16] is actually the second phase already, from about 1910. Before this there was f[in] d[e] siècle, new truth, building up the world.

This phase was subject to overseas influence. So this was more advanced then?

By a few years. There the problem was not solved either.

The movement became shallow there as well. But this was concealed because as yet there was no collapse.

(That would be *Redeemer* I, II. Then would come *Catacomb* when a root-and-branch attempt at salvation was made once again.)

In 1870 a great European organism had been constituted. In 1890 this underwent its spiritual crisis. Up till then, degeneration of a tradition that had simply been taken over (in the struggle against business enterprise and initiative and the intoxication of the aftermath of war); around 1890 "labor pangs" of its own soul *Redeemer*-"Idea" around 1910 already represents resignation. One of the reasons for turning to religion is because the synthesis of soul and "ratio" was unsuccessful.

That then leads on to the war.

Thus the history of Germany is only a paradigm of world history. More visible because the organism is new.

{Germany as a model for the world that is the idea of the *Catacomb*.} [. . .]

Narrative technique. The usual course of events longitudinally through time is actually a compulsion. Narrate straight down the path along which the problems happen to take shape in Ach. One has a notion that is decisive for one's life. X years later one takes one step forward or backward in this. These two events belong one after the other. What lies between them is only mentioned in so far as it is of significance, for example, a dream, the first car journey and the second. [. . .]

Satyr[ical], narr[ative] technique. Can usually be expressed in the formula: "pretend to be stupid." Narrate with assumed naïveté. (Sterne's[17] way of never bringing the preparation of the narrative to a close also belongs to this category.) That is also the nature of ironic people when they make polite remarks that one doesn't know how to interpret.

Dr. P. rounded this up into a formula: "imitate imperfectly." One exaggerates something, for example, in legal processions by adding a couple of words too many. Or when depicting a soldier by emphasizing, or suppressing, certain aspects. Then the familiar figure is somehow wrong and one is compelled to reflect.

Next formula (by me): loosening of the bonds that habit and necessity entail. In the *lettres persanes*[18] [. . .] French conditions are presented using Persian names. That suffices.

These points of view are also applicable to the accustomed contexts of causality and fate.

The Annina[19] generation. [. . .]

That human life is not sacred in the slightest runs just as much against the grain of conviction for Gaetano[20] as it does for Annina. My generation was anti-moral or amoral because our fathers talked of morality and behaved in a philistine and immoral fashion. The present generation of fathers talked of the immorality (of the war) and behaved in a philistine and moral fashion (shoulder to shoulder). So, from the same oppositional stance that we had, children today are moral, but want people to be serious about morality.

A positive and negative deflection around truth. How is one to be successful with truth! [. . .]

Satyr. narr. technique.

Fragments of the life's work of Anders. Has reached a standstill at the point where he did not break through, for example, right at the beginning with the dream:[21] theory of the dream. What significance does this dream have, then? One comes up against the individual element that cannot be subsumed under any rule.

The adventures are instances of standing still in the grander perspective.

He knows so much about the characters because he has studied them.

One could follow up immediately on the dream with an episode with a psychoanalyst. Then only afterward say that this took place 18 months later. Thus one could pretend to be a stupid narrator and, in so doing, introduce the new narrative technique that is completely spiritual, factual and inward. [. . .]

Edition of my essays. Title: Detours.

All the published essays came about by chance and therefore their form is also dictated by chance. The idea of collecting them does not appeal to me. The thoughts they express are often better in preceding drafts. It is with these thoughts that I am concerned. For various reasons I cannot carry them out. But I can lift them up from where they originate, set them next to each other according to their natural groupings and add some explanation. Questions and inadequate answers on creative writing.

Satyr. technique. Even what that one loves must be thought through and mastered to the extent that it appears satirical.

The times (after revol.)[22]

The relationship of someone from the middle ranks of business to someone with pots of money is the same as his relationship used to be to the ruler and to the authoritarian state. One perhaps feels that these people are standing on our shoulders but they are also responsible for everything being properly run. This is the reason for the fanatical defense of capitalism by people who do not gain anything from it whatsoever. They are against the Socialists in the way that the bourgeoisie were once against agitators and subversives. However much the workers demand in wages, the entrepreneur, the middleman, etc., gets more, and the various layers of society have a certain stability. That is the invisible and mighty reign of cash.

The times: capitalism is simply the same pessimism as militarism. [. . .]

Germany's collapse was not brought about by her immoral, but by her moral, citizens. Morality was not undermined but proved to be hollow.

Anders, {soon to be} the right hand of Harrach[23] who enjoys giving {a certain amount of} protection to a bourgeois intellectual who is passionate about science [. . .], makes him into a kind of secretary of the Campaign.[24] Because of this everything goes via him.

And because he is a bourgeois all those people of higher standing who want something or other turn to him. Those lowlier people, like stenographers, or those who seek healing in nature,[25] etc., are brought to him by Redbeard.

He receives invitations from all quarters, etc.

He gets to know the rest through the Moosbr[ugger] affair, through Ag[athe]—Foerster and the struggle with Lindner.[26]

Ludwig [Sütterlin], *The Contemporary German Language—Its Sounds, Words, Word-forms, Sentences,* Voigtländer, Leipzig, 1910.

Polis, contest, military competence, art, beauty, mysteries, tradition—on all of these are focused the unbroken instincts of the Greeks before Socrates.

Plato-Socrates posit the following: a human being wants to achieve happiness through his actions; if he does not achieve it this is due to mistakes in his handling of the means. (Virtue = reasonableness = infallible path to happiness because reasonableness makes any mistake impossible.)

Even the anti-intellectuals who want art in the community go back, in emotional terms, etc., to Nietzsche.

Diotima: she likes to say "altars," for example, "altars of sentiment." "Silence is the element in which great things take shape";[27] instances: her pretentious indecisiveness; "Let us not yet speak—rather give me your hand."

"The word, too, is great," she says, "but there are things that are yet greater." {This is where D[iotima] and Arnh[eim] find each other. Reasons. Intuition.}

"The instinct for the superhuman truths that resides within us all shows us that it is dangerous to be silent with someone whom we do not wish to know better."

"To listen to another soul and to bestow on our own a moment of life."

"The depths of the sea of beauty within us," {she said.}

"Minutes in which suddenly all hidden jewels are laid bare."

"The kiss of silence in misfortune—for it is, strange to say, in misfortune that we are kissed by silence—" (Misfortune: her husband) "one can never forget thereafter."

"The mystery of silence in the face of death or of love is the same for king and slave."

"Try to be silent with me; there are beings with whom the greatest hero would not dare to be silent." {D[iotima] to A[rnheim]}

{She has suddenly become unhappy with her husband. This makes the sensual side of A more powerful. To this are added dialogues about eroticism.}

Soul[28]
The word is the servant only of unreal communications. One speaks in those hours when one is not alive. As soon as we speak, doors close. The silence of a crowd is an inexplicable weight. People gather only in order to speak.

This means: the thin barque of the rational in which we row on the irrational. {[. . .] impression that Ag[athe] calls forth again.} The true truth [*sic*] between two people cannot be expressed. Every kind of exertion intrudes. The souls unite when lips are apart.

Everything in life proceeds according to a prior consent of which not one word is spoken. (These are the people whose lives are immediate and present at every moment, encircling them.) [. . .]

Diotima:
There will perhaps come a time—and there are many signs that it is close—perhaps there will come a time when our souls will see each other without the mediation of the senses.

Occult powers are waking round about us: magnetism, telekinesis and levitation. And[ers] finally takes D[iotima] to such seances. Scientific spiritism—materialization.

If you are not good your presence reveals this today to the awakening soul in a far clearer fashion than in earlier centuries: positively an incentive not to be good. [. . .]

"We never step outside the little circle of light that our fate draws around where we tread, and one might say that the most distant people know the coloring and extent of this ring that cannot be crossed. It is the color of these spiritual rays that they notice first, and this makes them reach out their hand to us with a smile or timidly withdraw it. We all know each other in some higher region and the image that I have of someone I have not met is in direct contact with a mysterious truth that is deeper than the material truth. Who among us has not experienced these things that occur in the impenetrable spheres of a humanity that belongs, almost, to the stars?"

Ag[athe]

Presentiments, strange impression of an encounter or a glance; a resolving,[29] one knows not why.

Who among us does not spend the greater part of his life in the shadow of an event that has not yet taken place?

Never are those we embrace the object of our most profound love. {Prelude D[iotima]—Arnh[eim]}

Thoughts give an involuntary shape to the invisible movements within. As soon as we say something we devalue it in some strange way. One can call for suffering in order to find a more real self within it. (Emerson) {M[ein]g[ast][30] Ag[athe]'s parallel to A[nder]s' being evil.}

Sins do not reach the soul. "The soul of the sodomite could pass through the midst of the crowd without sensing anything and in its eyes would be the innocent smile of a child." "*All depends on an invisible principle.*" {Basic idea. They vacillate between this and marriage.}

Love: the realm of unmediated certainty—this is right. {The realm of kindliness (even when one offends)}

Here, souls do nothing other than recognize each other again, observing, admiring.

Lovers are emissaries whose paths cross at a predestined moment. (She must become certain of this for the first time in the encounter with Anders. Now her empty former life receives its justification.)

A woman submits to predestination with greater simplicity, she never resists it openly. For this reason she gives a man a presentiment of a life that is not the life of the phenomena.

Thoughts, words, but also deeds are nothing in love. They do not reach as far as the soul. So neither does infidelity.

{A woman does not take actions, words and ideas into account. She believes only the first glance.}

(Anders' mistake is that he takes her completely away from Lindner.[31] Even she would do something to him eventually. But some element of friendship and sympathy ought to have remained. Beginning of her destruction by Anders.)

———————

Diotima
The silent child is a thousand times wiser than Marcus Aurelius speaking. (Admittedly, M[aeterlinck] remarks, the child would perhaps not be as wise if Marcus Aurelius had not spoken.)

———————

Ag[athe]
The psychology of passion basically does not concern us. One can commit a crime without being affected by it (the younger one is, the less one is affected; it is only with the passage of the years that one subjects oneself to the convention of taking these strong emotions seriously. R M.)[32] On the other hand, a glance, a minute without any sound, can raise a terrible whirlwind and flood one's life. (Couldn't one say: we possess a completed personality and one that is always in a process of emerging. The first has passions, thoughts, etc. The second is the unformed substance of humanity, the person minus the influences that have shaped him, that which might also have come about in a different fashion.) {(That is the person with ideas who is changed by motives.)}

"Which angel will ask Titus why he did not marry Berenice and why Andromache promised herself to Pyrrhus?"[33]

Mysterious powers in us seem to be in collusion with adventures in the outside world. We all carry enemies in our soul. Whenever they lead us toward the event their communications are indistinct, not clear enough to stop us but sufficient, nonetheless, to make us regret that we did not pay more attention to their vague and mocking advice. What impetus is behind these forces that after all share our doom?

In the hour of misfortune we are seized by a whirlwind that has taken years to weave.

––––––––––––

Diotima
Star, too. Connection with the astrologers.

––––––––––––

Ag[athe]
We are never so intimately ourselves as on the day after the catastrophe. Before, there was a huge exertion, of which we knew nothing, to avoid it; but when one is lying at the bottom of the abyss one feels a strange peace, a mysterious sense of relief.

What is the point of cultivating an "I" on which we have almost no influence whatsoever? We must watch our star—(changing fortune and misfortune, the circumstances of our misfortune . . . ? The piling up of events—their connection with certain people . .)

The power of the unborn and the power of the dead rules over us (Schopenhauer: species).³⁴

––––––––––––

Up till now have always drawn Promethean people. Couldn't I also love frivolous ones (*Peer Gynt*)³⁵ and criticize life [by depicting a character] who does not take it seriously and has something of the engaging rogue about him?

––––––––––––

Raw asparagus shoots, lying loose: these somewhat misshapen ovals. These flat phalluses, bent in many different ways, standing erect. With three-edged armor-plating. {Knotty.} Recurring at the point but like a flower. {Tapered. More delicate.} Violet flesh tints. Hard stems.

Studied by two women-friends. [. . .]

––––––––––––

Fishing on Usedom.³⁶
On the beach a little hollow is scooped out by hand and, out of a sack filled with black soil, the fat earthworms are tipped; the loose black soil and the

knot of worms make a loamy, uncertain, intriguing ugliness against the bright sand. Next to them is laid a {wooden} tray {that looks like} a proper table drawer, long, but not very wide, or like a money drawer {full} of clean yarn, and an empty tray {is laid} on the other side; the hundred hooks that are attached to the yarn are arranged neatly along a little iron rod at the end of the tray and are taken off, one after the other, and bedded down in the other tray filled {at one end} with damp sand. While this is happening 4 long, lean and powerful hands {as careful as those of children's nurses} are ensuring that each hook gets a worm.

Two men crouch down on the sand on their knees and heels. They have powerful, bony backs and long, kindly faces, a pipe in their mouths and incomprehensible words that issue as softly from them as the movements of their hands. One of them takes a fat earthworm in two fingers and, gripping it as well with {the same} two fingers of the other hand, tears it gently into three pieces, {gently and precisely} like a cobbler clipping off the paper strip after taking measurements, while the other one, gently, attentively, pushes these writhing pieces down over the hook. When that has been done they are {regaled with water and} bedded down into rows of small {dainty} trenches in the {tray with the} soft sand so that they will stay fresh. This is done silently, delicately, and the coarse fingers seem to walk quietly on tiptoe. The matter demands close attention. Above this, the sky has stretched a blue vault, and the gulls are circling high above the land like swallows.—(Fishermen poetry on U[sedom].) [. . .]

Anders[37]

Meeting with sister is first event in the narrative proper.

Up till then description of the man. Do not simulate narrative.

House and street: situation that no one can master, whatever kind of person he is.

{One sits at the edge of a mass in chaotic motion.}

The state of isolation, observation post, also simply follows on from that.

The logician by training. The man of precision with the awareness that precision does not lead to happiness.

A host of contradictory qualities can be explained in this way, for example that a university lecturer is a boxer. Remnant of a wish for greatness made up of boyish elements. Later this has turned into a means of contact with humanity. Happy in brawls. {(Perhaps start with such a brawl. Then the house on the following morning.)}

Perhaps here, too, the impossibility of fitting out a house.

Leona and Bonadea,[38] two forms in which an inability to establish relationships with human beings finds expression. He is very unhappy in all his wrongdoings.

The letter:[39] shadowy intuition of the extent of his own physiological conditioning. At the same time, anti-traditionalism.

Moosbrugger sets various reference bells ringing all at once.

Visit to G[raf] St[allburg]: finished reality and the unfinished individual. {(Actually {Graf} B.[40] with his "We are making history" ought to be the subject of an earlier stage of the narrative. Provides the focus.)}

That everything is "other" is a peripheral conception in young people with talent. State, morality, etc., senseless. {Suitable for the climax would be the will and testament.}[41] But he does not have the resources to fill the void. On the contrary, he recognizes that, as he dogmatizes, he is becoming impoverished. That is the critical point. Two paths: have recourse to love or anticipate cynicism that gives wings to the pen. L[eona] and B[onadea] were half-baked things; the "Collateral Campaign" makes itself available. [. . .]

The non-alloyed nature of the two sides within him.[42]

It is true that he has power over women but he makes very sparing use of it. Repugnance predominates. He lives in a withdrawn, hyper-"I"-oriented way. Waiting for the total solution.

What then happens is, in fact, only a reduction in the strength of this demand. He takes a little more interest in people and it is their stupidity that provides the impetus. This is so with Diotima, and also Arnheim, who is interested in him from the outset.

Example of the style: A[nders] had been interested in the theory of legal accountability.[43] Here there are principles like . . . And this winds its way back to Kant, {Fichte}, Pufendorf[44] and Aristotle. Was this the very life substance of the two old men?[45] What name does one give to this relationship to life? The senile squad? Moosbr[ugger] seen from that angle was only as lacking in accountability as a woman, etc.

He leafs through the papers among the estate.[46] (Medal) The schism within himself becomes recognizable. He is seized by monstrous fear. Then

Agathe comes . . Agathe is his autism. Describe something of what that is.
[. . .]

   Possibly insert here the beginning of the Collateral Campaign without
him. "We are making history" Graf B had said. So, for the time being, they
are making "history" without him, he could be there with them, he would
like, after all, to know what that is.

Roundabout on Usedom. {People flying}[47]
There was once a time, when one rode round in a circle with pedantic precision on a little horse as stiff as a ramrod and, using a little stick that was
straight as a die, thrust out at copper rings that a stiff wooden arm held out
as you passed by. These times are past. Today the fisherlads drink champagne with brandy. And, on 30 times 4 little iron chains, hang little wooden
swings—all in two circles, one within, one without—in such a way that
{when one flies around next to one another} one can catch hold of hands or
legs or aprons and let out terrific yells as well. This roundabout stands on
the little square with the monument to the fallen warriors, next to the old
lime tree where, usually, the geese are to be found. It has an engine that occasionally drives it and chalk-white searchlights fixed above many little
warm lights. When one feels one's way closer in the darkness the wind
throws snatches of music, lamplight, women's {girls'} voices, and laughter in
one's direction. The organ dances {shouts} and sobs. The iron chains squeal.
One flies around in a circle, but also if {when} one wants, upward and {or}
downward, outward and inward {each into the other's back or between
each other's legs}. The lads whip their swings high up into the air and pinch
the girls' legs as they fly past them or make them scream out as they are
pulled along with them; the girls, too, snatch at each other in flight and then
two of them scream at once just as if a man were there {as if one were a
man}. So they all go swinging through {the cones of} brightness into darkness and are suddenly hurled back into the brightness, in different pairs,
with foreshortened bodies and black mouths, racing bundles of illuminated
clothing flying by on back or belly, or diagonally toward heaven or hell.
{But} After quite a short spell of this wildest of gallops the organ abruptly
falls back to a trot, then to a walk, just like an old circus horse, and quickly
stops. The man with the pewter plate goes round the circle, but {after all}
they remain seated or at most change girls. And, it is not like the city where
different people come to the roundabout over a period of several days, but
{for} here it is always the same people who ride {fly} from the time when
dusk descends for two to three hours, throughout the whole week or fort-

night, until the man with the roundabout {and the pewter plate} senses that enthusiasm is waning, and one morning has gone on his way.

Anders
He wants to become a great person. Also has the makings of one. Soldier, engineer are first attempts. In the way he carries this out there are indications of talent. Religious systems, philosophical reflections when still a boy, betray great potential. At the same time, a strong, autistic component. But this can also be explained by his being an only child.

Becoming a great person: how does one go about that? Here lies the satirical side. However strong the demand for great people may be, no one knows how they become great. Clearly in the most varied kinds of ways; but these beings who are wise by accident are put forward as being of the greatest significance. Diotima, Gerda,[48] Bonadea are different versions of greatness. Nietzsche, Carlyle, Marx, Christ: individual variants, not the thing itself. In fact success is decisive only "post festum." It is only afterward that it arrives. That is the principle of evil. {The individual is a fool if he strives for something general.}

The sea:[49] it is probably the great size and sweep of the outline? This far-ranging certainty {encircling, not with a thousand hands but with one arm and no brain} that is superhuman. Or {only}, filled with an unusual color, this barrenness? Or the bell of heaven that {nowhere else in this way} sits immediately over it, {over life}? Or air and water, about which one never reflects, set up to display their immeasurable significance for human life?. [x]% of us consist of water, and the soul is breath. One becomes so small {once one has left the railway train}, for hundreds of thousands of years, since the time of the first myths, no essential progress has been made. And these [myths] with their immense progress: is there not some revelation behind this? Is there not, after all, intuition within us? {Arm in arm. Sky and sea flowed together in them. Love, greatness flowed through them.}

And next to them this immensely blessed life of laurel, gorse, bees. . . .

Anders
The love of brother and sister must be strongly defended. A[nders] perceives it as something deep, as something connected with his rejection of the world. The autistic component of his nature is here fused together with love. It is one of the few opportunities for unity that are given to him.

In the house of death[50] there is only a shimmering anticipation of this. [. . .]

The unfortunate tendency of our times to form sects is an evil dreamlike structure set up over the fear of death, over the separation of the individual from the generality and the horde.

Incest is an expression of the fear of death; roughly according to Jung. [. . .]

Motif:

A man wants to enter a monastery. Tired of this life. Dawn is breaking; bench next to the monastery wall. A cocotte has attached herself to him even though he finds this irritating.

Then a monk makes good his escape over the wall. Coarse peasant type. Longing for cinema, newspaper and brothel.

They exchange clothes and roles.

At the end the former wants to get out of the monastery, the second wants to get back in. (Title: "Carnival") [. . .]

Anders.

What it means I have no idea.

He was a very masculine man. Muscular, daring, adventure loving, circumspect, a conqueror and hunter of women. But when he was a little boy, in the years when they still wear girls' clothes, he had {himself} the secret wish to be a {this} girl. At such moments he felt that he was leaning against the door of a room filled with miracles but could not open it. Since the difference in the sexes is not clear to someone of his age, reality was certainly insuperable, but its blood-warm resistance, unhampered as it was by any reflection about how it might be realized was transpierced by his wish. Perhaps the only thing that happened here was that the soul of a girl that he may well have borne inside him still, was yearning for the boy-soul in him and for minutes on end submerged the other one.

He did not desire as a man desires a woman, but as a woman desires, and this was confirmed by what he later experienced when he truly fell in love for the first time.

(This "goodness" of love as sisterliness, obscuring of the polarity of the "I," etc.)

And this was further confirmed by the way that "sister" as a notion, despite all sexual experiences, retained for him a strange magic. [. . .]

Reunion.

4 people, who had once been young together, meet again.

A creative writer and his wife. Once they were "in love." Then treated each other "badly." The woman deceived him, he was jealous, possession had taken possession of them. They held it against each other that they had fallen out of the state of love.

Today all the writer's powers are spent. He has written many things, but not the book of love. He realizes that he has failed in his work.

In material terms too, both are finished. The writer, close to fame, has used up all his means and those of his wife (in actual fact the husband preys as a parasite on the lovers). He loathes the thought of writing something new.

They go to a sanatorium. Want to kill themselves. Suspicion that this is caused by nerves. Want to be certain that they don't do it from neurasthenia. And, moreover, want to enjoy the last weeks.

A friend of their youth was an academic {sthenic type} then became second doctor in a sanatorium. Is disappointed by scientific pursuits. With him, the faithful wife who still loves him; but with her, too, no happiness is to be found.

They decide to experiment, once more before they die, as a foursome, of living "in love."

All this takes place in a sanatorium and, seen from there, is an insane affair. A sick fancy. The most important thing in the world! [. . .]

Otto Gruppe, The Greek Cults and Myths in their Relationships to Oriental Religions. All attempts at Interpreting the sagas up to 1887, 300 pp.[51]

De Jong, The Nature of the Ancient Mysteries. (Review of the secret rites.)[52]

Burckhardt, The Time of Constantine the Great.[53]

Anrich, The Nature of the Ancient Mysteries in their Influence on Christianity.[54]

Franz Cumont, The Mysteries of Mithras (translated by Gehrich).[55]
Mogk, Germanic Mythology.[56]
Robertson Smith, The Religion of the Semites (translated by Stübe)[57]
J.G. Müller, History of the Primitive Religions of America.[58]

Reference books:
    Preller, Greek Mythology.[59]
    Roscher, Encyclopaedia of Mythology.[60]
    Pauly, Encyclopaedia.[61]

Bruno Schindler, The Magic Life of the Spirit, 1857.[62]
Görres, Christian Mysticism, 5 vols.[63]
Laistner, The Mystery of the Sphinx—Basic Elements of a History of
    Myths, 1889[64] (Connection with dreaming).
Mannhardt, Cults of Wood and Field, 2 vols.[65]
Pfannenschmid, Germanic Harvest Festivals, (Holy Water in Hea-
    then and Christian Cults).[66]
Rohde, Psyche.[67]

N[ietzsche], Birth of Tragedy.
J.J. Bachofen, Mothers and the Law.[68]
    The Symbolism of Graves in the Ancient World.[69]
    The Lycian People.[70]
    The Saga of Tanaquill.[71] [. . .]

Priests: the homosexual element in religion: God "overpowers," enters into the believer, "fulfils," "weakens," "ravishes" him, etc.—nothing but examples of "surrender," of imagined corporeality in relation to which one's own is feminine. Belonging here is the exclusion of women from church. They are a complicated, petty element. The believer goes among them, fulfilled by his God. But this behavior is very autistic and is usually directed against those who share one's religious belief. Church people are accordingly not disposed to speak well of this matter and try to make religion profane.

In the post-war decay, this behavior is like an island.

Anders

When L[eona] has stuffed herself full of food, A[nders] reads. Then there is also the game with antiquated sexuality, something verging on perversion, a withdrawal from ever directly touching each other, a sense of repugnance for human beings. This had led him over to his other mistress.[72] This is like a cabinet full of rare things, a collection of porcelain—he doesn't feel quite comfortable with them, his muscles tell him they were made for something better.

When, at a later stage, real, animated experiences are depicted, the difficulty that then arises is that I do not actually take them seriously. But no person takes them seriously and that is the essential aspect. One cannot live without reading daily in the paper about adventures, but it is only as one reads about them that they are exciting; when they are actually being experienced they seem antiquated. This source of illumination should be directed toward the lack of seriousness of politicians, of adventures, and finally of the war as well. Also on the way that a group of people is centered on the newspaper reports about M[oosbrugger].

L. Lévy-Brühl, Thinking of Native Peoples, Braumüller, 1921 (Les fonctions mentales dans les sociétés inférieures, 1910)[73] [. . .]

Peschuèl-Loesche, The Loango Expedition, 1907.
Preuss, K. Th. The Spiritual Culture of Native Peoples, in From the World of Nature and Spirit, Vol. 452. 1914.
The Origin of Religion and Art, Globus, Vol. 86.
The Beginnings of Religion and Art, Globus, 92 (Vierkandt).
Preuss, Phallic Fertility Demons as Figures in Ancient Mexican Drama, Archive for Anthropology, New Series, I.
H. Reich, Mime
E. Grosse, The Beginnings of Art, Freiburg, 1894.
Developmental Phenomena in the Ornamentation of Native Peoples, Proceedings of the Anthropological Society, Vienna, 1892 (Hjalmar Stolpe, Degenerative Sequences)
A. Vierkandt, The Problem of the Rock Paintings, Archive for Anthropology, New Series VII, 1909.
Koch-Grünberg, South-American Rock Paintings, 1907.
R. Thurnwald, Researches on the Solomon Islands and the Bismarck Archipelago, 1912 (Hornbostel)

Vierkant, Cultured Peoples and Native Peoples, 1896.
Groos, Karl, The Games Animals Play, Jena, 1886.
F. H. Cushing, Manuel [sic] Concepts, in American Anthropologist [sic], V, p. 291ff.[74] [. . .]

Behind a coffin:[75]

Remarkable condition days afterward: he[76] can emphasize objectively her bad qualities, even say that some malicious expression was made involuntarily or make a joke; indeed, he believes she was bad; and the next moment tears burst from his eyes.

Dreadful condition: one would like to do or say something kind. One refuses to grasp that this is no longer possible. {After all} I did not take my leave, it is not finished; for me it is not over, only for her. Those who watched her waste away are better prepared; there is an element of release in this for them as well.

As a child I prayed: "Unknown higher being, make me and my parents live for ever." Now that, as a man, after a long absence I have begun to turn my steps toward him and have prayed: "Give me a sign," he makes her die.

At a subjective level, the plea seemed to have taken effect since there was some remission, her condition stabilized with hope for a half-measure of improvement until, all of a sudden, came the collapse. "In objective terms," Dr. Mager says, "if we had not given her the insulin injection, she would have died two months earlier."

I greet those present in the name of my father. I have to go in the first rank behind the carriage, with two much older gentlemen on either side of me. It is an act of representation. "The people" look on. I can understand the feelings of a successor to a throne to whose shoulders power has been transferred. Such a death was rendered weightless by the consciousness of the act of state. The successor has already taken the place of the dead man; one does not stare into this horrific hole.

But occasionally I look into the reflecting glass panes of the carriage and see my head, hat and shoulders.

Here and there, flakes of wax on the ground that have not been swept up. It is a soft, clear, magnificent winter's day.

It is only to Julie,[77] of all the people present, that I want to say a few kind words.

In the mortuary there are at least a dozen coffins. Big ones, small child-sized ones, some elegant, some simple. A label: "Hermine Musilova." Factory[-made coffin]. When we walk to the mortuary, at ground level to one side on the right, the upper part of a window in the hospital is open. Heinrich points it out to me. "This is the room where she died." And his feelings "burst" forth; his lower jaw is pushed out like a hook.

Unimaginable: behind these six planks, there she is.

A post mortem has been carried out on her: pancreas, bleeding into the brain. Not sewn up properly, no doubt. Behind the planks, this cadaver, barely sewn together; in front of the planks, solemnity and illusion.

Papa and Mama do not believe in life after death. What happens to the dead body is of no consequence. The burial is of the cheapest kind. No priest. No one informed. Only a few friends. The coffin is lifted into a wagon at the shunting-yard. Freight, not express goods. No one travels with it. From Saturday morning to Tuesday the coffin goes wandering along the tracks and through stations. In Reichenberg[78] it is put in the oven. Ashes to lie there for one year in an urn, then scattered.

Papa does not wish to be comforted with possibilities. His pain is that this will never be again. Everything that reminds him must go. "I have become a hermit with her," he says, "Don't take it amiss, I even prefer it if you are not here."

After the arrival, walk through the familiar town.[79] Is it possible that she is not there? All these sensations are banal and unbelievably strong.

At home, remarkably, her absence is not felt. I can scarcely imagine where she found space, although the house is, after all, hardly a small one. I tried to imagine her in all her favorite places, but as yet I cannot account for this very clear sensation.

The agent from the funeral parlor. Thickset Jew with blond moustache. With a form in his hand like a travel guide. Examines this and that. Climbs into the wagon. He's everywhere.

"'She's a thief!'[80] dear Mama said," Papa tells me, and is so moved he begins to weep; all the while, there was not a shred of substance to this and it was not an act of kindness but rather one of antipathy. During her illness she often fell into a rage. She had Heinrich[81] turn over the pillows 15 times, one after the other and with increasing anger. He imitates the way she snarled at him, baring her teeth, both jaws pushed forward, and he is touched at the thought.

Over the last three days, her senses dulled and she was very disturbed when she woke up. On the last day, in her sleep, convulsive twitching.

"Doctor, must I die?" was the question she asked when she was brought to the hospital. "The mousetrap" was her name for the hospital. But her consciousness remained hopeful. [. . .]

"*New Irony.*" The social mores, the morals, etc. are totalities in which individual things appear to be determined. In world-historical terms, however, these are "Gestalt" forms shaped by the trial-and-error that is life, in just the same way that it has shaped the dinosaurs, etc., that succeed each other like failed experiments. When one looks at life in this way one arrives at an absolute (religious) lack of respect. [. . .]

In a tram. Girl, perhaps 12 years of age, with a very young father or elder brother. In the way she enters, takes her seat, casually hands the conductor the money, she is quite the lady, but without any affectation. She is miraculously beautiful. Brown-skinned, full lips, strong eyebrows, nose slightly turned-up. Perhaps Southern Slav. Her features are in advance of her years, and yet this is not the face of a dwarf woman but that of a child.

One can fall passionately in love with such a girl, madness from the very first glance—components of sexuality that have not been satisfied.

(A[nders] at a moment of retreat in the face of order.)

Story about cannibals and consumptives.

Girl or young woman. In the first days after her arrival, only a soft mountain of air upon her. Then the sun sends a hail of little darts into her torso. One feels that it is like the dry body of a violin. Anxiety: will things get better? Shame as one looks into the face of the doctor when one puts this anxious question, as all of them do.

She notices a neighbor. He nods to her. She knows nothing about this person. Her husband has deserted her—though this was what he had to do. She has entered the life of those exposed to die. A human being—this man next to her—may be warm and engaging, without one knowing anything about him.

They help each other to pass the time.

He was a journalist. Much traveled. Concessions toward public and publisher—for the sake of success. How far back in the past it all was.

They speak about the difficult position of humanity. They are fellow countrymen, Germans.

He says: every state of mixed feelings is normal; only from the perspective of one element developed to an extreme does the extreme development of another element appear monstrous. One has within oneself more possibilities than can be guessed from the normal state of rest. [. . .] And these have not been exploited; the woman has felt envious of this man who has seen the world. If we subtract the environment from ourselves, what is left over is something without shape.

Or he doesn't say that at all—or only a part of it. And he tells her the story of cannibalism. Every evening, lying in the dark clinic. And they become "without shape," come out of themselves; one does not know if they just tell this to each other or whether they experience it. It must be ghostly, they are already living an "other" life; the whole world seems to have come under their sway, these consumptives are stronger than the passionate shapers of the world.

Then they are separated since the woman's condition has improved and his condition has remained serious.

Motif: a profiteer who is a supporter of K[arl] Kraus. [. . .]

Image of the world:[82]
A particular mass of ideas forms a group around the most probable mean-values as in kinetic gas theory. It is of no consequence what one does or propagates, only the mean-value emerges.

It is very seldom that a new idea is added or an old one is extinguished. These ideas always come about in connection with external events, for example, the scientific *Weltanschauung* is derived from that of the Church not via polemics but via the findings of research, technology, etc.

At most, there emerge certain "directions" in ideas, certain groupings.

The mean-value shifts only very slowly whereas the oscillations that are grouped around it are of extreme violence.

Figure; an anarchist who believes in God? [. . .]

Krausians.
Bettauer[83] treats Kraus, who once pilloried him "unjustly," with pained reverence.

Kraus is positively developing into a complex.

The journalist takes the slovenliness of style and the lack of moral substance about his profession and sets it as something objective outside himself. Kraus is the redeemer figure; Kraus, by simply being there and pouring out abuse, makes everything good again. Objectified bad conscience. Of course, this effect is not a favorable one.

Kraus' opposition to war is, in moral terms, just as sterile as the enthusiasm for war. [. . .]

Mariazell:

The church is in an elevated position on a square that slopes downward. The area in front of the church is edged with trees and walls. In the direction of the slope, a set of stairs, two angels on columns. In the other recesses in the walls, saints on columns. Below, built against the wall, the shops for the pilgrims. Almost all selling gold and silver goods. Christ chased the merchants from the temple but they stopped at the wall. Next to the feet of the saints is written, in large letters, "Gold and Silver." Catholicism says: "When the heart is purified one likes to give one's loved ones a present."

The "other"[84] is not felt by the thick-skinned. After the procession into the church there follows a gathering with a political speech, then gorging. {Covetousness, gluttony celebrate triumphs in M[aria] Z[ell].}

The church is a basilica with a Renaissance facade between whose cupola towers a higher Gothic tower has been inserted: compression.

In the evening, the procession, with its red lanterns, rhythmic bleating and muffled music, comes swaying on like a file of poor souls. Slowly this traces its steps around the basilica, then snakes back and forth across the square like a heating-element. Suggestive means.

At the end they pray for the Pope and for Seipel.[85] Then the priest gives the command: "Put them out. Tomorrow, etc. . . ." Some want something else (to be taken into the open, illuminated church, or something similar). Coarse as a corporal, the priest says: "Finished, I said. Put out candles. 'Finished' means 'finished'." {In the tone there is something from the past like "His Majesty, our Most Elevated Lord in Battle, Hurrah! Hurrah! Hurrah!"}

At the head of the procession, two groups, each of four virgins, carry two wax statues of the Virgin Mary with rich vestments. These life-size figures are remarkably small. Stunted and beautiful. These are similar to each other but not the same. Strange notion: Mary is present in two figures, she is this one, and that one, too. Like in a sex dream.

{On the other hand: a strange Mary who has herself carried every day by different people, wearing white confirmation clothing, with thread-gloves, and hearts throbbing from the experience.}

The "simultaneity" of Catholicism. Above the wall, a procession of pilgrims is led around, below it, a man buys a pipe or a ring.

By the way, these smaller processions are extraordinarily slovenly; "rabble." With umbrellas, in disorderly bunches, they trudge behind the priest in his white-red-gold vestments.

Re: evaluation: how much more perfect are the ceremonies of the primitive peoples.

There are so many dogs that this could only be a market in Styria. All impossible hybrids. But they do not become embroiled in mutual butchery as they do in the Valley of the Enns, but their dealings with each other are loving and friendly. Even the stranger does not find himself surrounded by canine mistrust.

The coffeehouse is busy from one morning to the next. At night there are card games. In the afternoon the "Goal-Game."[86] Regulars arrive with a leather glove on one hand. A girl, no longer so young, hangs off her stool taking aim and fires off one shot after the other from the gun, with contorted face and blouse escaping from her skirt. The whole thing is a boys' war game. Preparation for fighting.

One woman says that she thought the Virgin Mary was quite good, "But the clothes weren't at all nice; they ought to be blue and red."[87]

They are the same kind of people as those who splash out on decorated hackney-cabs during confirmation festivities in Vienna. Big fat necks, bellies, sub-alpine East Berlin.

Demonstration of how the popular economy works: not all robbery takes place on a grand scale. [. . .]

Motif (novella, perhaps drama later) {Ed.}[88]

Young worker pulls himself up by his own bootstraps, acquires theoretical knowledge, finally prepares for matriculation in order to be able to take higher-level examinations. As he crams, nervous breakdown.

Through history we create a sense of the locality of the point where we stand, which is similar to that which emerges in our continuous orientation in time and space.

Just take historical data and change them round as you will. The Battle of Cannae is followed by the Peace of Versailles. Emperor Max[imilian] of Mexico was the son of Napoleon I, and suchlike. What changes take place? Things that have happened fit firmly to other things that have happened, the motivating transition falls by the wayside as unnecessary and illusory. The immense importance that we attach to existence, when we see it in terms of historical derivations, makes a mockery of itself. One comes up with the kinetic gas theory.

This man, naturally, fails his exams, eventually ends up in an asylum for the insane. A professor, whose dismay makes him ridiculous, represents, in contrast to the man [in the asylum], the unshakeable bastions of spiritual order. [. . .]

On the psychology of deep feelings. About a year on from the days when Mama lay dying; we are in Brünn, with Heinrich describing exactly what went on a year ago today. "This is how it was, for three whole days." My feelings in real, deep turmoil; for the outside world, too, in deep mourning. Toward the end of the actual day of her death—Mama died in the following night—I become aware that it is almost more than I can take. I did not force myself to go through this mourning, it came about quite naturally, and yet it is like being bent double all the time, something that starts to become unbearable. I sleep the whole night through and next morning am in a decidedly cheerful mood. "Now her sufferings are over," people say, but in actual fact it is our sufferings that are over. How wise is the Catholic Church to repeat this on a large scale and to have the Festival of Easter follow the time of Lent. [. . .]

Socialism: a fine, new, comfortable means of transport: one is happy to spend 1 Schilling when one has occasion to use it and, moreover, is pleased about the progress it represents.

The same transport—for 20 Groschen, or indeed free—but set up by raising taxes only provokes disgruntlement and criticism.

For any expenditure of money or effort one expects something in immediate exchange, or at least some tangible "quid pro quo."

That is the great incentive—it is difficult to replace—of capitalism.

The question of capitalism is not how to educate new people who, because they see things from a broader perspective, voluntarily take on unpleasant tasks; rather it consists in finding the compensating quid pro quo and taking account of human nature.

{Story}

In the evening, walk on the Währingerstraße.[89]

Women like flowers floating down a river in the dark.

His attention is caught by a girl on the pavement next to the wall, walking in the same direction as he is. He notices an inexpressible torment about the way she moves. Her limbs hesitate, her feet falter. Both legs try to lift at the same time or both stop at the same time, the wrong arm tries to swing forward, the right arm goes off in the wrong direction, tension makes the shoulder shift out of line, the will suffers untold efforts to disentangle this confusion and the body, sick with exhaustion, totters against the wall.

Even before he had recognized how strange this all was, he thought the woman had suddenly felt nauseous and was about to leap to her aid. Then he saw the soft and beautiful girl's face.

At this moment he was himself transfixed by a memory that came from dreams of which, until this moment, his waking self had known nothing. But it was his dream: to walk just that way, and suddenly not to be able to move one limb without moving all at once, and to be able to move one leg slightly further forward or bend a finger only by dint of debilitating exertions. He knew that this was what he was always dreaming. Now his dream had been sent to him here.

"May I help you?," he asked, pushing his arm under that of the sick woman. He trembled, anticipating a hysterical scene, something destructive, explanations to a crowd of people. But nothing happened. His arm was accepted as self-evident. This is how abnormal people recognize each other. "I have always dreamt about you," he said. "Where may I take you?" If she wasn't also aware of everything, then this ridiculous form of address would certainly meet with some protest or an equally ridiculous answer. But she simply continued walking, holding his arm, and now with complete assurance, and the confidence of her arm flowed like a nuptial celebration into his. "I don't know anything about medicine," he said, and felt glad. "It is not as bad as it looks," the girl answered quietly. "I love you, of course," he said . .

Morning in late autumn: silver-white mist, golden sun, grasses turning numb with cold, long shadows. Mulberry-colored shadows.

Boarding-house: a man who always has to whistle when his wife uses the chamber pot so that the gentleman in the adjoining room doesn't hear it through the connecting door that doesn't shut properly! [. . .]

Family group at the Achensee in Austria: Hermine Musil, the mother (on the left-hand side), Alfred Musil, the father (standing), Robert Musil as a boy (on the right-hand side), Heinrich Reiter, Hermine Musil's friend (sitting beside Robert Musil).

Robert Musil, in 1901 (with a mustache).

Martha Musil, Berlin, in 1905.

Robert Musil as a lieutenant, in 1903.

17

NOTEBOOK 25
1921 TO 1923?

[*This notebook, a collection of notes for essays, is concerned with ideas. Musil was educated, as we saw earlier, in philosophy and psychology at the Humboldt University in Berlin at a time when this institution was preeminent in German, indeed in European, thought. This education left its mark on Musil's thinking; to this are added other vital concerns: Musil's preoccupation with morality and ethics and his fascination with the mystical. Musil develops his distinction between the moral and the ethical.*

"Morality" for Musil relates to the kind of acts that are considered fitting in a given society at a given time. Precepts and injunctions reinforce behavior deemed to be good and pillory behavior held to be bad. "Morality," though presented as absolute, is, in fact, arbitrary and relative; it is nothing more than a system predicated on custom and usage. Being "moral" often involves disregard for what is right in favor of actions that society approves. To do the "moral" thing may in fact be wrong while what appears wrong may be right in all but the (wrongheaded) judgment of society. The above-mentioned judgments are derived from the realm of what Musil understands as ethics.

Where "morality" is concerned with rational calculation, with justifications in relation to a system, the ethical is free of rules and free of all hard-headed assessment. Though the realm of the ethical is accessible to all, access is commonly denied by the conventions of the "moral" life. The "moral" person is made uneasy by the spontaneity, the sleepwalking certainty, of those whose actions are prompted by an innate sense, by the feeling "This is right for me now," a move that takes no heed of what the world may think. Musil was concerned, throughout much of his creative writing, to celebrate the ethical state, to which he gave the name "the 'other' condition"; he was convinced that conduct was only right if prompted by instinctive behavior whose source rose in the realm of the ethical. Of all the characters brought together in the earlier parts of MwQ, Moosbrugger, the madman, is presented as the one with the greatest capacity to experience this realm. But contemporaries, with their feet firmly planted in "reality" (whose substance Musil calls into question in his narrative) misunderstand and mistreat Moosbrugger. He loses his grip on things, slips into paranoia, and commits murder. In the later stages of the novel, Ulrich and his sister Agathe attempt, as the subtitle of part III indicates, a journey "Into the Millennium," where goodness without moral regulation and love without the need of possession are coextensive. This notebook provides aspects of a theory that helps to explain Musil's intentions in MwQ.]

25.

?Robert Musil?

Attempts to find an "other" person.
?by
Robert Watt?
25

"I" will mean, in this book, neither {refer to} the author, nor to a fictional person invented by him, but rather a changing mixture of both. (I have often been advised to collect my essays in a book, but I have never done so, for they are pieces of work that specific occasions and circumstances prompted me to write; for that reason, at least half of what they contain is determined by the stimulus and at most half by me.)

In other words, I have neither the supra-personal nor the im-personal intention of speaking the truth—perhaps I simply lack the capacity to do so— nor the intention of putting forward my personal conviction, for I have no such thing {it is of no interest even to me}, nor the intention of making myself into a figure from a novel, which would mean that I would have to be a character {would have to be sure of myself, which I am not}; for I do not wish to be one. So, {But rather} in the way that a bad person is a more dar-

ing speculator when he uses someone else's money than he is when spending his own, I want to follow my thinking out beyond the border of those
things that, whatever the circumstances, I could justify; that is what I call
"essay," "trial." And since all that is good has rules, but evil {as yet} possesses no system and is treated {as} an exception and so always remains personal, the only thing I am able to do, since I am neither a scholar nor a
character {nor, in this case, want to be a creative writer}, to give to my
thoughts an "I"-context; this is demanded by the matter itself, not by me.
This "I" is not me—this much is probably evident—but neither will it be a
figure, for I want to put in place only as many fictional-biographical elements as are needed to provide a shortcut to understanding certain ideas.

One may imagine the hero of these thoughts as a man who raced through
the grammar school, but then became an engineer, and who would actually
like to be a philosopher or a creative writer, which is the reason why he is
satisfied with {why he values} neither philosophy, nor creative writing, nor
his profession—which is just how most people feel.

I must show first why I think in an "other" way. This comes from my being
an engineer. When a bricklayer is unable to fit a brick into place lengthwise
he tries to put it in at an angle. The same is true of a serving girl with a
gnarled lump of wood that she cannot push through the door of the stove.
Even a dog, unable to get a stick that he is carrying in his mouth between
two obstacles, moves his head around until he finds the right angle. It seems
that these unplanned changes and later planned trials represent one of the
qualities to which mankind owes its ascent.

Only in the realm of law and morality is this not permitted.

Only in this realm do the rigid and the unchangeable count as sacred. {At
mass} the priests wear the vestments of magicians, while professors wear officers' uniforms. {Laugh at the vestments of the sacrament and the uniforms
of civil servants and professors.}

Our morality possesses—or would at least like to possess—a highest
good. Or an all-embracing moral law.

Or it proceeds empirically {This kind of morality is crippling. It excludes
the individual. And the individual—so we feel intuitively—is a source of
ethics. Morality is "dead"}, then it adopts several such individuals.

Reasons: the old delicate and deductive arrogance.[1]

Perhaps there is the fear that, precisely in this realm, anarchy would
emerge if one is [sic] not strict.

By analogy with the princ[ipium] ident[itatis], the need for an Archimedian place to stand.[2]

But that indicates lack of the strong imagination that would work out systems of thought.

One of my earliest—and, I might almost be tempted today to believe, instinctive—attempts at thinking was to distinguish between a moralist and an ethicist.

The moralist adopts an existing corpus of moral precepts and arranges them in logical order. He doesn't add value to these values, rather he adds to them a system. Basic precepts, principles . . . are relationships, positions within the system. (Though normally a rigorous absolutist, he is in fact a relativist with respect to [a given] position.) His primary drive is logical. He makes use of ethical precepts only to the extent that they are amenable to logic. All those philosophers for whom ethics is a corollary of theoretical philosophy tend to do this. They make do with very few notions and usually the cardinal one among them is that of setting things in order. The majority of philosophers belong to this group.

A fruitful special case are the researchers for whom morality is a research field in which their interest centers on its relationships with other fields. Sociologists. Even psychoanalysts. Here, too, the type of activity is rational.

Typically different—namely different in terms of their type—are the ethicists. Names: Confucius, Lao-tse, Christ and Christianity, Nietzsche, the mystics, the essayists. {Stoa,[3] epicureanism}[4] They are different in type, not in principle. They are related to the creative writer. (Recognized by Dilthey,[5] analysis of man in the 16th Century.) Their contribution to ethics is concerned not with the form but the material.

They have new ethical experiences.

They are "other" people.

With them belong, finally, all anonymous forces that transform morality.

They teach human beings.

There is no teaching about human being. No ethics.

The teaching is present in subjective bondings. From scattered individual cases through to ideologies (pseudo-systems). Often only in facts (of life or of fiction). As such their effect is felt through millennia, so they must have a degree of objectivity.

Preliminary questions;
   What is an ethical experience?

     2 groups of experiences: those that can be fixed and tranferred;
                                  those that cannot be fixed and transferred.

These also called "ratioïd" and "non-ratioïd."
More simply: experiences that are of the understanding and those that are of the emotions?
Here the issue is how one goes beyond logic and epistemology without making mistakes! It is only a question of the difference.
One cannot assert that sense experiences are transferable, but they can be fixed. A red of x μμ is certainly different subjectively, but it is fixed.[6] Fixing by means of measuring. The concept "water," if in this instance I disregard H_2O, etc., is fixed in terms of the constant reference to the object "water." I can read off its qualities from the experience and the experience is repeated with sufficient constancy (damp, fluid, transparent . . .) Exceptions (non-transparent, for example) can be traced back without difficulty to "causes" (this is almost the sole function that has survived for the concept of cause).
Concepts concerned with characteristics such as "damp" do not rest on repetition of the experience (this, by the way, also holds true for the preceding cases), but of the character, or kernel, or whatever, of the experience.
(One would have to run further through the concepts in terms of categories.)
By the way, language points out everything that we need. Unambiguous words like "dice." To each word a particular group of objects is assigned.
Words like "damp": when a new experience of a thing is added, a new kind of dampness, this can be assigned to its proper place. The group of objects is not complete, but is capable, in principle, of becoming complete.

{"That pleases me" is not only subject to change from the perspective of the "that," but also from the perspective of "me"; different things please, there are different kinds of pleasure; what is common is something as vague as liking something. Here the uncertainties of the common type of psychology of feeling are of value.}

Words like "good." "That is good." Since they are understood there must be something common to them. "Approval," "being content," "being reassured," "norm," "goodness," {But that is like a spectrum—it turns corners and is not as unambiguous as things experienced.} {It is said that a practical approach enforces unambiguity. In that case, this ought then to be all the more applicable in the case of evaluating. But perhaps it is precisely here that the difference between morality and ethics arises.}

{False conclusion: because "good" is something we understand, there
exists a general good;
because "tree" is something we understand, there
is only one tree.}

Probably also a specific experience that something moral is being fulfilled.

It is a historical one-sidedness to emphasize the generally binding nature of this ethical mode of experiencing. Wherever there are people one finds, admittedly, the experience of the good and it will be possible to distil from this a definition of some kind of universal character; but all finer kinds of ethical judgment are not based on this common character but on the nuances of the objects that are described as "good." In ethics, we still keep a hold on scholasticism, but we must learn from nature.

Excursus: rigorous characters and reasonable ones.

Value of moral rigorism?

      Police. Melioration.

      Fanatics.

? The ethical experience is transferable, but cannot be fixed (to the object).

What appears to one person as good, appears to someone else as bad: that is less important because it can be brought into the system of ethical circles.

But just as if we had to say of something: "It is damp; no, it is just slippery, or perhaps smooth, or perhaps cold"—that is what it is like. That is the essential aspect of the ethical experience. Not the value-element but the qualitative element on which this is founded. And if something general within us were performing the evaluation then it would, after all, first be necessary for what was to be evaluated to have been firmly established!

But how do we judge actions, sentiments, and suchlike?

How do we understand them?

Youthful level of wanting to be good. Associated with concepts of love. In these, love is a general essence of the maternal, feminine caressing, softness, warmth. Since, as yet, no concrete wish-fulfillment is conceivable.

Through unskillful religious instruction in morals, "being good" becomes something ridiculous, unmanly. At the same time, probably veneration of the ideals of manliness. In this hybrid creature there stirs the caricature of a man. The code of conduct of a school also represents goodness, a sense of being bound by rules, etc. in its bleakest form. Both in and after this phase, a person is anti-moral. (If, that is, particular family influences do not work against this.)

When, in a third phase, the mature person becomes good again, then this comes about through business sense. And also from opposition to young people and from a need for moral peace and quiet.

Average people are talented in areas that interest them. All that needs to be done is to make them interested in spiritual matters.

Individualistic anarchism states: "Thou shalt not obey any law." The technical point of view: "There is no law."

In terms of the need to regulate behavior without laws, the two coincide. But I shall not make it so easy for you as call this "New Stirnereanism"[7] or "Sciencism" or suchlike. You will understand it only when you no longer expect unified formulae.

{Doing something "for the love of it"}
Genetic introduction:

When they were young, many people were once "in a state of love" (which is different from "being in love").

Main radiation: this depends on something quite "other" than usual.

Expressions: people ought to "meet in goodness"; this is a state, virtually a local environment.

Desire to bestow, not to have.

The moral relationships are "other"; the crucial and the incidental change places.

"Wanting to be good" means "giving," "bestowing," "communicating," "overflowing."

Related to this is the condition of the poem.

Now, instead of saying: "He was in love" which is somehow eccentric, one can take this "other" central point seriously and make it the axis of one's whole world.

All quarrels, all ambition, all relationships, are as nothing "since what matters is an 'other' kind of thing."

One does not want to possess even the loved one but to live together with her in this newly discovered world. {"Be mine": connection between love-rationalism-capitalism. The "other" attitude demands that one does not treat even one's own notions as possessions—one does not store them in the thesaurus of the "I"—but they are common goods of the people who love. It is possible that this causes ideas to grow in a totally "other" way. Certainly one is weakened by "not keeping oneself firmly in hand," but one also stimulates oneself to transcend. There is something dynamic about it, one simply has to continue moving forward to keep one's balance.}
etc. Valid at least for contemplative dispositions.

This was later joined by rational education. Scientific love of evil, etc.

Result: the asking of the question.

———————

Things are "other," because the attitude I take to them is an "other" one. It is less a question of my perceiving "other" sides to them, but rather that, in general, I "perceive" less, and instead adopt an ethical attitude. Not: "What is that?," but "How am I to relate to it?"; and not in practical but in contemplative terms. But what is "contemplative"?

But I can only reconstruct this now in fragments and only with considerable effort.

———————

"Contemplative" is a mode of behavior. One can very well understand that the mystic says: "I perceive 'other'." [*sic*] But that is too narrow and should be expressed as: "I am 'other'." It becomes what is supposedly an "other" kind of perception only through prior theological assumptions.

It is my theory that the "contemplative" is a special case of the n[on] r[atioïd].

Round out one's own experience with historical examples.

These should not offer, for instance, an exhaustive overview since, wherever it appears, the problem should, after all, only be hinted at.

The notes on intuition that are filed with the novel describe this far better.

———————

I remember that, at a very early stage, I had the impression that it is more valuable to express things via theories and in essays than through artistic creation. That one cannot create anything that has not been expressed somewhere or other. Expressing, rationalism, sensitivity to stimuli; it is enough if someone presses somewhere not too far away from the button; in-souciance, transcending. Rather like the essay writing of R[obert] M[üller].

Blei: I am a Catholic and an atheist. I have no relationship to God whatso-ever, no need for him; what a proper religious experience is like I do not know. But I am a supporter of the Church.

"Who is there then, today?!"—this pessimistic judgment on the value of contemporary creative writing, including mine.

Reasons: related to the longing for the "Redeemer."

Twofold, given the lack of unity in the times. 1. One cannot fulfill all the different wills. 2. The individual has no idea what he wants.

At the same time the average standard is decidedly high.

Two reasons: literati who have lost their way; people who would like greatness to be spoon-fed to them through art.

Blei: "There is no progress." Proof: letters from ancient times. (? Light from the East? 1911?)[8] Separate off: absolute?

Relative to my position at this very moment?
In scientific terms, in the sense of the principle of entropy. Ethi-cally; whose entwinement with the world of science can scarcely be avoided.
(Increase, decrease, etc., ethical concepts.)
In purely ethical terms these are probably identical with the state-ment: "There is no final value."
But it is possible to set a goal. Relatively free, relatively compul-sive. X-times unfree system as in mechanics.

Given today's counterreformation, one will probably have to follow two lines of development:

1. of the soul versus the understanding.
2. of the demand for order. Systematizing.

The whole task is a life without systematizing but, nonetheless, with order. Self-creative order. Generative order. An organization that is not determined from a to z, but one proceeding from n to n + 1.[9]

Perhaps also direction instead of order. Or rather, being set in a direction.

The belief in the value of art is an offshoot of the belief in the value of reason, etc. This stems from the sphere of the emancipation of mankind from religion. {Natural moral law, and suchlike.} This is why people today, quite rightly, look down on art.

{We need an "other," quite different, attitude to art.} [. . .]

Progress:

Does the modern house with 6 rooms instead of 3, with 2 bathrooms, warm water, vacuum cleaner, etc., represent progress when compared with the old house with high ceilings, thick walls, beautiful vaulting? It has + and –.

Railway—stagecoach route. Power-driven machinery—handicrafts.

Is it better to cross the ocean in 6 days or in 6 weeks? It depends on the particular need.

Progress has advantages and disadvantages. These cannot be reckoned up in one calculation. Rather, needs have changed. And needs are created.

In technology: the diesel engine was not predestined to find one of its main areas of application in shipping. The development of the idea, its refinement in actual engines, and the coincidence of circumstances, brought this about. Similar to the way the course of a stream develops when it is not on a steep gradient. {The development reaches a different goal from the one that was planned.}

Mathematics, physics: today they have grown significantly. (But perhaps there is less uniformity.)

But what happens if a long-sought-after solution is in fact discovered? There are, of course, instances of wishes being fulfilled. There is greater justification in speaking of "development" and even of "epochs" than of "progress." But at least a greater store of problems solved, of fulfilled wishes, is laid up.

Everywhere the development runs along 2 tracks: one ideological, one "à la baisse."[10] E.g., usefulness of ethnic German[11] politicians in Czechoslovakia.

But only accompanied by the simultaneous extension of the idea of supra-nationality. Or, as the case may be, the connection is reversed: the idea that I put forward is right, but since ideas never achieve a breakthrough it would have only a debilitating effect and would not reach maturity if it were not complemented by a movement of rank stupidity.

―――――――――――

The anti-humanism, anti-Europeanism, anti-idealism of the youth of today is not necessarily a bad beginning. Those who are idealists from the outset later grow soft and spout rubbish.

―――――――――――

"Other" cond[ition]:[12]   on the one hand with motor
feeling is connected: organs, on the other hand, with
                                sense organs.

Active and passive components. Active person and "other" person. Partially coincides with man–woman.

Switching off the motor element: "contemplatio." The automatic side of the motor element continues. Complete switching-off: death. = relationship between death and ecstasy.[13]

But what about orgiastic ecstasy?

Every feeling has motor and sentient components.

On the path between the world as active agent and the world as passive object of activities (even if only through locomotion) lies the "I"; switching apparatus with a dark glow from her (?) If one of the two parts is in the ascendant, then the "I" is sucked up and blotted out.

If this part is the sentient part, only the world remains and our feelings are in the things. If it is the motor part (dance, fight, complaint, singing, mass psyche, {?}) then the "I" is sucked up by the actions and they, too, seem to proceed as if of their own accord. This is the second form of ecstasy.

But where does the joy of ecstasy come from? In the first case one can still understand this to be the sensitive world, but what of the second?

Here the old metaphysical solution beckons: the "I" is something unnatural; in ecstasy, it dissolves (is torn to shreds).

If one does not make a metaphysics based on suffering must this extinguishing then have a particular advantage?

Motor ecstasy: the personality is dissolved in the activity of its muscles. (Dionysian rites, person running amok [. . .])

The pleasure-bringing aspect of this activity consists in exploding or dissolving the intellectualized, voluntarized normal relationship between "I" and (physical, social) world.

On the basic attitude: it is not a question of making the "other" condition into a support for the life of society. It is much too fleeting. Even I can scarcely recollect it accurately. But it leaves traces in all ideologies, in the love of art, etc.; and the aim is to stimulate awareness of it in these variants, for it is there that we find the life of these phenomena that are in the process of petrifaction.

I. Ethics and Morality. (The morality of the creative writer)
   The difference as found in some examples from literature. (Kassner)[14]

   Morality as a special case of specifying, quantifying, unambiguous behavior.
   Ethics as a special case of the "other" behavior. Rule and absence of rules.
   The opposition between rule and individual. Morality: morality of the creative writer.
      Mathem. morality as experiment.   Anti-rationalism.
      Morality as cause of disorder.   Intuition.
                                          History and science.

II. The "other" condition as basic state of ethics.
               .   Creative writer and direction.
               .   Creative writer and socialism.
         Evil as necessary complement.
         Evil as motor force and principle of order.

III. Problem and illusory problem, of the times.
      Reduction of the various illusory problems.

Impossibility of any other than a successive solution.
Progress and pessimism.

If a problem is recognized it can also be solved. Here lies progress. Progress can be effected. Even if, when that happens, the horizon of a new problem is moved further back.

IV. Experiment in a non-petrified morality.

Creative writing, essay, philosophy, history, as fields of operation.

The "other" position and treatment of the creative writer, of the theater, etc., that stems from this. The utter topsyturvydom of present conditions. World [as?] Theater.

The bureaucrat in the state, in the Church, in socialism: arch-enemy. But a personified, human quality, that of not always being able to be spontaneous, etc.

The "other" attitude:

According to Bergson, conceptual thinking—setting something down in words and suchlike—is a falsifying of the original experience. He, too, relates it to the practical sphere. [. . .]

18

NOTEBOOK 26
1921 TO 1923?

[Like the previous notebook, this one is concerned with essays. From the earlier part of the notebook it is apparent that Musil may have been working on the introduction to a collection of essays on related themes (that he would never actually publish). Reading the notebook is analogous to seeing a civil engineer's sketch of the load-bearing structures of a building whose external fabric will hide these from view. Essays are important within MwQ as transitional texts that join separate narrative segments; but the experience of writing essays is itself used to explain the force that shapes the life of the central protagonist, the so-called utopia of essayism. (This is expounded in part II, chapter 62: "The earth too, but especially Ulrich, pays homage to the utopia of essayism.") The contemporary world lacks any coherent structure within which individuals might shape their own lives, since there are no guiding principles, no system of ideals and expectations within which one might orientate oneself; because this is so, the lonely intellectual essays an approach to existence in a way similar to an author projecting thoughts in the provisional and nonassertive form of an essay. In fact, in part I and part II of MwQ, Ulrich "essays" one life—the project of a year's living without final commitment (his "year's leave of absence from his life")—before essaying another, more significant life, the journey with his sister "Into the Millennium." In the introductory pages of this notebook the essay as a projection of tentative ideas is linked to the life of an intellectual as a projection into reality of a provisional mental plan. This is not mere analogy; the family resemblance of one to the other reveals a genetic link.

Here in Notebook 26 the themes under discussion include the "sentimental education" of a German who can be seen as broadly representative of his gen-

*eration. These include: the war as an event that brings many Germans close
to religious experience; heroism and bestiality; social organizations as frame-
works; nationalism; internal groupings within society; cultural influences;
other groupings under such heads as tradition, morality, custom, and so on.]*

————————

Essays
1
26
Plan.
Introduction.
    The situation.——The last essay rounded out by the other ones.
    The search to find a human being.
    Concluding remarks.

————————

Subject: the image of the life of the creative, {and of the semi-creative?} and
the uncreative human being. For it depends just as much on the latter. They
had the war in common. [. . .] {The human being who is normal, abnormal or acclimatized to the norm}

————————

Introduction
    The individual and the whole.
    Analysis of the ideological situation.
    Deeper meaning of complaints. The "other" condition.
    The creative writer in these times.[1]

————————

Title: Attempts to find an "other" human being.
Or: The German human being as a symptom.

————————

Intr[oduction]:
When, in this introduction, {or in what follows,} "I" is mentioned, this does
not refer to the author as a private person; nor does it mean a fictitious "I"

as in a novel: what is important to me is not the way that the ideas and feelings to be delivered are connected in one person—so not in my person either—but only their connection to each other.

But I am not in a position to make a philosophy out of this. The material that I have before me is in fragments. Perhaps one can sense the whole to which they might belong, and one piece may be seen, intuitively, as a continuation of another; but I am forced to fill in whatever lies between them with "I think," "I say," "I want to"; what I say is not real but imaginative; and so it is "I" who speak and not fact.

Of course, in times like these one could pass this over without a further thought. The words that Hume wrote nearly 200 years ago in his preface to *A Treatise of Human Nature* have a strangely contemporary ring to them: "There is so much quarreling that it is as if everything were uncertain, and this is carried on with as much heat as if everything were certain. In this ranting and raving it is not reason that wins the day but oratory, and no one needs to despair of finding supporters even for the most daring hypotheses if he only possesses skill enough to present them in an advantageous light. Victory is won not by armed men bearing pike and sword, but by the trumpeters, drummers and musicians of the army." So, in times like ours, one could heedlessly present something one does not know as objective truth and could reasonably expect a greater degree of success—providing it is done in an elegant, offhand way—than for a hesitant speaker. On the other hand, since we have in Germany the ideal of a specialist philosophy written for specialist philosophers and that keeps itself aloof from all contact with the joys and sorrows, the blithe babble of life, one cannot even take it seriously amiss that, next door, a "sort of newspapers and magazine philosophy" has set out its stall, a philosophy of "things seen in the most advantageous light" in which the hands of literary jugglers send flying through the air just about everything that can be shaken out of the volumes of an international philosophical library if one cuts open {loosens} the spines. I shall have something more to add about this later; suffice it to say, for the moment, that it may be more modest to speak of oneself than to speak of ideas.

But if there is no satisfactory context for the ideas—and if one scorns to provide, as context, the person of the author, namely any kind of personal brushstrokes from, or indirect sketching by, an interesting author—then what is left is neither a subjective nor an objective context but rather one that might be both of these, a possible image of the world[2] and a possible person, and it is these two that I am seeking. What I have to say will display my mistakes, and, to the extent that I am not a fool, my advantages, but what should be at issue here are not the specific features of the person but the substance of the context. But where the context within the substance itself does not become sufficiently hard, it is likely that the personal one will show through;[3] but then it should be expanded into a utopian dimension and should not sketch an image of what the author is, but of what he loves. "I love something" contains as much of the subjectivity of the "I" as of the objectivity of the "something"! This is the way to pursue one's thinking, and there is no need for it to be either a personal thought belonging to my "I" nor a completely impersonal one, for which the impersonality of truth is appropriate.

It is with such thoughts that, in my view, essays are written.

I have been urged to edit those of my essays that have appeared over a period of ten years in a variety of literary journals; I have not been able to make up my mind to do so because I feel far too strongly how elements in them that are connected beneath the surface were shaped by the particular occasion that provided me with the stimulus, even though I did not actually feel that I was ready to write; thus what for me was essential always found a home in something peripheral.

Today I am attempting to place this in the context that is appropriate to it. I know that I shall only succeed in giving some intimations, and I am not trying to do any more than to draw a line under much of what I have already written, and to determine the "balance being brought forward." I am not a philosopher, I am not even an essayist, I am a creative writer; but for years I have been in the midst of the "struggle of the spirits" or whatever the term for this may be in Germany, and since people have paid me some attention, I assume that the ideas that I wish to account for, and the compulsion to think them, do not belong to me alone.

I confess that, however strong my conviction may be that personal achievement involves a scarcely perceptible change in the store of spiritual riches that one inherits from others, however strongly I believe that the above holds good not only for one's debt to the high traditions but also for what one draws in with every breath, I have nonetheless felt just as strongly—throughout my life in the Germany of today—that I am an "other" person, and I know that, within contemporary literature as well, I am opposed as something alien, am misunderstood, or judged inferior. Accordingly, this book is a polemic, even though it is not names that I am fighting, but conditions.

The precept "artist, create; do not talk" is sound advice not only aesthetically, but also politically. The confession, "Here I stand and have been unable either to go on further or to find a different way," has, in the last few years, left many a writer of confidences rather exposed and I am convinced that I shall not be able to protect myself from sustaining harm.

I hope that some will be willing to take my part.

Another possibility: leave the essays as they are and provide a commentary.

I have often been urged to edit these essays but I have always refused. I don't actually like the man who wrote them. He gives me the impression of a man who always wrote things and did things that were different from what he wanted. All his essays have something opportunistic and inopportune about them. It looks as if he has been urged to write about a pair of culottes and he, a man who could otherwise never decide to write anything, does so because he has been invited to—but he makes use of the opportunity to add in something of the things that he can never decide to write about. And this is what happens even when he writes about something as important as the fate of his nation. He starts off, and one feels that a man wants to speak; but before very long it is the things that speak. He moves into sociological or socio-philosophical ideas. They are not without originality; but what one finds here are just like "Collected Writings" of scholars, but in reverse—they are opening gambits, idea-stumps. Perhaps one or other of them would be worth executing in full, but then they would become a book, a project for several years, together they are the work of a lifetime. One feels that that was not what he wanted; he only wrote it down because no one else wrote it. There remains something beyond the range of proof about the attitude of this person but there is also, constantly, the compulsion to turn to the resources of proof. What does that mean? And time and again, with a certain degree of power, he pulls himself back into the objective world, into what is actually happening now, back to himself; one cannot overlook the following: behind this war game with the impersonal, behind what is not self-expression but rather a being-press-ganged-into expression, there hides something personal. One might almost say that is an intellectual[4] imagination. But yet not only the first stage of scientific activity, scattering the seeds of ideas, but also the final stage of artistic activity, the formal binding into a unity. They contradict one another to a certain degree but, in a shadowy way, they belong to each other.

At last I felt my interest in what would actually transpire in the process gaining the upper hand. So, just as one does in the preparation for any immanent critique, I disassembled the individual pieces and put things that belonged together, fitting them into the context that this process provided. Via precise study, it seemed to me that certain common strands continue through the whole enterprise, but these are often subterranean and it is not impossible that, now and again, I suppressed what was of greater importance. This is why I point to where the originals are to be found, in case anyone is interested enough to want to look for them—which is frankly something I do not assume. I have put together an image of the person and his position in the times and I act accordingly; in other words, in a somewhat arbitrary fashion but from the desire to stimulate interest in an incomplete person by recourse to the interest that is due to an epoch that, in terms of its peculiarities, has a very distinct profile.

For all the things that the man whose work I am editing has to express are, indeed, very incomplete. But they—or I, or the times?—have the peculiarity that, as yet, they are apparently incapable of reaching perfection. Since this state of affairs has forced me to be modest, I have quoted as much as possible in the original version and merely spun out the little that, as the older man, I know more of today. This is also why I have also quoted a great deal from the originals because, as is well known, one cannot tear thoughts of this kind from their context without changing oneself.[5] Just as they are, they form a whole, and the length of a nose depends on the face to which it belongs. One cannot lay hold of such assertions, one has to look them in the eye. Since this, not infrequently, is a face that seems immature to me, particularly in the works of youth, I have tried, in addition to ordering them in terms of their subject matter, to keep to a kind of biographical context; so what I want to offer is a kind of "biogram," the line along which certain ideas have developed in the course of a young life, or perhaps only a way of approaching these ideas at an oblique angle. Where I was able to, I have then also added the likely direction for any continuation.

I scarcely need to say that I am editing the work of a dead man. One will see that, according to his own definition, he was already dead when he wrote down some of his ideas.

"An 'Other' Person": explanation of the title.

Might actually be the heading for all my work, so that what is here is only one part of what I have attempted.

Young people feel that the facts of contemporary life have outgrown the concepts of the old.

This feeling of youth has survived from former times. What I have seen of more recent "youths" appeared to me rather to modify the thinking of the old than to adapt to the new facts. I have the feeling of standing in the midst of a belletristically eclectic and uncreative epoch. (Better than cursing one's opponents!)

Remember those who also want an "other" human being—the revolutionaries. In many respects I'm grateful for their holy ardor, but they believe that the new human being is merely an old one who has to be set free.

II. Title: Hölderlin: "In Germany there are no more characters, only professions."
{II. = An average German and what he experienced.

A normal German, an abnormal German, and a German who is acclimatized to the norm.}

I

Let us consider a German taken from the ranks of the broad average.

He should be neither stupid nor without character. Our satirists have so far made things too easy for themselves. "Satiram non scribere" is only "difficile"[6] because it forces one to mirror oneself in the person who is being reviled. {So it ought to be a normal person.}

In his childhood, our German went through experiences about that we can say little.
A diffuse, delicate eroticism.
Perhaps an "other" way of reflecting the world (eidetics) {and psychoanalysis. Since knowledge of it is widespread and, in any case, everyone chooses from it whatever he needs, there's nothing to be said about it. But eidetics ought be explained as one possibility for understanding oneself. Either in the form of *references* by the editor at the end, or after each chapter. Or, together with Köhler,[7] Allesch,[8] etc. as approaches to the new image of the world in a separate chapter?}
An "other," heroic, non-analytical attitude toward ideals (note about Foerster's son).[9] Something, so it emerged, that relates to the creative writer.
But also attacks of unspeakable cruelty and coarseness (phases anticipating the masculine behavior. Boys' games.)
Either a delicate rocking in the tender cradle of childhood or a tormenting impatience to be free of it. {Differences between the 3 Germans possibly in terms of vitality and the content of feelings—we have no knowledge of these—the abnormal German will probably reflect more or have a more active imagination than the normal one. The difference, however, in all {later} phases, too, remains fluid to the point where one consciously lets oneself go.}
Our German started school:
A rational world, drawn up with a ruler, was foisted on him. A world that has emerged from practical needs is driven home to him in theoretical terms before he gathers any experience of life.

Let us assume that, as an average person, he comes through this well, then he has to learn a mass of things with which he has no relationship. How is he to understand the complexities of mathematical and scientific reflections? He is taught questions of aesthetics and ethics by people—most of whom are not well-versed in these themselves—and he is taught them in a completely inadequate, pseudo-rational manner. He would like to be "initiated" into life, and is instructed in fragments of the most complicated artifacts of life. {(Fragments of the work of people whose life is behind them.)} {At the same time, through praise, punishments, ranking, a metric-moral form of behavior is produced.}

Whatever is to be said about the influences of the family will be repeated when he himself is the head of a family.

Outcome:

in the course of this period, there takes shape within him the idea of a profession to which he aspires.

{(a)} Either this profession corresponds to one of the subjects at school. Then a natural centering takes place {Ethics is centered inwards to become morality}; up to the point of matters of *Weltanschauung* everything is grouped in a more or less natural fashion around this. {It is always a chosen profession!} (Bourgeois professions)

α) An "acclimatized" human being takes shape in the case of a rational profession,

ß) An "abnormal" one, if he has something to do with the soul; art, religion, politics, partly business as well. But this is also the division between bourgeois and non-bourgeois professions.

More correctly then:

1. The young person is always heroic and enthusiastic. He wants to be chosen. He wants to be either a great, or a good, human being.
2. In school he begins to adapt to society.
3. Case a) happens;[10] or case b). a) and some of b) are bourgeois professions. In b) many an oppositional element is concealed that will later be reabsorbed.

1. But one can also divide according to α and ß. Whereby a part of b is also bourgeois.
2. There is also the case of particular talents in "a" and "α." That is a one-sided person and one-sidedness is always soul as well.

Even more simply:

1 and 2 as above.
3. Either strongly defined talents
    a. School subject. Bourgeois profession
    b. Not a school subject. Bourgeois profession
    c. Non-bourgeois profession.
4. Or not}

{(b)} Or it does not correspond. The determining influences lay outside the school. It is a "practical" profession {(remnant of the bourgeois professions)}. Then school learning is acquired partly in terms of a goal, partly with reluctance. Often there is a strongly oppositional element in this choice of a "school-free profession"; often leaving school early to join the army, to enter business, to become a farmer, etc.
But let us treat two special cases separately:
The conception of the profession develops, it is true, but it does not greatly inspire. {This is simply the case of non-correspondence. The case of the literary person is that of a mismatch in an attempt to correspond; remarkable only as a source of resentments that have, socially, very damaging effects.}
Then sport, student ideals, and suchlike, come leaping in. His will is not so much to be a member of a profession as a man. In my experience, here we have a prototype of the person who pursues politics.
The second special case comprises all those who wish to become literary people but who then do not, or who do but give up after some time.
    Our German enters life.
    {Follow up:
    Cases 3a, 3b and 4 from the last classification.
    Case 3c is a separate one.}
An important circumstance is that for almost 20 years spiritual goods have been stuffed into him and he is now left on his own with them. (Main meal in the morning.)
Things start to crumble away. In this process, individual things become linked with new impressions. Usually coincidentally and impersonally.
The centering factor becomes the profession:
A spiritual creative profession: specializing.
A practical-bureaucratic profession: like a facility with the hands. Men speak of "profession." Professional interests span the whole world.
{As the main means of education, the newspaper.}
    What happens with the soul?
A small part is bound by the profession, and the profession also develops the soul in different directions. Exactitude in the direction of pedantry, danger in that of recklessness, etc.

Another part is absorbed into the so-called principles. Rules of life—regularity of life: this is where the function of the principles lies, ideals, of the character and of social adaptation. In them—as we shall see—there is no more soul to be found, but they lay claim, in the way they appear, to be the soul. They also include joining a political party, a club, and suchlike.

A third part is consumed in the friction of nervous disorders, turns into tics, into character anomalies, typical kinds of disgusting behavior, etc.

A fourth part is kept alert by moral conflicts; it is probably the case that it can scarcely be distinguished from the others.

A fifth part is catered for by art and the newspaper.

{This would be the place to remember "rumor" as a condition. The lad forms his notion of sexuality by means of rumor. This is where its attraction lies.

In terms of rumor, too, he forms his view of all things that are not part of the immediate area. But this holds true just as much for evil rumors as for attractive ones. This is a characteristic of the condition in which abstract notions like "Empire" or "Emperor" can have such a powerful effect. A condition that includes a never-saturated yearning for a higher social stratum. In which antipathies such as nationalism, anti-Semitism, anti-pacifism, etc., swell up.

To this part that has {thus} been absorbed there also belongs unrequited love that is considered a youthful foolishness.}

I shall express things briefly:

Neither art, nor the newspaper, is taken seriously.

In both one looks for vindications.

Both, in absolute terms, are labyrinths {of oppositions} in which one has no signpost.

Both are a chaos of contradictions.

But this human being wants something like a heaven over his head, something like walls that surround him. These are not there. That, in spite of this, they are not missing is a remarkable social-psychological phenomenon {illusion}.

2

This human being was subjected to surprise attack by war. Then came the well-known summer-experience in the year, 1914, etc. DNR 1921/XII–II.[11]

This was related to religious experience.

{Cases 3a b, 4 and 3c were joined together.}

All peoples were touched by something irrational but gigantic, something alien, not of the accustomed earth, later explained as a hallucination.

Notable parts of this experience: for the first time everyone had something in common with everyone else. Dissolution into an impersonal happening. One feels the very body of the nation. Primal mystical experiences as real as factories. An "other" relationship with death. Specific to the average person: feeling that something great is being experienced.

One cannot simply call that drunkenness, psychosis, suggestion, mirage, etc.

Something related to this was repeated at the end of the war. The Easter world-mood. This, too, was not an illusion, etc.

It was like a Trojan Horse: a deception—but with the outlines of a divine experience.

3

But we also experienced quite "other" things. The whole idea we have of our civilization broke down.

If anything about it at all was firm then it was that of performing useful work, that existence had embarked on a trend of improvement and, simply, of becoming civilized. People had become very uncertain and indolent with respect to the so-called "divine" questions, and had become rather skeptical or brash in those relating to pleasure, but they were probably convinced that good would come of proper doings and dealings, indeed that things would get better and better; they believed in progress without having any conception of a goal.

And just as a person who has important things to do does not take the time to divest himself of the irritating foibles that have been with him from his youth, so these times—which in their essential drives were peaceable and were not particular about the kind of amusements they pursued—tolerated the splendid show of armaments {and tolerated in just the same way the occasional warlike remarks that went with them} [and] half-failed to register the empty revolutionary phrases of social democracy.

{This person is suddenly transformed not only into a hero but also into a beast.}

This was, I believe, the warm mist through which the larger part of the world was striding—and that, in political terms, is not without interest. In it there lay a degree of pride in the years from 1914 and a certain confidence in the world as a whole, a sense that things would work out well without any particular organization being necessary. This is not intended as a sketch of the situation—which, at a subterranean level, had quite different fissures—but only a widespread and important feeling that people had about themselves (and that probably, despite all that has happened, they now have again).

For this same person changed soon afterward not only into a hero, but also into a beast.

The measure of heroism set in train by the war—even if one disregards the passive, questionable heroism of "Machine Man" and restricts oneself to what, in the primal sense, were real deeds of heroism—was something that had never been seen before. The degree of bestiality almost reached the levels of the greatest models from the past.

The cruelties practiced in various revolutions must be judged as being even worse than the war and worse still were those that took place during the counterrevolutions, just as the behavior of France in the Ruhr is more base than that of Germany in Belgium—viewed from the perspective of civilization that no longer sees itself threatened by an acute seizure but from a disease that will not heal.

{Powerlessness caught between League of Nations and revanchism, capitalism and bolshevism.}

Thus this normal person had a mysterious experience and could not hold onto it, he went through one of the most heroic phases in world history and could not actually perceive any change in himself at all. Earlier he was a busy bourgeois and then became . . . and did not actually experience anything at all.

III

{The individual and the whole.}
Once I said the following about these experiences:

How wrong . . . NR.IV[12] Let us examine this "It." {"It" = the question: to what extent are we what we do and live, to what extent are we not those things? A crucial religious question, e.g., saying by Luther.}

It is clear that this "It" is the (political and social) organization.

The will and the characteristics of an organization are not the average of those who belong to it. This "It" is a new whole (like a melody, a figure, or suchlike.) If I were a sociologist I could probably explain this in terms of the most varied examples, from the crowd in a street to the Catholic Church.

{But show, for example: influence of the cost of sending letters on the individual nature of refuse disposal in Berlin and Vienna, and the example of a joint-stock company.}

In those days I was content to list some of the things that occurred to me with respect to the formations "state" and "nation" and I shall first repeat this.

IV

Are these institutions the bearers of particular characters? (of state or peoples . .)

They are, after all, pan-white civilizational.

Therefore the division that emerges must be attributable to some special factor.

Character of external borders.

Emergence of {national} characters.

{Apparatus [of state]. Just letting things happen.}

{V}

Borders within. Party literature, differences in education: same phenomena.

The ruthlessness of the internal struggles not less intense than that of external ones.

State, nation, Church, profession, class, gender, etc. The individual cannot fully belong to any of these groups because they are in conflict with each other. Here, too, the issue is one of struggles between different kinds of apparatus.

VI

Necessity of the apparatus—inescapable cruelty of the kinds of apparatus today—the whole is a question of organization.

Up till now the human being has had two inorganically connected histories: that concerned with the forms in which he was organized and that of his spirit.

VII

Even the {unorganized} influences of culture can broadly be understood as functioning as an apparatus.

Not the poem that I read but the fact that I read it is apparatus.

So the relationship of individual to apparatus must be taken one level further down.

Question in pencil one sheet above.

Theorem of shapelessness.[13]

VIII

Once we have tuned in to the "apparatus" we notice a group of influences that are not, and yet are, part of it: tradition, customs, moral system, in summa, ideology.

Without ideology the individual is a nothing.

Ideology as airspace, and ideology in special cases. Moments of elation: times of greatness.

The ideology of state, nation, race, Church, etc.: collectively regressive character; institutions, suggestions, suggestions of power.

Ideological development: a continuous stream through the ancient world right up to today, knotted in institutions. Atomism and ossification as phenomenon of civilization.

19

NOTEBOOK 28

1928 TO JUNE 1930

[During the period when this notebook was being written, namely, 1928 to 1930, Musil was working on the completion of the first volume of MwQ. The effort seems to have been reflected in the actual handwriting that Adolf Frisé describes (in the companion volume of annotations to his edition of the Diaries) *as "nervous, distracted, aged" (p. 479). It is interesting that despite his creative effort Musil still found time to note down ideas for other satirical work. A sharp ironic edge is evident in the pages of MwQ completed during this period; though the satirical novels with their extraordinary inventions were never to be published, they make themselves felt if only in the style of Musil's major work. In this notebook Musil drafts ideas in the tradition of Swift's* Gulliver's Travels, *by presenting the foibles of contemporary society through grotesque distortions. The satires depend on various literary conceits: on descriptions of life on a planet discovered circling the Earth at the South Pole, on libelous representation of the Prussian Academy of Arts (The Academy of Conceit City), and on extrapolations from Musil's own experiences as a librarian in Vienna for The Archivist. An impression of what this latter work might have been like may perhaps be gained from a delightfully comical chapter in MwQ in which General Stumm von Bordwehr (who was originally to have been called "Stumm von Bordsprung"—a mischievous name suggesting an eccentric naval ceremony in which, without a murmur, a senior officer leaps over the side of his ship!) makes his acquaintance with scholarship. (See part II, chapter 100, "General Stumm invades the State Library and learns about the world of books, the librarians guarding it, and intellectual order.") Sandwiched between*

*other entries more appropriate to the overriding theme is an eloquent ac-
count of Musil experiencing writer's block!]*

28

The Academy of Conceit City[1]

Archivist,[2] Planet Ed,[3] and literary satire to be fused into one work.

Beginning of Archivist—focus to be on individual-psychological treatment.

Post-war world. World being forced into a different shape.[4] Victory of
war jargon. The archivist who doesn't achieve anything.

Excursion to Ed.

From there, observation of the earth through instruments that are somehow free of contemporary prejudices. Object under scrutiny: the Academy
of Conceit City—i.e., the spirit takes on solid form; what does that look
like? For this, the Academy is representative. (One might have believed that
nothing is as compromised as the spirit of the past, for example, morality
that has not stood the test of time; but this is not the case.)

Bourgeois Th[omas Mann], the voice of the nation.

Tinny H[einrich] M[ann].

Kitschy W[ildgans].[5]

The bon-vivant President;[6] etc., a literary overview of the essential, of
meaning.

Prof. Specht.[7]

Prof. Becker,[8] the democratic Minister of Culture.

Begin with the "Journey into Childhood."[9] Steyr, the city for old people,
with the arms factory. He was born here. Werndl[10] has a monument. What
an unsuitable choice of father it was for any attempt to liven up the art business. And then these patricians and their attitudes . . The Man without Success said to himself: sometime I must get right to the bottom of all of this.
Possibly an episode from the parents' life around the 80's. Ironic-romantic
autobiography of an unsuccessful man (myself). The more colorful the better as a setting for the satire.

A *contemporary* [. . .] accompanied by the request to excuse me for being one myself, which is something I regret most deeply.

Selected chapters from my life. {For example, the real milieu of the Institute.[11] [. . .]}

The main matter in hand: a kind of biography of my ideas. [. . .]

Raven[12]

Besides being a pioneer, the following basic idea as well: strange type of person who is of great value but has never done anything. One finds good creative people everywhere. But there is a dearth of good uncreative ones, and the uncreative ones who are there bring about the failure of the world! [. . .]

South Pole.[13]

Includes the following kinds of experiments: husbands or wives who {only} live as long as dogs or horses. This intense attachment lasting 8 or 14 years. What forms does love take? Or other ones who live as long as trees. [. . .]

For example: she life-span of 300 years, he 10–16; but, while she is small, delicately made, agile, he is mighty, warrior-build. [. . .]

Important: represented without any mercy, my relationship to Rilke.

The first love with the Worpswede book.[14]

The indifference later.

Annoyance and love via Allesch.[15]

The indifference later.

Love after his death.

And then still hesitations: to what extent am I to expose him, to what extent extol him? These are the kind of uncertainties that are involved.

This is also where the idea belongs that you only learn what you know, etc. This is the young person and also a basis for generations.

And one does not do anything genuinely new.

. . . .

Writing poetry is sitting in judgment on oneself—with the certainty of acquittal![16]

Contemporary

An "other" shape: the archangel. Intelligible or intended shape of the "I." Was destined for a career as archangel, is rather indignant about the empirical "I." Conversation between the two about everything that worked out and did not work out. Or rather it is always only the angel who speaks; to the recipient R[obert] M[usil]: "Dear RM, on 6.XII.30[17] you will be . . . , etc. This is going to take such and such a course, so we want to make a start today to consider the position." Seen from the viewpoint of the angel, not from the empirical "I," from the "I" that has actually been reached, but from its enhancement via literature.

The angel came approximately in the 17th year in place of another one. He is bound to the empirical person and, for this reason, is not all-knowing but makes assumptions, weighs up, etc.

Contemporary:

I was born on . . . . which is something not everyone can say of themselves. The place, too, was unusual: Kl[agenfurt] in K[ärnten];[18] relatively few people are born there. In a certain sense, both of these are intimations of my future.

Contemporary: 3.I.29. Another title might be sought in the general area of "Talking to Oneself." "Confessions" but not by the "I" to the world but rather head-to-head confrontation between the "I" and the world within one head.

Inhibition: 5.I.29. Of course, on starting to write out the fair copy.[19] First chapter to be rewritten; 3 days ago, satisfied that I had the right idea; began yesterday, first part went well: inhibition sets in. How did it come on? I also have in my head a concluding section and a main section of the first chapter which satisfy me. I continue the first section in a way that appears formally clumsy, and cross it out. It occurs to me to insert at this point the unused depiction of the sounds and speeds of the city. I have a vague sense of how this is to go over into the final part. But it's imprecise and indeterminate. Now the classical situation is created: two fixed supports and, between them, a transition that refuses to take shape.

I push it in and am only partially successful in making it fit. I cross out and try a different way. Dissatisfaction comes creeping in. I lose the line of the whole. I get stuck on stylistic details, on the links between subordinate and main clauses.

Dejection. If things go on at *this* rate I'll need a year for the fair copy.

Nonetheless take comfort from all that has been completed. If that were not there?!

Evening has come, I leave things as they are, I read. At the moment when I go to turn out the lamps, as often happens, it occurs to me how it might be done. I make a note of it.

Added later: it bothered me that I did not earlier make a note of how I see the transition. It would have bothered me just as much if I had noted it down.

My sleep is undisturbed. But as soon as I awake, before I can tell myself that all is well under way: the pain.

Not quite pain although it is a physical sensation in the head. The best expression for it seems to me to be "intellectual despair." It is powerlessness mingled with a dreadful loathing (similar to that which one feels when utterly fatigued) at the thought of having to go back to the thing.

Quite understandable that I used to think that this condition was brought on by fatigue.

Similar situation when, earlier when I was packing, I let my hands drop and could not decide what to start with. In that context it looks like a failure of the will.

But it can be influenced from the perspective of its intellectual functioning. I recite to myself the simile of the mouse-hole. And now it becomes clear to me—and that is the main reason for writing this down—that a false kind of objectifying is involved. I attempt to create a situation that is external to me. All my efforts go in this direction when my writing is flawed. I am no longer the person who is speaking; it is rather that sentences are external to me like a material, and I have to manipulate them. This is the situation I try to create. [. . .]

Conceit City or The Contemporary.

Zarathustra, the lonely man in the mountains, somehow runs counter to my sentiments. But what position must one adopt in order to come to terms with a world that has no fixed point? "I do not understand it," that's the way to do it!

It is possible for physical courage to be accompanied by intellectual cowardice: one doesn't know what to start with. In minor, as in major matters. This is a personal shortcoming.

For the most important creative writer there aren't 5000 schillings to spare,[20] while money is spent on sport, on clubs, etc. The minister receives the boxer. [. . .]

Conceit City

The woman of the future as traveling companion alongside the old-fashioned type of aunt—muscular, trained, aggressive, but at the same time nervous, unstable, prone to hysterical mechanisms. Actually—horribile dictu—my own type. [. . .]

Learn to Read and Write. Title for the lit[erary] essays.

I have learnt that the German people is incapable of this, at least as far as "belles lettres" are concerned. [. . .]

South Pole. Increase the speed of human history one hundred fold and describe what happens in the process.

14.IV.1930: work-inhibitions are perhaps the same thing as my vertigo. Recently I was physically indisposed and to this was added an external source of literary annoyance, and, although I had only a few pages to write to reach the end of Volume I, my immediate feeling was: "You'll never get past this point!"

27.IV. Just as with mountain vertigo it is no use (or little use) to me if I reproach myself with how groundless this is. All that needs to happen is for some deadline to be set, 8 days before a journey, for example, and then I get stuck. I have met with a surprising degree of success with Chapter 116, which I am working on at the moment, although none of the drafts was right; but I cannot get beyond the last section.

28.IV.

Title for an autobiography: My Father Was Younger than Me.

[. . .]

I had the reputation of being an obstinate child. It took me roughly to the age of 50 to realize that this is not a mark of distinction.

10.VI.

South Pole. Make the framework autobiographical and contemporary!

[. . .]

20

NOTEBOOK 30

CIRCA MARCH 1929 TO
NOVEMBER 1941 OR LATER

[This notebook starts with one or two entries in 1929, then moves directly on to 1930, the year in which Musil was struggling to complete the first volume of MwQ. It reads for the most part like an orthodox diary; impressions from meetings, accounts of activities, reflections, and some indications of how the work on MwQ is progressing (or not, as the case may be—he uses a train journey to Berlin to reflect once more on what it is that occasionally prevents him from writing). The single-minded drive to complete the novel leads to a drying up of income from occasional writing for newspapers and to consequent shortage of money. Some signs of failing health are appearing: sleeplessness, digestive problems. His teeth cause trouble and the necessary treatment is documented in excruciating but fascinating detail. Then, after September 1930, there is a gap of some two years. The diary picks up again after the publication of volume I of MwQ and Musil's move to Berlin in autumn 1932, then jumps ahead to March 1933 shortly after Hitler's seizure of power. Musil's entries on politics, particularly those that have a bearing on intellectual affairs and culture in a broader sense, are expressed in cautious, sometimes covert terms. Musil must have been worried about what might happen if his notebook came into the hands of the authorities; his concern, however, about what is happening is clearly formulated: the loss of media freedom, the brutality of the new regime, the failure of liberals to respond adequately to the threats to democracy. After a number of entries in 1933 Musil makes relatively few notes on subsequent years in this

notebook. Entries on politics become more infrequent as Musil's attention moves to other matters such as literature, Christianity, psychoanalysis, a dream, the atom, anti-Semitism, and smoking.]

---

30. [. . .]

Friday, 22 March 1929.

We are without service. The water has been turned off again. But full spring warmth; the weather has moved without transition from unseasonable snowfalls to mature spring air.

I'm marvelous at cleaning shoes.

Frau Stanek[1] ("Kiss your hand") is helping Martha.

In the *Tag* in the morning, read about the fuss over the "Day of the Book."[2] The whole thing is nonsense and concern for externalities. Fontana[3] is maneuvering himself skilfully upward. I have felt irritated about him for days now. The basic characteristic of his being is the desire to get on in the world. By and large, by decent means. Whenever he doesn't behave as he ought—as was the case in the action he took against me when he succeeded me in the SDS[4]—it is perhaps because he has a thick skin and partly, too, because he is blind to what he is actually doing; an action performed with unintentional intent. Deserves reproach for having an urge to rise in society that is stronger than his talent. Or that, at least, runs on ahead of it. Probably his talent will take its revenge. But not on his success, since this is quite secure in the city of Julius Bauer.[5]

23.IV.1929.

Completed the L[eo] F[ischel][6] and family chapter with a great deal of effort, and too late.

In the morning, received a check for 66 Mk 25 groschen for 10 performances![7]

Have given extensive information to the SDS. Answered briefly Hildenbrandt's[8] rather unfriendly letter.

Day of rain.

City of Conceit and South Pole.

In every organism there are functions that are degenerating and ones that are being newly formed. Thus it may be God's will to allow spirit on earth to degenerate in order to create an industrial planet. That would explain why he doesn't treat R[obert] M[usil] any better. [. . .]

———————

1930.

———————

6.I. Since the start of the year I've been wanting to write things down. Aim: to record how my 50th year of life turns out! But also, in a quite aimless fashion, to record facts. I have become too abstract and would like to use this method to help me retrain as a narrator by paying attention to the circumstances of everyday life.

This is why I am writing about how we spent New Year's evening through to about two in the morning with the Fodors. Fodor is a journalist, a Hungarian Jew by descent and a mining engineer, correspondent of the *Manchester Guardian* and an American paper. No doubt my interest in his job is not a direct one, nonetheless one that is somehow there "for all eventualities"; so it would be advisable for me to be a little more restrained in the satire about "Great Writers" than I actually am. But I do like this kind of person, too, though I know very little about him apart from the following: he calls himself a "progressive journalist," he is pleasantly plump, prefers good literature to bad (I don't know if he can tell the difference between them), and he exudes a pleasing, matter-of-fact calm.

I know him from the "Tuesday evenings" of last year.

His wife is very thin (daughter of an Austrian officer)—in spite of this, speaks German with an English accent. Explains that a visitor is a "protégé of my husband and Mr . . .'s." Somewhat asthenic in appearance, she takes on quite an "other" expression when she sets her chin on her violin; energetic, almost tragic.

Gramophone music, which makes such soirées much more relaxed.

In addition to Lukács[9] and Frau Lorenz, nothing but Americans {and Hungarians}. English is spoken or Hungarian. When, out of politeness to me, there are passages of German, I get a shock.

A figure worthy of particular attention is Dr. Intrasz. Pupil of G.E. Müller,[10] works here with Bühler,[11] but makes his living as correspondent of a reactionary Hungarian paper. People make excuses for him. He has a touch of gentle malice about him, a diffuse air of evil. Perhaps this is just something that I am imagining. He is young.

Martha in the old satin dress that Frau Stanek has modernized. Poor Martha!

Frau Lorenz in an off-the-peg, but very elegant, evening dress with black lace braiding or suchlike, had her big day. Never before have I seen her looking so pretty. The long dress and the deep neckline at the back made her figure look quite different.

Two days ago I wrote to S. Fischer about the Hauptmann Prize,[12] since Herr Wasservogel and all the trustees are playing dead. Großmann,[13] who has up till now played a very positive role in this matter, has now given up and has advised me, since he has to go away, to let Hauptmann know about the affair. We have only enough to live on for a few weeks. Martha wants me to take note. I have postponed things until the point when the answer from Fischer either arrives, or fails to arrive.

Of late, the weather has been warm. Today it's still one degree above freezing.

Over the last few days both Martha and I have had a good deal of pleasure reading *Zeno Cosini* by Italo Svevo.

My condition is such that I would certainly have suffered a severe breakdown in the last few days if I had not got as far as Chapter 111 and did not have the prospect of finishing Vol. I.[14]

6.I. Yesterday before our meal we spent one and a half hours walking in the Prater [. . .] The temperature is between 1 and 3 degrees above freezing. A few days ago we had mild spring weather. Not a trace of any snow left.

In the evening, during a walk through the streets, met Gergely, the painter, on the way to Richard Götz's[15] house. Since, for some days now, I have not been able to decide to thank G. for his New Year's greetings either by phone or in writing, I went up to his house with him for a moment. Told him that I shall lend him the Spengler and Europe essays[16] for a few days. Met there his young friend with whom he wants to set up the journal.

Worked at the Ge[rda]-H[ans]S[epp]-U[lrich]-Chapter;[17] approximately 6 (prepared) pages.

In the evening, read some of the Sulfmeister-type novel by Scholz.[18]

7.I. The usual walk in the Prater. In the evening only as far as the cinema at the other end of the Landstraße and back.

Read, with repugnance, Scholz, *The Way to Ilok.*

8.I. Answer from S. Fischer from San Moritz. On his return to Berlin wants to urge Wasservogel once more to look for more benefactors for the Haupt-mann Prize. More than we expected. M[artha] nearly collapsed after the tension of the last few days; had to sit down. F[ischer] in the meantime has his publishing house send 250 marks.

Otherwise, day like all the others.

9.I.

Since yesterday evening Martha has had something like a tooth abscess or a fistula, inside her lower jaw, on the right; but not in any pain. Went to Piwniezka:[19] suppuration of the tooth sockets. Rare condition, connected with the loosening of the teeth. Treated this with an injection and removed the acute symptom.

Thanked S. F[ischer]. Returned the New Year's greetings of Dr. Elert and Schwarzschild.[20] Agreed to give a lecture to the College of Adult Education on the 24th of this month, at 8 p.m.

10.I. In the morning, the money from the S. F[ischer] publishing house.

The usual walk in the Prater. Light covering of cloud, temperature about zero degrees.

Since the day before yesterday have been reading "The Last Days of Mankind."[21] Martha is reading Svevo, *Senilita*, but is by no means as delighted as she was by *Zeno Cosini.*

Yesterday I didn't go out during the day because I had a chill on my stomach; in the evening, just as we were about to go out,[22] Helene came. Stayed for quite a long time, we accompanied her home and my hunger was sharp to the point of pain.

Her daughter has not yet married because she still hasn't passed her subsidiary examination in philosophy. Has chosen for this child psychology after Frau Bühler's[23] book (examined by the male Bühler). Today these young women prepare themselves thoroughly.

H. looks better than usual. Was in a particularly good mood because she was returning from Dr. Müller who declared that there was absolutely no further danger of blindness.

13.I. Wonderful spring morning, +8 degrees. I have forgotten exactly what happened in the course of the last two days. In external terms, they were like the others. In the evening read Kraus, Martha read *Schweik*[24] as well. Had a rest at 12.00 noon. I needed a whole week for Chapter 111 (Ge[rda], H[ans] S[epp] U[lrich]) although the work went relatively well; it became one of the longest; at any rate the amount of time used up was not scheduled.

Both of us slept badly last night, I'm beginning the big U[lrich] chapter,[25] but intend to shave and get dressed soon to take advantage of the weather. Walked along R[ustenschacher]—, H[aupt]-Allee down to the junction with lower Fahrstraße and back. In the afternoon under pressure from M[artha] who wants to return the books, read Kraus.

14.I. Afternoon, rested. Drafted 3 pages of the U[lrich] chapter. Walk in the Prater. In the evening at Josef Adler's[26] house. Room with work by Kokoschka, Schiele, etc., but the furniture, both in terms of selection and arrangement, feebly bourgeois. Similarly, while their response to art is of a high level, they nonetheless conduct their dealings with each other with a bantering interfamily tone.

15.I. Fontana is canvassing support in the *Tag* for Ihering[27] and Diebold[28] as the only Burgtheater directors who could save the institution! "[The Burgtheater] . . . can only run successfully under a director who is a leading figure in the realm of dramaturgy and possesses a ruthless sense of purpose . . . I see in the field of the German theater only two such men who, in addition to the coherence of their plans and the firmness of their character, have the further advantage of being familiar with the difficult circumstances in Vienna and have practical experience of work in the theater. Their names are H.I. and B. D. If it wishes to put the epoch of dead time behind it, the Burgtheater must choose between them."

Walking through the outer reaches of the Wurstelprater bordering the main avenue, discovered a downbeat nightclub with old-fashioned pictures of artistes decorating the exit.

In the evening read *Schweik*. Confirmed receipt of the money to S.F[ischer] publishers.

Drafted the chapter on Bo[nadea] in the final block.[29]

21.I. No idea what happened in the intervening time except that yesterday evening Regina Ullmann[30] came to visit. Martha has a cold, and apart from that the days were all alike. A head scarf suits M. very well indeed.

It's M.'s birthday today.

Freezing, slightly overcast weather. Yesterday evening I went for a walk on my own. I am struggling with the 10 concluding chapters and fear that I won't finish on time.

What I thought at the time about R.U. came back to me: she often speaks like a writer in a family magazine, but in her case it has a sense of authenticity and a touch of genius.

25.I. Yesterday I went over to proofreading because, in the course of the final Ge[rda] chapter,[31] I lost all desire to continue writing and take this as a sign that it is time for the last revision.

At 8 o'clock in the evening, gave a reading at the College of Adult Education on Ludo Hartmann Square. In the tram, beforehand, sat opposite a woman who appeared to be an elderly spinster, reading a copy of the edition of *Grigia* published by Müller. An unusual experience for me. Bright and shining building, full of warmth and activity, elegant room for the senior staff, the library run by volunteer assistants. In the audience a {young} blond, Jewish intellectual with a bullet-shaped head and spectacles, who listened to me with benevolent severity, petit-bourgeois matrons, some young men with faces from the suburbs and the superiority conveyed by a *Weltanschauung.* Given a nice welcome by members of the audience rising to their feet in silence when I arrived. I read the first chapter, the 3 officer-engineer-mathematician chapters on U[lrich],[32] and the first Bo[nadea] chapter.[33] Feldmann, Head of the Literary Division, and the Librarian who stayed in the hall (which was like an amphitheater), were very surprised at how well I read. In the course of the day I myself had been greatly surprised at this when I tried out the length of the chapters. The audience followed quite well, with the exception of the beginning which fell flat because I had forgotten to prepare the ground for the mixture of irony and seriousness. Applause very lively, but fell short of an ovation. I can imagine how different it would be in the case of Werfel[34] and, indeed, I can understand it. However nice it may be to present to these people all kinds of creative writers, the overall effect is to promote very straightforward narration of very well-known things.

After the reading, met Götz[35] in the Pilsenetzer.[36] Went home on foot dragging my unwilling companion as far as the Wollzeile.

Over the last few days had an attack of pharyngitis that looked really bad; traces of it have been there for weeks; sensation of foreign body in the throat, discharging, discolored mucous membrane. Was about to visit the doctor with the gravest fears, but it was probably nothing but an irritation from the nicotine-free cigarettes. For two days I have been smoking normal ones and have to keep a very strong grip on myself in order to be moderate. (Only one cigarette an hour.)

Have heard that the Radio Advisory Board, when issuing invitations to give readings, proceeds according to a political ratio: conditions seem to be set up approximately as the specialist professional advisers in the War Ministry had wanted them to be.[37]

30.I. The proofreading—50 pages a day are supposed to be completed—is not going as I want. At the beginning there was only a daily deficit that I hoped to make good, but then the water chapter[38] alone held me up for two days. Now it is finished, not quite as I want it, and my nerves are on edge. Have had the fat doctor call on me; pharyngitis; I had almost feared something worse. Blei sent me Broch's outline of his novel;[39] intentions that touch, in part, on mine. I have written to Rowohlt[40] and still not received an answer. The League of Culture is constantly inviting me to attend its lectures without inviting me to give a reading myself. In the newspapers that I read, the debate about the Directorship of the Burgtheater is continuing; Wildgans has now moved to center stage.

Morning, walk in the Prater broken off because of stomachache.

Afternoon, Ungar. Rennweg, Borhaveg Landstr. Rested. Proofread the first 150 pages.

Look at your problem this way: that you are not famous is natural, but that you do not have enough readers, etc., to make a living is disgraceful.

2.II. Yesterday, or the day before, an essay in the *Tag* by Juvenal[41] on the 60th birthday of Adler. The way Freud, Adler and Schoenberg are treated in their homeland!

I still haven't reached p. 200 with the proofreading.

3.II. Yesterday evening I read some of Gide's autobiography,[42] the evening before that, some of Sudermann's *Lithuanian Novellas*, over the previous few evenings Bernanos' *The Sun of Satan* and once, in the midst of all this, I again read a few chapters of [*Wilhelm*] *Meister*.[43] It is my intention, in these entries, to avoid anything to do with the spiritual content of my life and to note down only the physical circumstances. For this reason I note that the temperature outside is +7 C. and that since yesterday light, warm rain has been falling intermittently. As it falls, I hope that eventually the wet, grey roof of the Palais Salm and the Baroque roof of the Palais Rasumofsky with its crumbling red tiles will again rise up before my eyes.[44]

———————

4.II. Yesterday evening I again read Gide. I have the impression that the French landscapes that he and Bernanos describe are the land that I yearn for, which can scarcely be right in the case of B. since he chose an ugly landscape. As I went to bed I imagined a manor house in Austria with 4 low round towers, moat and massive walls; I think that I was reminded of E.? {?Eichhorn} near Brünn where Heinrich[45] used to shoot roebuck. Impassive ugliness. But then it occurred to me that if I had grown up there, I would perhaps have fallen in love with it and that if I were to portray it, then it, too, would be beautiful. In this way I passed on to the reflection that all the things one loves become beautiful in art. Beauty is none other than an expression for something that is loved. This would be the only way to define it. For this reason, too, the growth of satirical sentiments would be very dangerous. And beauty would be connected with [the "other" condition] even if it is only civilized love that brings it about. At this very moment as I write this up I do not know if it has any value; it doesn't really belong here but, for the moment, I do not have any other notebook in which to record it.

For this reason I shall also include a sketch by Polgar[46] that I intend to cut out of yesterday's newspaper. Polgar is fortunate in that the books he likes are, above all, books that have appeared with his own publisher. But I have cut out this review of Hemingway because his style, which P. praises, is precisely the recipe of Impressionism, and it can serve as an example in the critical essays that I want to write. (As an example of a typical mistake.)

In the evening, posted a letter of reminder to Row[ohlt].

———————

5.II. Some kind of parade or other: musicians in greatcoats resembling frock coats with broad sashes from shoulders to hip. Fat gentlemen in top hats, at the head of the procession and for a further few rows marching two by two. Some rows consisting of clergymen in twos. Some nuns in twos. Then, slender and black, like leaves: half-grown girls. Down as far as the clergy, they take the bend into the sidestreet in a sharp wheel in an exaggeratedly soldierly fashion; thereafter, gently.

Before the evening meal, in the Rochus cinema. Film script by Viertel.[47] Film tastefully made; leaves behind no aftertaste of aversion.

[. . .]

In the evening we were supposed to meet Lukács[48] but he made his excuses via the servant girl {of the sister} of Gaetano's[49] girl-friend.

―――――――

6.II. Thick fog with temperature of 5 degrees above freezing. My digestion has not been functioning properly for two days; probably a chill.

mU[50]

A man, fetched from the public house by his common-law wife, carries a small child on his arm, and with the free one presses the woman against some boarding and boxes her ears. (This from a courtroom report. He then stabbed a man who came to the woman's assistance.)

It has also been reported in the paper today that, on account of the new laws, the Constitutional Court has been staffed with new people. Instead of the two famous lawyers, Kelsen and Layer, there is a Christian-Social university professor, then Head of Section Hecht, Christian-Social ministerial civil servants, and suchlike. Only this morning I was thinking that an association ought to be formed to combat the spread of stupidity.

Just this evening I have been reading some of Gide's *Let it Die* again and came to a halt at a place on p. 251 where young Gide behaves in a very exaggerated way for no very good reason and beseeches his comrades to avoid a certain alley; he has heard a dark rumor about the alley that has frightened him more in terms of the brutality of his imagining than through its unknown sexual connotations to which he is indifferent. "Suddenly I felt a nameless, religious panic and fear pouring out into my heart, and, sobbing, I threw myself on my knees before my comrade: 'Bernard! Oh, I beseech you: don't go down this path!' My agitation necessarily aroused an impression of hysteria, indeed of insanity . . . But Bernard Tissaudier, who, like me, had enjoyed the advantages of a puritanical upbringing, was not deceived for a moment about the source of my fear . . ."—and he brings him down to earth with a calm, rather cynical reply. One page later, Gide calls this: "an attack of that deep, churning, mystical apprehension . . , to which I was subject at certain moments and whose manifestations shocked me so dreadfully!" Subsequently this happens more frequently, but the attacks are milder. "And soon I recognized that this spiritual drunkenness was nothing but poetic inspiration and that the moment when this fever took hold of me announced the approach of Dionysus and his bliss." pp. 251ff.

10.II. I didn't get round to making any entry. I am rewording Chapter 61 and separating it into a Chapter 61 and 62;[51] I'm adding to part of it, and this is proving to be very time-consuming but also very important for the novel because now the U[lrich] problem will be virtually complete except for the turning point at the end.

The weather has changed now, −5, −3, and suchlike; "inflow of a cold front," as it is called. It was possible to watch the fall on the thermometer.

I'm reading Chesterton at the moment. "What is wrong with the world" essays, in addition to Gide and Goethe. Extraordinary similarities with me.

Written a few words to Blei and sent back the Broch outline.

Once again, am not answering any letters.

Wildgans now really does seem about to become the artistic consultant to the Burgtheater.

Yesterday I felt excessively weary after quite a long walk, went to bed early (10 o'clock), took a lot of "Formamint" pastilles and today it had passed.

11.II. Yesterday evening met Lukács and Frau Lorenz in the Café Herrenhof and the Americans came along too.

Now Heinz Ortner[52] is being made an artistic consultant to the Burgtheater as well!

In the *Tag*, lament about the Constitutional Court, the University, the Burgtheater. Nowhere does one find objective standpoints anymore, nowhere respect in the face of spirit and achievement! And what about in the *Tag*?

13.II. Neither any news from S. F[ischer][53] nor an answer from Rowohlt.[54] For days now I have been under the greatest possible nervous strain without being able to defend myself, because a reminder to SF would be embarrassing to me and I am at Row[ohlt]'s mercy. I also tell myself that it may be that my agitation is disproportionate to any effect of his hesitation, it is rather the return of that kind of negligence that so profoundly annoys me and that makes me fear the worst; the row in the summer and reconciliation in the autumn seem to have been utterly futile. My nerves have again shown themselves not to be able to cope with this situation; my digestion is irregular and, as far as the novel is concerned, I was not able to finish the rewriting of Chapter 62. At noon, yesterday, because of my condition, I only walked along the Weissgerber Lende; in the evening, Kärntnerstrasse, Hoher Markt, the Ring as far as the Wollzeile.

Nice weather, temperature just below freezing, in the daytime a little above that.

In the evening I read, by turns, Gide and Chesterton. [. . .]

16.II. Since, as long as I have not finished, I cannot undertake anything with respect to R[owohlt] I am trying for the time being to resign myself to the situation.

Yesterday evening I was at Eckstein's house[55] (last time was about 2 months ago). Those present: Herr and Frau Flach,[56] Dr. Schmidt, Miller-Fülops.[57] A number of times, so Martha insists, I interrupted Herr M. F. most discourteously. He, for his part, called Chesterton and Claudel[58] "probably the greatest" without having the slightest idea that I might presume to feel insulted.

Frau F[lach] admired him because he works ten hours a day. Asked me about recent literature, but he took a good deal of pleasure in indicating that he would probably take any advice from Fülop more seriously. She doesn't seem to have ever heard the name "Döblin"[59] before, but reads Leibniz. Her work on color is supposed to have been successful. She doesn't want to start work again immediately, but to study. Attends lectures by Pötzl,[60] among others. Strange marriage: he is managing director (of a factory) in Brünn.

Before our meal today, we visited the Waldmüller Exhibition[61] of the Hagenbund, returning with that feeling of purity and friendship, which is imparted by contact with a person from a high order of humanity. The tradition that W. is predominantly a genre painter is reversed by the impression one gains from this exhibition. He is, first, a landscape painter, then only a portraitist. His portraits are not among—s[it] v[enia] v[erbo[62]]— the historical elite of this school, but sometimes come close to it. With few exceptions (as, for example, the portrait of an old, once beautiful, rather malicious lady), color is missing, a bright reddish-brown covers up the faces; the characterization is extraordinarily distinctive; a calm eye that lays everything bare; but this eye lacks the idea or the prejudice that runs counter to contemporary prejudice, it is implacably true to life but not prophetic; it was probably the disfavor of the Viennese "Biedermeier" era that prevented this. Much more vigorous is the painterly quality in the landscapes and the way figures are interwoven with the landscape (for this is not window dressing). In his later pictures, W. was probably influenced by the French; but the intuitive awareness, the half-recognizing and gradual attaining runs (in a way similar to Pettenkofen)[63] through the whole of his work. Already in pictures, where the figures are still arranged to balance each other according to the scheme of academic painting, the image is dominated by an "illuminated figure." Then, later, he turns to landscapes in which the painting is wonderful and rather in the style of the early Impressionists (reminding me, most of all, of Monet) except that they lack the sense of dissolving in the outdoor light. The colors are simply sated with light, they swim enclosed in light, they are clear and translucent, but not blurred. Then, from this high level he takes a further step; in the exhibition there are a few landscapes painted throughout in bright colors that have the effect of tempera, and the people in them are entwined with the trees, etc., to form one "Gestalt," with the effect that, when viewed from a few paces away, they are completely absorbed even though, when seen close to, they are painted exactly. That was, in fact, an independent solution of the problem of the times—which was clearly ousted by Manet's more paradoxical solution that, in its transformation of the charm of Paris, was more original, more exotic, or at least more stunning—and has, in fact, to this day not reached the level of consciousness. A sad and strange fate for ideal conservatism!

What strikes one about the genre paintings is, in those with a wealth of figures, the way the throng of heads resembles a bed of tulips,—one has almost the impression of a textile—while what stands out in the simpler motifs is the delicate handling of bright illumination.

By the way, the effect of all his pictures is heightened from a distance of 5–10 paces; this, too, is evidence of the Impressionistic element. This view in close-up and from a distance is like a material that can be worn on both sides. But to wear the material inside out—this demand made people more excited.

His self-portrait (reproduction) reminded me, despite the lack of outward similarities, of the inward Gide-type.

———————————

17.II. I forgot to mention that the observation of W.'s late landscapes comes from Martha. In some way or other, the execution of the curves also reminds me of Böcklin,[64] only they are much better; poor W.

In the evening, a conversation with Martha from one bed to the other. M. tried first to explain the deficiencies of his portraits by reference to the fatal situation of having to paint portraits for money. Finally my counterargument won the day to the effect that, if that was the case, then why hadn't such a purist painter at least painted his housekeeper in a way that suited him?

My thesis ran as follows: he sees the people of his times with an objectivity that lays them bare, but he does not feel the need to "let them know just what he thinks of them." He is not aware in any final sense of who it is that stands before him. The last step in the synthesis is not taken, it is not centered on a great, if unspoken conviction (although, as a person, he probably has fragments of this, perhaps a cutting sense of humor or suchlike). He does not quite objectify his feeling. This, in broad terms, seems to be the psychology of this painting.

If this were not the case he would have to give his feeling some kind of expression in his painting. Some richness of color or an optical shortcut to represent this would have to make an appearance. Now he paints in a single layer and nowhere in this surface of color is there any source from which come waves cutting across at an angle.

18.II. Somehow or other the whole thing is wrong. W. must, after all, have learned something from the school of Barbizon.[65]

Democracy: today, something important in the *Tag*—an article that is half in favor of Zeileis.[66] A certain number of spas have set up forms of treatment that follow his system. So that's the economic dimension then! [. . .] Monarchy was a wrongheaded ideocracy, democracy has no ideas at all.

I fear that the following thought (in the afternoon, on the sofa) does not belong with my essays but to my biography: God, according to the normal idea of the relationship of the spinning electron and the body as a whole; what significance does it have for him if one builds Gothic or some other kind of structures? Spiritual differences do not have any effect on the laws of nature; if the human being is not to be more superfluous than a pendulum, then the superstructure of the whole is spiritual. To be precise, it is probably the next level in the superstructure. Aside: a finalistic observation of this type is not prohibited to any greater degree than the causal kind that leads to a prima causa. Is it forbidden altogether to draw conclusions by means of analogies? Does one not come closer to God through induction than through speculation?

Yesterday, before supper, we went to watch an old Chaplin film in a cinema up on the Landstraße. His balancing on board a rolling steamer is an act of genius. The way his legs fly out sideways is both priceless and graceful.

Weather +4 degrees, wet remnants of snow and puddles.

This evening we are invited to a film première in Rothgasse.

My position and the matter of how I'm to behave vis-à-vis R[owohlt] and F[ischer] are causing me great anguish; each time I discuss this with M[artha] I am very irritable (she is too). I draft and reject letters. Sent off a letter to R[owohlt].

19.II. Dreadfully boring film. Our seats, with the enticing name "Circle," were in the front third. Taking our seats, seeing Salten[67] holding court at the center toward the rear, and asking for those in charge of the seating arrangement—all these steps were as one. Gave my name and gave back our tickets; apology, short wait in two wicker chairs in the foyer, seats in a box. Twice Salten's eyes met mine but no acknowledgment; stupid how I cannot bring myself to adopt an easy social manner in such matters. After the showing we went to the Café Wollzeile.

A box next to the screen with the word "Welcome" and some kind of arabesques on a piece of cardboard. Announcement that the film actress Evelyn Holt (who was in the film) would greet the audience. "Dear film friends, I am pleased to see you personally, here in beautiful Vienna . . ." etc. Hint of a Berlin accent, voice of an actress who plays walk-on roles. Then she sat near to us in a magnificent evening dress.

Significant, the extent to which films project an ideal of Jewish beauty. E.H., for example, is a blond Jewess. Old Götz, who cuts such a nice figure on the streets, is presented in close-up, with his elephantine ears and the clever eyes of an old Jew.

And in the coffeehouse I read: "First interview with the {new} Director of the Burgtheater, A[nton] W[ildgans]." The 6 o'clock paper is very proud to present the first. The interviewer seems just like a creation by Wildgans, and the two together seem as if they'd been created by me: W. lay on the sofa (he's not well) and one saw that he was weighing up every single word. Before he goes to sleep at night, he directs his last glance toward St. Othmar's Church.

21.II. Situation unchanged. The big D[iotima]-U[lrich] Chapter (67–69) finished. In the evening went to a Buster Keaton film. Then in the Café Kolowrat. Eggs in a glass and chocolate.

25.II. At last finished proofreading the third folder yesterday, all the while turning over the question of Rowohlt, Fischer, *Frankfurter Zeitung*, etc., without coming to any conclusion. I am extraordinarily nervous and am sleeping badly even when I stop thinking about anything at all. The thread on which our life hangs is already extraordinarily thin. This morning I decided that I would write, and what I would write, today.

Friday, 28.II. The day before yesterday and yesterday morning proofread some further chapters, then set the work aside and wrote to Fischer in the afternoon, a few lines to Bermann,[68] too, and drafted a few other letters from the large supply of unanswered ones that I still have to think about. This tiny break in my work left me with the feeling of being on holiday—quite remarkable. Proof of the senseless weight of the pressure of work. I asked S.F. in confidence if it is really the case that he doesn't want me back.[69] I'm expecting a rejection because, from his point of view, what reason would he have for taking into his fold an aging author who is both difficult and who, in addition, doesn't have any particular reputation at the present time? And I am also aware of how badly he behaved toward me and of how much I disliked him—far more so than the feelings I now have for Rowohlt. The only positive aspect is a ridiculously romantic sense of pleasure that I felt after the half an hour I spent with the Fischer family last autumn in the Hotel Imperial;[70] this had something of the air of resignation of old people reunited after futile stormy quarrels. For all this, I have not forgotten that he is a hard business negotiator and (when he sees no hope for large profits) rather petty—as in the case of the few thousand inflation-marks that brought about the wreck of the reunion all those years ago.[71] The right thing to do would be to enjoy the feelings of growing older in their own right and not to have any business connection with him, except under quite altered circumstances! To express this without emotion, that I am offering myself to him is a humiliation—a plea for peace on the part of the vanquished. What is more, the plea is in vain; and even if it is not quite in vain, it is then only a prelude to new annoyances. What, in spite of this, impels me to write is that I do not set much store by my future as a creative writer and assume that, when the novel is finished and has boosted me a little, I shall try to earn my bread as an essayist; in this context, the modest security that is offered by the House of F. is to be preferred to the insecurity of R.

At the same time I have also written to Dr. Reifenstein[72] with reference to the *Frankfurter Zeitung*.

The day before yesterday, in the evening, Lukács called to take us to the café of the American journalists. But Fodors were still in Czechoslovakia, and only Mr. Bath was there, with someone with the name of Dr. Rosenbaum, or something similar. Runs a concert agency, earlier a lawyer. Radiotelegram to Mr. B. "How many people have been unemployed in Austria over the last few months?" Probably needed for a leading article. People confer, telephone calls; there's nobody who is able to supply the information off the cuff, and Mr. Bath doesn't want to wait until next day. Whether they finally found someone who knew this I did not find out. The last thing that happened was that Lukács took him off to his home to look up some statistical reference source but then L. returned on his own. Strong impression that was left on me by this abruptness. (Mr. B. is of medium height, generously upholstered in flesh. When I got to know him his coat had burst under the arm and his shoelaces were not properly tied; he was also wearing a Havelock cape. Roughly speaking, the sum of American provinciality and Austrian small-town life. But he also possesses better suits. It is only about the neck that he's always rather untidy. He has a handsome, sharp, short profile. Very white, even teeth and black hair. Expressive eyes. A Christian with brown hair. He's always merry and gives the appearance of lacking determination; but, as has become clear, he's very sharp at what he does.)

Through the intermezzo about unemployment we found ourselves alone in the company of strangers who were the latest arrivals. I was next to a young German-American (perhaps also Jewish) actress, with magnificent red-blond hair and covered in paint, but young. A beautiful face, the features finely drawn in within a square. I got into a quarrel with her over Liebstöckl[73] (I only found out later that she is his girl-friend) because she declared that "he at least" was an incorruptible critic. I was only a hair's breadth away from telling something of the dirt that is circulating about his affairs but fortunately I couldn't remember them accurately enough. What I said later is of no consequence; the figure of "this Zeileis,[74] of the Viennese scene" receded into the background of my thoughts; the only remarkable thing is that she loves Liebstöckl and Altenberg. Later on I became more deeply embroiled in a quarrel with her husband. He looks a little like Sonja Bogs;[75] fine limbs, anaemic, slender, and expressing himself with delicacy and cunning. Correspondent of the Hearst press. Before this was a correspondent for the Ullstein group in America. I must find out about him. He spoke to me in a very offhand manner and I was rather sharp. I had recourse to the rather unfortunate distinction between literature and journalism, roughly in the sense of two categories that, despite all the points where they cross, have nothing to do with each other. (As I write, a criterion occurs to me: things that one has collected and that one can still read after two years are not merely journalistic.) As usually happens in debate, I didn't have the right reasons to hand; I was forced to speak circumstantially about bad literature and good journalism—things that did not affect the distinction; I was also unwise enough to mention the droplet of lyricism that made something into literature, and so forth. (A further simple distinction would be the one that can very readily be checked between the intellectuality of a researcher and that of a journalist. The speed of the writing and the immediacy of the reaction determine a position from which little good can come.)

What was interesting about my opponent was only his type. He sees Shaw as the peer of Aristophanes and above all the others. But, for him, in spite of objections that he concedes, Liebstöckl is frequently a writer of spirit. Even Julius Bauer,[76] in his view, sometimes writes with spirit. Descriptions of journeys by Erich Salzmann[77] he sees as the equal of similar works by creative writers or, indeed, better than those. He speaks in a reserved manner and with a smile. With every word, one feels that he believes he is the advocate of the new spirit. (An Ullstein service to humanity!) It occurred to me that this is what second-generation Ullstein looks like. A mixture of what they consider "neue Sachlichkeit" and the incapacity to detect the stupidity of an L.

Yesterday, toward evening as I was preoccupied with putting a new ribbon onto my machine, Götz arrived; alarmed by my terse note, he had come to make his excuses. I shall now fill in the details: I had invited him on the 25th of last month to come and see me in the next few days in order to speak about the two essays. For 4 weeks he did not follow this up. I tried in vain to reach him by telephone. Well, he certainly had all kinds of other things demanding his attention. But at any rate I let him know, and not without some justification, that I was annoyed. He apologized and we arranged the matter for some time after 10th March, after he had straightened out his affairs. It was certainly the case that he had been negligent; the strange thing about it was that I was firmly convinced (M[artha] against this view!) that Fontana was behind this; and secondly that, for quite a while now, I have been haunted by the superstition that this matter had to be cleared up first before progress can be made on the others! Last night I dreamed of unadulterated filth; vederemo!

Yesterday evening I read some of *Olaf Audunssohn* by Sigrid Undset, a fat tome that M[artha] had brought home with her. I hate this woman but she has something Homeric about her—in the effortlessness and plasticity of her narrative. If she were even one short step closer to being clever—and it is almost a matter of chance that she is not—then she would be immense. She has the rare gift of describing landscapes, and occasionally people, too, in such a way that one can really see them. She doesn't thrash away at detail but usually narrates in an epic rhythm. (Another example for this concept is found in the narrative parts of *Wilhelm Meister*). After reading her, before going to sleep at night one sees figures, images, events. She sees life. When the two "children" run away from the farm and make their way to the town by land and water, one can see what they are doing, from the time they put on their clothes to the time they come back home; one could tell the whole story again in broad terms—it is charming right the way through. At the moment I can scarcely say what I have against her. Is it the case that we miss, amongst all this magnificent evidence, a sense of the problematical side of the Middle Ages? Does she completely fail to see each human being as a whole while making every detail so plastic? (For example, in the few aspects of the meal after the revenge when candles are brought into the hall and -?- is sitting on his seat, with his blond hair that grows down over his forehead, {a man in his prime} seemingly ruddied by the open air and by an inward intoxication, as well as by the self-infecting wound.) [. . .]

---

3. March, Monday. I'm bringing this record up to date: Grimme, the Prussian Minister for Culture, has said that his predecessor, Prof. Becker, was the last representative of an individuality that is dying out; today, he said, every functionary was only conceivable as the exponent of some power-grouping. (From a report by Olden)[78]

Just this minute—I'm writing this in the morning before I start work—have had a reply from Fischer. Letter dictated with speed and determination. W[asservogel] is not answering him and W. is the source of money, so this makes it impossible for him to do anything, he says! It is transparent that he is turning down my offer; unfortunately, he said, this came too late—recently they have made considerable commitments.

For the moment this news leaves no resonance whatsoever in me, except that I have an indistinct awareness that the catastrophe has now arrived. I haven't yet even copied up and sent the letter to Reifenstein I mentioned on the 28th of last month; this is the next thing I shall do.

9.III. Sunday. Things have gone very badly for me, little sleep, heart very unsettled. The most unpleasant aspect is a condition in which one doesn't have any physical sensation but the spiritual pain (the feeling that life as a whole holds no pleasure) sits close to one's heart like a wound; it is just as I describe it, though it seems impossible.

Then, the day before yesterday, a telegram from the publishers, yesterday a letter from Row[ohlt] himself. He is on a journey, excuses, misunderstandings! A good thing that I did not lose my temper. I had already been to see the lawyer (Breuer).

I am now embarrassed about a remark I made about R. in my last letter to S. F[ischer], I shall have to put this right.

Fragments of dialogue: "As far as getting people to pay their bills is concerned, one needs to take a hard-handed approach!" I look up—two Jews are passing close by to me, the older one, portly, barely of medium height, is saying this.

Vienna: "Atten—tion! Atten—tion! The future program includes. . . ." The so-called "Talking-film interludes" in the small cinemas are gramophone records. These are the reason why they have taken the bread out of the musicians' mouths and increased prices. Here, through some kind of megaphone, the owner announces his program; I recognize his voice. He's a fairly tall, well-upholstered man, Jewish, about thirty years of age, and slurs his words slightly as he speaks through the "radio."

Yesterday evening a nice invitation by Sinsheimer[79] who is now with the B[erliner] T[ageblatt], to write something for page 3. Don't know what that is.

10.III. Monday. Yesterday evening I made a resolution that I entered under today's date in the notes for the essays.

Since Row[ohlt's] letter I have lost the thread of the novel. It may also, however, have something to do with my reading 300 pages of proofs and that, beyond this, I was looking for something in the novel and am depressed because it is too abstract.

13.III. Thursday. On Tuesday we went with Lukács to the café of the Americans. To be precise, most of them are Hungarians or Yugoslavs. Fodor wants to put me in touch with a journalist who works for a major Christian Science paper and who wants to write about me. A blond young man with a face like a potato; but we were sitting far apart at opposite ends of the big table-arrangement and I only registered the intensity with which he shook my hand when he had to leave early.

I have worked through my correspondence. Among them, one to S. F[ischer] to whom I have now said that, in my view, the trustees of the G[erhart]-H[auptmann]-Foundation have to assume liability for the promise that was made to me. I expect an explosive riposte.

I have despatched 600 pages of manuscript to Row[ohlt] and told him to expect a further 100, to be despatched at the end of the week. But that seems to have been too much of a commitment because I still have to think about, and draft, the chapters I have not yet written before I can get round to giving the definitive form to pp. 600–700. But, by and large, after one lost day, things are going well again.

Yesterday it snowed while the temperature was +4. Dry, whitish-grey spots in thick flurries against dark {blackish}-grey air. Before supper we went to the nearest cinema. Snow-filled air from the mountains was arriving throughout the day with the wind.

In the evening I read Carlyle, *The Diamond Necklace*. M[artha] insists there is a similarity to me. I can see this, but only in the mistakes: he also tends to preach and his method of narrating is just as if someone were rolling and kneading a prune in dough until it is in the middle of a dumpling. And he also has such a curious way of designating things; it's a bit like the cultural arrogance of Social-Democrat philistines, when he skewers his object, points it out, heaps scorn upon it or anoints it with statements about the beginning and end of all things. But there is no doubt that he is an important man.

Yesterday a program of action from Wildgans: on contemporary creative writers, above all Csókor![80] [. . .]

16.III. Sunday. I felt ill yesterday, I couldn't move either forward or backward in my work; I thought a flu was on the way. Toward 4:30 p.m. we visited the "New Gallery" to have a look at the exhibition of a negro painter. Of no interest whatsoever. Incidentally, I behaved badly and, on entering, mentioned my name and refused to pay the entrance fee; I declared that one should either invite me to attend as someone from the world of art or not invite me at all. Since I was only speaking to an intimidated employee this was naturally not the right way to behave; I really ought to post the 2 schillings to them today, retrospectively, and make a written complaint, but I'm too lazy.

We then went on foot to the Café Museum in the hope of meeting Morgenstern;[81] I wanted to tell him about Frankfurt. But, to our surprise, we met Frau Kirsta.[82] They are now living in Berlin and things don't seem to be going right for them. She noticed that I was in a bad mood. Introduced briefly to Hans Richter, the director of "Avantgarde Films" who was at her table. "The greatest filmmaker in Berlin," as she puts it. Max Mell[83] type, but softer, more relaxed, more sensual. He is said to have many adventures of the heart and not to be able to part from any lover.

I have read the amusing book by Mrs. Sheridan.[84] Unsurpassable, the inner pose of these politicians from Lenin to Mussolini when a pretty woman tempts them to reveal their sweetness. This is worth reading again. Also the friability of the aristocratic elite that permits a seamstress not to release a dress that has not been paid for, and yet still does not boycott her. I shall ask Blei to get me a copy of the book from the List Publishing House.

You can easily narrate something real—even a real conviction.

---

26 March. The previous hasty note was one that I made since the last full entry; I had no time to write any more. Work. In the meantime I have sent 600 pages to Rowohlt and have not got as far ahead with the rest as I had hoped.

My nerves are miserable. I fall asleep late and wake early. My heart hurts.

Yesterday, or the day before yesterday, spent some time with Morgenstern in the Café Imperial.

No answer from the *Frankf. Zeitung* because Reifenberg is going to Paris and is handing over the literary review to someone else.

On the other hand, have received a book from there with the request for a review. Did not want to do it but would like to now; don't know what I'll do eventually.

Received a "chain letter"; intensely unpleasant feeling at such presumption; then experienced a certain degree of euphoria on deciding not to comply. But I ought to render to myself a detailed account of how such superstition meets with God's displeasure. I had Anna Leznay[85] to thank for that.

---

30 March, Sunday. Yesterday evening, for the first time in my life, I took bromide. I was concerned that the preparation, which was a year old, might be spoiled, and perhaps it was this that made me feel a little agitated. Then I also imagined that I was experiencing a sensation rather like being forcibly pressed down into sleep. Jolts in the head as if something were making sudden attempts to empty out the blood. Expected an unpleasant final moment as with anesthesia. With all these imaginings, I took quite a while to fall asleep. And in the morning did not sleep any longer than usual. But was thoroughly rested experiencing a feeling of laziness, a sense that I could not bear to leave the bed, that is otherwise alien to me. All seems smooth within. Because this is such a different sensation, I realize that my normal state is one of agitation.

---

4 April, Thursday. Just what have I been reading since the book by that Sheridan woman? Part of Hauptmann's *Book of Passion.* (Rogu[86] tears the lending library books away from me when she has finished hers.) No doubt it's something that he wrote in an earlier period. Admirable for the way in which it is always presenting new manifestations for the single theme of this love affair. Magnificent descriptions of objects (the naked loneliness of the stormy sea that is depicted with antipathy). Powerful scenes, as when the married couple burn their love letters in the garden and the children leap around the fire and run to catch papers as they go flying away and take them back to the fire. Very informative with regard to H.'s nature and stronger than the artistic creations that he has shaped from such feelings.

François Porché, *The Life of Baudelaire.* This man was treated outrageously by his contemporaries. Like today! Discouragement was the cause of his downfall. The fact that, in his despair, he applied to be admitted to the Academy.

Jean Martet, *Clemençeau speaks.* In French reviews it is said that the book stands alongside Luther's *Table Talk* and Goethe's *Conversations with Eckermann.* Typical errors of judgment. He was a juicy fellow; a touch eccentric with those quickly formulated ideas about paleontology or Greek art; hypomanic; irascible, stubborn; capable, on occasions, of producing work in which ideas and expression {for example, p. 85 on his sculptors} were both outstanding; but nonetheless a long way from real greatness of spirit!

On p. 88 he gives a definition of action that is like the one that I am trying to formulate in Vol. II.

And then I read *Gerber, the Schoolboy, has Matriculated,*[87] but I have to write about that anyway.

The *Frankfurter Zeitung* has deigned to declare that it will examine the manuscript.

My book is to be printed at Hegner's[88] and Row[ohlt] has sent me samples. I chose the largest of the types that he described as acceptable and suggested an even larger one. That was yesterday when I had to write him a long letter about all these questions. (Hegner doesn't want my dashes, preferring quotation marks[89] for stylistic and aesthetic reasons, and to save space.)

I was pleased by an open letter to me from Prof. Norman Linker[90] in the *Österr. Schriftst. u. Künstler Ztg.* that was earlier called *Der Pfeil*. He had sent me an issue of the "Pfeil" that pleased me most in terms of its anti-corruptionist tone (and unfortunately also for some remarks criticizing Wildgans), and I had thanked him in a friendly, but mildly sarcastic fashion, asking him, with reference to the content of the article, whether he counted me among the "shadows of yesterday" or the people who are not yet of any consequence. For a long time he gave no answer, then this one.

Several times we went to the cinema, which is the right kind of pastime for this style of living. The weather has been fine, by and large; indeed it is unusually precocious. There are 700 pages of mine waiting in Berlin, and today I have made a start on the continuation.

Though I am not suffering from sleeplessness, I am sleeping very little again and don't feel at all well.

It is not right to have any time to think of God; not being able to spare a thought for him is the way to live that is most pleasing to him!?

From science I bring the regular work routine, from creative writing that of waiting for floodgates to open; this is one of the reasons for my difficulties. I now believe that one should talk oneself out of any thought of inspiration because this is merely a means of preventing inspiration; but what is the meaning of these moments of special happiness in spite of all this?

21.IV. Easter Monday.

Find things that you can narrate (cf. 16.III);[91] the wit[92] will arrive of its own accord as you narrate. The other way round is very difficult. That is the experience from Vol. I.

The feeling that I am not giving personal expression to my personal affairs in such notes makes it difficult for me to write up my diary. Nor can I find the time because I never get through what I intend to do. So I'm only making brief entries using key words. Postponed Berlin visit to the 28th. Row[ohlt] at moment with Ludwigs[93] for their Silv. Wedding. Read some things to Götz for the Easter number;[94] he seemed to be very taken with them. Was unnecessarily annoyed about the announcement of the Easter issue (my name next to Fontana's, after Mell), telephoned Koller[95]—he was charming but probably a little surprised; on the next day I had been put next to Schnitzler, before Hofmannsthal; felt a little embarrassed now that the smoke of my anger has dispersed.

Went to a tea given in honor of Tairoff by the "Society for the Promotion of Relations with Soviet Russia." His face is like Castiglioni's,[96] but around the eyes a touch of sultry charm, a boyish deficiency of character. Frau Dr. Halle[97] showed little interest in our presence. On the other hand, to my great surprise, Professor Specht[98] was clearly anxious to greet me.

26.IV. "More than 100,000 people filed past the bier of the great Russian author, Vladimir Mayakovsky, after he took his own life a few days ago" writes the *Tag* to accompany the picture by M[artha] showing an energetic, somewhat limited head. A few days ago I also read about him in the *P[rager] [Presse]*; he seems to belong to the species somewhere between *Action*[99] and Becher.[100] At any rate, all the journalists know just as little about him as I do but the predicate "the Great" is bestowed on him because the Communist Party members call him this, even though people are against the Communist Party. A complicated absence of points of reference, at the end of which emerges what is called "the epoch" and suchlike.

I have read *Lincoln* by Ludwig. It has been written in such a perfunctory manner that a raft is given a ship's side, and similar things. Fate is added by the ladleful. But it achieves its effects with a confident touch. And Lincoln, the man, gripped me. Here the circumstances of life shape a character, the character shapes the intellect. I felt a desire to change my way of representing people and to turn my attention to the problem of character. If I do so, I shall return to L. His style of writing, sometimes extraordinary, is characterized by drastic similes and thinking by means of examples. He traces complicated situations back to simpler ones—something that is possible in psychotechnical terms. And he always goes straight for what he wants or what he wishes to destroy. In some sense, this style of his is imperiously negligent, which is what makes it so simple. When I compare it with myself, the difference in kind lies in the riches of ambivalence. (This means that the appropriate way is to get rid of them.) But something else is added: he wants what he wants, but in each instance he feels himself into the opponent or recipient, imagines what the effect will be and so has what is probably, at root, a kindly attitude. So, to this straightforwardness, kindliness must be added. I shall take note of this recipe.

28.IV. Monday. Today I'm traveling with Martha to Berlin. Because of this I've had ample opportunity to concern myself with writer's blocks. The following are the main findings.

There seems to be a similarity between mountain vertigo and a work block. In both cases the idea appears that you will never get beyond this stretch. This idea, for its part, has a numbing effect. Sometimes during the work itself it is accompanied by a physical sensation (an inner pain, perhaps an aching confusion)—talking things through sensibly is of no help in the mountains, but it does help a little with work. This time it was particularly noticeable because there could be no question of any real fear of not finishing at all, at worst (and this I have long since recognized) of not finishing before departure. In spite of this, the idea was there in finest and fullest form and linked with the state of dejection. This is so stupid that I thought it could only be explained, finally, in ps[ycho]analytic terms!

(I have just realized that I did not write up a dream that was both drastic and naive that I had some time ago when I was unsettled by the nervous heart condition: I am walking with Martha and a gentleman in a wood. Climb up on a smooth tree with strong branches all of which are a long way from the others. Put on something of a show. Climb higher than I intended, led on by my success; or, to be more accurate, the portion that I have climbed up grows insidiously; it suddenly becomes clear that I have come much further than I can cope with, I do not dare to go back and have a panic attack with strong palpitations. At the end, probably as I examine the dream on waking, I realize that the tree was a beech (book!)[101] and the gentleman was a friend from my youth, Herzfeld (heart-flaw!)).[102]

Since the impression that my inhibitions might fall under the heading of psychoanalysis, I have made the following countersuggestions to myself: the uncertainty that arises is none other than the nervous uncertainty that I feel when I play tennis, or fence, or type while someone is watching me or I resolve to do something particularly well. This phenomenon is widely known. This would explain the efficacy of tranquilizers (bromide), the effect of diversion, or indeed of everything that dissipates the attention when it has become overfocused. Take, for instance, the cold, indifferent feeling when writing that is particularly favorable to me. Relaxation of tension, interruption, taking a walk. But there must also exist some hardening technique to make one resist.

Yesterday I faltered because of the impending journey, and, near to the end of the chapter—after I had completed more than ten pages, and very much to my satisfaction—, got hopelessly stuck; however, the inhibition was lifted immediately when I made a definite decision to break off my work and turned to the business of setting in order all the remaining papers that

I had not yet dealt with, in readiness for the interruption by the journey. This ordering straightaway became a continuation, and a working mood returned.

But ordering also possesses another kind of value beyond its effect of calming and diverting, and this is in fact the distinctive one: I have reduced this to the formula "divide et impera" or, expressed in a more vulgar fashion: "One at a time, please, and don't push!" It is perhaps not right at all for me to speak of ambivalences, although it looks like one when several things occur to me and I cannot decide on any one. But this ambivalence-equivalent does not come from an emotional disposition but simply from impractical behavior while putting things in order. I have the feeling that I have a swarm, a cloud of possibilities in my head, and resemble a man who wants to tie up a bale that is bigger than he is. So I must make the task easier for myself and divide it up! One at a time. This is the case in all things. It is likely that I shall not have to set things out in an objective and correct fashion at all, but only set myself up correctly! Divide the task up into subtasks.

I finally set down what also occurred to me in the course of the last few days: when writing difficult passages, first do the easy part in key words, but pay detailed and correct attention to the knotty intersections and transitions in order not to be tired before I arrive at them.

Furthermore: never draft something out just to the end but always go one step beyond the end, and into the next passage. If I don't do this, too much gets stuffed in between the start and the finish and tends to spread out.

On reading Zschokke:[103] do not say "avalanche" as if it were obvious what is meant by that. But describe it as if it were an unknown happening! He stepped on the snow, the snow began to shift, etc.

Of what significance is it that religion is supposed to be of {equal} use to all people, and that the religious man can derive no more benefit from it than the non-religious one?

Funny trait: I began here with descriptions of the weather and now I'm making entries in 4 notebooks with no precise system!

The be-all and end-all of all writing is: take pleasure in doing it! If you are not convinced of something you make a botch of it whether you are jumping or writing.

Whit Sunday, 8 June. Under the trees at the edge of Jesuits' Meadow[104] found a nestling that had fallen from, or been thrown out of its nest. No one took any notice of him. As we approached he looked at us and made no attempt to get out of our way. It had tiny little wings and the gaping mouth of young birds. If I hadn't seen it at the very last moment we would have trodden on it. The look it gave us was one of tired indifference, tired fear, tired hopelessness. Because of the many dogs in the area I should have liked to put it up on a branch but there was none within reach. I don't know how to rear such a creature. And, since there was no way I could help it, I left it to its fate. But I don't feel right about this.

26 August. Tuesday. This evening I finished the manuscript of Vol. 1.[105]

27 August. One of the reasons for not continuing with these notes[106] was because the attempt to note down the weather and walks appeared just too foolish to me and these would have taken too much time away from the more important internal processes, etc. Despite this, I intend once more to record the factual memories but this time in larger-scale summaries.

At present the dominant feature—apart from finishing the first part[107]—is the problem with my teeth. On the upper jaw on the left side 3 teeth that were capped by Dr. Katzer have developed cysts over the decades, one of which has penetrated quite deeply into the maxillary sinus. Approximately a week to ten days ago, this was discovered by Dr. Petrik when, as he drilled into a root canal, unusually large amounts of pus and serous liquid were released. The epithelial lamellae that are characteristic of the formation of cysts were not to be found in the secretion. It was confirmed that an x ray was necessary. Most well-known radiographers were away. P. telephones around. We consider Dr. Isaac Robinson, a consultant. In the evening I went to ask Koller whom he knew of. Only R.! Immediately a letter of recommendation to ensure that he does the work for nothing or at cost.

30.VIII:

I am received most warmly at R's rooms, but afterward it emerges that he was under the impression that a dental technician, Koller, had recommended me—someone who is, I assume, an old friend of his.

I didn't like the letter of recommendation on my behalf, it was bumptious, saying that he had no need to introduce me and indicating that I should only have a significant income after the appearance of the book, or something of the kind.

R., after assuring me that he would be as accommodating as possible, starts friendly negotiations once the treatment is finished. The cost was 60 Schillings (in reality it ought to be 90S) would 40 be too much? I don't say yes, I don't say no, and eventually we arrive at 20S, i.e., cost price. I offer Koller's services to R. by way of compensation, he says he has no need of these, at which I try to limit his concession to the medical insurance rate but he is no longer willing to accept this. (In Vienna it is custom and usage or a customary abuse, that newspaper-people have favored treatment in all kinds of undertakings—an arrangement that is somewhere midway between payment of dues, bribery and respect for the spirit. Since I receive comparatively small honoraria for my contribution to *Der Tag*, and the eternal lack of money is demoralizing—and also because Koller is very kind and forthcoming with offers of assistance—there have been occasions—very rare occasions—when, as a freelancer for *Der Tag*, I have taken advantage of this abuse.) Afterward, further discussion between Robinsohn and me. His appearance is halfway between Max Reinhardt[108] and Rudolf Kasper. He knows nothing of my work. Only reads for entertainment. His highest achievement is Ginzkey.[109] Looks at things from the perspective of race, wants me to characterize the literary species to which I belong as a special case, derived from my racial mix, etc. Asked for a copy of my book, saying he would like to continue the discussion when he has read it.

The photographs make up a little album, no less. Among them, my skull, taken in profile, quite large. Looks rather like I did, a while ago, after the big operation; very much a Slav, of the elongated type.

I don't much like my face but this skull, remarkably, inspires me with a certain vanity. But, on the other hand, this coquetry with death is something that I don't like at all.

The most important thing is that I have known for about a week now that I have to have the operation. (2 or 3 cysts have to be scraped out of the maxillary sinus, root resection for one tooth, extraction of another. If one of the cysts has broken through into the maxillary sinus—which has a slight shadow on it—it will be necessary to follow up with an operation to cut through from the maxillary sinus into the nose.) The surgeon, Privat-Dozent Dr. Hofer, first-class, the procedure is guaranteed to be painless. But over-work, {months of} high temperatures, and all the difficulties of the last few years have made me very nervous.

If I reproach myself with the thought that the procedure will be positively impersonal, the sense of unease is concentrated on the process of being anes-thetized. {(I have been told that this will probably be external via the joint of the jaw.)}

Whenever I have managed to persuade myself that this, too, is of no con-sequence, then I start to be apprehensive about the fear that I shall experi-ence immediately beforehand. Now fear of fear is decidedly a process affecting the nerves. Genuinely not of the realm of reason, it cannot be taken in hand. Recedes when individual psychological measures lay bare this nonsense. Is, however, fed anew by agitation of heart and colon.

Tricks of fear: perhaps, in spite of all defensive measures, it will become overpowering at the last moment? How humiliating! Of course, only an at-tempt to move it out of reach of reason.

Another trick: I change the countermeasures. Since none of these satisfies me, fear that, at the last moment, all will be caught up in a vortex that will make me powerless. (Set in motion by my original intention to take my mind off things by counting {throughout what had been estimated to be about 30 minutes}: but I dropped this plan as unworthy of me, and did not practice regular counting.)

In amongst them, moments of total indifference and calm. Sense that I'm really quite indifferent to the whole thing, etc.

I mobilize the notion that I have already been through the experience of cutting open the jaw and clipping off a piece of bone.

But all of this leads to such a theoretical concern with the whole affair that, suddenly, the practical implementation appears to me as something to-tally new to which these thoughts have contributed no relief whatsoever!

The notion that "This has to be!" signifies a degree of relief but touches, perhaps, on the childlike resistance to having to do something, precisely to being dragged along against one's will, etc. In addition, it strengthens the sense of unpleasantness.

A better way is the positive notion of usefulness, of avoiding more serious harm later. One has, after all, to be thankful.

―――――――――――

The following is of particular interest to me: I have a previous experience of a root-canal treatment. This sense of delving into the finest channels of the

"I" (and this is just what this involves, on the first occasion), a notion that is almost as unpleasant as that of being cut or chiseled open. Later this becomes part of the complex—"root-canal treatment"—that is accepted as a totality and that, as such, is no longer disturbing. The same thing would occur if one were to experience such cyst operations frequently. And it is a completely routine phenomenon. We shape, so to speak, a closed superficies out of everything that concerns us. Or a smooth one, with nothing protruding. Our [best] interest demands that we avoid analysis and we are only reconciled to analysis when it promises to provide a better synthesis. This explains the public's distaste for an author like myself, and the reproach that I am analytical and subversive. One ought really to take this into consideration and always arouse, as well, a sense of optimism that synthesis is possible. For it is really loathsome to be made uneasy. This antipathy toward such "stirring things up" in existence is justified.

Paradoxical reaction on the eve of the treatment: "Thank God, now this bleak business is at last going to become reality; now, at last, the unpleasantness is {actually} going to start." Immediately, general state is sober. Cf. unpleasant thoughts at night. Things shrink down to their natural dimensions. The state is oriented more toward action than to letting things happen.

Conclusion drawn: this is why a human being loves descriptions of events and loathes reflection and analysis!

Reason and the causality of things are pushed out by imagination; this must be Adler's feeling of community. But why then does one start thinking at night, for example? {(They appear of their own accord!)}

---

19 September. In retrospect.

Took place on 1 Sept. at 8 o'clock in the evening.

From three days beforehand, completely master of myself. Stopped the prophylactic course of the sedative and tranquilizer "Sedormit"; with a kind of pride. Only my digestion was a little out of sorts and on the last day I had no appetite whatsoever.

My appointment was for half-past seven, at Josefsgasse, a small private house. Traveled on my own in order to concentrate entirely on my psych. preparations. Was not necessary, however. But, on arriving at 7.25 p.m., I walk a few paces to and fro rather than ringing the bell before half-past.

Servant: "The gentleman has an appointment for an operation?" A small jolt.

One leaves one's coat in the foyer adjoining the stairs. Large, low salon with some kind of stylish furniture.

After a while Dr. Petrik's voice outside. I smoke a cigarette with him. Hofer drinks a black coffee in the cafe between operations.

Arrives, we greet each other. Mid-thirties, tall, lean and powerful build, clean-shaven, well-dressed, long peasant's face. Take a strong liking to him.

Small, quite modern operating room; I was able to see into it as soon as I entered the foyer. The gentlemen stand at two adjoining sinks and spend an eternity washing their hands right up to the elbow and using endless quantities of soap; they talk as they do so, lecturer and disciple, academic gossip. The nurse takes forceps, chisels, knives, syringes, etc., from the container with boiling water and lays them on the sterile serviette. I watch her and envy the doctors. This quarter of an hour is rather limp but runs calmly past in its factual flow.

I am then transformed into an operational area. Apron made from Billroth-batiste, or some such material, my arms are pinioned by this. "It will not hurt, but this is so you aren't able to make any involuntary upward movement with your hand" or some such remark from the nurse. Cloth over the head and parts of the face. Beforehand I have removed collar and tie.

eu—ei—ei—i: man boring a hole in a stone. [. . .]

---

4. VIII.32.[110]

Herr Doering, presumably sports editor of the *Lokal Anzeiger*, reporter on the Olympics, states in an essay that pays tribute to the significance of the pentathlon and the decathlon that, for these events, a prize for the Perfect Human Being should be instituted. For, he wrote, it involved not only the greatest degree of physical versatility but also the greatest spiritual concentration, receptivity, etc.

October 32.

During the proofreading of Vol. II of the *Man without Qualities* found the words "Glücke" ["joys"][111] and "Zwänge" ["compulsions"]. Justified by the location. Avail myself of the chance to strengthen my knowledge of grammar; look up words that form no plural. As I do so, it occurs to me that the plural to be improvised might be "Glücker."

"Ah, What 'Glücker' there are, and—" a verse {-fragment} from a non-existent costume drama takes shape. Doesn't only give me pleasure, it provides me with an intuition of the person who I might be if I were able to write in verse. From a single inner gesture there emerges—only held at one corner and, of course, even then only as a vague intuition—an inner world. *This* is where the actual significance of writing verse lies, something that has been lost today. {i.e., a single word makes the whole human being "other."} (Possibly also Hauptmann's[112] capacity to inspire respect even though his verse is not particularly special.)

Co-responsible for this, reading of Cassirer's *Philosophy of Symbolic Forms*; assertion that, in each spatial or temporal detail, the system of spatiality or temporality is co-projected.

———————————

A few days later, on a similar instance: if one writes using incorrect grammar, for example, idiomatic Austrianisms, one usually defends this to the last and is inexhaustibly inventive in discovering the advantages of one's error. (For example, the hint of the future tense in "würde" when used incorrectly.) If one then, after all, follows correct usage, it is as if one were used to living in another area. What was impossible becomes indispensable etc. I have just read Freud, *Introduction to Narcissism* and thus became aware of the connection with the feelings of the "I."[113] This unconditional love for linguistic errors and, in a broader sense, linguistic usages, points toward the close connection between language and the "I." Grammar is the spirit of the public at large, or an important part of it.

From this one can conclude that the Germans are a people who do not write correctly, indeed who feel that to write and speak correctly is an affectation! [. . .]

———————————

One might criticize Th.[omas] Mann on the ground that he reminds one of a boy who has practiced self-abuse and later becomes the head of a family. The knowledge of immorality and how the normal person comes to terms with it, this immorality—which has lost all danger and yet can be called to mind with a raised eyebrow—in the work of Thomas Mann can be traced back (virtually) only to that source. And what does his problem child, Castorp,[114] do in all that time on the Magic Mountain? Obviously he masturbated! But M. removes the private parts from his characters as if they were plaster-of-Paris statues.

November 32.

Something is well-written if, after some time, it strikes one as alien—one would be incapable of writing it that way a second time. Such an idea (expression) did not come from the fund that is available for daily expenditure.

Guillotining. Conceivable that, one moment after separation, "I" functions are present both in the head and in the body (sub-cortically). A "What is happening to me?"—then the human being is truly double.

Conclusion from this: "I" consciousness is a function of a relatively independent totality. It does not have the significance that it arrogates to itself.

Transitions to formation of buds, finally to procreation.

The "I" does not divide, become extinguished, emerge, but is rather—simply part of the given whole.

March 33. Three days ago the Reichstag went up in flames. Yesterday the emergency regulations to eliminate the Communist party and the Social Democrat Party appeared. The new men don't wear kid gloves. In the circles with which I have some contact there was, at first, a general feeling of indignation, an instinctive response to this blow in the face for truth, freedom, etc. It is the reaction of the liberal education in which people have grown up. Yesterday, after Goering[115] set out the measures in a radio broadcast, with a calm, friendly, masculine voice, Frau Witte is already starting to waver! "If it is true what the Communist Party was up to, then things are really in a dreadful state!" The hypothetical part of this statement is shrinking. The feeling is growing that the new arrangements will not be so bad after all and that, overall, there will be a liberation from many of the things that were felt, at an unconscious level, to be oppressive. An impression of decided rejection comes only from the serving girls, even though they keep silent.

Spirit itself, at its highest level, felt as late as two or three days ago that one "had to" make oneself available, it was essential to kill G.;[116] today, already, its view is that cooperation with Communists is out of the question, that it is essential, if one wants to make a contribution, to drive them out— so the new people know what they want, and if they also knew this at a higher level then this might be an intermediate link in the chain of history that makes sense. One way to view it might be that, by the time that history declares it [National Socialism] redundant, a higher level of socialism could develop than that via the dictatorship of the proletariat that is suddenly causing widespread destruction. Spirit, at the highest level, is just a bourgeois who is unaffected by any existential fears during the time of upheaval.

Freedom of the press, of expression of any kind, freedom of conscience, personal dignity, {freedom of spirit} etc., all the liberal fundamental rights have now been set aside without one single person feeling utterly outraged, indeed by and large without people being strongly affected at all. It is seen as a spell of bad weather. The average individual does not yet feel under attack. One might feel most profoundly disappointed over this but it is more correct to draw the conclusion that all the things that have been abolished here are no longer of great concern to people. This was indeed so. Did a person make use of his freedom of conscience for example? He had no opportunity whatever to do so! Nor did he trouble himself over this freedom in the way people did in the Biedermeier age. The newspaper did this for him and everything that the newspaper did he accepted with a degree of unease, even though it was seemingly indispensable to him. Seen in this way the discipline of the "fascio"[117] is indeed a creation that goes unerringly to the core of man's instincts.

From this is derived the present tendency to form organizations; the individual is beginning to recognize himself and wants to be led, to take a lead from someone, to be brought together with others, included and enveloped.

On the 1 March (in other words immediately at the beginning) in the offices of the Central Organization of German Citizens of Jewish Belief a house search was carried out by the police and the S[turm] A[bteilung].[118] [. . .]

Klaus comes to Auguste in tears: "I'm not there anymore, Ine has eaten me all up!"[119]

Auguste: "But I can see you, you're still here, here you are still!"

Klaus: "Am I really here then?," calms down, runs back to Ine: "Ini, Guste says, I'm still here!"

(Ine, whom he was annoying, had said to him: "Now I'm going to eat you up!")

When Ine was painted, he was frightened, that she would have to stay there (in the picture).

On reading a pamphlet: this uninhibited cursing of the opponent is a saturnalia. In private everyone curses this way, wishing death to his enemy. Today, in the social context, this is a stream in the wilderness that has not been dammed up.

———————

By and large, the following can be stated: if emotions go uncensored, as they are in dreams, they then create radical images. The person against whom one's anger has been directed has to die, and suchlike. This is just what is happening today in the political field. The victory of the parties of government expresses (apart from the influencing of the elections) the latent sense of unease that the idea of a Soviet Germany called forth. Many of those who felt that reason obliged them to incline toward such a Germany are now suddenly abreacting.

———————

Democracy has been laid bare to the very bone. Dogs that bark don't bite. Whoever spends his whole life talking is not a man of action. But the experiment is not yet finished because Ns. [Nazis] have so far both barked and bitten.

———————

The only steering of events—of the kind that many "progressive" people expected and that was actually an imponderable possibility—lay with Hindenburg, the Reichswehr,[120] the influential bureaucracy. If any change had come, or if it were still to come from those quarters, in the event that something failed to go smoothly, it would be brought about by a general spirit of moderation: proof that the task of the people of spirit[121] is not one involving activism, placing them on the level with the parties, but is a purely objective one.

———————

The experience that the only way to deal with Comm[unist] intellectuals is to place them behind bars. [. . .]

———————

Election day in the streets where the middle class live: an image of mobilization. It was a war mood with victory guaranteed, patented satisfaction of a deep-seated need, a minor, more successful repetition of 1914, so to speak.

Min[ister] Frick[122] is supposed to be an affable man; but in a speech he announces that Communists are going to be given, in concentration {labor} camps, as much time for contemplation as they need to mend their ways. In former times one would have called that forced labor or work on the galleys. What is remarkable today is the sober, natural way in which the announcement is made, without any kind of reference whatsoever to actions dictated by a state of emergency, or any suchlike.

Theater manager Barnay[123] in Breslau (according to a report in a right-wing paper) is abducted in a car by 5 men in uniform, forced to get out in a copse near the town, and beaten up. The local party leadership condemns this action without trying to find the culprits.

There are hundreds of examples of such happenings. Earlier a case such as the one just mentioned would have started a blood feud; today all those things that affect personal dignity and freedom, etc., are not motives for serious resistance any longer. The general feeling is: it isn't as serious as it sounds—a process of "making-things-less-serious"! The personal element in all this is that the person who is a helpless coward is perhaps the same individual who was really brave in the War. Possible explanations for this: degeneration of the race—hardly!; beginning of the decline of a class finds expression in the decline of its ideology; optimistic—emergence of the ant-person. Outside the range of its function such a person is a failure. "Nationalism," "nation,"—these are formal concepts.

H[itler]: a person who has turned into an emotion, an emotion that can speak. Arouses the will without having an aim.

Uncanny impression: late in the evening a police car with swastika flags and singing officers, speeding down the Kurfürstendamm.

It is alarming that Germans today possess so little sense of reality. On the Day of Remembrance for those who fell in the War, many cars with delegations, flags, students in full ceremonial uniform. Intoxicating victory mood where, in fact, work is only about to start. Family-magazine writing, too, has no sense of reality.

———————

One man has conquered a people! (Christ with radio, car, and membership of an organization.)

———————

A *satirical point of departure: "The fellow traveler"* (The intellectual is a born fellow traveler.) A painter who has experienced Expressionism, indeed has been involved in it, suddenly discovers that Franz Hals and formal unity are mere painting and nothing more, believes that the present has brought forth nothing whatsoever, that Picasso is only a neurasthenic, having no intuitive link with the contemporary context. Another says: "H[itler] has opened the eyes of the people; now the time of Stef[an] George is approaching!" (Ewers[124] and Bloem[125] do not disconcert him.)

———————

In exactly the same fashion, explain, once again, the downfall of democratic culture; thereby give comfort to those who are genuinely moved. This theme cannot be displeasing to the new leadership and permits double-edged satire.

———————

Note: Dr. Goebbels is a pupil of Gundolf.[126] The connection with George-ideology is indeed supposed to be acceptable at the highest levels of the State. But at the same time the Horst-Wessel-Song is the official anthem.

———————

In the midst of the initial oppressive uncertainty, An[nina] and Otto[127] have invited friends around; gramophone, dancing. An individual sense of "Oh, what the hell!"

With this magnificent "Kaiser weather" the streets are full of people. "Life goes on"—even though, each day, hundreds are killed, imprisoned, beaten up, etc. This is not frivolity, but is rather to be compared to the helplessness of the herd that is slowly pressed forward while those at the very front go to their deaths. The herd sniffs the air, senses what is happening, becomes uneasy, but has no stored psychological response, has absolutely no defense against this situation. Thus one sees, here too, how crucial are the kinds of social behavior that have developed. One sees the nature of the "steering." N[ational] S[ocialism] is right to despise the leaderless masses.

Stef. George and family-magazine writing have in common the rigidity of their morality!

A fine picture:—Deputy Kardorff[128] indistinctly illuminated by two standard lamps, burying his face despairingly in his hands. All ideas have collapsed around him. He is ashamed of the nation. He is very tall, lean and powerful, has thick, greying hair with a parting, and an aristocratic face.

In all those who oppose what is happening the insight is dawning, a "restitutio in integrum" is inconceivable.

The individual human being was founded on a basis of order in public life; this is why he is helpless when he cannot recognize it anymore.

Anna {girl in the boarding house} (what party did she vote for earlier?) extremely excited: "It's supposed to be wonderful, the festival in Potsdam![129] People are paying 300 Marks for a seat!"

Definition: the modern person is a coward but likes to be forced to perform heroic feats.

The Germans like to be ruled by fools: William II,[130] Otto of Bavaria.[131]

In the early morning military marches boom out from the radio.

The accursed era. Since when? Generation [18]70? From [18]66? From [18]48? [. . .]

The defections, the crumbling support (example of Gulbransson[132] who is supposed to be presenting himself as a victim of Heine),[133] demonstrate how everyone picks out a few plums from *Weltanschauungen* and political programs and accepts the rest as part of the package. A person can find what appeals to him just as much in B[olshevism] as in N[ational Socialism]. But the conclusion to be drawn from this is that new political formations have, of necessity, to run their course along a non-spiritual path. Force, suggestion, and suchlike.

In Germany, there used to be (now it's dissolved) an "Imperial Association for the Regulation of Births and Social Hygiene," an "Association for Sexual Reform," a "League for the Protection of the Mother and for the Social Hygiene for the Family," and others.

From a private letter from Erna Morena[134] *to Duchess D.:*
   "You have no conception of how serious a time this is. It is 'idealism rising up in outrage' (as one Italian put it). The Jews see everything from two sides, but one can't run politics that way. {Politics needs restrictions.} They had to atone for this. The Jews are three-quarters guilty for everything that has happened—or at least half-guilty. Corruption stank to the heavens."

Can one credit that Germans who are alive today, who were born after 1860 and have been involved in all three major European wars {and add to this the emergence of the theory of class struggle} are not supposed to have known that politics involves the use of force? And yet this is indeed so with respect to that majority that has declared its support for democracy. [. . .]

Lukács told of a woman friend who was married to a sculptor, pretty as a picture but frigid. She to him: "Please go ahead, if you want to; it is a matter of complete indifference to me." [. . .]

March 1934. Given the present state of education it would be more reasonable if one were to send future scientists to grammar school and future humanists to technical school. (On reading Vögelin, *The Idea of Race in Intellectual History*)[135] [. . .]

Film and literature Anne Bernstein travels round Europe searching for material for films on behalf of Metro Goldwyn. The criteria she gives for suitability in America (and {at the same time for Europe in general}) are: the subject matter must have an intrinsic drawing power for as broad an audience as possible and, for the roles, suitable actors must be available. {By and large one can say that, both in Europe and in America, the audience only wants material that either has such an immediate human impact that it has something to say to everyone (for example, Werfel's novel on Armenians) or works that focus on a towering personality—this may be a historical one— and offer this or that artist the opportunity to put on a great acting [performance] (for example, <Marie Antoinette> by Stefan Zweig).}

One may say that these are principles that are diametrically opposed to those that give rise to creative works. [. . .]

June 34.

In Austria, a transitional constitution has put an end to the principle that judges cannot be dismissed. There are plenty of reasons for non-Nazis [to voice their dissent?] In spite of this, one more pillar of individualism topples. Now the police, without any warrant from a judge, are able to conduct house searches, to make arrests, and similar things. It looks as if people, with the exception of political opponents, are quite unconcerned about it. Furthermore, nothing is lost because a person's rights have not affected the person. One can only say that things should never have been allowed to come to such a pass. But even under the monarchy the judges took the part of the monarchy. The epoch of individualism has brought forth few individuals. [. . .]

Books seen at H[eller's][136]
Karl Menger, *Morality* . . , Julius Springer, Vienna, 1930 (6 M 80 gr.)
Carnap, Rudolf, *Outline of Logistics*, ditto, 1929 (10 M. 80 gr.)
Schlick, Moritz, *Questions of Ethics*, 1930 (9 M. 60 gr.)

Race. Reflection

My {old} essay, according to which there are only individuals and race is "something to do with individuals" is not quite tenable. See the old criterion of reproduction in Vögelin. So one has to say that a person, on the one hand, passes on his genes, on the other hand, acts as a channel through which part of the family's genetic makeup passes. In terms of purpose, one can explain it to oneself as nature's striving for stability. It is not only the case that the acquired characteristics are only passed on in a restricted form, if at all; but also the individual variant that is handed on from the parents is constantly being corrected, in a conservative direction, by means of the breaking through of characteristics of ancestors prior to the parents in the process of hereditary transmission. To a certain extent—and within bounds that are open to question—nature wishes to maintain the constancy of the species. Thus the species, too, are, to a certain extent, a reality and not merely a collective concept. [. . .]

Observing the movement of a punch in a training session for boxing: it is not the deep {meaningful} things that make life so fine but those without meaning. No spirit could have dreamed up this beautiful movement, it came about only through the silly bits and bobs of sport. [. . .]

Space.[137] In terms of naive thinking, space is that which is between things; it is that which is not a thing—that in which the thing stands. Space, in its original representation, (appearance), has only inner borders. And, for this reason, philosophical thinking is unable to conceive of it as finite. The representation of the external boundary is not connected with it. [. . .]

Dream. M[artha] a young woman. Country house built of reddish wood. I say goodbye because I have to go away when an acquaintance arrives (but whom I do not know). Am jealous, hesitate. See both of them standing within the frame of the front door. He is bent over her in urgent discussion. Then they go into the house. M[artha] has obviously given way after all. I see them at the end of the corridor in the middle of the house with its wooden floor, disappearing into the bedroom. Then somehow see M. alone in her nightgown. Feel: so now it has happened irrevocably; with this comes pain, then I awake.

Basis of the dream: I received, on the previous day, a good, powerful impression from the Lichtenberg's story about the Blocksberg[138] in which the cuckolded partners can see what is happening while remaining invisible to each other. So this is a dream of adultery. But—it occurred to me—that also means: "Unlucky in love, lucky at cards." I had, after all, been concerned, shortly beforehand or afterward, with dreams about numbers. Question: the pain of jealousy was genuine and, despite this, is supposed merely to be there to screen off the desire to win money. The real feeling, which does not actually make an appearance, is supposed to produce an intense illusory feeling? [. . .]

Beginning of January, [19]36. Remarks on *Niels Lyhne*.[139]

It is at least the third time in my life that I have read this novel but I have no idea what happens in it. Only one place, {the fact that during} the scene between Lyhne and Frau Boye where the servant girl {outside} is polishing the door handles, has always stayed in my memory; and, as I now see, this memory was incorrect {to the extent that it made the detail much more important than it is}. [. . .]

From Ludwig Ullmann's epilogue for Karl Kraus.

". . In the world of royalties, film honoraria and a literary journalism that, despite his efforts, continued its indestructible glitter, he valued a comma in one of his manuscripts more highly than the question of circulation figures" . . . "Probably not the least of the reasons for his campaign against the sleight of hand, facile practices and shallowness of the trade was that no one, after Balzac's gigantic example, had performed the 'drudgery at the desk' as he had, caught up in the intoxication and exhaustion of the chase and flight of formulations, changes, improvements and corrections, a work-ascetic, a master and slave of language [."]

13.IV.38. During the dire time of Hitler's march [into Austria] with all its consequences I read again *Joy* by d'Annunzio. It is one of the books through which, 40 years ago, I first made the acquaintance of the "Modern" movement, and it is one of the first that exerted an influence on me. I would give a good deal still to be aware of what this influence was. Probably a general immorality and an equally general aestheticism. [. . .]

Carlyle [Hitler][140] might say: one wanted to drive out the Jews, that is conceded. If one were to let them emigrate with their capital that would cause damage that would be difficult to repair; and to sacrifice the individual to the whole has become customary since the war. So one took their capital. And because that would have looked bad, one had to make of this crime of self-interest a crime of passion. Hence the wild, unrestrainable anti-Semitism. In honor of the Fatherland. [. . .]

C.: a) Beyond the pale of any discussion and inferior. Class terror. b) It emerges that he is something quite different: true rule by the "demos."[141] [. . .]

Morality. Genius: What does this mean? We Germans brought forth the greatest moralist {of the second half} of the preceding century and are today bringing forth the greatest aberration in morality that there has been since

Christendom? Are we monstrous in every respect? Or is it chance that brings this about? Are we lax, perhaps?

—————————

Nietzsche wrote dramatically. On the stage. Is that one of the secrets of his influence?

—————————

Pessimism: switching effect but "cum fundamento in re"
  "Your friend betrays you; your lover deceives you; your wife does not want you but a child" (Shaw). "The drive to procreate deceives you, and perhaps her, too" (Schopenhauer).[142] You deceive yourself.
  Primitive form: "The world is bad, but you are good."
  "You, too, are a 'swine,' or you would be if fate did not protect you" is more correct.
  "Ideals are only the illusions of emotions" is perhaps the most general form of this skepticism, and also its modern form.
  "Morality is there to stop us being worse than we are." Or in order for us to be able to make good excuses for our bad deeds.
  "That man is supremely great who, despite all this, pulls a people up to the heights"—unwelcome consequence. [. . .]

—————————

C. [Hitler]. You must believe either in the future of N[ational] S[ocialism] or the downfall of [Germany]. At any rate, in a break in the tradition in which I know I am embedded. How is it possible still to work when one is in this position?
  For one's pleasure? I have never done so. I write whole paragraphs simply from conscientiousness and no one will thank me, after all, for such amplitude.
  The effect one has even on individuals functions only via totalities. The interest in Euripides presupposes interest in the Ancient World, (in addition to that for the "Modern Movement"). My homegrown theory—about transcending the conditions and questions of the time through mental leaps leading to indirect influence on people who are practically involved in creative work or on later spirits—is rendered invalid by this idea. [. . .]

—————————

Hitler Youth, running along the streets shortly before 10 p.m., making a lot of noise. All that was needed was for the moon to be shining or a boat trip on the Danube to be in the offing. Compare with the dejected, pale, re-pressed grammar-schoolboy of earlier years, full of fragmentary ideas that never turned into anything coherent. Today they are already much more powerful and self-confident, so it seems to me, although in this (given the short time span) the optical effect must play its part. They remind me vividly of our military colleges. And then, of course, I am reminded of the empty melancholy that lay beneath this spirit of enterprise. [. . .]

C. Isn't it best in every kind of (literary) representation to adopt the pose of benevolent irony along the lines of passages conveying the thoughts of the Gn.?[143] After all there is something right in everything. [. . .]

Books have to be bought for one to read them enthusiastically. Even I treat with indifference those books that arrive unsolicited. In spite of this I write my books as if no market existed. A contradiction; or should I simply say, a failure to take advantage of additional energy?

The "mass" was something that I despised as a beginner; later I considered that to be a youthful error; now I'm probably moving back a little toward the original position? But probably more in the direction of an object of study? (For example, wild outbursts of enthusiasm at major festivals). What kind of thoughts may these most skillful manipulators of the mass have about such things?

Fascism something that is evil "a priori"? To think that I should have to love democracy more. But "a posteriori," in details, in little things! In flattery, for example? [. . .]

Why do old people sleep less? Because it's easier going downhill than uphill. [. . .]

C. Juvenile lack of respect for what exists. Attraction exerted by retarded people on those who are not fully formed. Isn't it remarkable that the latter are taken in? If nothing else were involved, this would be scarcely conceivable. [. . .]

Basic feeling of the human being before [19]14. "I can go where I want. I must, of course, to an extent take institutions into account but they, for their part, may not trouble me with excessive demands. Today, by contrast, everyone feels that such demands are justified to a certain degree, e.g., that it is unjust that rich France is available only to a few people whereas next to her crowds of people have to scramble for a crust. Or the justification for states to place strict controls on immigration so that the composition of the nation does not suffer any harm. Or the view that a good upbringing is a problem. So it is not possible for you to make a free choice of a marriage partner—in a liberal fashion—etc. This loss of inner freedom is part of the rejection of "liberalism" that is so widespread today.

Freud: insights of great importance intermingled with things that are impossible, one-sided, even dilettante—see Vol. I[144] on the way that great things today are born by breech delivery. So is this generally the case? Is this "the" distinguishing mark of the present day and should it therefore be subjected to closer examination? Or is the criterion of exactitude wrong and is this tendency for things to be flawed being seen from a false standpoint? [. . .]

"He slept in her arms" has become a hackneyed phrase and is usually understood as coitus. But it actually means something about a woman that is touchingly like a little girl, the childlike expression of her tenderness that, when she is in bed, even when she just wants to go to sleep, makes her wrap her arms around what she loves, pressing it to herself. Whether this is her doll or her husband. [. . .]

Democracy is consumed by concern for herself, and wherever possible, paralyzes all who are energetic and capable of wielding power. [. . .]

Boarding house walls are often positively riddled with holes that transmit sounds; this is why I choose them as an example for creaking beds. If your own creaks when you turn over again when half-asleep that doesn't disturb you in the slightest. But if the neighbor's bed on the other side of the wall creaks it tears you, despairing, from your slumbers. What is this an example of? {of anti-altruism} I forgot what I wanted to say as I wrote it down. At any rate, an example of the functions of the "I." And for the elemental nature of love and hate.

Concern and consideration: sectarianism in capitalistic liberalism. It is essential either to dissolve, or to break the recalcitrant and usually narrow-minded stubbornness {of all these sophic cliques and Christian sects or even of the "free" spirit} (but democracy makes no moves whatsoever in this direction). This is the nature of N[ational] S[ocialism]. National Socialism is right to take the crudest kind of action here—or at least partly right. If one wishes to criticize the movement for that, one must know some other solution!

He who indulges his drives in order that they should not be aroused is a type. He eats in order that he shall not get hungry {and} makes love so that desire will not trouble him. He anticipates his drives. [. . .]

Duel: concepts of honor: throwback to the rutting contests: such notions, however, are to be treated with a certain humor because they are incomplete! [. . .] Humor as a sign of modesty.

Language wearing down: {I don't want to get close to you!} instead of: {too close to you.} Such irritating sloppiness completely alters the linguistic sense.

Gordon W. Allport, *Personality—a Psychological Interpretation*, London: Constable, [19]38, is supposed to contain a good presentation of all approaches.

Fingerprints as a means of identification were already in use in China and Japan more than a thousand years ago. In Europe it was only around 1880 that one had the idea. An example of the way that the development of culture, when it neglects or loses something, is by no means able to reach it along other paths within a short time! [. . .]

The charm of growing old, of involution: scales fall from one's eyes. You see those you love and activities in a merciless light. [. . .]

Ambiguity. It has seemed to me, quite spontaneously, a symbol of presumption and ignorance—moreover, as an involuntary one—that the Berlin "students" rode in ox-carts when they set out to burn the books. Only now does it occur to me that young people who burn the false and obstructive wisdom of the past, may also give rise to a sense of pleasure and to the impression that a new start is being made.

It seems sensible to interpret this example in terms of the ambiguity of the spirit; between 1890 and 1910 one would have said that spirit was "false-bottomed" like some cabin trunks.

In truth this is an example of the way that, in the field of morality, it is not a matter of the "what" but of the "how." This "how" would have probably been identifiable through accompanying circumstances, faces, what was said, but in the main it comes about through what happens next and later developments.

How is it possible, however, if one always allows consequences to decide, to adopt a particular mode of behavior? Should one surrender to one's emotions while reserving judgment? Certainly not. . . . etc. [. . .]

Radio: Frau Frischen, who has her own radio and always arrives at table 5 minutes after the others because she listens to the "foreign news" and then hands out this or that tidbit to her favorites, tells us all with joyful excitement, as she crosses the room to take up her place: "The Queen has had a son!" Whereupon everyone wants to know: "Where?" and "Which queen?" Mrs. F., in consternation replies: "Well, just fancy that, I've forgotten!" But the radio has fulfilled its function, and the newspaper does just the same.

Fame would be the title of a little book that might be subdivided into "The Great Author" and the "Mann Circus."[145] It would also refer to H[itler].

"Humus" and "Post-humus" would be another subdivision. Cf. the aphor[ism][146] about eclecticism. Another functional description. It is usual for death to bring forth a pinnacle of exaggeration in a reputation. Then further attempts are made with editions of collected works and literary estates; then, gradually, grass grows over them all. What is actually happening here? Think of Hofmannsthal and George. A parish is scattered to the four winds, i.e., a community with different concerns held together by a common focus of interest. What was probably common to all was the way they all "clung like vines to the trunk" of this man, the creative writer as a climbing pole for the critic, historian, publisher, etc.—even for the more or less political and social group (like, for instance, Th[omas] M[ann] and the bourgeoisie). A further point is probably "Speaking from the Heart," for example, Th. M.—anti-Semitism—the Joseph novels. Novels, in general, that are born of the times. It must certainly be the case that, in order for someone to become famous, a host of uncertain factors, are afforded organization and support in this fashion. The relationship between admirer and the person who is the object of admiration can be thought of in terms of a "High School play." The same variety of "concepts hanging loosely around." [. . .] A need for superlatives (from Aeschylus to Wildgans [. . .]) Cf. also the need for applause. (Chapter on exhibitionist in Vol II of MwQ.)[147] But with reference to the "post-humus" growing of the grass, one ought to say, in addition to this natural explanation, the following: perhaps the relationship was ambivalent and something happens that is analogous to the way disciples desert their master. In my own personal case, the opposite happens: I become loving; others apparently become indifferent. A load falls from their mind (cf. the commemorative stone in monuments). Perhaps, in other words, the man disappears from life.

But how then does his second career begin? Let us disregard those who write about historical epochs. I imagine myself reading Hofm[annsthal] or George afresh. Does that reach down into a deeper level? In the process, does the creative formulation become separated from the content? I don't know. I could imagine, in the case of Hofmannsthal, that all his attempts to be a great link in the chain of tradition fall by the wayside as shortcomings and snobbery; but passages remain where he has succeeded in an involuntary way.

Moreover, when one reads something, the relationship with a leader has a part to play,—with Goethe, for example; also the admiration for the perfection of an exemplary figure. The man of letters is by no means totally subsumed in literature; by no means is his work merely an instructive example. But what is the primary factor, for instance, in the influence of Shakespeare? [. . .]

A conservative and monarchist writes (and for him conservative sentiments are only possible when they are monarchical) that the new political form requires Christianity as a moral[148] support. But {against this one might argue, for example,} that a) it {the Church} is totalitarian b) it has used for too long the methodology of force c) Is this vocation of Christianity not a shining confirmation of the modernity of N[ational] S[ocialism]? Is it possible today for a people to be Christian instead of incidentally Christian? Is a historical process in evidence here? Perhaps, expressed in simple terms: Christianity contains too many non-contemporary features and elements. Its relationship with knowledge is out-of-joint. Lack of breadth of spiritual heroism. Moral law too rigid (and here one can even speak of the law of statics and of the absence of a suitable form for the dynamics of spiritual development). (Is this last point prejudice on my part or can the mass really no longer be governed in this way?) (The bad, the indifferent person. Is it not the case that any political organization must build using him?)

Starting point for reflections on politics:
Things have to be looked at from a practical angle. All my ideas are ideological.

Right then: the basic element of all German (West European) politics is the petit-bourgeois. The worker is, in essence, a petit-bourgeois or a variation on one. The rural population is on the way to being so.

What does the petit-bourgeois want (need)? He wants to cope. Wants an activity that brings in some money. Some pleasure and variety. In sum, freedom from envy. In sum, the possibility of feeling satisfied. A degree of emotional stability under the guidance of some idea or other, just like any other person. An honor. Here, perhaps, is the right place to ask the general question: "What is it that a person wants?"

The petit-bourgeois proletarian is Christian and chivalrous with respect to the morality with which the surrounding atmosphere is imbued. (See

Coudenhove's[149] definition of this concept) He also possesses a "bon sens," a truth-core of unspoiled innocence, a vestigial link with the people of the kind that is deposited in proverbs and expressions. His moral sensibility is usually more accurate than that of educated people. But he lacks intellectual agility whether for good or evil. He is prone to stuffiness and his intelligence may not stretch far enough (cf. those cultural clubs of earlier times that were really dreadful).

What would need to be done to make of him, as the predominant type, a spiritual elite?

Who should undertake this, if not himself?

Life has always been shaped by a master-caste or a hierarchical system of figures in authority. Where is this to come from in the future? [. . .]

Politics. Caricature of creative politics. It would be possible to consider it to be creative. Nothing stands firm, every promise is broken, all goals that are indicated are relinquished at any time for the sake of other ones. Morality has not the slightest binding force.

What is involved here are the principles of creative morality. The artist-politician. This makes one believe that he is really considered by many to be a genius. {This might also be dealt with from the perspective of the "revenge of art" on society.}

The unmasking must come from that angle. Distinction to be made, for example, with respect to the relationship to justice, to the capacity for forgiveness, etc. The creative factor and its caricature? Is the difference between an aristocratic quality and resentment, and similar distinctions, of greater significance here? Are there certain things that "one" simply doesn't do? Are details typical of the whole?

That would be the way to tackle this!

Ps[ychoanalysis]: autumn in Velden came to my mind again. I was probably somewhere between 18 and 20 years of age. Walks in the moonlight along the road lined with poplars. Mist coming from the lake. I wrote poems, prompted by the yearnings of a melancholic disposition, they were of little value.

This disposition—it was completely determined by sexuality, by the woman one loved whom one wants to have despite the base possibilities that are available. (It is part of the overall circumstances that one carries on some activity of equal value, something that is analogous to the "loneliness of the neurotic person." In this insubstantial, nonetheless quite unambiguous situation, the mother exerts a disruptive influence. She makes claims on one, at least on one's soul. She draws the whole aura of woman into the realm of the impossible. The instinct for poetry is disturbed by her. Thinking more crassly one may add the following: sexuality loves unappetizing things. {Or that which is not particularly appetizing}. The smell of the vagina, which is after all a suspicious smell, becomes a source of ecstasy. Lack of inhibition in private will afford release. The extreme dubiousness of physicality demands the highest degree of idealization. All that is in the process of developing is unrealized and under intense pressure. What stands in its way is the asexual physicality of the mother. The voluminous, non-transfigured shape. The smell of the aging skin. Is that not an extremely annoying and challenging barrier? Instead of Oedipal sensations, do not irritation and rejection make their appearance? Is that not the truth—the sad and healthy and non-invented truth? It is the opposite of ps[ychoanalysis]. The mother is not an object of desire but a mood-barrier, a stripping away of the mood of every desire, should chance present the young man with any sexual opportunity. [. . .]

Martha: How well she sees things—qualities, weaknesses of a head, whether real or drawn from life. In addition, her capacity to form judgments of creative writing, based on feeling. How deep and broad is her talent for this. When I put this capacity in the context of her abstaining from work she answers: "Basically I've always been too shy." [. . .]

From the time of my youth I have considered the aesthetic to be ethics. [. . .]

English joke: "The Irish don't know what they want, but they want it passionately!"

This can be applied to the various types of creative writers who are concerned with politics, indeed to creative writers without exception!

Also to men of action: it is simple to be an active person; it is difficult to look for a meaning behind action. MwQ II, p. 121.[150] [. . .]

How fortunate that literature (art) is not involved in any progress when you consider, for example, the structure of a molecule of any kind of organic or industrial nitrogen compound; when you think that the whole of physics today is derived from remote, indeed positively self-effacing corners of the physics that was taught while I was a student; when you think that there is an "International Association for Documentation" (without it being possible to define properly what D. is) in which libraries, and the administrations of public bodies and industrial concerns, etc., participate. [. . .]

———————————

Appetitive: the classical triangle of the mother in her mid- to late thirties, the daughter of seventeen or nineteen, the mother's lover who is engaged to the daughter. Occurred to me when observing Frau Olch[151] and her daughter. Based on the assumption that the affair starts at approximately the time when a closer relationship develops with the daughter.

And now: the daughter witnesses the mother kissing her fiancé or fiancé-to-be. It is the kiss of a woman who is not familiar with such experiences, and the kiss assails the woman with the wild abandon of a developing taste for love so that she is the more active participant in this kiss. The daughter is taken aback. Up till now she has only known a woman's kiss as a tentative gesture; but this is like a dog sinking his teeth into another—which is something she once saw—or when a lion at a zoo seizes hold of the piece of meat that the keeper holds out to it.

This is how the first acquaintance with the appetitive nature (part) of the emotional life appears.

———————————

The relationship between speaking and understanding, translating out of, and into, a foreign language is also found in one's own—to be precise, with all out-of-the-ordinary expressions and forms. (Struck me with the word "Staffel" ["baton," "squad," etc.]) The secure store of words and forms that is part of understanding is smaller, the meanings vaguer. The relationship overall is not exact: in childhood development, speaking often takes greater steps forward than understanding, I believe; it is also the case that one learns foreign languages partly though one's own activity . . . I am not informed about the issue.

The writer, in relation to the reader, writes a foreign language. [. . .]

———————————

Thinking in a dream. Observed this in myself again in the early morning; unfortunately have forgotten most of it.

This is something half dreamed, half thought: dreamed but not without the guidance of the will, such as one experiences in daytime.

It was something to do with nicotine. I had woken up, and under the influence of some physiological impression or other, had been turning over the intention of smoking less for one day. Then this slid back again into a doze, and then, suddenly becoming clear again, apparently awakened by the interest itself, I wanted to take particular note of something. It was a frightful word designating the effect of nicotine; some hours later, all that remains in my memory is the notion of the kind of model of a body—which I assume permeated my brain—made up of wires or threads, which is used in a geometry lesson, and a word for this that possessed dreadful penetrative power.

I believe that my first recollection of this was no different; I only caught the tail or the backwash, as I so often do.

Then a reflection made its appearance that I can remember in part. This was that it is not the case that such words, from some affective reason or other, are "occupied" by feeling, and they derive their excessive effect, their thunderous impact and hyper-significance, from this source; on the contrary, whatever they are, they are definitely half-formed emergent thoughts, notions in the process of taking shape; but they fall into an adulterated state of consciousness.

In other words, they fall into a state in which the determinants, the coercive powers of waking thought are not at work; into just that state of somnolence that resembles a state of tiredness or of inspiration. (I am thinking of the "sphere" that Kretschmer talks of in his Medical Psychology.)[152]

There is certainly a separate category of dreams proper; but this other kind also exists. And it is probably down to my individual constitution that I experience more of the latter than the former.

Then to this was added an idea of how "consciousness"[153] might be defined.

Not starting with the "I" and the distinction between dream-"I" and conscious-"I," but from the determinants and coercive forces (see above). Also in the following manner: the dream does not present contents that follow one after the other in a sequence of images. (At least, I shall leave this possibility to one side.) There is neither a dream-"I," nor a waking-"I" there, nor any dreaming or thinking. Rather there exists an "apparatus for occasional use" like that which is found with more or less common sequences of body movements that one learns to perform. The notion (aside, once again: Where does this come from?) is caught up in this; the notion and its setting form a whole that can be of varied degrees of robustness. As the notion (similar; notions that boys experience; onset of tiredness) is caught up in a whole that is both transitory and soft and blurred, dream-thinking takes shape in which the notion is momentarily preponderant then quickly disappears.

I don't now know any more than this. The important factor seems to be a characteristic of thinking in general: varying kinds of apparatus for occasional use that are of varying degrees of fixity, i.e., whether isolated or not, depending on whether they form part of a frequently practiced, wider apparatus or not. Let us call them functions of the waking "I"; but the "waking 'I'" is only present in relative terms, what is given is a "Gestalt" function. Partial and complete transformation into crystalline form.

"Prima Vista." I made the objection to myself that I have the tendency to reduce everything to a "Gestalt."

A particular kind of dream-thinking is the verbal one, in which one experiences everything in an arrangement similar to a pseudo-contract or a pseudo-treatise. The whole in this case would be imagined writing or speaking. The writer's disposition coming into play etc.

By the way, à propos "play": the whole may be related to play, but the fashion in which this is taken up into the dream in a partially creative way is serious, if incomplete. This is also of importance for aesthetics. [. . .]

[. . .] Re U[lrich] and Ag[athe]: coit[us] as a remnant of the trance.

The trance belongs with the magical effects of the real world. Thus it is logical that Ag and U. do not want coit. The contemplative [element] {of the "other" condition} is, however, something different from the trance, and in addition is less of a surrogate for behavior overall. It is a European attempt without loss of consciousness, etc. Thus it [the contemplative element] could probably—given a priori indeterminacy of the achievable level—seem possible as an experiment and be willed. [. . .]

Psychologia phantastica: this is the way to summarize Klages, {partly to some extent} Freud, Jung. My instinctive enmity because they are pseudo-poets and deprive creative writing of the support of psychology! [. . .]

A real upheaval in recent times has been brought about by anaesthesia; it has removed a somber element of uncertainty from life. I note that this is also true of contraceptives. Getting a woman with child, this wild, agitated recklessness of the man is on the wane, and with it the {remaining} notions of violence, of throwing {laying} the woman down, the concept which is central to seduction, the mistrust of each sex for the other, the finding a way past objections, the weakness of the woman, to some extent, the strong and the weak sex, the tendency toward baseness on the part of the male, the strong man, etc. [. . .]

Re: atom physics. "Atomon," the indivisible, as a conception belongs in the category of the "thing" but, of its basic nature, contradicts it. In just the same way, it contradicts experience at the macroscopic level. Distinguishing between the nucleus of the atom, proton, etc., takes things further into the category of "things" that at best can only be an approximation derived from the macroscopic perspective. The dual image of wave mechanics is none other than this contradiction. Not so much directed against classical physics as rather linkage between phenomena and the category of things. That which is only explicable in terms of "waves" and "quantum theory" involves a different linkage between phenomena. It is no contradiction if, according to Mach,[154] one does not demand anything more than some kind of unambiguous linkage. Of course, it will then only be with some reservation that one may talk of "projectiles" and suchlike. The difficulties emerge from the search (whether justified or not) for a model based on "things." Grasping, in conceptual terms, the smallest particles as "divisible" and "indivisible." [. . .]

On association: I go outside, see that the stairway is wet and register a sense of unease. It is only then that it occurs to me that I have forgotten to put my galoshes on in the hallway. According to associational psychology this would be an intellectual connection; but really a feeling is interposed that caught my attention. [. . .]

Belief: I have no spark of religious genius—excuse for: "I do not believe." Be convinced—that way insights would follow.

Difference between "belief that . ." and "belief in"; belief that God exists and believing him, or rather, believing in him. Belief that one derives from something, and belief that one brings to something.

Thus it is understandable that one arrives at the formula for belief which says that the most important thing is to love God. What is this love? Clearly intuition is still too intellectual, it is rather the case that something like complete abandoning of self is necessary.

On anti-Semitism. Basic formula adopted without any concern: cross-breeding, assimilation.

A convinced Jew, on the other hand, values precisely what is specific. He dislikes the characteristics of the assimilated Jew and finds edifying the things that I may find antipathetic.

It is similar to the specific taste of a national cuisine that has powerful connections with homesickness and love of home.

Similar to cheese that, for one person is loathsome, for another a complicated pleasure. Like tea, laced with sugar (and rum), and bitter tea. Like the connoisseur's delight in decay. Similar to sexual-symbolical smells from secretions in tabooed zones of the body, according to whether they are perceived sexually or not.

The last example leads to the connection between smells and the relationship to the self. Deviant forms that are frowned upon, sympathy for what is one's own.

Smell as a sign of being in heat. Vanilla smell of the vagina. Is the beast in us to be overcome, or is it right to return to nature? Is preference for one's own smell degenerate or is it the basis for the awareness of race? Is it possible to answer these questions?

These anti-pathies and sym-pathies are capable of sublimation and shape the spirit. Is it dangerous to examine them via reason?

So would it be permissible to subject the question of anti-Semitism entirely to reason and, with complete enlightenment, allow every aspect to come into its own? Certainly one would like to do so but one also has reservations in this matter and to surmount these sensibly is scarcely possible in an impromptu fashion.

Perhaps by starting from the angle that the man who "can smell a Jew" displays such and such degenerative symptoms; or, from the viewpoint of the Church, one must love even the lepers. This has been downgraded to the level of an image. There is a difficult problem of mutual tolerance. Its history? From passion to empty tolerance, thence to what kind of substantial tolerance? [. . .]

The lady wife: when men are interested in each other, a tendency arises to avoid the wives. This holds more strongly in the case of a wife than with a lover who is merely a kind of extension. Men are more involved, more interested, more sincere, {more natural} when the wife is kept out of things; they are younger. Things are almost as they were when one left one's parental home in the evening. Areas of the "I" that were colonized are set free. The wife annexes, and even if one lends one's support to this process, one does so grudgingly. Or: a wife makes someone into a man, makes him a worthy, so what now happens is like taking off some state regalia. Or: sexuality groups so many feelings and emotional states around itself; it is the worst form of gynocracy (?) Or: ambivalence? [. . .] (The way that, as happens with rogues, the soul always winks its left eye when it raises its right hand to swear an oath.) [. . .]

The melancholy male. (Swiss choler)

R[obert]: Ah!
M[artha]: What are you annoyed about, then?
R: I don't know. But it's bound to be something or other! [. . .]

A *further entry on smoking:* see the concept of the "replacement act" in the excerpt from Levin.[155] Add to this the torture of boredom, which even Goethe said he suffered from a great deal. Boredom is one of the main sources of tension forcing one to work. One can rush headlong into one's work through boredom and also because one's nerves have had an excess of rest—and then they are completely free from strain.

The replacement act is smoking. It calms one down, relaxes tension; the boredom, the state induced by excessive rest, are set aside by a single cigarette.

And instead of gaining something that can keep despair at bay and impart a sense of self-satisfaction—and that is of undoubted importance and, in short, the biological goal—one spends a little time manipulating one's nerves! [. . .]

Assimilation: when this is the object it is better if Jews convert to Catholicism than to Protestantism. It is more rural, at least in Southern Europe, and above all, it is more external, it nourishes gesture, the mimetic and an indigenous language.

But against this: Protestantism nourishes the intelligence of the laity and would be able to offer Jewish cleverness a task that would keep it safe from journalism in the broadest sense of the term.

———————

Smoking, an idea: melancholia, melancholic dissatisfaction: deep suffering. Best countermeasure: to have some small achievement to one's credit. Work instead of smoking: in this way you will furnish yourself with the greatest pleasure you can have. Fight it (see above) by striving for a particular pleasure. [. . .]

———————

Theology for a lay person [. . .]

The power of prayer! U.h.W.![156] Help St[alin]! Help H[itler]!

If I *myself* had the power would I be sure of what I ought to do with it? God ought to know this; but how can I ask him and what shall I ask?

At best, he gave his commandments: the believer can remind him of this. But is he[157] sure about their interpretation? Otherwise he might perhaps do something out of love.

Perhaps feeling, too, gives [him] a sense of certainty.

Otherwise it would say that he who is beyond the reach of understanding should do what he wants. But how is it possible to reconcile the qualities that form belief in God with such moral indifference!

To put the question in this way is to seize the bull by the horns! [. . .]

———————

From the homeland of A[dolf] H[itler]. This occurred to me when I noted down 33/189 [reference to Notebook 33, Entry 189]. The slogan, "Father . . God the Father" denotes the changes in politics as well as the cultural guide-feelings. There the immediate crisis was that of the principles in a family. In a third or fourth generation the H[itler] era would surely issue forth from this.

But the headline here has a different intent: on occasions I wanted to write letters to a young man who lived eighty (to a hundred) years after me. Instead of that they might be directed to a young American of our time. In them, I treat America with the respect due to an advanced era that I do not know and will never get to know. And I depict for him the <homeland> he has heard about and that he cannot consider innocuously indifferent. Partly respectful, partly not with regard to A. and vice versa for the old homeland.

Not least—it might *captivate* attention in A. [. . .]

"Great Writers." Last night M[artha] had a dream—A[nnina] was to marry O[tto]. The wedding ceremony was to be in St. Charles' or St. Peter's Church. She just wanted to hurry off with A. to fetch (it's typical of her) some red silk laces for her shoes. On the way she buys a midday paper and, feeling on my behalf a keen sense of neglect, reads the words: "Wedding of the son of Thomas Mann in the Church of" etc., and the full newspaper treatment. But not a word about his marrying the daughter of R[obert] M[usil]. In anger, is about to go with A. to see Fontana, then wants to telephone him to prevent the insult to me, etc.

As M. was telling me this, it occurred to me that it would be possible to treat the subject of the Great Writer in a satirical fashion: a confidence trickster pretends to be Th[omas] M[ann]'s son. What the papers then have to say about this scarecrow. (See also Klaus Mann).[158] The stories they would tell, etc. If I wanted to make him A's bridegroom, and thereby, up to a certain point into the real O., I could work into this the motif of Kulka's[159] plagiarism of Jean Paul. In order to take the overvaluing of M[ann] to the extreme of absurdity—in other words, in my interest and in order to introduce himself both as a literary figure and someone who is worthy of A.—he lights upon the idea of plagiarism. [. . .]

Theology of a lay person: if God wants to create and develop the spiritual through the agency of humans, if the spiritual contribution of an individual is of any kind of significance, then suicide is a deadly sin, a refusal to serve God, the creator.

Theology of a lay person: immortality. One still feels desire long after one has ceased to be desirable. The body becomes old and the soul stays young. Sexuality is beset with the most durable kind of human complications. Does this offer, in the midst of life, a glimpse of what immortality is like?

Theology of a lay person: if one makes the assumption that God might set some store by the MwQ or such things, if one places so excessive a value on soul activity, one is forced to kill oneself if progress comes to a halt. On the other hand, [. . .] given this assumption, it would also be wrong to take one's own life! [. . .]

21

NOTEBOOK 31

7 FEBRUARY 1930
TO SPRING 1936

[Despite the title, this notebook is not just concerned with essays. Its main focus is literary figures and literary issues. Musil is both intrigued and depressed by the success of some contemporaries whose work he considers inferior. This prompts one or two ironical remarks (which are all the more understandable since a survey of contemporary Austrian writing by a leading Germanist fails to mention him at all). Musil continues to think about satirical works such as Ed (notes for which are interspersed with other entries here) through which he evidently finds an outlet for his bile. He unleashes private scorn on leading authors, including the Expressionist Franz Werfel, Hermann Broch, a distinguished fellow Austrian novelist, and the director of the Burgtheater in Vienna, Anton Wildgans.]

31.

Notes on the Essays.

7.II.1930.

Look up Hans Naumann, *German Literature of the Present-Day*, J.B. Metzler, Stuttgart, 4th edition, 1930. From a note in the *Prague Press* I understand that there is a piece about "Neue Sachlichkeit" there. Hofm[annsthal],

George, Binding: hero-worship. Goering's *Battle at Sea*[1] as an Expressionist precursor of Brecht's *Lindbergh Flight*,[2] Bronnen's *OS*,[3] Renn's *War*,[4] etc. I am convinced that there won't be even 5 lines about me there. Typical of the "quick sketch" historian. [. . .]

8.II. "Art has to have an immediate effect!" This is one of the most dangerous prejudices. Yet it remains a goal that one constantly tries to achieve. After all, it wouldn't be difficult to analyze what is required for something to have an immediate effect. The most difficult thing about this is somewhat like a meeting. The immediate impression that some people give is that of peace, sublimity, etc., and this is what is demanded of art. People want to be won over from the very first word, etc. This is not completely unjustified but leads to neglect of books that are demonic, Titanic, {unpleasant}, and so forth.

My difficulty: what is there for me in a world in which Werfel finds people prepared to promote him!

12.II. Life at its limit of maximum load (which I discuss in Chapter 61 of MwQ)[5]—that is the principle that I have always applied in my writing!

13.II. Yesterday, reading Chesterton was of immediate assistance to me in finding a freer and more relaxed expression for something. His drastic, hammering examples took effect on me. But even the most incisive comparison could discover no similarity between what I wrote and what I read. The influence is not one of content but of gesture, similar to the sense of release that comes from a person who behaves with freedom and self-assurance, without our feeling pressure to imitate him. This is the connection in the case of Stendhal who read the "code Napoléon" before he began work. It is related, but not identical, to the effect that reading *M.L. Brigge* had on me that I noted at the time. One might define a group: "Mimetic Influences of the Author on the Reader" or simply "Personal Influences."
    Retrospectively, I want to indicate more precisely that the influence of Ch[es-terton] is expressed in a process of "sobering up." "Write in a state of sobri-

ety!" is a message that I wrote down weeks ago and that lies before me as a warning; occasionally I forget it. Ch. merely supplied the necessary gesture.

16.II. Spoke with Martha about translating. I: "Anyone who is able to read as you do, can also write." M: "No. I cannot imagine writing with the facility of a journalist." I: "That isn't writing—it's some kind of obscene activity." Indeed, some of the admiration for poor writers comes from people who are amazed at facile and prolix writing. One ought to examine a group from Wallace[6] to Feuchtwanger[7] or Neumann[8] from this angle. [. . .]

The utopian: "I give you the rule that will be valid in 2000 years' time." Christ: "I give you the rule that will be valid for 2000 years."

18.II. Transferred from an old note:

What does it mean that, in the long term—from the perspective of literary history—by and large a just evaluation emerges? (If that is the case at all?) This is a process that could be analyzed. If one knows it then one can probably produce it in 10 years, instead of in 100?

Usually it is not a pleasant experience when writers philosophize and formulate their thoughts directly. False to draw the conclusion that the creative writer should not be allowed to do this!

19.II. It would be possible for me to replace what in Chesterton's essays is occupied by orthodoxy (and, by the way, I am orthodox, too, {but orthodox in scientific terms}) by democracy; in other words, I would formally assert that I was a democrat—which is probably correct—then, starting from that point, would speak like a heretic; in other words, I would mean an "other" kind of democracy.

22.II. Ullstein:[9] don't say: "Ullstein-ization." Say: "Industrialization," "Epoch of High Capitalism." In creative writing, too, one is passing from handicraft to machinery.

Isn't that right and proper? Isn't there something within me that agrees with this?

Precursor of collective achievement. Criticism of this to take account of its potential.

But what does this look like in concrete terms?:

A. a public that does not know what it wants.
B. a team of workers who are always required to find something new.
C. the shallowness—a factor that presents the first point for attack—is perhaps merely a secondary phenomenon, a kind of brake. The force that actually drives it forward lies in b). From b) alone, a great deal can be derived. [. . .]

2.III. Term for Sigrid Undset: "Auntie Homer."

9.III. Yesterday evening I had the following train of thought: I'm correcting a passage in the proofs, get stuck, and note down around 5 variants, none of which pleases me. After a walk, the whole thing—which has already upset me—seems a matter of no consequence, and I feel I'll probably find the right course without difficulty. The same experience, writ large, when one sets aside a completed piece of work for a few weeks. It is evident that one then looks down upon the work, as it were, from on high. What is the psychological significance of this?

In emotional terms, it means freedom from ambivalence. One had started to be uncertain, beset with a host of little vacillations that eventually made a disproportionate impression—very similar to hesitating for too long before going along a dangerous path. One has, so to speak, subjected the situation to emotional overload. One frees oneself by renouncing the situation?

But it appears that an intellectual process takes effect in the same sort of way. An insight that eluded one in the course of the day may come during the night; or, generally, the way a reflection "sits itself down and sorts itself out."

This even seems to be something physiological, for the same thing happens when one learns new movements.

In other words, switch the brain to a state of rest; introduce spells of relaxation according to the Kogerer method;[10] take one's mind off things? But at which point? Make oneself indifferent. Clearly this only works when one has come halfway to achieving something.

————————

Another train of thought: yesterday I had to check quickly through the proofs of 300 pages and was depressed about the way the novel is overburdened with essayistic material that is too fluid and does not stick. As I worked, it occurred to me that I can remember next to nothing of the book by Chesterton (see diary of 10.II)[11] although, in personal terms, it is so close to me; on the other hand, I could relate whole pages of events from *Olaf Audunssohn* by Undset. It is true that I only read this book in the course of the last fortnight but the distinction goes beyond this.

We remember more about facts:

1) probably because we do not store intellectual material in objective form but classify and file it away within us.

2) perhaps also because reports on factual things address a much more primitive attitude or function. Response to danger: primeval man has to take precautions if it is reported to him that at such and such a place something has happened. It is possible that the shape of this reaction is still preserved within us. Admittedly I cannot quite imagine how. Perhaps there are different centers that participate in the reception of stories?

Then there is also the following question: if the exposition is addressed to the intellect, and if the story works in the way just described (then there would be the additional matter of "imagination," or, more accurately, surrogate experiences through the medium of imagination), then what does an essay address? Does it fall between two stools? Does it take immediate hold of the reader's creative functions and disappear within them? [. . .]

————————

10.III.

In future, in my creative writing, put myself only in the position of a minor character, a spectator. In the novel I stand in the middle, even when I am not depicting myself, and that inhibits the "telling of the tale"; it is possible that absolutely everything depends on this kind of basic perspective. Already when one is working out the story itself one should put oneself in the role of an observer. I am writing this down here[12] because it probably has significance for the understanding of the process as a whole. [. . .]

19.IV. L[eonhard] Franck, the creative writer, who has all his power available to describe the external world {for external description} because the inner world is of absolute banality.

Today, while working on the end of Chapter 115,[13] I had the following insight: it is built on the reflection on dream and analogy [. . .] and this can be given a broader base as follows:

The kind of behavior that I once called, provisionally, "ratioïd" and "non-ratioïd" refers to the two underlying modes of conduct, which are given with human history—namely, the mode of the "unequivocal" and that of "analogy."

The unequivocal is, in fact, the basic principle of logic and as such it does not originate in something "a priori," but simply in the dire necessity of life that would lead to destruction if conditions were not both recognizable, and actually recognized, without equivocation. (By the way, equivocal worlds are conceivable.)

The second basic principle is that of analogy. The logical remainder of the dream, of religious feeling, {vision}, (intuition), of the a Z.,[14] of morality, of creative writing.

This is now the binding standpoint both for the essay about the a Z. and for the one about lyricism.[15] [. . .]

Ed:[16] technological man. First false hair, then false teeth, then false complexion, artificial organs—he gets older and older—and finally all that remains is the sexual organ that, at the end, is also artificial. The human being dissolves totally into illusion. [. . .]

Ed. Amandus and Amanda—a modern pair of lovers. She has taken on masculine attributes, he is tinged with homosexuality. Sentimental, touchy.

Sexual love has snatched hold of all available tenderness, now homosexual love, too, binds up to itself all those things that are still to be found (if only rarely) in the relations of man to man: fidelity, surrender, admiration, etc. This is the actual significance of homosexuality in today's evolution!

Notes for later

3.II. 32.[17] A ruffian is given a state funeral. Coffin solemnly displayed in the cathedral for several hours.

The following are being considered for the post of acting Reichskommissar for the Prussian Ministry of Culture:

Prof. Bäumler, follower of Nietzsche at the University of Dresden.

Prof. Krieck, one of the precursors of the new movement of National Pedagogy, edits the *Sun*, a paper for promoting ethnic religion.

Schoolteacher Rust who is endeavoring to win spiritual circles over to the National Socialist movement.

Arbeitsdienst [work-service]:[18] a young man with a doctorate in chemistry gives up a good job to go to the Arbeitsdienst, just as men once went to war. He cannot look those without a job in the eye. He does not want just to talk about this. What he wants is to do more than simply earn a proper salary. The young German who wants to pass inner muster in the face of his people; to do his duty by his people. To know where one stands is a source of joy and strength. The time of the "I" (Liberalism) must be taken and buried. (From the *Daily Review*, 3.II.32.)[19] [. . .]

Kisch[20] about my book—he says it's counterrevolutionary. {This has been said of me before.}

The answer would be that a monkey puts all things into its mouth to test if they are of use; it knows no other kind of use. [. . .]

Christian and Jew:

It is conceded even by opponents that the individual person may be of this kind or that, the question is whether there are "bunchings," whether average values deviate from the mean. Is it not a more promising approach to consider the way that the so-called Aryan originates, either directly or at short remove, from peasant stock? (Is that correct? Population movement in cities? Do new peasants arriving outnumber the city families? Are the latter not preponderant for very long?) The peasant (in what way different from the Jew?) is a brawler. He is atavistic, in respect of both good and evil; is it not possible to detect this still in sublimated forms? Moreover, the peasant does not like talking a great deal. Or does he? (In the inn.) But at least he distrusts people who talk even more. Distaste for parliament even though he is democratic. He likes higher things to be arranged in a dignified and non-oppressive manner. This is why he leaves them to the clergyman and the officials of the Kaiser. He is less religious than people think. It has already been shown that even his feeling for the dynasty was only an illusion.

One has to seek to understand the elements of National Socialism. Among these, the fact that whoever terrorizes others is himself a democrat. [. . .]

Göbbels [*sic*] on culture and will of nation or something similar (first radio *lecture*)

> The intellect is nothing (understanding, reason and intellect)
> Understanding sees everything from two sides.
> The intellect can never be creative. Or: in the int. there is nothing creative.
> The reason does not produce anything new.
> Asphalt literature
> L'art pour l'art is quite wrong; superseded. [. . .]

H[itler]-scholasticism. The title of a really good essay by Paul Fechter in the *German Review* is: "From Wilhelm Meister to the Sturm-Abteilung"

On the sixth page an idea of H[itler]'s—one that is full of theatrical pathos—to touch the standards that are to be dedicated with the old bloodied flag of 1923[21] is described as possessing profound feeling for the subject of the essay, which is concerned with the significance of the theater for education or, rather, with the significance of the "mimetic." Thus it is that everyone in Germany manages to add in some [. . .][22] and an obeisance. We see the first signs of that fixation that, at maturity, will be scholasticism. In scholasticism, propositions are derived logically from immovable basic principles; in the contemporary case something similar is running its course in the area of feeling. The basic premise, however, is only a desire to experience emotional conformity, a search for points of contact—an unsystematic prototype for a system to appear later. Difference—the Middle Ages revered the "logos."

Morale in wartime. In wartime a process developed whereby, at a time of general slackening, a brave company might flee; it had to be intercepted, and then became brave once again. This refraining from acts of individual heroism (with certain exceptions, the significance of which must be determined afresh!), this collective bravery that is a mixture of individual components of different kinds {of bravery and cowardice} has emerged under the influence of war, and politics has simply taken it over. In this sense, N[ational] S[ocialism] really is the continuation of war, and H[itler] possesses an instinct for the times. [. . .]

"This is the place where Spartacists are made into liver-sausage and blood-sausage," or words to this effect, was written in chalk on the gate of Stadelheim prison after a report by Toller.[23] That was the time when much of what is happening today came bubbling up from its source. One can also say that each generation of young people derides, and makes fun of death and horror—this is, in other words, a primeval human need. Today such things are not tied down into any cultural context and this is one of the reasons for the unrestrained cruelties.

Broch:[24] leaning [on someone].[25] When one leans up against a wall one's suit ends up all covered in patches of whitewash—without plagiarism being involved. [. . .]

According to the cultural theories that take precedence in Germany today, it is supposed to be impossible to make another people understand the best of one's own achievement. This seems to be one of the points in which the German revolution has so far proved right. In spite of this I am trying . . . [. . .]

Executioner posts were advertised in Prague, Budapest, Vienna [. . .]. Among the applicants a large number of academics, bank officials, former officers. And a woman.

The living Unknown Soldier—H[itler]. The idea was originally a virtually inimitable French gesture—one that was copied by everyone, finally copied even by us. This was what the loss of the war, in moral terms, actually meant. Now we have a living one. It is only now that we have him. We have an original and powerful gesture. This is what many Germans feel and say: "the unknown German soldier of the World War—H[itler]." [. . .]

The correct anticipation of unknown reactions of *Rathenau* from known ones of *Arnheim*[26] is not a mystery but something like the prophetic gift of a correct *theory*.

Discipline.

The main weakness of the democratic system is the decay of discipline. Is it then the case that fascism, in the excessive stress it lays on this principle, is not only understandable but also a correct instinctive defense mechanism?

Why is it that some creative writers have to be 20–100 years ahead of their time? [. . .]

The unnatural has always given people pleasure. Ring through the nose, hairstyling, makeup in the hollows of the eyes, Rococo, etc.—and today, lips. [. . .]

The stupid woman: she was slim and soft, her body seemed not to have a firm hold on itself; it bent forward a little in the middle and she probably did not fully straighten her knees when she walked. Curls of blond hair peeped out from under her cap, her nose was long and narrow and her face always wore a smile; to be precise, it lay before her face. Her calves covered by brown stockings were soft, their curves barely noticeable; they reminded one a little of darned stockings. She was a servant at the X's house. One day Herr X was alone with her in the house and she had pleased him. He quite gently placed his arm around her body and kissed her. She seemed to have expected it without having ever shown her feelings. She neither resisted nor responded. But when Herr X's lips came down on hers, her lips relinquished their reserve and opened into the kiss. One might have believed that she was letting herself be kissed like a woman of wide sensual experience, but she was a virgin and it was only because her understanding was weak that a deeper or older instinct pushed it gently aside. Herr X exerted a pressure on her in the direction of the sofa. . . . "But you must [. . .] take off your drawers!" he explained to her then. Pleasant and painful sensations were intermingled. She stood up in just the same undetermined way that she had allowed herself to be laid down. None of the words that they spoke after that were of any consequence. They saw each other each day as usual. She smiled as she always had. Her memory held nothing of importance. She would not even have been able to say that it had been beautiful or even particularly pleasant. But from day to day her body waited with increasing intensity for it to be repeated. This did come about just as, after sunset, the moon makes at first a modest entrance, but at last, full and shining, dominates the heavens. [. . .]

Germ[any]: according to the *Hour*,[27] Reichswehr Minister Blomberg said in an address to the Reichswehr after the Saarland had been reintegrated into the Reich: "We soldiers shall delight in this victory and take as our model the tenacity of the people of the Saarland. Those powers of the soul that brought the peaceful battle on the banks of the Saar to a happy conclusion are the same as those that we soldiers will have to demonstrate when we are tested under fire in actual warfare." A people is divided up into an officer corps, NCOs (N[ational] S[ocialists]) and soldiers.

Germ[any]: according to the same source, all the papers that had demanded the resignation of Furtwängler after his article in support of Hindemith[28] expressed overwhelming joy and satisfaction about his imminent return as conductor of the Philharmonia, after he declared that his comments had been made merely from a musical perspective without taking matters of cultural politics into account. First stage in the emergence of the future state: by means of suggestion one generates the desired feelings; second stage, one no longer needs to generate them, it is sufficient to express a wish. Provided that the center conducting this process possesses genius, what a possibility this is! A people evolves with a sense of power, uniformity and creativity.

N.b.: re the two previous notes. How happy the spirit [Geist] feels that it-self does not have to give shape to life, but receives it. It gladly takes second place, indeed perhaps it is degeneration and utopia to lay claim to first place? [. . .]

22
NOTEBOOK 34
17 FEBRUARY 1930
TO EARLY SUMMER 1938

[*This notebook contains heterogeneous material in which Musil takes the pulse of contemporary intellectual and cultural affairs by means of wide reading in newspapers and journals and extensive quotation from these sources. He remains alert to politics and general developments in Nazi Germany. He continues to make notes for satirical works; these include some for* Ed *and for the so-called* War Diary of a Flea. *Among the books he reads are Goethe's autobiography,* Fiction and Truth, *and Tolstoy's* War and Peace.]

34.

17.II.1930. Chesterton's representation of "woman" which largely runs counter to my own, has led me to reflect on my own. Timely for Ag[athe].

A major difference: need of the man to "speak his mind." That of the woman to refrain from doing so.

The same difference can already be seen in sexual matters. The man shows his excitement, the woman allows hers to be torn from her.

The man feels flattered when he shows his anger; a woman uttering oaths is obscene.

In the case of fear it is the other way around: the woman flirts with fear, the man, who is no less fearful, conceals his fear.

With vanity it is halfway to being the other way around.

The man is generous, the woman thrifty.

One might, of course, say that both put on show what they consider to be their virtues. But, after all, human beings are not simply a product of their social function. What functions are involved?

{?Genesis: would like to—is not able to—projects this into the ideal image of the other—fixes the other.

Or all is contained in the notion that the woman tends to hold back more (because she is weaker)?

Or the man conceals what are allegedly female qualities, the woman conceals allegedly male ones?} [. . .]

––––––––––

12.III.31. Funeral car taking away the old woman from the ground floor.

There it stands with the rear door wide open. At the front, next to the radiator, is a group of children.

"That's a Steyr," says a boy.

"No, a Daimler," says another.

Then two attendants carry the light-colored coffin out of the house. A packing slip has been stuck under the cross that is mounted on the lid, and a red label of some kind has been glued onto the wood of the coffin. Then the two attendants put their furs back on and exchange a few good-natured words with the chauffeur.

The car has the registration number A 81805.

––––––––––

12.IV. Ed.[1]

The difference between male and female sexuality can be traced back, in the main, to abreaction through ejaculation which is {after all, in part} absent in the woman. In the case of coit[us] interr[uptus] where the spermatic cord has been tied off or manually constricted a similar state is produced in the man. The high-point of arousal is not followed by a sudden fall in tension, but rather the pent-up pleasure sinks back again and is dispersed around the body. The lips seem swollen, the eyelids hot, the sexual organ is tired but sensitive and prepared for a renewal of effort. The psychic state is warm, lustful, diffuse, clinging to the other and, to a certain extent, at the other's mercy through the immediate response to stimulation. But that is the female mode of reaction. The only kind of women in Ed are those who take over from the man the thankless task of earning a living. They are able to do so because they take everything much less to heart than men do, they don't make so much fuss. The man is the one to make difficulties, he is the deep one; it is the woman who is better suited to the busy life of today. In sex, too, she doesn't make much fuss. "Come here!" she says. He, in his state of lustful absentmindedness, tends to want to do housework. The one with the greater capacity for release of tension—and, all things being equal, the woman is better equipped for this because she is, in general terms, more labile—dominates the other sexually; she is able to switch immediately to quite different thoughts and moods. [. . .]

Ed. A fairly young officer, pensioned off, a commercial traveler, cleans three pairs of shoes every Sunday morning at the window in the corridor. The people from the riding school go by on their horses. One of them, returning from the Prater, has pushed back his hat and put his legs up on the front ridge of the saddle. The officer suddenly shouts out: "You pig, you Jewish brat, how dare you sit on horseback like that!" and so forth. Explosion of post-war tension. {It is relevant that this officer is probably only a lieutenant in the pay corps or something like that!}

Ed. Idea? 5 or 7 brothers—the most gifted one is a failure—the others are representative figures.

One is a confidence trickster, has spent time in prison, given up by the family, becomes a great director of "talking films."

Begins in the hallway of a hotel, the gifted one is waiting for Mr. X., his long-lost brother;—the family has sent the gifted boy to see him.

Ed. What if one observes people from the perspective of animal psychology, e.g., that of a dog?

On a Sunday evening, for example: they bark, play with balls as a dog does with a stone; they feel they have reached their goal when they have a female with them, and vice versa; they seldom pay particular attention to the breed of the other; eating and drinking are among the most important activities.

It is probably possible to transfer the whole of the structure of the animal soul to that of the human being.

Study of this possibility on a farm.

Or ironic reversal with the effect that, in their life together, the dog has become the human being's teacher. [. . .]

Ed. The leading actors at the Burgtheater earn monthly fees of 4000 to 5000 schillings and are outraged because it is proposed, at a time when all of us face difficulties, that this minimum be reduced. The directors, senior management, accountants, etc., probably all earn similar amounts.

There is a "Richard Schaukal Society"[2] of which university professors are members!

?

There are two things that one cannot fight against because they are too long and too fat, and have neither head nor foot: Karl Kraus and psychoanalysis.

Wildg[ans], in one of the events in the "Austrian Festival Weeks," is reading from his works in the "Urania." [. . .]

Guide to contemporary literature—this would provide a perspective. Preface: my situation as a seventeen-year-old in front of the bookcase at home when I had lost contact with books. Individual phenomena and elements relating to the formation of judgment. [. . .]

Ed. To describe, in the contemporary epoch, a chaste woman (aunt) is an ironic technique, similar to the description of the G[eneral] in MwQ.[3] She is right to the extent that life needs inhibitions!

Ed. Plan: the situation today is similar to that in Plato's Academy during the years when Aristotle was withdrawing. Contrast the Academy of Conceit City with the Platonic! [. . .]

Ed. A town like Marienbad or Karlsbad that lives off the defecation of its visitors. [. . .]

The Hegelian conception of thesis, antithesis and synthesis[4] fits spiritual history and, in particular, the history of art (in this process, however, the synthesis is deficient). Why does it fit? Because the human being is, by nature, ambivalent and antagonistic.

(The human being shapes his objectification in his own image?)

Reminded of the Isis-Osiris poem.[5] It contains the novel[6] "in nucleo." A charge of perversity has been leveled against the novel. Counter this as follows: the archaic and the schizophrenic find convergent expression in art, yet, in spite of this, are totally different from one another. In just the same way, the feelings of brother and sister for each other may be perverse, or may be myth.

(Aside: a myth of today contains elements of ideas. The myth contains a "partial solution." A myth must be cred-ible, "worthy of belief." But today it is not believed in its entirety. Was this ever the case? Probably not. It will always have been something half believed, for human beings would not have been able to live the kind of practical lives that they have always led if they had believed implicitly in gods and demons.) [. . .]

George: one of the few examples of morality[7] but, ultimately, an archaism?
   Heroism of the spirit. On a false trail with respect to the second component.
   The only non-disciple of Nietzsche.
   The man who did not understand the aesthetic law of prose? Nor the path of great prose. That is why he is a romantic figure. [. . .]

The soul does not grow old? At least not in a constant way. The protective shield, the body, grows old, what is protected and enwrapped does not. Or at least they grow old in a different way. We see the colors, hear the sounds, smell and taste in approximately the same way when we are old as we did when we were young. The understanding does indeed change, but tends rather to increase than decrease in capacity. The sharpness of the senses decreases, but that can easily be made good, and is not so much a process of growing older as a sudden change. In short, the well-known experience that a youthful soul is still present even in an old body. Indeed, in some respects, a childish soul.[8]

The material in the memory increases, at least potentially. Are there permanent losses in what can be remembered? Yes, there are. For example, things one once knew by heart.

Spiritual ability is also lost. Mathematics, for instance, and scientific thinking. Not only ability, skills, too, to wax and wane.

But there are such things as a young soul, a mature one, and an old one.

But soul is something quite different from body. (After Nietzsche turned our attention to the way that, to a certain extent, soul = body.)

And what about the bones? Don't they have a graph of development that differs from that of the flesh? And the hair ages suddenly over a short period? So there are quite different processes, among them the one concerned with the nerve substance? [. . .]

Compromise: a person who does everything right according to principles, who wants to set everything into proper moral order, muddles everything. The consternation that I caused in my Company! I, myself, not some pedant. People who order things practically are always improvisers. The human world a constant improvisation. Does this have some link with average education? [. . .]

Hospitality and willingness to help, on farms in South-West Africa that are about 30 kilometers from each other (in an area of desert), are, so it is said, positively boundless in European terms. But these are immigrant settlers, in other words they are the same Europeans who in their {old} homeland have almost completely lost these virtues. Is it the case then that each situation gives rise to its own morality? Are those lost European virtues no longer needed in Europe? Or is it {merely} this: a fellow human being as a scarce commodity as opposed to the same offered cheaply, someone whom one would not want even if one were given him for nothing? Virtues offered for sale at prices that depend on how good the ware tastes; and this in turn, depends on the frequency with which it is eaten? [. . .]

Creative writer and nation. What I present in the novel will always remain a utopia; it is not the "reality of tomorrow." But it is probably the case that the inadequate relationship between Germans and their literature, together with the literature itself, is a phenomenon that forms part of a "whole." Without H[einrich] M[ann?], for example, A[dolf] H[itler?] would have emerged in a different fashion.[9] [. . .]

Creative writing and philosophy are both neglected in our time. (Compare the effect of Kant right up to the previous generation with the effect he now has). And here the extent to which they belong together is apparent. [. . .]

Tolstoy's morality, in relation to me. I say this in advance so that I shan't forget it. The morality of "Resurrection" is not without flaws, in theoretical terms his thinking is less precise than elsewhere. I consider my own version of the problem to be a legitimate continuation (love of one's neighbor, etc.). But he is not looking for any theory, he is looking for an answer to questions that shake him to the core! This human dimension takes hold of people and drags them along with him, even if they are not prone to such reflections. And it is a matter of indifference whether the reflections are more, or less, accurate.

My particular danger is to get caught up in theory. Always work back toward whatever it was that led you to these theoretical and provisional investigations! [. . .]

Breakfast terrace: two old women of exquisite ugliness; a third one, of similar appearance, arrives. One of the two says to her warmly: "When you come, the sun rises!"—which is what that untouchable star is doing at this very moment.

The critic is supposed to form his judgment immediately after reading a book, the theater critic straight after seeing the play, whereas everywhere else in life the rule holds that one should give oneself time to form a judgment! (This may well be connected with the "immediacy" of effect that Impressionism has demanded of us.)

Judging a person correctly is something that often takes a whole lifetime.

How often have I changed my judgment of Rilke, of Hofmannsthal. The popular conclusion to draw from this is that there is no such thing as "objective judgement," only a "living" one.

The stinking, lying blabbermouth of our times. [. . .]

Tolstoy's morality. In Chapter 28, pp. 403 ff:[10] as long as one is concerned with oneself, one has too much time on one's hands, feels bored or angry at everything and racks one's brains about what to do next. If one acts on behalf of others, everything is appealing and one is never short of things to do; one is usually in a happy mood.

Then, with respect to the things with which N.[11] occupies his time, a confrontation with the law. "What is the nature, what is the purpose of . . this strange institution that is known as the penal code, and what are . . all these places of confinement, from the Fortress of Peter and Paul through to the Prison Island of Sachalin . . ?" T. divides the "criminals" into 5 categories:

1) victims of justice that "according to the prison chaplain number about 7% of the prison population . . ."

2) Those punished for actions that were committed in exceptional states of mind—anger, jealousy, intoxication, etc. One might say with near certainty that, given the same circumstances, these actions would also have been committed by those who passed judgment on them and punished them. More than 50%.

3) People punished for actions that, in their own opinion, were perfectly proper and even good. Secret dealing in brandy, smuggling, collecting wood, stealing grass, non-believers stealing from churches, Caucasian mountain bandits. Here T. does not indicate any percentage.

4) Those who are only treated as criminals because they are on a higher moral level than the social mean. Members of sects, national rebels, socialists, strikers. "According to N.'s calculations, the percentage of such people was very high."

5) People to whom society had a greater debt than they had to society. Socially deprived. Those who had degenerated through being led astray and through constant oppression, people who are driven to crime systematically, through pressure of the conditions under which they are forced to live.

"He had also seen a tramp and a woman, both of whom were made to seem repulsive by their dull wits and apathy, but . . . he saw in them only human beings whom he personally did not like, just as he had also met some who belonged to high society and wore tails, epaulettes and lace who also aroused his antipathy."

Why are all these categories of human beings thrown into prison whereas other human beings, of precisely the same kind, walk about in freedom and, indeed, even sit in judgment on them? [. . .]

My memory: I would be able to describe the people I knew during my childhood, but I know nothing of their lives, where they came from, and what has happened to them. This predisposition of my memory is some indication of the way I write! [. . .]

Th[omas] M[ann] and similar authors write for the people who are there; I write for people who aren't there!

Enthusiasts,[12] basic difference: most dramatists write as actors speak; I demand that they speak as I write. The former results—with the exception of Naturalism—in something {empty and} unnatural; the latter is intended to lead to a higher form of nature. [. . .]

Jewish concept of wisdom: correct perception of God on the basis of his revelation in the law which gives the law its inviolable standard.

Greek concept: autonomous perception of thinking without presupposition {Meyer, Vol. II, p. 104, Note 3).}

The former is thus the more N[ational] S[ocialist], the latter is the {Jewish} one. [. . .]

I have, in this struggle, a remarkable stance. The love of a people for a spir-itual leader—this thought occurred to me while reading Bernhard's remarks on Augustine's influence on all epochs in the preface to his selection pub-lished by Kröner—is disavowed by Hitler, Hindenburg, Bismarck. Despite this, Th[omas] and H[einrich] Mann both strive for this kind of influence, and with some degree of success. They want to stand in his place, that is the essential significance and the good conscience of their struggle. And that is not what I want. I am convinced that this is not the right thing, etc. [. . .]

Retrospective glance: ethnologists say that the Paleolithic rock drawings—and today negroes still make similar ones before they go out hunting—were intended to work magic. According to them, art originates in religion and magic. This is the same as my now deceased companion on a short stretch of the way, v. H[ornbostel][13] once proved about creative writing, which I have already made use of in the essay[14] . . .

This view matches my experiences and my feelings. But the (weak) out-break of religion that is locked away in my childhood happened in my 10th or 12th year, and neither before nor after . . . until . . ?

Art and religion, then, are related (For this reason they also compete with each other.) {I don't know more than this.} I can still remember Dilthey's claim (where was it that I gave an account of this?)[15]

This is the wretched state of a man who, on occasions, has been honored by the praise bestowed on his spirit. Art, of course, has become independ-ent; one might come across, in the field of art, some clues about how reli-gion would have to look today if it were not lived out historically, but treated in a contemporary way. I believe that this, too, is one of the supports on which my house stands. [. . .]

Ley, Leader of the "Work Front,"[16] said that the Jew has been chosen to murder and destroy the peoples of the earth. The fighting in Spain, the sub-jugation of Russia, he said, was the work of the Jews. "The Day," 30.IV.1937.

On the previous evening, Frisch[17] (at Frau Schnitzler's)[18] told of his stay in Poland, saying that each Jew has a completely personal relationship to God (a relationship involving responsibility, with God, too, being made re-sponsible, if I am not mistaken)—something that a non-Jew could not understand. And even Beer-Hofmann[19] was non-Jewish or non-orthodox in a Jewish fashion that only a Jew could grasp completely. I do not remember the content of these assertions, but what I do remember is that I said "So the Jews, in your opinion, are a chosen people?" and that F. did not deny it. Postscript: throughout the whole history of the Jews, and only through their history, runs this moral relationship to God—I have just now remembered this fragment of what F. said. But they don't think about it at all, so self-evident is it to them. [. . .]

Average people: they tell each other in precise detail what was on their boarding house menu.

Love of an old man for a young girl. That would be a practicable form for a fruitful comparison of the present epoch with a past one. A substitute, and more than that, for components of a description of life. This occurred to me as I contemplated a picture of old Montmartre that I enclose. It had that unmodern beauty that was found even in the shabby remains of old Vienna that are today being torn down for being "in the way of the traffic." This was a delicate enclave in Paris. Artists used to live there not only because it was cheap and had its local café, but above all because it was beautiful. With odd angles, trees. At once modest and rich. Today it is an attraction, but touches the memory only in one or two places. Like the Prater, the Danube, the Viennese cuisine, and the Viennese bread roll. But even in those days it was no longer innocent; it already had the reputation of being the place where the rise to wealth began. They did not sing as the bird sings . . . , but with one eye to success. In this "already" and "not yet" lies the tension of art that drives one upward in a bourgeois age.

Of this, and similar things, you young people have no idea at all. You don't know how poor you are, even if you complain. What kinds of industrialized foodstuffs are used to feed you? You have only the empty shell of being younger, of beginning—, even that is an incredible amount! Recently I envied a calf its frolicking!

A young girl who loves the grand old man as Bettina did Goethe.[20] And he no longer had belief in life. And he does not want to give complete expression to the conditions under which he would like to believe; for it is in youth that one experiences the incalculability of life, its real irrationality.

10 letters, hardly more than that! [. . .]

Ed. The woman, quite dreadful! No loyalty to nothing [*sic*]. Everything about her pure vanity. Her interests are hypocrisy and play, a sexual role that she takes upon herself. She betrays every idea for the sake of a dalliance. If she grows old, she suddenly becomes stupid; a crumpled, sullied paper husk is all that remains of her: just for once, let a misogynist speak from the heart! And in Ed the attempt is made to found a state, not on anti-Semitism, but on misogyny. [. . .]

Ed + autobiography (27 August 1937) The unpleasant thing about an autobiography is taking oneself so seriously, and yet everyone feels the urge to do so. Even this cursing of just about all and sundry is both ugly and indispensable. But if I describe my life as being exemplary, as a life in this age that I want to hand down to later ages, this can be toned down with irony and the objections raised will then fall away. And this epoch deserves to be handed down just as it is (not in the distanced mode of MwQ but), seen in close-up, as a private life. It can have the charm of intimate historical finds. My probing of conscience, contemplation of my shortcomings and the like, will also find their place here as a reproduction of the times. Then Ed would have two parts and the first would be this one, ending somewhere or other, or breaking off at a point where I simply couldn't go on. A major advantage is to be found in the way the two volumes can run in parallel and also do not need to be finished.

This allows me to start soon.

. . .

The Spanish Civil War, the contrast between China and Japan, between England and Italy, etc., the way that all of this is only the background to a biography, is a human (or bourgeois) aspect. In addition, it is subsumed under the question: "Why apolitical?"

. . . .

It is already apparent that the first part will be more extensive and more loosely structured than the second and will contain a good deal that has no significance for the other. But that doesn't matter!

[. . .]

But the mode of writing in the first part is a biography or a *bogus* autobiography. [. . .]

Ed. If any metaphysical problem impinges on our lives today then it is the sense that the earth is getting too small for us. At the same time we all have the feeling that the reduction in the number of children is decadent. It is also quite natural, however, that it is precisely those in higher positions, with their more extensive view of things, who instinctively go on forward in this direction. Propagation to achieve strength in battle: this "solution" marks a gigantic step in the wrong direction: one breeds in order to destroy instead of making plans to restrict numbers. Breeding for talent is the correct solution. A frivolous decision to renounce having children and similar notions also represent a false solution. N[ational] S[ocialism] has intuitions of many things, but in a distorted way. Jews as the victims of a false solution. War the unintelligent solution, the primitive reaction. The Church as an obstacle.

"Flea" (War diary and description of the life of a . .) (Experiences and thoughts.)

One character is a waiter with the High Command of the Army. (Head waiter at the Hotel Thalhof.) In his discreet and independent fashion, he looks after everyone and enjoys their trust. The flea has chosen him as his permanent quarters but, as far as is possible, takes his nourishment from orderlies and obnoxious persons. It is only rarely that he has recourse to a favorite as a delicacy.

For he knows that he is unpopular, a pest, a parasite. He has come as far as to appreciate this himself. He is weighed down by the history of his people—even though his old and highly developed race is capable of miraculous achievements. When a sentimental mood possesses him it makes him feel ill to be a nomad. But "blood" and "soil"[21] imbue him with heroic attachment to blood. {As far as blood is concerned he possesses the learning of a haematologist.} It saddens him that he is a burden to all. He hates the lice, those parasites without talent, who are spreading so quickly in wartime. He takes cognizance of the extermination of his people: he is an individualist. Gives melancholic and ironic consent to the way that "progress" is connected with a battle against his people. Mussolini is driving the fleas out of Italy. Even their old seat in Turkey is being contested. In his youth, at a college, he was an orderly or serving girl; he knows today's dictators from the time when they were at school.

He himself, in the introduction, complains about the hero of his memoirs being a flea. But every epoch has its memoirs and he is a solitary individualist.

(I am a German flea. I have an intimate connection with German blood. And I am a flea in your ear.)

Name for the waiter: Herr Kreuzeder (this is the actual name of a servant on the domestic staff in the Thalhof.) [. . .]

Woman: there is nothing unusual at the way we put our finger, hand or arm in something; we also "poke our nose into something" or put ourselves, or other humans, into a dress, bath, prison, etc. But having something put into us, well that's quite out-of-the-ordinary; and this exception to human behavior is the norm for women. [. . .]

Long before the dictators, our times brought forth spiritual veneration of dictators. Stefan George, for instance. Then Kraus and Freud, Adler and Jung as well. Add to these, Klages and Heidegger. What is probably common to these is a need for domination and leadership, for the essence of the savior. Do leaders also have character traits in common as well? Fixed values, for instance, that nonetheless permit different lines of thinking? [. . .]

Youth and changing times. Today even professional philosophers who happen to have aesthetic leanings quote Kierkegaard. I don't like him, I never liked him, and I don't need him. How did that come about? Perhaps as follows: the positive element that people derive from him today was formerly part of the atmosphere of the times and I did not need him to supply it; thus I am aware only of the negative and unpleasant elements, those that resemble the fin-de-siècle type. [. . .]

Simile. Differences between the poetic or creative ones that develop freely and the sort that emerges under the compulsion of an idea, the psychoanalytical, for example, seeing the rim of a fountain as a vulva.

Aristocracy is, a priori, the best form of government. So I thought when I was young. For the unpolitical person, the problem of politics is easily solved. [. . .]

Nietzsche. Did I absorb, in my youth, even as much as a third of him? Despite this, a decisive influence. [. . .]

What democracy spat out. It is not possible to polemicize against Emil Ludwig, Stefan Zweig and Feuchtwanger—that would be a tempest in a teacup—but all three together, these beneficiaries of emigration who have now become the darlings of the whole world, while good writers can scarcely steer clear of destruction, all three together are a tremendous symbol of the times. President Roosevelt, the man of the Brain Trust who has E. L. listen to the processes of government in the mask of a portraitist! The fortune that shines on N[ational] S[ocialism] made it remove these people. [. . .]

The spirit says: it is unimportant whether you are on the side of good or evil. [. . .]

Max Scheler:[22] fiery professorial stallion spoiling for a fight, with the strangest feelings spurting from his nostrils. But still a great wealth of material that has been thought through (with varying degrees of intensity). [. . .]

"Extra-territoriality of the spiritual person" is the correct term in this epoch of "blood," "soil," "race," "mass," "Führer" and "homeland."

The age of the actor: I have repeatedly referred to this prophecy of Nietzsche's that has actually been fulfilled.[23] Toward an understanding of this phenomenon: what is characteristic about the exaggerated importance of the actor is the immediacy of the effect involved and that this effect is not developed nor indeed capable of development; this, in turn, is connected with the widespread sense that the aesthetic means enjoyment, experience, etc.; in other words, malfunctioning, or absence, of any system of ideas.

N.b., the film was a present for this age—it was not born of the age, rather it has been an addition that arrived for heterogeneous reasons, but it is, in its effect, like a prestabilized harmony; and what does that mean? This occurred to me while listening to an example of how one simply needs to speak to people from the heart in order to receive the most sublime praise from them. (Schuschnigg[24] speech.) [. . .]

Psychological thought: started out by reflecting that a very mobile spirit has difficulty in occupying a secure position when this is necessary, and has found peace in cool disdain for any particular insult—until now I would have said "a stabilizing feeling." But it is more correct to say that our memory, our life, our thinking fills in outlines. I find a form, and if it is a good one, everything comes and fills this in. Just now it was memory that did so. I can, for example, suddenly read French when I am interested in something and need to do so. Nothing has been added to me, it only a form, or a dynamic principle, or an organization. (See the question of whether a "Gestalt" possesses its own energy. But it is probably the case that it is more than merely a "Gestalt"!) [. . .]

{Carlyle} [Hitler] teaches us to understand ancient peoples who worshipped a bull. [. . .]

C [Hitler]: he has united people, but on what a low level. [. . .]

Spirit and Jew are both "stateless persons"; nowhere in the world do they possess a country "of their own." [. . .]

23

NOTEBOOK 33

1937 TO
ABOUT END OF 1941

[*Here Musil collects material for an autobiography; he starts work in 1937 and continues making entries until the end of 1941, only a few months before he died. The notebook contains references to, and reflections on, matters of importance in his life and on those people who were vital to his development. These include (in approximate order of their appearance in the notebook, which does not follow any chronological order): thoughts on his mother and father and on his own temperament and physical makeup; potential careers as university lecturer and librarian, both of which were open to him shortly before World War I; some notes on ancestors; Martha; creative writing; various childhood experiences; his feelings about death, with reference to service at the front; memories of educational institutions he attended; his love as a youth for the beautiful daughter of one of his father's colleagues and how he associates her with Elsa, the older sister who died before he was born and who influenced the development of the brother-sister theme in MwQ.*]

33.

1) *Lucky numbers and colors:* a suspicious matter. The lucky number 6 comes from November 6th being my birthday and June 6th having been

considered my Name Day for a long time. The lucky color red comes from father's tales of the horses he rode [. . .] (Love of self and love of others.)

I can remember a game with racehorses with a course with hurdles and horses cast in tin; one threw dice to move them forward. It emerged that I was more successful with number 5 than with 6. It caused confusion and has still not evened itself out to this day.

---

2) *My father:* a quiet, rather anxious person who knew no fear of death.

{[. . .] He wasn't cowardly but anxious or fearful, no more and no less. What does that actually mean? Of a yielding and easily cowed disposition, overlaid with higher traits. I have something of this from him, mingled with the quarrelsome nature inherited from my mother.}
[. . .]
{There was greatness in the manner of his dying after Mama's death—it was quite devoid of any belief.

Did the renaissance of the stoa in the seventeenth century (see Cassirer on Descartes)[1] work its way through as far as the peasantry by the nineteenth century? The attitude to life of which I speak was stoical. This generation, which was submissive to government and was not enthusiastic about progress (it was perhaps only in the middle of the century that the emancipated Jews took this attitude), adopted a stoical point of view, without much differentiation. This needs to be checked!

[. . .]}

---

3) (Re: 1) One will see in this the expression of a powerful love of self and (I am immediately prompted to add) of few other people and this cannot be seen as correct. I would, myself, like to know what functions are involved. I have been capable of loving others, not often, but very intensely: unhappiness that came with the idea that my father was mortal—homesickness in Eisenstadt[2]—the Valerie experience[3]—Martha. With the little girl whom I brought home from Kindergarten[4] there is the intimation of an "other" component. I traversed the stage of love of self very quickly: hero of the first fantasizing, vanity in dress and my relation to it.

---

4) The two most beautiful moments in my career as a writer[5] (I don't know if they really were the most beautiful but this is how they have been recorded in my memory).

I had given up the engineering profession, had moved from Stuttgart to Berlin, had registered at the University, was preparing for, or had already passed, the grammar school matriculation, at any rate I wasn't attending many lectures and had made use of the time to complete the *Confusions of Young Törleß* which I had started in Stuttgart. When I had finished the manuscript, several publishing houses returned it to me with compliments and a rejection. Among them were Diederichs of Jena, and I also remember Bruns in Minden, and Schuster and Löffler in Berlin. These were houses, particularly the two former ones, which I had chosen with feelings that stemmed from the spiritual realm of childhood and, as is the case with children, my sympathy was not founded on sound knowledge. I was somewhat perturbed that all three, and all three with the same alacrity, examined and rejected my work. In those days, I wanted both to become a creative writer and to qualify as a university lecturer in philosophy, and I was unsure of how to judge my talent. Thus I came to the decision to ask an authority to judge.

My choice fell on Alfred Kerr—and there was something remarkable about that. I had perhaps read some of his reviews, which in those days appeared in the Berlin paper *The Day*; his style of writing appeared particularly mannered to me as a South-German (it both attracted and excluded me like some strange carnival) but I sensed the solid foundations of the language and of the judgments. But I think that the real reason lay in my familiarity with his little book on Eleonora Duse that had appeared in the series *The Fruitbowl* (published by Barth)—and the real reason wasn't the work as a whole but, as I remember, it was just a little group of two to four sentences that had aroused my "sense of belonging." I had read this little book when I was still in Brünn and the memory of it is connected with the "Esplanade," a tract planted with trees where, on Sundays and to the accompaniment of military music, people used to promenade up on the one side, down on the other. Why this was connected with the book on Duse I no longer know, but I think that I can clearly remember that this was light-grey in color with gold lettering and the format was small-quarto, (Check this!) and that it was somehow linked to the Esplanade. It may have been as follows: on those dreadfully boring Sundays one tried to make contact with life and everything was, well, just as it tends to be in quite small towns, and I had probably tucked the book under my arm to play the part of the interesting young man. This was the way that I came to choose Alfred Kerr.

---

5) I want to achieve too much all at once! This serious flaw is to be found in my writing in the first few essays, in "Unions," etc., almost through to

the MwQ. What emerged from this was something cramped and contorted. {When I wrote *Törleß* I was still aware that one needs to know how to leave things out.}

{Additional point: I too seldom know what it is that I want. In me there is no vestige of the preacher, appellant, executor of an inner preordained course.} [. . .]

---

8) My father often requested that I explain some aspect of what concerned me: I was never capable of doing so. I still have the same difficulty today; if I wanted to explain to someone the chapters on feeling that I have now been working on for so long[6] and with something approaching success, I would quickly become confused and come to a halt. Seen from the perspective of self-love, this might be considered the basic quality of an MwQ, setting me apart from the writers who see all things clearly before them—"formative" thinking in the place of purely rational thinking. But it also has to do with the lack of clarity that looms so large in my life. It is hardly right to call me an unclear thinker, but nor am I a clear thinker. Expressing this indulgently: the capacity to clarify is well-developed, but the mists that obscure what needs clarifying lift only for points of individual detail.

My father was very clear, my mother was curiously confused. Like hair covering the pretty face of someone sleeping.

---

9) In "The Blackbird"[7] I was not successful in expressing my mother's strength that seemingly had no substance. But it might be expressed approximately in the way that Lewin did: strong tensions. Often there was a high emotional pressure behind her reactions, a pressure stabilized in principles that were both noble and engaging. Unfortunately, this was also at the mercy of her "nervous disposition."

---

10) The relationship to politics.

Reising,[8] Boineburg:[9] today's dictators in nucleo. Also the conception of the "mass" as a being to be subjugated.

Between 17 and 20 the involuntary affection for the Gentz principle.[10] The unscrupulous spiritual individual.

And today I am again on the point of guiding the important individual away from the generality. This is, of course, impossible because even the genius is more indebted to others than to himself. (More correctly: this cannot be measured, but both are indispensable.)

I belonged, peripherally, among the class dictators.

Seldom any talk of politics in my parents' house.

I don't wish yet to sit in judgment on myself, I only want to weigh up how things were.

The child's fear of the Russians and the workers had no influence later. But worth considering how it was that good people like my parents felt, in advance, that the striking, rebellious workers were evil. What joy when soldiers were sent to Steyr.

What was our attitude to politics in the military institute? Revolutions appeared to us as disorder; I, at least, had not the slightest degree of sympathy for the French Revolution (although we were scarcely subjected to any influence whatsoever). I believe that the decisive influence came from the figure of Napoleon; not from him as a person—and I still know too little about him to this day—but from the disdain for the world and from the force, etc., that he embodied. As I reflected on the matter, it occurred to me that aesthetic elements probably also exerted a decisive and immediate influence on us: the solemn blowing of the horns, drum rolls, the closed mass ranks. We were neither dynastic nor very patriotic in outlook; but certain moments sent shivers along our spines and right down into our feet. What prospects for Germany today?

Later in Brünn it was probably my adopting the stance of young outsider that made me sympathize with socialism—though rational considerations were, of course, also in play—so that I was very close to making my literary debut as the theater critic of *The People's Friend*. What a joke of fate that the theater committee, at that very moment, canceled the paper's reserved seat![11] The visit to Deputy Czech,[12] the lecture in the workers' hostel, the musty atmosphere—here, too, aesthetic elements were decisive in turning me away.

---

11) At some time between the ages of 5 and 10 when I enthused about {was fired with passion for} all that was noble (or was it stories told by friends, or warnings from my mother that were responsible? But I think that I had an urge to set things in motion for it was then that I also "abducted" the girl from the Kindergarten), I flung myself headlong into every battle. I once defeated one {more than one!} "giant" who was up to three years older than

I was, he was probably a lad who had shot up in height; I can still remember the place where this happened and the negotiations in which we became involved since I had wrestled him to the ground but then did not know what I should do next.

It must be characteristic of me that I have always wrestled, but was reluctant, or uninspired, as far as fistfights were concerned.

I was small and stocky and my arms are rather short.

I was always the youngest in my class and once, on the way home from school with a brother of one of my classmates who was two or three years older than I was, I got into an altercation that, to my surprise, ended abruptly when I found myself being thrown to the ground. I was full of shame and fury, but did not have the courage to retaliate. It was hopeless; the issue was sealed.

In Brünn there were two places for fights on the way to and from school; here there were battles with other schoolboys and with the "outlaws" of the Augustinergasse, as it was then {the street leading to Getreide Square}. This was the place for stone throwing and boxing matches. I once received a blow to my kidneys that put me out of action.

Every life has something of the sort and, in a biography, it is either overlooked or painted in loving detail {harmlessly} as typical of youth. But, in the end, it seems perhaps to have shaped the nature of people today, their capacity for boundless indifference in their treatment of their fellow human beings?

---

12) I must have caused my parents great concern over the violence of my temper that was, however, a response to the violent temper of my mother, and that was also connected with a touchy self-importance. This explains why, despite their spoiling me in other things, they let me enter the military college that was, in truth, anything other than an educational institution. So I was difficult to educate as a child and I know today how helpless one is in the face of such a person; in those days, one could not have recourse to findings that have since become generally accepted. But were they, before our times, perhaps dispensable?

---

13) After the death of my parents, Martha and I suddenly wanted to keep their house and move to Brünn. But the owner of the house—the ownership had changed a few years previously—now also laid claim to it. He was a

businessman who had grown prosperous, a clever, modest, serious-minded Jew who went firmly on his chosen path; he came to see me and explained to me what he wanted, together with the supporting arguments. I took the matter to court, lost in the first instance, and then gave up my plan. We Romantics, of no fixed abode, had troubled this circumspect man in vain, and been taught a lesson for doing so. [. . .]

---

15) I treat life as something unpleasant that one can get through by smoking! (I live, in order to smoke.)

---

16) [. . .] I fear that even my fidelity involves a "lack of desire for living." Here, i.e., in the Thalhof {I must date these entries. Until further notice these are being written in the Thalhof, in the months of June, July and August of 1938.},[13] there was a Hungarian baroness; at the outset she emphasized her status as a woman on her own and had nothing to do with anyone, smoking cigarettes and spending the whole day in a reclining chair set up a little way apart from all the others. Her mouth was like a slit, though she wore lipstick; as I remember, it was rather beautiful, at any rate sensual {and} an invitation. It called the vagina to mind, though only when one had got used to the woman as a whole. For she appeared grotesque, with her slightly up-tilted nose, her dyed blond hair and the ravaged hollows of her eyes, which may have been caused by vice or illness. She was, from the first glance, an erstwhile beauty who is trying in vain to tart herself up again {wanted to reestablish her looks}. I saw her in another light only when she came to a table in the garden in a very lightweight beach costume. Her figure was as beautiful as—let us say, as a 40-year-old spruce. Perfect from the soles of her feet to her chin. I could, admittedly, not gain a clear impression of her bosom. This was somewhat more than a good average size and, as I suspect, both rounded and elongated. The skillful design of the culottes that seemed to consist of virtually nothing at all, left this uncertain. But I must not forget: the white skin was of the most beautiful texture. Judging by this, the woman was certainly less than forty years of age; she might even have been only thirty.

I am only setting all of this down in order to record what memory happens to supply; my subject is a different one. I had quickly become aware that this woman, in her intense boredom, had "noticed" me and knew that I had noticed her. At every encounter our glances touched in passing. The probability was great that we would not have spent much time waiting if I had been on my own. And now I said to myself: "You only need to speak to her. She will invent some excuse that will guide you to her room, or you will invent something to test her willingness. When you have gone as far as that, all that remains is to maintain a degree of composure as you fall." And I could see all of this vividly before my eyes. Life is so simple and eager. Then I realized with this offer—"You can have it straight away"—that I do not want to have anything. And that, as I have said, fidelity is, among other things, no more than the absence of a will to live. (Incidentally, I have resolved to think of this example when considering the difference between the two passionate kinds of people, the appetitive and the inward-looking.)

---

17) Since yesterday—I add the date, 22 August 1937—I have been reading, as far as time permits, Scheler, *Forms of Sympathy*, Cohen, Bonn, 1923 (2nd extended edition of *The Phenomenology of the Feelings of Sympathy*, 1913); this is the book that I have now to tackle quickly before I can send the chapters on the theory of love in MwQ, Volume II, second part,[14] to the printers. As I read, the following occurred to me:

---

18) It appears as if my natural development ought to have taken the following course: acceptance of the university position in Graz;[15] patient fulfilment of the boring duties of an assistant lecturer. Taking part spiritually in the transformation of psychology and philosophy. Then, after having had enough of that, a natural breaking away and attempt to move over to literature.

Why did this not happen? Our desire not to move to Graz after getting married could have been overcome. What was decisive was that I had naive hopes about the way my career as a writer would develop; decisive, too, was that I had no idea how dangerous it is in life not to exploit the chances that present themselves. (I was magnificent—in a provincial context, magnificent—in the realm of dreams. All this was a consequence of the security of my youth.) A decent reason was that I felt that, in psychological terms, I lacked experience and I took little pleasure in psychological experimentation; even during my time in Berlin I had steered clear of direct involvement. A stupid reason was that I did not give credence at all to the notion that one works one's way into the material with the energy that life happens to place at one's disposal; instead, I only invested energy in the things that I chose myself. It was important that I had always wanted to become involved with ethics, but knew of no suitable means of access. In other words, the important point was that I hadn't studied enough! {Scheler, after all, found a means of access!} It was significant, too, that I had imagined it to be more important to take whatever one wants from one's own self, and only to seek advice when one wants advice and further information. The first trial that life brought caused this strategy to collapse. One might also say: the dreamer tripped up the thinker.

Once again, a little later, I might have chosen to go down the natural path if, as a librarian, I hadn't tortured myself with creative writing without having the necessary tranquillity, but had rather said to myself that it was also possible to become a scholar outside the university as well. The time and the library were available. But I laid stress on the creative writer and, although I tried to keep in contact with psychology, I drifted away from it. Reason: division of interests whereby the major concern was with literature. The second cause that had an important part to play in the first case as well: my tendency to lack expedition when I have no particular goal, and even, on some occasions, when I have. High melancholic viscosity. Lack of curiosity "to get to know" what is happening, which is a quality that a scholar needs in large measure. I have never "taken a look around" my spiritual surroundings but have always buried my head in myself.

The other side: if, instead of collaboration in the *Vagabond*[16] and beginning the *Enthusiasts*, I had studied, made excerpts, even published, I should possibly, indeed probably, have moved away from literature and become an Andrian case.[17]

---

19) My tendency to read slowly has, in many respects, determined my fate. In spite of this I have, or at least I had, a capacity to assimilate quickly. [. . .]

---

24) I am debarred from becoming a creative writer in Austria:

My father {see 3)} spent his whole childhood and youth in Graz; he went to school there, from Kindergarten right through to obtaining his engineering qualifications; throughout his life he felt that he was a son of Graz, and what caused him the greatest pain was never being called to a Chair of Technology there. But he was born, by chance, in Temesvar and died in Brünn as an involuntary member of the Czechoslovak state.

His father came to Graz in his prime, choosing this as his home, practiced as a doctor there and then took up farming on an estate close to the town. But he was actually born in Rychtarow in Moravia.

My father's grandparents on his mother's side lived, and died, in Salzburg; my grandmother on my father's side was born there.

My grandmother on my mother's side is buried in Salzburg, so that three of my ancestors lie in the graveyard there.

My mother was born in Linz.

Her father was one of the four men who built the Linz-Budweis railway and later he was manager of the railway; I can still remember the grand house set in beautiful gardens in which my mother was born and where she spent her childhood. But this grandfather, whose connections with the local history of Linz are evidently of some significance, was born in Bohemia.

I myself was born in Klagenfurt.

I spent my childhood in Steyr—they spoke there the coarsest kind of Upper Austrian dialect that one could possibly desire.

Even Rosegger[18] was a relation of mine by marriage.

But none of the Provinces of the Federation lays claim to me.

---

25) Why not? Because they are too provincial to know me and nowhere is there a member of the family who would give a little help. But can I deny that the German Academy of Literature also failed to make me a member? It is said that, when a minority proposed me, the majority really did turn this down on the strange grounds that I was too intelligent to be a true creative writer.[19]

So there seems to be something about me and my life that has an influence on such things. "Man with pockets buttoned up . . . ."! But can one make deals with such people!

And yet by no means do I measure people who approach me in friendship with the same severity as I do strangers. Here there is an inconsistency in me that needs to be examined.

I show the same indifference whether I am behaving in a friendly or unfriendly way. It is only at the periphery that I behave in one way or the other. I can be very obliging—but is this for the right reasons? All my life my disposition has remained unstable, etc.

---

26) Let us start with the temperament. I am very taciturn, then suddenly words may come flooding out of me.

---

27) Ironic introduction: since criticism is forbidden[20] I have to indulge in self-criticism. No one will take exception to this since it is unknown in Germany.

---

28) I am, after all, quite naively convinced that the creative writer is the task that faces mankind; moreover, I want to be a great writer. How well I conceal my self-love from myself! [. . .]

---

30) On money: Martha, the poor orphan from a rich family, had just enough money to have about her the advantages of coming from a "good family," and too little money to be spoiled by it, as is usually the case with rich women. [. . .]

---

31) Again, on money: as a boy and a youth I held the rather naive view that money was a family possession and that, though it might be enjoyed by the parents, it had to be looked after in such a way that it would, in the course of time, come to me undiminished, or even increased. So I, too, made claims on the money and it seemed quite natural to me that I should devote myself exclusively to my education, up to the age of thirty. Having me as a son was not pleasant.

---

32) My father and his brothers, on the other hand, had renounced their portion of the inheritance from their father in order to increase their sister's dowry. As I write this, it occurs to me that my father was one of the last outlets of the Romantic movement.

---

33) [. . .] The way in which I laid claim to my wishes being fulfilled was that of a person of strong drives. I am "egotistical," albeit in a way that is restricted to certain themes. It is remarkable, at any rate, that I am now writing the MwQ chapters on feeling, with their renunciation of the drives.

---

34) At the age of 5 or 6 Martha had read the whole of Schiller, and every day, at the age of 7, was reading two novels from the lending library in Leipzigerstrasse[21] that she fetched for her grandmother and read quickly herself before she handed them over.

Her mother went walking a good deal and took little care of her. "But that was fine as far as I was concerned because I always did {was always able to do} what I wanted." At the age of ? she bought her clothes on her own.

This child's trait—doing what one wants to do, even if it is forbidden, keeping it out of the reach of criticism—has become a permanent trait in her life. Powerful instincts and secretive.

Another trait, unusually powerful in both of us, is that each wants to have the other entirely to him/herself.

---

35) Once, about the time when *Törleß* appeared, or only after that—at any rate at the time when he took some trouble over me—Kerr said to me that it was necessary for me to "allow my own style to write its way into the open," so to speak: he expressed this in the way that the French are supposed to say: "se faire la main." It is probably characteristic of me that I have to do this anew with each new book. I am unable to calculate in advance the length of any plan[ned work] if I have not written my way into it. [. . .]

---

37) Development of language: at the outset, excessive use of foreign words and nouns. {Retrospectively, I note how bad is the German of the translation of *Piacere*,[22] indeed what seductive weaknesses are to be found in the language of Nietzsche!} If challenged, I would probably have replied that this was "modern." Look for examples in old notebooks. First overwhelming experience in Stuttgart or in the first years in Berlin; I believe that the journal was called *Arena*[23] and that it published 2 or 3 sides of good prose from former times without giving the authors' names—these one had to guess. It was then, in this journal, or in a publication by Avenarius (competition within the memory), that I also found the explanation of the importance of the verb for style and the condemnation of substantivizations as an instance of contemporary decline;[24] I know that this was a revelation to me but that I found great difficulty in following the advice and was unable to make the necessary adjustments. Second influence: Kerr's careful criticisms at the proof stage of *Törleß*. Third: proofreading of the first volume of MwQ.

Typical of me that I never carried out any systematic studies and still work with very few reference works.

---

38) It is curious that Martha says she would be capable of stealing, but, at a spiritual level, she is enchantingly honest. Her existential technique is based on taking detours to find a way for her wishes.

Someone who was ill-disposed toward her might say that our life was built on the illusions of sexuality, on typical patterns of overvaluing and wanting to be overvalued. Both of us do indeed have a strong, inward-facing sexuality that is capable, however, of facing outward in a "headless" (that is, soulless) fashion. [. . .]

---

41) Relationship to politics: not even science is safe, let alone the creative writer. At some point or other—with regard to disinclination toward military drill, for example—he must always rely on his feeling. More correctly: the decision about what I believe is made in the act of writing. Beforehand, I believe that I believe many things, but, at the very moment when I represent something in words, it becomes impossible. This way of behaving is doubtless a source of error, but one has to take the creative writer just as he is—the state must either show tolerance or will cause creative writing to dry up.

---

42) Apolitical, too, from indifference to external circumstances. In other areas it is expressed in the way that I both loathe the literary film and am a "founder" of a society for its promotion.[25] (Karl Kraus would never have done anything like that.)

---

43) I left Vienna in 1931 because "Red" and "Black" agreed that, in Wildgans, they had lost a great Austrian writer.[26]

---

44) Yesterday (end of October 193[. .])[27] I had to make an extensive search in the second volume of MwQ and, in the evening, felt unhappy about my

botched art that comes from not being able to allow the manuscripts to ripen; this, in its effect, in terms of what is bequeathed to the world, is beyond the reach of any kind of excuse. Because I do not know what will happen, I weave the same words around every move between U[lrich] and A[gathe], and this is like a thick mixture, carefully applied, though its constituents are just a little different in each passage. The only hope is that this has involuntarily helped to produce something of epic scope; perhaps it is really like feeling one's way forward in life, just as one does in a conversation. But if only it had not yet been printed, and there was still an opportunity for cutting and tying together!

---

45) I am both well known and unknown, and this doesn't result in a midpoint "half well known" but in a remarkable mixture of the two.

---

46) When I was writing *The Enthusiasts* I deliberately didn't go to the theater. I wanted to make my own theater. The success of the play was in proportion to this intent.

(I am impressed at the way that Hofmannsthal—in Volume Two of his "Letters"—is at pains to do justice to the theater and to be a link in the great tradition.) [. . .]

---

48) It occurred to me, as I was listening to a lecture by an assistant of [. .] Schlick[28] on the application of "physicalism" to psychology, how, in Stumpf's[29] institute, everything was done in a far more precise manner. All credit for the sober, scientific atmosphere was due to this teacher and it was not by chance that his were the most important pupils. [. . .]

---

52) On 7.XII.37, gave a reading to an audience of 400 in the L. Hartm. Sq. Again had the impression that there is not much point to the authors of difficult works giving public readings if these are not preceded by explanatory courses—and even those would probably be of little use. It is likely to be a feature of a "free" educational system that people cannot assimilate what is offered to them. The superiority of a real university does not only con-

sist in the educational level of the audience and the quality of the academic staff, but much more in the coherence of the scheme of study and, preeminently, in the learning program that every student is set by the profession to which he aspires. Even a student can only absorb parts but he possesses his own "structure of intentions" into which he fits these parts.

---

53) Although I have never given as good a reading of "On Stupidity"[30] as I did yesterday, I became sharply aware both of its weaknesses and my own. This might be expressed in the following way—all my creations fail to say anything like: "Now you simply must listen to this!" Though they are born of the sternest kind of self-imposed inner compulsion, they do not have any urgent appeal; the will, which in the individual context {creative work} is strong, remains weak overall {with respect to communication}; it might also be said that this careful act of formulation is unable to discover the gesture appropriate for complete expression. To put this another way, I remain ensnared in the effort of thinking and do not lay stress on how to apply it. My spirit is not sufficiently practical.

---

54) In this context, the following thought occurred to me: dramatic form is strongly coerced—if it is to respond adequately to the requirements of the stage—into paying attention to a "receptive balance"; to take stock of itself "in actu"; to present something that is both beautiful and tightly knit. Nowhere in the drama should there be anything left over to drag behind and flap about; it should stick to the point, and the point has to be directed straight toward the audience. It is extremely sensitive in respect to the relationship between performance and reception by the audience. It is really necessary for a "whole" to emerge that does not tolerate even the quietest interruption (with the exception of the spiritual interruption).

From this perspective, even I can concede a high status to dramatic art and can understand a number of things that I otherwise fail to understand.

---

55) The compulsion that is exerted on any work—on the novel also—by the act of preparing the fair copy is not inconsiderable. What I write for the printing of the book itself is very much better than what I still allow to pass at the galley-proof stage. (MwQ Chapter, "General Stumm drops a bomb.")

Now the intention is firm and uniform; at last it excludes everything that, though it is equally justified, does not quite "make it," and this sets all the rest in the correct order. (The sequence also works in reverse.)

---

56) To learn a language completely involves a theatrical achievement. Language shapes character and bearing. It is not possible for me to speak as politely as a Frenchman and to be as stubborn as I am.

Or does the explanation lie in the way that, when abroad, we do not make the acquaintance of those spirits who correspond to ours, but come into contact with convention? [. . .]

---

58) (Variation on entry no. 53) Upon finishing each of my works, I fail to ask again: "Why am I producing this for the public?" and "What is it that I want?" And then, starting out from the answer to these questions—as long as it is not too arbitrary—I should work through the whole once again.

---

59) Sword and pen. To wield the pen like a sword is the ideal of many writers. Probably stems from the '48 period. But I grew up with the sword and am suspicious of this exchange. I know that I would have to fence with a wax candle!

---

60) Possible title: "You and I" (Community-Individual)

Compensation at the level of a historical unconscious for the upsurge of collectivity: individual psychology and psychoanalysis. Never before was there so much concern for the dear "I." It is true that religion, too, used to be concerned, but only under the supervision of a moral code. Only the authoritarian states are compensating for this.

---

61) After the death of d'Annunzio, flags were at half-mast throughout Italy and Mussolini journeyed to visit the bier with his general staff. Sinister paying of respects under orders.

I would put it as follows: he was a good patriot to the extent that he was a good creative writer. But people reverse this, saying that he was a good writer because he was a good patriot. Is it only Fascism that does this? With Th[omas] M[ann], under modified circumstances, the same thing would happen!

———————

62) I have a minimal need to communicate: I am a deviation from the standard type of writer.

———————

63) I am ungrateful. [. . .]

———————

65) My morality has probably always been that which was hinted at in Volume I as "the morality of the gentleman."[31] Irreproachable in everyday matters but, at a higher level, immoralism. But now the cry is: "Decide!" This is the effect of these decades that are the stuff from which history books are made. [. . .]

———————

67) In the course of the 10 or so manuscripts for what are only 200 pages of the first part of MwQ, I have reached the significant insight that the most appropriate style of writing for me is that of irony. It is on a par with the importance of the break with the ideal of depicting larger-than-life examples. [. . .] On a par, too, with the insight that a creative writer should not go so far as to produce a philosophic system (nor is he able to do so). [. . .]

———————

69) One of the main ideas, or illusions, of my life has been that spirit has its own history and, without regard to everything that happens in practice, rises higher step by step. I have held the belief that the time of its catastrophes is past. It is from this angle that my relationship to politics is to be understood. [. . .]

———————

70) As a young being, you find yourself one day in an unknown region of which only the most immediate parts are familiar to you. There are people with you who point out to you the paths to be taken next and then leave you, even though they occasionally return. In this region, which contains things that tempt and things that frighten, you now begin to lay cautious hold of whatever attracts you, and to come to terms with whatever frightens you. Thus you start to construct a relationship with the world that is at once active and soulful. I believe that that is the usual point of departure at which a human being finds himself and that, for most creative writers, represents the beginning of their activity. Traces, for example, in Th[omas] Mann.

Different in my case.[32] Began aggressively and found my bearings by forcing the image of the world into the highly imperfect frame of my ideas. I mean, of course, only that I did this to a greater extent than others. The desire to dictate the law is distinct from the desire to find a favorable position for oneself and different from the astonished question: "How is it that I came to be lying here at all?"—the notion might be expressed in roughly these terms.

Only within the context that one has previously shaped for oneself does the strong realism of thought find expression in words.

And it is only in my mid-forties that I caught up with the astonished questions: "How have I become who I am?" "Have I come out right?," etc. [. . .]

---

72) One of my "aesthetic" principles has always been the following: the opposite, the contradiction of every rule of art is also possible. No artistic insight can claim to be the whole truth. Or something like that.

Since I am nothing if not a skeptic I proceeded thence to attempts at formulating concepts such as "Ratioïd" and "Non-ratioïd," and later to the manifold relationship of feeling and truth that is intimated in MwQ. {Indeed, I have built up a whole philosophy of life on this.}

But my life so far has lacked any confrontation with academic aesthetics, e.g., with the concept of judgments of taste.

"It doesn't concern me at all!" which is the artist's view of art theory, remains an issue that I have largely failed to resolve; this instinctive reluctance.

---

73) Yesterday evening I read the beginning of *Niels Lyhne* and, yet again, could not remember anything at all about it!

This beginning contains much that is very beautiful, but I could hardly stand the methodical way in which he carries out his descriptive program. I fear that this will also be said of me when the reasons for the detail—ones that I myself create—have aged and turned to dust.

The only elements of lasting value would then be realism and temperament (meant in the sense of Nietzsche's aphorisms) and yet, if something is restricted to these, immediately a yearning for more spiritual substantiality appears! How can this problem be solved? [. . .]

---

75) Whoever reads *Attempts to love a monster*[33] and similar pieces might believe that I found inspiration in Tolstoy. Appearances do really argue this. So it is remarkable that, though I liked *Resurrection* when I was young, the whole of Tolstoy's religious side was of complete indifference to me. It was only when I read *War and Peace* in the course of working on the second instalment of Volume II of MwQ that T. took this side of me by storm—for, in the meantime, such a side had grown within me. [. . .]

---

77) The relationship between the creative writer and his times. That one does not move in step but stays behind, loses contact, does not contribute, and suchlike. I was receptive, in a specifically literary way, to Dostoievsky, Flaubert, Hamsun, d'Annunzio, and others—there was not one contemporary in the whole group! They wrote 20–100 years earlier! [. . .]

---

79) When I think what successes I have had to watch! From Dahn[34] and Sudermann[35] through to Stefan George and Stef. Zweig![36] And they explain it away as snobbery or decadence when one despises the public! Explain to yourself how things really are. [. . .]

---

81) [. . .] Shouldn't it be admitted that I simply lacked the courage to present those philosophical matters that concerned me as a thinker and in works of scholarship? And shouldn't it be said that this is the reason why such things break into my narratives "via the back door," making them impossible? This occurred to me once again in the context of the "theory" of

opinion (and thus also the theory of feelings) as I was sorting it out in my mind for the final section of the second instalment of Volume II.

I could make the excuse that philosophy did not provide me with the foundation; but it is also an expression of my nature in which both interests are united and are perhaps not properly defined in relation to one another.

It occurs to me that, in my youth, a ban on all "instructive material" was part of my aesthetic "medicine chest": anything that can be expressed better in rational terms, indeed anything that can be expressed in rational terms at all, should not form part of a creative work. It seems that, in that respect, I have later made some compromises. [. . .]

---

86) [. . .] The young girl, the woman-child in MwQ,[37] has often given me pause for thought about whether inclinations like this are perverse. Today, as I observed children who were seriously disrupting my work, I have come to see things clearly.

Girls between the ages of 11 and 15 have beautiful legs. They are long, good at running, and do not have the solidity that comes later when they will have to carry the heavy, voluminous sections of belly and buttocks. The hair has the sheen of youth. The face is pure and often indicates the beauty to come without being spoiled by the expression of pettiness, self-centeredness and retarded spirit. The eyes are full of dreams and fire, i.e., they still have the idealism of youth, while the emptiness of the idealism is not apparent. See the remark on art and infantilism. The thighs, though they already have some female fullness to them, are magnificent.

The weaknesses of the body, i.e., at this age the chest and the child's belly, are concealed by the clothing that suggests the adult shape.

In other words, these children are really lovable, and it is not in the least perverted that they provoke this feeling.

Perversity only makes an appearance if a person feels a desire to abuse this dream of form in reality. Then he has to disregard the spirit and innocence {or helplessness} of the child, and also the absence of a sexual response; it is as if he wanted to go to bed with a doll or like a rutting frog, clasping a piece of wood. [. . .]

---

88) My concept of literature, my support for it as a whole, is probably the counterweight to my aggression toward individual creative writers. It is certainly true that, wherever I approve of someone, I do so without reserva-

tion; but I am much more often repelled than attracted. In the course of time this may have turned into a bad habit. This is why I have formed a utopian concept of literature.

When I eventually find time to write about the matter I must make this central to my approach: always give to literature what I deny to the individual writer! [. . .]

---

90) *Unions*, access: a writer, an epigone in the best sense of the term (i.e., an unblemished traditionalist, untroubled by anything out of place) wrote a review, saying that I had no understanding of the nature of the novella as this was expressed in the simile of the falcon. (Probably meaning that in a well-fashioned narrative the sense had to rise up, at the decisive moment, like a falcon—according to C.F. Meyer[38] or Keller).[39] He had no inkling of the distaste for the act of narration that lay behind these two novellas. Against narration, against pseudo-causality and pseudo-psychology. And thus about the path toward the principle of the "movere" motif and the extreme form that its structure took on. But where did the mistakes come from? From the meticulous work of not-being-caught-up-and-carried-along-oneself. From the mismatch between the interest in the project and that in the execution. From the (not ignoble) principle of the heaviest load placed on the shortest step forward. But this can then lead to the derivation of a moral code, a morality of time at rest.[40] See the analogous remark on the sheet with the principles of the MwQ. Thus the main mistake was that the principle was not developed. Antidote that this is to be elicited from the work. *Unions*, then, is also [a] link in a chain of development.

---

91) How little pleasure I derive from dividing up the day I am describing into tenths of a second! Which is the reason why I have sometimes been compared with Proust. The optimum of essentiality is rather different from a maximum amount of time filled in, or from detailed analysis. The difference is similar to that between meticulousness and logical precision.

Whoever fails to see the embattled nature of my work will not see its precision, but only something that can be confused with precision.

Objection: is the imperturbability of the lion always distinguishable from that of the nibbling mouse? [. . .]

---

94) The story of my life ought to be interesting—although I am a very disciplined writer, rigorous in my approach, there are all kinds of defects in my ancestry. My quiet grandparents. Their "original" sons. The epileptic son who died young and had an "insular" memory for figures. The ancestor who suffered from insanity—at the moment I do not know whether he is part of the genetic line or an offshoot of it.

Transmitted to me psychically by my mother. I shall fulfill her wish and not speak ill of her. The heroic and noble side of her character, her childlike love of father and brothers. What else can be said of her. Nervous constitution very vulnerable to stimulation; violent temper and tendency to worry away at an irritation to the point of explosion. Temper giving way to convulsive sobbing. These events dependent on inner ones. Days of intense happiness or comparative harmony, followed inexorably by one in which she drifted toward an outburst. What connection this had with her marriage is unclear. She held my father in high regard but he did not match her inclinations—she was attracted more by the masculine type of man. Later she developed some protohysterical traits. But she was conspicuously incapable of deceit, or of putting on an act. So, in her case, it was probably more a nervous failure to come to terms with something that in turn led to a kind of convulsive reaction (of the sort that is found in weak individuals even if they do not suffer from hysteria). This was the nature of her struggle to win my love and admiration as a son.

But there was never any quarrel between the parents over which of them was to hold sway over the child.

Always took the form of an outburst of temper. On the one hand my response came from the same disposition; I, too, am vehement by nature, I, too, am prone to nervous intensification of feeling instead of reaching a calm decision. I have never become acquainted with this latter reaction, which is the normal one. My father only attempted to influence me by benign admonition. I always had the impression that he stood to one side during these quarrels. As if he did not want to give a ruling. He was a strange person. On the other hand, I was also under the influence of the boyish-masculine realm and did not want to cede this territory in a quarrel with a woman. So the relationship also possessed, without our noticing it, a kind of sexual polarity. When I was about ten years of age these scenes became so intense (an intellectual protest was probably also involved; I wanted to have "spiritual" independence, and it was a recurrent reproach that I was not childlike and loving) that, with all three of us agreeing, I was sent to a college.

One of the considerations, as far as my father was concerned, was the prospect of a career.[41]

Continuation. Clear traces in the spiritual constitution.

95) The description of an "Imperial and Royal Military Institution for Instruction and Education" {Post-classical, Stifteresque or similar designation} would be strange enough, even without regard for the importance of boarding school pupils for politics later on.

The transformation in *Törleß*.

The truth—does this belong in the era of Franz Joseph or is it of earlier origin? There was still something about it of the principle that the officer should emerge from the ranks. 48? Spirit of the frontier? Same idea as the old cadet school? I would need to read up about this. "Spartan," let us say.

{Suddenly today, I remembered being surrounded by a lot of artillery officers at the academy. Love of this uniform that is brightly colored but restrained; but in those days I didn't feel any love.}

With the exception of my time at the academy, my education was best suited to N.C.O.s. The teaching assistants and the class sergeant (and my opposition to him). The rig-outs and the shoes. The parade uniform that didn't fit properly and the school outfits that defied all description. Worse than convicts. The washrooms and the disinfectant capsules. The latrines.

Together with this, an image of the school field in Eisenstadt with the pupils doing gymnastics all over the place.

Is the concern for cleanliness that I still have today an overcompensation?

Why didn't my parents protest? Still incomprehensible today. My God!

96) It was often said to me when I was a child and a youth "You are like your grandfather (on your father's side)" In other words: stubborn, energetic, successful {too}, awkward in company—but this said with an undertone of respect. It was never followed through into matters of detail, never explained and assessed. It always gave me pleasure to hear it. Such remarks made to children are important; they change imperceptibly into guiding stars, give fruitful support to one's love of self, etc. The remarkable aspect is the part played here by things only half expressed, that stimulate the imagination. This has something of the nature of a literary comparison.

97) The mountain in Steyr, the Kirchberg. The big, (probably) young and heavy horse that, (probably) in play, lunged at my chest with its muzzle or at least made as if to do so. The enormous fright I got, pressed against the side of the house with no opportunity to get out of the way since the pave-

ment was very narrow. Probably surprise affected me as well. Stayed with me all my life as timidity with horses (indeed with animals of all kinds). The aftereffects of such moments are said to be so very decisive. (Came about mainly because I was not taught straightaway how to handle horses, though my father would have been able to do this.) [. . .]

---

103) I remember that Hofmannsthal praised "Grigia" highly, but objected that, in his opinion, it was regrettable that I had not paid more attention to the construction of the story, to the frame. I remember that I answered that I had done so deliberately—and I probably explained why as well—without going any more deeply into this question.

Today it occurs to me that I have always considered his objection to be right and criticized myself for the same failing; haste and, in part, indifference have become fixed in the memory as causes for this.

But this story belongs to the same period as Alpha[42] which was even more of a disaster, and some kind of principle could also be set up in front of it (for willing judges! Just think that Werfel's *Weltanschauung* has found people willing to promote it!) For example: a picture in which all the light, all the power of color is concentrated on particular parts and all the rest is diffused (e.g., as with Munch, into peripheral perception). The accentuation comes not through accumulation but neglect. This is represented. Of course, it would be possible, with the same intention, to insert poor verses into a poem! The principle is probably wrong. But as something transitory, subjective and one-sided it could serve as a source of some interest.

And one somehow works with different degrees of intensity and depth. One does this involuntarily, and the so-called "principle" would only be an exaggeration.

It might also be said that it has something of the alternating of light and dark, picking out detail and smudging over, forte and piano. At the moment I am completely unclear about what this means and what its limits are!

---

104) This is partly an unintended continuation of the last note. I have had a copy of *The Enthusiasts* sent on to me [. . .], and am sending this to Lányi;[43] I have leafed through it for the first time for years and read some passages again. I was surprised by the beauty and power of the language and also by the strong sense of a guiding principle at the beginning. In their

day they caused quite a stir, but today they are as good as forgotten—what an injustice that is! For, however many mistakes they may have, they contain elements of the great continuum that makes only rare appearances!

Then I tired of reading (even I got tired!) and now I ask myself whether I made a serious mistake and, if so, what it might have·been. I set down here what I noted immediately after reading the work:

The execution,[44] the "engine," has no "neutral." But the layout of the characters and problems can be grasped quickly—probably because it makes such a strong impact—and the actual execution does not add anything essential to this. This is why the latter is so bothersome and tiring.

But the execution, for me, constantly added new, essential elements, indeed this was precisely the law behind it. So a rift must have opened between what was essential for me (which may even have been intrinsically essential) and what was essential for the reader or audience.

Before my eyes hovered the law of the higher life itself—this was my intention. It is said that, wherever there is a confrontation or a decision has to be taken, no moment can be empty, no link can be slack. Life should be motivated [. . .] to the highest degree, as should dramatic art, too. That was the view I held, and still do hold, to a certain degree. In my eyes, it is precisely here that the importance of *The Enthusiasts* is to be found.

Confronting this are the "laws of dramatic art" that I have so often mocked as "suitcase" and "cookery book dramatics." Probably the onset of fatigue that sets in is its revenge. A drama has to have passages where it runs "in neutral," places where one rests, adulterations, etc. And, corresponding with, and counterposed to these, it must have points of concentrated illumination, etc. This may well be linked to the everyday psychology of comprehension, but the purpose of a drama is not, after all, like that of a religious or philosophical document.

In any revision of the work I shall probably have to start out from this contrary principle and then compare the results. [. . .]

---

111) My grandfather[45] was a man who had broken out of his circle and, in so doing, achieved success. My father operated entirely within the context that was set for him, adapting to the opportunities that were available, and only in the latter stages (Vienna, Graz) did success elude him. Alois shared the same fate as my grandfather, his great-uncle.

---

112) "On the sidelines," "living 'on the sidelines'"—or some such term—as a title would fit—at least inwardly—the nature of the work and the attitude to the powerful actions that happen in the contemporary world. It also fits the relationship to literature, and now, finally, this experience of being thrown out.

Title: *Sketches of a Writer.* [. . .]

---

114) "He is the greatest creative writer alive today!" They ought to say: "the greatest I can understand!" [. . .]

---

118) One no longer speaks about oneself (as one did when young) but about the things with which one is concerned. Talking about politics, for example, is the equivalent excess in manhood. In both cases one speaks far too much. Of young people's interest in themselves it might be said that it is interest in the instrument.

---

119) a) He: belongs to the type that is "fire smoldering in the ashes." Characteristic expression would be: "I told you . . years ago that the way you walk is most beautiful!" As far as he is concerned, that is that; there is no need for it to be repeated.

b) She: she finds it right and proper that people are less interested in her than in him. But anyone who likes her she repays in kind.

Sometimes she is irritable and aggressive for no reason—just like some children who only show affection after they have been beaten. But watch out if she really meant it and felt that she had a reason! Then she would not forget a harsh rejoinder.

---

120) What an error it was to feel flattered when philosophers and scholars sought out my company and set greater store by my books than by others! They were not appreciating the philosophical core {(meaning)} but were thinking that here was a creative writer who understood theirs!

---

121) I do not enjoy talking (nor, in any spontaneous way, do I like writing)—what a paradoxical quality for a creative writer! But, unlike philosophers, I don't preoccupy myself with things that are totally burned to a cinder. I am like a dog, taking his bone off to a quiet spot, in that I allow the things I have thought over (either in the course of conception or in the process of perception) time to settle; often they are never seen again, sometimes they wait until appropriated by some new insight. One might call such a person, in some measure, "imaginative." But there are two kinds of imagination: the active and the utterly absorbed. Mine was the imagination of the quiet child, utterly lost within himself and transfixed by a tendency to make up stories. [. . .]

---

123) "I do not know what it is that makes life worth living" might be the way to put it. What appeals to others does not appeal to me. This has been so since childhood—with few exceptions. This is the joyless and "nonappetitive" human being. According to the psychology that predominates at present wouldn't one expect me to take my pleasure through the medium of writing? But I do not enjoy writing, though I write with passion. Probably one has to love life in order to write with facility. It has to exert an attraction, partly via a detour through the satisfaction of writing. What kind of special case is a human being who takes no pleasure in that? [. . .]

---

125) M[artha] is reading the *Country Doctor* (*Le Médecin de campagne*) by Balzac. We speak about how knowledgeable he is in a wide variety of areas. Then I say: "This is often the impression that a writer gives—he grasps a handful of knowledge and one thinks it is much more than it is." It is more a case of intensity of narration than of knowing. So this characteristic belongs in the realm of the aesthetic.

---

126) A childhood trait was my brooding in the melancholy of the room, perhaps one should mention that this usually happened with a beloved toy or some such object. This was the root of the "mani di stoppa," the offhand treatment even of spiritual matters and the theory of the "other" condition.

---

127) (End of September 1939 in Geneva.) Yesterday while looking for something I leafed through many notebooks, and this ended in deep depression. Sometimes a good idea, hardly ever any progress. Admittedly this is partly because whole notebooks are concerned with some special situation, with *Unions* for example. But I have never taken anything beyond the opening stages (though I have finished the books that have the scars to show for it). It would have been so easy to arrange the reflections in proper order; these would have made treatises or books that would, together, have amounted to a modest life's work. But I didn't want to do that, nor do I feel capable even today of doing this. That is how Note 126 emerged. Yesterday I had the impression of a person who is of no value and who was not destined to achieve anything of importance.

---

128) [. . .] It occurs to me, that, if there is any chance of redemption, then it should come not by using these notebooks as a source for what I write, because I shall never be able to bring these thoughts to any conclusion, nor even to a state where they are of significance; I must rather write on the subject of these notebooks, judging myself and their content, depicting aims and obstacles. That would unite the biographical with the factual, these two plans that for long have competed with each other.

Title: *The Forty Notebooks*[46]

Attitude: that of a man who doesn't agree even with himself.

---

129) I'm appending 3 papers that have had a profound affect on me:

"Mort du prof. Freud" (good overview).

"Cournot and the Philosophy of Mathematics."

"Modern Polish Philosophy." [. . .]

---

132) My modesty: I am a person who possesses a multifaceted ignorance of things. (This, on specifying my reading requirements to a librarian.) ((My lack of knowledge has very many facets to it.)) [. . .]

---

134) One of the strongest old impressions from the War gradually crept up on me [. . .]—that I was suddenly simply surrounded by people who never

read a book; who could not imagine that writing any kind of books other than those concerned with a particular specialism could be a respectable activity; and who considered reading the newspaper, and nothing but the newspaper to be entirely proper. I believe that there was at most one man in every battalion who knew what reading is about. What an unexpected and wide-ranging contact with the life of average people! (See the note on the specialist advisory committee that did nothing but read the newspapers of large political parties.) [. . .]

---

136) A stove (porcelain or tiled stove) cannot be opened at whatever time one wants to do so—explanation of why the work, even when it is only creeping forward or when I am not working at all, does not permit one to write a letter.

---

137) It seems to be a typical situation in my life: here I am in Geneva and nobody knows me; I am not invited to any event that has anything to do with art; Prof. Bohn [. .],[47] the petty Pope, cuts me. And the situation is similar throughout Switzerland. It is reminiscent of Brünn in my early youth where Strobl was held to be a phenomenon of the very highest promise, and I was just a hack churning out paraphrases.[48] [. . .]

---

139)[49] In the morning had the spontaneous idea (that actually belongs to one's 40th or 50th year, but not to the 60th): who, what manner of man are you? What are your principles? How to you propose to round things out?

At any rate, a writer of the present epoch. With great success and little success. That much is interesting.

Often, the strong need to break off everything I'm doing. At such times, consider my life a failure. Have no confidence in myself, but drag myself along with my work, and every two or three days, for one moment, what I'm writing seems to me to be important. The way that I formulate the questions about my experiences and principles has also to conform to this condition. Not because it might be interesting but because it happens within an existential crisis. That would shed enough light onto the surrounding epoch.

Decision (how long will it survive?): this is the way I want to write the book for my 60th year! This is the way I could draw up the opening lines. [. . .]

142) How much more afraid of death one is when one is young! At night in my room as a child, the idea of its inescapability. The plea for eternal life for oneself and one's parents and the comfort that came with facile belief in eternity. And, beforehand, the annihilating pain of the idea.

When only 17 years of age, fear of the fortress-artillery because one is inescapably trapped in the building and one renounces the imaginary possibility of taking evasive action and starting a counterattack. In hand-to-hand combat one could be happy and skillful.

In 1914 and as early as 19. ? . [sic] (Bosnian mob[ilization]) it was different, it was "other." The atavistically mystical experience of mob[ilization] in 1914. In the War itself seldom any moments when one feared death. On going to sleep in the midst of houses on the Isonzo, some of which had been destroyed. Awareness in the Val Sugano that a new long-range artillery piece was trained on us (at night). But on the other hand (Lago d'Ezze near Palai), fell asleep in the sun in a clearing that was "under observation." More frequently than moments filled with the fear of death were those of joy in death. See the description in "Grigia." Avalanche and hobgoblin-light. Marching up to the positions on the Isonzo.

One might also think of how nocturnal or nervous fear dissolves in the face of reality; as with operations.

Also, the older one gets the more one comes to terms with things.

One is less attached to life (one is fed up with it). On the one hand because one knows its sadness, etc., on the other because the drives are no longer so hungry and keen (sharp knives) as they are in one's youth. Also, with time, one adapts oneself to what is inescapable. That is a great salvation.

To what extent does a relationship emerge that is both positive and under the influence of the metaphysical? Change came with the death of my mother.

(Most of this holds true for mankind in the two Great Wars.)

---

143) "Common-law wife"—during the time when it was in power, social democracy produced (along with many quite dubious existential ideas) this expression and this concept. "Wife" without any sacrament or state compulsion. Just dignity of human life. Sharing joy and sorrow over the course of many years is not a passion but something that pertains more to the constitution—being destined to bear life together. Its enormous ambivalence and unreliability. One is destined, from childhood, for such a sharing. One wants to have the "common-law wife" before sexuality is in place and ready

for action. Such people can be destined for each other. Sex is one of the natural forces to which they are exposed together. They do not arouse it in one another, they receive it from one another. It is good if they did not meet as virgins. They transform treachery into trust. Neither robs the other of a piece of the world. It is part of the situation that one admires the other to the extent that each requires. Or that, if this is not the case (beauty, lyricism), that this is understood. Or that they share their amazement [. . .] at sharing each other's lives. "Complementing each other" is pleasant, but admiration and amazement must be present as well. Yielding in such a way that one's stubborn will does not feel insulted that the yielding is too general, etc.—here there are many individual aspects. I knew a happy marriage: he was ambitious and successful in a theatrical way, her ambition took the shape of intrigue, she promoted his interests by repeated acts of adultery of which he knew nothing except for his wonder at the {miraculous} successes. In general, partnerships are better when the adultery and suchlike has happened beforehand.

---

144) I shall at some time be forced to explain my interest in "shallow" experimental psychology while Freud, Klages, and even phenomenology do not. [. . .]

---

145) In the field of technology, too, I have come into contact with some important developments through the course of my life. My teacher, Wellner,[50] with his glider wheel construction and the studies that accompanied it; forgotten today, but it is not beyond the bounds of possibility that these ideas could be of importance in the future. (Look this up and write about it.) The development of the turbine, from the one that my father could not quite get to work in Klagenfurt to its present importance. Possibly, the last design my father made for a [turbine?] control system, which was unsuccessful. (Ask Zeis[51] if this is registered with the Patents Office?) Kaplan,[52] Diesel,[53] and my father. The development of electrotechnology has occurred almost exclusively in this period, and so has that of synthetic chemistry. [. . .]

---

147) At the age of 17 and 18—probably under the influence of the books I was reading (it was the period of transition when the "barbarian" turned to

culture)—I imagine the powdered [. . .] Rococo to be very beautiful; woman as spirit, illusory sheen and sexuality. A certain degree of satisfaction with this triad has remained with me right up till now. In order to understand how things were originally I must add that I could not have given any account whatsoever of my sense of beauty. For me, the beauty of a woman did not exist, it had not yet been determined. I was not able to imagine how the kind of woman I wanted might look. That was probably connected with my lack of talent in the realm of the plastic arts, but in the main it was the absence of any experience of beauty. Out of different shallow experiences of what I liked, only disparate and non-binding details were left that were distressingly insubstantial and incoherent. It is probably the case that only the full factual experience of love, the calm that comes with "faits accomplis" (in other words this is all guided by the sexual urge), fixes the response to certain stimuli. (By the way, the ideal Libussa type—Jarmila Novotná[54]—that emerged under those original conditions has to this day {the capacity} to work a kind of spell on me.) [. . .]

---

149) It is part of my relationship to politics [. . .] to be dissatisfied. Dissatisfaction with my fatherland has been precipitated in the gentle irony of MwQ. But I am also convinced of the unviability of capitalism and the bourgeoisie without being able to make a decision in favor of its political opponents. Certainly it is in order for spirit to be dissatisfied with politics. But the spirit that does not know how to compromise will appear too individualistic to men who attempt to find a balance.

---

150) M[artha]'s mother deceased, her aunt did not prepare her for anything. Severe bleeding and pain on the wedding night. Even beforehand she had imagined it would be like going to the dentist. This most sensual creature experiences yielding to the lover for the very first time as something very unpleasant to be simply endured.

[. . .]

Unimaginable, the posthumous idolizing and love; but perhaps as a consequence of the beautiful memories, sexuality is more strongly focused, with less freedom for, and compliance with the drives.

---

151) At the age of 11, despite all her reading, M[artha] had no clear idea of sex. Heine's "I want to put my finger in your wound" seemed to her to have significance of some kind.

R[obert] was 4 years old at that time.[55] [. . .]

---

153) To start out from reality: the coexistence of interests within me that have quite different dimensions. The future and the guilt of Germany and of the world, and my need to present my work in the right way. This may be troublesome but it is, at the same time, the real point from which I start out.

Sketches of just one writer would be to express this impersonally. But I would also need to have some way of taking, if not my work, then at least my (erstwhile) intention seriously. To the extent to which this leads to the present set of problems grouped around the MwQ this would be comparatively easy. But how are the older things to be dealt with? Non-contemporary writer, famous and unknown in equal measures? Overall, the opposite of the "Great Writer"? Or simply reconstruction of the almost incomprehensible path. Starting out from the period of youth that feels the stirring of genius within its body—that force that makes every thing "other" than it is? But, for that, it would be necessary to determine the endpoint, the condition in which the process of writing things down would take place. Am I under the sway of hope—and what kind of hope—or of fatigue? The truth is, probably, that I have had more than enough. But that is not a state for creativity. The truth is that I do not lay claim to success. But why don't I? I am so close to it! The answer would probably lead to utopia or to the utopian preconditions of my work. {The individual works were always set in motion by some chance factor!} It would lead to: literature as utopia, to the human being who is non-appetitive but contemplative—and there is much that provides biographical support for this. The way to complete this would have to be to determine his function and task in the real world. (See Hexner's[56] repeated question: "But how do you envisage that in real terms?" The author's evasion in some partial solution.) There follows from this, finally—the—?—[*sic*] {ecstatic} society that I touch upon in various places in the current sections of MwQ.

In essence this would be a long essay; an essay that would be given its precise contours in the attempt to write it up. How it might be divided up into aphorisms is a matter for later; also what similar questions there might be to round this out.

It's probably best simply to make an attempt. [. . .]

155)

[. . .]

It is remarkable that I have never had any sense of dance rhythm. It is not clear to me why this is so.

My first memories have something to do with hopping, but there is no detail.

It was probably the dancing lesson at Alber's place.

He was the builder of whole streets after the style of the Pforzheim silver. Later he probably had to live in much reduced circumstances, but in those days he lived in two floors of a three-storey house that he had built for rental. It was in his house that I saw the first inside staircase. My physical memory of him tends to merge a little with those of pictures of Wagner.

Children of professors and the like, and textile barons.

At the beginning I chose Elsa v. Czuber as my love. Emanuel (?) v. Cz., Professor of Mathematics at the Technical University in Brünn, later in Vienna. I later read a book by him about probability calculus. His daughter married an Austrian Archduke who gave up his peerage for her. Her feelings for me were ones of utter indifference.

I retain a memory of the beautiful growth of her long, dark-blond, silk-soft, well-brushed hair. This memory has clearly been absorbed into the MwQ.[57]

But her name was Elsa, like my sister who died before I was born and who was the object of a kind of cult of mine. Evidently there are connections here! (In truth, I did not carry on any cult; but this sister interested me. I sometimes used to wonder what it would be like if she were still alive— would I be the person who was closest to her? Did I put myself in her place? There was no motive to do so. However, I do remember from the time when children wore a smock that I, too, sometimes wanted to be a girl. I tend to see this as a reduplication of eroticism. But the most probable connection is one with my later conduct at balls. [. . .])

Even as an engineer attending the first balls, I didn't enjoy dancing, even though I was not particularly bad at it, but liked withdrawing with a dancing partner to one of the adjoining rooms or refreshment areas, quite indifferent to the way this compromised her. What I experienced was, in fact, a literary situation (literature then?); it was not a real personal relationship at all.

---

156) Part of a biography:

The {A} town without Jews. (Steyr)

Brünn (The wisdom of that old animal (Austria)). The juxtaposition. The very slow filtering {and other principles (selection of professors, etc.)} With which the wisdom of the old animal failed to come to terms: Czechs, self-confident social democracy. How I was saved from disgrace and B[rünn] did not get me as a theater critic.

M[ährisch]W[eißkirchen]-Hranice[58] (The arsehole of the Devil.) {cf. 163).}[59] Cavalry cadets and pupils at a technical school for the military. The true story of Törleß. The old N.C.O. spirit of military education. Different in the Academy and sudden difficulty in taking leave of it.

Possibly the year of military service[60] and later the famous Major B[echer][61] through to Head of the Department of the Praesidium.

Berlin before 1914. The impassive faces of the students, and the Institute of Psychology.

---

158)

I would not be certain that I was another person when I first set about reading Dostoyevsky's *The Player*, then found that I didn't enjoy it beyond the first ten pages, and did not read any further. That was several years ago. Now I am reading it with great pleasure. The opposite experience (*Vanity Fair* for example) is seemingly more comprehensible.

"Oh, how I loathe all that! How much pleasure it would bring to turn my back on it all!"[62] This cumbersome kind of moral rejection is Russian and—Czech. Today it reminds me of the impossible tone of Russian newspapers.

Moreover, throughout this whole novel, the talk is of an overcompensation for the Russian feeling of inferiority.

And, in the face of this love that he depicts so superbly, I repeat, full of enmity: D. did not have a trace of love within him when he wrote that. (And I am much too closely identified with my "ultimate love story"!)[63] [. . .]

---

164) [. . .] God: how, instinctively, the formula takes shape: "Unknown, higher being, I set down my thanks and my pleas in the furthest corner of the outermost forecourt!"

Given that the relationship to God is shaped after the image of a human relationship, which one is this then?!

Given that it is only the expression of a feeling (the feeling of a need), then a feeling only takes its expression and its organization from experience (in the way that I describe it in Tb I).[64] Whence does the need for God take on the specific form in which it is expressed?

Throughout my life I have neither felt any antipathy toward such humility and modesty, nor have I considered it to be necessary—so where did the idea of such a superior being come from and why was it seen as natural to subject oneself to him?

Is there an urge to subjection and self-abasement? The skeptic says: "infantile reminiscence." But is such a firmly organized feeling conceivable without prior experience or merely on the basis of childhood experience? Or is it no more and no less than just a particular feeling, one of a kind? Does not the maintenance of the childlike relationship (the theologians speak of being "children of God"!) also require an explanation? Perhaps it lies in our failing, in this matter, to get beyond childlike belief and through to knowledge? These are, admittedly, strong doubts! [. . .]

---

166) Indecisiveness: the quality that has caused me most suffering, and that I fear the most.

---

167) My exclusion and self-exclusion from Germany can be partly explained in the following way: in 1914 I was in a crisis. I did not like the way I was expected to progress—by concerning myself with young writers whom I was to promote with the *Neue Rundschau*.[65] I was suffering from the aftereffects of *Unions*—the effort and then the flop. *The Enthusiasts* were a fog of spiritual material with no dramatic skeleton (see the first drafts). My essays[66] gave me no satisfaction, the notes to various subjects were perhaps not uniformly uninteresting, but nothing gave the impression of being vital.

The War came over me like a sickness, or rather like the accompanying fever.

For its duration and afterward I had so much on my hands with the *Enthusiasts* and the emerging MwQ that at least half of me had no connection with what was emerging in the world.

I have a volume of the *N[eue] R[undschau]* in my hand [. . .] with the essays on Goethe's Jubilee;[67] among them the one on "Nationalist Youth" by Friedr. Franz v. Unruh.[68] For the first time I realize that I would necessarily have been disliked by up-and-coming writers, even though they would not have been unaffected by my work, and I realize why this would have been so. If this author had taken any notice of me at all he would certainly have misunderstood every word I uttered; I have committed my old error of not concerning myself with what the others want, and not reading them at all.

---

168)[69] [. . .] I review the main points of misunderstanding in the order in which they occur to me:

Desperate situation of German youth in 1919: disarmed, and weighed down with intolerable burdens until they reach old age.

Their urge to make their mark looks for some avenue of expression. Hence the formation of groups—in particular those with an air of being distinct. In nationalism the young person proves his competence by the fact that he exists; school bench and study, the demand for mere ability are seen, in the light of this urge to be somebody of consequence, as obstacles.

The soldier who has served at the front stands in the way of the urge to be somebody. Astonishing: the young say: "We would have held out, you were deserters and cowards!" They feel suspicion and contempt for those who were soldiers.

Those teachers gain in influence who say that the love for the Republic and for peace is mediocre and against good blood. They say that bad blood lacks the capacity for dedication and the readiness for sacrifice.

Organization and disorganization (U[nruh] does not see it this way). Above all, the NSDAP. German National Association of Shop Assistants (several hundred thousand members)—not affiliated to any party, but nationalistic. Publishing houses that are of similar leanings: G. Müller, Albert Langen, Hanseatische Verlagsanstalt; the journal *The German People and their Culture* [*Deutsches Volkstum*]; writers of similar persuasion: Wilh. Stapel, A.E. Günther, Hans Blüher, Aug. Winnig; precursors: Moeller van den Bruck.

Small groups: O. Straßer with Herbert Blank (W. v. Miltenberg).

Circle of Friedr. Hilschers (originated in the Erhardt group), journal *Das Reich*. Ernst Jünger and Schauwecker belonged to this.

Tat circle (similar to the Strasser [*sic*] group) around H. Zehrer. {Then all the other ones as well: the guilds, journeymen, volunteer corps, leagues of pupils and students, rings, eagles, falcons, werewolf.}

In this way there develops:

the basis of a *Weltanschauung*: the most implacable enemy, as far as nationalism was concerned, was pacifism. (Cult of cowardice, selfishness, degeneration, biological plague.)

Will to self-defense despite horror of war is characteristic of healthy blood. Beyond that, war of revenge and, further still, war in itself. To live is to kill. It is only in war that the human being comes into his own, and such-like.

Marxism is said to have undermined the spirit of self-defense. Its materialism is despicable. Material things are not without importance but economics must not become fate. The human being has to create the conditions not the other way about.

But the main obstacle for the unification of Germany is liberalism. Those who are addicted to humanity. There is no such thing as international understanding. Ethnicity[70] sets barriers. Justice, "League of Nations" are dreams—hollow, westernized jargon.

Wherever advantage is decisive, Jews are the leaders.

Liberalism is *relativism, objectivity*, business cycle, worldwide bourgeoisie, *intelligentsia*. All these things fill German youth with loathing. Relativism is countered with [proper] attitude. The liberal, the pacifist, the Marxist, the Jew—they all think in a rationalistic way; the ethnic thinker[71] sets, in opposition to *"ratio,"* the *irrational* and religion, counter the individual with the community.

In opposition to reason are set instinct and feeling. It is only when thought is permeated with the blood of feeling that it becomes organic.

The scientific/academic approach, grinding life down into concepts appears as the servant of liberalism and of its quintessence, "ratio." This approach sieves and describes phenomena, divides them into groups, unravels their fibers; anaemic specialization, brain work without any obligation to evaluate and to synthesize. By contrast, "organic thinking" disputes the capacity of thought as logical function to have insight into the world. Novalis: "How can a human being have a sense of anything if he does not possess its germ within him? What I am to understand must develop organically within me; and what I appear to learn is only nourishment of the organism." The world view of organic thinking does not set one thing next to another but sets each part in an organic relationship to the whole, it becomes universal. In just the same way, the "I" is set in the context of its people.[72] It is only from the natural unity of the people that the individual can fulfil his organic function. Therefore, this obliges him to sacrifice himself for the people should this be necessary. (A people that is born to authenticity has a people-spirit[73] like the bees' state. In this way the nation becomes mythical. [sic]

Refers to Romanticism. Is right to do so insofar as it, too, seeks a manner of thinking that is underpinned with feeling. According to the ethnic[74] approach, Romanticism, too, sought the myth of the nation. (Novalis, C.D. Friedrich, Schelling, Adam Müller—he saw individual and community thus—, Fichte.)

But, within this view, as oppositions: national bolshevism and bourgeoisie with their greed for possessions (Hans Grimm, *People without Space*); socialism and misanthropy; community and aristocratic individualism; Protestant sobriety and Roman Catholic romanticism.

In another passage, U[nruh] says roughly the following: the heart of the young is in ferment and *it hates* those *who offer them only self-satisfied intelligence and irony!* (They want instinct, heart, idealism.)

---

169) I can't work in any public library because I'm not allowed to smoke; set that to one side. But when I read at home I don't smoke; and often for longer periods than I have set my mind to. So how would it be if I were to work (to write) with the same degree of interest? Is it the case that I do not start to write with sufficient interest? Instead of all my attempts to fight against smoking ought I not to change my attitude to writing? I always lack the impetus and fervor, the conviction that this has to be. That approach has had much to recommend it; but is it not time for a synthesis?

---

170) My "barrenness" as a creative writer that so often causes me pain; that, quite apart from lyrical poetry, sets me so far below Goethe. [...] Whoever has, and foresees, many such insights, is not barren at all! And just remember the good example of Flaubert (provided I have not misunderstood him; I know too little about him!); what a mistake it was to see the fertility of a creative writer in terms of the quantity of what he produced! By the way, to go to the opposite extreme was a youthful characteristic of mine; perhaps not culled from the epoch of exactitude (in the way I depict this in the MwQ),[75] but explaining why it lasted for such a brief period!

---

171) Father: his fine progress to the point where he was called to the Chair at Brünn. (The qualities that smoothed his way: model schoolboy without the usual drawbacks; but somehow his spirit lacked any volcanic quality. Perhaps, too, mistaken in his choice of profession; cf. his aptitude for descriptive science.) This also all happened at the time when a new type of technical university was emerging. His dislike of mathematics even though he had been a model schoolboy in that area as well. The failed attempt to make it to Vienna and Graz, his becoming stranded in Brünn, the loss of am-

bition, or something of the kind. Sometimes I imagine that somehow I might be like that, too. The small, neat, domestic qualities win the upper hand. [. . .]

———————

174) Never felt comfortable in the lap of the family—tended rather to look down on it, or at least to judge it in objective terms. Never, with certain reservations, made a present of my feelings as, for example, Goethe did with Lavater and the Stoltenbergs. (See, with reference to this example, T[ruth] and F[iction].)[76]

For this reason, not indulgent, tolerant, uninhibited.

A start of a line that diverges from reality. [. . .]

———————

179) I consider it to be more important to write a book than to rule an empire—and also more difficult. Burckhardt[77] certainly sees this differently.

———————

180) Have appended a review article {on Bergson}.[78] [. . .] A further two on his death. See, particularly, at the end on his concepts "morale close" and "morale ouverte."

I will be accused of being influenced by him.

But I was never able to read him because I was held up by details, mainly by his concept of "durée créatrice" and the way he applied this to the distinction between space and time. In the same way I am opposed to his connecting space with science, and time with philosophy. Where I appear to say something similar to him, the meaning is, in fact, quite different; I have never dealt with him properly. This should be made good in the form of an essay.

———————

181) Probably my father had an unfulfilled leaning toward religion. This would explain his words: "Ah, why bother! Burn and scatter!"[79] Similarly, the stoicism with which he lay down to die after losing Mama who never quite returned his love. Once it was not given to him to realize his original yearning for religion he preferred to feel that he had been rejected and left without an answer. [. . .]

184) Eisenstadt marked the decisive change—I wanted to go there in order to wear long trousers. Papa was in favor because he remembered Uncle Rudolf[80] and was calculating that at the age of nineteen and a half I would be a lieutenant, would earn my own keep and, with the help of an affordable sum of pocket money, would be a man of means whose future was secure. Mama seems to have had the idea that it was wrong to let me have my way in everything. Perhaps on some occasions she was severe or lost her temper and this offended my boyish dignity and triggered a reaction of rage. I did not allow myself to be educated, and certainly not by force. In this way we were all in agreement about parting. But this had scarcely happened when, in E[isenstadt], I was seized by the most passionate homesickness! Passionate child. [. . .]

188) The youngest child[81] with the ambition to hold her head up high in the company of her elder sister and brothers, and also to stand her ground spiritually and as a character.

From this came her assertiveness. See her influence on Mattia,[82] Heinrich[83] and Eduard.[84]

This urge foundered on her son. The natural love of the son for his father is greater than that for his mother.

But why? Something else comes between them. Why did she not surround her son with tenderness and direct his tenderness toward herself? At the latest in his fourth or fifth year the conflict begins.

Stubbornness against stubbornness. Not a trace of the erotic.

(The possible hint was the warning always to keep the hands over the covers of the bed, for reasons that were not quite clear. But this was successful and took hold of the disposition—easy as it was to set aflame—so that the memory is still tinged with gratitude and trust.)

Perhaps jealousy because the tenderness of the son was focused more on the father.

The moment when the conflict burst out is present in conscious memory: walk; field of stubble (I can still remember a stream with willows and "dog violets"); the boy five years old at most; had apparently been disobedient and bad-tempered; had gone into the water in his shoes or something of the kind; as punishment, had to go on walking barefoot; some kind of memory that pricks the soles of the feet; at home the solemn punishment. A cane is soaked in water; Papa extraordinarily polite and serious—I believe that he was almost weeping when he gave his warning, and the whole affair was rather elaborate.

Evidently carried out at the initiative of the young mother. And this is the reason why the whole incident implies earlier conflicts (probably disobedience and loss of temper). The boy did not offer any resistance, Papa simply convinced him. No memory of pain, no screaming out. Probably bit back tears, probably, too, a very mild caning.

But what horror! I believe that the parents, too, were shocked by it all. {Almost feverish.}

And at the age of ten the bad-tempered scenes were repeated, became routine.

Once more, attempt at caning, but this time resisted.

---

189) Father, father of the country, God the Father: this was the musical scale of Old Austria when my father was a child. And, just as the impressions of youth are repeated in the character, so this trait remained in his. He was an implicit believer in those in authority; it was natural for him to ask the authorities to fulfill his wishes, and he was deeply hurt when his life did not continue along a successful course after the call to the Chair at Brünn. Witness his journeys to Germany and England on scholarships; the relationship to his protectors, Baron Frei and Court Councillor von Grimm; his disinclination for, indeed his incomprehension of, politics.

Be good, be diligent—after all you have talent and the right diplomas. This was the kind of advice that Grandfather M[usil] gave. An exception to this (or was it an exception?) was the harsh attitude to Viktor.[85]

Grandmother M[usil] seems to have been a good-hearted woman, because her sons loved her so much. Her consideration toward Grandfather even though the family fortune may have come from her—for how was he able to acquire an estate[86] while still relatively young? Perhaps she was never sugary-soft but knew how to maintain her composure, and subordinate herself voluntarily. What doesn't quite fit into the picture is the a-Catholicism, indeed the a-religiosity of the family. Perhaps a kind of theism reigned, a kind of adherence to goodness and order; perhaps, too, a shyness about mentioning God too often; perhaps, too, a kind of treaty between the more gentle mother and the father who was influenced by Darwin.

(In my case, this well-ordered family inheritance was joined with the more stormy one from my mother's side. I do not know which of my ancestors this goes back to.)

And while the children were growing up, Old Austria was changing; God the Father impaired the authority of the father of the country. The principles that I found in place were already less secure. [. . .]

195) Usually, even when I am telling myself the story of my military youth, it is with the justification of the long blue trousers, and similar things. But when I left home I was in fact guided, if only vaguely, by the idea of a life in which the spiritual was chosen as the highest good. And, conversely, I was probably attracted to soldiering by a sense of some Napoleonic quality, or something of the kind. [. . .]

24

NOTEBOOK 32

CIRCA SPRING 1939
TO ABOUT END OF 1941

[This notebook is concerned with the interrelations between culture and politics in the broadest sense. Two of the speeches to which reference is made were delivered by Musil some years before he started the notebook. The first of these, "The Creative Writer in the Present Epoch," was very successful as demonstrated by an effusive review in the Viennese newspaper Der Wiener Tag, published on 16 December 1934: "The ceremonial address itself, [. . .] repeatedly interrupted by storms of applause [. .] was delivered by Robert Musil on the subject 'The creative writer in the present epoch.' It was a storm of accusation of the most subtle kind, directed against the 'Ungeist' [literally the unspirit, *namely, the anti-intellectual, anti-spiritual mood] of the times. Crystal-clear thoughts in crystal-clear sentences. Logic of mathematical precision. Sparkling irony [, . . .] unfettered commitment to humanity. [. . .] The speech of one of the greatest creative writers of his nation." The second, a lecture in Paris in July 1935, was not well received. There are several reasons for this: non-German-speaking delegates were given copies of the translation of another speech; Musil himself, an incorrigible bourgeois, immaculately well-dressed and groomed, was out of place in the predominantly left-wing gathering. But no doubt the main reason lay in some of the formulations in the speech itself. Culture was, as Musil put it, "not tied to any political form"; he further alienated the audience by tarring National Socialism and communism with the same brush in the words "part of the distaste for strongly authoritarian state forms, bolshevism and communism, is attributable to our being used to parliamentary*

democracy." At this point, many of those who understood German started to whistle their disapproval. Musil, though unhappy with the way he had expressed some of his ideas, insisted that he stood by the content of the speech with its insistence on the separation of culture from politics.

In 1938 Musil left Austria and emigrated to Switzerland. He received some funds through admirers and well-wishers. (Thomas Mann was one of those he approached for help with obtaining financial support in America.) But his fate was typical of many emigrés, namely, poverty and crippling uncertainty about the future. His finances had been ruined by the drying up of income from his writings—it appears that MwQ was banned in Austria in 1938 and later throughout Germany. Under this pressure Musil continued work on MwQ, and though the novel was never to be finished it became an expression of the will both for personal survival and for the survival of the view of culture and of politics that Musil advocated.]

32.

> *Search for the Title.*
> The public task of the creative writer.
> The creative writer in the present age.[1]
> The free spirit and politics.
> Difficulties of a satirist—see 28.[2] The ravaged temperament of a satirist.
> Difficulties of a humorist in the contemporary world. [. . .]

---

1) *Basic idea:*

1. Spirit: politics = theory : practice. Where would it lead if a craftsman or someone from an applied science were to prescribe which theoretical developments are permitted! [. . .]
2. The importance of individuality; after the Paris lecture[3] and its additional notes.

1. The role of assumptions in induction. Impossibility of a non-deductive code of living. These demands are to be reconciled.
2. Equation 1) is only partly right. What is missing is the emotional preamble. In loose connection there develop, from the de facto condition, the ideas on which the next condition is based.

2) An attempt has been made, and not without some justification, to characterize N[ational] S[ocialism] as a religious movement and a type of sect. The truth, however, encompasses more {and less} than that. Our period offers an analogy with the religious movements of the 16th century, but here it is non-religious belief that is disintegrating within it. This occurred to me when I had a chance encounter with psy[choanalysis]. These dozen concepts that its registered members use to explain the world. Any other scheme at all could probably achieve the same effect. It would be worth the effort to construct such a one. That which has been explained is then left completely barren and there is not a single path, however narrow, that leads on further from there. (Total explanation as a bad sign.) In a minor key, the Kraus sect, the Klages sect, Jung, Adler. The "materialistic interpretation of history" also had the same function.

Knowledge by halves, then, as an analogy for belief. See also MwQ, Vol. I.[4] Every truth is born today in the form of two half-truths. [. . .]

---

8) Macchiavelli who provided today's state with its spirit or at least with its good conscience, its self-confidence—this same M. was the poor sad man who played cards in village inns with the peasants and who gave his book the touching dedication "To -?- Medici" because he had been banished and was not able to apply his politics to his own life.

What a symbol for the relationship of spirit to politics and might!?

---

9) It is remarkable that today's authoritarian states are: the Italy and Germany of the despotic little courts, Tsarist Russia and Poland, the Turkey of the Sultans, half of feudal Hungary.

Does it mean anything to have had experience of freedom? To have gone through a particular evolution a hundred years ago? Is it predisposition, is it tradition? Or did the others have too little time to adapt to life in freedom and to make this life secure? Or were the times no longer right for it?

---

10) Creative writing is not merely description but, in the first instance, interpretation of life. (In life, anything at all can happen; what matters is the sense behind what happens.) If one interprets it by using the concepts and

prejudices that people apply, then refines these a little as Th[omas] M[ann] does, then one becomes the teacher, philosopher, etc. Far be it from me to overlook the high degree of certainty, composure, and suchlike, which such a procedure bestows on one. [. . .]

---

16) I do not fight against F[ascism], but fight within dem[ocracy] for its future, so I also fight against dem[ocracy]. [. . .]

---

18) Inseparability of politics and spirit: this is demonstrated by the quality that those who wish to reshape the field of politics must possess, namely courage. Do not forget how, in the last days of September, 1938, Chamberlain and Daladier came to negotiations as men who had been defeated in advance, and H[itler] achieved everything because he was determined to go to the very limit.

And courage is necessarily attached to other qualities.

---

19) "The end justifies the means": because whatever commands admiration and whatever inspires loathing come together in the unity that is a person to form a moral unity as well. This totality of the views of one person, however, does not mean that the person is infallible in matters of detail. This is the last stronghold for the defense of spirit against politics, but it is extremely difficult to fortify.

---

20) Is cowardice an inherent feature of pluto-democracy? {see 42}[5] In that case, is all the talk of its spirit being the agent of its moral destruction also correct? Are there any signs of the birth of a new, powerful setting for the spirit?

---

21) What an experience Czechoslovakia had after the rather childlike dream among the superpowers. Deserted by all, exposed, betrayed. The annihilator greeted with rejoicing for his moderation because he left a small number

of them untouched. Quite apart from the injustice done to the Czechs, what a lesson in justice, what a lesson, overall, in human behavior!

---

22) I do not know where it was that I read that Mr. Ch[amberlain] had saved "peace morality" and that this was his greatest achievement; but it is a characteristic statement these days.

It is not the role of a statesman to save "peace morality" but rather—if this is what he wants—to save peace itself. It is common for democratic politics to borrow from morality {and suchlike} and to apply what it has borrowed in a one-sided way, making it banal in the name of morality—indeed, it is so common that, where decisions are required, it really does confuse the statesman's task with the moral task. A major symptom of decline.

{This might be formulated as follows: Don't look for morality among the statesmen (for then you will arrive at . . .). Look for it among the moralists, in the area of religion, among the few creative writers . . . ! And since I am a creative writer this comes back at me from the opposite direction: "What have you done to creative writing? Just look at the consequences!"}

---

23) "Realpolitik." The treatment of Sch[uschnigg],⁶ reminding one of Genghis Khan and Tamerlane, is supposed, in the eyes of a conservative statesman, to make one incapable of conducting negotiations—just the treatment on its own. That the opposite happened is extolled as "Realpolitik." In this context, G[raf] L[einsdorf]⁷ occurred to me. Is "Realpolitik" not a favorite word of the noble senility and of those who are incapable of dealing with the realities of the contemporary world? "Realpolitik" as a sign of lack of spiritual orientation in the real world. Boldly capable of all kinds of surrender since, after all, everything {in this world} is so different from what one senses oneself.

---

24) [. . .] The philosophers who ruled after Plato:

They would have been Platonists. They would have treated the Aristotelians in a friendly and paternalistic fashion but later would have become jealous and suppressed them as subversives. And what of Leibniz, Kant, etc.? Does that not take the idea to limits of comical absurdity?

Catholicism—imperialism of the spirit carefully built up and extended, yet good only when on the defensive. Became far too conservative in order to preserve its rule.

Another approach: many of those who speak of spirit profess their allegiance today to a political system that they wrongly imagine to be its guardian.

What conclusions are to be drawn from this, what assumptions are to be made?

The function of spirit is to give nourishment, it offers countless possibilities. It does not have the function of providing practical organization.

It is the function of politics to make things really happen. What is to be realized and how is it to be done?

To be possessed by spirit is not the main thing; this process takes time; politicians of an all-too spiritual disposition are dangerous. They are either weak or they make their spiritual part into a whole.

The politician must be aware when something has reached maturity—when its turn has come.

Is it the case that politics must make the spirit of its age a reality? No. If one assumes that the Grand Duke[8] had begun to realize Goethe's ideas {from *Wilhelm Meister*},[9] then Goethe would have been deeply alarmed even though his ideas were entirely focused on the creation of a vigorous, integrated scheme of education. The Grand Duke would have had to modify these ideas himself. In other words, he would have had to have spirit—but a spirit that was oriented toward the practice of politics.

Does that not mean: thinking of everyone, not only the great spirits?

Is this not what politics is about?

But it is usually about being concerned with anything but the great spirits.

Let us stay with this formula for the time being.

And with this simile: hurling oneself against the wall in a rolling barrel to determine the course that it takes. That is politics. The barrel is spirit.

[. . .]

---

25) Is that which has caused the turbulence in the world simply the final collapse of the old religiosity and the beginning of a new kind? One that is, however, destroying its deepest foundations through the activities of research, etc.? This at least would be an apological [*sic*!] and ironic means of proceeding. Broken open against a particular instance of politics, namely the suppression of Germany and its false ideology, as resistance to all old ideology. [. . .]

28) In a heavy moment when I could not come to terms with my inner turmoil (MwQ banned;[10] negotiations with Claassen[11] or Swiss publisher dashed; T[homas] M[ann] and all the others having let me down; favors heaped upon T.M. in America while I seem to be a complete unknown there;[12] sense of inner opposition to friends and enemies; no desire to be either here or anywhere else while still complaining of being rejected both here and everywhere else) roughly the same thought occurred to me (and such thoughts are preferable to complaining or investigating to what extent the faults are of my own making) as the one I had before I made up my mind about Vol. I of MwQ and that made a further appearance when I left Austria out of anger about the mourning for Wildgans[13]—namely that I have to be an ironist, a satirist, or something of the kind.

In my serious mode—with my first group of books—I do not get through. To achieve this I need a pathos, a conviction, that is attuned neither to my "inductive modesty" nor to my intelligence that moves in directions that contradict each other—an intelligence in which enthusiasm and vehement passion have, as their indispensable complement, irony. One might also say "philosophical humor," etc. {For the world itself is not yet ready for seriousness.}

At that time, then, I made a decision in favor of irony. It is true that the work on Vol. II[14]—which is almost entirely positive—and also the preparations for the aphorisms[15] have not made me forget this decision, but have robbed it of its efficacy. Now it suddenly occurs to me again and affords me comfort as does every thought that sets things in order. Now the reversals of fortune are nourishment to me; now the feeling that I never quite fully belong either here or anywhere else is not weakness anymore but strength. Now I have found myself again and also my way of facing the world.

Irony has to contain an element of suffering in it. (Otherwise it is the attitude of a know-it-all.) Enmity and sympathy.

This is the way in which the essay about the creative writer is to be written. Not a complaint that I am being unjustly treated but description and explanation of the fate of someone who is in two respects an emigrant, etc. In the way I am treated and in world history, too, the same thing is happening, the good is not so different from the bad as it thinks, etc., and it is not the position of the creative writer vis-à-vis politics but the double exile of the type that I have to describe that sets the tone.

Addendum: the "Great Writer" might fill a small volume. The superficiality of the world, the Anglo-American world that is. Including St[efan] Zw[eig] and Lion Feuchtw[anger]. Including the love of Masaryk,[16] of social democracy and of psychoanalysis as the three superficialities. (As far as

analysis is concerned this would have to be put in a more circumspect fashion—it is not so much analysis as the "Great Writer's" relationship to analysis that is superficial.) The German group could follow as the KPQ.[17]

Postscript: Frau Dr. Krs.[18] told me about the Hesses.[19] Her cousin, an art
historian, revered him since she was a girl, seized her opportunity—which
came when he married a mistress for the sole reason that he wanted to find
a decent way to bring the relationship to an end—and became his wife.
House in Montana,[20] 2 bedrooms, 2 bathrooms, library, guest room, etc.—
gift from Hans Bodmer[21] accepted as a loan so that he pays the taxes. The
difficulties that H. causes are mainly the foibles of a famous man who has
to defend himself [. . .] from German visitors from the Reich. She has to
keep them away from him, and then he discovers that he would have liked
to talk to one or other of them; he cannot stand any noise in the house, no
irregularities in the daily divisions of work, reading, walk, meal and night's
rest. All this is very understandable; the only funny thing about it is that he
has the weaknesses appropriate to a greater man than he actually is. Today
one is a "Great Writer" without possessing a great gift for writing. [. . .]

----

32) It seems that I was not wrong to assume that, where a political movement is involved, no moral starting point can be too low, no relationship to
spirit can be too wide of the mark. For what happens in the case of an individual? One has no need to know what it is that one wants, or alternatively one can be mistaken in what one wants; if a direction has been
set—i.e., when certain emotions have a set direction—all the rest comes
streaming along as well, and gradually conforms. This is the creative process
proper, which does not work out in advance what is going to happen.

Without doubt it is often wrong to compare social processes with individual ones, but one must also know the extent to which they may coincide.
Here it is not a question of ascribing the unity of one personality to a whole
people, however, the way a momentum is generated in a people is similar to
the same operation in an individual. The vague setting of a course in the direction of ethnic[22] achievement and greatness may be sufficient to make
those forces and ideas that happen to be available stream along with this
course. Admittedly one has to ask which forces have been stifled. That is a
separate question. Other questions are: "What is the minimum amount of
spirit necessary for this?"; "How long is it right for the period of politiciza-
tion itself to last?"; "What damage does this cause?" etc. But this has to be
considered impartially. Another question, however, involves the change in

values. But this is a matter of chance. And where the others are politically decadent or weakened this may not become an issue of current debate.

---

33) Have the ideals of the 19th Century (possibly the 18th Century as well) collapsed? No, it is the human being who has collapsed under the ideals! [...]

---

36) [...] The essential beauty of narrative lies in the surroundings. I have made fun of the notion that creative writing should be repetition of life.[23] And yet, by doing just this, it makes life beautiful. I had the notion of telling the story of a widely admired love affair and marriage that was then continued in aversion and disillusionment. Was it the story of my father? And, as I thought about it, my interest centered not on the moral issues to be identified but simply on the descriptions of the circumstances, in other words, on the act of true narration. [...]

---

41) {According to the official public orator (Schtscherbakov) speaking on the fifteenth anniversary of Lenin's death (21.I.39)} it is now said in official speeches in Russia that Lenin was the "most powerful theoretician" whereas Stalin is unsurpassed in the way he directed practical politics. It has to be said that the second point, whether it is true or not, is natural enough; the first subverts the spirit. But what is the purpose of preaching that it is an abuse to make spirit into a function of politics (and how tame is the spirit to whose realm Lenin is relegated)! Today that has no effect at all. To put it both correctly and succinctly, whoever wields absolute power, also possesses absolute wisdom and absolute goodness. This deification is common to all dictators and is also (given that, in private, one sins and curses and blasphemes against God in all those areas beyond his reach) a mark of the times. Is it possible, by the way, to draw conclusions from the present conditions of church belief for the future of the autocracies? [...]

---

48) Aside: creative writing is a battle to achieve a higher species of morality. [...]

54) The anti-fascist "front line of the spirit"? presupposes that there are such things as the True, the Good, the Beautiful. Only the Catholic Church is justified in this presumption. Hence the horrifying thinness of dogmatic liberalism. One might almost formulate it as "those things against which the others are building moral and spiritual foundations." More correctly: a building whose foundations will follow later—here lies the deepest paradox of the free spirit. (The spirit is in the world. Does it have a final principle out of which the right world might be constructed? This question must be asked.) Until something else turns up, however, the whole of history depends on the luck of circumstance, and whether this luck holds or fails will later be declared to have come about through necessity! [. . .]

56) One does not need a public but one does have to have some kind of image of one's social function and position. [. . .]

65) Think, in order to act; act, in order to think[24] One's individual life sometime carries one somewhere or sets a task that has the gradual effect of rearranging the way one functions within (however, this happens with less frequency the more constant and comprehensive one's activities are)—consider, in this regard, the following: the job to be done, the task set, opportunity, temptation, the whole field of what remains relatively impersonal and subject to chance. This is somewhat similar to the function of politics. What politics "does" cannot be derived from thinking alone. Not even the love between two people will have a determining effect on the whole of their lives without their de facto coming together. The political leaders would thus seem to be substitutes for chance, creating from countless possibilities the task that is set. [. . .]

70) Democracy: the notion that the will of a people can be ascertained through voting in a democracy is, of course, an illusion. But when one observes at close hand the attempt to decide the questions of divergent interests by means of a vote rather than with knife and pistol it is evident that this is a more human and civilized procedure. [. . .]

72) But what is the purpose of this human and civilized procedure? The opposite way is a guarantee that one is fit to rule. (Take, for example, the fighting for the sultanate among the sacred baboons.)[25] At least it guarantees that one has the capacity to rule. But this does not mean one will rule with wisdom—it means only that one will rule with might. One may be a very successful politician even if one has to fritter away a large portion of one's strength on problems connected with affairs at court as Bismarck did. So why not fritter away part of one's strength on humanitarian problems? This will probably add wisdom to the other portion of one's strength. [. . .]

74) Flatterers and those he [Hitler] has convinced say: each expression by him is absolute; his is also the spirit that sends the law out into the world. Or, at least, all is permissible for him because he is a genius. A critical observer on the other hand might say: assuming he is a genius, then his ruthlessness, his total identification in each instance with what he pledges and then breaks, is coextensive with the creative drive, the uninterrupted process of genius; quod erat demonstrandum. Even a conservative opponent could say: the genius of the people chose and understood this creative man even at the time he could not be distinguished from a confidence trickster; e.g., in the demand for an omnipotent state when the genius could not be seen (but only guessed at) and the negative manifestations of genius were in the foreground. [. . .]

78) The spiritually creative person lives in totalitarian states as in times of the Inquisition. The Catholic Church, as well, is thus not without guilt in this respect. Of the democracies one might say to a high degree: serves them right!

How does one come to terms with the Inquisition and yet remain creative? See Descartes [. . .] However, in those days there existed a very precise dogmatics (after several centuries!)

79) "The nation as ideal and reality" is to be found in the N[eue] R[undschau], December, 1921. Cf. 81) below. [. . .]

81) [. . .] Today I received the essay under 79) and leafed through it. Contradictory impressions: I don't like what I read at all, but I don't have any desire to change it. Thought and expression suffer, at individual junctures, from a tendency to overelaborate. I would like to disclaim the whole piece; and, for all that, it is in its own way an achievement that would be difficult or impossible to imitate.

I think that I have this or similar impressions with everything of mine that I reread at a later date.

I am a total stranger to myself and could be either a critic or a commentator of my own work.

Conclusion to be drawn: any rewriting is out of the question. But nor would I want to disown these works. They would have to be published just as they are. And what does one have to do with a thought-experiment that does not bring satisfaction? One keeps on thinking! Extend this with new essays on the same theme, on themes that develop out of them—this is the positive solution. They are just opening chapters! (But one can also take into consideration that much of what is contained in them is not as it might be.)

82) Is it right to say that I have a deep hatred of everything revolutionary? I don't like it whatever the form happens to be in which it emerges. Its content always seems to me to amount to the same; I don't like the kind of things it expresses, this sense of "humanity in the throes of revolution" with all its typical spiritual consequences. But nor do I like stasis, or the conservative principle. The mentality of the Swiss bourgeoisie, for example, with its cemeteries for particular classes of taxpayers, its hatred for socialism, its planning of towns for the sake of those who own cars. I have never liked the idolatry of the family, this whole ridiculous superstructure for procreation, this coloratura of egoism. I would have liked to see children brought up in an incubator, and even to arrange for them to be born there.

What is the consequence of these two elements? Is it an "evolutionary" cast of mind?

83) The German doesn't know which he likes better, Heaven or Hell. But he is definitely thrilled with the task of bringing order to one or the other—and probably he slightly prefers the task of setting Hell in order. In other words, to stand together in fraternal union with Yesterday's Enemy No. 1 is some-

thing profoundly German. Contrary to appearances, H[itler] was never more popular than when he made his volte-face toward the Bolsheviks, since it was assumed that he was bringing German efficiency to bear on what they were doing. One can call this, if one so wishes, an act of genius. [. . .]

---

88) On the utopia of literature. Virgil, Dante, Homer . . . set them to one side. A certain degree of illusion and a certain love of their surroundings is an essential element in the love one feels for them. But what of Balzac, Stendhal, etc.? Just imagine they were alive and were "colleagues." What a weight of loathing for Stendhal, the scribbler, and Balzac, the gusher! Their imaginary worlds would be mutually incompatible if one did not think of them as being set in different places and epochs. Can they be added to each other or are they mutually exclusive? What is the nature of the problem that the sharpness of effect is toned down in the reception of an artist from a past age together with his epoch. (As far as the first idea is concerned, I am not even capable of formulating the question properly.) [. . .]

---

92) Diplomat, politician: man who swallows everything because he knows what he wants.

He will also continue to want, but he will forget how to know. For example, the way religiosity has taken flight from the Catholic Church. One cannot refute and still be creative.

A servant of the Church can constantly tell lies ad majorem dei gloriam; an author cannot.

So one can only lie (make concessions) for as long as the stamina of the will lasts out. [. . .]

---

96) Decline of art. The human being who is at present emerging is interested in philosophy and film. This struck me after what B[arbara] von B[orsinger] de B[aden] told me about her assistant gardener, a lad who asks her for books about philosophy and who despises novels. She was astonished when I mentioned that I nearly became a university teacher of philosophy.[26] She seems partly to share his view; it is, however, not without a certain pride that she mentions that her brother, a writer, has a job with the Federation that has something to do with films (and that he has been a film critic).

97) Would you be willing to kill yourself in order to help me in my career? Probably not. Would I do it for you? I would probably not do it either.

But on the spur of a moment of pathos I *would* do it.

And in a society where "nobility of mind," "magnanimity in sacrifice," "love beyond the grave" were on everybody's lips we would both do it.

Today the individual virtues and aims are all lame. That is why H[itler] is right in this respect as well. [. . .]

104) The petty-bourgeois happiness that is social democracy. Mixed in with the Rubiner-L[eonhard] Frank-Werfel epoch[27] together with a pinch of love for all humanity. But in the case of Sorel,[28] and as far as the proletarian states are concerned, still with property as its foundation. [. . .] Journalistic origin, owes its spirit to newspapers. Even where this spirit is right, it is unfortunate that it is right. Basing the human being on the principle of might has not been thought out beyond Nietzsche. Lenin? 18th century skipped over. [. . .]

111) The German: "Impressive what the red brothers are managing to do!" This sentence was (perhaps) spoken in burning Witebsk (in July 1941). The men—emaciated from lack of food, sweaty, exhausted—were receiving refreshment in a sidestreet from medical orderlies offering field flasks, something to sate their hunger, stimulants, and so forth, all of which looked really good. For all the troops the most important thing was to take off their helmets and cool their heads. It may have been the one who was in his late thirties who spoke the words. He was nearly bald and had lost a lot of weight.

These words are almost tender and express professional respect; they give voice to the knowledge that one's own capacities are themselves substantial. Characteristically German.

They would be capable, on the very next day, of fraternizing with the enemy who defeated them. They murder without enmity. They place their lives in danger because it would be shameful to do anything less than that.

The German is, among other things, an MwQ. Sole aim? To contribute his share.

? Is it necessary to give the Germans something to aim for? The average German has no other aim. [. . .]

Abstraction. The displacement of whole industries, whole peoples, for good, for evil; it is a variety of abstract thinking. But one must perhaps distinguish between abstraction and superficiality and the latter's temerities. [. . .]

25

NOTEBOOK 35

6 NOVEMBER 1939
TO 6 NOVEMBER 1941

[In this last notebook Musil moves from politics and culture to a more intimate realm. The title is a reference to Musil's birthday—he became 59 on 6 November 1939. In straitened circumstances—Musil and his wife are now distressed gentlefolk subsisting on charity from organizations that help emigré intellectuals and artists—Musil becomes absorbed in his immediate surroundings. He records details of shrubs in the garden, contact with neighbors and their children, the sexual activities of the local cats. Entries toward the end of the notebook seem touched with the anticipation of death.]

35.

[. . .]

6.XI.1939. In the morning the weather was overcast. In the afternoon we went to the "cinema." Lazing about (both spiritually and physically). I now have no more recollection of particular details and understood very little of the dialogue. But if one were to examine this proffered spiritual activity in which people indulge, one would say the following: those who indulge are really no better than card players and drinkers in public houses. That is one's immediate impression when one has not been to a film for a year and is going through a difficult time.

When we came out it was pouring, and it took quite a long time to find a seat in a coffeehouse. Then, somewhere near the [Place du] Molard,[1] we found a quite cozy place to sit in a corner among a crowd of people and drank a strong light-colored filter coffee. We had previously taken flight from the boredom and arrogance of Mäder's coffeehouse and cake shop.

When, in the black of night, we reached our house (Chemin des Grangettes, 29) we were rather damp. Read one or two scenes from Racine's *Andromaque*. Needed hardly any help to understand it, then went through it again with M[artha].

A few days ago she came across a cheap edition of some of the older French authors and Corneille is making a strong impression on her; this is important to me because I am reading, intermittently, E. Cassirer's "Descartes" and have found that my conception of the theater needed him as an example. I have now come to believe that the "dramatic art in the *Enthusiasts*" would derive substance from him. This would then serve as a corrective for the influence of Lessing who was responsible for German literature becoming starved of ideas. (But my edition of Lessing is on one of the bookshelves in Vienna.)

In the morning wrote to Lejeune,[2] since permission has arrived from the Foreigners' Department of the Canton police for me to await the decision of my application in Zurich (!) Then also to [. . .] Prof. Hunziker[3] whose invitation to me to give a reading or lecture in Winterthur has arrived.

7.XI. [. . .] Before my eyes, part so to speak of the backdrop of the garden, there are four young spruce, 5 to 6 meters tall, dominated by two slim birch trees that stand between them and whose colors are now a very yellow yellowish-green and a bright grey with a yellowish-green tinge. At a distance of ten paces directly in front of me is the semicircular fountain with its low stone edge, forming half of an ellipse, whose backrest is quite covered with trailing ivy. The ivy leaves seem to me to be smaller and more clearly defined than those I am used to. Standing a little closer to me, and to one side of the fountain, is an arbor with a low stone bench. On the other side, the same distance away as the well, is a bush whose name I do not know, but that I like very much. It has the shape of hair brushed down but with no parting, a vigorous confusion that is broader than it is long; cocoa and red wine mixed together might come together to form a similar color—this seems to come from small, dark, shining leaves and many tiny, elongated fruits. {Looked at close to, the leaves are a dark Bordeaux red and bright wine red—perhaps in a ratio of 1:20 to these there are small, dark-green leaves.} [. . .] A narrow bright-green growth of leaves with bleached cinnamon-colored tufts crowns its center and is bent over a little by the rain.

Next to it an unknown bush {shrub}, almost as tall as a man, with about ten stems; all the charm it possesses—apart from this it has none at all—lies in the form of a shallow heap, latticed with the horizontals of the foliage as a whole (this in spite of the disorderly way the leaves have grown) and the verticals formed by the stems. In front of it is an area of lawn with vigorous grass and on the left a tree with layers of wild, then mild, wine red that has perhaps absorbed some white or yellow; {In the sunshine it gleams like varnish. It should also be said that, wherever it gleams, it is like crimson madder varnish, wherever it sits in its own shadow it is bluish-red. Or, perhaps more simply: it is pure red, now brighter, now darker; a red red—red and nothing but red. It may be something rare.} I cannot describe it even though its impact is as strong as a blow. On the right-hand side, however, there stands (though I have forgotten to mention it up till now and though it is set back a little) the queen of the garden, one of those splendid trees that one finds in Geneva that in summer have big white blossoms like magnolias or water lilies, with big, shining, dark-green, lancet-shaped leaves; the twisting, greenish-black branches perhaps remind one of the snakes in images of Indian gods. Behind all of these, with a reddish-black tiled roof and today wreathed in mist, lies the brown-ochre Pouponnière,[4] with tall birches and a kind of cypress to one side, that in other respects is a solid construction in the Zehlendorf style,[5] or something of the sort.

My study had two tall windows and a glass door; it is at ground level, on the same plane as the soil in the garden, and is painted bright cream with green, new-old-fashioned furniture, a fireplace and a big desk from which I can see into the garden. Rather archaic-looking, primitive stone columns and a {stone} balustrade enclose a flagged corridor that runs around our flat. Vines, figs and all kinds of other things grow up into the archway; but there is enough light.

Once—it was about three weeks ago—I got up between three and four o'clock in the morning and went out into the garden to find out what had caused a strange noise. The moon had already gone and the dawn was not yet breaking. The garden looked like a sketch drawn by a somnambulist, and painted in by the same artist, though without any of the colors of the day.

I write so much about the garden because it makes us happy, and I intend to add to what I have written.

The War entered a dormant phase some time ago and so we don't have to think about it.

In the afternoons the weather turned clear and beautiful. Before our meal we walked to Chêne-Bourg;[6] when we got into the [bus] to return home we had a chance meeting with Holitscher.[7] In the afternoon we walked along the Ch. d. Grange, {-Falquet} Ch. de la Gradelle, Ch. de Grange Canal; it was remarkable that, for almost the whole duration of the walk as we discussed questions of how to behave toward the others (Fräulein von Borsinger, the sculptor, Dr. Bouvier),[8] we were annoyed with each other.

Today I wrote to the Wotrubas[9] and Dr. Rosin.[10] [. . .]

9.XI. The red bush has turned brownish-red, but there is no question that the red remains.

I don't sleep for long enough. I don't know why I cannot manage to write. I seem to be under a spell. Soon I won't know where to turn for lack of money; this seems inevitable to me, even though I don't spend much time thinking about it. And for a long time now I have felt that I am ready to write.

10.XI. When little Nardja comes into the garden she takes pleasure in screaming with all her might. If one gestures [. . .] to her she goes silent and withdraws. If her mother were to find out she would shout to the child "Don't take any notice of the strangers!"

We once sent a message upstairs—via Frau Morand[11] who is on very good terms with the family—because the dear little child was tearing through the house at such a rate that no one below could stand it. The consequence was a screeching in the stairway for the benefit of all and sundry.

The garden—I still have to finish what I wanted to say—is, with respect to its other larger portion (from the narrow side of the house, next to the "winter garden"), also very beautiful. In the corner are a few tall birches, a big lawn and some old apple trees—in fact they are quince trees. Beyond them, sky; the feeling of looking out over a high plain covered by trees and bushes, and, in the background, high mountains, now quite white, that one can hardly see at all in the summertime. {But} this is the kind of garden one might also find in Upper Austria.

We have large numbers of birds: finches, tits, linnets, and four very domesticated pairs of large blackbirds. From time to time the beautiful and elegant magpies make their appearance. [. . .]

27.XI. Typically, time has been slipping away. I know that on many occasions I wanted to make an entry, but did not find the right moment.

[. . .] In so far as I turned, in my writing, either to matters of detail or to broader issues I felt comfortable and in control; but as soon as I try to make progress, step by step, toward completing the work I feel I'm lost in a desert without trees or shelter.

In the meantime the so-called "mine war" has begun. I shall note down the following floating ideas about this:

Not long ago, foreign journalists asked Goering why the Germans had not made use of the secret weapon that H[itler] had mentioned; he replied with cruel humor: "It's simply because we are humane." One may draw the conclusion from this that it is not simply a case of drifting mines that would be no more than a military aperçu.

The English, taken as they are by surprise, seem (to judge by the newspapers) to have settled on the theory that this all has to do with mines being guided electromagnetically by the metal hulls of ships—a German invention made in 1935 that was then dropped. But this seems a cumbersome device. It may have been significantly improved in the meantime. But it might also involve bulky listening devices that automatically lock a torpedo onto the sound of propellers.

The great demand for platinum that is supposed to restrict production to only a limited number of electromagnetic mines—the number has even been announced and people are waiting for the frequency of their use to be reduced—might have been met by Russia; this would have justified major political concessions. [. . .]

At any rate, the Germans are unexpectedly demonstrating great efficiency. None of the things that can be leveled against N[ational] S[ocialism] as a philosophy and morality seems to inhibit its efficacy.

Once again, the moralist has to wait for further developments.

On a private level, this is what has happened in the intervening time: two married couples, the Rodas[12] and the Holitschers have paid us an afternoon visit. Astonishing encounter with H. at the terminus in Chêne.

200 francs from Lej[eune], of which 100 came via Marian W[otruba]. Final refusal by Opr[echt].[13] For the moment we are secure, but my view of the future is one of deep pessimism.

The Pen Cl[ub] in London deems it appropriate to drop the action in my favor at this juncture. Olden,[14] who sent me the letter, enclosed copies of letters to the P[en] C[lub] from Arnold Zweig, Broch, Rob. Neumann, Th. Mann. I am touched, particularly by Th. M. to whom I have often been unjust. I am also flattered.

Walk around the end of the Route de Malagnou and the edge of Chêne with a view out over the magnificent plain that stretches to [Mont] Salève. [. . .]

I still have to make an entry about the view from the bedroom. A greenish-blue house, taller than it is wide, five-angled gable with barge-boards. Tall, narrow windows let into the end-elevation and set out irregularly at different heights. Framing it, about four or five black-green spruce. The blue-green sky that, in the evenings, is always interposed before the Jura. Once, beyond the mountains, the sickle of the moon; the same sight, once more, in the morning. The rest, houses and bushes, confused and inconsequential. The whole like a noble head set on ugly legs. A fairy tale on a very ordinary base. Probably caused by the gradations of colors and light. Individual detail is ordinary, the whole indescribably whole. [. . .]

14.I. The day before yesterday the cats started a season of love. Because of the position of my room with its big windows I am, so to speak, on the same level as they are.

The big, good-natured house cat. Striped in two milk-coffee colors: also in tan and milk-froth. A pretty beast, a little faded—she has been a mother several times over. One would estimate her age—if she were a woman—as late forties. But she is visibly alert to the wiles of her sex.

The beautiful stranger. The surface of her hair has a clear porcelain sheen. Two shades of grey; or white with brown-grey layers; or greenish-brown layers. A charming little nose. A soft, no longer girlish shape; one cannot say that this is "of perfect beauty" since it is, after all, an alien form of beauty for us; one might say, rather, that it is beautiful in its perfection. Everything about her is uniform, slow and supple. Her eyes are of shining green. They are too indifferent to be called "radiant." She is quite large. She has a small head. I do not know who it was who painted women like her. Botticelli, perhaps. She would be in her mid-twenties.

On the first day, a small, dirty, white tomcat paid court to her. He is no youngster. Not strong, but well-made. They met each other time and again as if by chance. If he was not there, she went to look for him. When he came, she sat down unintentionally in his path. He sat down close to her. He made music. He is a courtly singer. She listened attentively to him; but in the fashion of a lady who does not indicate what it is that moves her. She bestowed on him her favor—her attention, that is—and also the friendly desire to share his company. After his song, which is passionate and melancholic, he stood up, moved a little further off on stiff legs as if the excitement he had endured had made him slightly lame. She, too, went away and, as if unintentionally, they met again in another half an hour.

She is not frightened or inhibited when one goes to the window. Looks up, and her gaze is soft and friendly, but unattainable since it comes from another life that now has nothing to do with the life of humans.

In the intervals she also occasionally goes after a bird.

He withdraws into a prickly bush as if doubled up in pain.

The second tom is young, his body, despite having the clumsiness of youth about it, has the air of a virile and powerful young nobleman. He reminds one of a two-year-old racehorse (or is it one-and-a-half or two-and-a-half? I mean the time of the first races that do not properly count). He has brown-grey stripes; has a bold bad gaze and a mustache like a Japanese knight; promises to become a light-heavyweight.

17.I. We are in Zurich, at the "Fortuna Boarding House." I did not experience the "season of the cats" right through to the end. [. . .] On the third or fourth day, already, things became rather vulgar. The old beauty, the yellow house cat, lay under the white tom. I do not know what led up to it. He held her firmly but quite gently by the scruff of her neck, but her hind legs were stretched out back along the ground (splayed out) in a position in which she was totally helpless, really wide open. One could see the hair on the thighs in the shape of "mutton-chop" whiskers, and the vagina was extremely accessible. The tom stretched to reach the right place but was apparently too short. This happened without words and without music as she worked her hind legs like oars to bring them back beneath her. When, at last, she was successful she shook off her partner with scarcely any effort and gave a couple of rather obtuse little jumps to one side while he withdrew in shame.

Soon after that fur flew all around when the magnificent female and the beautiful young tom were rolling about in the grass. Apparently he was trying to roll her onto her back but she was too strong and put up too serious a resistance. They parted in anger. The female then returned to no avail.

The next day she came past our door with a remarkable expression as if, in the meantime, far too much had happened to her. She no longer seemed to have stepped from some fairy tale, but had a distracted air about her and also that unwashed appearance that made her look as if she had been on a railway journey.

A big, very bad-tempered and masculine-looking three-parts-Angora tom-cat can be observed in the neighborhood. [. . .]

Cat music. [. . .] At some time or other I decided to append a chapter like this to the "journey" one.[15] The biological travesty, nonetheless very touching, that is love. I add [. . .] to this: the beautiful female cat has a less beautiful double; since the time when she was knocked about I can't tell the two apart. In the same way, the "Minnesänger" tomcat has a fatter and unappealing counterpart. This makes the general principle tangible.

If circumstances prevent coitus (or even coitus interr.) there is a residual need—quite separate from soulful tenderness—to snuggle up close, to touch, to catch hold of some of the softness and warmth. There is something similar to this in the way cats behave when they content themselves with following each other at a distance or sit down five paces apart. This is the first physiological step leading to much that is human. The tender dependence of the child on the mother; its desire to snuggle close and be warm; its happiness when it does so; this non-sexual eros that Freud interprets as sexual. It may be in fact the physical continuation of whatever it is that cannot be finished physically, or of whatever cannot be carried out immediately.

15.II. Yesterday I had the idea of narrating the biography of the Raven[16] in the first person—with a female body and spirit. To do so would certainly be to kick over the traces and break the rules and I have been right not to yield to this side of my talent. But for once, and as compensation for the excess of reflection and ratio, one ought to let these demons loose—in the way that some people (and not {always} the worst) have done, even though they were undisciplined characters.

Eros, in my case, is still a realm of illusions and lyricism. For once it would then be treated in a realistic fashion. That, too, would be important.

This moral development is also worth examining from the point where a strong drive dominates up to the point in one's life where one reaches maturity and, partly too, resignation. Somewhere or other there is a note stating roughly the following: "From 'enfant terrible' of the epoch to pioneer."

Great goodness, the good female-companion, emerging naturally from a disposition that appears to contradict morality.

Then it also seemed to me that in the second part it might take the form of a narration of my own biography, giving expression to my own advantages and weaknesses.

I also find it interesting to record a life with no achievement and no intention of producing spiritual work; much more clearly expressed than with Agathe.

Title: "A Raven." "Self-help and self-education." "Sketch of the Raven's Life." [. . .]

N.b.: My confrontation with myself as a person would come via such a work, and only factual details would be available for the aphorisms.

At the same time, this fictional biography would perform the task of being M[artha] in the form that she would have to see things today if she wanted to set any kind of romanticizing {completely} aside.

A few inventions could be added, for example the notes about figments of jealousy.[17] The real heroine rejects them, after all. Homos[exuality] is not completely alien to her but sexuality immediately alerts the defenses against it. All the same, for once, another approach would be conceivable.

The individual love affair involves being dazzled by the beauty of a drive. In retrospect, both can be called to mind: the dazzlement, which is today an object of scorn, and the sense of how beautiful it all was. This beautiful nonsense of life at the side of Robert whom sense tortures and twists out of shape. Despite all the love and closeness she sometimes feels, here too, as if she were someone in a picture book.

He has written "Claudine"[18] and, on one occasion, she commits a moral misdemeanor. One has to do the same thing again. He almost discovers it.

(This would, by the way, make for a far more realistic version of the deleted final section of Ag[athe] and U[lrich].) [. . .]

Mai, 1941, Champel, Chemin des Clochettes.[19]

I was born in 1880, I'm 60 years old, and the year is 1940.

There seems to me as if there were some significant congruence here.

Perhaps someone will discover what such things mean. Astrology, graphology and suchlike have been practiced with extreme foolishness. Perhaps someone will develop some great theory that will also explain my psychological weakness that has become apparent through my observations. Explanation of a spell of number mysticism.

I, myself, have the impression that some kind of end is beckoning. [. . .]

6.XI.1941:[20] a morning, companionable, tender, in fact, but no c[oitus].

What was it like in all those days through all those years? Where were the beds placed in all those rooms? What was it that took place as an unquestioned preamble? Was there no sense of satiety, of surfeit? Sometimes one or two signs of this, but post [coitum]. How did the transitions take place?

At any rate, the marriage that is still intact after decades serves as an example.

Few details remain in memory. Those that do remain have become lyrical: the golden "fruit of the fig" on the white sheet in M[artin] L[uther] Street.[21] The greenish-blue blanket beneath it. The gaslight. The scarlet chalice of blossoms. See the poem,[22] the passage in "Grigia" with its lyrical effusion.

The black hair on the white pillow in Weißgerberstraße.[23] The head with the black plaits one morning at the window in the next room in Lofer.[24] Nothing at all of many places: Venice, Lavarone, Pergine, Schlüsselgasse[25] and Schlösselgasse,[26] Koserow,[27] etc.

In spite of that, no doubt about being sexual and erotic people.

It has become smooth and leveled out, even statistical.

What does it look like in retrospect? This is part of the meaning of life itself.

We reawaken ourselves to ourselves in what is virtually a statistical sense. We observe ourselves according to the characteristics of the average. Occasionally enlivened by the way that spirit, too, has had its share of life.

[. . .] Personal history with the history of the "Idea." The appropriate moment in Switzerland during the battle for Moscow.[28]

In what way can we identify what is statistical about us in relation to what is individual?

A perspective of general interest: how does a relationship that is under the influence of sexuality change between youth and old age?

The expressive and most beautiful female body. (Reflection in some poems.) What it has to suffer. As a substitute, belonging together. The tenderness of life afterward. The importance of delicate skin and other things. Cf. the successes of old N[inon] d[e] Lenclos.[29] What is lost when beauty disappears; what, even in physical terms, is more permanent, indeed more important than beauty.

When one is young, one is more demanding, more critical—and more susceptible to disappointment. What inhibits me is that damned poem by Goethe in *Faust*, Pt. II, "Philemon and Baucis." [. . .]

NOTES

PREFACE

In working on this preface I have had recourse to many sources. Among the most important are the following:

The second volume of the German edition of the diaries: Robert Musil, *Tagebücher*, ed. Adolf Frisé, two vols. (Reinbek bei Hamburg: Rowohlt, 1976); Karl Corino, *Musil: Leben und Werk in Bildern und Texten* (Reinbek bei Hamburg: Rowohlt, 1988); David Luft, *Robert Musil and the Crisis of European Culture, 1880–1942* (California: University of California Press, 1980); Sibylle Mulot, *Der junge Musil: Seine Beziehung zur Literatur und Kunst der Jahrhundertwende* (Stuttgart, 1977); Marie-Louise Roth, *Robert Musil: L'Homme au double regard* (Paris: Balland, 1987); Hannah Hickmann, ed., *Robert Musil and the Literary Landscape of His Time* (Salford: Department of Modern Languages, 1991); Silvia Bonacchi, "Robert Musils Studienjahre in Berlin, 1903–1908," *Musil-Forum*, Beilage 1, Saarbrücken, 1992.

I would like to thank colleagues at the Arbeitstelle für Robert-Musil-Forschung at the University of the Saar for their generous help in providing some of the materials for this introduction, and to make special mention of Silvia Bonacchi, who gave valuable advice on the manuscript. Any remaining mistakes of substance or interpretation, however, are the result of oversight or stubbornness on my part.

1. Musil was in the front line from 1915 to 1916 when he was hospitalized for infections of the mouth and throat; 1916–1917 he worked on the Army newspaper, *Die Soldatenzeitung*; from 1918 to the end of the war he was attached to the War Press Department.

2. I have in mind such figures as Ernst Mach, Hugo von Hofmannsthal, Arthur Schnitzler, Franz Kafka, Sigmund Freud, and Rainer Maria Rilke, who all first made their mark in the reign of Franz Joseph; Ludwig Wittgenstein, Hermann Broch, Karl Kraus, and, of course, Robert Musil came to prominence after the end of the imperial era.

3. They included Franz Blei, Alfred Polgar, Franz Czokor, and Oskar Maurus Fontana.

4. The first performance was only much later, in Berlin, in 1929.

5. This is referred to below as MwQ.

6. Dr. Frisé has kindly given me permission to make use of his notes; this use is so extensive that I shall not acknowledge each instance. My debt to Dr. Frisé remains, like that of so many others who have worked on Musil, immense.

7. *Heft* (Notebook) 31, p. 827. This and subsequent page references are to the 1976 Frisé edition of the *Diaries*.

8. Elias Canetti, "Memory of Musil," *Merkur*, 39 (February 1985): 142–47, at p. 142.

9. Adolf Frisé, *Plea on Behalf of Musil* (Reinbek bei Hamburg: Rowohlt, 1987), p. 72.

10. *Heft* 30, p. 722.

11. *Heft* oNr. (Notebook without a number), p. 344.

12. *Heft* 21, p. 584.

13. *Heft* 17, p. 299.
14. *Heft* 8, p. 420.
15. *Heft* I, p. 315.
16. *Heft* 4, p. 13.
17. *Heft* 3, p. 101.
18. *Heft* oNr., p. 346.
19. *Heft* I, p. 307.

20. In one of the later notebooks—*Heft* 33, p. 917—Musil makes quite blatant assumptions about the character and proclivities of a Hungarian baroness who is staying at the hotel where Martha and he are on holiday.

21. Karl Corino speculates, however, that Musil may have had a liaison before World War I with the actress Ida Roland (see *Musil: Leben und Werk in Bildern und Texten*, p. 187).

22. See Emanuela Fanelli, "Als er noch Fräulein Valerie liebte."—"Musils Valerie-Erlebnis: eine biographisch-kritische Korrektur," *Musil-Forum* 19–20 (1993–1994): 7–30.

23. *Heft* I, p. 314.

24. There is a hint of regret at a relationship that was clearly marked by inhibitions on both sides: *My father often requested that I explain some aspect of what concerned me: I was never capable of doing so* (*Heft* 33, p. 914). Despite a suggestion that Musil felt that his father should have been more forceful in his relationship with his wife, he evidently feels deep respect for the way his father conducted himself at the end of his life, praising *the stoicism with which he lay down to die after losing Mama who never quite returned his love* (*Heft* 33, p. 960).

25. *Heft* 3, p. 96.
26. *Heft* I, p. 315.
27. *Heft* 5, p. 226.
28. *Heft* I, p. 306.
29. *Heft* 7, p. 269.
30. *Heft* 33, p. 952.

31. Musil was very proud of his physical strength and performed daily gymnastic exercises to keep himself trim throughout his life.

32. This state of mind is so vital in Musil's thinking that in my view it gives his use of the adjective *anders* ("other")—even in what appear at first glance to be neutral contexts—an extra weight of significance that I have rendered throughout by placing "other" in quotes where appropriate.

33. *Heft* 11, p. 151.
34. *Heft* 4, p. 8.
35. *Heft* 33, p. 943.
36. Moritz Schlick (1882–1936), founder of the Vienna Circle school of philosophy.
37. *Heft* 33, p. 925.
38. *Heft* 30, p. 790.
39. *Heft* 21, p. 638.

40. This is a complex play on words: someone who has second sight, a "seer," is a *Hellseher*—literally, "bright-seer" in German; Musil here replaces the verb "to see" with the verb "to hear" and comes up with an abstract noun implying the possession of "second hearing"—an acoustic faculty of prophecy. Yet there is a further level of ambiguity, for the adjective *hörig* has an extended meaning of "being in fief to." Thus we have a faculty for prophetic hearing allied to the conception of being enslaved—in this case to the woman who has not yet come to bed!

41. *Heft* 7, p. 286.

42. See Karl Corino, "'Zerstückt und durchdunkelt.' Der Sexualmörder Moosbrugger im 'Mann ohne Eigenschaften' und sein Modell," in *Musil-Forum* 10 (1984): 105–19.

43. *Heft* 8, p. 400.

44. *Heft* 4, p. 2.

45. *Heft* 5.

46. *Heft* 19, p. 527.

47. *Heft* oNr., p. 324.

48. *Heft* 8, p. 353.

49. *Heft* 28, p. 680.

50. *Heft* 31, p. 813.

51. *Heft* 31, p. 826—the wall in question is, unsurprisingly, Musil himself!

52. *Heft* 34, p. 845.

53. "What strikes (and moves) me [. . .] is [. . .] a kind of fullness, even a kind of joy simply at being alive in the midst of concrete things that are observed, certainly with sharp attention, but without being separated from them" in Marie-Louise Roth, *Robert Musil, les oeuvres pré-posthumes—biographie et écriture* (Paris: Recherches, 1980), pp. 7–8.

INTRODUCTION

1. According to Elias Canetti, access to Musil after his marriage was jealously guarded by his wife, Martha.

2. Adolph Frisé comments that there is no actual evidence for Herma's death. Philip Payne, who concurs, believes, however, that "she probably died as Tonka does in the story modeled after Herma."

3. Philip Payne cautions me when I speculate on a later passage in Notebook 11—dated after January 1908: "Probably here, as with other real characters who live on in Musil's creative imagination, the references to Herma are made after the actual relationship has ceased (indeed, in this case, possibly after the other's death). It is interesting, and perhaps significant that, in the middle of this entry, Hanka/Herma becomes 'Tonka' which is, of course, the name of the fictional character who is based on Herma."

4. This circumstance, of an otherwise bourgeois home, his mother's friend, Reiter, ever present, accompanying his father and mother on trips, Robert wondering who his real father is, certainly had its effect on Musil's work. The *Diaries'* excerpts about Gustl Donath and his wife Alice, and their transformation into the Walther and Clarisse of *The Man without Qualities,* demonstrate how powerfully Musil's thoughts turned on the *menage à trois,* his attraction to Alice, Alice's to him, and Gustl's position in this. Many details of Musil's life, first with Herma, his mistress at the turn of the century, then with Martha, who would become his wife, depend on the magnetism of the triangle, even as he seeks a moral definition of life.

5. Frank Kermode expresses this succinctly in his introduction to the *Five Women.* "Grigia. . . . The climax of the tale has an insoluble ambiguity; but it is worth noting that ambiguity is a property not only of the narrative but also of the texture of the book. . . . Tonka steadfastly *is* Tonka, the 'nobly natural' shopgirl who has nevertheless quite certainly been unfaithful. These ambiguities reflect the ambiguities of human reality; Musil once wrote that he saw no reason in the world why something cannot be simultaneously true and false, and the way to express this unphilosophical view of the world is by making fictions. As Tonka's lover notices when he debates with himself the question of marrying or leaving her, the world is as a man makes it with his fictions; abolish them and it falls apart into [']a disgusting jumble.[']"

6. Can a life of the spirit overcome the limitations of man and woman's existence on earth? Is there an adventure or journey that will carry us beyond the bounds of death?

◆ ‖ I ‖ ◆
NOTEBOOK 4

1. The notion of intellectual vivisection was borrowed from Friedrich Nietzsche, whose influence on Musil was profound. This entry was probably written before 1900.

2. A highly seasoned hors d'oeuvres with pepperoni, onions, etc., in vinegar.

3. Here is an early glimpse of the theme of the murderer-visionary—the best-known embodiment of this kind of figure in Musil's work is Christian Moosbrugger in MwQ.

4. At some time around the turn of the century Musil contacted several publishers offering them his *Paraphrasen*, a collection of literary pieces evidently inspired by his first major love affair, with a woman called Valerie; he was not successful in placing this project.

5. Herma Dietz was a young woman from the working class who lived in Brünn where Musil's father worked as a professor at the Technical University. Musil probably met her in 1901 and she became his mistress. He rented a room for her in Brünn and when he moved to Berlin Herma accompanied him. Herma is frequently referred to in the *Diaries* until her death in 1907. Tonka, the central figure of Musil's story of the same name in the collection, *Three Women*, is based on Herma.

6. Christmas roses are not roses but a hellebore (*Helleborus niger*).

7. Hauer and Hannak were probably friends with whom Musil studied in Brünn from 1898 to 1901.

8. *Einfälle*. *Einfaelle*, the plural form of the noun *Einfall*; this is derived from the verb *einfallen*, which expresses the notion of an idea occurring spontaneously to someone. In the present context *Einfaelle* has the extended sense of some kind of poetic idea that can be worked up into fiction. The translation of *Einfaelle* as "ideas" may be bland, but in the context, "inspirations" would be too much.

9. See preface note 22.

10. *Einfälle*.

11. In MwQ, chap. 10, parts of this entry are used and developed.

12. *Lust*.

13. The syntax of Musil's sentence appears to be broken.

14. *Geist*—though the range of meaning in Musil's use of this word is somewhat different from that of the English word *spirit* I have consistently translated *Geist* and its derivatives *geistig*, *Geistes*-, etc., with "spirit," "spiritual," etc. Though this occasionally results in phrases that sound a little odd in English I felt it was important to retain in the English text something of the resonance of *Geist* in Musil's lexis since it is so crucial to his thinking. (On the few occasions where I have used, after all, another English word as an equivalent, I have indicated this in a note.)

15. Musil tends to see the realm of the ethical as being that of ineffable experience, a fire of goodness; morality, by contrast, he sees as systems according to which human beings regulate their lives. Morality is more rational, ethics more mystical.

16. A literary journal, founded in 1896, to which Hugo von Hofmannsthal contributed.

17. Here Musil touches on two themes that he would develop in MwQ, the "garden" and the "asylum." A garden is presented as a special environment, often in the midst of a city, that gives scope for intense reflection, contemplation, or dialogue; in the lunatic asylum contemporary society confines men and women whose visions or actions it condemns, instead of trying to learn from them.

18. See note 17.

19. Gustav (Gustl) Donath (1878–1965) was Musil's boyhood friend; his father, Professor Eduard Donath, taught at the Technical University in Brünn with Musil's father; Gustl was later portrayed in MwQ as Walter, the oldest friend of Ulrich, the central protagonist.

20. This is an excerpt from an unidentified work.

21. Jakob Wassermann, *The History of Young Renate Fuchs* (Berlin, 1900)—a novel.

22. Rudolf Stratz, *The Foolish Virgin* (Stuttgart, 1901).

23. Musil is evidently being ironic: he will examine, in later years, the way that journalists appropriate words such as *genius* and apply them to the latest sporting sensation.

24. Evidently here an older Musil is commenting on his more youthful self who wrote the earlier part of the entry!

25. *der Verstand.*

26. In MwQ Musil explores what he calls the "Utopia of Exactitude" that appears to have been based on some kind of experiment of the kind to which he alludes here.

27. In this entry Musil uses several terms derived from the noun *Intellekt.*

28. *das Verstandliche.*

29. Stefanie Tyrka-Gebell (died 1949) ran a small salon in Graz that was attended by musicians, writers (including Musil), and officers. Diotima, the salon hostess in MwQ, may be based in part on Frau Tyrka, and the social milieu around Tyrka, the model for Diotima's circle.

30. Musil was a cigarette smoker throughout his adult life.

31. *Geistiges.*

32. *Eigenschaften.*

33. This last, incomplete section is Musil's own variant of part of the previous sentence.

34. The original German word is *Seelen*; as in the case of *Geist* ("spirit") I have chosen to translate *Seele* as "soul" even where the English equivalent sounds somewhat out of place in a given context—wherever I depart from this practice I mention this in a note.

35. This "monster in the mind" is Musil's reference to the human capacity—which, in normal people, lies dormant but remains accessible in their imagination—for violent or otherwise socially unacceptable actions.

36. Musil borrows this heading—which is in English in his text—from Emerson. It is the title of a work published in 1860.

37. Hermann Bahr, *Dialogue on the Tragic* (Berlin, 1904)—the following entry consists, apart from the opening paragraph, of Musil's commentary on this work.

38. Some details in the following piece are products of Musil's imagination—he had, for example, no brother—but much, possibly most, is based on personal experience.

39. Here Musil substitutes in his diary the name of a character from MwQ—Clarisse, who is Walter's wife—for the name Berta (which was in fact the name of Musil's nurse when he was an infant). Clarisse, based on Alice von Charlemont, has a vital role in the novel.

40. In MwQ the name of Clarisse's husband, who is based on Gustl, would be spelled "Walter" without an "h."

41. Hugo is another name of the central protagonist of the novel, based on Musil himself. Bertha becomes, as we have seen, Clarisse, Gustl becomes Walter, Robert becomes Hugo (not to mention one or two other, later names!).

42. Herma, Musil's mistress in early manhood, becomes Tonka, in the short story of the same name.

43. Another name for the central protagonist of the novel Musil was working on at this time that ultimately became MwQ. *Anders*, the German form of Andrew, means "other" or "different"—this was one of the reasons why Musil chose the name, marking the attempt of the hero to set himself apart from the contemporary world.

44. Homo, the hero of Musil's short story "Grigia," is a mining engineer.

45. *Geist.*

46. Musil mentions Anna for the first time around 1907; hardly anything is known about her except that she may have been considered as a possible match for Musil. It appears that

Musil was reading through this entry after some years had elapsed and that the relationship with Anna is on his mind.

47. The Romantic author Friedrich von Hardenberg.

◆ ‖ 2 ‖ ◆
NOTEBOOK 3

1. *geistig.*

2. Shackerl and Frau Ali are evidently two of Musil's acquaintances from Brünn where his parents lived.

3. A provincial military academy that Musil also attended.

4. Josef Popper (1838–1921) used the pseudonym "Lynkeus"; he was an engineer, literary author, and essayist.

5. Frommann's was a publishing house that brought out a series of German classics of philosophy around 1900.

6. Berlin, 1869.

7. Herma Dietz, Musil's mistress for several years when he was in his twenties.

8. Literally, "Court Councillor."

9. Commentators have suggested that this may be short for "Minette," which is some form of sexual activity.

10. Styria.

11. One of the circle around Musil's psychology professor in Berlin, Carl Stumpf, was a student of medicine and psychology called Oskar Pfungst [*sic*]. It is apparent from later entries that Musil was using this particular man as his model when drafting this fragment, which he probably intended to include in a novel.

12. Lake Garda, Italy.

13. Nicolaus von Cues (1401–1464) was Bishop of Brixen from 1450 to 1458.

14. This is yet another name referring to one of Musil's central protagonists.

15. Musil met Johannes von Allesch (1882–1967) when they were both studying psychology in Berlin and they became close friends. Indeed, the relationship was so important in Musil's life that one wonders why Musil did not portray von Allesch in his prose writing. However, some of the characteristics of Paul Arnheim, the businessman and intellectual who has a vital role in the first volume of MwQ, may have been borrowed from von Allesch, though the figure of Arnheim as a whole is modeled on Walther Rathenau, who turned to politics after a successful business career.

16. See notebook 4, note 29.

17. In MwQ Paul Arnheim falls for Diotima who, as previously suggested, may have traits from Frau Tyrka.

18. See entry in Notebook 11 for 13 June 1905.

19. Alice von Charlemont, Gustav Donath's wife, is, as we have seen, the model for Clarisse in MwQ.

20. In MwQ Musil explores the triangular relationship among Clarisse, Walter, and Ulrich, on the basis of the feelings and tensions among Alice, Gustl, and himself.

21. Ellen Key (1849–1926), a Swedish essayist and mystic whose works Musil read with interest mingled with skepticism. Her influence is evident in some of the effusions of Diotima in MwQ.

22. See reference to the (hypothetical) brother in the draft in Notebook 4.

23. This is apparently a reference to Heinrich Reiter (1856–1940), who lived with Musil's parents in an eccentric ménage à trois. This permanent houseguest gave Musil's mother the

close emotional attention that his quiet and reserved father was unable to supply. Though Musil was unable to find evidence that Reiter and his mother were lovers, he was obsessed by this question.

24. Thomas Mann, *Fiorenza* (Berlin, 1906)—a play in three acts.

25. This was Alice's younger sister.

26. One of the cast of minor characters in MwQ was Meingast, who was based on the philosopher Ludwig Klages. Klages knew the members of the von Charlemont family and though Musil apparently did not meet him personally, he was evidently fully informed about what had gone on between Klages and Alice and Lili von Charlemont. In different notes and drafts for the novel Klages is given different names—"Rössler," "Urbantschitsch," "Sziezynski," and ultimately "Meingast." Later in this entry it appears that Musil refers to him by S., perhaps short for "Sziezynski."

27. See note 26.

28. Hanna was possibly Hannah Poltzer, the daughter of another painter; Musil used her as a model for Clarisse's sister in MwQ.

29. See note 26.

30. This is clearly not the "Bertha" who is the forerunner to Clarisse in early drafts of the novel.

31. Lake Millstätter, a vacation resort in Carinthia.

32. Perhaps this is a slip of the pen for "S."?

33. Jules Bastien-Lepage (1848–1884) was a well-known portrait and landscape painter; his fame came not only from his painting but also from the account of his relationship with another painter, a Russian, Marie Bashkirtscheff (1860–1884), which she recorded in her diary. This was published in German translation in Breslau, 1897.

34. A park in Vienna.

35. Styria.

36. Raoul Auernheimer (1876–1948) worked for the Viennese newspaper *Die neue freie Presse*, and wrote short stories and plays.

37. See note 23.

38. As indicated in chap. 1, note 42, Musil based his story "Tonka" on his affair with Herma Dietz. The story starts with the death of the grandmother of the male protagonist—Tonka has been her maid—and ends with Tonka's death.

39. Vienna.

40. This sentence is the point in Musil's story where Tonka, without speaking, accepts an offer of protection from the central protagonist; it is significant in that it marks the start of the affair.

41. This is a character in "Tonka"; he is a tenor and Hugo, the central protagonist, suspects he may have had a relationship with Tonka.

42. In MwQ van Helmond [*sic*] is the name of Clarisse's father.

43. The Austrian painter of the Romantic school, Moritz von Schwind (1804–1871).

44. Though this may refer to Alice it is possibly a slip of the pen and should have been "H[erma]."

45. Elements from this passage are transposed to a scene in MwQ where the central protagonist, Ulrich, goes for a walk with Diotima. Such transpositions are common in Musil's creative work.

46. Nicolas Edme Rétif de la Bretonne (1734–1806) was a French novelist who popularized the ideas of Rousseau.

◆ II **3** II ◆
NOTEBOOK 24

1. Musil invented a machine while a student in Berlin; this so-called *Variationskreisel* was used to help in investigating perceptions of color. Later he did apparently receive a sum of money for the patent, which was eventually produced commercially. This did not, however, bring him financial independence—in other words, this entry has some basis in fact but is certainly, in parts, fiction.

2. Musil did indeed qualify as an engineer in Brünn at the age of 21.

3. *alles Seelische.*

4. The critic, Alfred Kerr (1867–1948), was a decisive influence on RM when he was attempting to establish himself as a writer. Kerr was deeply affected by Musil's novel *Young Torleß* and was a source of psychological support for Musil as a young author; when Kerr rejected Musil's next work, *Unions* [*Vereinigungen*], Musil was deeply depressed.

5. Here and in later notes Musil reflects on aspects of his reading of Edmund Husserl, *Logical Investigations* (Halle, 1900).

6. See on this instrument: Silvia Bonacchi, *1903–1908: Robert Musil's Studienjahre in Berlin, Musil-Forum*, Beilage 1, 1992, p. 14. The tachitoscope was an instrument used in psychological experiments to measure the extent of a human being's optical attention and range of perception.

7. Though the context of this entry is provided by Husserl's *Logical Investigations*, it is illustrated with a topical reference Musil makes to the "securing of peace." (In 1905 the Russo-Japanese War ended with a peace treaty negotiated between the hostile parties in the American coastal city of Portsmouth, New Hampshire.) This illustrates clearly Musil's habit of thinking through the implications of what he read.

8. The implication is, since Dresden is on the line between Berlin and Vienna, that A. has not yet reached Vienna.

9. Gustl?

10. Robert?

11. Here Musil is making notes on his reading of Maurice Maeterlinck, *Le Trésor des humbles* (1896), from which the quotation from Plotinus in this entry is taken.

◆ II **4** II ◆
NOTEBOOK II

1. This seems to refer to Musil's intention to subject feelings and other aspects of human life that had hitherto been considered unsuitable for scientific enquiry to rigorous systematic research.

2. Leipzig, 1920. Ricarda Huch (1864–1947), neo-Romantic poet, critic, and historian; among her works is the book on the Romantic movement to which Musil refers in this entry.

3. Franz von Baader, a philosopher whose collected works came out in Leipzig in 1851.

4. In many cases Musil uses the adjective *anders* ("other") in an unusually deliberate way. It then refers to a mode of perceiving the world that is quite different from the norm—in which the individual loses that sense of his or her separateness and, becoming submerged in experience, is overwhelmed by a feeling of the oneness of creation. Musil calls this "der andere Zustand" ("the other condition"); this is associated with mystical experience. Though there are many cases where it apparently does not point to the "other condition," in cases where I believe it does I have signaled this by placing the word "other" in quotes.

5. *Gehalt.*

6. The philosopher Friedrich Schelling (1775–1854).

7. Reference to a particular group of Romantics based in Jena.

8. The aesthete and writer Gabriele d'Annunzio (1863–1938).

9. *in der Moderne.*

10. *Durchgeistigung.*

11. *weder punkto sentio noch punkto mens.*

12. Franz Grillparzer, "Selbstautobiographie," vol. 19 of *Collected Works*, ed. August Sauer, 20 vols. (Stuttgart, 1893), pp. 9–168.

13. Probably a reference to a Brünn contemporary, Eugen Schick (1877–1909).

14. Musil refers to his novel *Young Törleß.*

15. *die Geburt der Moderne.*

16. Friedrich Leopold von Hardenberg (1772–1801), the German Romantic author, wrote under the pseudonym "Novalis."

17. In fact Musil wrote *"Werther"* by mistake here.

18. *Ein Dilemma* (Berlin, 1898).

19. This refers to Heinrich Reiter, Musil's parents' houseguest.

20. Near Vienna.

21. *seelisch.*

22. The publishers, J.C.C. Bruns Verlag, Minden.

23. A novel written in 1880.

24. Presumably the Institute for Psychology run by Professor Carl Stumpf.

25. My English rendering exaggerates the ineptitude of this poem; however, the original is not very good at all. The critic Wolfdietrich Rasch judged it to be an attempt by Alice von Charlemont to write something in the style of the poet Stefan George (1868–1933)—he suggests further that the influence of George was mediated by the philosopher Ludwig Klages (1872–1956) who, as we have seen, knew Alice well.

26. Cf. some of the reflections on triangular human relationships in Notebook 3.

27. This is the essay "The Unfolding of the Soul Through the Art of Life" in the literary periodical *Die neue Rundschau*, June 1905, pp. 641–86.

28. See references to Valerie in chap. 1 (Notebook 4).

29. Reference to the period he spent as an assistant at the Technical University in Stuttgart.

30. Dr. Friedrich Schumann, an assistant at the Institute for Psychology at the University of Berlin.

31. Karl Hans Strobl (1877–1946), an Austrian author.

32. Carl Stumpf (1848–1936), Professor of Psychology at the Institute where Musil studied.

33. Richard von Schaukal (1874–1942), poet and writer.

34. Peter Altenberg (1859–1919), a Viennese poet.

35. *Eigenschaft.*

36. This entry is Musil's paraphrase of a section of Ellen Key's essay mentioned earlier.

37. Carinthia, on Lake Wörther.

38. Gustl's father-in-law.

39. Reference to *Human, All-Too-Human.*

40. A character in Thomas Mann's novel *Buddenbrooks*, whose name was misremembered by Musil.

41. A school in Vienna for the children of the nobility.

42. *das stets andere Denken.*

43. *Alle hochgespannten Seelenzustände.*

44. The interplay of fidelity and infidelity will be the theme of Musil's story "The Completing of a Love."

45. *Seele.*

46. Musil himself punctuates, as I have done, with two dots.

47. Probably a Musil-persona.

48. Herma Dietz.

◆ ‖ **5** ‖ ◆

NOTEBOOK 15

1. Very little is known about Anna beyond what I have reported in my introduction.

2. Edward Munch (1863–1944), Expressionist painter.

3. Lovis Corinth (1858–1925) was a painter who taught Martha Heimann, who was later to marry Musil.

4. Paul Cassirer, the cousin of the philosopher Ernst Cassirer, founded a publishing house in 1908; in 1910 he cofounded *Pan,* a journal to which Musil contributed.

5. Father Erich Waßmann (1859–1931), zoologist and entomologist.

6. Erich von Hornbostel, musicologist and psychologist, who collaborated with Carl Stumpf, Musil's Professor of Psychology. Von Hornbostel's wife, Susi, is mentioned further in the text.

7. This is where Musil regularly took his meals.

8. Musil eventually obtained his doctorate in March 1908.

9. See note 11 in chap. 2 (Notebook 3).

10. A Berlin coffeehouse frequented by literary people.

11. Possibly "Hartmann"; the Hartmanns were acquaintances from Brünn.

12. Berlin art dealers.

13. The Jugendstil artist, Gustav Klimt (1862–1918).

14. Anna?

15. The critic Alfred Kerr—see note 4 in chap. 3 (Notebook 24).

16. See page 109, entry for 14.II.

17. Martha Marcovaldi, née Heimann (1874–1949), would later marry Musil.

18. Aubrey Beardsley (1872–1898), the artist.

19. Joseph Lanner (1801–1843), Viennese composer of popular music.

20. Thibaut IV, King of Navarra (1201–1253), French poet of courtly love.

21. One of the themes of Musil's MwQ would be the love between the central protagonist, Ulrich, and his sister, Agathe; it was a theme that preoccupied Musil for most of his adult life.

22. Frau Sanitätsrat K.

23. Per Hallström (1866–1960) wrote *An Old Story* in 1895; it was published in Germany in 1903.

◆ ‖ **6** ‖ ◆

NOTEBOOK 5

1. These were Martha's children from her marriage with Enrico Marcovaldi.

2. A reference to negotiations with Enrico Marcovaldi about the divorce. Musil eventually married Martha on 15 April 1911.

3. Musil had published a story entitled "The Enchanted House" in 1908; he was reworking this and it was later published in *Unions* in 1911 as "The Temptation of Quiet Veronika."

4. This was the other story in *Unions* that was published in 1911; it deals with infidelity in a love affair based on the relations of Musil and Martha.

5. Martha's sister, Hanna, married an art dealer and publisher, Jacques Casper.

6. Reference to the stories of *Unions*.

7. *gedanklich*.

8. For the first thirty years of his life Musil had depended on financial support from his parents; now his parents were beginning to put pressure on him to earn his own living.

9. A novel, published in 1890 (German translation published in Munich, 1895).

10. Stephanie Tyrka-Gebell, who ran a literary salon in Graz, made an anthology of work by Keller, Strindberg, Hamsun, and others, introducing each extract herself; the anthology was published under the name *Silhouetten* in Munich in 1902.

11. Reference to the story "The Temptation of Quiet Veronika."

12. Reference to the story "The Completing of Love."

13. Musil refers to his use, in "The Temptation of Quiet Veronika," of an extended passage from "The Enchanted House," the original story.

14. The reference is to Alice's state of mental health, which, as becomes clear, was unpredictable.

15. Georg Bernhard (1875–1944) was on the staff of the Ullstein publishing house to which the *B.Z.*, a popular newspaper, belonged. Musil evidently wanted to discuss with him the founding of a literary journal, *Pasquill*.

16. In December 1906 Alfred Kerr had published a very complimentary review of Musil's first novel, *Young Törleß*.

17. A reference to the plan to become a librarian in Vienna.

18. Musil would later rework the material in this entry for drafts of MwQ. It appears, however, that he originally intended to make it into a story.

19. Alice's brother was named Faust.

20. Emil Kräpelin (1856–1926) was a Munich psychiatrist.

21. Adalbert Stifter (1805–1868), the poetic realist author.

22. Reference to a sanatorium near Dresden.

23. *das Intellektuelle*.

24. Evidently Musil originally intended these entries to form the basis of a story.

25. Musil here refers to a set of highly technical notes on perception that he had drafted; it is difficult to imagine how they could have been worked into a story or novel.

26. A technical term for hyperactivity.

27. This theme will be taken up in MwQ.

28. A reference to "The Completing of Love."

29. Franz Blei (1871–1942), a gifted satirist, was a close friend of Robert Musil and a member of the small literary circle in which Musil felt at ease. He published a number of important pieces by Musil in journals he edited.

30. See earlier entry in this notebook for 12 August 1910.

31. A reference to the novellas.

32. Musil here refers to a theme from "The Temptation of Quiet Veronika."

33. *eine Vereinigung*.

34. A quotation from "The Temptation of Quiet Veronika."

35. See p. 122, also note 16, notebook 5.

36. Martha's children, Gaetano and Annina.

37. This essay, entitled "Obscenity and Sickness in Art," was published in *Pan* in March 1911.

38. The German is *Der Lose Vogel*—literally, "The Loose Bird"; a loose bird in German is a reference to someone of frivolous disposition: it is the name of a journal edited by Franz Blei.

39. Wilhelm Herzog, co-editor of *Pan*.

40. A play by Gerhart Hauptmann, first performed in 1911.

41. A reference to an article by Musil's friend von Allesch in an art journal, published in 1910.

42. Kerr was protesting about the seizure and confiscation of an earlier issue of *Pan* on the orders of the police.

43. Musil's father, Alfred Musil (b. 1846), died in October 1924, eight months after his wife.

44. Easter, 16–17 April 1911.

45. A reference to Musil's starting work as a librarian in Vienna.

46. Emma Rudolph (1875–1953) was an intelligent woman of striking appearance—she was one of the central figures in an artistic circle—who was to marry Musil's friend, von Allesch, in 1916.

47. Gerhart Hauptmann, *Michael Kramer* (Berlin, 1900); a play.

48. See p. 133.

49. This probably refers to Karl Wolfskehl (1869–1948) at whose house members of the circle around Stefan George used to meet.

50. "Raven" was Musil's pet name and symbol for Martha Musil; it is also a heading for a set of literary drafts by Musil.

51. Flat where the Musils lived for a while.

52. This observation resurfaces in Musil's play *The Enthusiasts* (*Die Schwärmer*).

53. The central character of *The Enthusiasts*.

54. Max Wertheimer (1880–1943), one of the founders of Gestalt psychology.

55. This refers to Musil's decision to turn his back on a career in academic psychology and devote himself fully to literature.

56. This relates to the notion—see entry in this notebook on 5 September 1910—that the author should express himself only *through* his characters.

◆ ‖ 7 ‖ ◆
NOTEBOOK 6

1. Musil had moved to a new flat in Vienna not far from the Prater.

2. Nietzsche's autobiographical extravaganza.

3. A quotation from Goethe's *Faust*, "Prologue in the Theater," spoken by the Fool.

4. The following draft is evidently related to a contribution to Franz Blei's journal, *Der Lose Vogel,* entitled "Religion, Modernism and Metaphysics," in 1912–1913; it is also related to work on a novel about a Catholic priest that Musil did not finish. (The translation reproduces the tenses as they stand.)

5. *Unzucht.* The German word is of etymological interest and Musil seems to play on its ambiguity. *Zucht* refers to the process whereby discipline is instilled and also the breeding of animals. *Unzucht* has come to mean obscene sexual behavior.

6. This paragraph is evidently an alternative draft of the reflections in the previous one.

◆ ‖ 8 ‖ ◆
NOTEBOOK 7

This notebook covers less than a year just before World War I.

1. Musil is in Vienna; he is visiting the Psychiatric Clinic of the University where Otto Pötzl (1877–1962) was a neurologist.

2. *Geistigkeit.*

3. Probably refers to Gustav Klimt, the painter.

4. This refers to Martha Musil's first husband, Fritz Alexander (1870–1895), who died of typhoid fever in a hotel in Florence after only ten months of marriage.

5. These are places close to Vienna.

6. Ida Roland (1881–1951), an actress.

7. Musil's friend, Franz Blei, the satirist.

8. This entry was found in 1980, sewn into the lining of a coat that had belonged to Martha Musil.

9. Musil's stepdaughter.

10. On the eastern edge of the Vienna Woods.

11. The Theresianum was, as we have seen, a Viennese school for the children of aristocrats.

12. In November 1921 Musil was to move to an address in Rasumofskygasse that became his permanent residence.

13. This stands for the name of the hero of the novel *Spion* (*Spy*); this was, first, "Achilles," later "Anders."

14. Musil is here describing a scene not far from the flat where he was then living.

15. A penciled "1913" stands next to "September."

16. This is a reference to Quirino Sergi, whose father was the Director of the Anthropological Institute. The Sergis lived in the same house in Rome as the Marcovaldis, the family into which Martha Musil had earlier married.

17. Wilhelm Wundt (1832–1920) founded in Leipzig the first Institute of Experimental Psychology.

18. A lunatic asylum.

19. "Outside the gate of the city."

20. Martha.

21. Versions of this entry would later be published in a number of newspapers and in Musil's anthology of short pieces, *Pre-Posthumous Papers*.

22. Musil uses a northern dialect spelling for what in standard Italian is *gioco di pallone*, some kind of game played with a large ball such as football, handball, or volleyball.

23. Walther Rathenau (1867–1922), the Jewish intellectual, businessman, and politician, evidently made a very profound impression on Musil. The son of the founder of the AEG (General Electric Company) in Berlin, Walther Rathenau eventually became Foreign Minister of Germany. He was assassinated by right-wing extremists. Musil used him as a model for the Jewish intellectual and entrepreneur Dr. Paul Arnheim, who is one of the major figures in the so-called Collateral Campaign in MwQ. It appears that Musil was actually introduced to Rathenau on one occasion and took an instant dislike to him.

24. See note 23 this chap. with reference to Musil's use of Rathenau as a model for Arnheim in MwQ.

25. This will become Soliman, Arnheim's black page boy, in MwQ.

◆ ‖ 9 ‖ ◆
NOTEBOOK 17

1. 24 May 1914.

2. Suburb in West Berlin.

3. This was evidently the source of the text "The Blackbird" in *Pre-Posthumous Papers*.

4. Probably a reference to Musil's essay on the war and national identity, "Europeanness, War, Germanness," published in 1914.

5. Professor Oskar Bie (1865–1938), musicologist and critic, who edited a journal, *Die neue Rundschau*; Musil worked for a few months before World War I on the staff of this journal.

6. "Memorial Church."

7. A conservative newspaper, the official organ of the *Reichspartei* ("Empire Party").

8. Though the identity of this person is not certain, it may be Albert Einstein's cousin, Alfred Einstein (1880–1952).

♦ ‖ 10 ‖ ♦
NOTEBOOK I

1. Musil adapted this entry for his story "Grigia" in *Three Women*.

2. This entry refers to Martha's first husband, Fritz Alexander, who died only months after their marriage.

3. Anselm Mornas, a character in Musil's play *The Enthusiasts*.

4. Leo Slezak (1873–1946), Viennese tenor.

5. Musil uses this exchange, virtually unchanged, in his story "Grigia."

6. Musil's memory from childhood of the smell of a chinchilla fur that belonged to his mother—see further reference in this notebook.

7. Randaschl was Musil's orderly during the war.

8. This refers to anti-personnel darts that were dropped on the enemy from aircraft.

9. This, the second part of Maxim Gorky's autobiography, was published in Germany in 1916.

10. A lake to the west of Klagenfurt in Carinthia, Austria.

11. A town in Upper Austria.

12. A city in Romania.

13. Apparently, at about the age of three or four Musil abducted a small girl from the Kindergarten in the same building where he lived and announced that henceforth she would share their home!

14. A reference the Psychological Institute in Berlin University where Musil studied.

15. Julius Carl von Bach (1847–1931) was the head of the Engineering Laboratory at the Technical University in Stuttgart, Germany, where Musil worked from 1902 to 1903.

16. Carl Stumpf was the Professor of Psychology at Berlin who supervised Musil's doctoral dissertation.

17. This and subsequent titles in the text refer to projects for novels that Musil did not write.

18. *der Geistigen.*

19. A post-doctoral dissertation written as qualification for a permanent university post in Germany and Austria.

20. A parish in Vienna.

21. An Austrian political party founded by Karl Lueger that was anti-liberal and anti-Semitic—it counted among its admirers the young Hitler, who acknowledged in *Mein Kampf* that he had learned much from its tactics and propaganda.

22. A. P. Gütersloh (1887–1973), Expressionist painter and author.

23. G. K. Chesterton (1874–1936), author of the Father Brown stories.

24. Cardinal Newmann (1801–1890).

25. Catholic monthly, founded in 1903.

26. The Catholic Cathedral in Vienna.

◆ ‖ **II** ‖ ◆
LITTLE NOTEBOOK WITHOUT A NUMBER

1. Probably Cristoforo al Lago di Caldonazzo.

2. Northeast wind.

3. This is probably a reference to Musil's friend, Johannes von Allesch, whom he had met when they were students of psychology together in Berlin.

4. In March 1916, Musil, who had an infection of the mouth, gums, and throat, was transferred to a hospital in Prague.

5. Musil originally misspelled *Faradization* by using a double "r"; he evidently has in mind some form of electric shock therapy that took its name from Michael Farady (1791–1867), a pioneer in the field of electromagnetism.

6. The following appear to be extracts from soldiers' letters that Musil, as an officer, was required to censor.

7. *Minasch* possibly for "ménage" and, by extension, "food."

8. Evidently Musil was unable to make out a word here.

9. A reference to an incident when Musil had narrowly missed being killed by a dart dropped on the Austrian lines from an enemy plane.

10. *Panama* was the name of a novel Musil planned to write about his experiences during the war at the headquarters of the Austrian Grand Duke Eugen—the Panama Canal had been constructed in the last decade of the nineteenth century and was a byword for corruption.

11. As a child Musil had been fascinated to learn that he had had an elder sister who had died in infancy before his birth; Musil's relationship with Martha brought into play some of the emotions that were focused on the sibling whom he had never known, and occasionally he would refer to Martha as his "sister"; the experiences portrayed in the relationship between Ulrich, the central protagonist of MwQ, and his sister, Agathe, were based in part on Musil's life with Martha.

12. E. V. Zenker (1865–1945) was a journalist in Vienna.

13. Dr. Benno Karpeles founded the weekly *Der Friede* (*Peace*).

14. This is a play by Musil based partly on experiences of his life with Martha before World War I.

15. A reference to the Hapsburg monarchy.

16. The organ of the Austrian Social Democratic Party.

17. Egon Erwin Kisch (1885–1948) had been a soldier under Musil's command during the war; in 1918 he led the Red Guard in Vienna. After the war he became famous for his journalism.

18. Probably refers to the Prague-born Expressionist poet and writer Franz Werfel (1890–1945).

19. References to the fig tree, etc., as in many other cases throughout the *Diaries*, are probably instances of Musil returning to ponder earlier experiences that continue to feed his creative work. The particular matter of his account of revolutionary Vienna was evidently derived from firsthand experience. He had moved to Vienna in March 1918 to be editor of a newspaper for the armed forces called *Heimat* (*Homeland*).

20. Possibly Cina di Vessena.

21. Gillian Farrar (1882–1967), American soprano who starred at the Royal Opera in Berlin from 1901 to 1907, then at the Metropolitan Opera in New York.

22. Musil's personal cross-reference to his entry about the horse in Notebook 7.

23. This is the pet form of "Grigia," the female character in Musil's story of the same name, which had been based on experiences of his in the South Tyrol during the war. The

character, Grigia, was based on a local woman who was probably Musil's mistress—Lene Maria Lenzi (1880–1954).

24. *Vereinigungen* (*Unions*).

25. The Emperor of Austria-Hungary.

26. Erich Graf Kielmannsegg (1847–1923), a leading Austrian politician.

27. Title of a planned novel.

28. The central protagonist of *The Spy*.

29. This refers to a scene planned for this novel, the execution of the murderer Christian Moosbrugger, a character who would ultimately appear in MwQ.

◆ ‖ 12 ‖ ◆
NOTEBOOK 8

1. There is evidence in this notebook of Musil integrating more insights into politics, social and cultural life in general into the pre-war corpus of psychological, philosophical, and more narrowly focused literary concerns of the pre-war period. There are ambitious plans for a whole bookshelf full of novels—some of them ironic or satirical—he is consciously seeking out a range of potential characters, and he is developing his powers of fixing in his mind, and vividly reproducing, physical settings.

2. In MwQ Ulrich intercedes on behalf of the murderer, Moosbrugger; it may be that this is a reference to an earlier variant of such a scene.

3. Reference to the White Terror after World War I.

4. "Graf Harrach" was the name of a character who became, in MwQ, "Graf Leinsdorf," the originator of the "Collateral Campaign" or "Parallel Action"—Musil's fictional plans for the celebration of the seventieth anniversary of the Emperor's accession in 1918.

5. "K" is an abbreviation for *Katakombe* (*Catacomb*).

6. Hedwig Courths-Mahler (1865–1950) was the author of more than 200 popular novels.

7. The anthroposophist Rudolf Steiner.

8. *Katakombe* (*Catacomb*), a draft novel.

9. Musil appears here to be commenting on an essay by Robert Müller in *Der neue Merkur*, December 1919; Musil collected quotations, etc., that caught his eye and incorporated them into the text of MwQ, often in modified form.

10. The countries defeated in World War I.

11. An experiment that conclusively proves, or alternatively conclusively disproves, something.

12. This story was contained in a collection of strange narratives put together by Karl Blöchlinger; it was entitled *Strange Supernatural Events from the Lives of Famous People* (Leipzig, 1901); Friedrich von Matthisson (1761–1831) traveled through the Tyrol, Switzerland, and Italy, and some of his experiences were recorded by Blöchlinger.

13. Julius Glaser (1831–1885).

14. Ludwig Fulda (1862–1939), dramatist and novelist.

15. A Viennese club for journalists and writers.

16. The play (German: *Reigen*, 1900) by Arthur Schnitzler (1862–1931).

17. Wilhelm von Humboldt (1767–1835), scholar and educationalist who founded the University of Berlin.

18. Erich Schmidt (1853–1913) was from 1886 Professor of Philology at the University of Berlin.

19. Samuel Fischer (1859–1934) was the founder of the S. Fischer Publishing House in Berlin.

20. Hedwig Fischer (1871–1952), wife of Samuel Fischer.

21. Privy Councillor.

22. Robert Müller (1887–1924), who was one of Musil's circle of friends after World War I; he contributed essays to leading journals.

23. Moosbrugger, the murderer in MwQ, was a carpenter.

24. The title of a planned satirical novel.

25. Robert Müller.

26. Excerpts from an article by Robert Müller, published in June 1920.

27. Kurt Hiller (1885–1972), a revolutionary writer who published in various journals, including *Pan* and *Die neue Rundschau*, and had some influence on Musil.

28. *Geistesgeschichte*——literally, "history of the spirit."

29. Gaaden lies to the southwest of Vienna, near Mödling.

30. *anti-häuslich*—"anti-domestic"—however, the root of *häuslich* is *Haus* ("house") and "anti-domestic" would lose the reference to the theme of "house" in the text following.

31. An age of domesticity after the defeat of Napoleon and the putting down of revolution, when society turned inward and became submissive to authority; the period spanned approximately from 1815 to 1848; it is associated, among other things, with heavy domestic furniture and stolid conformity.

32. A famous monastery near Vienna.

33. Musil uses the French word for *ceiling* here.

34. Giovanni Giuliani (1663–1774), Italian sculptor who did some of his work in Austria.

35. Martin Altomone (1657–1745), Italian artist who painted altars and ceilings throughout Austria.

36. Jacob Jordaens (1593–1678); the picture of Moses to which Musil refers exists in two versions: one, on canvas, in the State Gallery, Kassel; the other, on wood, in the Karlsruhe Art Gallery.

37. Houston Stewart Chamberlain (1855–1927), racial theorist who influenced Adolf Hitler and others.

38. Cecil Rhodes (1853–1902), British imperialist after whom Rhodesia (now Zimbabwe) was named.

39. At the beginning of World War I.

40. This refers to three drafts by Musil of his piece "The Inn in the Suburbs" ("Vorstadtgasthof").

41. This may refer to the attempt by protagonists of Musil's novels and MwQ to live a life of single-minded rationality; in MwQ this theme is treated with ironic detachment by the narrator.

◆ ‖ 13 ‖ ◆
NOTEBOOK 9

1. In South Tyrol.

2. Many of the figures in this entry are identified further in the text where they are portrayed separately.

3. "Kralik" refers to Richard K. Ritter von Meyrswalden (1852–1934), a Catholic lyric poet and dramatist.

4. *Meh* is referred to further in the text as "May."

5. Karl Hollitzer (1874–1942), a well-known Viennese painter who also sang in nightclubs.

6. Sibylle Blei, daughter of Musil's friend, Franz Blei.

7. As we saw earlier, "Concordia" was a club in Vienna for journalists and authors.

8. Karl Kraus, the Viennese satirist.

9. Made in 1919 by Abel Gance, the film criticized the Germans.

10. Archduke Leopold Salvator (1897–1958).

11. Further in this notebook, Musil quotes from Fritz Zerner's article "Die vorbereitende Revolution" ("The preparatory revolution") in *Der Strahl*, vol. 1, no. 2, January 1920.

12. Reference to the academic assistant to a university professor.

13. Musil here continues his paraphrase and quotation from Zerner.

14. "The Ray."

15. See reference further in this notebook.

16. Reference to a word portrait of New York by Robert Müller in *Der neue Merkur*, vol. 3, no. 8, January 1920.

17. Johannes Fischer (1888–1955), an Austrian painter.

18. Evidently a reference to the philosopher.

19. An unidentified acquaintance of Musil's.

20. This may refer to deserters from the Imperial Austro-Hungarian Army.

21. Probably a reference to developments after World War I when the Austro-Hungarian Empire was dissolved and a number of new states were set up.

22. Max Weber (1864–1920), the sociologist.

23. The person in question has not been identified.

24. Ea, the wife of Musil's friend, Johannes von Allesch.

25. Apparently a reference to the servant in Musil's parents' house in Brünn.

26. Erwin Ritter von Kratochwile-Löwenfeld was a fellow pupil of Musil's at the Military Academy in Mährisch-Weißkirchen.

27. I have not succeeded in getting close to the terse resonance of the German: "Schieben bildet!"

28. Heinrich von Treitschke (1834–1896), historian, politician, and supporter of Bismarck.

29. A reference to a famous saying by a member of the German Reichstag in January 1910 to the effect that, at any time, the German Kaiser could have the Reichstag sent home by a lieutenant and a detachment of ten soldiers.

30. This concept, which Musil also uses in MwQ as representing a widely held view, refers to an approach to human affairs that proceeds from a fundamentally pessimistic assessment of mankind and its potential. In dealing with people, all appeals to "better nature" are to be avoided; force is, from this perspective, a more reliable strategy.

31. Presumably this entry refers to an article Musil read somewhere.

32. A reference to Kant's concept according to which each individual has an innate sense of what is morally required in any given situation.

◆ ‖ 14 ‖ ◆
NOTEBOOK 10

1. Presumably a reference to early novel plans including *The Spy* and *The Redeemer*.

2. Probably the novel *Panama*.

3. Presumably to be based on Martha Musil's experiences.

4. Ernst Zahn (1867–1952), Swiss author who wrote stories of peasant life.

5. Walter Bloem (1868–1951) wrote about simple folk from a nationalist perspective.

6. Paul Ernst (1866–1933), neoclassical author of novellas and plays.

7. Eduard Stucken (1865–1936), playwright and author of stories many of which were concerned with legends.

8. Ernst Hardt (1876–1947), neo-Romantic author of plays and poetry.

9. Reference to the hero of Dostoyevsky's novel *Crime and Punishment*.

10. *Hannele's Ascension to Heaven* is a play by Gerhart Hauptmann, published in 1894.

11. A novel by Heinrich Mann, published in 1909.

12. Reference to Maurice Maeterlinck, *La Sagesse et la destinée* (Leipzig: Eugen Diederichs, 1899).

13. Presumably a reference to the kind of experiments in aesthetics that Musil's friend, Johannes von Allesch, conducted in Berlin.

14. Björnstjerne Björnson, *Selected Works*, ed. Thomas Schäfer (Berlin: Peter J. Oestergaard, 1910), vol. 1, "Village Tales."

15. Helene Alving, the central character of Ibsen's *Ghosts*.

16. Helen Keller (1880–1968); Musil is evidently referring to her being blind and deaf.

17. Musil was fascinated by time lags between the act of willing an action and the action actually happening. One example is turning over in bed at night. See, for example, MwQ, part III, chap. 10—MoE, p. 737, also notebook II, p. 101.

18. *Gleichnisse*.

19. Ludwig Klages, *Vom kosmogonischen Eros* (*Of Cosmogonic Love*), 1922.

20. The Samuel Fischer Publishing House in Berlin.

21. Reference to *The Enthusiasts* (Dresden: Sibyllen-Verlag, 1921).

22. At this point Musil makes notes on a work by Thomas Mann, *Reflections of a Non-Political Man* (Berlin: S. Fischer, 1918).

23. Reference to a novel by A. P. Gütersloh, *Die tanzende Törin* (Munich: Georg Müller, 1913).

24. Theodor Däubler (1876–1934), literary author; this entry refers possibly to notes on his travels.

25. Alfred Wolfenstein (1888–1945), Expressionist lyric poet.

26. Kasimir Edschmid (1890–1966), Expressionist writer.

27. Musil had written reviews of R. J. Sorge's play *The Beggar* in *Die neue Rundschau*, Berlin, January 1913, and of Alfred Wolfenstein's collection of poems, *The Godless Years*, in the same journal, June 1914.

28. Here *singular* used in the sense of "relating to an individual."

29. In MwQ Musil explores the way in which the processes of justice inexorably move toward a definite answer to the question "Is this individual responsible for his actions or not?" and condemn or absolve accordingly. The creative writer, by contrast, seeks to reconstruct the total context in which the event took place that has led to a trial.

30. 1900.

31. (Paris: Delagrave, 1879–1882).

32. (Hamburg, Leipzig, 1862–1864).

33. (Leipzig: Günter, 1892–1897).

34. See previous reference to work by H. S. Chamberlain.

35. A work quoted by Chamberlain: Rudolf von Ihering, *Prehistory of the Indo-Europeans*, ed. Viktor Ehrenberg (Leipzig: Breitkopf & Härtel, Duncker & Humblot, 1894).

36. "Sexus."

37. Musil makes a play on words with *ringen*, "to wrestle," and *erringen*, "to achieve by effort" or "to wrest."

38. (Munich: Langen, 1914).

39. Regine is one of the main characters of *The Enthusiasts*.

40. Next to these doses of poison Musil drew a large cross to indicate their lethal effect.

NOTEBOOK 19

1. The German is *denke ich mir die Sache anders*; since Musil often uses the adjective *anders* with a special weight of meaning (as I believe he does here), I have placed the translation "other" in quotes to give it special emphasis. Musil's expression "Der andere Zustand" ("The 'other' condition") refers to a mental state in which the selfhood of the individual merges with the universe as a whole. This state is so central to Musil's thinking that it seems to color his perception and usage of the adjective *anders* even when "der andere Zustand" is not directly mentioned.

2. Wilhelm Wundt (1832–1920) who, as we saw earlier, founded the first institute for experimental psychology in Leipzig.

3. Karl Lamprecht (1856–1915), historian of culture.

4. Houston Stewart Chamberlain (1855–1927)—Musil makes notes on his work *The Foundations of the Nineteenth Century* further in this notebook.

5. This may refer to *Letters Concerning Toleration* (1632–1704).

6. To a United Kingdom reader, the image and thereby the sequence, is clear. The penny-farthing was an oddly shaped two wheeler with a huge pedal-driven front-wheel some 5 feet in diameter and a miniscule rear-wheel to give minimum stability. (The image implied in the name "penny-farthing" is that of the front wheel as the "penny," a large coin, while the back wheel is the "farthing," a tiny coin worth one quarter of a penny.) The penny-farthing was hazardous to ride and the next bicycle in this technological progression, with its two more sensibly sized wheels, was a "safety cycle" by comparison.

7. Reference to the Vienna School of Philosophy, the "Verein Ernst Mach."

8. In this entry Musil makes notes on, and excerpts from, Chamberlain's work.

9. (1881–1888).

10. (1879–1894).

11. *History of Scientific-Academic Instruction in German Schools and Universities*, 1885).

12. (1860–1864).

13. Woodrow Wilson (1856–1924), President of the United States from 1913 to 1921.

14. Theobald von Bethmann Hollweg (1856–1921) was from 1909 to 1917 Imperial German Chancellor.

15. K. H. Helfferich (1872–1924) held senior ministerial posts in Imperial Germany, including that of Deputy Reichskanzler.

16. J. H. Heinrich Graf von Berstorff (1862–1939) was Ambassador in Washington from 1908 to 1917.

17. Nikolaus von Horthy (1868–1957) was in 1918 in command of the Austro-Hungarian Fleet; he led the Nationalist Army, which was in action in Budapest against the Communists in 1919. Musil's comment on the speech in question was that, like others, it contained "not a single word that belongs to the present."

18. Reference to the shooting of hostages in Munich on 30 April 1919 during the period of Communist rule there.

19. Ludwig Rubiner (1881–1920), a revolutionary activist and Expressionist.

20. Reference to a newspaper article by Guttmann about the psychology of the cinema.

21. Emil Fey (1886–1938) founded in 1919 an anti-Communist self-defense organization, the "Heimwehr"; this became very important in Austrian life.

22. A reference to the separatists who supported an Independent Province of the Rhine; this was set up in 1923.

23. Leopold Jessner (1878–1945) was a highly innovative general director of the Berlin State Theaters.

24. Kurt Eisner (1867–1919) became the first minister-president of the Bavarian Republic and was later murdered.

25. Musil is evidently mistaken about this "murder." Georg Ledebour (1850–1947) was an Independent Socialist and member of the Reichstag.

26. (Stuttgart, 1919).

27. Anton Graf von Arco auf Valley (1897–1945) murdered Kurt Eisner in 1919—see note 24 this chap.

28. As a twenty-year-old grammar school boy in January 1920, von Hirschfeld made an attempt on the life of the Center Party politician, Matthias Erzberger.

29. Rudolf Eisler (1873–1926), Austrian writer on philosophy.

30. "In this sign you will be victorious."

◆ ‖ 16 ‖ ◆
NOTEBOOK 21

1. Gustav Donath's father.

2. Leopold Kunschak (1871–1953), Austrian politician who founded the Association of Christian Workers.

3. Georg Kerschensteiner (1852–1934), schoolmaster and activist for educational reform, whom Musil would use as a model for Agathe's husband in MwQ.

4. Friedrich Wilhelm Foerster is to be found in MwQ in the figure of Lindner, the pedagogue who falls in love with Agathe.

5. Either a deliberate or an unintended reference to another writer, Wilhelm Meyer-Förster (1862–1934).

6. In the Berlin Zoo.

7. Heimann was Martha's maiden name.

8. *The Catacomb*, one of several planned novels, was to have as its central character Achilles, an anarchist.

9. There follow quotations from works by Kerschensteiner that will ultimately find their way into MwQ.

10. This evidently prefigures Rachel, Diotima's Jewish serving girl in MwQ.

11. This is paraphrased from Foerster's *How to Live One's Life*.

12. Richard Dehmel (1863–1920).

13. Musil writes "Anders" with the first letter in uppercase; he thereby seems to indicate that the choice of the name "Anders" ("Andrew") for the hero of earlier drafts of his novel has absorbed something of the mystical quality that is often present in Musil's use of *anders* as an adjective elsewhere.

14. Ferdinando Galiani (1728–1787), Italian economist who influenced Karl Marx.

15. François Quesnay (1694–1774), French economist and philosopher.

16. As we have seen, *The Redeemer* is the title of one of the novels Musil planned.

17. Laurence Sterne (1713–1768), author of *Tristram Shandy*.

18. Montesquieu's *Lettres persanes*, in which the author provides a critique of contemporary France disguised as travel correspondence.

19. Musil's stepdaughter.

20. Musil's stepson.

21. A reference to the planned opening of the novel.

22. Apparently a reference to the German Revolution in 1919.

23. Graf Harrach, who later became "Graf Leinsdor" in MwQ.

24. The "Campaign" or "Parallel Action" is an enterprise Musil invented for satirical purposes in MwQ: a year of celebrations is planned to mark the seventieth anniversary of Francis Joseph's accession to the Imperial Throne—in fact the anniversary will fall in 1918, the year in which the monarchy collapsed.

25. This is a reference to the groups of people who seek to promote their particular interests through the campaign in question.

26. Musil changed his fictitious names around in different drafts; probably "Lindner," in this entry, refers to the character based on Ludwig Klages.

27. This and subsequent quotations attributed to Diotima are derived, sometimes with small adjustments to the German translation, from Maeterlinck, *Le Trésor des humbles*.

28. This and the following entries, through to the one on Agathe that ends with a reference to Schopenhauer, contain further quotations from Maeterlinck.

29. *Entschließung* can imply both "resolving" and "opening."

30. "Meingast" appears here to refer to the Ludwig Klages character in MwQ.

31. Adolf Frisé believes this to be a reference to Agathe's husband. In the final version of the novel, Musil has changed the name to "Hagauer"; this Lindner/Hagauer character is based on the educationalist, Georg Kerschensteiner, while Foerster, mentioned in note 4 of Notebook 21, influenced the character who became Lindner in the last drafts. A note of danger for Agathe is implicit in Musil's remark that it was a "mistake" for Ulrich to take his sister "completely away" from another sphere of male influence but the remark could apply to either of these men.

32. Possibly a reference to Robert Müller.

33. Here Maeterlinck is referring to Racine's tragedies *Bérénice* and *Andromaque*.

34. This appears to be a reference to the view expressed by the philosopher Arthur Schopenhauer in *The World as Will and Representation* that, while individuals have a transitory existence suspended in illusion, the species is permanent, indeed eternal.

35. The central protagonist of the play by Ibsen of the same name.

36. In 1922 Musil spent the month of August on holiday at the Baltic coast on the island of Usedom; he sent a sketch based on this draft to the newspaper *Prager Presse*.

37. Many, indeed most, of the themes touched on in this entry survive in some form or other in MwQ.

38. Both of these women are mistresses of Anders.

39. A reference to a letter to Anders from his father that brings the former into contact with the campaign, thus setting a main theme of the plot in motion.

40. "Graf Bühl," forerunner of "Graf Leinsdorf" in MwQ.

41. Reference to the will of Anders's father.

42. Anders.

43. A theme that finds a point of focus in the question of whether Moosbrugger, the murderer, is accountable or unaccountable for his actions.

44. Samuel von Pufendorf (1632–1694), who in his main work, *De iure naturae et gentium*, was an advocate of natural law.

45. Surviving into MwQ is the bitter legal rivalry between two lawyers representing different positions in jurisprudence; one of these is the hero's father.

46. The hero's father has recently died.

47. Title of a piece in *Berliner Börsen-Courier* of 24 December 1922.

48. Gerda Fischel, a young woman who falls in love with the central protagonist of the novel.

49. This whole paragraph relates to the segment of the novel *The Journey to Paradise*.

50. In MwQ the hero meets his sister, Agathe, in the house where the body of their recently deceased father lies, awaiting burial.

51. The books in this entry are taken from the bibliography to Ludwig Klages, *Vom kosmogonischen Eros* (Munich: Georg Müller, 1922).

52. *The Nature of the Ancient Mysteries, Illuminated by the History of Religions, Ethnology and Psychology* (Leiden: Brill, 1919).

53. 1853.

54. (Göttingen: Vandenhoeck & Ruprecht, 1894).

55. (Leipzig: Teubner, 1903).

56. (Berlin and Leipzig: Sammlung Göschen, 1913).

57. (Freiburg: Mohr, 1899).

58. (Basel: Schweighauser, 1867).

59. (Berlin: Weichmann, 1894–1926).

60. (Leipzig: Teubner, 1884–1937).

61. (Stuttgart: Metzler, 1894–1968).

62. (Breslaus: Korn, 1857).

63. 4 vols., 1836–1842.

64. (Berlin: Hertz, 1889).

65. (Berlin: Bornhaeger, 1904–1905).

66. (Hannover: Hahn, 1878).

67. Erwin Rohde, 2 vols., published in 1890 and 1894.

68. (Stuttgart, 1861).

69. (Basel, 1859).

70. (Freiburg im Breisgau, 1862).

71. (Heidelberg, 1870).

72. Her name is Bonadea.

73. The following bibliographical notes are taken from the footnotes to Lévy-Brühl's *The Thinking of Native Peoples*.

74. The reference is to an article by Cushing, "Manual Concepts. A Study of the Influence of Hand Usage on Culture-Growth" in *The Anthropologist* 5 (1892): 289–317.

75. This entry is concerned with events immediately after the death of Musil's mother, Hermine, on 24 January 1924.

76. This may refer not to Musil's father but to Heinrich Reiter, the man to whom Musil's mother turned for emotional support and who, as we saw earlier, lived with Musil's parents in Brünn.

77. Musil possibly refers here to his mother's cook.

78. Northern Bohemia.

79. Brünn, where Musil spent much of his youth.

80. Possibly the mother was talking about her maid, Marie.

81. Heinrich Reiter, the male companion of Musil's mother.

82. *Weltbild.*

83. A Viennese journalist.

84. *Das Andre.*

85. Ignaz Seipel (1876–1932), Catholic theologian, Christian-Social politician, and—from 1922 to 1924, 1926 to 1929—Federal Chancellor of Austria.

86. In English in the original.

87. In the original, Musil attempts to reproduce the local dialect.

88. A satirical novel about a fictional planet.

89. One of the main streets in Vienna.

♦ ‖ 17 ‖ ♦

NOTEBOOK 25

1. Here Musil plays on the chance resemblance between the verb *deduzieren* ("to deduce") and the adjective *zierlich* ("delicate"), coining his own adjective *deduzierlich* ("delico-deductive").

2. This is apparently a reference to Schelling's philosophy in which thought and existence are identical; the discovery of this identity would provide the Archimedean place to stand and lever the world off its axis.

3. School of philosophy founded in Athens circa 300 B.C.; the wise man, from the perspective of stoical philosophy, is one who keeps his emotions under firm control and accepts whatever experiences fate has in store.

4. The Greek philosopher Epicurus (341–271 B.C.) taught that lasting happiness comes only from the imperturbability of the soul and the limitation of desire; the absence of pain was inseparable from virtue.

5. Wilhelm Dilthey (1833–1911), the founder of the school of the philosophy of life and experience in Germany, whose approach to philosophy was opposed to the scientific psychology of Wilhelm Wundt and his followers.

6. Among the experiments carried out in Stumpf's Institute in Berlin during Musil's time as a student were those that involved investigating the subjective responses of different individuals to an identical, precisely measured color stimulus; it turned out that these responses varied considerably.

7. Reference to Max Stirner (1806–1856).

8. This is a reference to a book, *Life in the Ancient World Seen Through Letters*, ed. Alexander von Gleichen-Rußwurm, 1911.

9. See also MwQ, part III, chap. 10, "The Morality of the Next Step."

10. This refers to a category of thinking for which Musil borrowed a term from the stock market: speculating "à la baisse" involved a pessimistic assessment of the future direction of the majority of shares; philosophical speculation "à la baisse" is Musil's shorthand for philosophy based on a pessimistic assessment of the prime motives behind human action.

11. The original word is *deutschvölkisch*.

12. These notes are prompted by Musil's reading of Ludwig Klages, *Vom kosmogonischen Eros*.

13. Musil has set out these words in the form of an equation.

14. Rudolf Kassner, *The Morality of Music*, 1905.

♦ ‖ 18 ‖ ♦

NOTEBOOK 26

1. This was the title of a lecture Musil gave on 16 December 1934.

2. *Weltbild*.

3. The original here is possibly flawed.

4. *intellektuell*.

5. Perhaps this is a slip of the pen and should read "without changing them."

6. One wonders what Musil meant by this.

7. Wolfgang Köhler (1887–1967) was one of the founders of the school of Gestalt psychology.

8. Musil's friend Johannes von Allesch, also a psychologist.

9. In MwQ the educational theorist Friedrich Wilhelm Foerster was portrayed in the figure of Professor August Lindner; Musil delights in portraying some of the problems Foerster/Lindner, the educational theorist, has in the practical upbringing of his own son.

10. Perhaps Musil's lettering for the subdivisions is inaccurate.

11. Here Musil refers to the second part of an essay, published in *Die neue Rundschau,* no. 12, 1921.

12. Further reference to the essay in *Die neue Rundschau.*

13. Reference to a theme of the essay *The German as Symptom.*

◆ ‖ 19 ‖ ◆

NOTEBOOK 28

1. Plan for a satire on the Section for Creative Writing that was affiliated with the Prussian Academy of Arts in March 1926.

2. A planned novel.

3. Another planned novel.

4. The original German is *Umschiebung;* this means, literally, "pushing around" but the root verb *schieben* refers by extension to activities on the black market.

5. Anton Wildgans (1881–1932), a writer who also became Director of the Burgtheater in Vienna.

6. Reference to Ludwig Fulda (1862–1932), who wrote poems and plays.

7. Richard Specht (1870–1932), author of poems, stories, and plays.

8. C. H. Becker (1876–1933) was from 1925 to 1930 the Prussian Minister for Arts, Science and Education, whose decree brought into existence the Section for Creative Writing of the Prussian Academy of Arts—see earlier.

9. This was a draft of Musil's short story "The Blackbird."

10. Josef Werndl was the maker of the "Werndl Gun," which was made in his factory in Steyr.

11. Possibly a reference to Musil's experiences as a student at the Psychological Institute in Berlin.

12. This is a reference to Martha Musil, who had black hair.

13. This is another novel project: *The Land over the South Pole.*

14. Rilke's book of this name, published in 1903.

15. Musil's friend, Johannes von Allesch.

16. Reference to a verse from a poem by Henrik Ibsen.

17. Musil apparently meant to refer to November, not December: 6.XI.30 was the date of his fiftieth birthday.

18. Carinthia, Austria.

19. Reference to the fair copy of MwQ.

20. This may refer to financial problems that led to Musil's not receiving the money that should have accompanied the Hauptmann Prize for literature, which he had been awarded.

◆ ‖ 20 ‖ ◆

NOTEBOOK 30

1. Frau Stanek is probably the wife of the caretaker of the flats where Robert and Martha Musil lived—Rasumofskygasse 20 in Vienna's third district.

2. This is a reference to a report and leading article on the "Day of the Book" that appeared in the Viennese newspaper *Der Tag,* 22 March 1929.

3. The Viennese author Oskar Maurus Fontana (b. 1889).

4. SDS is the acronym of the "Schutzverband deutscher Schriftsteller" ("The Association of German Writers"), which had been established in 1912.

5. Julius Bauer (1853–1941), a theater critic and editor of the *Wiener Extrablatt.*

6. Leo Fischel, a Jewish banker, is a character in MwQ. The reference here is to MwQ, part II, chap. 51.

7. References to performances in Berlin of Musil's play *The Enthusiasts*.

8. Fred Hildenbrandt was editor of the review section of the *Berliner Tageblatt*.

9. Dr. Hugo Lukács (b. 1879), a psychiatrist of the Adler school whom Musil consulted in the 1920s about his difficulties in overcoming writer's block.

10. G. E. Müller (1850–1934) was the cofounder of Experimental Psychology.

11. Karl Bühler (1879–1963), a pioneering educational psychologist at the University of Vienna who later emigrated to the United States.

12. Musil was to have been awarded the 1929 Gerhart Hauptmann Prize but apparently Herr Wasservogel, who is mentioned later in the text, failed to provide the corresponding funds.

13. Probably Stefan Großman (1875–1935), who was the editor of the weekly *Das Tagebuch*.

14. Reference to the first volume of MwQ.

15. Richard Götz was editor of the review section of *Der Tag*, a Viennese paper.

16. Reference to two essays by Musil: "Spirit and Experience" and "Helpless Europe."

17. MwQ, part II, chap. 113.

18. Wilhelm von Scholz (1874–1969) was a former president of the Prussian Academy of Arts; the reference to "Sülfmeister" is to a short story by Julius Wolf entitled "Der Sülfmeister," which was written in 1883.

19. A Viennese dentist.

20. Leopold Schwarzschild (1892–1950) published the weekly journal *Das Tagebuch*.

21. A play by Karl Kraus.

22. Helene has not been identified.

23. Charlotte Bühler (1893–1974) was the wife of Karl Bühler, the psychologist—see note 11 this chap.

24. Reference to Jaroslav Hasek's novel *Good Soldier Schweik (The Adventures of Brave Soldier Schweik)*, which was made into a play by Erwin Piscator and later adapted by Brecht.

25. MwQ, part II, chap. 116.

26. Josef Adler, a bank official and acquaintance of Musil.

27. Herbert Ihering (b. 1888) was theater critic for the *Berliner Börsen-Courier*.

28. Bernhard Diebold (1886–1945) was Berlin theater critic of the *Frankfurter Zeitung*.

29. MwQ, part II, chap. 115.

30. Regina Ullmann (1884–1961), Swiss author.

31. MwQ, part II, chap. 119.

32. MwQ, part I, chaps. 9–11.

33. MwQ, part I, chap. 12.

34. Franz Werfel (1890–1945), an Expressionist poet.

35. See note 15 this chap.—Richard Götz, who was a literary editor for the Viennese newspaper *Der Tag*.

36. A beer hall selling Pilsner.

37. Musil refers here to the time after World War I when he worked for the War Ministry.

38. MwQ, part II, chap. 28.

39. *The Sleepwalkers.*

40. A reference to Ernst Rowohlt (1887–1960) who, with an agreement in 1923, became Musil's publisher.

41. Pseudonym of a doctor, Benno Juhn, who wrote a popular medical column for the newspaper.

42. The French title is *Si le grain ne meurt*, the English title *Let It Die*.

43. Novel by Goethe.

44. Reference to the view from the window of Musil's flat.

45. Heinrich Reiter, the family friend who lived with Musil's parents.

46. Alfred Polgar (1875–1955), Viennese author.

47. Berthold Viertel (1885–1953), who directed Musil's play *Vinzenz and the Girlfriend of Important Men* in 1923.

48. Musil's psychiatrist—see note 9 in this notebook.

49. Martha Musil's son by her previous husband, Enrico Marcovaldi.

50. Symbol referring to something Musil wished to keep secret.

51. References to MwQ, part II.

52. H. H. Ortner (1895–1956), Austrian playwright.

53. The effort to finish MwQ had meant that Musil had lost potential income from other sources and was running out of money. He had been awarded the Hauptmann Prize but the foundation was in financial difficulties and Musil had not received the money due to him; he had written to his former publisher, Samuel Fischer, to see if he could help in any way.

54. Robert Musil's publisher in 1923—see note 40 in this notebook.

55. Friedrich Eckstein had a reputation as a man of unusual breadth of knowledge.

56. Herr Flach owned a factory in Brünn.

57. René Miller-Fülop was the author of a book on the Jesuits.

58. Paul Claudel (1868–1955), French poet and playwright.

59. Alfred Döblin (1878–1957), author best known for his novel *Berlin Alexanderplatz* (1929).

60. Otto Pötzl, a Viennese clinical psychiatrist.

61. F. G. Waldmüller (1793–1865), an Austrian painter, precursor of realism.

62. "Forgive the expression."

63. August von Pettenkofen (1822–1889), Austrian genre painter.

64. Arnold Böcklin (1827–1901), Swiss painter.

65. A village near Fontainebleau that is associated with a school of painting that influenced Pettenkofen who is mentioned earlier by Musil.

66. Valentin Zeileis, a doctor whose supporters were convinced that he was capable of performing near-miraculous cures.

67. Felix Salten (1869–1945), Viennese author and literary editor.

68. G. B. Fischer, son-in-law of the publisher Samuel Fischer. After Samuel Fischer died, the son-in-law founded the Bermann-Fischer Publishing House in Vienna in 1935. A continuation of MwQ was actually typeset by Bermann-Fischer in 1938 but did not appear.

69. From 1914 to 1920 Musil's work had been published by Samuel Fischer.

70. Hotel on the Ringstrasse in Vienna.

71. Reference to negotiations with Fischer in 1919–1920 over a contract to continue publication of Musil's works.

72. Apparently Musil was mistaken in the name—Benno Reifenberg [*sic*] (1892–1970) was from 1924 to 1930 editor of the literary review of the *Frankfurter Zeitung*.

73. Hans Liebstöckl (1872–1934) was editor of the Viennese journal *Die Bühne* (*The Stage*).

74. See note 66 in this notebook.

75. Sonja Bogs was the actress who played the role of Regine in the production of Musil's play *The Enthusiasts* in Berlin.

76. See note 5 in this notebook.

77. Erich von Salzmann had published a book on China in 1929.

78. Rudolf Olden (1885–1940), journalist in Vienna and Berlin, one of Musil's supporters.

79. Dr. Hermann Sinsheimer was in charge of the literary review of the *Berliner Tageblatt*.

80. Franz Theodor Czokor (1885–1969), Austrian author.

81. Soma Morgenstern (1890–1976), Viennese cultural correspondent of the *Frankfurter Zeitung*, who arranged for his paper to publish several chapters of MwQ in the period from 1931 to 1932.

82. Possibly the wife of the painter Georg Kirsta.

83. Max Mell (1882–1971), Austrian playwright.

84. Clare Sheridan, *I, My Children, and the Major World Powers* (Leipzig, 1929).

85. Anna Leznay, a Hungarian painter and poet who lived in Vienna.

86. Family name for Martha Musil.

87. Musil's review of this work appeared in the *Frankfurter Zeitung* on 11 May 1930.

88. MwQ was printed by Jakob Hegner of Hellerau near Dresden.

89. The quotation marks were so-called goosefeet (arrow marks)!

90. Norman Linker taught at a Viennese grammar school.

91. Musil's cross-reference to the entry made on 16 March.

92. The original is "das Spirituelle."

93. Emil Ludwig (1881–1948) and his wife. Ludwig, a biographical novelist, was one of Rowohlt's most successful authors.

94. Reference to the newspaper *Der Tag*.

95. The editor of *Der Tag*.

96. Camillo Castiglioni (1879–1957) was one of Austria's leading financiers.

97. Frau Dr. Fannina Halle, the widow of a manufacturer, was an art historian and author of a book on women in Soviet Russia.

98. Richart Specht (1870–1932) wrote poems, stories, and plays.

99. *Die Aktion* was an Expressionist periodical edited in the period 1911 to 1913.

100. Johannes R. Becher (1891–1958), the Expressionist poet who joined the Communist Party and eventually became Minister for Culture in the German Democratic Republic.

101. The words are very similar in German: *Buche* is "beech"; *Buch* is "book."

102. *Herzfeld*—literally, "heart-field"—sounds rather like *Herzfehler*—"heart-flaw."

103. Heinrich Zschokke (1771–1848), Swiss realist author.

104. This is in the Viennese park the Prater.

105. This, the first section of MwQ, was eventually to appear at the end of 1930.

106. Musil made very few entries in his notebooks for the months of June, July, and August 1930.

107. The first section of the novel to be published contained part I and part II.

108. Max Reinhardt (1873–1943), theater director in Berlin and Vienna.

109. F. K. Ginzkey (1871–1963), Austrian author.

110. This entry is made nearly two years after the previous one—in the meantime Musil has moved to Berlin, where he lives on the Kurfürstendamm (No. 17) in the Pension Stern; the move is intended to give him the critical detachment to finish the novel.

111. *Glück* ("happiness") in German does not usually have a plural form—hence Musil's questioning of the hypothetical plural ending *Glück-e*. The reference is to MwQ, part III, chap. 19.

112. Gerhart Hauptmann (1862–1946), the Naturalist playwright.

113. The standard English translations of Freud render *Ich* as "ego" rather than "I."

114. Hans Castorp is the central protagonist of Thomas Mann's novel *The Magic Mountain*.

115. Hermann Goering (1893–1946).

116. Goering?

117. This is a reference to the root of the word *fascism*. The "fascio" or bundle of twigs symbolized the power of the Roman consul over life and death.

118. This was the paramilitary wing of the National Socialist German Workers Party.

119. Klaus and Ine were the children of Martha Musil's daughter, Annina; Auguste was a maidservant.

120. The German Army.

121. *der Geistigen.*

122. Wilhelm Frick (1877–1946), Minister for Internal Affairs.

123. Paul Barnay (1884–1960), director of the Breslau Theater, discovered Marlene Dietrich and Carola Neher.

124. H. H. Ewers (1871–1943), novelist associated with Nazism.

125. Walter Bloem (1868–1951), author of nationalistic novels.

126. Friedrich Gundolf (1880–1931), one of the leading Germanists of his generation, taught in Heidelberg and, for a while, was a member of Stefan George's circle of admirers.

127. Annina, Martha's daughter, was married to Otto Rosenthal; at this time they were living in Berlin.

128. Siegfried von Kardorff (1873–1945) was a member of the Reichstag; Musil was quite well acquainted with his brother, Konrad.

129. The ceremonial opening of the Reichstag in March 1933, shortly after Hitler had come to power.

130. Wilhelm II (1848–1921) was "Kaiser Bill," Emperor of Germany at the time of World War I.

131. Otto of Bavaria (1848–1916) became King of Bavaria in 1886 even though he had been insane since 1872.

132. Olaf Gulbransson (1873–1958), Norwegian graphic artist who worked for the German satirical magazine *Simplicissimus.*

133. T. T. Heine (1867–1948), leading caricaturist of *Simplicissimus.*

134. Erna Morena (1892–1962) was one of the stars of silent films in Germany.

135. *Geistesgeschichte.*

136. A bookshop in Vienna.

137. This entry probably arose through Musil's reading of Cassirer's *The Philosophy of Symbolic Forms.*

138. Reference to a story about the Blocksberg by the German physicist and author Georg Christoph Lichtenberg (1742–1799).

139. *Niels Lyhne* was a novel written in 1880 by Jens Peter Jacobsen (1847–1855), a Danish writer influenced by Naturalist theories and who in turn influenced literary impressionism.

140. Musil uses "C." (relating to "Carlyle" or possibly, on occasions, "Caesar") as a covert sign for "Hitler."

141. *demos* is "people," "plebs."

142. Reference to Schopenhauer's *The World as Will and Representation,* vol. 2, chap. 44.

143. Reference to General Stumm von Bordwehr, a character in MwQ. Musil's novel has recently appeared in a two-volume edition by Burton Pike, translated by Sophie Wilkins and the editor (New York: Knopf, 1995). Further references are to this new translation.

144. MwQ, vol. 1, chap. 72.

145. Reference to the several members of the Mann family who were authors: Heinrich and Thomas, Erika and Klaus.

146. Musil planned to write a book of aphorisms.

147. MwQ, vol. 2, chap. 14.

148. *sittlich*.

149. Richard von Coudenhove-Kalergi (b. 1894) founded the Pan-Europe Movement with the aim of bringing about a European federation.

150. "Our era is dripping with the energy of action. It's not interested in ideas, only in deeds" (MwQ, vol. 2, part II, chap. 10, p. 804); "It's so simple to have the energy to act, and so hard to make any sense of it!" (p. 805).

151. Adolf Frisé believes this may refer to a Frau Olschki (*sic*), the wife of the director of a Berlin bank; he moved in the same circles as Musil and may have belonged to the group that gave Musil financial support to help with the completion of *The Man without Qualities*.

152. Ernst Kretschmer, *Medical Psychology* (Leipzig, 1921); see particularly part II, chap. 3, section entitled "The Sphere."

153. Musil separates the two elements of *Bewußtsein* with a hyphen thus: "Bewußt-sein"; *bewußt* means "aware," "conscious," while *sein* is "to be" or "being." In this way he reminds his reader that consciousness is "being-aware."

154. Ernst Mach (1838–1916), physicist and philosopher, whose theories Musil examined in his doctoral dissertation.

155. Reference to an excerpt from a work by Kurt Lewin (1890–1947), one of the leading Gestalt psychologists. Musil misspells the name.

156. Abbreviation for "Unbekanntes höheres Wesen!" ("Unknown higher Being!")

157. It is not clear from the context whether this "he" and subsequent ones in the passage refer to "God" or to "the believer." My own impression is that "he" refers to "God."

158. Klaus Mann, one of Thomas Mann's sons, was a writer—see also note 145 this notebook.

159. The Expressionist lyric poet Georg Kulka (1897–1929) published in 1919–1920 a plagiarism of a work by the novelist Jean Paul Richter (1763–1825).

♦ ‖ 21 ‖ ♦

NOTEBOOK 31

1. Reinhard Goering (1887–1936) wrote his tragedy *Battle at Sea* in 1917.

2. A radio play.

3. Arnolt Bronnen (1895–1959), Expressionist author, wrote a novel about Upper Silesia (*Oberschlesien*—abbreviated O.S.).

4. Ludwig Renn (b. 1889) published in 1928 *War*, the diary of a soldier at the front.

5. MwQ, vol. 1, chap. 61.

6. Edgar Wallace (1875–1932), author of detective stories.

7. Lion Feuchtwanger (1884–1958), novelist.

8. Alfred Neumann (1895–1952), novelist.

9. A Berlin publishing house.

10. Probably a reference to the work of the Viennese psychiatrist and neurologist Heinrich Kogerer (1887–1958).

11. Reference to an entry in Notebook 30 (chap. 20).

12. Musil here evidently refers to the Notebook itself, entitled "Notes on the Essays."

13. MwQ, vol. 1, part II, chap. 115.

14. With the abbreviation "a Z" Musil refers to "der andere Zustand" ("the 'other' condition"). This is Musil's private code for a state of mind, frequently alluded to by mystics, that is associated with the most intensely spiritual experiences of love, in which the individual ceases to feel any sense of separateness from the world at large and loses selfhood in ecstatic union with all things.

15. The essays in question are "Points of departure for a new aesthetics" and "The spirit of the poem."

16. "Ed" refers to a planned satirical novel, *The Planet Ed.*

17. The date is probably wrong; more likely Musil has in mind the year 1933 and refers to the state funeral of an SEA man called Maikowski in Berlin Cathedral.

18. From 1932 a so-called Freiwilliger Arbeitsdienst (FAD)—a work service in which volunteers did menial work for very modest pay—had operated in Germany.

19. Here, too, the date should read "1933."

20. Egon Erwin Kisch (1885–1948), a reporter; Kisch, a Communist, knew Musil quite well—they had met on active service in the Austrian Army.

21. Probably a reference to the failed 1923 Munich Putsch when Hitler and Ludendorff had tried to overthrow the Bavarian government.

22. The original is indecipherable.

23. Ernst Toller (1893–1939), a Communist writer and member of the 1919 revolutionary government in Munich, spent a number of years in various prisons, one of which was Stadelheim.

24. Hermann Broch (1886–1951) was a leading Austrian novelist.

25. The German term used here is *Anlehnung*, which means in this context "borrowing," in the sense of one author "borrowing" from another; in using the term Musil plays on its root—it means literally "leaning on" or "leaning against."

26. As we saw earlier, Musil modeled the MwQ character Paul Arnheim on the Prussian-Jewish intellectual, businessman, and politician Dr. Walther Rathenau (1867–1922).

27. The following is an extract from the Viennese newspaper *The Hour*, 2 March 1935.

28. Wilhelm Furtwängler (1886–1954) had been forced to resign from his post as conductor of the Berlin Philharmonic Orchestra because of his support for the composer Paul Hindemith (1895–1963).

◆ ‖ 22 ‖ ◆

NOTEBOOK 34

1. "*Ed*" refers to Musil's projected satirical work whose plot centers on a hitherto undiscovered planet in orbit around the Earth.

2. Richard Schaukal (1874–1942), writer; the society to which Musil refers was founded in 1929.

3. Reference to General Stumm von Bordwehr.

4. See Musil's essay, translated as "Mind and Experience," in Robert Musil, *Precision and Soul: Essays and Addresses*, ed. and trans. Burton Pike and David S. Luft (Chicago and London: University of Chicago Press, 1990), pp. 124–49, at p. 142.

5. Musil's own poem "Isis and Osiris."

6. MwQ.

7. Stefan George left Germany for Switzerland in 1933 after resisting the attempts of the National Socialists in general, and Goebbels in particular, to obtain his services for their cause.

8. *Seele.*

9. This entry comes not long after a reference to 1934 and may well have been written in that year. It seems likely that Musil's reference to Heinrich Mann and Hitler in this entry is influenced by the following events. In 1931 Heinrich Mann, a radical democrat and Thomas Mann's elder brother, was elected chair of the creative writing section of the Prussian Academy of Arts; his appointment led to protests and the resignation of two nationalist authors.

At the beginning of 1933 Heinrich Mann was still chair of the creative writing section. Two weeks after Hitler came to power Heinrich Mann signed an appeal to the Social Democrats and the Communist Party to join in a united front against Hitler; copies of the appeal were posted on advertising display columns throughout Berlin. He was then forced to resign by the National Socialists' threat to dissolve the Academy if he did not step down.

10. The reference is to Tolstoy's novel *Resurrection*, which was brought out in German translation in 1899.

11. "N." probably refers to Nietzche.

12. Musil refers here to his play of this name.

13. Erich Maria von Hornbostel (1877–1935), musicologist at the Psychological Institute of the University of Berlin and a colleague of Carl Stumpf, who supervised Musil's doctoral dissertation—see note 6 in chap. 5 (Notebook 15).

14. Reference to Musil's essay "Man of letters and literature [. . .]."

15. In fact it was in Notebook 25 in a note relating to "Confucius, Lao-tse, Christ and Christianity."

16. Robert Ley (1890–1945), responsible for the dissolution of the trade unions in Germany in 1933 and the formation of the "Work Front."

17. Possibly Efraim Frisch, who edited *Der neue Merkur.*

18. This may refer to Olga Schnitzler, the widow of Arthur Schnitzler.

19. Richard Beer-Hoffmann (1866–1945), creative writer and friend of Hofmannsthal and Schnitzler.

20. A reference to the love affair between Goethe and Bettina von Arnim.

21. "Blut und Boden" ("Blood and soil") was a slogan of National Socialism.

22. Max Scheler (1874–1928), a philosopher influenced by Husserl and phenomenology.

23. Musil refers in Notebook 4 to a passage from *The Case of Wagner* in which Nietzsche discusses the nature of the actor.

24. Schuschnigg Kurt (Edler von) (b. 1897), Austrian Christian-Social politician and Federal Chancellor from 1934 to 1938—he was imprisoned by Hitler from 1938 to 1945.

◆ ‖ 23 ‖ ◆
NOTEBOOK 33

1. See Ernst Cassirer, *Descartes: Teaching, Personality, Influence.*

2. Musil's first boarding school was located at Eisenstadt.

3. This refers to Musil's first experience of ecstatic love—apparently Valerie was an accomplished pianist in her late twenties whom he met on a holiday in the mountains before he was twenty.

4. See reference to this episode in chap. 10, note 13 (Notebook I).

5. Musil writes of "two moments" but subsequently refers to only one.

6. These are to be found in MwQ, vol. 2, chaps. 52, 54, 55, 57, 58.

7. "The Blackbird" appeared in Musil's collection of short prose pieces, *Pre-Posthumous Writings.* [Posthumous Papers of a Living Author]

8. Jarto Reising von Reisinger (b. 1878) was the model for "Reiting," one of the characters in Musil's *Young Törleß.*

9. Von Boineburg-Lengsfeld was the schoolboy behind the portrait of Beineberg in *Young Törleß.*

10. Friedrich von Gentz (1764–1832) originally supported the principles of the French Revolution but later became an arch-advocate of conservatism.

11. See also the further reference to this in entry No. 156.

12. Ludwig Czech (1870–1945), a lawyer who became Chairman of the German Social Democrat Workers Party in Czechoslovakia.

13. Musil apparently wrote down the wrong year. The next entry is dated 1937.

14. See MwQ, pp. 1176–1211.

15. The psychologist Professor Alexius Meinong offered Musil the chance of a university position in Graz in 1908 but Musil turned this down in order to devote himself to literature.

16. This was a journal (German title: *Der Lose Vogel*), published by Musil's friend, Franz Blei—see note 29 in chap. 6 (Notebook 5).

17. A reference to the author Leopold von Andrian-Werburg (1875–1951), a friend of Hugo von Hofmannsthal and Stefan George, who worked as a diplomat, later as director of a theater in Vienna—presumably Musil implies that Andrian's commitment to writing was compromised by official duties.

18. Peter Rosegger (1843–1918), folk author from Steyr.

19. There is evidence that in 1932 there was support for making Musil a member of the German Academy of Literature in Berlin.

20. Reference to Goebbels's decree against "destructive criticism."

21. In Berlin.

22. Gabriele d'Annunzio, *Il piacere* (*Happiness*); the original novel appeared in 1889, the German translation in 1898.

23. The first issue of the journal *Arena* appeared in Berlin in April 1906.

24. I have attempted to reproduce in the English translation Musil's ironic use of substantivization!

25. Musil was one of the founders in 1936 of the "Society of Film Friends of Austria."

26. Musil is evidently mistaken, since Anton Wildgans died in 1932.

27. Musil left a gap for the exact year; in fact it was 1937.

28. Moritz Schlick (1882–1936), neopositivist philosopher who belonged to the Vienna Circle.

29. Reference to Musil's professor in Berlin, Carl Stumpf.

30. Musil's lecture "On Stupidity" was published by Bermann-Fischer in 1937.

31. See MwQ, vol. 1, chap. 40.

32. Musil's words here are *Anders ich*, literally, "Other, I." It is not unlikely that this is a wordplay on the name of the hero of an earlier draft of MwQ who was called "Anders." This name, in turn, echoes "der *andere* Zustand" (my emphasis), "the *other* [mystical] condition."

33. A chapter from the unpublished drafts of Musil's literary papers—MwQ, part III, chap. 63.

34. Felix Dahn (1834–1912) wrote historical novels.

35. Hermann Sudermann (1857–1928), author of plays and novels.

36. Stefan Zweig (1881–1942), Viennese author.

37. See MwQ, vol. 2, chap. 28, pp. 1023–24.

38. C. F. Meyer (1825–1898), Swiss author known above all for his novellas.

39. Gottfried Keller (1819–1890), Swiss writer, famed for his novellas of Poetic Realism.

40. The two short stories in *Unions* are concerned with the process whereby the two central female characters make slow, indeed virtually imperceptible, psychological-emotional moves toward sexual experience that would be condemned by conventional moral codes.

41. Once he had graduated from the college—which offered training for the military—the young Musil, so his father thought, would be well placed to pursue a career in the Army.

42. Alpha is the heroine of Musil's comedy *Vinzenz and the Girlfriend of Important Men* (1924).

43. Jenö Lanyi, an art historian, married Monika Mann, one of Thomas Mann's daughters, in 1939.

44. The word Musil uses is *Ausführung*, literally, "carrying out"—this evidently refers both to the writing of the play and to its performance. I have rendered this "execution" both here and later in the text.

45. Matthias Musil, a medical doctor.

46. There were originally forty diary notebooks, but some have not survived.

47. Possibly this refers to Gottfried Bohnenblust, who was president of the Geneva Society for German Art and Literature.

48. At the very start of his literary career in Brünn, before he published anything, Musil worked on a manuscript called *Paraphrases*—see Notebook 4.

49. This entry can be dated precisely via a cross-reference from another note; it was written on 8 December 1939.

50. Professor Georg Wellner was one of Musil's engineering lecturers at the Technical University of Brünn.

51. Franz Zeis was an engineer at the Patents Office in Vienna.

52. Viktor Kaplan was a professor of mechanical engineering at the Technical University of Brünn.

53. Rudolf Diesel (1858–1913), inventor of the diesel engine in 1892.

54. Jarmila Novotna (b. 1903), a Czech opera singer.

55. Martha Musil was born early in 1874, Robert Musil late in 1880.

56. Erwin Hexner (1894–1968) combined wide practical experience of administration with a gift for theoretical reflection—he had worked in the iron industry and taught administrative law at the University of Prague. Musil admired him for his skill in bridging the realms of theory and practice.

57. See the description of Agathe, the sister of the central protagonist, Ulrich, in MwQ, vol. 2, chap. 2, pp. 734–35.

58. The second military college Musil attended was at Mährisch-Weißkirchen.

59. A reference to entry No. 163 in this notebook.

60. Musil spent a year of voluntary military service in Brünn from 1 October 1901 to 30 September 1902.

61. Maximilian Becher (1878–1955), a distinguished officer Musil met during World War I who became acting head of the Department of the Praesidium after that war.

62. Here Musil is quoting from the third book of Dostoyevsky's novel *The Player* (1867; German trans., 1888).

63. A reference to Musil's work on the continuation of MwQ. See, e.g., MwQ, part III, chap. 46—a chapter that was not published in Musil's lifetime.

64. Musil refers to another draft chapter of MwQ, part III, chap. 50.

65. For a short time before World War I Musil had been employed by Samuel Fischer on his journal *Die neue Rundschau*.

66. Musil published a number of essays in various journals between 1911 and 1922.

67. The issue in question was that for April 1932, no. 4.

68. The following entry—No. 168—contains in note form some of Friedrich Franz von Unruh's ideas in the essay to which Musil here refers.

69. See note 68 this chap.

70. *Volkstum*.

71. *der Völkische*.

72. *Volk*.

73. *Volksgeist*.

74. *völkisch*.

75. Reference to MwQ, vol. 1, chap. 116.

76. Reference to Goethe's autobiography.

77. Carl J. Burckhardt (1891–1974), who was the president of the International Committee of the Red Cross in Geneva.

78. The French philosopher Henri Bergson (1859–1941).

79. Reference to Musil's father's wish to have the ashes of his wife disposed of with minimal ceremony.

80. Rudolf Musil (b. 1838), who became an officer of the General Staff of the Austrian Army.

81. Reference to Hermine Musil, Robert Musil's mother.

82. Matthias de Gaspero (1858–1937), a friend of the Musil family in Klagenfurt.

83. Heinrich Reiter.

84. Eduard Donath, who, like Musil's father, was a professor at the Technical University of Brünn; the two families were very close, and Gustav Donath (Gustl) (1878–1965), Professor Donath's son, was Robert Musil's oldest friend.

85. Viktor Musil (b. 1840) was Robert Musil's uncle; he worked as a bookkeeper in Graz.

86. The estate was Plachelhof near Graz.

◆ ‖ 24 ‖ ◆
NOTEBOOK 32

1. This was the title of a lecture Musil gave to the Federation of German Writers in Vienna in September 1934.

2. Reference to entry No. 28 later in text.

3. A lecture Musil gave in Paris in July 1935 at the International Writers Congress in Defense of Culture.

4. Chap. 103.

5. Entry No. 42 further in text.

6. Reference to the bullying by Hitler of the Austrian Chancellor Schuschnigg at Berchtesgaden in February 1938.

7. Graf Leinsdorf is a character in MwQ who makes the central protagonist, Ulrich, his protégé in matters of cultural politics.

8. Goethe's friend, Grand Duke Karl August of Saxony-Weimar.

9. This is the title of Goethe's "Bildungsroman" ("novel of education").

10. In 1938 Musil's new publishers, Bermann-Fischer, informed him that his book had been banned by the National Socialists.

11. Eugen Claassen (1895–1955) was in charge of the H. Goverts Publishing House in Hamburg, which he took over himself after the war. Claassen conducted negotiations with Musil in 1938 with a view to Musil's joining Goverts.

12. Musil attempted to obtain financial support via fellow German authors with contacts in America.

13. See note 26 in chap. 23 (Notebook 33).

14. Reference to MwQ.

15. Musil planned to publish an anthology of some of his aphorisms.

16. Tomas Masaryk (1850–1937), the founder and President of Czechoslovakia.

17. Abbreviation for "Kriegspressequartier," an army group dealing with the press to which Musil was assigned after World War I.

18. Frau Dr. Nellie Kreis worked for the Comité International pour le Placement des Intellectuels Réfugiés in Geneva.

19. Hermann Hesse (1877–1962) and his third wife, Ninon.

20. The house was in fact in Montagnola, Switzerland.

21. Hans C. Bodmer (1891–1956), a well-known collector of manuscripts.

22. *völkisch*.

23. See earlier in this Notebook, entry No. 10.

24. This is a variation on Goethe's words "Thinking and doing, doing and thinking are the sum of all wisdom"—in *Wilhelm Meister's Years of Wandering*, vol. 2, chap. 9.

25. In Ancient Egypt, baboons were sacred to the Moon God.

26. The woman in charge of a school for young children's nurses; Robert and Martha Musil lived for a while on the grounds of this school during their stay in Switzerland.

27. Here Musil refers to the following authors: Ludwig Rubiner (1881–1920), Leonhard Frank (1882–1961), and Franz Werfel (1890–1945).

28. George Sorel (1847–1922), French sociologist.

◆ ‖ 25 ‖ ◆
NOTEBOOK 35

1. A square in the center of Geneva.

2. Robert Lejeune (1891–1970) was a parson of the Evangelical Church in Neumünster, Switzerland; he became a friend of Musil's and helped to organize material support for him and Martha.

3. Rudolf Hunziker (1870–1946) taught at the grammar school in Winterthur and was active in the town's literary association.

4. A building that housed a school for infant children's nurses.

5. A suburb in the west of Berlin.

6. A suburb of Geneva.

7. Arthur Holitscher (1869–1941), journalist and literary author.

8. Dr. Auguste Bouvier was director of the City and University Library in Geneva.

9. Fritz Wotruba (1907–1975) was a Viennese sculptor—one of his works was a bust of Musil.

10. Dr. Arthur Rosin, an acquaintance of Musil, formerly a bank director in Berlin, was interested in science and the arts.

11. Frau Morand was Barbara von Borsinger's cook.

12. A. F. Roda (1872–1945) was an Austrian who wrote literary reviews.

13. Emil Oprecht (1895–1952) was the founder of two publishing houses in Zurich.

14. Rudolf Olden (1885–1940), journalist in Vienna and Berlin, tried to solicit assistance for Musil from the Pen Club in London.

15. This refers to a section of the MwQ, the "Journey to Paradise," where the love of Ulrich and Agathe reaches its climax; extracts of this are found in MwQ, vol. 2, pp. 1450–74.

16. This was a pet name of Musil's for Martha.

17. Among the drafts to which Musil refers is the entry entitled "Dream" in Notebook 30, p. 387.

18. This is a reference to Musil's story "The Completing of a Love," in Robert Musil, *Selected Writings*, ed. Burton Pike (New York: Continuum, 1986), pp. 179–222; the narrative traces the path from the experience of marital love at a pitch of emotional-spiritual intensity to an act of adultery.

19. This was the Geneva address where Musil and Martha lived from 1 April 1941.

20. This entry was found in 1980, sewn into the lining of a coat belonging to Martha Musil.

21. An address in Berlin where Martha lived after her separation from her second husband, Enrico Marcovaldi.

22. This refers to one of the very few poems Musil wrote, entitled "To a Room."

23. Weißgerberstraße is in the IIIʳᵈ District of Vienna.

24. Lofer is in the Tyrol.

25. A boarding house in Vienna.

26. Another Viennese boarding house; it was run by Theodor Seleschan—Musil and Martha stayed there in 1910.

27. Koserow on the Baltic island of Usedom, where Musil spent a holiday in August 1922—see, e.g., the entry "Fishermen on Usedom" in Notebook 21.

28. Reference to the attempts by the Wehrmacht to take Moscow in World War II.

29. Ninon de Lenclos (1620–1705), whose name evidently was a byword for a lady of fashion who retains her attraction after beauty has faded.

LIST OF OMISSIONS

The omission mark "[. . .]" has been placed beside or beneath the appropriate entry in the main text of the English translation at all *major* points of abridgment; in some cases (because they are trivial, a few letters of abbreviation, etc.) not all omissions indicated in the text appear in the following list.

To identify the position of each omission I have given the last three or so words of the translation of the previous entry in quotation marks thus: "is the end."

After identifying the position of an omission in the main body of the translation I have added (in square brackets) after a reference to the German edition, brief details about the content of the missing section, thus: [AF 819–822: various short entries, mainly on literary matters.] The designation AF refers to Robert Musil, *Tagebücher* [*Diaries*], edited by Adolf Frisé (Reinbek bei Hamburg: Rowohlt, 1976, rev. ed., 1983).

NOTEBOOK 4

4   "one's own companion." [AF 3: entry entitled "M.l.v. als Erzieher" (M.l.v. as educator).]
8   "the Turkish cigarettes." [AF 7: two paragraphs of m.l.v. draft entitled "Die Geheimnisse des Lebens" ("The mysteries of life").]
8   "hold of me" [AF 8–10: reflections entitled "Aus dem stilisierten Jahrhundert" (On the stylized century) based on the theme of a street.]
9   "positively unnerving." [AF 12: "The stranger"—Musil quotes a translation of Baudelaire.]
12   "a precarious thing.>" [AF 14–15: entries on sensations, on time spent with Gustl, a few lines in the second person familiar addressed to someone who is not identified.]
12   "forgotten its base." [AF 16: entries on ideas and on Musil's "new concept of art."]
12   "are so possessed." [AF 16: on certain sciences that are "of little or no use."]
14   "us to adopt." [AF 18: brief note on style and psychology.]
19   "any great loss." [AF 23: entries on jealousy and on aphorisms by Nietzsche.]
21   "just his philosophy." [AF 25: entry on romanticism.]
22   "necessarily decadent itself?" [AF 27–32: a number of entries, mainly quoting from Nietzsche.]
23   "of this philosophy." [AF 32–34: more quotation and brief notes on Nietzsche with relation to decadence and "conduct of life."]
23   "Path to Express[ionism]}" [AF 34–36: several entries on aesthetics, one on religious contemplation.]
24   "for the interpretation." [AF 37: further entries on aesthetics.]

NOTEBOOK 3

39   "burden to her." [AF 50: entry entitled "Eccentric people."]
40   "but no one goes in!" [AF 51–71: various entries including observations on attitudes and aesthetic matters—including Aristotle on tragedy, the Renaissance, notes on books, including the diary of Marie Bashkirtseff, which had been translated from the original French in 1897.]
43   "their simplest form." [AF 75: fragments of a poem, thoughts on the Romantics and their women, two epigrams.]
44   "activity at all." [AF 76–77: notes on theme of "Causality—teleology."]
45   "in May 1903." [AF 79–80: narrative describing an encounter outside a grammar school; note on Grauauge and Herma.]

NOTEBOOK 24

NOTEBOOK II

NOTEBOOK 15

No omissions

NOTEBOOK 5

NOTEBOOK 6

NOTEBOOK 7

NOTEBOOK 17

NOTEBOOK 1

LITTLE NOTEBOOK WITHOUT A NUMBER

NOTEBOOK 8

210   "in natural activity." [AF 358–359: entry on *The Spy*; further short entries, one on France.]

210   "moral decision making." [AF 359–364: entries on expressionism, on revolutions, reviews of articles on the collapse of Germany and the "curse of objective spirit"; further fragmented entries.]

211   "Illusions: realities." [AF 365–367: various entries including ones on France and England, notes on an obituary of Prince Alois Liechtenstein.]

211   "'Experimentum crucis' for God." [AF 368–369: entry on ghost stories; related entry on *The Devil*—a projected novel; brief bust in words of Pflanzer-Baltin.]

211   "eagle of Zeus.)" [AF 370: diverse entries with observations of individuals.]

212   "is very contented." [AF 372: entries on trade union priests and quoted criticism of university education, which is compared unfavorably with activities of worker-intellectuals.]

213   "as a tutor." [AF 373: short entries including ones on liberals and Kisch.]

213   "in the right." [AF 373–379: various entries mainly on ghosts and like phenomena.]

214   "of Erich Schmidt." [AF 380–383: various entries, one or two perhaps character/plot studies for the novel *The Spy*.]

215   "scents from the garden." [AF 383–388: various entries probably intended for use in literary work; on gall stones, on homeopathic medicine, political observations, etc.]

217   "not lasted either." [AF 390–391: entries on the life style of workers, on capitalism, on novellas by Per Hallström, etc.]

218   "of the personality." [AF 392: reflections prompted by an incident on a tram; quotation on finance and administration with comment.]

218   "ghostly form of life." [AF 393: three brief entries relating to literary projects.]

218   "to the public." [AF 393–394: short entries on literary projects, including a fragmentary one relating passages from Nietzsche to the portrait of Clarisse.]

219   "explosivity of youth." [AF 395: remainder of entry on bank director; brief entry on the present time and *Catacomb*.]

219   "past 30 years." [AF 396–398: various entries including one on astrologers, notes on phraseology, on creating a world language, on the "will of the amorphous."]

220   "without deflection, to warn." [AF 399–400: entries on priests, Stendhal, Pflanzer-Baltin, expression, etc.]

221   "an ironic way." [AF 400–401: two entries, one on *The Land over the South Pole*.]

222   "than in ours?)" [AF 402: fragments, an entry on *Blind Alley*, a novel by W. L. George (1882–1926) about the political situation in England.]

224   "that of pariahs." [AF 404–405: brief observations on various subjects.]

224   "metaphysical belief." [AF 406–407: entries on the crushing of the middle class, on civilization/culture, on *The Spy*, etc.]

225   "New ones arrive." [AF 408: entries on officers of the high command, socialism, a dialogue with a virgin.]

226   "ripple on the waters." [AF 409: entry on the "bureaucratic spirit."]

226   "a 'soul' exists." [AF 409: short entry on love.]

226   "hold me back." [AF 410–412: various entries including extensive quotations from *Staatswehr* (*Defense of the State*), which identified itself as a "weekly paper for matters of military policy and economics".]

227   "expr[essionism] belong here." [AF 413: short entry on *The Spy*.]

228   "descriptions of landscapes." [AF 413–414: observation on Frau Reichle, a Viennese society woman.]

228   "out her task." [AF 414: entries on German youth, a headmaster, etc.]

228   "avoid any quarreling)." [AF 415–416: entries including extracts from a soldier's monologue, from "post-revolutionary-bureaucratic phraseology," etc.]

228   "tendency toward homosexuality." [AF 416–419: entries include portrait of a Marxist intellectual, mental maths at night, the sense of fate in relation to one's understanding of the passage of time, Expressionist works, etc.]

229   "under his coat." [AF 419–420: brief entries including one on *The Spy*.]

229 "how unprepared!" [AF 420–423: various entries including "spirit today," *South Pole*, extracts from Babylonian law, excerpt from Old Irish poem.]

NOTEBOOK 9

237 "an educational experience." [AF 431–434: entries on homeopathic medicine, on the H.Q. of the Austrian military press, on bureaucracy.]

238 "civilian influences." [AF 435–436: entry ends with a list of acquaintances and historical figures representing different types; further entries on Holitzer and an Italian female acquaintance.]

239 "struggle against materialism." [AF 436–444: further entries on religion including notes on a book on exorcism; notes on an essay on national politics by Robert Müller; various notes, some of them fragmentary, on individuals, etc., evidently intended for use in novels.]

NOTEBOOK 10

242 "Stucken and Hardt." [AF 444–446: plans for an essay on, or overview of, aesthetics/literary criticism.]

244 "relationship is missing.)" [AF 448: two short segments on aspects of literary aesthetics.]

245 "a commonplace feeling." [AF 449–450: further notes on literary aesthetics.]

247 "warmth of the center." [AF 451–452: the entry continues by saying that Heinrich Mann will be used as an example—but there is no example.]

249 "of turning over." [AF 453–470: reflections on psychological stimuli; notes on a book on revolutionaries; fragmentary records of broadly philosophical concerns; an entry on probability and induction; list of book titles under the heading of "probability"; further notes on probability; an essay on, or study of, probability in six segments; record of books on Bismarck and an epigram by Treitschke.]

250 "love at a distance." [AF 471: entry on Alfred Döblin's novel *Wadzek's Fight with the Steam Turbine* (Berlin: S. Fischer, 1918).]

251 "or a *Weltanschauung*." [AF 472; two entries relating to a work by Heinrich Gomperz on Greek philosophy.]

251 "to do with repertory." [AF 472–474: plan for a book on successful authors.]

255 "synthetic technique exists." [AF 477: further entries, most relating to the reading of Thomas Mann's *Reflections of a Non-political Man*.]

256 "outside the sum." [AF 480–489: further notes on reading of Thomas Mann, *Reflections* [. . .]; quotations from Rudolf Kassner, *The Morality of Music*; various other brief entries; notes for an essay on "The progressive and the conservative principle in literature"; a series of notes on early Christian sects derived from a German translation of Gustave Flaubert's *The Temptation of St. Anthony*, short entries on various subjects followed by one on "The nature of creative writing" and another with reflections following a reading of a work on Duns Scotus.]

256 "sociological one, too." [AF 490: the final paragraph seems obscure.]

257 "the finished society." [AF 491: brief notes relating to reading matter; entry identifying a number of Germans who saw the aesthetic sense as marking out mankind from the animal world.]

258 "of the Indo-Europeans." [AF 492–494: various entries, including one on "Aesthetics"; reading on Copernicus, entry on Raabe's story, *Pfister's Mill*; further brief entries on reading matter.]

259 "reflect about creating." [AF 495–518: entries relating to reading Schiller's essays on the theater; evidence of further reading from journals, including extensive notes on essays on consciousness and a sense of self; entry on mathematics and logic; entries on Stendhal and Stumpf (on the human voice); notes, derived from essays in journals, concerned with language—these include erotic-metaphysical words; the Minnesang and the German language; under the heading "Psychology of literary success with the masses," quotations from, and notes on, a newspaper article; critical notes on an article on "The problem of Germany" dealing with overriding philosophical attitudes in French, German, and British culture; summary of ideas from journal article on the sociology of times of crisis.]

260 "and Existential Organization." [AF 518–523: various entries including ones on Neurath and on the psychology of intention and motivation.]

260 "Vertebrates, Stuttgart, 1912." [AF 524–525: entries include one on ornament in relation to evolution of prehistoric pottery, etc.; notes on Erwin Schröder writing on the laws of the atomic world; entry on Cassirer, Descartes.]

NOTEBOOK 19

266 "History of World Trade." [AF 532–539: several pages, most of them with statistics relating to society in Germany in the years before World War I (including details of population, marriages, employment in the main sectors, pupils in the different levels of the education system, criminality, etc.)]

267 "they are minds." [AF 539–540: extract from a speech by an Austrian military commander, Nikolaus von Horthy.]

273 "we have access." [AF 545–546: extracts from a Viennese workers' newspaper on relative salary levels; brief entry on the theme "The human being is good."]

275 "how it emerged." [AF 548–552: entries on various subjects: ideologies; statistics; politics in Czechoslovakia, South America, and Hungary; how to make literature interesting in schools.]

275 "with this morality." [AF 553–568: most of the remaining pages in this notebook are taken up with draft material for a satirical play; he summarizes the plot succinctly—AF 553: "Love stories in the second instance; in the first, satire on conditions that will come."]

NOTEBOOK 21

278 "The 20 Works III—" [AF 569: brief entries on *The Spy* and *Catacomb*.]

278 "are 18–20 today." [AF 570–575: various entries, most relating to novels; these include two on psychopathic behavior; one on journalism; several on Kerschensteiner, the educationalist; one on the view of a Christian socialist and a Marxist socialist.]

280 "those of reading." [AF 577: brief entries on disparate matters.]

280 "One deludes oneself." [AF 578: fragments of ideas.]

281 "right to do so." [AF 579: very short entries including one on a mother who is cruel to her child.]

284 "idea of the *Catacomb*.}" [AF 582–583: entry containing a review of key ideas, etc., for a novel, cross-referring to entries in notebooks.]

285 "successful with truth!" [AF 584: short entry on a book by a Christian author about mankind's capacity for goodness.]

287 "pessimism as militarism." [AF 585–586: entries on satire, *Panama*, *Catacomb*.]

288 "moment, encircling them.)" [AF 588: fragmentary note setting out juxtaposed pairs for a novel draft—A[nders], Ag[athe], D[iotima]-Arnh[eim].]

291 "by two women-friends." [AF 591–596: entry on *Ed*, excerpts from book on English democracy, entries on *Panama*, children's games, Agathe, on drama, overview of contents of book on evolution of life on earth: F. Müller-Lyer, *Phasen der Kultur* (*Phases of Culture*).]

292 "(Fishermen poetry on U[sedom].)" [AF 597: fragmentary entry on Clarisse.]

293 "makes itself available." [AF 598: fragmentary entries.]

294 "what that is." [AF 598–599: entry on communist party members and military action.]

296 "anticipation of this." [AF 601: two short entries.]

296 "according to Jung." [AF 602–608: various entries including the following: entry on Alexander von Humboldt in South America; reading of Maeterlinck's *Life of Bees*; fragments on Agathe; notes for literary work under the heading "*Schildkröte*" (*Tortoise*); two entries on Anders.]

296 "(Title: 'Carnival')" [AF 609–612: draft scenes and narrative plans for a play about a man exchanging places with another, a monk.]

297 "a strange magic." [AF 613–614: entry headed *Little Napoleon*, evidently plans for a play.]

297 "thing in the world!" [AF 614–623: brief entries including ones on Agathe, *Tortoise*, *Catacomb*, followed by extensive notes, headed "'Other' Condition," on Ludwig Klages," *On Cosmogonic Eros*.]

298 "The Saga of Tanaquill." [AF 624–626: various entries including one headed *"Archivist,"* another "Anders," another "Gaming clubs".]

300 "[*sic*], V, p. 291ff." [AF 627–628: entry on language with reference to Levy Brühl and Alfred Döblin; entry on "Priest novel"; extract from essay by Max Mell; further short entries.]

301 "consciousness remained hopeful." [AF 630–631: short entries, one on "The 'I'-form in the drama".]

302 "lack of respect." [AF 631–632: short entries on the theater, etc.]

303 "supporter of K[arl] Kraus." [AF 633: three entries, one dealing with journalists.]

303 "believes in God?" [AF 634: entries on *Tortoise* and women prisoners serving life sentences.]

304 "enthusiasm for war." [AF 635: entry entitled "The evil person" evidently for the *Tortoise.*]

305 "a grand scale." [AF 637: statistics on books published in Germany and elsewhere in Europe.]

306 "of spiritual order." [AF 638: entry entitled "Cruelty" on atrocities committed in warfare; three further fragmentary entries.]

306 "time of Lent." [AF 638–639: several entries including ones on *Archivist, South Pole, Little Napoleon.*]

307 "doesn't shut properly!" [AF 641: entries on *The War Diary of a Flea,* "expressions," *South Pole.*]

NOTEBOOK 25

318 "attitude to art.}" [AF 653–658: notes on a book by Paul Honigsheim on the history of the philosophy of education; fragmentary notes on "rat[ioïd]—non rat[ioïd.]."]

321 "the practical sphere." [AF 661: fragmentary notes that mention Schopenhauer, Spengler, and Bergson.]

NOTEBOOK 26

No omissions

NOTEBOOK 28

339 "of my ideas." [AF 678: two entries on the draft satire, *The Academy of Conceit City.*]

339 "of the world!" [AF 678–679: notes on *The Contemporary* (evidently a kind of autobiographical novel?)]

339 "mighty, warrior-build." [AF 679–680: entries on *Ed, The Contemporary, Inventor.*]

341 "try to create." [AF 682: fragmentary entry on *The Contemporary;* entry on *Conceit City;* summary of report on actual court proceedings where the accused shoots his accuser, the "Pöffl Trial."]

342 "receives the boxer." [AF 683–684: further note for *Conceit City.*]

342 "my own type." [AF 684: entry *"Conceit City* Essays."]

342 "'belles lettres' are concerned." [AF 684: entry on author who has been decorated by the Austrian Republic for his services to literature.]

343 "autobiographical and contemporary!" [AF 685: entry on *Ed.*]

NOTEBOOK 30

346 "30." [AF 687–691: mainly entries on *The War Diary of a Flea.*]

347 "M[usil] any better." [AF 692: brief entry evidently relating to literary plans.]

356 "Gide and Chesterton." [AF 701: entry for 14.II. on medieval malpractice.]

363 "the self-infecting wound.)" [AF 708: copy of seventh-century Latin poem and German translation.]

365 "above all Csókor!" [AF 710: a list of politicians and literary figures who have been honored by having streets, etc., named after them.]

376 "in a stone." [AF: 720–721: very brief entries.]

379 "the S[turm] A[bteilung]." [AF 723: one short entry on special public collections arranged by the National Socialists.]

380 "place them behind bars." [AF 724: brief entry on *Ed.*]

384 "From [18]48?" [AF 727: entry reads: "Inn-keeper peoples, but not domestic-servant peoples."]

385 "support for democracy." [AF 728: two entries entitled "Natural Law," one on *Ed.*]

385 "indifference to me." [AF 729: entry on the feelings of an acquaintance for a woman who has recently died.]

385 "*in Intellectual History*)" [AF 729–730: entry on Lloyds of London.]

385 "to creative works." [AF 730: two brief entries.]

386 "forth few individuals." [AF 731: brief entry very critical of a polemical article in the National Socialist paper *Der Angriff* (*The Attack*); another brief entry on a Viennese journalist; brief entry referring to Ernst Cassirer.]

386 "a collective concept." [AF 732: three brief entries.]

386 "bobs of sport." [AF 732: quotation and comment on an article on Pavlov.]

387 "connected with it." [AF 732: two short entries.]

387 "intense illusory feeling?" [AF 733: entry on organizations connected with Richard Wagner.]

387 "more important than it is}." [AF 733–736: further commentary on *Niels Lyhne*; excerpt from a newspaper on a famous Burgtheater actor.]

388 "equally general aestheticism." [AF 736–740: the entry on d'Annunzio continues for two more pages; several entries on various topics including ones on Stendhal.]

388 "honor of the Fatherland." [AF 740–742: Various entries including one on the earlier Stendhal, prohibition of making a rogue into a literary hero; on the psychology of a radical swing in feelings for others, optical inversions, and the like; on the "other" condition; on fashion.]

388 "by the 'demos.'" [AF 742–743: short entries on Nietzsche, one on Shelley; an entry on the "Lion of Aspern," referring to a victory by Archduke Charles over Napoleon.]

389 "heights—unwelcome consequence." [AF 744: brief entries including one on women's intelligence, one on the experience of satisfaction from a psychological perspective, one on Hitler.]

389 "invalid by this idea." [AF 745–746: entries on novel by Selma Lagerlöf, on optimism in creative writing, on Jews, etc.]

390 "spirit of enterprise." [AF 746–747: extract containing quotation from an American journalist critical of moral decline in his country, with Musil's commentary; extract on Nietzsche and Wagner.]

390 "right in everything." [AF 747: entry on the Wohnküche ("Live-in kitchen").]

390 "flattery, for example?" [AF 748: short entry.]

390 "downhill than uphill." [AF 748: brief entry on art.]

391 "be scarcely conceivable." [AF 748: short entries on cubism and the feeling of being one among millions.]

391 "a false standpoint?" [AF 749–750: several brief entries, including ones on a petty "Caesar" and on compulsive hand-washing and an entry commenting on a novel by a Swiss author, Paul Ilg.]

391 "or her husband." [AF 750–751: various short entries including one listing books, a note on "veneration of race" as "veneration of the average," on "un-happiness" (*sic*).]

391 "of wielding power." [AF 751: entries on old age, and on gloomy feelings as a German characteristic.]

392 "anticipates his drives." [AF 752: brief entry on infidelity; entry on journal essay on Hölderlin.]

393 "within a short time!" [AF 753–754: further entry on fingerprinting; two entries on Hegel.]

393 "a merciless light." [AF 754: four brief entries.]

393 "Certainly not. . . . etc." [AF 755–765: entries on a variety of subjects, including the following: notes on "Rewriting history" (an essay in the *Neue Zürcher Zeitung* by Karl Löwith); list of books; excerpt from another on the author Ernst Gläser; details on earthquakes; excerpt with commentary from an article on "F. W. Murnau, a classic filmmaker"; thoughts relating to earlier essay on nation and race; on Anton Wildgans; excerpts, with comments, on an essay on Byron; excerpt from Jean Paul; entry on Eugène Delacroix; on pianos; entry in which Musil, on meeting,

in Swiss exile, the sculptor Fritz Wotruba, is moved to reflect on an alternative twist to the plot of his earlier story, "The Completing of Love."]

395 "influence of Shakespeare?" [AF 767: two entries, one on aphorisms.]

396 "in the future?" [AF 768–772: entries on various subjects, including the following: palindromes (with Latin examples); statistics on Jews in Austria before the Anschluß; a vivid reconstruction of an accident with an elevator and its consequences.]

397 "any sexual opportunity." [AF 773: entry on attempts to inhibit an emotion.]

397 "been too shy." [AF 774–777: entries on various subjects: on actions performed involuntarily; an account of the sexual behavior of a black female dancer (evidently recounted by an acquaintance); on Swiss-German; on Honoré Daumier, the artist.]

397 "to be ethics." [AF 777–779: the entry continues with extensive, but compressed and only part comprehensible notes on aesthetics with cross-references to other notebooks.]

397 "MwQII, p. 121." [AF 780: brief note on Swiss countryside.]

398 "concerns, etc., participate." [AF 780–781: short entries on Galicia and on a review on a book about the British Empire; fragmentary entry on an article on racialism by Julian Huxley; etc.]

398 "writes a foreign language." [AF 782–784: various entries, some short, on a military funeral, on consciousness, on Lord Halifax, on early film and on theater, on the study of art, on the concept of abstraction with reference to the behavior of dogs, etc.]

400 "importance for aesthetics." [AF 786: excerpt, entitled "Trance and coit[us]" from an article on dances, etc., on Bali.]

400 "and be willed." [AF 787: Wissenschaft (scientific/academic research) in Germany; observing himself as he reflects on a female acquaintance whose life is in ruins and who is fatally ill.]

400 "support of psychology." [AF 787–788: the news that very long books are again in fashion in America prompts critical entry on what would happen to book publishing in Germany if books were taken more seriously.]

401 "the strong man, etc." [AF 788: brief entry referring to book by William Stern on general psychology.]

401 "'divisible' and 'indivisible.'" [AF 788–789: entry on trees, on Ernst Jünger and Martin Heidegger, on plays and scenery.]

401 "caught my attention." [AF 790–794: various entries including reflections on a sculpture by a contemporary, and excerpts from an anti-militaristic article by a Swiss Christian author.]

402 "of substantial tolerance?" [AF 795–796: short entries including one on coitus, another on the notion of God as the all-encompassing power, love, goodness.]

403 "swear an oath.)" [AF 797: fragmentary entries.]

403 "something or other!" [AF 799–801: various entries including notes on an essay in a journal, observations on an acquaintance, Professor Keller, and an entry referring to Ibsen, Dostoyevsky, and Hitler.]

403 "manipulating one's nerves!" [AF 801–802: various short entries, several on smoking.]

404 "a particular pleasure." [AF 803–805: various entries, including a short one on Rilke, and one with observations on the Swiss.]

404 "bull by the horns!" [AF 805: several entries under the heading "Theology of a lay-person."]

405 "*captivate* attention in A." [AF 806–807: entry on Switzerland; note evidently relating to Hitler's military campaign in Russia.]

405 "idea of plagiarism." [AF 808–811: further entries, including one on "Theology of a lay-person"; one on canine behavior; one on sculpture; one with some references to work on MwQ.]

406 "take one's own life!" [AF 811: brief note on Switzerland; short entry on smoking.]

NOTEBOOK 31

409 "from this angle." [AF 814: entry on Emil Ludwig.]

410 "can be derived." [AF 815: entry entitled "1.III. Ullstein service to humanity."]

411 "disappear within them?" [AF 817: two fragmentary entries.]

412 "as a whole." [AF 817: entry for 15.III. on theatrical matters; for 28.III; why readers enjoy certain kinds of writing; for 30.III, 4.IV, 6.IV, 10.IV on various literary matters.]

412   "one about lyricism." [AF 819–822: various short entries, mainly on literary matters.]

412   "totally into illusion." [AF 822: entry on *Ed.*]

413   "*Daily Review*, 3.II.32.)" [AF 823: fragment.]

413   "kind of use." [AF 823–824: two entries, one with newspaper extracts, on the crisis in the Prussian Academy of Arts in 1933.]

414   "himself a democrat." [AF 824–825: brief notes for a novel, further brief notes on several topics.]

414   "quite wrong; superseded." [AF 824–825: brief notes on several topics.]

415   "instinct for the times." [AF 825: possible title for edition of essays: "Far from today."]

415   "plagiarism being involved." [AF 826–827: various brief entries including note on votes in a referendum in Germany in November 1933.]

415   "I am trying . . ." [AF 827: entry on "average people".]

416   "World War—H[itler]." [AF 827: note on creative writers.]

416   "ahead of their time?" [AF 828: entries on *Ed* and "Martha."]

416   "and today, lips." [AF 828: entry on *Ed.*]

417   "dominates the heavens." [AF 829–832: several entries on *Ed*; entry on "spying chapter," entries on other subjects, including music and Schopenhauer.]

418   "to first place?" [AF 832–835: various entries, including an extract from an interview between a journalist and Charlie Chaplin about silent films, an entry relating to Hitler, several brief notes for *Ed.*]

NOTEBOOK 34

420   "allegedly male ones?)" [AF 837–843: a number of entries for 1930, including some with reference to *Ed*, one on *South Pole*, one on General Stumm and Middle-Eastern oil interests.]

421   "thoughts and moods." [AF 844: an entry on Heinrich Mann, three on *Ed.*]

422   "human being's teacher." [AF 845: brief entry.]

422   "in the 'Urania.'" [AF 846: entry on music.]

422   "formation of judgment." [AF 846: short entry on *Ed.*]

423   "with the Platonic!" [AF 846: remainder of *Ed* entry; another brief entry.]

423   "of its visitors." [AF 846: reference to a book.]

423   "gods and demons.)" [AF 847–852: expressions taken from Goethe's autobiography, *Fiction and Truth*; other mainly brief entries on various subjects.]

423   "a romantic figure." [AF 852–855: excerpts from journal articles on legal and socio-political questions relating to National Socialism; further short entries, including comparison of individualism and collectivism.]

424   "with the nerve substance?" [AF 856–857: various entries, extract from Tolstoy, *War and Peace.*]

424   "with average education?" [AF 857: further quotation from *War and Peace*, several entries on literary matters, on pessimism and politics.]

425   "it is eaten?" [AF 861–862: on keeping diary records of the weather; entry on the Devil; two other short entries.]

425   "a different fashion." [AF 862: remainder of entry; further brief entries.]

425   "together is apparent." [AF 863: various entries, including one on Tolstoy, one on politics, freedom, and culture.]

425   "and provisional investigations!" [AF 864: entries including one on the Alpine landscape, another referring to Faulkner, Dostoyevsky, and Conrad.]

426   "*of our times.*" [AF 865–870: various entries including excerpts from a report about Schuschnigg, extract from a newspaper article about the Olympic Games, excerpts from Tolstoy's novel *Resurrection*, details of Schubert's life and works.]

427   "judgment on them?" [AF 871–879: various entries including extract from a speech by Mussolini, on the use of the comma, judgments by authors on forgotten books, on travel to the moon, on life in Greenland, extract from a review of *As You Like It* at the Burgtheater, further quotations from Mussolini (with comments), reflections on the qualities of a European adventurer who lives by his wits and fighting capacities as a gangster in China.]

427   "the way I write!" [AF 879–880: various entries on themes including football, solidarity between Germany and Austria, communism as seen by the Pope.]

427   "form of nature." [AF 881: short entry on conscience.]

427   "the {Jewish} one." [AF 881: short entries, one on Arthur Brisbane, a highly paid American journalist working for Hearst newspapers.]

428   "not the right thing, etc." [AF 882: entries on young people's attempts to gain acceptance and make progress, and on *Ed*.]

428   "my house stands." [AF 883: two short entries.]

429   "self-evident is it to them." [AF 883–887: various entries including the reputation of Stefan George and Rilke, commentary on the account of a sexual encounter in a work by Jules Romains, on "Burgtheater authors," on grammatical speech, on imagination as the basic characteristic of literary creativity, some references to Goethe.]

429   "hardly more than that!" [AF 888–889: entries on the "unity of science," on *Ed*, on politics in England, etc.]

430   "but on misogyny." [AF 889–891: a series of short entries, most on *Ed*.]

430   "a *bogus* autobiography." [AF 892: two entries, one on Austrian authors who will tour Switzerland, the other comparing the verse of Bettina Brentano and Goethe.]

432   "in the Thalhof.)" [AF 893–895: various entries including several brief ones on *Ed*, on the destruction of some old buildings in Vienna, and the installation of harsh lighting, on music.]

432   "norm for women." [AF 895–896: entries on impressionism and naturalism, on meaningful writing, on the persecution of a man by local villagers, and his revenge.]

432   "lines of thinking?" [AF 896–901: entries include one on British and American foreign policy toward Japan, on politics and culture, on advertising, on aphorisms and epigrams, an account of the experiences of an officer in the High Command of the Austrian army.]

432   "the fin-de-siècle type." [AF 902: several short entries including some on aphorisms.]

432   "is easily solved." [AF 903: brief entry.]

433   "a decisive influence." [AF 903: entry on Sir Robert Vansittart, as politician and creative writer.]

433   "remove these people." [AF 903: entry on the Grillparzer prize.]

433   "good or evil." [AF 904: various mainly brief entries, including one on "spirit."]

433   "degrees of intensity)." [AF 904–5: entry on fidelity as "duplicity by sexuality in extremis."]

434   "(Schuschnigg speech.)" [AF 905: four short entries, one on an advantage of aging.]

434   "merely a 'Gestalt'!)" [AF 906: mainly short entries on a variety of matters, including fame, on gallows humor.]

434   "worshipped a bull." [AF 907: brief entries on various matters, including spelling reform.]

434   "a low level." [AF 907: two brief entries.]

434   "country 'of their own.'" [AF 907–909: various entries, including cruelty in history, anti-Semitism, etc.]

NOTEBOOK 33

438   "inner preordained course.)" [AF 913–914: entry 6) on Musil's sense that anything he wrote should contribute something new; entry 7) on the letters between Bettina Brentano and Goethe.]

441   "for doing so." [AF 917: entry 14) on Musil's notion of living as a peasant.]

443   "to assimilate quickly." [AF 919–920: entry 20) on gardens; entry 21) on Musil's irritation at the success of a literary rival whose work he considers inferior; entry 22) continues the theme of 21); 23) a fragment.]

445   "self-love from myself!" [AF 921–922: entry 29).]

446   "my way into it." [AF 923: entry 36).]

447   "that is, soulless) fashion." [AF 923–924: entries 39) and 40), the latter on Martha's criticism of her earlier drawings.]

448   "the great tradition." [AF 925: entry 47) on his distaste for Expressionism.]

448   "most important pupils." [AF 925: entry 49); entry 50); entry 51) on the high, stiff collars Musil wore in his youth.]

450 "contact with convention?" [AF 927: entry 57).]

451 "I am ungrateful." [AF 927: entry 64) on his emotional response to addressing someone as "Dear friend" in a letter.]

451 "books are made." [AF 928: entry 66) referring to reading of d'Annunzio.]

451 "able to do so)." [AF 928: entry 68).]

452 "come out right?, etc." [AF 929: entry 71) referring to literary work of his earlier period.]

453 "problem be solved?" [AF 930: entry 74) on nervousness and melancholy.]

453 "grown within me." [AF 930: entry 76).]

453 "20–100 years earlier!" [AF 930: entry 78) on provincial authors.]

453 "things really are." [AF 931: entry 80) on the distinction between "interesting" and "classical," apparently with reference to literary work.]

454 "made some compromises." [AF 932: entry 82) and entry 82a) on classical sculpture; entries 83), 84), 85).]

454 "a piece of wood." [AF 933: entry 97) quotation from Hans Carossa on Thomas Mann.]

455 "the individual writer!" [AF 934: entry 89).]

455 "the nibbling mouse?" [AF 934–935: entries 92) and 93) with reference to Thomas Mann.]

458 "able to do this.)" [AF 937–938: entry 98); entry 99); entries 100) and 101) on lectures; entry 102) on learning grammar, military fashion.]

459 "compare the results." [AF 939–940: entry 105) quotation from Nietzsche; entry 106) quotation from Kant; entry 107) contrasting science and art; entry 108) on Aristotle on art; entry 109) on *The Enthusiasts*; entry 110).]

460 *"Sketches of a Writer."* [AF 941: entry 113) quotation from Hofmannsthal.]

460 "I can understand!" [AF 941–942: entry 115) on aesthetic experience; entry 116); on his response to a verse by Rilke.]

461 "make up stories." [AF 942: entry 122).]

462 "Modern Polish Philosophy." [AF 944: entry 130) on Corneille; entry 131) on his tendency to be a negative critic of literary production.]

462 "many facets to it.))" [AF 944: entry 133).]

463 "large political parties.)" [AF 945: entry 135) on his monogamy.]

463 "churning out paraphrases." [AF 945–946: entry 138) on a journalist, Josef Koller.]

463 "the opening lines." [AF 947–948: cross reference to other notes; entries 140) and 141).]

465 "of synthetic chemistry." [AF 949: entry 146) on wanting things and on imagination.]

466 "spell on me.)" [AF 950: entry 148) on the large quantity of literary output and the small amount of quality work.]

467 "old at that time." [AF 951: entry 152) on the need to distinguish between "Hitlerism" and Germany.]

467 "to make an attempt." [AF 952: entry 154) on Jules Romains.]

468 "155)" [AF 952: reference to a cutting from a Swiss newspaper.]

469 "'ultimate love story'!)" [AF 954–955: entry 159) is a postscript to 158), entry 160) on his shyness, entry 161) on his father's side of the family, entry 162) on the law, entry 163) on *Young Törleß*.]

470 "admittedly, strong doubts!" [AF 955: entry 165).]

474 "the upper hand." [AF 959: entry 172) cross-refers to entry 138) on Koller; entry 173) on "painting" ("malen") as an earlier expression for "writing" ("schreiben").]

474 "diverges from reality." [AF 959–960: entry 175) on asking important questions of himself; entry 176) on *The Enthusiasts*; entry 177); entry 178) on giving "stage directions" to himself.]

474 "article {on Bergson}." [AF 960: cross-reference to other note.]

474 "without an answer." [AF 961: entry 182) on spiritual success in Germany; entry 183) on Thomas Mann.]

475 "homesickness! Passionate child." [AF 961–962: entries 185), 186), 187).]

476 "already less secure." [AF 963–965: entry 190); entry 191) with self-critical comments on his work on MwQ; entry 192); entry 193) on Dostoyevsky; entry 194) dialogue with Martha on his predisposition as author.]

477 "something of the kind." [AF 965–966: entries 196) and 197).]

NOTEBOOK 32

481   "of two half-truths." [AF 968: entry 3) on violence within the law; entry 4) on cohesion in nomad groups; entry 5) on poetic justice; entry 6) and entry 7) on politics and spirit.]

482   "bestows on one." [AF 969: brief entries 11), 12), 13), 14) on National Socialism, 15).]

482   "fight against dem[ocracy]." [AF 970: 17) on politics.]

484   "all old ideology." [AF 972: entry 25) speculates on whether the current turbulence in the world is the effect of the death-throes of an old form of religion and the beginning of a new form; entry 26) examines the word *Jüngling* ("youth" or "young man").]

486   "gift for writing." [AF 974: entry 29), entry 30) on hatred, entry 31) on form as principle of exclusion.]

487   "under the ideals!" [AF 975: entries 33), 34), and 35).]

487   "of true narration." [AF 975–976: entry 37) on Wilhelm Tell; entry 38) on artists and democracy; entry 39) on rebellion of the masses; entry 40) with varied reflections on Malthus and population.]

487   "of the autocracies?" [AF 976–977: entry 42) Voltaire quoted by Emerson; entry 43) on freedom and leadership; entry 44); entry 45) on political ideologies; entry 46) on uninhibited action and Germany; entry 47) on drifting and leading.]

487   "species of morality." [AF 977–979: entry 49); entry 50) on the incapacity for assassination; entry 51) on the tendency to think ill of fellow human beings; entry 52) on pessimism; entry 53) on a leading Italian journalist, Virginio Gayda.]

488   "about through necessity!" [AF 979: entry 55) on "predator states".]

488   "function and position." [AF 979–981: entry 57) on belief in progress as a potentially unpleasant goal; entry 58) on prophecies of Jacob Burckhardt; entry 59) also on "predator state"; entry 60) cross-reference; entry 61) on books about art that inhibit art; entry 62) on the way political systems incorporate anachronisms; entry 63) brief thoughts on organizing a projected publication; entry 64) with extract from a speech by v. Brauchitsch, from the German High Command, together with Musil's comments.]

489   "task that is set." [AF 981–982: entry 66); entry 67) on the views of J. J. Bodmer (1698–1783) on literature and art; entry 68) on resignation as the basic tone for his aphorisms; entry 69) reference to book on Daumier by Robert Lejeune.]

489   "and civilized procedure." [AF 983: entry 71) comparison of election of a Pope with the democratic electoral process.]

489   "of one's strength." [AF 983: entry 73) on the concept of dignity.]

489   "in the foreground." [AF 984: entry 75) on art at a time of dictatorship; entry 76) on the relationship between politics and spirit (Geist); entry 77) on mass movement of population.]

491   "an act of genius." [AF 986–987: entry 84) on the injustice wrought in Germany; entry 85) on parliamentary democracy; entry 86) cross-reference; entry 87) on the treatment of Germany.]

491   "the question properly.)" [AF 987–989: entry 89) on early Jesuits; entry 90) on Casanova's memoirs; entry 91) on rereading literary works.]

491   "will lasts out." [AF 989: three brief entries 93), 94), 95).]

492   "respect as well." [AF 990–992: entry 98) extensive extracts from, and summary of, a book by Friedrich Grimm, *On the Meaning of this War*; entry 99) with reference to National Socialism; entry 100) on Ernst Wiechert's novel, *Die Majorin (The Major's Wife)*; entry 101) on Goethe's *Fiction and Truth*; entry 102) reference to Goebbels; entry 103) on the financial support, etc., received by the great French moralist authors.]

492   "century skipped over." [AF 993–994: entry 105) quotation from Schiller and reference to Descartes; entry 106) critical remarks on position of immigrants in Switzerland; entry 107) reference to René Clair; entry 108) on his attitude to H[itler]; entry 109) on the capacity of National Socialism to enthuse average people; entry 110) reflections on the government of states, large and small.]

492   "has no other aim." [AF 995–996: entries 112) and 113) on great artists; entry 114) on the decline of the middle class and the "astonishing achievement of Russia"; entry 115) on attempts to create a new world order and reference to Heydrich and to the philosophy of the S.S.; entry 116)

on his sense that the world is undergoing revolutionary change, with references to America, Russia, Switzerland, and Hitler.]

493   "the latter's temerities." [AF 996–998: entry 118) in which he finds an echo of his work *Unions* in a story in a newspaper; entry 119) on Chiang Kai-shek; entry 120) on Rommel.]

NOTEBOOK 35

498   "and Dr. Rosin." [AF 1001: short entry for 8.XI.]

498   "make their appearance." [AF 1002: entry for 12.XI on visitors; brief entries for 14.XI. and 16.XI.]

499   "stretches to [Mont] Salève." [AF 1003–1004: brief entry for 8.XII; entry for 4.I.1940 on Christmas celebrations; reference to sinking of the battle cruiser *Graf Spee*.]

500   "whole indescribably whole." [AF 1004–1007: various entries, including the following: on tensions and war as a background to his life; some cryptic references to personal erotic experiences; on mines and the war at sea, and on the way that war has forged German unity.]

501   "in the neighborhood." [AF 1009–1010: entry for 29.I. [1940] on a lecture he gave; entry for 30.I with retrospective remarks on the lecture; entry for 5.II on a cat; entry for 7.II on an approach to autobiography; 9.II. on the theme of "genius"; entries for 13.II and 14.II.]

503   "of Ag[athe] and U[lrich].)" [AF 1012–1025: entries for the following days: 22.II. [1940]; 7.VII (with reference to the cessation of hostilities between France and Germany); entries for 9.VII, 12.VII, 13.VII, 14.VII, 17.VII, 19.VII, 22.VII, 25.VII, 28.VII, 31.VII, 3.VIII, 5.VIII, 7.VIII, 8.VIII, 10.VIII, 15.VIII, 19.VIII, 20.VIII, 29.VIII, 20.IX, 20.XII, with close observations of acquaintances and recording of what they say and do.]

503   "end is beckoning." [AF 1026: entry on a dream of Martha's.]

504   "Philemon and Baucis." [AF 1027: brief note on the Wotrubas.]

Made in the USA
Lexington, KY
17 June 2016